Voices from *Night Lessons*

"The parchment that bears true and simple lessons burns easily in the fires of pride and impatience"

– Angelo

"The caddie's essential skill: Sooth their nerves, coddle their confidence and keep the damn fools' eyes off the cart girl"

– Billy Kurtez

"Stop whining about injustice. Your opponent gets a few breaks and you start thinking it's divine retribution...now you're playing against God Almighty and sure as shit he's always on the other guy's side"

– Wedgy Byrne

"Remember: The Bank of Life don't take cash"

– Howell Juitt

"The game's hopeful purpose often lays obscured beneath its opaque numbers... but its difficult grace offers solace to all who surrender, whether they be stymied in the rough or staggered by a more profound tragedy"

– Ricky Cloudsborough

NIGHT LESSONS

Don Anslow

 Lucky Bat Books

A Lucky Bat Book

Night Lessons

Copyright © 2016 by Don Anslow

Cover Design: Brandon Swann

Book design, format and programming by Joan Pinkert
About the Author and On the Road photograph by T.C. Brown

ISBN: 978-1-943588-19-0

LuckyBatBooks.com

10 9 8 7 6 5 4 3 2 1

Published and printed in the U.S.A.

 Lucky Bat Books

Night Lessons

Don Anslow

2016

Acknowledgments

Special thanks go to my friend and assistant, Joan Pinkert, for eternal optimism and boundless energy. This book would be impossible without you. Thanks to Louisa Swann for editing advice and to the transcription crew: Tom Gossart, Adriana Buer, Chris Ritter, Martha Amick, Robin Hammond, the late Rosemary Hurdle, and the always-gracious, immeasurably generous Meredith Hildebrand for your labor.

Thanks for the good humor and contributions of my usual partners on the turf: TC Brown, Mike Hurdle, Joe Otnes, Bill Curtis, and Travis Dawson. You all make the game of life that much more fulfilling.

Special affection and appreciation go to my original—and still favorite—playing partner and son, Faron Anslow. Thanks for great words and for helping to squeeze all the light out of twilight rounds and for enjoying shag-bagging from center field as much as teeing it up at Bandon. And to that shining pillar of courageous creative fire, my daughter, Nellyda Anslow, goes a mighty nod for ignoring the bars that so many of us struggle to clear.

A special word of thanks to Larry Bergman for aeronautical advice and to Tulley Long for helping Shara and me conjure Rama Schwain from the carefree summer skies above British Columbia.

Finally, I mustn't forget to mention the late Helen Shaw, who made the world a wonderful mystery.

—•—

In Memory of Guntis Turks and Jesse Rogers

Don and Shara Anslow at a roadhouse in eastern Washington.

To my wife, Shara, who endured many lonely hours as her husband pursued the adventures of his cast across an imaginary stage, goes my deepest thanks and ever-growing love.

Night Lessons was written mostly in the dark of night, and in the course of its creation, some nights were far darker than others. Her willing counsel and complicity in the realization of this work were invaluable and are never to be forgotten.

Too often she bore the burden of second fiddle to Rama, Hank, and company but always did so without complaint, even as the myriad costs and distractions ringing up in this endeavor must have appeared an endless folly.

Talk may be cheap, but the phrase "follow your dreams" is worth more than gold when uttered from the lips of such a sincere and faithful partner.

Thank you.

Chapter 1

"God-damned bugs!" Hank strangled the steering wheel and plunged into a storm of locusts. "The bastards are gonna plug the radiator," he cursed as the horde, flickering with the beat of a billion brittle wings, swept past his road-weary eyes.

Hank's young passenger hardly noticed the insects; he was miserable and just wanted out. The boy pressed his forehead against the window and strained to remain patient, but the car's steamy cabin didn't make waiting any easier. The highway simmered with heat and humidity, yet the windows of his father's '56 Ford Wagon were raised tight against the afternoon's swarm.

Through the fuzz of his breath against the glass, the boy watched as the insects and a sea of sage streamed by, and tried to forget how badly he had to piss. He hated to pester his father again. He'd asked to stop several tedious miles ago, but the wagon had never slowed or strayed from its course. Eventually the bashful eleven-year-old's discomfort prevailed.

"Dad, anywhere will be okay…"

"Hang on, Rama, just hold it another minute…at least till these GD hoppers blow through." Two thunderstorms now separated them from Texarkana, and Hank was determined that this damnable storm would soon fall behind as well. They continued west.

"I'll think twice before I get you another damned Coke. Sons-of-bitches go right through you."

Hank looked over at his son hunkered uncomfortably against the door. The boy's thick brown hair was growing damp. "And, Jesus, they're up to a dime now."

Rama pressed his knees together and fidgeted with the door lock. Click up. Clump down. Click up. Another miserable mile crawled by. Click. Clump. Click.

"Okay, okay, Chief. Hands off the damned lock. I can take a hint. I'll find you a good spot. It's bad enough just drivin' out here through the middle of nowhere to bet on your uncle's damned horse, but plowing through this…"

Hank gestured at the storm. "This plague, that's what the Bible would call it, just for a few lousy bucks? Hell, I should turn around right now, or have my head examined."

Rama relaxed, grateful that his message was getting through. His mother would have stopped right away, but Rama guessed his dad just wasn't used to having a kid around. It was already a year since they had last been together.

Another minute passed, but Hank never touched the brakes or budged the wheel. He strained against the incoming hoppers to spot a stretch of firm shoulder, even as he entertained a Cecil B. DeMille vision of a black insect swarm venting God's wrath upon the luckless. Hank pressed the washer knob several times and sent a feeble stream across the abstract green composition growing on the windshield, but with little effect.

"Christ," he groaned, as he set the wipers into a futile, slimy sweep.

Rama leaned forward and strained to see through the arcs of insect essence.

"Don't worry, Chief, I'm looking," declared Hank. "You've gotta be careful about pulling off the road in this sandy shit…there ain't no shoulders. And wouldn't your mother bust my chops if she knew I'd sunk the Ford up to the axles on our first road trip together? She's not all that tickled about me hauling you this far from Memphis."

Hank chuckled at his wife's reluctance to let their only child venture into what she saw as his sketchy world. She would never have imagined his destination was the horse track in Ruidoso, New Mexico, and he never dreamt that locusts in west Texas might stymie his intentions.

"But it's gonna be worth every damn mile. If your uncle Henry knows what he's talkin' about, his pony is gonna win us some real do-re-mi…at least until those fools in New Mexico catch on."

The thought of the inside track on a long-shot winner and an inevitable harvest of cash swept Rama's discomfort from Hank's head. "Before this trip is over, we'll get a little fishing in. Catch a few bass. Maybe hike down into that cave at Carlsbad. What do you think?"

Click…clump…click.

Hank returned to the races: "Odds are, those fools in New Mexico won't know squat 'till Henry's little wonder is running their hopeless nags into the ground." A bead of perspiration broke from Hank's damp black hair and trickled down his face as he pictured a payday materializing like a mirage somewhere far down the road.

"It's gonna be like shooting fish in a…"

"Dad. Over there!"

Rama cut Hank's rhapsody short as he stabbed a finger across the dusty dashboard in the direction of what appeared to be a water tower looming up through the insect cloud—a large white sphere poised about forty feet above the ground on a rusting steel column. Through the spattered windshield he could see a gravel road heading out toward the curiosity.

"Yep, that'll work." Hank cranked the wheel left.

The crunch of gravel replaced the whine of asphalt as the Wagon lurched onto the road. As the tower loomed ahead, Rama could make out a pattern of dimples painted across its surface. Long exposure to the Texas sun, hail, sandstorms, and a lightning strike or two had taken a severe toll on the paint, but the carefully rendered dimples and the giant tee formed by the sphere's supporting structure left nothing to the imagination. It was a giant golf ball. If you were looking for a round out on this dusty brown landscape, somebody had gone to great lengths to ensure you wouldn't pass it by. In fact, a weather-beaten sign invited you further:

Mesquite Creek Golf Course and Aero Park
Grill Room Cafe – Public Welcome

Rama didn't care about golf or grill rooms. A quick rest stop on the gravel drive would be good enough for him. He gripped the door handle and waited for the brakes, but the drive dropped unexpectedly into the first steep folds of a hidden arroyo.

"Hang on another second, Chief," said Hank, tightening his grip on the wheel. "Ain't stoppin' now 'til we get to that golf course down there."

Hank and Rama Schwain certainly weren't looking for a place to tee off. Neither father nor son had ever touched a club, but the Grill Room Cafe held out the promise of a good hamburger and a cup of coffee. Rama relaxed as much as he dared; he could wait another minute. He was relieved that his father wasn't upset at being interrupted in mid-ramble. Talking and dreaming were important to his dad, especially when the subject was race horses and winning big—a payday, Hank called it. To an admiring son, races were for fun and paydays were infrequent but memorable events, like Christmas.

⌐•⌐

It had been too long since such a Christmas had come to their house, but Rama remembered it well: a balmy July evening about five years earlier. His father had arrived home late, and with a shout had tossed his cane to the floor while dancing around the living room on his good leg as he happily sang the chorus to his favorite popular tune. The sloppy rendition of "Luck Be a Lady Tonight" had awakened Rama and sent him running down the hall to peer around the doorjamb into the living room. Rama recalled being apprehensive at the sound of his father's voice howling with such abandon.

From the doorway that night he saw his parents as never before: His father was balanced on the sofa like a crazy acrobat, dancing deliriously for his wife, Doris.

Only a few minutes earlier, she had settled in for another quiet evening alone. Now, clothed in her housecoat, she sat quietly on the edge of the coffee table—an unusual posture in light of Hank's wild behavior. Rama wondered if his mother were enjoying the entertainment. He couldn't see her face, but her body seemed poised somewhere between joy and restraint, as if she couldn't decide whether to laugh or scold her husband.

Rama slipped back into the door's shadow, sensing that this was some kind of grown-up rite and he didn't belong. But then his mother let out an odd yelp of a laugh, one he'd never heard from her before—tentative, short gasps followed by longer more confident notes. With these more concerting sounds, Rama stepped from the shadows, just in time to see his father reach into his jacket and produce a thick green stack of fifty-dollar bills. With glee, Hank tossed the stack onto the table with a thud. Then thump, another stack hit the table, nearly sending Doris's favorite teapot to the floor. A third bundle landed on the *Saturday Evening Post*, obscuring President Eisenhower's balding head.

Hank lurched from the sofa to the antique hutch where they kept their liquor. He opened the beveled glass doors to extract a decanter and a couple of glasses—rare crystal, like the exotic perfume bottles on Doris's vanity—jewels reserved for special occasions. The glasses were raised, and in a moment the hi-fi needle dropped upon Duke Ellington.

"To those beautiful ponies," offered Hank.

He and Doris sipped through smiling mouths. For a second the house was quiet as they savored the antique liquid, and then with breaths held too long, they burst back into laughter. Doris had joined her husband in his toast to good fortune and God only knew how much cash. Yet she celebrated with the reticence of one who had seen both sides of the beautiful ponies. In fact, only a few minutes earlier as gingerbread cookies baked in the oven, she had angrily complained into the stillness of her Friday evening kitchen: "Hank Schwain, a couple of races couldn't take this long. It's my Friday night, too." But by eleven o'clock, with the music, the cocktails, and the smell of baking still hanging in the air, all seemed to be well.

Rama recalled listening from the darkness of his bedroom as his parents' happy voices moved together from the living room to their end of the world. Switches were thrown and doors softly closed. Their happy chatter and the Duke's enchanted rhythmic pulse rang into every dark corner that night.

The house would never sound the same again.

—•—

The Ford Wagon growled in protest as Hank and Rama descended to Mesquite Creek, but Rama's memory still lingered on that special night. From the perspective of such a happy occasion, he had always believed his dad's interest in a payday seemed as reasonable as his own interest in a bright new bicycle, but Rama hadn't yet glimpsed the black vein of avarice that had begun to poison Hank.

Chapter 2

The harrowing plunge momentarily forced Rama to forget his urgency. The deep arroyo was the only feature that had enlivened the day's grind through the east Texas Blacklands and out across the relentless plains. Below, inviting in its contrast, lay Mesquite Creek—not just a name penned by an overly optimistic cartographer but an actual twinkling stream that rambled through dusty bottomlands and across its namesake golf course.

At the drive's end, a whitewashed adobe clubhouse lay serenely in the shadows of several sheltering ash trees. The structure was roofed in shining green tile, punctuated by two large gables, and crowned by a widow's watch. A wide, welcoming veranda wrapped around the building's sunny sides. Beyond the clubhouse, spotty grass fairways separated by hedgerows of cottonwood wound along the creek, then turned eastward behind a red rock butte. To the west stretched an overgrown airstrip. A faded orange windsock fluttered uselessly from a staff atop a derelict hangar. Hank noticed how tightly the neglected trees encroached on the strip.

"Rough damn place to land," he muttered as the hair on his neck stiffened at an old and painful memory.

Rama looked away uncomfortably. The rare references to his father's disastrous airborne exit from the war were fraught with explosive emotion—best avoided like the blasting caps he and his friends occasionally found in the limestone quarries near his home on the outskirts of Memphis. His eyes traveled aimlessly up the rocky walls of the arroyo, but stopped abruptly as they encountered an indistinct figure of a man on horseback peering down from the shadows of a ledge. Rama's attention snapped into focus. Although vague, the man appeared to wear an odd, flat-brimmed hat from beneath which his hair hung in a thick white braid. Even at a distance it was clear—the horseman was intently watching the descent of Hank Schwain's Ford Wagon.

Rama shivered.

"Okay, Chief. Out you go," barked Hank as he guided the wagon to a stop in the earthen lot. The din of the Ford's V8 dropped away, and the angry buzz of hummingbirds battling over honeysuckle and wild rose pierced the lazy afternoon. The wagon's dust cloud swept past like a spirit, to dance on the vivid green before whirling out across the empty course to be diluted into nothingness.

Apprehensive, Rama waited for his dad to make the first move. But Hank went nowhere as he fiddled to extract a stubborn ignition key.

"I thought you had to go *numero uno...pronto,*" he said when the key finally slipped free. Hank watched as Rama leapt from the car and darted with purpose across the veranda, as if he already knew the way.

In a moment Rama stood before two large weathered doors that had once served as the club's formal entry. As urgent as his condition was, he paused. A neglected bronze plaque greeted him as it had once greeted patrons in Mesquite Creek's glory days. A phrase lifted from golf's most venerable clubhouse at St. Andrews demanded his attention: *For as we breathe, there's hope.*

Rama mouthed the words, nudged off-kilter by wisps of deja vu. The phrase seemed so familiar, yet standing at the portal he felt like an intruder. He had felt this way once before back home in Memphis, when one bright Sunday morning he had been caught peeking through the hedge surrounding a supremely private golf course.

That course, to the chagrin of its most effete members, had been forced by geography to run grudgingly along Crutchfield Lane—a public road. To protect their privacy, they had planted a dense laurel hedge backed with a bamboo thicket. To a young boy, the barricade served to make the game being played within irresistibly mysterious. In one spot, a gap yielded views of a gracefully sculpted landscape with blazing white patches of sand nestled into the flanks of an impossibly smooth green. Rama often rode along the lane, stopping sometimes to peer through the gap. Occasionally he would spot a player or two—older folks mostly—putting on the green. Fearful of intruding, he had never lingered to watch until the morning his mother, Doris, tucked two quarters into his hand and sent him down Crutchfield to fetch a quart of milk.

With the fresh new tread of his tires singing, Rama stood on the pedals and floated down toward the course. Gleaming fairways flashed at him through the foliage as he sped past. Ahead, through the gap, he caught a glimpse of the putting green and its snappy checkered flag waiting in the early sun. The flag lay in stillness along the shaft; no one appeared to be golfing that morning.

In silence, he coasted to a stop and walked the bike to the break in the hedge in hopes of stealing a good long peek into the forbidden world. Just as his vision focused on the blazing green, its white sands and red geraniums, he felt as if he were about to faint. An odd sense of vacancy overcame him—as if his spirit were falling into a different domain. In seconds the feeling passed and he returned his attention to the course. As he did, he noticed a spark of white against the sky.

A bright, incoming golf ball flashed in the sunlight as it fell toward the green. It flashed again as it leapt up from the green's emerald fringe and bounced out onto the putting surface. Spellbound, Rama watched the ball settle into a purposeful roll toward the flag. A sparkling rooster tail rose as the ball scribed a graceful curve in the silvery morning dew before being blocked from his sight.

Rama spread the foliage for a better view. A perfect record of the event he had just witnessed was drawn out in the moisture on the green below: Dot. Dot. Dash. Dasshhh. The long, final dash arched gracefully across the turf to the ball, which was clamped tenuously between the flagstaff and the lip of the cup.

The dewy curve had perfectly graphed a complex expression of velocity, angular momentum, gravity, slope, and friction. But it took no understanding of physics for the enthralled young boy straddling the Schwinn Phantom to know that he had been fortunate to see that rare streak etched like a meteor before his eyes.

A warm gust rustled the oak leaves above him and the checkered flag came to life. As he watched, the flagstaff rattled once and that falling star tumbled to the bottom of the cup.

Rama looked up to see who had hit the ball, but there was nobody nearby. In the distance the fairway curled east toward the morning sun, then disappeared around a knoll alive with flowering dogwood. The course appeared vacant, but as Rama turned his interest back toward his milk run, he saw a golfer just cresting the knoll. The fellow wore white slacks and a pale yellow sweater vest pulled over white sleeves. With the morning sun blazing up the fairway behind him, the golfer glowed in a bright corona. Even the faithless might have mistaken him for an angel that Sunday morning, except that he towed a decidedly earthly black leather golf bag strapped to a rickety trolley. Behind the shining figure, his trolley's earthbound tracks straddled a set of footprints that rambled back into the sun.

The white figure made Rama uneasy. He jerked the Phantom's handlebars around, preparing to continue his ride, but a shaft of light caught the bike's shiny chrome fender and shot a signal out into the golf course. Alert from his morning round, the golfer's eyes readily caught the glint from the hedge and the scuffling of a skinny young boy preparing to flee on his bicycle.

Something had dazzled the golfer that morning, something more than the brilliant sun. He had just hit the most pure, miraculous shot of his life—he could feel it—yet he had no clue why or where the ball might have landed. The hole was a par five, and the amazing shot had been his second: a reasonable iron intended only to put him within a full wedge of the green. He had never considered trying for the green, but moments ago as he took a stance above his ball, a vacant sensation had overcome him. In the fleeting void, reason collapsed. In the instant that he swung, he was released from a mistaken faith in the impossibility of such a shot. Anything became possible. Incredibly, he now feared he had hit the ball *too* well and that it had flown through the dogleg into the creek beyond. Maybe the kid could help out.

"Hey there. HELLO," he hollered at Rama.

Rama Schwain, son of a used car salesman at Big Muddy's AutoTorium, was surprised that a wealthy golfer from Bluff Meade Country Club was actually addressing him.

"Did you see my golf ball? My BALL," the man called again.

Rama felt uneasy interacting with strangers, particularly the rich folk who frequented this place. He had watched them through the laurel; sometimes he had heard them celebrate a holed putt or curse a missed one, and he had even seen members of the civilized gentry angrily throw putters at their terrified caddies. From his vantage in the hedge, Rama had always felt embarrassed at secretly witnessing their emotions spilled so uselessly over such a trivial pastime. Now he had been discovered.

"Over there," Rama responded as he pointed across the creek to the checkered flag.

"Where's there?"

"The GREEN," Rama hollered.

"On the green?" the man questioned in disbelief.

Rama's right foot settled on the pedal. "Yes. I mean no...it's in the hole," he shouted. Rama cupped his hands together to form a circle and held them above his head in the light slashing down through the branches.

"IN THE HOLE."

Suddenly the man in white realized what Rama was signifying. He paused, threw his head back and shouted with abandon to the great blue sky.

"Praise the Lord!" He paused for a deep breath and to grasp the moment's reality. Thus assured he wasn't living a lucid dream, he resumed rejoicing at what was the rarest shot in all of golf.

In a few more steps, the jubilant golfer could see for himself the track of his shot through the dew to the base of the flagstick. He looked over at Rama who was now within speaking distance across the creek.

"My God, son, do you know what that was?"

Rama, who had been growing increasingly impatient to ride, was uncomfortable with such an obvious question. *That* was a ball rolling into a hole. Simple. He had seen it a million times at Putt-Putt miniature golf. He didn't reply.

"That was a double eagle." The man answered his own question triumphantly. "My God...a two-hundred-and-fifty-five yard draw. Cut off the dogleg with a pretty 3-iron."

The golfer was a tall graceful man, the kind of loose-limbed fellow who might pull off such an athletic wonder. A comforting smile illuminated a kind face beneath a shamble of tossed white locks.

"The shot of my life. I don't even know why I tried it. Just had a *feeling*."

Rama had no clue what a draw, a dogleg, or a 3-iron were or how they could be pretty, but he knew the elegant arc across the green, the little rooster tail like the spray of a thousand minute diamonds into the crisp morning air, were beautiful things. He guessed *double eagle* was good, too. Then as Rama prepared to return to his milk run, the golfer spoke again.

"Thanks."

A single, sincere word from a stranger. It startled Rama, as if the fellow were somehow suggesting he had contributed to the incredible stroke.

Rama said nothing further. He didn't wait for the man to pluck the miracle ball from the cup, but dropped his feet to the Phantom's pedals with all the force a boy could muster. He still had milk to buy that morning.

———•———

"Damn, you're liable to hurt yourself if you pinch that thing off much longer, Chief. I thought you had to take a leak…or are you gonna stare at that door all afternoon?"

Hank stood beside the station wagon, carefully applying the red coil of the cigarette lighter to a long-awaited smoke. He exhaled a thin blue cloud that followed a dust devil across the green. "Go on. I'll bring up the rear, soon as I pick these damned hoppers from the grill."

Rama grabbed the door's handle, a club head that had been sunk impossibly into the dense black oak panel like a sword in an anvil, and slipped behind the adobe walls.

Chapter 3

As Rama disappeared into the clubhouse, Hank's attention was drawn to a screeching in the sky. Above him, perched atop the widow's watch, a copper weathervane forged in the likeness of a bag piper played a sour metallic note as it turned on a rusty shaft to face dusty winds spilling down from the plains.

"Jesus, someone oughta give that thing a shot of grease," Hank grumbled as he struggled to slam the wagon's door over the resistance of corroded hinges. "Too bad to let a nice place like this run down."

With lowered expectations, he turned to face lunch at the grill room, already forgetting that he had assured Rama he would be right behind.

Rama's apprehension lingered as the great doors closed behind him. To eyes dazzled by the afternoon sun, the foyer was surprisingly dark. As he listened for his father's steps, the rich odor of mesquite embers drifting from the grill room barbecue reminded him of incense at his mother's church. For a moment he was at peace, but the urgency that had driven him there returned abruptly when, as his eyes adjusted to the light, he discovered he was not alone. In a moment of panic, he jumped back as a tusked creature materialized from the gloom.

A stuffed wild boar—Mesquite Creek's menacing mascot—had been strategically placed in the shadows to greet unsuspecting visitors. At first glance the animal appeared threatening, until one noticed the plaid tam-o'-shanter resting askew on the critter's prickly head.

Rama didn't linger to appreciate the humor. He shot down the hall where, with sneakers squealing, he slid to a stop at the rest rooms. But rather than plunge immediately into the welcoming facilities, he paused in deliberation. The appropriate gender on the two adjacent doors was, by someone's typographic wit, denoted as *Ladies* and *Laddies*. Rama pondered the choice; only a single letter separated him from potential embarrassment.

He was spared agonizing deliberation when the *Laddies* door burst open and a lively, deeply tanned man almost bowled him over.

"Whoa there hombre," blurted the fellow, deftly stepping around the unexpected obstruction.

Rama could feel the heat of self-consciousness flowing into his face on a tide of embarrassment, that he, an intruder, had almost tripped up a bona fide golfer. But far worse was the feeling that he was on the very brink of a far greater humiliation.

"Maybe they should've put *glass* doors in here, eh amigo?" With a flourish, the man pushed the door open and Rama shot through.

In seconds he stood in a private stall, staring into a painting hung just above the water closet. In relief, his eyes played across the canvas. There, in an absurd Grand Canyon landscape of cliffs and chasms, an old cowpoke wielded a hickory golf club and leaned at a gravity-defying angle out over the edge of an abyss so deep that its bottom was obscured in a blue haze. A fall into this gorge would be like falling into the sky. Only a taut rope, fastened around the cowpoke's waist and secured to the horn of his faithful old pony's saddle, prevented a fatal plunge.

The object of the daredevil golfer's attention was a ball perched on the top of a prickly pear cactus growing defiantly out over the precipice. Thus suspended, the cowboy golfer clutched a crooked wooden shaft with a rusty iron head and lashed at the ball—forever frozen in mid-swing.

"Play It As It Lies" read a title scribed into the picture frame.

Rama's interest in the painting suddenly vanished as he felt an unmistakable sensation on his left leg. He looked down in alarm and discovered that he had neglected to raise the lid.

Rama yelped in despair and the stream stopped with youthful immediacy. But the damage had been done. The splattering from the lid had dampened his jeans in an incriminating stain. He tried to fathom the depths of ridicule he might suffer if he encountered a member of the golf club on the trek back to the grill room. All eyes would fall accusingly to that damned spot.

He stepped cautiously from the stall. An electric hand dryer hung on the wall nearby. Saved, he thought. Rama shuffled over to the appliance and turned the shiny nozzle down. He raised his damp leg as high as he could, then slammed the silver button, but the nozzle was too high; it blew uselessly above the troublesome target. Rama grabbed a small waste basket and flipped it over to make a stool, scattering paper towels, dog-eared score cards, and the sports page in the process. He quickly resumed his pose at the blower, thigh pressed against the nozzle as he braced himself with both hands against the tile wall.

Rama punched the button again, and within seconds the spot began to fade under the machine's hot breath. Above the fan's roar, he did not hear the click of metal golf spikes on tile behind him. Without warning, a ponderous patron crashed through the locker room door like a bulldog and discovered the young man posing awkwardly before the hand dryer.

———•———

T. "Boney" Carlisle was a regular at Mesquite Creek, although he would be considered highly irregular in most respects. Despite the nickname favored by his friends and golfing buddies—in his case, two distinct groups—he was anything but bony. He possessed a large, compressed physique that somehow produced speed and grace against all odds. Although his golf game was reasonably competent, Boney's real claim to fame was his ability to drink at least one can of beer per hole and consume half as many Little Debbie Brownies per round while maintaining a prolific stream of rude one-liners and less-than-enlightened observations on his playing partners' swing deficiencies.

Boney's slashing golf swing was stitched together into a reliable quilt of swing thoughts, routines, rules of thumb, blind confidence, and luck. Yet, impossibly, Boney's game held fast under the onslaughts of heat, fatigue, frustration, inebriation, and—on this day—grasshoppers.

Boney was taken aback, but only for an instant, at the sight of the mortally embarrassed young man humped over the dryer. "For God's sake, son, the damned blower is for your *hands*."

Rama was frozen in a self-conscious nightmare. He had no insight into the implications of his posture at the dryer. In his innocence, he only knew he had been caught with piss on his pant leg and was responsible for the trash strewn about the locker-room floor.

"Sorry s-s-sir," he stuttered. "I just needed to dry…I mean, I spilled some…" Rama choked off the hopeless explanation and jumped down from the basket to begin collecting the trash, under the amused and puzzled gaze of Boney Carlisle.

"Aw, Christ, don't worry. I was a randy little shit when I was a kid, too. Your secret's safe with me." Boney wheezed like a broken bagpipe as he chuckled at Rama's predicament but quickly abandoned the line of blow dryer innuendo.

"C'mon, I'll help you tidy this crap up before the vice squad arrives." Boney picked up a page of the sports section and prepared to toss it into Rama's basket, but he couldn't avoid the headline: *Rain Forces First Sunday Finish for US Open – Casper Leads.*

Boney had just walked through a lucrative but grasshopper-infested round of Saturday golf and still felt sporty. "Hey kid, slide that basket over there," he said, pointing to the farthest corner of the locker room. "Might as well make a game out of it, eh?"

Rama said nothing but nervously obliged, tapping the basket into position with the tip of his tennis shoe.

"A buck says I can toss this paper into that basket," he proclaimed as he crumpled the sports page into a ball. "You in?"

Rama had always been told not to talk to strangers, especially in bathrooms, so he remained silent. But Boney didn't really expect an answer; fishing for a bet was just an old habit. Without another word he took his shot. The wad caught the edge of the basket and bounced to the floor.

"Crap," he mumbled. "Now you."

Rama made fleeting eye contact with the bear-like fellow. The big man's cheeks were burnished from wind and sun, and his grin was wide and friendly though smeared with traces of a brownie consumed moments earlier on the eighteenth green.

Rama considered an exit strategy, but Boney interceded.

"Alright, make it *four* bits. You just toss in a wad of newspaper and you've got yourself fifty cents. Ain't you ever gambled?"

Gambling, thought Rama. Wasn't that what this trip was all about?

Although his dad was after bigger stakes in New Mexico, they often played rummy for pennies. Rama grabbed up the last remaining sheets of the sports page and formed a decent projectile.

"It's not gambling if I don't bet, is it? Anyway, I've only got a quarter."

"Heee heee, a hustler," laughed Boney. "Well okay, then we'll just call it two-to-one odds. I'll take your quarter if you miss."

Without thinking Rama launched the paper into a trajectory that arched from his fingers to the confluence of the tile walls just above the basket. The missile caromed between the walls and down into the can.

"A double banker. Damn, I should have known," cursed Boney.

He flipped a Lady Liberty over to Rama, who snagged it out of the air without thinking.

"Nice shot," Boney said as he lunged toward the nearest stall, the same one in which Rama had just executed his sloppy performance. As the door slammed shut behind the big man, Rama made his escape—half a dollar richer and sporting a diminished damp spot that he still considered incriminating.

Although this exchange was less lofty than the double-eagle moment he had shared with that angelic player years earlier, Rama had already traveled a path familiar to those who embrace the impossible game—a route that so often plummets from the sublime to the ridiculous.

—•—

Rama followed the smoky scent of Texas barbecue back to the grill room. A cocktail lounge lurked along one wall like a grotto. From its inviting depths the glow of illuminated liquor bottles winked in soft ambers, burgundies, and electric blues. Across the room, broad windows blazed in a green and blue panorama of golf course and dazzling sky.

He recognized the profile of his father seated in a booth beside the sunny windows. Hank stared intently into a racing form. The paper was folded into a sturdy sheaf as if ready to swat flies. His right hand rested idly on a glass of iced tea.

Rama made his way to the table, walking crab-like to keep his damp side from view. As he shuffled past the bar, he noticed three men hunched in conversation over a pile of cash and another scribbling at a scorecard with a tiny pencil. Across the grill room, an agile woman with stylish silver hair carried a shiny steel coffee pot in one hand and plate of lemon pie in the other. The waitress looked to be about his grandmother's age, Rama guessed. She wore a light green uniform with white trim and what appeared to be an insignia of a wild boar embroidered above her blouse pocket.

Hank looked up from his form as Rama arrived. "Feel better now, Chief?" he smiled. "I was 'bout ready to send the Texas Rangers out after you."

Rama slid into the booth, glad to be home free. His father's fingers still rested on the glass, having just traced a dollar sign on its frosty surface.

"Did you see that big pig in the front room, Dad?"

"No, Chief. I came in the other door." Hank absently gestured out toward the course with his racing form, then glanced up as his boy's words settled into place. "Why the hell would they keep a pig in there?"

"No, Dad, I mean a stuffed pig. A big one, too…with tusks."

"Stuffed…oh yeah, probably a boar," replied Hank, returning from the land of odds. "Guess a real one would mess the place up, now wouldn't it?" Hank chuckled. He raised a damp finger to summon the waitress.

Rama relaxed with the humor in his father's voice. It had been a long time since they had spent this much time together. In fact, this was the first time since Doris had insisted on a temporary separation, that she had consented to Hank's taking him for more than a weekend. She knew that between Rama's shyness and her husband's attention to other matters, her "boys" had grown too distant. She hoped that confined for a couple a weeks to that cozy old station wagon, a few budget motel rooms, and a procession of cafe tables, the elusive bonds that she knew needed to be formed might grow. If she had to die early, she didn't want to leave Rama with only a *figure* of a father.

Hank Schwain was, in the forgiving words Doris had so carefully chosen to inform her son of his dad's failings, "a dreamer." His dreams had taken him into worlds that Rama didn't know and eventually into places that Doris couldn't accept. Sometimes the distant look on his face, or an irrelevant response to a question, made it seem to Rama that his dad carried his dreams with him everywhere. Unfortunately for Rama, *everywhere* didn't always include the dinner table, the ballpark, or his bedside.

The truth was that Hank had a prospector's soul and for years had mined the thin air at race tracks, pool halls, and card rooms for a single lucky vein that, like a dream, would allow him to fly freely above the unrewarded labors of a mundane life.

It was not that he couldn't or wouldn't work. With his Electrolux Demonstrator Kit he had once trod the heartless sidewalks of spanking suburbs with news of amazing new housecleaning technology. He had hauled a heavy valise of Colliers Encyclopedia samples up a thousand dirty brick stoops to offer the unenlightened a chance at education from *A* to *Z*. But the grinding procession of tasks that presumably led one to the promised land of financial security proved futile. Hank sought a shortcut through what had become a passionless life. But it had not always been that way. He had once aspired to the heights—to flight—picturing himself content in no other endeavor. It wasn't just a dream; it was a full-fledged passion he had nurtured since boyhood. By the time he turned nineteen—July 5, 1942—and with the smell of gunpowder still fresh on the cardboard husks of last night's fireworks, he resolved to put the wheels of destiny in motion by applying for agricultural flight training at Duster Enterprises. But one hot day later that summer, another set of wheels rolled up to his mailbox and bumped him from that hopeful path onto a new and tragic course above the roaring carnage of Omaha Beach.

Rama waited for the waitress to respond to his father's signal, and in the silence he groped uncomfortably for a new topic. He watched the hopeful figure on his father's glass evaporate as Hank's eyes drifted away.

———•———

The dust behind the postman's old Buick still curled into the September sky as the rattling six-cylinder disappeared down the dirt lane from the Schwains' farm to the village of Othello, Washington. The sound of the mail carrier's rig was only a murmur—and fading fast—as Hank stepped from the shade of the porch into the silence of the bright, rolling landscape. Its emptiness collapsed upon him like a wave.

The road stretched fifteen miles across three hilltop horizons on its course back to town. When not churned by the vibration of pistons and the crunch of worn tires on gravel, the sonic signature along this lane was that of wind hissing through the hairy heads of mature wheat in summer, crying amongst lifeless stubble in autumn, or howling over the icy, broken fields in winter.

On the day the letter arrived, the hissing was just turning to tears.

Two months and ten days had crawled by since his resolution. In the wake of the postman's departure, Hank could see that the red tin flag on the mailbox had been lowered. His chances were promising. Finches trilled from a roadside thistle at the scuffling of his boots along the stone path to the box, a path he had trod many times before while his imagination churned with ever-rising expectations at the arrival of his Preflight Kit from Duster's Sacramento office.

Hank had read and re-read their advertisements in *Popular Mechanics*: The message—*Learn To Fly Them*—leapt from magazine pages stacked like dry leaves out in the Schwain privy. The ad's crude lithograph depicted a Waco biplane suspended forever above the last row of some forgotten crop. Two plumes of white dust fell away like ropes cast from a ship as the powerful aircraft swooped up to clear a cottonwood hedgerow by inches.

Three Weeks To A Career In Aeronautics, read the copy, and Hank dreamt it to be so. He knew he could not follow his father to the endless fields forever. His destiny would not allow it. The wind sweeping across his old man's soil blew with gusts of fortune, bringing welcome wet weather from the west or arctic misery from the north. It could scour away the very soil on which families' lives were founded. Its turbulence could even wear a young man's dreams away. And with the sharp edges of his imagination blunted, a fellow might stop picturing any vision beyond what he already knows—beyond what he can lay his hand, his eyes, or a spade upon.

The whirlwinds dancing for no one across fields of freshly turned sod spoke of loneliness, but Hank was determined to step beyond the empty routines of the wheat lands; its open space was suffocating. The pre-destiny of his friends' lives, like the cattle he and his father tended, seemed pointless. They never questioned their fates, but he would certainly question his. He knew that the farms over in Yakima Valley would soon demand crop dusters just like they were using out in Texas and down in California. Soon as the war got over, he guessed, a whole crop of flyboys would be coming home and grabbing up those jobs. He was going to get in on the action while the getting was good.

It wasn't only clever career strategy that inspired the young man walking out to the mailbox that afternoon. More than any other reason, passion fueled his desire to fly. A hundred times he had kicked the tractor into neutral just to watch a hawk rising high on thermals swirling up from the baked fields. Over the soft chugging of the diesel, he imagined the sound of air moving through stiff feathers. And once, while deer hunting alone in the lee of a high ridge, he had nearly touched a Golden Eagle. The huge bird had ridden a wave along the ridge's crest and at the sight of prey had dropped, passing only a few feet above Hank's head. For a moment he heard the very sound of air supporting the great bird: the hiss through polished barb and the unexpected slapping of ragged trailing feathers. The spellbound young hunter even thought he heard the tips of talons tearing at the sky itself.

At dusk on late summer days, with dew already settling on grateful growing things, swallows would patrol the air space immediately above his mother's lush backyard. Hank would walk the lawn just to watch the little birds fly at impossibly slow speeds, only inches above the grass, to intercept invisible insects his feet had scared into the air. The swallows' magical flight—so low and so close—and Duster's hopeful advertisement still tucked in his wallet had served to bring his dream within reach.

With the mail carrier's dust just settling back to earth, Hank felt his future might begin at any second.

The rusted steel latch on the gate squealed in protest as Hank stepped from the front yard out to the galvanized mailbox teetering on its post. A tangle of morning glory clung to the box and one curling tendril tried to block his access to the lid, but to no avail—the mail always got through.

Hank threw open the box, and sure enough, a single letter addressed to Mr. Henry Schwain Jr. lay there like a thin white wafer in a hot oven. He had expected the Preflight Kit to be much more substantial. Hank snatched the envelope from the box. Its white paper was almost blinding in the summer sun, so he held it in the shade. His young eyes quickly adjusted as he read the return address:

United States Government
Department of Defense

And so it was that the draft board got to Hank Schwain before Duster Enterprises. Standing beside that empty road with a torn envelope dangling uselessly from one hand and Uncle Sam's greetings held up to questioning eyes with the other, Hank was frozen at a juncture of possibilities. One hopeful route would have led him to buzzing the tops of tall hedgerows and scraping the bottom of drifting summer clouds; the other to a less lofty place—one, that with a war raging in Europe, was far less certain in its outcome.

After reading and re-reading his orders to report for induction in Yakima, Hank had guessed it was a safe bet he could kiss his flying dreams good-bye. But that would have been a bet lost. The arrival of his draft notice that distant morning had interrupted his soaring plans, but it had not robbed him of his opportunity to fly. In fact, eight months after being swept into the service, Corporal H. Schwain had earned his wings, and fly he had—not swooping over lazy summer hedgerows, but gliding helplessly over Normandy's coastlands in the dead of a treacherous night, the pilot of thirteen doomed participants in the silent airborne invasion of Europe.

Chapter 4

Hank's crippling memories always began at the mailbox in Othello where, years before, his destiny as a grandstanding crop duster began to evaporate under the heat of international conflict. The recollection would usually skip the draft notice, the frantic run through boot camp, and his headlong entry into an airborne troop carrier unit. His mind would leap past the sketchy training flights where potato sacks stood in for condemned troops, and would jump directly to 3:45 a.m., June 6, 1944.

He remembered checking his watch on that fateful morning. It was at least an hour before first light and they were finally aloft. Unlike thousands of terrified troops facing the bloody cacophony in Omaha's surf, he had earned the privilege of entering the great liberation on the rush of air beneath a glider's fragile wings.

Hunkered over the stick in the dark of that moonless night, Hank had rejoiced that he was finally *really* flying. The sound of the glider's rippling canvas skin and the craft's softly roaring slipstream rose above the heaving breath of twelve troops huddled behind him in the dark.

Only a few weeks earlier, a request had been issued for volunteer pilots in the Army Air Force's newly formed Troop Carrier Command. Three days later, Hank had stepped from a bus with thirty other anxious candidates at an improvised training facility in the farmlands of Sedalia, Illinois. The scent of manure hung in air alive with the frantic energy of a new military endeavor: glider infantry assault training. Hank soon learned this wouldn't be crop-skimming aerobatics, but it *would* be flying. But sadly, very little flying. With less than a half-dozen short flights above the lush spring pastures of the heartland, Hank was on his way to a nameless, makeshift airfield the Brits had carved from an ancient golf links somewhere along England's southern coast. He would take up temporary residence in a rotten canvas barracks and begin the nerve-wracking wait for Ike's call to action—a single, powerless flight to glory.

The plan was to hop from the old links, out across the black waters of the channel, to the soft welcoming fields of Normandy, and to secretly deliver twelve troops behind the lines of the German coastal defenses. The mission would be flown in the dark and would be stripped of all essentials. There would be no landing lights, no radio, no airstrip, no engine, no prop—and no second chance.

—•—

"Need a refill on that iced tea yet, Sweetheart? Looks like you were mighty dry."

The voice of the waitress in the pale green uniform jolted Hank back to the bright grill room windows. He focused on the woman. She was talking to him, but looking at Rama.

"You said your boy would be along shortly, but you didn't say what a handsome fella he was." She smiled sincerely, then lowered her glasses to the end of a delicate chain in order to have a better look at Rama.

"Have you all been here before?"

Hank and Rama both shook their heads.

The waitress seemed troubled at their response, but quickly snapped back to the task at hand. "Alright," she said. "Your papa had iced tea…what are you drinking, honey?"

Hank sensed a confident spark in the woman. He guessed that she was in her late sixties, but thanks to a commanding, energetic presence and her tasteful makeup, she could easily have passed for her late fifties. Her gray hair looked like fine platinum wire, carefully styled a la Jackie Kennedy.

"I'll have a Coca Cola…please."

Hank groaned, fearing another piss stop down the road to New Mexico.

The waitress didn't acknowledge Rama's order. Hesitating in recognition of something familiar in this boy's manner, something just beyond understanding, she raised her glasses again as if to focus on her order pad, but her eyes returned to Rama's face.

"You haven't been on TV or anything have you, sweetheart?"

Rama shook his head again.

The waitress drew a set of menus from beneath her arm and tossed them on the table, attempting to shake free of the disconcerting feeling. "We've got a Mexican fella cookin' and nobody makes better brisket. Can wrap it in a sandwich for you if you're in a hurry. One dollar fifty and it comes with potato salad and beans. She touched a pencil to her order pad, certain in the effectiveness of her sales pitch.

Hank lowered the racing form and looked across the table at his son. "So what do you feel like eating, Chief? That sandwich sounds pretty good to me."

"Me, too," said Rama. He really didn't care, as long as he got his coke.

Hank smiled up at the woman. "You heard the man, make it two…we'll eat 'em here. Take your time, ma'am, except for my son's drink."

Hank was in no hurry to get back on the road. Not with the locusts swirling up on the plains or with the steel pins in his leg beginning to act up. He straightened out the sore limb and rested his foot on the seat beside Rama, then flipped the racing form back open.

From across the table Rama could see the grainy photographs of horses and the dense tables of numbers. Awfully boring news, he thought, and turned his interest out beyond the bright windows. At the top of a grassy bank, a couple of men were hitting golf balls out onto a range lying just beyond his view. More fun than horses, he thought, as he watched them swing.

Suddenly, a familiar voice booming with disdain drew Rama's attention back inside. It was Boney.

"Okay, which of you sloppy sons of bitches pissed all over the floor?"

Chapter 5

Boney Carlisle strode purposefully toward the three men huddled together at the bar. "It's bad enough you damn duffers can't get the *ball* in the hole." The men hardly looked up from their calculations. This was business as usual with Boney. He was a regular and far-too-familiar member of their weekend foursome; it would take accusations far more serious than inaccuracy in the restroom to rattle them.

Rama felt differently. He was stricken by a strong desire to see for himself what the two golfers on that bank were shooting at. Hank, now fully engrossed in the racing form, only grunted as his son slid from the booth and disappeared into the welcoming afternoon.

Rama ascended the path to what turned out to be Mesquite's practice range, then paused to watch the golfers in action. But the action wouldn't last long; both men had nearly exhausted their supply of balls. Rama recognized one of the golfers: It was the man who had nearly run him down outside the locker room door. Apparently the fellow was content with whatever swing flaw he had come to iron out, for he slung his clubs over his shoulder and plopped a straw cowboy hat on his head. His clubs rattled as he returned to the golf course.

The remaining golfer casually tapped at his basket to coax the last half dozen balls onto the grass at his feet. Rama watched silently as the fellow took a stance over one of his last remaining balls. Something must have been on the man's mind, thought Rama, because a fierce concentration consumed him. It seemed as if he were trying to remember something, the birth date of a distant relative, perhaps—one that he didn't particularly like. The fellow froze over the defiant ball for what seemed like minutes.

Suddenly the man came to life. In a spasm of unnatural motion he drew the club back and threw himself into a vicious assault on the golf ball. The sphere, spanked rudely in its arctic latitudes, buzzed like an indignant hornet out toward a tattered white flag—never rising more than ten feet above the dying turf. The ball never reached the flag, but executed an abrupt course change to the right and dove rapidly for cover in the chapote and poison oak thickets along the range's perimeter.

Rama winced instinctively at the ugly shot but felt a powerful, unwarranted compassion for the golfer. He didn't know the man. He shouldn't have cared, but he absolutely *believed* better shots still lay at the golfer's feet. Inexplicably, goose bumps tingled up his arms. He wanted to help, but he didn't know how, or why.

"Tempo. Tempo. Tempo, you idiot!" the man scolded himself. The fellow could not have been happy with the last shot, but he appeared blasé. He had been through this fruitless drill before.

In fascination, Rama stepped closer.

Another ball was soon in position at the golfer's feet. But somehow, even after a basketful of demoralizing shots, the man was awash in an unlikely flood of confidence. It was as if his preceding fusillade of foozles had been heroic, towering lobs across St. Andrews' Valley of Sin.

With sudden clarity of purpose, the fellow stepped back from the tee and slipped his driver back into the bag. He pulled a persimmon 4-wood. "Why make life difficult?" he whispered. For no apparent reason, the hands that had just strained at the driver's grip now softened on the four, as if they were holding his new daughter. Her tiny face filled his mind. She was only seven months old, born on Christmas Eve—his life's greatest moment. The treasured feeling obscured all thought of swing mechanics as his club went back slowly to the perfect perch above his shoulder. When a natural rhythm urged go, the club fell easily into the elusive, invisible slot that ensures glorious contact. The rich "tock" of a well-struck wooden club ringing above the scruffy range was proof enough of such glory.

Rama didn't understand the mysteries of a proper swing, but he knew good when he saw it. Just as it wasn't necessary to understand baseball to realize that when a shortstop backhands a bullet destined for left field and throws a strike to first base against all forward momentum, you have witnessed a great fielding play. He watched the yellow range ball speed up and away from the uncoiled golfer, rising gracefully, for seconds longer than seemed reasonable, before eventually returning in a puff of dust a few paces ahead of the most distant flag.

"Mother of…what was *that?*" The man gasped as he held his follow-through pose for half a minute. He savored the sensation, like cognac too wonderful to swallow. After hitting another half-dozen similar shots, he stood in mute amazement as the final ball soared to a dusty landing far down-range. He wondered how could it be that so suddenly he had found seven diamonds after years of dull stones?

No one's going to believe this, thought the golfer, as he shoved his 4-wood back into the maw of a leather bag. He resigned to keep this transformation a private miracle, to be sprung with maximum effect on his unsuspecting golfing partners.

Rama, still watching nearby, wondered why the man didn't finish. Perhaps the fellow had found the swing he sought. Perhaps he didn't want to leave on a bad note and dared not risk another shot. Whatever the reason, with three balls still lying on the grass, the golfer turned to go. With renewed lightness, he lifted his bag from a sunburned wooden bench, and as he swung it to his shoulder he noticed he had a witness.

"Hope you saw those last few, kid," he called to Rama. "Timing is everything, and mine's usually way off, but those…whoo-whee! Best damn shots I ever hit. No shit, even *with* these piece-of-crap range balls. What did you think?"

"They looked…" Rama paused, on the spot now. "Pretty," he said recalling that angelic golfer's description of his double eagle years ago.

"Pretty?" The man laughed at Rama's choice of words, but then he thought of his daughter. "Yeah, I suppose they were. But, if you wanted to see some real *pretty* shots, you should have been watchin' that Mexican guy, Lee Trujillo, who just left. Now, *he* hits some beauties. Comes up from El Paso every once in a while just to kick everyone's ass. In fact, he's got a big money match here tomorrow."

The man shoved his arm through the strap of his old leather bag and pulled it tight around his shoulder. He looked straight at Rama. "If you're here to hawk up some free range balls, let me warn you. There's nothing but rattlesnakes and scorpions out there," he said, nodding toward the range. "Don't get too greedy. Then with a chuckle and a clattering of clubs, he walked unknowingly away from the best thing that ever happened to his game.

Rama found himself alone on the range and was about to head back to lunch, when he noticed sunlight twinkling from the grass; someone had forgotten their golf club. Its forged steel shone like chrome on a new Cadillac. When he retrieved the prize, Rama was surprised to find that the club's smooth shaft felt cold, even though it had been left lying in the sun. It was obvious that somebody treasured this club and would regret its loss. He guessed that if he took it back to the grill room, the waitress could find its owner. But before he left the range, Rama found his fingers curling around the lost club's leather grip. It rested comfortably in his uncertain hands. He had held baseball bats and hockey sticks, but no tool had ever felt like this. After a few crude swings he could feel its potential to take a small effort and add to it. When he raised the arc higher and his wrists began to flex in response, addition turned to multiplication.

Rama took a dozen cuts at the savory summer atmosphere, content to produce a satisfying swoosh at a phantom ball. He imagined sending shot after shot far into the sky before he remembered the three balls still lying on the grass. In a few seconds he was balancing one on a cracked rubber tee while his heart pounded in anticipation of his first real golf shot. This would be easy; there was just no way the ball *wasn't* going to explode deep into that prickly range.

But soon other thoughts intruded: How close should the ball be? Should he even be touching this club? Was his father getting anxious? The club answered with lifelessness. Unlike those glorious practice strokes, the club scuffed the ground several inches short of the ball, then skipped up to deliver a diminished blow across the top of the yellow sphere. The golf ball managed to travel about thirty-five earthbound yards, not what Rama had envisioned.

Two balls remained. He had only two more chances; then it was back to a golfless life. He tapped the next ball into place and looked up-range, but instead of the vision of a soaring ball, he could only imagine the poisonous creatures scuffling about the desert floor.

Timing was everything, the previous golfer had said. Rama had assumed he meant the beat of the swing, but maybe he had something larger in mind. As Rama looked up toward the distant flag, the wondrous white form of a whooping crane floated majestically from behind the rusty crags looming over the range and glided on slow, powerful strokes out and beyond a grove of cottonwoods along the creek.

Rama was mesmerized by the regal creature. With its serene passage above the range, so, too, did the noisy thoughts fly from his mind. In the quiet, the club returned to life. On the next swing, its forged steel never touched the ground, nor did Rama remember its impact, yet the faded yellow ball shot up steeply and spent a couple of happy seconds looking down at the Texas countryside before falling reluctantly to earth just shy of the white flag.

—•—

"Almost look like a golfer there, amigo." A voice startled Rama from behind. "Except maybe for those tennie sneakers."

Caught in the act. With the incriminating club dangling from his hand, Rama turned toward the voice. To his surprise, he faced the man in the straw hat again—the fellow the last golfer had called Lee.

"Son of a gun, you're the kid I 'bout bowled over down in the locker room. You're still as red-faced as you were then." The kind, broad smile that flashed at Rama in the doorway of the locker room bloomed again. "Are you feeling okay?"

Rama held the wonderful club out to Lee. "This was just lying here, so I thought…"

"That you'd give it a few whacks. Who wouldn't?" Lee laughed. "Who cares? As long as you didn't take a divot. This concrete they call turf up here could do some damage. I don't suppose that club would happen to be a Walter Hagen 6-iron would it?"

Rama held the club up to have a closer look at the script etched into its toe. "I don't know if it's a nine or a six."

Had it not have been for Rama's honest response, even the affable owner of the club might have mistaken him for a smart-ass. But Lee realized the boy knew nothing of clubs, despite the fact he had just hit a fairly decent shot a third of the way up the range.

"Well, amigo, it's a six. You just hit a pretty good-lookin' shot there. How much you golf?"

"Never."

"Ever?"

"Well I hit another ball just before you got here," Rama said innocently.

"Whoo-whee, that would make two," cried Lee. "You mean you hit the second shot of your life almost one hundred and forty yards—with this *blade*?"

"Is that good?" Rama asked.

"Well, let's just say I'm about to call *Ripley's Believe It Or Not!*"

Lee took the iron from Rama and looked it over carefully to make sure two swings at the hands of a novice hadn't damaged it. He scratched a few grains of sand from the grooves with his fingernail, then motioned for Rama to yield the tee box.

"Fade or draw?" Lee asked. But realizing Rama's inexperience, amended his question: "Right or left... do you want me to turn the ball right or left? And don't think about it too long, I've got a foursome to catch."

"Left," Rama replied.

"Good. That would be a draw...and your name would be?"

"Rama Schwain."

"Now that's not your run-of-the-mill sort of name, huh? Okay, Raja, this one's for you," laughed Lee, and before Rama realized it, the club—now in the hands of a master—was in motion again. Lee's powerful brown arms brought the shiny club through the ball in a graceful, explosive instant.

Rama had seen cartoons in which the fleeing mouse or pursuing cat would elongate to illustrate speed. This yellow bullet appeared to stretch out, Walter Lantz-style, to an impossible velocity in its flight above the hostile range. The ball started on a slight diagonal toward the poison scrub on the right, then arched up and turned obediently left before crashing home within five feet of the bamboo shaft supporting the two-hundred-yard flag.

"Jeez, two paces from the flag...that would work on tour."

Lee seemed surprised at the results of his demonstration shot. He held the club head up for a close inspection: "Purest damn 6-iron I ever hit...and with these crappy balls. I'll be go-to-hell. I'd like to put that shot in a bottle."

Rama was amazed too. He gazed after the ball as if he could still see its slipstream hanging in the air. "Cool" was the only word he uttered.

"Okay, amigo, your turn. Why don't you take another whack at it?" Lee suggested. He reached into his back pocket, produced a new white ball, and tossed it to the ground, then handed the club back to Rama.

"This should fly a lot better than those old range rocks. But you only get one shot, 'cause I'm sure as hell not fetching it back from that damned snake pit. Here, take the club. I'll show you a couple of tips to give this ball a nice long ride."

Rama tried to relax as Lee guided his fingers into a proper grip and his legs into a reasonable stance. He felt awkward in his attempt at recreating the mysterious golfing posture, and guilty at so readily obeying the instructions of a stranger when he should be eating lunch with his father.

"One more thing, Rajah. I know you want to knock the crap out of this poor little ball. Am I right?"

"Mmm…yes sir." There was no doubt about it; Rama wanted to make the dimpled sphere whistle down the range just like he had seen a moment earlier.

"Good, but that doesn't mean you start fast." Lee grasped the club below Rama's anxious hands and guided it straight back from the ball. "Now take it back slow like this here, then turn your shoulders and lift that club up with a nice straight left arm…and keep that blasted right elbow close to your gut." Lee guided the club through a ninety-degree rotation skyward and set Rama's wrists in the proper position.

"Now you're ready to take a serious whack at it," Lee said happily. "But here's what you don't expect, amigo. The knockin'-the-crap-out-of-it part doesn't begin up here with your hands all cocked up."

Lee patted Rama's clenched fingers. "If you think you wanna tear the cover off that little thing, you've gotta start slowly…down here." Lee tapped the side of Rama's left knee. "Get the knees in motion and start turning your hips back toward those flags."

Lee demonstrated the action he was describing. "Now drop your arms into the swing. The club is gonna follow straight down. Once it does, swing the bejeezus out of it at the bottom! Ka-bong," he bellowed. *"Comprende?"*

Rama, still coiled into a frozen backswing smiled awkwardly, thoroughly confused.

"Okay," said Lee, "Lesson's over. I got a tee time comin' up. Crank out a few swings for me, pronto." Lee stepped back and watched Rama unleash several violent lashes at thin air.

Rama felt the difference in delaying the swing while his body turned. The club whooshed mightily. He expected the disturbance to spin little dust devils out into the dry range.

"Damn nice." Lee interrupted Rama's thoughts again. "All right, hit that ball for keeps now or I'll take it back, too."

As comfortable as Rama was becoming with Lee's club, the panic at performing stopped him. "My dad's waiting for me." He held the club out to Lee. "Here…thanks."

"It's only a game, Rasa, but, okay…if you're that shy, I'll just look away—promise—and you can knock the damn thing to kingdom come in private."

Lee turned away. Rama couldn't argue and he dared not delay. He stepped up to the ball and before another thought entered his mind the club started back slowly. Then, as advertised: ka-bong, and the ball was on its way, following a flight path similar to the one Lee had produced except some fifty yards shorter. Instead of bouncing beyond the blue flag as Lee's had done, Rama's first shot with a fresh new ball was snatched out of the air by the frayed white cloth of the 150-yard flag.

Four hundred and fifty feet away, Rama almost pissed his pants…again. He turned with new confidence to Lee for some praise, but the teacher was still looking back down the slope toward the clubhouse as promised. Rama felt foolish that he had been so bashful, and was disappointed that Lee hadn't seen the shot.

"Sir," Rama said humbly, "here's your club back. I hit it good."

Lee turned back around. A grin pushed his cheeks back up toward his bright, smiling eyes. He carefully lifted his club from Rama's happy hands.

"Yeah you did," Lee said. "By the *sound* of it, about one-hundred-fifty yards…maybe with a touch of a draw in it, too."

Lee returned the club to his bag and prepared to leave but stopped when he noticed his pupil's hand was raised.

"I suppose you're looking for a reward?"

"No…no, sir. But are you a pro?"

Lee laughed. "Working on it…Raja. Hope I'll get on the tour one day. But I earn what I can these days in home-grown matches, if you know what I mean."

"Like the one tomorrow?" Rama remembered the words of the man whom he had first watched on the range.

"Well, shit, how'd you know about that?" Lee's bronze cheeks creased as he smiled. "Now I bet you're gonna ask me how much I'll win."

Rama remained silent.

"Well, I sure as hell can't tell you that…depends on the bets." Lee looked curiously at the innocent eleven-year-old. "Why? You know somebody who's a gambler?"

Lee slung his bag to his shoulder and winked at Rama as he returned the straw hat to his head. With his quiver of clubs rattling behind, he hurried down the slope to catch up with his lucky foursome.

As Rama watched Lee go, he wished his father could have seen his last shot. But his pride was quickly trumped by his appetite and the thought of a brisket sandwich and an icy Coke. He trotted down from the range with good news for his father burning within him like his grandmother's ginger beer.

Chapter 6

Rama returned from the range with chimes of accomplishment ringing in his head. He had touched what had always seemed an unapproachable game, and at that touch, something within him stirred. But the chimes yielded to a melancholy not unlike what he had felt when he noticed the rider watching from the ledge earlier.

The sensation of his ball rocketing from Lee's six-iron—a strange, startling blow executed under the discerning ear of a master golfer—had changed him, but as he stepped back into the grill room no one seemed to notice. Boney and his friends were still huddled at the bar. Their voices had quieted under the spell of cold beer and boiled peanuts. His father hadn't moved other than to cast the *Racing News* aside in favor of studying a *Texas Road Atlas*. A lunch platter of Mesquite's signature brisket lay half-eaten beside him.

Rama slid into the booth and attempted to draw his father's attention from the map.

"Dad, guess what…I hit one real *pretty*."

Hank's eyes traced the blue highways, never rising to acknowledge Rama's pronouncement. "Pretty? Hmmm…I suppose that's golfing talk." With his attention still focused on the map, Hank caught the eye of the waitress. He whirled his finger for a reprise of lunch and pointed to Rama.

"So, great, now I've got to keep a golfer fed. I hear you folks are finicky eaters." Hank chuckled and pushed the platter across the table. "Have a taste of this while you wait."

Rama took a small piece of meat and dipped it in the barbecue sauce. The dense, smoky flavor was completely alien, but its richness hinted at wonders awaiting discovery.

"Best I ever had."

Hank laughed at Rama's reaction, sensing its humor. "Well good, you'd better get your fill of this Texas chow 'cause it looks like we might be heading home sooner than expected."

He tapped his hand on the *Racing News*.

"Somebody spilled the beans on our little pony out there in New Mexico… the damn odds fell back to earth. Christ, she could run away with that race now and about all we'd wind up with would be a couple of bucks and old Harry bragging his fat ass off about his three-year-old. Anyway, it ain't worth it to drive out there through all these damn bugs just for a social call with Uncle H, and I'm sure as hell not going there to bet on that horse to *lose*."

Hank searched his son's face for understanding. Rama looked unusually happy; he guessed that was good enough.

The waitress arrived with a platter in one hand and a cold bottle of Coca-Cola in the other. "Aren't you going to finish your lunch?" she scolded Hank. "As slow as you're eating, your boy's liable to beat you to the check. I know he's hungry after hitting balls up there with Lee."

"Lee? You know everybody around here?"

"Everybody knows that Trujillo fella'. Lee…he'll be famous one day," she replied. "Now, didn't I tell you my cook makes the best brisket in Texas?"

"Best I ever had," Rama tried his line one more time, and bashfully raised his green eyes to meet hers.

The tableside chatter stopped abruptly. The waitress froze. As steam from the hot platter curled into the sudden stillness, she felt a disconcerting jolt of recognition. She looked back into Rama's eyes as if a clue to something lost was written on his retinas.

"Now there's a boy who knows what's good…" She set Rama's lunch before him and turned quickly for the kitchen, nearly stumbling over an impossible truth.

— • —

Hank raised his eyes at the waitress's sudden departure, then turned back to Rama. "Like I was saying, since the race is off, we've got a couple of extra days and a few bucks to blow. Maybe go look at the Alamo, or head down to Corpus Christi? What do you think?"

Rama took a hearty tug on the Coca-Cola. The cold soda sizzled in his mouth and provoked an impressive belch.

Hank didn't wait for a more articulate answer. He pushed his plate away and swung his aching left leg around to dismount the confining booth. With the help of his cane he rose to his full six feet, then brushed the crumbs from his shirt.

"Now don't go wanderin' on me, Chief. I'll be back directly. I'm gonna work the kinks out of this damned leg…maybe get some cold bubbly of my own."

Hank left Rama in the booth and limped out to the veranda that overlooked the golf course. The clatter of the grill room yielded to the silence of the course. His vision was drawn into tranquil green spaces meandering out into the rugged landscape, and he forgot the stiffness in his leg. Thoughts of splattered locusts and lucrative bets that might have been faded into the peaceful afternoon.

It wasn't long before the taste of an Old Crow on the rocks called Hank back from the veranda, but as he prepared to test Mesquite Creek's bar, a flash of orange in the distance made him pause.

Beyond the fairway, on a pole above a forgotten wooden hangar, he noticed the tattered orange remnants of a windsock fluttering uselessly. Hank shaded his eyes for a better look at the traces of Mesquite Creek's neglected "aero park." The sight intrigued him, as things aeronautic always had. An icy glass of whiskey vanished from his mind as his thoughts fell—as they often did—back to watching gravity-defying crop dusters barnstorm the fields and windbreaks of his father's spread in Othello. Then, as they often did, the bright memories of flight turned dark…to the dead of night: June 6, 1944.

———•———

It had been fifteen minutes since the C-47 Skytrain had tugged Hank's and two other gliders aloft. He had barely a moment to ponder the line of silver breakers churning below as the Dover coastline quickly disappeared into the blackness of D-eve. Landing would be in another twenty minutes.

Keep the tow at 12 o'clock high. Stay light on the pedals.

Hank had hoped the instructions, drawn in stubs of chalk on a slippery blackboard back in Sedalia, would burn forever into his memory. But as hungry dark waters waited below—extinguished of all navigation lights under war's black hood—he struggled to recall the landing procedures.

Nose up, release tow, nose down, bank left—and then the crucial final step: *Pick out the steeple of St. Claude and commence downwind approach.*

They were words to live by, and Hank knew it. But following the instructions in daylight would have been tricky enough. Gliding to a successful touchdown—let alone surviving this crazy mission against darkness, anti-glider poles, hedgerows, and a swarm of terrified, marginally trained pilots all scrambling to grab the best landing spots—appeared to be more a matter of *chance* than procedure.

Would the steeple, his only reference point to ensure that he wouldn't miss the "safe" landing areas or land directly into the hands of the German troops, be there? That was up to the tow pilot's navigational skills and his own ability to follow a heading pointed out by the green glow of a radium compass. Tonight, in the dark on an ever-descending flight path, all success hinged on that heading and that landmark. Would he see it? Would he remember what to do next?

Those thoughts cycled through his mind even as faint twinkles signaled habitation and the approach of the continent. Several miles ahead, the headlights of a German supply truck flickered as it bumped down a dirt road atop the coastal bluffs, its driver unaware that he traveled on the very brink of history. There would be only a few more peaceful seconds before the C-47 would cut loose its cargo and take the incriminating howl of its engine back to Britain. The release signal from the tow pilot could come at any instant, and when it did, it would be irrefutable.

Then, bingo, there it was: The wings of the plane waggled. It was time.

Hank pulled the stick and sensed the glider's nose rising. He yanked at the release lever and felt the aircraft's frame shudder with the loss of tension as the line fell safely away and the Skytrain disappeared into the night. Now, with the towline intercom disconnected, there could be no farewell salute. No blessing from the tow pilot for a safe landing. No human touch.

Nose down. Left turn. Level out.

Hank squinted at the compass and banked slightly until the heading was as planned. Then he could only follow the flight plan *faithfully* and pray for the steeple to show itself; otherwise, he was absolutely lost. It was a matter of faith indeed: The young men sharing the night sky with him trusted that they would be delivered safely to the war. Hank remembered thinking it funny that somewhere below slept the congregation of St. Claude. For years they had looked to their church for deliverance, and now, slipping silently like a dark bird through their moonless sky, he did, too.

Hank ran through his mental flight plan and the words of his instructor:

On a southern heading with the wind off the channel, pass right of steeple. Look for statue of Mary on the west side. Make thirty-second left turn back up-wind to hay fields east of church. Hold it level. Wait. Flare out and the turf will drag you to a safe stop.

His instructor had turned from the blackboard to face his anxious students and added his own warning: "*And keep your god-damned heads down. There'll be fuckin' Krauts everywhere.*"

Hank peered down from the canopy. A darkened village had materialized from the gloom and was passing beneath the shivering aircraft. For a moment, with his vision fully adjusted and his eyes raised from the stingy instrumentation, Hank suddenly became aware of the true sensation of flight. It wasn't green and bright like he had dreamed, but even in fear, it was a greater feeling than he had ever imagined.

Towering trees foreshortened into menacing dark shapes drifted dangerously by. He could make out the faint pattern of a plowed field draped like corduroy up and over a gentle hill. Almost directly below, a man carrying a lantern cycled along a lane in a pool of amber light. Even as the powerless craft floated overhead, the cyclist never looked up. In that moment, Hank had been aware only of suspension in the silent night sky. He had forgotten gravity and the terrible danger. He knew only the fleeting joy of a dream realized.

Hank almost smiled as he recalled the sensation from the safety of Mesquite Creek's broad veranda. A cocktail awaited back in the grill room, but the remainder of that flight haunted him in its horrible immediacy. He couldn't let it go.

—•—

"Hank, it's at 10 o'clock…about a minute out," whispered Walter Crow from the seat beside him.

The voice of his co-pilot startled Hank from his reverie. They called him "navigator," but after half a dozen rudimentary compass and celestial nav briefings, he didn't know any more about navigation than did Hank. He, too, had jumped at the chance to volunteer for tonight's adventure but, unlike Hank, Old Crow didn't give a shit about flying. All he knew was he sure as hell wasn't *wading* into Europe.

"See it?" he repeated. "The steeple of Saint Clod or whatever they call that damned church. That's it…I think. That should put us near Carentan…our objective."

Hank peered ahead and thanked God out loud. For the first time he could discern the form of a fine Gothic spire to the southeast. Somewhere along its flanks, the stony face of the Holy Mother looked west and across their path. Behind her were the promised fields of Carentan and Hank's best chance at delivering himself, Old Crow, and his terrified cargo to the liberation of Europe in a single breathing piece.

"Shit, I thought we'd be higher," Hank cursed. "Hang on, Crow." Without a precious second's delay he threw the stout glider into a steep left bank and counted out a fifteen-second turn. The sudden bank incited a volley of curses from the troops tucked into the dark reaches of the glider's plywood gut. They had held their breath far too long. Enough was enough!

Forty seconds ahead and maybe two hundred feet below, the Holy Mother and her steeple assumed a ghostly silver form. Hank cringed at their rapid approach. "How'd we get down so fuckin' fast? Crap!"

What Old Crow lacked in navigational skills he made up for in common sense. "Hank, put this thing down quick while you can still get upwind a little."

"Upwind? Christ, Crow. You think I can see a windsock down there?" The steeple was nearly on them.

"Hank, the winds are *always* off the channel. Another 90 north, ASAP!" Crow was nearly shouting now.

"No can do, damn it," Hank barked. "There's too much crap down there." Indeed, the land on the west side of the church where Crow hoped for a landing appeared to be torn for some future construction. They were sinking fast. With the steeple's threatening cross dead ahead and rising, and the wind out of the north, Hank had to gamble. He could take his chances with a dive to the broken ground or try to hold on a few more seconds, then pivot sharply around the spire to get a chance at the soft, survivable hay fields beyond.

Old Crow wasn't a religious man, but suddenly he was signing himself with one hand and bracing himself against the airframe with the other. A prayer played across his taut lips.

Hank had been brave to try for the steeple, and had been a good soldier for trying to stay on the flight plan, or so said his fiancée, Doris, when he returned, broken, to Othello. But Hank always wondered, and questioned even now as he lingered alone on Mesquite Creek's quiet veranda, if a few seconds less entrancement with the thrill of flying would have made the difference. Perhaps he should have landed, regardless of the risks, without hesitation when Crow pleaded. At least Old Crow had seen the end coming and had gotten a prayer in. That was more than could be said for those other poor soldiers.

The last images in his mind before being wakened on the damp grass of St. Claude's graveyard by the searing pain of a shattered leg were the pitted granite face of the Virgin Mary looking sadly up at him from a dozen feet away and the spire's bronze cross flashing like a knife as it severed the left wing and disemboweled the glider. The last sounds he heard were far worse: the uncomprehending gasps of men falling from the sky and the awful thud of flesh through the chapel's slate roof or onto its unforgiving marble crypts. These memories would sound like artillery long after the war had been won.

—•—

A growing thirst muffled the cannon. The tickle of insect legs reminded Hank that he was back in Texas and the tail end of its damned locust plague. He flicked an offender from his arm and raised his foot, but he couldn't bring himself to crush the creature.

Chapter 7

Hank left the wreckage on the veranda and took a place at the grill room bar. With an Old Crow on the rocks and an animated Bavarian beer clock to entertain him, he sipped in silence, only vaguely interested in the friendly disagreement brewing between two members of the foursome seated nearby.

"For Christ's sake, Boney, damned bugs got to count for something. At least a couple of strokes anyway. This is bullshit!" complained the thinner of the two, Mirage Jimson. "You saw it. The little bastards swooped in on the tenth green just as my ball was rolling toward the hole—and *you know* it was a good putt.

"Lousy critters bumped me off my line," Mirage continued. "I shoulda got a do-over right then...especially with six skins on the line. Or at least a stroke credit right now...it's only fair." He slapped a gaunt hand on the bar, bouncing a couple of peanuts to the floor.

Somewhere around puberty, Mirage—they called him Michael back then—had become enamored of the flattop and had developed an aversion to real food. In the fifty or so years since, the malnourished golfer had not reconsidered his hairstyle nor had he gained any more weight, even though he had added several inches to his height.

Mirage was a lot like a creosote bush: No one really knew how he survived. But he did—with piss and vinegar to spare—on a diet of Nesbitt's orange soda, Longhorn jerky, and Abba-zaba taffy. Freckles up and down his arms and across his leathery face had long ago turned into a dense mineral pattern that defied the crippling west Texas sun to raise even a hint of a tumor.

They called him the Mirage, not because he was so ethereal but because his swing, his game, his humor, and his luck—the whole golfy enchilada—could vanish in an instant like a wavy desert apparition. During spells like these it was best to treat him like a molting rattlesnake. The irony was that this skeletal fellow wasn't nicknamed Boney like his rotund golfing nemesis with whom he was vigorously debating the consideration of insects in the rules of golf.

Mirage tipped the bottle back and drained his orange soda with a heaving of his goiter. "And besides, Boney…those bugs were *Outside Agencies*. I know my rules. On the green I can replay the shot if an *OA* interferes while my ball is in motion."

Boney moved confidently into the fray. "Damn it, Mirage. You ever think about eating a pork chop or something? Some decent chow might keep you from getting all worked up like this. Might help your memory, too. You recollect your rules wrong. That'd be Rule 19-1 you're attempting to cite, and it *does* say you can replay your putt if any moving thing messes with your ball on the green. You got that part right, my friend."

Boney Carlisle took a long drag on his Garcia Vega and huffed out a couple of decent smoke rings, pausing to admire them for dramatic effect before moving in for the kill. "But the rule makes an exception for worms and insects. If those critters interfere, you are shit outta luck, or in this case…shit outta money. Those grasshoppers are in fact…" The big man paused to ponder one more drifting ring, "…insects," he proclaimed with finality.

Mirage looked pained over Boney's interpretation of the rules. They and two others had gathered every Saturday morning for fifteen years to take the air, to harangue each other viciously, and to greedily take each other's money. "Just to keep it interesting," they lied.

On this day, on hole number 10, the interest and the greed had escalated geometrically. The winner would pocket six 10-dollar skins grudgingly surrendered by each of his three competitors. That figured to be a $180 payoff at this hole, more than enough incentive for Mirage to question Boney's command of the rules.

"Where did you come up with that crap about worms and bugs?" Mirage protested indignantly. "This is golf damn it, Boney, not biology. Show me the rules or those skins carry over to number eleven, and you know who won that hole." Mirage tapped his chest in triumph. "And believe me…I can use the money."

—•—

Mirage's last word did not escape Hank Schwain. At the mention of money, he lost interest in Bavaria and turned his attention to the debate. While Hank watched furtively, Boney produced a tiny book from his hip pocket and tossed it on the bar.

"Ask and ye shall receive," he proclaimed. "USGA rules…somewhere about page 50 should put this issue to rest."

Mirage and the two equally-less-fortunate members knew Boney well enough to know he wasn't bluffing. He had won that hole, and Mirage's protests were bound to be in vain. No one touched the rules book, but they all reached for their billfolds.

"Okay, you SOB," conceded Mirage with some irritation. "Tally 'em up, Andy."

As a third member—Andy Whistler—huddled back over the scorecard, Mirage settled on his stool and peeled the yellow-and-black-checkered wrapper from an Abbazaba. After some mumbled arithmetic and a muffled curse at his own misfortune, Andy made the following pronouncement: "Boney eleven, Mirage five, Gabe two, and me three...CRAP!" followed by a statement of the damages: "Mirage owes Boney $60, I owe Boney $80 and Mirage $20 while Gabe owes me $20, owes Mirage $30, and owes Boney 90 freaking bucks."

With that, three hundred dollars materialized and, in a green dance of debits and credits, sorted itself out on the bar. "Don't worry, boys, you'll get yours one day," offered Boney in a cryptic toast to his wounded comrades.

Hank watched as the money changed hands. The scene was familiar: the numbers, the winners, and the losers. His gambling antennae had been tickled and he was drawn in. He took his cane, and slightly exaggerating his reliance on it approached the foursome to break the ice.

"Someone got lucky, eh?"

"Hell, it wasn't luck, buddy, these guys are just bad," Boney replied. Boney put his beer down and quickly sized up the crippled stranger. He had noticed the fellow reading the *Racing News* earlier and had pegged him as a hustler, but a golf hustler wouldn't have a bad leg so the fellow was probably a run-of-the-mill gambler. "Yeah, I got a few skins off 'em today, probably give 'em back next time though—you know how it goes."

"Well, not really, never played golf," replied Hank. He tapped his cane. "And probably never will."

"Oh shit, they even got guys with no legs play this game," said Boney. "It hardly matters, the damn game is kind of an equalizer—cripples everybody one way or another. The only good excuse for not playing is that you're just too smart to start."

The rest of Boney's group chuckled; they were more than ready to second that motion.

"Is that a fact? I never been around the game," said Hank honestly. "You fellas had a pretty good pot going there...how do you bet on it?"

"Well, I suppose I shouldn't tell a stranger anything about our little skins game," Boney said seriously. "There's folks around here that don't approve of gambling. You looked pretty involved in that racing rag so I'm laying odds you're not one of them."

Mirage joined the conversation abruptly. "That a war injury?" he asked, glancing at Hank's stiff leg. "You a vet?"

"Yeah, got shot down over Normandy," Hank lied. "D-day."

"Shot down, huh?" said Mirage. "Well, let's get old Boney here to buy a vet a drink...the bastard's got all our money anyway. What's your poison?" Mirage asked without concern for Boney's approval. "Didn't get your name, soldier."

"It's Hank Schwain. Old Crow…on the rocks."

Mirage signaled for Hank's memorial cocktail and beers all around. "Now what brings a fella' out our way in a swarm of god-damned hoppers?"

Hank explained about the trip with Rama, the race out in Ruidoso, and the downturn in the odds he had hoped to exploit. "Might as well make a little vacation out of it now," he concluded. The five men fell into easy conversation about war, weather, insects, and Ike. The duffing ex-president led them back to golf and eventually to gambling, including an explanation of skins, Calcuttas, greenies, presses, and pushes. If there was a new way to gamble, Hank Schwain was eager to learn.

The wagering workshop was progressing nicely until the waitress, who had been tacking purposefully across the grill room, stopped at the bar. "I've got a customer that needs to know if his Daddy can afford dessert," she nodded in the direction of Rama. "Says he is leaning toward the pecan pie."

With the horse race trashed, Hank had a few extra dollars smoldering in his wallet, so he felt generous. "How much?"

"Best seventy-five cents you'll ever spend."

"Make it two…a la mode. While you're at it, put another round for my friends on the tab."

"Now, you see that, Boney?" said Mirage. "There's a generous man. Nobody has to badger him for a drink."

Boney caved easily to Mirage's scolding. "Keep your money, Hank," he said, waving away the vet's offer like a fly. "I've robbed these boys enough today and sure don't need to take any of your vacation money."

Boney stepped from his bar stool and rested both his considerable forearms on the bar alongside Hank. "But, if you really want to put some of that money to work, we've got a little match goin' here tomorrow between me and a Mexican fella'. The guy's pretty damn good for a beaner. You might wanna buy into a little of that action."

Boney motioned outside to two large willows shading the putting green. Their feathery boughs waved sensuously in the south wind. "You see that breeze blowin' up? I got a good chance at making somebody some money tomorrow—probably better odds than that horse was ever gonna give you."

Boney lowered his voice conspiratorially. "See, I'm the underdog, sure enough, but he's young and doesn't know this damn track's quirky greens or how to handle the wind that's always blowin' out here like a curse." He smiled at Hank with the confidence of a salesman who truly believes in his product. "You know what I'm sayin'?"

The entourage at the bar all grunted favorably.

It would have taken a mighty pair of pliers to extract the hook Boney had set in Hank's mouth. Hank knew he was in; he just needed to know how and how much. "Well, what's the game?" he asked coyly. "It might be interesting."

"Match play, eighteen holes," interjected Andy. The statistician in the group eagerly jumped to the task of explaining the Sunday match. "Just two players: They will win, lose, or draw each hole. When either player gets to the point that he is ahead one more than the number of holes left…he is the winner.

"So…" Andy took a polite sip from his beer, "say Boney beats Lee in fourteen holes. There's four holes left and he has to be one up over that so he wins by five over four. We just say he wins five."

"And what about the bets?" asked Hank.

"First thing, everyone tosses in twenty bucks to make a purse; otherwise we'd never get any talent to come out this way. Then there's a pool for the bets. Carla holds the money and keeps the book. Folks figure the number they think their boy will win by, then bet as much as they want per stroke, but we always start at ten bucks. You like Boney in five and bet twenty dollars a point, you just wagered one hundred bucks. At the end of the game—after the winning golfer and Carla take their cuts—the winners split the remainder of the pool based on their portion of the total winning bets placed. The bigger the pool gets, the bigger the payoff, and the closer a guy bets to his golfer's winning score the more he makes."

"It isn't that complicated—about like a football pool," concluded Andy, "but you've got to have a good book to keep it straight. That's what Carla does, and she takes an eighth of the pool for her trouble."

Hank had forgotten about the pain in his leg. "How big does that little pool of yours get?"

"Oh, about seven or eight thousand bucks some matches," Andy said. "You just watch tomorrow morning how much traffic comes rolling down here. Won't be surprised if we get the pot over ten grand on this one. Folks are kind of worked up over this Trujillo kid."

"So much for the non-gambling folks, eh Hank?" observed Boney.

"Guess so," said Hank. "And who is this Carla? She'd be clearing over eight hundred bucks on a pot like that."

"Who's Carla?" Boney asked incredulously. "That's her serving your boy a fine-lookin' slice of pie."

Boney did a double take as he recognized Rama. He choked back the story of losing fifty cents to Hank's son down in the can. That could be dangerous territory to explore with a stranger, especially one teetering on the edge of plunging into tomorrow's pool.

"You mean our *waitress* keeps the book…and all the bets?" asked Hank.

"Well hell, why not?" interjected Mirage, "She's honest as the day is long, and besides…it's her damn golf course."

The concept of this slight, grandmotherly woman being the proprietor of a gambling operation seemed implausible to Hank. He'd have to see that to believe it, but this was Texas and this was golf—two concepts equally alien to him.

"I'd better get back to my boy and that ice cream while I can still eat it with a fork," said Hank. "When are you kicking off this little game tomorrow?"

"Eleven o'clock. Usually like to start a game earlier, but we gotta give those folks time to get over here from church," laughed Boney. "Jesus might save their souls, but he ain't putting anything in their pockets."

Hank planted his cane on the terra-cotta floor and tossed back the remainder of his drink. "Sounds interesting," he said. "Appreciate the whiskey… really do. Can't see as how I'd still be around here tomorrow, though."

Hank gave his new friends a so-long salute and began to walk from the bar, but the line on the hook Boney had set must have pulled taut, for his head jerked back around in mid-stride.

"How many holes you figure you'll take this Lee guy by?"

Boney never hesitated. He held up four thick fingers.

⬥

Rama watched Hank returning for dessert. The Wurlitzer had spun up a Hank Williams record while his father had been speaking with the men at the bar. The country singer's angular voice had cut most of the men's conversation to bits, but Rama had heard the name Lee and the word *dollars*.

"What'd I tell you? Mighty fine chow, eh?" beamed Hank, always glad to see his son happy. He had always worried that Rama was too sensitive for the world's rough edges, but his wife thought differently. She was glad to have a boy tuned to life's wonders and to people's feelings. What Hank saw as wimpy, she perceived as wise. What he perceived as being shy, she saw as being thoughtful. What he saw as silly, she saw as joyful.

Doris had always been impatient with Hank's effort to "harden up" the boy and with his contrived, chest-beating competitions. She guessed the world would temper the boy soon enough in its own way; the tide of testosterone and expectation could not be held back forever. Doris feared her failing health might one day force Rama into Hank's custody sooner than she had ever considered. She had raised Rama with a hearty helping of goodness and could only hope that he was prepared to absorb the type of growing up his father was likely to promote.

"He's our crown jewel, Hank," Doris reminded him just before they pulled from her driveway on the opening day of their trip.

Hank slid back into the booth. His pie awaited.

"Dad, are we really staying here tonight?" Rama asked in excitement. He looked forward to exploring the course. Maybe be would catch some frogs in the creek or hit some more balls up on the range.

"What makes you think we're stayin' here?"

"The waitress said so."

"Did she?" asked Hank. "What else did she say?"

"Just that you were staying for the golf game tomorrow between Lee and that big guy you were talking to," reported Rama.

"What the hell? I never even said I was..." Hank's voice trailed off in wonder. Carla really was an operator.

"She said she has a couple of rooms upstairs all fixed up for visitors," continued Rama, "and I can have the one right under the crow's nest."

Rama reached into his shirt pocket and pulled out a couple of keys attached to a leather tab in the shape of a golf bag. He slid the keys in front of his Dad's pie. "She said to settle up with her later."

"I'll be damned," Hank belched. The Old Crow and the pecan pie were in conflict. Maybe that was why he was feeling odd, or maybe it was his son. Somehow, the boy who had been begging to pee just an hour ago had damn near booked their lodging for the night. Hank recalled what Doris had often said: "Children grow up so fast...we're always a few steps behind."

"And Dad?"

Hank looked across the table at his shining son.

"A guy up on the range said that Lee was really good."

"Good?" asked Hank, remembering Boney's cocky four-finger prediction. "What else did he say?"

"Well, the guy said Lee kicks everyone's a-a...ass around here." Rama stammered as he ventured his first obscenity in his father's presence.

Rama felt himself blushing and turned away as if interested in the deserted range. He pressed his cheek lightly to the window. Beyond the cool glass, a late afternoon sun was patiently burning a soft orange swath across a hazy blue sky. Faint whirlwinds of tiny insects rose then collapsed in frantic dances along Mesquite Creek. Above the putting green, willows waved as new winds drove the last of the locusts north into Oklahoma.

Chapter 8

Dusk settled like fog on the eighteenth green as the day's last golfers completed their cautious dance with par. They lined up their chips and putts, oblivious to the scent of laurel and oleander rising from the thickets along Mesquite Creek and to the presence of a boy prowling its waters for tadpoles.

From his perch by a promising pool, Rama heard the metallic rattle of the pin jabbed exuberantly into the cup and the timbre of happy voices coming from the green. The sound comforted him like the familiar beat of a woman's heart in the ears of her unborn. The hearty laugher of one voice rising above the chatter told Rama that Lee must be among the golfers just finishing their round. From the sound of Lee's voice, Rama guessed, his game must have been good.

As the men vacated the green, the smell of a freshly ignited cigar drifted to Rama's hideaway. The scent of tobacco stirred an image of his mother and her secret vice. Her occasional craving for a late- night cigarette would sometimes betray itself on a current rising from her kitchen porch and up into her son's bedroom window. Rama would lie in bed and drink in the comforting smell of her bad habit. Some nights he couldn't sleep until she had finished her smoke.

Rama's tadpole search led him several hundred yards from the clubhouse. Looking back, he could see its lights glowing amber against the dusk. The gables over what Carla had called her guest rooms jutted westward; the window in one was illuminated. He guessed his father must already be settling in. Along the crest of the roof, the widow's watch loomed forlornly, its forgotten windows lurking behind broken shutters. Their vacant louvers reminded Rama of missing teeth.

With no mother to call him home, and with the evening chill yet to descend, Rama felt as if he could stay out on the course all night. The thought of the dark didn't bother him, but the image of Hank settling back with his whiskey and cola did. Rama began moving reluctantly toward the clubhouse before his absence might disturb his father's cocktail hour.

The wicker chairs up on the veranda creaked as Lee and his companions settled down to review the afternoon's game. Carla appeared at the grill room door with a tray of cold beers, and after satisfying her guests took a bottle for herself and sank onto her own rocker.

Rama made his way back to the clubhouse, and as he neared he noticed Carla dab discreetly at perspiration and exhausted makeup with the edges of her apron before taking her first grateful sip from the frosty bottle. Anticipating a good crowd for tomorrow's match, she had closed the grill room early and was happy to share in the golfer's gathering, even if their discourse was several notches beneath her dignity. She cringed at the filthy jokes and was pleased to find a reason to turn her attention away from the golfers as she noticed her intriguing young guest approach.

"Hope you're not coming round for more of that pie, Sweetheart," she sang out happily, "cause I've shut the kitchen and sent home the help."

Rama felt bashful and exposed, standing at the foot of the stairs before Lee and his buddies. "No ma'am."

"Carla, don't call him Sweetheart for God's sake," mocked Lee as the familiar grin grew across his face. "His name is Bama. He's the kid I told you about, the one that corralled my six-iron. Said he'd never played golf, then goes and whacks it 150 yards. Hell, he could be the world's youngest hustler." Lee winked Rama's way. "Ain't that right, amigo?"

"I don't know, sir." A familiar heat swept his face. "What's a hustler?"

The blush told Lee that Rama could use some support. "Oh, it's a fella who's got some game and takes advantage of those that don't. Like these boys here… they *think* they're hustlers," said Lee, tipping his bottle to his friends. "But hustlers can *really* play."

As his friends groaned in protest, Lee grinned mischievously at Carla. "Don't suppose I could talk you into bringing Rala a soda…on me? I owe him one for finding my club."

"Lee, Rama had pie ala mode just an hour ago, the poor boy's going to have so much sugar in him he'll be up all night." But Carla set down her beer. "Alright, gentlemen, last call. I'm not getting up twice." She stood up to leave, then looked at Lee sternly.

"And Lee, his name is Rama…with an *M*."

Lee looked at Rama still standing at the foot of the stairs. "Come on, grab a seat; there's nothing to be shy about up here."

Carla returned with a full tray and handed Rama a cold glass of Coke on the rocks—far more rocks than Coke, he noticed. Lee lifted his bottle to his companions and to the sunset. "To tomorrow, and to our new friend, Rama… the natural. Hope I got your name right."

With the sky darkening overhead, the group moved on to other matters. They commiserated over blunders, toasted their brilliance, and alternately praised and cursed their luck. They dissected one another's swings and the swings of the gods: Snead, Jones, Hogan, and Nelson. The rockers creaked as the men talked or jumped up to demonstrate footwork or wrist action. Rama was enthralled. He sipped his soda as the men and Carla tugged at their beers. He was part of a ceremony. He had been named, he had received his sacrament, and his presence was contribution enough in this club.

The men drew, cut, punched, faded, lobed, flopped, and feathered shots beautifully about the veranda's nineteenth hole—Mesquite's most receptive of greens. And in their camaraderie they received the real riches of the game: a fellowship more rewarding than score, strokes, or skins.

Eventually the bubbles escaped from the beer and the conversation. Lee rose to his feet. "Sorry fellas, it is adios for me," he announced. "My sister promised to make pozole tonight and I'm not so crazy that I'd miss a bowl of that even if you dudes were buyin' drinks all night."

Lee stopped at the top of the stairs and looked intently up the first fairway. A flurry of cottonwood tufts swirled through the air in the distance. He looked concerned. "You fellas think this wind will hold up tomorrow?"

The group remained silent; in this windy place such a question was pointless.

Lee faced Rama. "I hear you are sticking around for the match tomorrow."

"Yeah. I've never seen golf...well, I saw a double eagle once."

"Sure, and me and Arnie Palmer are drinkin' buddies," laughed Lee. "Double eagle...you say? So who do you think your pop is betting on?"

"I think it depends on the weather."

Lee laughed again. "See, I told you guys he was a hustler. Well, just don't let your pop put down too much *dinero* on old Boney, okay?" Lee's eyes sparkled as he shouldered his bleached leather bag and trotted off across the gravel lot to a dusty Chevrolet pickup.

The full moon peeked over the crags above Mesquite Creek. Carla looked up from collecting beer bottles. For the first time that afternoon she felt tired. "You'd better get moving, Sugar. The stairway up to the guest rooms is outside, just around the corner. You're in number two. Tell your daddy that we open up at 5:30 a.m. for the dew sweepers. The grill will be hot by six.

"Now get along," she instructed. "I'll be turning off the lights in a couple of minutes. We'll leave the course to Carlos and the coyotes."

Rama was seized with interest at the mention of Carlos but was too shy to ask Carla who the fellow might be that would roam a golf course at night in the company of coyotes. He guessed that was his cue. He said as manly a goodnight as a member of the club could muster and headed for the stairs.

—•—

Hank was sitting on the bed, head-down in concentration before a big-band-era radio set. A chaotic stream of sounds stuttered forth as Hank's fingers twirled the dial. Nothing in the rapid-fire sampling of pitchmen, preachers, country twang, Cajun fiddles, and hillbilly DJ's crowding the Texas airways seemed to please Rama's father. When Rama stepped into the room, Hank was cursing the lack of good sports broadcasting and the overabundance of "damned wetback and white trash music."

"Listening for the fights, Dad?" Rama asked.

Hank looked up. "Hey, Chief, I was 'bout ready to come looking for you." Hank looked back at the radio. "Yeah, the fights would be good."

Suddenly he dialed across 1570 and snagged a powerful signal from Mexico, a transmission that staggered him like a left hook. A tortured voice and a gut-bucket blues recording burst from the radio on the crest of 100,000-watt radio waves. The music slapped him directly in the ears and grabbed him by the throat. From that moment, a crazy DJ who called himself the Wolfman held Hank, Rama, and a far-flung legion of listeners agape with every gravely word. In ranches, roadhouses, shacks, shops, bordellos, and deep in Mesquite Creek's arroyo, the Wolfman's listeners lingered spellbound as he cued up rare and raunchy records beneath a full moon.

The irresistible opening licks of "Hootchie Coochie Man" leapt from the old radio's generous speaker.

"Jesus, I don't think there's any boxing tonight," Hank said, pausing to take in the primal music. "Muddy Waters…hell of a name, eh?"

"I kind of like it," Rama said.

"Yeah? Well pull up a chair, Chief, and we can go a few rounds of rummy with Muddy and the Wolfman before bed." He rapped a fresh deck of cards on the table as Rama took a seat.

Rama was fond of cards. He and his father shared their most congenial moments when engaged in card games the way other fathers and sons shared baseball or football as a neutral ground. On equal terms with the rules and the draw of the deck, he and Hank could be themselves…or forget themselves. Doris Schwain, though reticent at the direction cards might take her son, tolerated their games: "As long as you don't make the boy play for money."

"To fifty points?" asked Hank.

"How about a hundred?" replied Rama. "Penny a point?"

Hank recalled Doris's admonition, and winked yes.

As the moon climbed above Mesquite Creek, Hank and Rama played to the accompaniment of an R&B soundtrack conjured from a cinderblock studio perched above the Rio Grande. Thirty miles from Mesquite Creek, Lee Trujillo pulled the Chevy truck into his sister's drive. Soon he and his nephew, Donaldo, would settle at the kitchen table and savor the sounds of XERF and generous bowls of rich pork pozole.

—•—

Time passed quickly at the Schwain card table. After successfully outplaying his father, Rama felt sufficiently emboldened to ask his dad if he were really planning to bet on Boney like he'd said at lunch.

"Yeah, makes sense to me from what I've heard." Hank lowered his cards and stretched his bad leg away from the table. "Why you asking, Chief?"

"I don't want you to lose, Dad," Rama said, careful not to patronize his father. "Lee's gonna win…he can make his golf ball go wherever he wants it. I saw him do it." In the air above the card table, Rama scribed the trajectory of Lee's high, cutting fade.

Hank folded his hand. "That so? That skinny fella in the bar told me the same thing about Boney," replied Hank. "Now, how in hell are you gonna know who to believe?"

Hank yawned and checked the tally. "Damn, you waxed me tonight, Chief." He fished three quarters from his pocket. "By seventy-five points."

Rama stood up to head for his room, but Hank stopped him. "The shitter in your room is on the fritz, so if you need to go you can use mine. I'll leave my door unlocked."

With his dad's words and a Hank Ballard instrumental ringing in his ears, Rama grabbed the key and wished his father good-night. Alone in his room, he could still hear Hank's muffled radio. He could still make out the rustle of the evening breeze through the great cottonwoods, and the croaking courtship of some nocturnal amphibians. High above it all, the rusty squeal of the piper weathervane sounded a lonely counterpoint to the evening's music. Rama hoped the sound wouldn't keep him awake, but before he could even think about sleep he had to patrol his room. He looked under the bed and through all the drawers. He found a half-finished love letter in the Gideon's Bible, but best of all he discovered the kind of mystery a boy with a vivid imagination might hope for—a hidden door in the back wall of his closet.

The door was irresistibly intriguing: a secret passage to some creepy room up in the widow's watch. He pushed aside the empty coat hangers and examined the door; it had no knob, just a tarnished lock. The impression of lettering long ago removed left a shadow on the door's painted surface; the phantom letters read: Crow's Nest.

Rama's heart leapt; this was about as close to a *Hardy Boys* adventure as he was ever likely to get. He put his comb between the door and the jamb, but the door was locked securely—not even a wiggle. Reluctantly he abandoned the notion of exploring the dark mystery up the hidden stairs. Maybe tomorrow.

Once in bed, the shadows of cottonwood waving across the wall overcame thoughts of the Crow's Nest. Rama could not resist the hypnotic motion and was soon asleep, but the hypnosis wasn't powerful enough to overcome the urgings of his bladder. Carla was right; he'd had too much soda. Somewhere near the witching hour, Rama was wide awake and contemplating a trip to the bathroom. He tiptoed down the hall and paused at his father's door. The sound of snoring confirmed Hank was asleep. Rama grasped the doorknob cautiously to avoid waking him, but the door was locked. His dad had forgotten him… again. Rama headed outside.

The moon streamed brightly across the deserted fairways as Rama stealthily worked his way down the stairs and out into the shadows. He was ready to return to bed in a flash but was attracted by silver moonlight twinkling off the little metal flags on the putting green. Even though he was alone out on Carla's grounds, Rama felt remarkably at ease—at home, as if now that the night had shooed away all the players, the golf course existed for his amusement. He moved silently to the green; its fine, clipped turf felt cool under his bare feet. For a moment Rama lingered in the stillness, and as he did he became aware of two facts: that the three balls he had scavenged from the creek that afternoon still lay in his pocket, and that he heard the sound of hooves somewhere out in the darkness.

Rama held his breath and turned his ear toward the darkened course. Soon there was no doubt. A horse was slowly approaching up the path along the creek.

Chapter 9

Rama stood transfixed. He should make a run for the stairs, get back to bed where he belonged, but all thoughts of fleeing vanished when the horse emerged from the shadows. Rama froze. A shiver raced through him as he realized the horse carried a rider. His fingers clenched in apprehension.

The bright moonlight revealed a thin figure sitting high in the saddle. Even in the soft light, Rama could see that the rider, although wrinkled with age, carried himself with dignity. He wore a turquoise satin shirt and black leather trousers with silver studs. A thick braid of white hair fell from beneath a flat-brimmed hat; the braid glowed platinum in the lunar light. Rama recalled photos of cowboys from Argentina in a *National Geographic*. The rider looked like one of them—a gaucho. A ghostly gaucho. And he looked familiar, like the rider Rama had seen on the ledge that afternoon, or somewhere before.

Rama wished he weren't standing so prominently—so exposed—on the green, but it didn't matter now. The horseman had seen him long before; in fact, the old gaucho had imagined this encounter years ago. The ghostly figure reined the horse to rest beside the green, then, to Rama's amazement, addressed him in a warm, familiar voice.

"Dickey Stone, is that you?" The gaucho's wrinkled brown hands touched the points of the cross across his chest.

Rama was speechless except for a no strangled deep in his throat. He was at a loss for any further response and tried to act with indifference in hopes of avoiding trouble for trespassing in this strange horseman's world. Rama pulled the trio of balls from his pocket and dropped them to the green as a diversion.

"I was gonna practice a few putts…for tomorrow," he lied as casually as his nerve would allow.

Moonlight glinted from a golden tooth as the gaucho smiled. "Then shall you not need a club, sir?"

The rider reached down along the flanks of his mount and, to Rama's surprise, pulled a putter from his rifle scabbard. With a flourish, he presented the club to the bewildered boy. Rama stood frozen, uncertain. This moment seemed like a dream, yet the putter hovered before him. He hesitated, then drew it politely from the rider's hand.

"It is true then, you are not a ghost," smiled the gaucho. He exhaled as if he had held his breath for imponderable years, then offered an explanation: "You appear, sir, just as did Dickey Stone…upon this very green, in bare feet on nights just as this."

The gaucho seemed lost in recollection. "He was of your age, sir…and would putt at any hour."

Rama considered the putter now in his possession and replied timidly. "I thought *you* were a ghost," still not certain that the old horseman wasn't.

The ghost gaucho laughed warmly at Rama's point of view. "It is true, sometimes I feel as a spirit," he laughed. "But Carlos is flesh and bone—old flesh and bone." The horseman dismounted with agility belying his age and tossed his ends of the reins into a desert rose bush beside the green. He turned to Rama and introduced himself formally: "I am Carlos Taddio. I seek not to frighten you, sir."

Rama shuffled awkwardly. If not scared, he was certainly uncomfortable. "I'm Rama…but who is Dickey?"

The old gaucho looked at Rama intently…curiously. "Dickey *was* Chandler Stone's son." He offered no more explanation, as if he had said enough.

"Will you not try thee club?"

Rama relaxed at the invitation and lined up a putt to the nearest flag, but nervously snubbed the putter's face into the green. Carlos regarded the shaky stroke with little concern. He paused to roll a cigarette.

"I shall speak to calm you, sir," said the gaucho. "Chandler was my patron. He saved me—your servant, Carlos—from a life with thee cattle.

"Many seasons ago Chandler came from thee highlands—from Dornoch— to bring thee golf. Thee Yankees wished him to teach its secrets and to fashion their links. It was so that my patron loved thee game far more than thee flocks or thee fishes of his homeland, and he chose thee game for his life. And as did your Juan thee Apple Seed, Chandler grew golf upon thee land…upon thee land, sir. Together we fashioned this course."

The old gaucho bowed slightly in deference to Rama's attention span. "I speak too freely. Please…you may wish to try thee club again, no? Do not fear, thee briar is strong."

Rama tightened his grip on the wooden shaft and made a few airborne putting strokes under the watchful eyes of Carlos, then obliged the old fellow by sending a trio of balls skidding silently across the putting surface to within inches of the tiny flag.

"Ha. And a touch like Dickey's as well." Carlos crossed himself.

Rama collected the balls to try again but grew uncomfortable in the silence. He asked Carlos to continue his story. The music in the strange voice made him feel welcome. Carlos obliged.

"Chandler settled upon Mesquite Creek after meeting Señora Carla at a festival of thee golf in Fort Worth. At that time, these were her papa's lands and I bossed thee cattle. But our Holy Father took him, yet soon smiled upon Chandler and Carla in holy matrimony. They built this place," Carlos bowed at the memory, "with Carlos Taddio's humble assistance, sir."

Carlos drew on his cigarette thoughtfully, lost in his story. "Their children, Dickey and his twin, Glendora, were born even as thee greens were in seed."

Rama idly tapped the three golf balls as he listened to Carlos. The clipped grass under his bare feet felt lively; he realized he might never sleep that night.

"So why is Dickey a ghost?"

Carlos crossed himself once more. "Thee lightning," Carlos sighed, "took Dickey and Glendora on thee green of number sixteen. Our Heavenly Father's will."

The old man turned his face away for a moment. "Yet they were in my care on that day…" His voice trailed off with an old and tragic memory. "Thee children do not yet rest…not with their father, Chandler, still wandering."

Carlos turned his attention from the moonlit fairways and looked into Rama's green eyes. "Tonight you come upon thee green, after thee locusts as I have dreamed it…to startle Carlos with your spirit."

The old gaucho touched the back of Rama's left hand, still clenched on the putter's grip. "Yet, you hold thee club too tightly to be only a vapor."

Rama watched, entranced, as the sure old fingers touched him for confirmation. He noticed traces of bright color—oil paint, he thought—clinging to the old man's fingernails.

The old horseman grabbed the reins back from the rose and steadied himself to mount Niña. "Thee putter which you strangle, she must serve me at tonight's labors upon thee course. Carlos would be pleased of your company."

Carlos Taddio rose into the saddle and clicked his tongue. Niña started for the course, leaving Rama on the green with his head spinning. The implication that he—Rama Schwain—was a spirit was creepy, but cool in a "Twilight Zone" sort of way, probably just the musings of a crazy old man. What Rama didn't know, and what Carlos hadn't revealed, was that these musings were only a small part of Mesquite Creek's sad history.

The loss of their children had been too much for the Stones to bear. Chandler's spirit had collapsed and Carla, grieving and embittered, had embraced a more avaricious approach to golf than Chandler ever would have approved. She had placed bookmaking and liquor sales over her devotion to the game and over her attention to the land her father had once ranched. Carlos was left burdened with a leaden cloak of guilt for the children's death, and in his anguish could not resist Carla's blame nor guide her back to the pure spirit of the ancient game as her husband would have wished. Carlos realized he had become dispensable on the very course that he had constructed. In time he faded from its sunny fairways, seeking sanctuary in a camp carved deep in Mesquite's wildest barranca. He remained an invisible partner to Carla—a ghostly groundskeeper who refused to let Chandler's beloved Mesquite Creek, or the memory of the Stone family's happy days, wither away.

On summer nights such as this, Carlos Taddio patrolled the course on his horse, Niña, to nurture the turf under the forgiving cover of darkness. With a coiled hose, a putter and a hole drill slung from his saddle, Carlos would ride through the dark course like a conquistador. Tonight, before Lee and Boney's match, he would secretly scramble the pin placements and fuss with the greens' speed as he had hundreds of times before.

—•—

As Rama watched Carlos and Niña recede into the night, he considered the pros and cons of sleep versus whatever it was that he might do to assist the old gaucho. Charged with curiosity and a rising sense of adventure, he grabbed the trio of balls from the green and fell in behind Niña on a strange parade into the balmy night. At first he trailed by about a chip shot, but as they left the clubhouse behind, a pack of coyotes began an insane song just beyond the range of his moonlit vision. In an instant he closed the gap.

Carlos stopped at the first green and quickly put Rama to work. He directed his helper to attach the hose to a spigot hidden behind a boulder and deploy a sprinkler on the low side of the green. "We shall soften number one, so to lower thee players' guard tomorrow."

The trio continued along the silvery golf course. Rama dropped one of the balls to the turf and began putting it along, being sure to keep pace with Niña. Before they arrived at the next green, he was shepherding all three balls and hardly noticed when Carlos dismounted.

"Gather thee balls, my friend." Carlos had already grabbed the hole drill and a bucket from Niña's pack and walked to the center of the sloping green. "We shall not quench her tonight. Is been four days now and she shall be as granite. Tomorrow thee balls must be played below thee hole or no putts shall find thee cup. Carlos shall be stingy with this green."

Rama joined Carlos on the putting surface. The old gaucho took the balls from his hand and dropped them in a line, each about six feet apart. "Now sir, please...a soft putt for each down thee slope."

"But the hole is above us," Rama observed correctly.

"Si, and it shall soon be below." Carlos stood where he wished Rama to aim his putts. "Now, please, sir. Aim for my boots."

Rama tapped each ball as he had been told; they settled into a triangle near the low side of the green about three feet to the right of Carlos. "Aha, and that," Carlos announced gesturing toward the three balls, "is where thee pin is *not* to go."

Carlos pulled his pocketknife and dropped it into the turf between his boots. He fetched his bucket and drill and plunged the auger's tip into a spot about one foot closer to the triangle from his knife. "Carlos shall give them a foot of grace." He worked the auger until he had extracted a core of sandy Texas turf and had placed it in his bucket. In a moment the old hole had received the new plug and the new hole had received the cup. The morning's golfers would be surprised to find less than nine feet between the flag and the fringe. Carlos carefully trimmed the edges of the new hole with a pocketknife and rose with a popping of his knee joints.

"A struggle…but she is fair," declared Carlos with a grin.

Rama had no understanding of the grace of which Carlos had spoken, and he didn't care; the night was already full of mystery. Rama grabbed the bucket and followed Carlos, tethered closely by fascination with the stately old greens keeper.

The procession roamed from fairway to fairway, green to green, Carlos making some holes "curl up like a soft kitten" and others "tear at your throat like thee mountain lion." Under Carlos's scrutiny, Rama drilled holes, feathered bunkers, repaired pitch marks, relocated tee markers, and stroked test putts for his mentor into the dead of night. Eventually Carlos glanced at the height of the moon, then back to the course. "Si, I think thee lady will break many hearts tomorrow. What do you think, Dickey?" he asked, turning to Rama.

Rama was suddenly too uncomfortable to answer.

Carlos's face flashed with alarm, aware of his slip. "Please excuse me, sir…Señor Rama," he said formally. "Come, we shall skip to number sixteen, through thee barranca, and then shall be done."

The old fellow returned to his agreeable mount and swung up easily into her saddle. He patted her back and reached out to help his young helper aboard. "Take my hand, for you ride with Carlos Taddio now." Carlos cleared the stirrups for Rama's feet. "You shall not walk through thee barranca, for thee vipers shall be at your bare feet."

Niña found her footing along a narrow trail leading down through stands of prickly pear and saber plants. Carlos pulled a hand-rolled cigarillo from his shirt pocket and struck a match with his thumbnail. Without a word he handed the smoke over his shoulder to Rama, who paused in uncertainty before taking a shallow puff. Rama formed a question as an intoxicating dizziness and the herb's scent nearly derailed his train of thought. He imagined his mother at home alone and wondered whether she bothered to hide her cigarettes when no one was around?

"Mister Taddio, do you ever get scared down here…all alone?"

"Thee puma, thee scorpion, thee whirlwind, thee flood, thee falling tree—what is on earth I do not fear," replied Carlos, his courageous words floating on a cloud of blue smoke.

The riders rocked back slightly in the saddle as Niña began climbing the incline from the bottom of the barranca toward the dark silhouette of a butte rearing against the starry sky.

"But what is above...that troubles me, sir."

Niña emerged from the barranca at the fringe of the sixteenth fairway. To their right the butte rose about fifty feet. Rama could see a set of stone stairs leading up along its jagged outcroppings like a castle. Carlos helped Rama from the stirrups. As Niña busied herself with tuffs of grass along the fringe they lingered motionless in consideration of the steps leading toward the sky. Carlos slowly drew a lungful of smoke into his chest and listened to the evening. Niña, winded from her climb, breathed deeply as quail rustled clumsily in the brush and coyote's crazy laughter still confused unfortunate prey somewhere in the darkness. "Is a thing of beauty this night, no?" asked Carlos. "But from thee butte she is even more." He started up the crooked stairs.

The summit had been leveled into a fine flat plateau, which served as the farthest teeing ground for the sixteenth fairway. "Thee man's tee, my friend," Carlos observed. "Below...you see thee fairway under thee moon? She runs down and away to thee south 530 meters. With thee wind she can be reached in two blows...I have seen Chandler Stone do it so."

Rama strained against the gloom to gauge the enormity of the reach to the green, but illuminated by moonlight, the goal was too dim at that distance. He turned to the east and could see a few ranch lights twinkling across miles of lonely rangeland. To the north a ridge of low hills molded the horizon into soft, dark curves against the night sky.

"Where is Mr. Stone now, Mr. Taddio?"

Carlos took a short tug on the cigarillo and paused. "Perhaps with thee angels...is not known. Perhaps only lost. I should wish Chandler thee angels."

Rama noticed a smile cross the gaucho's face and a sparkle of moonlight glint from the corner of his dark eyes. Carlos smiled, not at Rama but at the constellations above as he continued speaking. "And if thee Holy Father is of good heart, it should be that Chandler walks thee links of Dornoch with Dickey and Glendora, even as we stand upon thee place of thee night lessons."

Carlos reached into his shoulder bag and withdrew a coffee can with a tin lid. "We have but little work here," he said and handed the can to Rama. "Please sir, cast these seeds upon thee bald places." With that instruction, Carlos disappeared over the edge of the tee box and down behind a fractured boulder. Alone for a moment, Rama heard a distant train whistle's song of industry on air currents sweeping up Mesquite Creek from the south. Then Carlos was back, scuffling up the rocky slope to the tee box with the aid of a golf club he used like a walking stick.

"You found a club!" exclaimed Rama. "Out here?"

"No, Carlos hid this club, sir, that there might be another *night lesson.*"

Carlos could see the confusion on Rama's face. "Let me explain, sir. On many bright nights as this, my patron, Chandler, and thee twins would come to this place for practice. Chandler said thee game was best played like thee puma—by instinct. And to teach these arts, Chandler's lessons were given in thee night.

"They would come to this place—God rest them—thee children with a sack of old balls and Chandler with this very club." Carlos held the persimmon club before him, searching for the moon's reflection in the finish of the old wooden head. "I am surprised to find her this night...it has been eleven years since I last returned to this blessed place."

Carlos waggled the old club a few times just above the grass. Rama could see the rusted shaft and weather-beaten head whipping to and fro. "Thee grip, she is dry like a relic," Carlos observed, "but she is lively still."

Carlos rubbed at the rusty shaft and looked at the rouge upon his thumb. "She is a brassie and was far too much for thee children's arms, but Chandler helped them *feel* for thee secret in thee swing.

"He spoke of magicians who could strike thee ball with perfection with clubs taller than a man, or with shafts of hemp or rubber. It was no matter once thee golfer had thee feel...thee understanding."

Carlos laughed out loud at the image of the Stone twins' awkward, ambitious swings with the brassie. "Upon this tee, Chandler taught thee children to play in such a way. It is thee feel that brings joy, and from joy thee game shall follow. These were Chandler's words: *Joy cuts thee waters of doubt like a prow, and fine rounds shall sweep behind as a wake.*

"It was his greatest gift...his night lesson." Carlos passed the club over to Rama, then cupped another flame against the wind to re-ignite a cold smoke.

"Ah, thee twins would swing that club into thee night, as Chandler had decreed, just for pleasure of thee striking. From thee grass, from cigarillo stubs, even upon thee backs of beetles did they tee their balls. Thee joy...it was Chandler's gift, and Dickey happily received it. And like a sacrament, he could pass thee spirit to others. It was so that even as a boy, Dickey became thee greatest caddie of Mesquite's links."

Carlos watched with interest as Rama absent-mindedly waggled the club. "From Dickey Stone thee gift she flowed like water. For his lucky player, thee impossible game was made possible. My patron, Chandler, would say his boy had thee powers to ease thee patience of players in a puzzling game on an angry environment." Carlos laughed softly. "Thee Gift promised joy and accomplishment in an endeavor designed to yield neither. And with no such magic, thee golf would yet consist of fools knocking stones into rabbit holes."

Rama's waggling morphed into a set of fully formed swings. Carlos sensed divine intervention; how could such a swing be guided by anything but the

Gift? It could not be luck or circumstance. Luck has no such sway in the mechanics of golf; its capricious benefits are confined to the bounce, the rub of the green. This was more. He vowed silently to linger on the Rosary before retiring that night.

Carlos considered the loss of the Gift. The spell conjured from the chime of ringing sweet spots, the startling bliss of green-side chip-ins, the gasp at improbable putts, the aroma of mown fairways, and the flask shared on a homeward hole had, with Dickey's death, left Mesquite Creek.

Could it be now, thought Carlos, that Rama harbored the Gift, the power to transform expectations into sparkling reality? He might never have doubted had he witnessed one extraordinary putting performance a month earlier at the Kings Kreek Miniature Golf Course near Rama's home in Memphis.

The carny who worked the booth at the King's course had become skeptical after members of Rama Schwain's foursome had returned eight times in the first dozen holes, each time to claim a ticket for having earned a hole-in-one. When Rama arrived at the booth for the ninth time, the carny was certain he smelled a rat and refused to award another ticket.

"Cheatin' little shits, we'll see about that," the swarthy fellow grumbled through a cheek of chew while leading Rama's pals to number fourteen, the barn-door hole. "Wasn't born yesterday for Christ sakes. Okay fellers, drop them balls down on the rubber…and you each take a putt through the barn while I'm watchin'. You make one, and you got another damn ticket. You miss…then you'll be givin' all them other tickets back or I'll whip the shit out of the lot of you."

The carny's threat hung in the air as he stepped back to judge Rama and his friends' efforts. The boys stepped to the rubber…after four strokes, the final ball lay upon the three previous balls nestled impossibly in the cup.

A voice interrupted Carlos's deliberations. "Did Mr. Stone play, too?"

Carlos recalled the night lessons with a smoky smile. "Like his children, Chandler, too, was happy to strike thee balls into thee night, even when blind to their landing."

"And Mrs. Stone?" Rama tried to picture the whole family who made a home at Mesquite Creek.

"No sir, but she would raise Hades at thee many lost balls. Carla is still thee tigress with money, no?" Carlos laughed heartily at the thought. "Chandler would give a nickel for each ball thee twins did find, and they did find many." He remembered smoking and sharing a cup of maté or a flask of Scotch whisky with Chandler on the tee while the children raced to shag what balls they could find. Even now their laughter rang up from the darkened fairways into the old gaucho's ears.

"But many balls did soar forever into thee chaparral beyond searching." Carlos's voice lowered at the conclusion of his tale. "Some nights Carlos shall still find thee old balls glaring upon him from thee fairway. How can this be? Perhaps thee ravens pluck them from thee chaparral and drop them...to remind Carlos of his sin."

Carlos tossed his cigarillo to the ground and crushed it dead beneath an ancient snakeskin boot. "Thee devils," he hissed.

With the night lessons club in hand, Rama remembered the shiny 6-iron he'd swung earlier that day. This club felt loose and spring-like by comparison and made a particularly satisfying sound as it parted the night air. The feel of the old brassie, together with the image of the Stone family happily launching balls into the night, fueled a desire to send his own shot down the moonlit fairway.

"Would it be all right if I tried to hit one?" he asked tentatively. "I'll be careful with the club."

"Of course, thee club was hidden upon this butte for this night, sir. It has awaited you. You have three balls with you still, no? Please, let Carlos tee one for you."

Rama reached into his back pocket and handed one of the balls to Carlos. The old man bent down and formed the discarded cigarillo into a tee that supported the ball a half-inch above the turf. "Do not worry of thee club, sir," said Carlos. "You will make her sing...I have heard it already. She is happy in your hands again." Carlos stepped back to watch, unaware of Rama's inexperience but prophetic at his potential.

Rama practiced the motions Lee had shown him that afternoon: parallel to the ground, then slowly raising it to a more vertical plane. He remembered tempo, and he heard Niña whinny anxiously from below the butte, a reminder that this moment could not last forever.

Rama imagined the spirits of Dickey and Glendora, lingering for years to race after this ball and collect their nickel.

Maybe it was the herbs in Carlos's cigarillo, but as Rama commenced to take the real swing, the breakers on his circuits of volition suddenly tripped off and the image of Lee's powerful swing took command. Like a spectator Rama watched the brassie start back, and he felt the swing coil impossibly around and above his shoulders. He noticed the crisp elliptical shadow the ball cast on the moonlit turf.

⌐•⌐

Ten miles beyond the horizon and two hours into the Lubbock run, an engineer on the Gulf-Colorado & Santa Fe pulled on the air horn lanyard to announce his approach to the Coleman, Texas, siding. The banshee in his horns screamed in jagged sound waves that pierced the Texas night. The train's thundering locomotives pounded at the rails as it roared westward. Jackrabbits cowering nervously in the desert panicked at the great machine's approach, darting foolishly from their cactus sanctuaries in crazy retreat.

But on the promontory tee at Mesquite Creek, far from the mighty engines, the air horn's shriek had mellowed to a sonorous longing note that arrived just as the persimmon face of Rama Schwain's brassie collided explosively with the ball perched atop its cigarillo tee.

Rama watched the ball rocket quickly into invisibility while the train whistle provided a perfect fading accompaniment. In the silence that followed, he listened for the voices of children.

Chapter 10

"Was worth thee wait, no?" The happy voice of Carlos Taddio filled the air after the train's whistle had died away. "Come, we have work below," he said, and turned to follow the steps down to Niña.

Rama still held the brassie. He thought he should return the old club to its hiding place, but the idea of disappearing into those broken boulders at night while his only companion in this foreign place was heading down the steps didn't appeal to him. Rama quickly descended from the heights.

Rama, Carlos, and Niña ambled along the sixteenth fairway for five hundred yards, then began to climb a hill upon which the green was perched. The upslope hid the putting surface from view; even in daylight a golfer could see only the top of the flag. It was, Rama would soon learn, a diabolical design.

The furtive green was kidney shaped, curving from right to left around a mound upon which a single yellow oak tree lorded over the green. The oak provided the only aiming point for a golfer attempting a blind approach from below, but should the shot stray left, the oak became an unforgiving obstacle.

As Rama began the climb up from the center of the fairway, the tree loomed large and forbidding. Niña and Carlos had taken a less-direct route up the hill along the fringe some distance away. Rama felt uneasy alone on the fairway. His fingers tightened on Chandler's club, and he hurried to reach the tree. As he waited for Carlos to catch up, Rama surveyed the odd green below. A rock outcropping rose ten feet above the putting surface—a dark, formidable hazard.

Rama yawned. His interests drifted to thoughts of a warm bed, when in a sleepy trance his eyes traced the outline of the rocks. Suddenly, a surge of adrenalin sent an icy shock through his body as the silhouette of a great cat—a puma—appeared on the outcropping. An ancient fear spurred his heart to a gallop and triggered an explosion of goose bumps down his frozen limbs.

The cat crouched on the rocks not more than forty feet across the green. Rama thought to call for Carlos, but his mouth was paralyzed. Instinctively, he raised the club in defense. His toes clung to the turf for better footing, and he waited for the cat to make the next move.

The predator regarded Rama with a feline logic that was incomprehensible but ultimately sensible. Is the prey too large? Does it have weapons? Is it alone? Am I hungry enough?

Rama was ageless before the cat. He could not know it, but being judged as a force—not as a boy, or a man, or the bashful child of a broken marriage— gave him new strengths, and what felt like fear at first was really an equation for living.

The cat turned its head imperceptibly, just enough for its eyes to catch a spark of moonlight. The puma watched for a sign of weakness but saw the menacing club rise. Then, in a signal of retreat, its green eyes blinked sleepily. A prairie dog or a juvenile boar seemed like better prey.

Rama saw the green eyes twinkle once, then close, and watched in relief as the silhouette climbed unhurried from the rocks and circled around the green to the farthest point below. Then, like a ball too eagerly struck, the cat slid over the edge and disappeared into the chaparral.

A folksong from the Pampas hummed from Carlos's lips as he arrived at the oak tree. He laid his tools on the shaggy grass beside Rama, then produced a dented Thermos bottle and filled its cup with warm maté. He held the offer- ing to Rama.

"You look cold, sir," Carlos said. A feather of steam drifted from the cup.

Rama was unaware that he was shivering. His instincts had returned to stand-by, but not without leaving their physiological effects. "Uh huh," he re- plied shakily, too drained to speak of the puma. The strange earthy flavor of the hot drink and the old gaucho's serenity comforted him beyond words. Rama sipped in gratitude.

"Thee maté shall not let you dream tonight, but nor shall you fall from Niña in sleep as we ride, sir." Carlos laughed softly and patted Rama on the shoulder as if the boy had just returned from a walk-off grand slam. A gold tooth gleamed from the gaucho's mouth. Rama sipped in silence. Soon their attention was back on the night's work.

"Is a great one, this green," declared Carlos. "She shall not give up her strokes easily." He pointed out the points of an imaginary compass spread upon the green below them. "Thee oak guards thee south, rocks protect thee north, west falls to thee barranca, and east gives only a false harbor.

"Is hard to land upon her, and tonight we make it harder." Carlos picked up his tools and walked in a curve that followed the perimeter of the green, downhill to the west and to the very spot where the puma had disappeared. As he neared the far end of the green, Carlos put down the bucket and drilled a new hole. After extracting the plug he walked back up the steep narrow section that joined the upper and lower surfaces. He directed Rama to place the cup and its flagstick in the new hole down below.

With the flag set in its new position, Rama stood at the bottom of the green with his back turned to the dark shadows of the barranca; the flag's yellow fabric hung limply above his shoulder. He tried to imagine the impossible line a putt would have to scribe to find its way down to this hole, but the thought of the cat somewhere behind him sent him quickly back up the green to Carlos.

"Mr. Taddio, this one is too hard unless you putt from the bottom."

"You learn well, sir," laughed the old man. "Si, who would try for such a hole without first a chip to thee bottom? Thee putt from above is impossible, no? So, too, Chandler believed." Carlos smiled at an old memory. "We fought like cocks over this one. Chandler said to test thee golfer here, but your servant Carlos begged for grace. So it was, we agreed to make it a puzzle."

Carlos lowered his voice, as if someone might overhear his secret. "There is a key to thee hole with thee flag as is now." The old gaucho grabbed the putter and told Rama to drop a ball on the fringe just below the oak.

"Now...behold." With the tree at his back, the flag sixty feet to his left, and the hole at least twelve feet below, Carlos tapped the ball directly and most improbably across the green toward the rocks.

"You see, sir? A stroke aimed with faith at thee highest rock will turn left and roll to thee narrows as if guided by thee Holy Father."

Rama watched as the ball followed Carlos's commands faithfully. "Now she shall lose her steam and make one lazy turn toward thee barranca...watch how she seeks thee cup."

And so she did: Carlos's impossible putt nearly stalled twice on its foolish charge toward the rocks and its plunge downhill, but ended up less than two feet from the hole.

Carlos pointed back up the fairway. "But, sir, our puzzle starts beyond...in thee shot before finding thee green. She must lay in perfection upon thee fairway for thee golfer to find a line to thee green without meeting thee branches above. That is thee key...yet thee secret is in thee rocks, for as you have seen, they shepherd thee ball to thee hole."

"Now sir, drop your last ball and try."

Rama did as suggested. When the putt had come to rest, it lay less than three feet from the hole.

"Chandler did his finest work here," said Carlos, collecting his tools. "Go gather thee balls please, sir."

The two companions climbed to the top of the mound beneath the oak. Carlos lit another cigarillo, then murmured a Hail Mary and crossed himself with a smoky hand. Rama noticed the gesture and recalled Carlos had mentioned that the twins had died somewhere on the sixteenth hole.

"Where did...?"

Carlos's hand was already raised to silence the inquiry.

"Is here, upon this high spot that your servant, Carlos, stood. Thee children were rolling many balls as we just practiced, sir, and had gone below to fetch them. A few had swept into thee barranca and a few into thee hole." The old man smiled at the thought of the balls falling into the cup, but his face collapsed as he was swept back into the terrible memory.

"I watch from above, and I hold thee flag and thee drill as tonight. Thee air is wild and lively with storm. I feel power in thee air. Thee children begin to climb, yet I tell them to stay below, there are many dangers above. I fear of thee lightning. Thee children they wait for me on thee fringe."

Carlos pulled on his smoke, then spoke through a cloud billowing from his mouth. "A cannon seems to fire beside me…everything is blue, and Carlos is thrown to thee grass. I have gone to thee angels perhaps, but my brain clears quickly. Thee children? I hear nothing."

Carlos's voice rose in anguish. "Why was Carlos not prey for thee lightning? It was I upon thee hill. I held thee steel shaft!"

—•—

Compassion washed away the adrenalin still coursing through Rama's heart after the puma encounter. His father's misfortune and its lingering damage entered his mind as Carlos's sad voice rose again.

"I turn to thee green and thee children are upon thee turf. Thee balls are scattered, some smoking. I stumble to reach Glendora, but she is with thee angels already. Her red hair is an ash, her feet are black, and like thee golf balls they, too, smoke. Dickey thrashes like a…" Carlos paused to compose himself, "…and his servant Carlos tries to hold him, but thee boy's fight is only mechanical. He, too, is gone."

Carlos turned to Rama as if the boy already knew the story. "Forgive me, *por favor*?" The gaucho looked back across the moonlit green, the oak casting a faint shadow on the turf. "You see, then, why thee ravens will not let Carlos rest? They remind me: I placed thee children in thee path of thee bolt. I brought them into thee sights of thee sniper."

"No, Mister Taddio!"

Rama's voice rung loud and with unexpected authority, like the precocious stroke on the sixteenth. His spirit cut Carlos's damning proclamation short. He spoke as if to console a faithful old friend.

"It wasn't your fault! You held the steel shaft like a lightning rod…you were in danger but you never dropped the club. You tried to protect them. How could it be your fault—doesn't lightning just go where it wants?" Moonlight illuminated the question in Rama's face.

"It was just bad luck. Luck can go either way, that's what my dad says. He knows. He crashed in the war and only he lived. My mom says there's a reason he is alive, and it turned out to be me. I bet there's a reason for you, too."

Rama's thoughts turned from his parents' simple logic, and he recalled the welcoming face and the warm words of Father Rulon, the portly minister who sometimes came to visit Doris on weeks when she was too ill to attend church. Reverend Rulon wore his hair in short white bangs and to Rama looked for all the world like Captain Kangaroo. But the holy man carried an authority beyond the Captain's—and knowledge beyond Mister Green Jeans'. This captain dealt in "holy mysteries," and Rama was always intrigued by a mystery. He had overheard many of their conversations, and it always seemed that forgiveness was a prominent subject. Rama never fathomed why God should care about people's crimes, but as he felt the crippling guilt in Carlos's story he was moved to pluck a leaf from Father Rulon's book:

"You are forgiven."

The words escaped into the night, as unlikely a statement from his young lips as a hole-in-one from his brassie. But like the mystery Rulon promised, these simple words were a manifestation of the Gift's power to strengthen a person, whether swinging a club or facing a sorrow. Indeed, they worked magic in the heart of Carlos Taddio. The evening's chill had begun to penetrate the old gaucho's wiry frame, but the words, uttered by one whom he had imagined to be Dickey's ghost only sixteen fairways ago, warmed him like liquor.

Carlos looked into Rama Schwain's eyes, but the boy looked away, embarrassed at his bold outburst. It was hard to square up any karmic equation that placed death behind such innocent green eyes, but Carlos felt as if the son of Chandler Stone had returned from the grave to comfort the spirit of a faithful, forgotten servant.

It was as he had dreamed one night in his shack, hidden deep in the barranca. In the eerie light of that vision he had seen the children—Dickey and Glendora—waiting his arrival on the sixteenth green. Dickey had spoken of returning one day in the heart of a good, young man. "You will know the time…when the locust swarms, and you will know the person when you sense the Gift. Bring him into a game on the site of our passing, and we will fly to our eternal peace."

Softly, the old gaucho began to pray:

My children that linger restless in death,
if thee lightning was but for thee grace of thee Holy Father,
and if Carlos be forgiven, then grant him this purpose:
that he shall labor to secure your rest before he finds his own.

It was a true holy mystery. Rama felt it now as the sorrow that had shrouded Carlos since he had spoken of the twins' fates lifted. The magic in the old man's voice shamed the slick shazam of every sideshow trickster or TV preacher Rama had ever seen. The old gaucho turned from his prayer and looked down from where he and Rama shared their maté. On the green below—on Chandler's best work—he imagined the children again. The cascades of Glendora's red curls were restored from ash, and the bright young girl stooped to help her drowsy brother up from his long sleep.

An ember dropped from Carlos's frozen cigarillo. The twins craned their necks to find their old friend sitting below the familiar oak. Happy smiles sparkled from eternally young faces as the Stone children skipped from the green and down into the moonlit expanse of that long, wondrous fairway.

Niña whinnied to call it a night.

The old gaucho puffed futilely at his cigarillo. Rama noticed the fellow's skin wrinkle with the effort, and he spotted the trace of a tear. Carlos Taddio scratched another match. "Sir, thee night is heavy with understanding." He grabbed his tools and nodded his head toward Niña waiting restlessly below the mound.

"Come, sir, let us leave thee remaining greens as they lay for tomorrow's contest."

Bouncing along to the rhythm of Carlos's reliable mount, the two friends made their way back toward the clubhouse. The light in Rama's window still burned bright. Luckily, his father's room was dark.

At the edge of the shadows surrounding the clubhouse, Carlos tapped Niña to a halt. He did not dismount, but helped Rama drop to the ground. The old man reached into his saddlebag and extracted a small brass object. Carlos spoke before Rama's inevitable question.

"You have asked about Chandler. Thee crow's nest can tell more than thee words of Carlos," he said, holding a bright brass key at arm's length.

"But return thee key to Carla with Carlos Taddio's salute before you continue your journey, sir."

Something—perhaps the odd formality of Carlos's words—made Rama feel lonely. He recalled the same feeling when he had said good-bye to his mother as she boarded a train for her first brief trip away from a young and troubled family.

"I'll see you in the morning, huh?" asked Rama expectantly.

"You shall know how our work tonight plays upon thee golfers in tomorrow's match, si," answered Carlos evasively. He smiled broadly, and Rama could see the glint of gold once again. Carlos extended his arm. "Thee ravens shall find no more balls for Carlos." He touched his forefinger to his eyebrow in farewell and gathered the reins.

Rama stood on the stone where he had dismounted. He held the old persimmon brassie tightly as he watched Carlos turn Niña's head back to the dark course and disappear.

Rama walked into the feeble light from the clubhouse as if returning from a dream.

Chapter 11

"**D**rop your cock and grab a sock!" Hank's familiar admonition penetrated to the depth of Rama's dreams. Since tip-toeing back to bed on grass-stained feet, the remainder of Rama's night had passed quickly. Neither Carlos's maté or the screeching weathervane had prevented him from falling into a deep slumber, but now, as his father bellowed the hallowed army wake-up call, he was instantly awake.

Excitement set in quickly. This morning's match between Boney and Lee, and the promise of his father's payday loomed ahead. And so, too, did the prospect of retracing his steps across Mesquite's enchanted course in daylight.

"Okay, Dad...I'm up," he lied. "Be there in a minute."

"Hurry on down, Chief," his father commanded, "I could eat the ass end out of a buffalo." The comforting smell of coffee brewed for the dew sweepers rose from the grill room.

Rama heard the hiccup in his father's gait as the hungry veteran limped down the hall toward breakfast. Rama pulled on a fresh shirt and slipped into the same jeans he had been wearing for four days. He poked his bare feet into a pair of sneakers and shot down the stairs, forgetting to brush his teeth and to pick up the brass key lying on the bedside table.

As sunlight torched the cliffs above Mesquite Creek, Rama rounded the corner of the clubhouse and found Carla Stone out on the veranda, savoring the final puffs of a morning smoke. She didn't notice him; her attention was focused up the bright first fairway and on the tracks of two golfers etched in the morning dew. As she gazed into the distance, she idly stubbed her cigarette into a coffee can.

Rama froze in fear of disturbing her meditation, but before he could back away, he saw her tuck the pack of menthols into her apron pocket and then, to his amazement, extract a small revolver. Peering over her glasses, Carla inspected the pistol carefully. She opened the cylinder and inserted several cartridges, then tucked the gun away. After brushing a few errant cigarette ashes from the railing she disappeared back into the kitchen.

Rama had often gathered with pals to watch TV westerns on his neighbor's new Muntz. Until now, he had been disappointed to discover that here, in the Wild West, folks didn't actually carry six-guns. Apparently Carla was an exception. But the thought of her toting a pistol proved more alarming than intriguing. He imagined that along with the wagering on her matches that had so attracted his father came certain dangers. He was right. Carla was determined that anyone expecting to steal a slice of her pie would have to tangle with her Smith and Wesson.

Because her bookmaking was illegal, these matches were officially only "friendly competitions" played for mere bragging rights. Carla knew she could not count on protection from the Rangers unless their money was on the line.

Rama followed the scent of frying bacon into the grill room. At this early hour, only four other customers shared the sunny room with Hank: a foursome of college-age Arnold Palmer aspirants anxious to squeeze in a round before Carla cleared the course for the Boney-Lee match. The group happily tore through their huevos rancheros while chatting with excitement about the beatings they were going to inflict upon one another. It looked like fun, but Rama was more amused guessing what Carlos's pin placements would do to their scores. He smiled with a trace of cynicism beyond his years.

In a moment Carla burst back into the room, working her arms into a stylish business jacket as she walked. She stopped briefly at the Schwain's table, still tugging the last wrinkles from the sleeves. "Well good morning, Sweet Pea, how's your appetite? I hope Carlos didn't keep you up," she joked.

"Well, he did sort of..."

Carla wasn't listening, and she wasn't taking orders, either. "Your daddy here said something about the wrong end of a buffalo," she reported with a laugh. "I bet you're hungry, too."

She picked Hank's menu from the table and handed it to Rama. "I've got to get to the office," she smiled. "The new girl will get your order in a sec."

Carla disappeared through a Dutch door beside the bar. In a moment the top half of the door swung open, revealing a set of bars like a teller's cage. Behind the bars, Carla fussed with the tools of an impromptu bookmaking office. Rama wondered where the gun was hidden.

"Never heard you use the pisser last night, Chief." Hank's voice startled Rama from thoughts of Carla's firepower. Hank reached across the table and mussed his son's hair. "I heard that damned weathervane, though."

"You were sleeping, Dad...you locked me out. I went out on the..."

"Oh, Christ...sorry Chief." Hank turned his eyes from Rama's and plunged into a dog-eared copy of *Life* magazine. From its cover, Ben Hogan waved through a storm of ticker tape at a throng of jubilant New Yorkers. Rama sat at the table in silence.

In a minute Hank lowered the magazine and slid it across the table to his son. "Here's something to read while you wait. No funnies, though...guess they can't get the Sunday paper this far out in the sticks! Check out this Hogan fella; they call him the Hawk. Arrogant bastard sounds like a barrel of laughs," Hank chuckled facetiously.

Rama smiled along. His father appeared happier than he had since Doris's health had declined. It had always seemed as if his dad felt responsible for her condition. But she had never held Hank accountable for her health, even though it was obvious she would not suffer his bad habits. It was a testament to her regard for Rama's and his father's relationship that she had approved this trip. Rama knew how uncomfortable she was with his father's gambling, but on this fine morning with the happy anticipation of a payday and a good sunny walk ahead, the habit didn't look so bad. Better still, he thought, with what he had learned on the course last night, he might even improve his father's fortunes.

Rama bubbled with inside information 'til he burst: "Dad, most of the holes are in new places now. That'll be better for Lee."

Hank looked up from his *Life*. "New? What do you mean *new*? What'd they do, dig new holes…overnight?"

"Well they don't dig them, they drill them." Rama was fearful of mentioning Carlos and last night's experience, but he wanted to help his father win, for once. "The new holes are in places that are gonna be hard to hit. And I bet Boney won't know them."

Hank Schwain looked at his son with increasing interest. "New holes, huh? Wouldn't you bet the holes will be just as hard for that Mexican fella, too?"

"Yeah, Dad," Rama agreed, "but that's why it'll help Lee *win*."

Hank looked at Rama curiously.

"Because Boney won't know the putts," explained Rama, "and Lee is better everywhere else. That's what I heard."

Hank sipped at his coffee and pondered his son's logic. The thin, shaggy-headed boy before him looked a little sleepier than usual. Hank wondered if Doris would approve of her boy's appearance. He pondered the wisdom in Rama's advice, and he thought of her words. She had once advised him that you are always a step behind your children…when you think you have a fix on their position, they have already moved on. Now he realized the truth in her insight.

"Hmm, sounds reasonable," Hank replied. "So you're still rooting for your beaner fella', eh?"

Rama nodded.

———•———

Carla emerged from her cage with a ledger book and a cookie tin, and took command of the grill room.

"Alright boys, sorry to make you wait." The college kids looked up from their table, but Carla was addressing only the Schwain "boys." With a snap of her fingers a shy young woman joined Carla at Hank's table. "Marcilla here's gonna take your order. Things will start getting busy here pretty quick—too busy for yours truly. She'll take up the slack. Order away…the hot cakes are real good this morning."

After Hank and Rama had ordered and Marcilla had slipped back into the kitchen, Carla pulled up a chair and got down to business. She opened the ledger to a clean sheet and popped the lid off the cookie tin; it was full of poker chips.

"Now, you don't think I put you up last night for nothing," she laughed. "Let me tell you how our book works for this match, and you can tell me how much you want to *invest*."

With pencil and paper, Carla covered the same ground that Andy had plowed yesterday afternoon in the bar. "This is match play, Mr. Schwain, so we don't care about strokes, just whether a player wins or loses the hole. One of these fellas wins the match when he gets ahead by one more than the number of holes left. For example: If he's ahead by three with two holes left he wins— we say—by three, and that's what you bet on. You place chips on the number of points your fella wins. I got ten-, twenty-, fifty-, and hundred-dollar chips.

"If he wins, you get all your chips paid back plus a percentage of the pot. Your percent depends on how many chips you bought per point. Of course, you're gambling by buying more chips: if your fellow loses you've lost it all, but if he wins…"

Carla glanced up from her diagrams and smiled at Hank. "Well, it can add up, Honey! You can place a bet now or you can wait till eleven and see how the pot is building; I'll chalk it up on a board by the cage." She looked at Hank with anticipation. "Of course, the sooner I get some numbers on that board the better…it's like priming the pump. What's your poison?"

"Well ma'am," said Hank diplomatically, "this is all new to me. But I don't think I can make a *financial* decision on an empty stomach. I'll tell you this much," Hank turned toward Rama and winked, "I'm leaning toward Lee, just ain't come up with a number yet."

Carla gathered up her ledger and snapped the lid back on the cookie tin. She rose with a perfunctory "suit yourself," clearly unhappy to leave left empty-handed. Although pleased at his dad's conversion to Lee, Rama felt a pang of compassion as Carla walked away with her ledger and her chips. He recalled Carlos saying that after Carla lost her children she had turned her back on the spirit of the game in favor of its earning power. Rama wondered if Carlos had spared Carla the terrible details of the lightning's aftermath, and tried to imagine if she still suffered.

Hank and Rama ate breakfast with few words. Rama ignored the *Life* magazine but absorbed himself instead in the "Pro Secrets" section of an old golf magazine. Like millions before him, he was quickly confounded by its impenetrable instructions. The swing, frozen in still photos and cold type, proved to be an impossible concept when explanations of less-than-intuitive actions were described with less-than-precise phrases, like: releasing the hands, on the plane, opening the stance, over the top, outside in, holding off, shutting the face, cupping the wrists, and chicken winging. Nowhere in the article was there a mention of feel or faith, the essential attributes of a good golfer that Carlos had said Chandler Stone so embraced.

Before long, the college boys had finished breakfast and were happily haranguing one another as they clattered out to the tee on noisy spikes like crabs. The room soon filled with hungry golf fans, the pleasant sound of silverware on china, and laughing breakfast chatter. Rama was content in the company of his father and the clamor of the busy room.

Hank noticed that the chalk numbers on Carla's board had begun to grow, and he felt his pulse quicken. He put an end to breakfast by pulling a large roll of bills from his jacket and peeling off enough for the meal and a little something for Marcilla.

"Well, Chief, I know you want to get out there...so scoot. I'll catch up to you when they start. Got some business now." Hank tucked a couple of dollar bills in Rama's shirt pocket. "Don't spend it all on pop," he said, patting his boy on the shoulder. Rama started for the door and the morning sun while his father made his way to the bar where a few of Boney's friends had returned to their stools like swallows.

—•—

Mirage and Andy welcomed their new golf fan back to the lighted liquor-bottle ambiance of their morning refuge. Mirage snapped to attention and offered Hank a tipsy salute.

"Good day, sir! You done the right thing by sticking around for this little get-together. Boney's got some game in him today, though, I'll tell ya. Drove up just now and damned if he didn't head straight for the range—never seen that before."

Mirage's skeletal face beamed with confidence below his flat top. "He'll be swingin' like Sneed today...oily. Our amigo from El Paso will be lucky to get past twelve holes."

"Christ, you fellas got some lingo." Hank seemed just as baffled by the game's odd terms as was Rama. "What the hell is *oily*?" he asked.

"Yeah, forgot you're a virgin," laughed Mirage. "It's the smooooth motion... the tempo, the way Slammin' Sammy describes it when he's swingin' real good. And believe me, soldier, Sam swings the best."

Andy Whistler quickly reeled off a statistical short list of Sam Snead's entire professional record like a human ticker tape.

"Damn. You got room for anything other than numbers in that noggin of yours, my friend?" Hank asked playfully. Although Hank laughed, he was truly impressed. He understood the value of statistics when it came to wagering. If it weren't for stats, thought Hank, he'd probably be throwing good money after a losing cause at the fairgrounds in Ruidoso right about now.

"What stats you got on Boney?" asked Hank.

Andy coughed up a USGA handicap, high-school tournament records, junior amateur record, and a murky semi-professional earnings number.

"And Lee?"

"Nothing," replied Andy. "He's flyin' below the radar screen so far. Probably knocking around as a loner. Could be a hustler. Got no tournament experience."

"No, and the son-of-a-bitch isn't on the premises yet either!" Carla cursed as she strode into the room. Her strident voice cut short any further statistical reports from Andy. "Any of you fellas seen Trujillo lately?" She didn't wait for an answer. "I've got one hour until tee time and thirty minutes to close up this book, and I've only got one golfer. There will be hell to pay if I've got to scrub this match."

Carla knew she'd lose an eighth of a pot that was already closing in on seven thousand dollars. But worse, she'd lose a reputation for running a good event, and in this sparsely populated country, that reputation was crucial. She was well aware that the owners of those cars and trucks crowding her lot had come a long, dusty way in faith that she would deliver a good match. No match just wouldn't cut it.

"If you see Trujillo's Mexican ass before me," she glared, "tell him to get it on over to my *office*." Carla gestured toward her cage and hurried away.

The men watched Carla storm off. Hank was impressed with the transformation from grandmother to grand dame. He instinctively respected her regard for her customers, but his companions at the bar were not equally moved; they had seen the metamorphosis before and they knew that she was ultimately only interested in her cut.

Andy watched her go. "Hell, she's lucky she got half this crowd. She's got competition today. I heard that the final round of the US Open out in New York got bumped 'til today by bad weather. It'll be the first Sunday round ever. I don't think she figured on going head-to-head with the fucking US Open."

Mirage softened the tip of a fresh Abba-zaba in his beer. "It wouldn't of made any difference, Open or no Open—not this year. This crowd here's all Texans," he said. "They were lookin' for Hogan to kick some ass again and he ain't even in the top ten. Who do they have out there at Winged Foot: Casper, Harmon, Rosburg, and Souchak? Christ, who cares about those hacks? Mesquite Creek folks would rather be here rooting for Trujillo and Carlisle."

Mirage looked at Hank warily. "By the way, flyboy—if you don't mind me asking—what are you putting down on our boy Boney?"

Hank sensed he might be stumbling into a faux pas and spoke judiciously: "Well, I have a beginner's hunch about Lee...no offense or anything, but I think it just might be his day."

"Oh Christ, man," Mirage blurted in disgust.

Like any good poker player, Hank projected confidence in his hand. But he wondered if his son's story about the new hole locations was accurate or if it really would make a difference. He preferred to believe Rama over Andy and his arcane numbers, reasoning that Andy's numbers reported the past while Rama's information somehow predicted the future. That was where he was putting his faith.

"A fool and his moolah," sighed Andy. He got up from his place at the bar and slipped a quarter into the jukebox. The cloying strings of Nashville's most bored violinists soon sounded the opening notes of a three-song Jim Reeves set. But before he had returned to his seat, the needle mysteriously skipped across Andy's beloved songs. The jukebox's mechanical disk jockey whirred wildly as it snatched his selection from the queue and replaced it with something more spirited.

"God damned gremlins," Andy swore, as "Ghost Riders In the Sky" took the Wurlitzer's stage.

"Gremlins, hell," Mirage mumbled through a wad of taffy. "It's damned Carlos again."

—•—

As the song faded, the voices of Hank, Mirage, and Andy joined the amplified crackle of the record's inner grooves. For a moment all was peaceful, but suddenly, as if Frankie Laine's fan club had taken command of the jukebox, the Wurlitzer roared back into the "Ghost Riders" opening hook for an unexpected reprise. Another two-and-a-half minutes later, the song's intro started again.

In a flash, Hank Schwain pivoted from his stool and lunged at the juke box with his cane. Several raps against the offending machine put the music to silence.

"Sorry, fellas. Two damned devil's herds across an endless sky is enough for me. Yippie ki-yay my ass."

The robot DJ in the Wurlitzer shuffled its vinyl deck and, as if nothing had happened, resumed the Jim Reeves violin intro right where it left off five minutes earlier.

Chapter 12

The activity around Mesquite Creek that Sunday morning reminded Rama of a school carnival. Folks flitted in and out of the clubhouse to place their bets and to satisfy their morning thirst. The crowd, already gathering at the first tee, buzzed in anticipation of the match and in the failure of one player to show his usually beaming face. A question as to the whereabouts of Lee Trujillo raced through the gallery like a virus.

Boney Carlisle's presence was never in doubt. In fact, the massive golfer's attire—black checkered sweater, red plaid knickers, and a sporty green tam-o'-shanter—left him unavoidably visible, a blinding visibility that turned the evolution of sophisticated golf attire back several notches toward The Three Stooges. Boney may have looked like a clown, but he frowned like Pagliacci at the absence of his competitor.

The question was soon answered in a plume of dust roiling behind an old Chevrolet pickup careening down the driveway's treacherous hairpins. The truck jerked to a halt and Lee Trujillo, accompanied by his sister's teenage son, Donaldo, climbed slowly from the cab. It was clear to Boney and the gallery that something was wrong. Lee attempted to smile as he crunched feebly across the gravel lot.

"We still have time yet, no?" Lee asked of the crowd milling about the veranda. Lee's usual cheek-to-cheek grin faltered; no cheerful buenos dias escaped his lips. He looked drained and apologetic for his uncharacteristic torpor. His nephew looked even worse. Donaldo's complexion shifted through shades of green as the young fellow struggled under the weight of Lee's bag.

Carla walked deliberately to the top step of the veranda and considered her subjects below. "God damn, Lee," she scolded, "how do you think you're going to make the big time if you can't even make a tee time. You're flirting with a DQ, you know." Carla couldn't show it, but she was happy to see the dusty young golfer; scrubbing the match would have been a costly disaster.

Lee was preparing to explain the reasons for his tardiness when Donaldo let the golf bag clatter to the ground and dashed to the far side of the old truck.

The sound of energetic non-productive vomiting was explanation enough: The duo was hopelessly ill.

Lee asked for a glass of water. Carla—grandmotherly for the moment—took him inside the grill room and drew a tall glass of club soda from the bar.

"Sorry, it's not my style to be late," apologized Lee. He was sweating and much of the bronze had flowed from his skin. He brushed the cold glass across his forehead and took a deep, painful breath as he prepared to tell Carla about tangling with a bad bowl of his sister's pozole, but the thought of food poisoning and the image of the pork belly in the orange broth nearly made him gag.

Instead, Lee exhaled deeply and squeaked, "I'm god-awful sorry."

Carla fetched half a dozen packets of Bromo-Seltzer from a display by the cash register and ordered Marcilla to soak some towels in cold water. She was not granting sick leave today. "You got plenty of water in your bag?"

Lee nodded. There would be plenty of water, but he grimaced at the thought of his nephew burdened with any extra weight.

"So be it, Lee. Freshen up and put up a good fight. I'll give you thirty minutes before your tee time…you know I can't call this thing off," said Carla. "I hate to see you like this, but if you don't put on a good show that crowd is going to demand their money back. That could get ugly." She patted Lee on the shoulder. "Damn it. I was hoping to see that clown take a whipping…of course, I am professionally impartial."

"Thanks," said Lee wiping down his face with a towel. "I'll see what I can do." He puffed up his best competitive face for the people outside and charged through the door to rescue poor Donaldo from his disgrace.

———•———

Hank had been nursing a cold beer back in the bar when the stricken golfer entered the grill room with Carla. He didn't like what he saw. It had always been his habit to place his bets at the last moment, and here was a good reason why. No matter what Rama had said about Boney losing his advantage with the difficult hole locations or Lee's familiarity with the wind, Lee's unexpected illness trumped any edge he may have had over his competitor. Now it was Boney's match, Hank guessed, by at least three holes.

Carla returned to her office and checked the lock on the safe. She unconsciously touched the pistol in her pocket and turned to close up her books when Hank stepped up to the cage.

She sighed and looked at her watch. "It took you this long to figure a number? What'll it be, I'm closing up right now."

"I'm takin' Boney in three holes. Five hundred dollars."

Fifteen hundred dollars was a substantial bet for her patrons, but Carla didn't flinch. She took the cash, marked the ledger, and handed Hank the chips. "Good luck," she said, "but it doesn't look like Boney is going to need much of that to win this one. Don't go crowing to anyone about making your wager so late; a lot of folks out there won't be too happy about getting locked into a bet on a lame horse."

Hank nodded, smug in his good fortune. He returned to the bar for a final morning beer and savored the calm that, like a junkie's rush, followed the placing of a bet. Hank always enjoyed the waiting. He reckoned that with the money already gone, there was nothing left to lose and everything to gain.

———•—•———

From his vantage on the veranda, Rama was also optimistic. He didn't understand the finances involved in the betting pool, but was confident that, even under the weather, Lee was the superior golfer. His father would still have his payday. Rama guessed happily that the extra money would be good for a few milkshakes along the road home and maybe a motel with a pool and those "magic fingers."

Rama recognized Boney's voice as it rung out above the crowd in a volley of dirty jokes. Clearly this fellow knew how to stay loose. Rama remembered how easily Boney had offered up a bet on a simple toss to the wastebasket. He had said he was always up for a game and apparently that was no exaggeration.

Lee, on the other hand, was keeping disturbingly quiet for the effusive character Rama had met under yesterday's healthier circumstances. The stricken golfer occupied a corner of the putting green in the shade of the willows and worked deliberately on a shaky putting stroke. Lee's wilted caddie clung to the leather bag for support like a withering rose on a trellis.

Rama had heard talk from the crowd that the challenger from El Paso and his young caddie had perhaps made a poor decision in last evening's entrée selection. Words like *trots*, *runs*, *two-step*, and *squirts* seemed popular in the analysis of Lee's and Donaldo's condition.

Rama wished there were something he could do. The only Christian gesture that occurred to him was to dash for the locker room and scavenge a fresh roll of toilet tissue. He caught up with Lee and Donaldo just as Carla was calling for the players to assemble on the tee.

"Good luck," he blurted as he extended the strange offering to Lee.

Lee was not too ill to appreciate a laughable anecdote for some future bullshit session, and accepted the surprising gift with a wan chuckle. "I'll be damned…toilet paper. If you'd given me a choice between this and gold, I swear I'd a gone for the lucky ass-wipe."

Lee realized the importance of being equipped with such a vital commodity on this especially challenging day. The four-mile course sported only one true *baño*.

The stricken duo left Rama standing alone for a moment in the willow's shade. He smelled the scent of the desert rose bush and recalled Carlos throwing Niña's reins into its thorny foliage the night before. He wondered if the old gaucho would turn up for the match.

—•—

The sputtering of a small engine approaching from behind startled Rama from his thoughts. "Hey, can you help me?" A pleasant female voice sang above the engine's growl.

Rama whirled around to see who needed help now. A tottering old refreshment cart had pulled up along the green; a young girl smiled from behind the wheel. After a streak of old men, bitter women, and sick golfers, Rama was grateful to meet someone about his age, especially someone as pretty as this girl.

Although Rama often found himself paralyzed by the opposite sex, he was not without interest, nor was he free of the occasional pang of passion. He secretly savored his standards of girlish beauty, figuring the perfect girl to be lithe, long-haired, and fair—even freckled. But the girl asking him for help was none of these things. She pondered him with lively brown eyes, set beautifully in a face tanned in a hue that spoke of Indian ancestors.

The lovely creature in the sputtering cart was absolutely feminine, though without an inch of ruffle or lace. Glowing skin flirted from her neck and arms, then dove beneath the coarse fabric of a green linen blouse. Her chest, in transition, supported the blouse easily with a hint of promise.

The cart girl sat comfortably, tapping one foot on the floorboards of the Cushman. Old sandals caressed her feet with soft leather straps. In the shadow beneath the dashboard, Rama noticed a splash of green glint from her toenails. She turned her head slightly to flick away an insect alighting on the peach fuzz of her forearm. The motion caused a heavy braid of thick black hair and its sloppy white ribbon to bob across her back. Rama quickly refigured his previous notions of beauty to match this stunning girl.

"Hey Dozy," the girl called again, slightly befuddled by the distant look in the boy's face. "Hey, they are about to start. Can you help me?"

Through the blushing heat of self-consciousness he found his voice. "Well, yeah…hi…what's…what's wrong?"

"It's this old wheel, it keeps running over thorns." The girl slid from the vinyl seat and kicked at the flaccid front tire. Her jeans were rolled up high, exposing ankles the same hue as her arms. "Those blammed stickers, they just like me I guess…I get all the flats around here," she giggled.

"Why don't you just stay on the grass?" suggested Rama. His words helped quench the fire in his face.

"I think they get me down in the barranca," she replied, "over by number sixteen. There's all sorts of trouble in there."

Rama remembered.

"Come look," the black-haired girl said. She quickly moved to the back of the cart and threw open a small compartment beneath the tub of iced beers and sodas. She reached far into the void to extract a spare tire. Rama noticed her arms were taught and graceful. She set the tire at Rama's feet and smiled back up into his eyes. "I'm not strong enough to change 'em."

Rama thought she looked strong enough to do almost anything. "What do you mean?" he stammered. "You look plenty...strength."

The girl looked at Rama with a disarming grin. The corner of a front tooth was chipped away, leaving an intriguing little dark triangle in the center of her smile. "Plenty strength!" she laughed. "You sound like Tarzan."

She noticed a blush overcoming the shy boy. His colorful madras shirt made his green eyes fascinating and intense, but they turned away bashfully. She wanted them back. She reached out and tugged at his wrist.

"Me Jane," she laughed again. She didn't release his wrist until he laughed along. "Come on, Tarzan, I really am too weak to take off the nuts. Grab the spare, I'll get the wrench. Carla will kill me if I'm not back on the job pretty quick."

The two knelt side by side and changed the flat front tire. Rama was relieved that he could get the nuts to yield. They didn't come off easily and he wondered if the pretty dark-haired girl could have put them on so tightly herself. Their shoulders touched as he worked the wrench, and he smelled the floral scent of shampoo in that thick braid. Rama was overcome with more questions than answers.

Out on the first tee, the voice of the crowd swelled again in laughter at another howler from Boney. The sound spurred the cart girl into action. She brushed off her hands and tossed the lug wrench back under the seat. "Hurry, put that old tire back in the trunk...Tarzan?" She paused, awkward that she didn't know her new friend's name.

Rama slammed the tailgate shut and stood, slightly lost, a few feet from the seated girl. She looked at him and felt an unexpected blush rise in her face. She wondered if he noticed. "Well thanks," she said. "So what are you doin' now?"

"Watching Boney and Lee."

"By yourself?"

"No, with my Dad...I think."

The girl pushed the starter button and the soft sputtering commenced again. She wiggled her hips slightly as if to make room on the seat beside her. "Hop in, we'll find him."

Rama grabbed the roof rail and swung himself into place by the girl. She pressed the pedal. "Hoooweeee," she cried in delight as the vehicle lurched toward the golf course. With his arm still clinging to the rail above him and his body bouncing on the seat, Tarzan performed his best impersonation of Cheetah.

—•—

The hands on the Bavarian Beer clock in the bar had nearly worked their way around its alpine panorama. When Hank glanced up for the time, the hands rested to the left of an icy white summit: 10:55.

"About game time," Hank said. Steadying himself with his cane, he dismounted the stool and left the bar in the good hands of two elderly dew sweepers. The old duffers were anything but interested in hiking around the rangy course again just to watch somebody else lose his money. As far as they were concerned, the sun burned most of the magic out of golf long before noon.

From the vantage of the veranda, Hank realized the scale of Carla's little enterprise. He reckoned that several hundred people had gathered around the opening tee box. Carla stood at the center of it all addressing the spectators—a queen bee to her drones.

Hank started down the stairs, and as he did he heard the sound of a Cushman engine. He looked up in surprise to see Rama approaching in the refreshment cart in the company of a girl, and a mighty pretty one at that. Hank remembered that Rama once had a crush on the girl across the street back home, but it was clear he was too shy to approach her. Doris had always assured Hank that Rama's time with girls would come. Well maybe it had.

"Where did you pick him up?" Hank asked the girl as the cart pulled to a stop. She looked like a tomboy in her jeans and old sandals, but he could see why his son would want to ride with her. He wished for Rama's sake that she lived across the street, not out here in the sticks.

"Hi, Dad. We fixed the cart...she gave me a ride," Rama said proudly, even if he couldn't introduce her without a name. He started to dismount the cart. "She's got to get to work."

"*He* changed the tire for me," the girl interjected with a little more clarity. She, too, found the lack of name awkward.

"Well I'm glad to hear he was helpful," Hank replied as a ripple of applause for Lee's introduction floated over from the first tee. "Hey, Chief, we got to get going."

Then to Rama's surprise, the girl asked if he could ride along with her for a few holes. Her smile appealed to all ages, and Hank, already taken with the thought of his son's inching one step up the ladder to self-confidence, was agreeable.

"Hell, I'd ride too if there was room for the three of us!" Hank winked his son's way, then tapped the fender of the old Cushman with his cane. "Just don't run off with him, eh girl? We're gonna be back on the road this afternoon... pronto."

"Yes sir," she said.

"Gotta see if that Boney fella can make me a few bucks," said Hank as he started away. But as he spoke his voice was consumed in a wave of laughter from the tee box—another Boney punch line delivered—and Rama did not hear his father name his newly chosen player.

As Rama watched his father limp back into the crowd, the refreshment cart surged forward.

"What is your name anyway, Tarzan? I'm Melyssa...with a *Y*."

Before Rama could reply, Melyssa had pulled the cart onto the hardened dirt path below the first tee box and throttled the motor back to a respectful idle. Above them, Carla Stone held a tee in her right hand—poised for the ceremonial toss. Now that Boney's wisecracks were finished, she recited the rules with emphasis on the fact that if any judgments were to be made, they were to be made by her.

Carla raised the tee and it became abruptly quiet in the unique way that the buzzing of a raucous golf gallery can be choked off in an instant with the wave of a marshal's hand—or released to a full roar at the impact of a ball.

Without another word, Carla Stone tossed the tee into the blue Texas sky.

Chapter 13

Carla's tee danced on the prickly turf, then pointed affirmatively toward Boney Carlisle. Lee and Donaldo receded from the tee box like spent waves, leaving the green stage to Boney and his caddie, Mirage. Boney looked to his undernourished caddie for a club but was met with what appeared to be indifference. Mirage made no move toward Boney's clubs but fiddled instead with the sticky, stubborn wrapper of an Abba-zaba.

"Don't suppose you had anything real to eat this morning, eh, Mirage?" asked Boney. "Damn candy's getting to your mind…aren't we forgetting a little something?"

Mirage responded with a substantial tug on his taffy, then slowly drew the driver from the bag. "Last thing you need to worry about is *my* diet. Hit away, Bones."

Boney looked anxiously up the fairway, a dogleg right, and exhaled mightily with relief. The match had been delayed far too long for his liking. "Christ, I've chewed at this bit long enough."

He curled his thick impatient fingers around the grip and pointed the club toward the dogleg, sighting down the shaft like a rifle. "Least I'm not hurting as bad as some folks…" He chuckled mercilessly at the thought of his opponent's food poisoning. Mirage did not.

Boney pulled a snow-white balata ball from his checkered shirt, and with agility defying his physique, quickly bent down and teed it up. Mirage backed away from the tee as Boney stepped into his stance and waggled the club.

"And no upchucking in my downswing, sonny boy," he cracked as he commenced a ponderous takeaway. Even locked in the rigid program of his pre-shot routine, Boney was not immune to yips of the vocal cords or lapses in good sportsmanship.

A ripple of laughter swept through the most heartless of Boney's supporters. Their man proceeded to crack a solid, high fade that soared easily on the wind, carrying well past a sagebrush-covered dune that intruded menacingly into the crook of the dogleg. The ball turned up the fairway, then settled into a fine position for his approach. Boney held his follow-through pose for maximum dramatic effect, then snatched up his tee with a swift, smug gesture before yielding the stage to his challenger.

Lee forced his face into a tight smile. "Decent, very decent," he congratulated Boney in a feeble attempt at gamesmanship. As he took his place at the tee box he knew he needed as decent an opening shot to make a statement—as much to himself as to Boney. As he visualized the booming drive that would announce his resolve to compete, a sudden gust of wind spawned a menacing plume of dust and sent it teeward. Lee backed away and wisely traded his driver for a 2-iron.

The rough-and-tumble golfer from El Paso tried to find comfort over the ball, trusting his routine to block out the pain in his gut and the slack in his normally reliable arms. But comfort was too much to ask, and Lee's misery worsened as Donaldo followed Boney's advice to the letter and wretched just as Lee's club dropped into the slot.

Nobody laughed at Donaldo's comedic timing or at Lee's truncated stroke. The ball, scalded badly on its northerly regions, screamed in pain and took a low route to a dense tuft of buffalo grass about seventy five yards out. Lee and the gallery groaned in unison; this was no way to begin a round.

Boney seized the moment to notch up the psychological attack. "Damn it, Lee, are you gonna scare up quail or are you gonna play golf?"

Plagued now with pain in his guts and damage to his confidence, Lee wasn't sure what he was going to do, but as he walked unsteadily to his ball, he had a moment to collect himself. He struggled to visualize his next shot: a low, hard fade around the toe of the intruding dune with sufficient top spin to penetrate far up the remaining fairway. After brushing grit from the 2-iron's grooves, Lee was over the ball again and redeemed himself slightly with what seemed like a great shot somewhere into the vicinity of Boney's ball; but when he arrived, he saw the orb resting defiantly in the meanest of Mesquite Creek's fairway bunkers.

No one called them sand traps at Mesquite Creek, because sand was the least component in their composition—ranking well below caked mud, pebbles, twigs, thorns, and a variety of animal scat. Even Carlos's midnight groundskeeping never got around to bunker rehabilitation.

To Boney's credit, he kept his comments on Lee's second shot to himself. While striding ponderously to his ball, he began deliberations with Mirage on club selection. The pin was center cut, the wind was at his back, and all was well with the world. He smiled as he drew the 9-iron back and beamed as he followed the perfectly struck ball's arc across the sky.

The essence of what attracted Boney, a diesel mechanic whose physique roughly matched the massive engines of his trade, to the most unlikely of pastimes in this marginally golf-friendly country, was the same thing that pulled golfers from warm beds to cold morning tees along the firths of

Scotland or the foggy headlands of Monterrey Bay. It was, and is, and always will be, the ball's magical flight.

Soaring high and far, beyond all proportion of effort, the ball, when struck purely, flies with a smudge of the golfer's spirit. Boney's ball, thus struck, flew optimistically from his club. He tracked its ascent, apogee, and descent with a curious fluttering of the eyes from ball to flag and back, hoping to predetermine from the diminishing gap a vision of a joyous landing. In Boney's case the magic worked; the ball dropped softly, against all aerodynamic principles, and came to rest about eight feet from the flag.

Hank had never golfed or even watched golf, but he knew a beautiful thing when he saw it. The curve the ball had scribed in the sky reminded him of flowing muscle in a thoroughbred's forelocks. Boney's crude confidence brought to mind the competitive fire in a winning horse's crazy eyes. These qualities mattered to him as assets matter to a banker. They were the clues to predicting a winner. Hank grinned with satisfaction. With the bets safely booked and Boney's skill in full flower, he reckoned he could just enjoy the walk and savor the luxury of a forgone and lucrative conclusion.

Similarly cerebral thoughts were not exactly sweeping Lee Trujillo to a golfing epiphany as he entered the parched bunker. The old scab of a trap had not seen new sand for years, which, in the case of the 150-yard shot he faced to reach the green, was a good thing. The bad thing was that he would be hitting off a virtual brick yet still had to find a way over the bunker's high, dusty lip only twenty feet ahead. The lie he was dealt and the loft required to clear the lip added up to a losing hand, but with a tremendous effort—like striking steel on flint—he scratched an open 8-iron's face across the bunker's bottom with a burst of sparks and amazingly elevated the ball enough to clear the obstacle and hold the right edge of the green.

Anyone privy to the condition of the lie and the gutsy club selection could have seen what a masterful shot it was and would have concluded that Lee had some game in him yet, even if everything else in him had recently been purged. To Hank it was just one stroke too many, and he was right. Lee fell immediately behind by one hole after failing to sink his thirty-foot putt from the right edge. The only good news for Lee was that Boney took two confidence-draining putts from eight feet.

"Damn gremlins been fuckin' with the green," he cursed as the first putt fell off line. The big man was mystified by how the speed of the greens varied so much from the previous afternoon. More troubling was Lee's shot from that hellhole of a bunker. The creativity in the stroke had not escaped Boney's attention; he had tried that very shot before with far worse results. Lee, without knowing, had fired a losing but effective psychological shot in the match's opening salvo.

Lee picked his ball from the green and handed it to Donaldo for a rubdown. As he rose, a swarm of stars darted across his vision like shiny minnows and he felt his knees wobble. The poisoned golfer crouched back down on the green and fanned himself with his cap, thinking of a thousand things he would rather do than drag himself to the second tee. Donaldo held the sparkling ball out for Lee with an unsteady hand, watching helplessly as his uncle suffered.

Lee looked up into Donaldo's damp face and smiled as a smidgen of mirth flickered in his brain. "Next time you think you're gonna lose it, son, lose it in one of those damned bunkers…no one will ever notice."

Donaldo considered the suggestion seriously for a second, then slung Lee's bag over his shoulder and headed toward the second tee.

By the time Lee and his gallery arrived, Boney was already teed up and taking aim. The hole was a short 380-yard par four that was bisected by a wasteland of prickly pear, saber plants, and other thorny species. A smartly hit drive carrying 260 yards would deliver a ball safely to the fairway beyond the prickly hazard. Such a drive demanded an accurate, shapeless shot to find the narrow fairway; anything drifting right would be swallowed by a hedgerow of hackberry trees that separated the fairway from the weeds of Mesquite Creek's abandoned landing strip.

Boney peered down-range. The green formed a receptive bowl to welcome incoming shots, but it would quickly spit them back out if they landed too high or if they had too much backspin. Today, the flag stood perilously close to the front fringe—closer than he had ever seen before.

"Gremlins again," he muttered. Boney knew too well the danger in that pin location, and he was aware that balls falling short could slide back down toward the wasteland or that balls putted from above could share the same miserable fate. The hole offered plenty of reasons to be cautious, but buoyed by his drive on the first hole and by his superior health, Boney decided he was in no mood to lay up. He waited impatiently for the crowd to settle down before taking his swing. He loathed waiting, fearful that excessive time for reflection might prompt doubt in his own strategy or erode the confidence in his swing.

"Any time now, Carlisle," urged Carla. She shared his impatience.

"Damn it, Carla, your customers are too jumpy," grumbled Boney. "I'll be damned if I'll shoot till I'm ready, and I'll be damned if I'm landing in Chandler's Garden." Boney knew that any reference to Carla's long-lost husband was bound to sting, but she deserved a little bite for hurrying him. Just to make sure she knew he wasn't going to relinquish control of his rhythm, he casually bent over, plucked up a few blades of grass, and tossed them ceremonially into the air as if to test the wind.

Boney wished, in retrospect, that he had taken that test more seriously, because the galloping blow he laid on the ball produced far too much elevation far too soon. With the headwind billowing beneath it, the ball floated up, then plummeted into the cactus patch. He looked at the inhospitable foliage in disbelief, waiting futilely for the ball to reappear by some impossible force or improbable bounce. But nothing emerged from Chandler's Garden except three terrified quail.

"Son of a bitch…just blew up on me," he cursed as he speared his club back into its bag.

"Carlisle, if you see Brer Rabbit down in the Briar Patch, tell him hello," Carla deadpanned as Boney stepped from the tee box. She wasn't going to relinquish any ground to the burly diesel mechanic-cum-golfer.

With as little wasted energy as possible, Lee stepped to the tee and slapped a fluid 3-wood into a layup about forty feet short of the hazard. He wanted to get this hole over as fast as possible and was more concerned about what privacy he could find in the brush beyond the green than what the outcome of the hole might be. With little hesitation Lee lofted his second shot high above—but too far beyond—the flag. The ball struggled to cling to the slope, but lost its grip on the shaved surface and inexorably sought the path of least resistance from the green to an awkward resting place several paces below the fringe.

After watching Lee's advantage roll off the green, Boney turned to deal with his own thorny misfortune. He grabbed a sand wedge and a 7-iron, figuring that if there was any chance of getting out of the garden without a drop, he could manufacture the needed shot with one of those clubs.

As the big man headed for his adventure in the hazard, Mirage stopped him. "Hey, Bones, don't forget your ball!" He reached into his bag and prepared to toss a new ball to Boney. "You can drop as far back up the fairway as you like. I'd say about 20 paces puts you right on the money for a lob."

"Shit, Mirage, you think I'm takin' a drop?" he looked at Mirage, infinitely discouraged at his caddie's lack of moral fiber. "Damn it, that ball might be playable."

"Hey Bones, I'm only carrying this bag as a favor," said Mirage. "You can't pay me enough to go rooting around in that crap. You're liable to hurt yourself in there." Mirage held the brand new ball up between his thumb and forefinger like a precious stone. "Take a drop."

Boney turned to the thorny tangle and started picking his way through the alien vegetation with an eye open for snakes, but even as he worried about fangs and venom, he suffered the strikes of spikes and spines. Above him he heard critical muttering from the gallery and the voice of Mirage imploring him to be sensible. He knew they were right; if he dropped he would lose one stroke but save himself from inestimable damage in trying to hack his way from the garden. But just as he was ready to cave to intelligence, he saw a ball lodged tightly beneath a creosote bush.

Boney surveyed the surrounding landscape: He was hidden from view by several rugged boulders and a healthy crop of cactus. Not accepting Mirage's advice would be a senseless waste of time and strokes, and an egotistical exercise at best, but what he did next was worse. Reaching under the bush with his 7-iron, Boney slid the ball into a clear patch of open sand and brushed the incriminating track away. Then he took several steps back into the brush and hollered up at his caddie.

"God damn it, Mirage," he bellowed. "Help me find this GD ball."

Mirage didn't want to irritate Boney any further, so he joined the hunt. After a minute, the caddie spotted the ball in its phony fortuitous lie. "I'll be go to hell, that cheating son of a bitch," he said softly to himself.

Then raising his voice for the benefit of the gallery, Mirage called loudly and convincingly: "Bones, over here, you're in luck."

———•———

The gaunt caddie's proclamation rang up into the blue above Chandler's Garden. The words of complicity in Boney's crime resounded to an invisible locale somewhere above the dry Texas turf. There, in the domain of the Golf Gods, in a place as mythical and unapproachable as Magnolia Lane, Butler's Cabin, or the Great Room above St. Andrew's hallowed first tee, the arbiters of golfers' fates begged to differ with Mirage's facetious statement. At that moment, as if to say "I wouldn't count on it, Bones," an unexpected clap of thunder startled the patrons gathered below.

Chapter 14

Boney had manufactured the best lie he could under the circumstances, but his next stroke was in as perilous a position as was his conscience. His lie left little clearance for a back swing, and the route forward to the green was blocked against anything but a perfectly executed, high-stakes lob, yet Boney was damned if he was going backward. He considered moving the ball a few beneficial inches away from the encroaching foliage, convincing himself that a second infraction stacked upon the first would be excusable, when Carla's voice rang out with a threat to come down there and make a ruling.

Boney knew he had to pull the trigger quickly and resolved to play the ball as it illegally lay. He tossed the 7-iron back to Mirage and took a hasty practice swing with the wedge, trying to imagine the motion he would need to get the ball up. As he swung, his right hand raked against a thorny branch.

"Fuck the luck," he cursed, adjusting the swing and trying again with the same results. Two wounds appeared as if he had encountered a snake. Boney cast his weight out onto his left foot in hopes he would take the club up steep enough to clear the thorns.

He came down hard. Had he known that one-quarter inch below the sand lurked solid rock, he might have relented and taken Mirage's suggested drop, but now, committed to this immoral course, he became the recipient of both damnation and salvation. His sand wedge might just as well have been one of Carlos's vipers for the bite it gave him. The ball emerged from the shot with little loft yet somehow found a favorable angle on the face of a boulder to deflect it upward and, against all justice, to the upper right edge of the green. The gallery clapped appreciatively for what appeared to be a magician's effort.

Mirage looked at Boney with contempt. "You lucky fuck…that was a phony damn lie if there ever was one. I got a mind to call foul on that one." Before Boney could respond, Mirage continued: "You remember the lousy outside agency ruling you called on my ball yesterday after I putted over that grasshopper?"

Boney looked at Mirage sheepishly.

"Well, big fella," Mirage winked, "then I'll be wanting my money back on that hole…six skins, I think it was."

Boney looked at Mirage and then at the ball sitting on the green, in what appeared to everyone else, in two. He wasn't about to argue; he had just abused the honesty that lies vulnerably in golf's rugged terrain. He was less contrite at his deception than he was at Mirage's blackmail. Boney knew that justice is not overtly served on the course. The score may appear to grant a transgressor his shining numbers on the card, yet detracts from the true game: an enterprise of the heart tallied in strokes of joy, humor, and humility and penalized in marks of guilt, loathing, and empty vanity.

Boney Carlisle was unconcerned with such abstruse values—low numbers were his only interest. Justice be damned, or so it seemed, because the "luck" he so skillfully manufactured under the bush carried unfairly forward. The scales of justice had been rudely tipped and weren't about to return to equilibrium directly. Lee's pitch shot from below the green, which seemed predestined to strike the heart of the cup, peeked over the lip instead and, repelled at the sight, spun out several feet from the hole.

Soon Boney stood above his ball resting sixteen feet from the hole, ten of which traversed a gentle down slope to the right. His shot would have to be on a high, bold line that would take it across Lee's position on its way into the cup.

"Get out your peso, amigo, you're gonna have to mark that one," he said. But before Lee finished scrounging through his pockets for a coin, a pang of guilt pricked Boney's heart and he corrected himself: "Aw damn, pick it up."

He calculated that conceding the putt to Lee would award him some capital that might be useful in bribing the Golf Gods down the road. After Lee had gratefully recovered his ball, Boney stroked his putt and watched calmly as it climbed, curled right, found the fall line, and raced inevitably into the waiting cup for a birdie. The Gods, Boney recognized, were either blind and stupid or damned gullible.

Walking away from the impressive, impossible birdie, Boney was feeling invulnerable and just a little blasphemous as he faced his incredulous caddie. "You know, Mirage," he said sarcastically, "God *heps* them that *heps* themselves." Wielding his putter, Boney took a roundhouse swipe at a ripe cactus blossom and sent it and an attending bumblebee into oblivion. He tossed the club into the bag—trading it for the day's first brownie.

If Boney's pronouncement was intended as a salve for the moral wound he suspected Mirage was suffering from his complicity in their deception on the previous hole, it had little effect. Mirage was rightfully impressed with his boss's up and down, but he could find no room for respect for the big fellow sucking brown icing from his sticky fingers.

"Bones, if God was *heppin'* you, he'd drop right down out of heaven and wipe that brown crap off your face."

Good caddie that he was, Mirage tossed Boney a towel. A skeletal grin escaped from beneath his flattop.

Boney's birdie pounded at Lee's confidence, but thankfully the hole didn't drag on, for Lee's next appointment out in the brush was nearly overdue. With Boney's ball still rattling in the cup, he was off. A cold shiver knifed through him as he found himself squatting in contemplation of that most terrible of decisions.

A few sagebrush away, Donaldo faced the same miserable purging options. Unfortunately, he didn't have much control of either outcome—the pozole had spoken.

Carla winced in sympathy and considered the thought of canceling the match. But such a move might instigate a riot in the prejudiced gallery. "Sicker than a dog" squared in her mind with the concept "rub of the green." These were the breaks; it certainly wasn't fair to penalize Boney for showing up healthy—not that she felt Boney deserved any favors.

She watched Lee and Donaldo return from the brush to the third tee. "You're gonna be all right now...aren't you?" as much a suggestion as a question.

Lee nodded, aware that he'd have to see this round through come hell or high water. All he lacked now was the high water. Donaldo just slumped.

"Alright, get on with it," she commanded. "Boney's honors."

Two holes later, Boney still hadn't lost a hole but had halved one after Lee made a miraculous chip-in on number three. Lee made another bid on the fourth hole by attempting to jump-start some magic with a forced carry across a creek where a decent lay-up would have been sufficiently heroic. But his swing lacked the required voltage, and he was soon fishing the ball from the water while his caddie slumped on the bank.

The score read: Boney three up with fourteen to play. Hank Schwain was learning to enjoy the royal and ancient game.

The challenger and his caddie trudged from the fourth green to their own private dirge. Lee was grinding hard to find a buoyant thought to lift him above despair. He had played some tough matches down in West Texas on some rugged tracks and against some rough opponents, but he had never backed down. Here in the grip of food poisoning he was still holding on, although the tally didn't show it. Dragging himself to another tee without having won a single hole, and with Boney's impossible luck at full tilt, was threatening his competitive spirit. Lee uncharacteristically flirted with thoughts of surrender.

Lee's caddie didn't even attempt to make it to the fifth tee. Out of the gallery's sight, Donaldo dropped the bag to the ground and settled down on it with his pale face buried in his hands. He cried in misery and humiliation. He was done for the day; if death wanted to take him now, so be it.

"Don't make me finish, Uncle," he sobbed. "Leave me here, I'm no help anyway." Tears and sweat rolled between his fingers and down his ashen face.

Lee's heart ached with empathy for the young man. He wanted nothing more than to slump into the shade and quit, too. Had it been any other match, he might have conceded right there and hitched a ride on the snack cart back to anywhere but the damned golf course. He had promised Carla his best, but that didn't mean he had to make life any harder on his nephew.

"Hey there, hombre, I couldn't have gone this far without you. Just hang back here…we'll laugh about this someday. Lay low 'til we all move on," Lee continued quietly, trying to spare his nephew any more embarrassment, "then head on back to the clubhouse when you feel better." Lee handed Donaldo his water bottle and his truck keys.

"Here, maybe you can listen to the radio while you wait. If you run across Oral Roberts, just lay a hand on the radio and ask God for some intestinal fortitude," Lee chuckled despite himself. "I'll get back soon as I can finish off this dude."

Lee did the math in his head and figured he could theoretically square the match in the next three holes, then take the first six of the remaining eleven to win in a 6 and 5 victory. "Hell, Donaldo, I could beat that lucky son of a bitch in nine more holes," he said betraying an embattled sense of optimism. "That'd get me back in ninety minutes."

"Sure," said the boy in disbelief. He stood to help Lee hoist the bag. "Good luck, Uncle," he added before sliding back down to lay in the grass.

"Don't need luck, now Donaldo," Lee said, forcing a taut smile under the strain of a new burden. "I need Kaopectate."

—•—

Carla watched with interest as Lee arrived at the fifth tee carrying his own clubs. She approached him with the air of a rules official. "Don't suppose you know the whereabouts of young Donaldo, do you?" she asked.

Lee slung the bag off his shoulder and let it slam to the turf. "He's done in, *struck down*…ain't going another foot today," Lee replied sternly. "There's nothing in the rules about him passing the bag to me…right?"

Carla didn't answer. She shivered at Lee's choice of words. The phrase "struck down" aroused memories tucked painfully away for, what had it been now, ten, eleven years? She dared not pursue the memory of that lightning further.

"Lee, you can't leave him there," she scolded.

Lee returned a weary look and a shrug that begged for an alternative.

Carla quickly scanned the gallery and found the snack cart idling just off the fairway. "Melyssa…front and center!"

In an instant the dark-haired girl and her passenger, Rama, were sputtering up to the gathering on the fifth tee.

"'Lyssa, hurry up and run Lee's caddie back to the clubhouse." Carla said urgently. "You tell him that if those old duffs are still in the bar, the bald one used to be a damned good doctor; he can help."

The delay in the game and the interruption in her refreshment sales were wrestling with her motherly instincts. "Go! Get going before I change my mind." Then with a waggle of her thumb she commanded Rama to dismount.

Rama climbed from the cart, feeling unreasonably jealous of the boy who would replace him beside Melyssa—never mind that the poor kid was wracked in misery. This new emotion caught Rama off guard, leaving him feeling awkward and selfish as Melyssa pushed the throttle. Before disappearing, Melyssa hollered back at Carla:

"Tarzan would make a great caddie."

As Rama watched the cart chug back toward the clubhouse, his runaway emotions were halted by Lee's weakened voice. "You heard her. Got anything better to do…Tarzan?"

Rama blushed. He did not answer.

"You probably wouldn't mind changing places with my caddie about now, would you?" Lee inquired mischievously.

"No sir."

Lee looked at Carla. "Any problem with Raba here carrying the bag?"

Carla was losing her patience. "Strap your clubs onto a blessed camel for all I care, Lee; let's just get this show back on the road. You know how Boney loves to wait…and damn it, Lee, his name is Rama."

Lee helped his new caddie adjust the straps to fit his shoulder. Rama could hear the labor in Lee's breathing and could feel the heat of distress. Sweat seeped from Lee's tangled black hair and zig-zagged down his pale temples. This was not the same Lee who had hit the incredible 6-iron for him yesterday afternoon.

"There we go," said Lee. "Now, if you really want to earn your keep, pull whatever club I ask for pronto, and stay close. God knows I don't want to walk any more than I have to today."

Lee gave Rama a sly look. "And keep the sixes and the nines straight, amigo."

Rama remembered. He smiled self-consciously, then followed Lee to the fifth tee.

—•—

Within shouting distance of the developments on the tee, in a camp hidden beneath a tangle of firethorn and mesquite scrub deep in the barranca, Carlos Taddio awoke from a daydream with the whisper of premonition in his ears. The vision had come again and stirred him like the track of a spider across his cheek.

The vision had first appeared many years earlier. Carlos had seen that the spirits of the children were not at rest—not with the soul of their father trapped somewhere between life and death or with their mother, Carla, locked in bitterness. But the premonition comforted Carlos with the knowledge that their spirits would find refuge in the heart of a charmed young man with whom they would one day return to the very place of their passing—the place of the lightning. There, on the sixteenth green, should their host be consumed in play they would be free to ascend to eternal peace.

Last night, with the coming of the locusts, Carlos had been drawn back to the lights of Carla's clubhouse, and like the curious Puma, had come to see who might bear the spirits of Dickey and Glendora Stone. He shuddered at the memory: He had sensed their spirits as surely as the beating of his own heart.

As the vision had promised, a young man was the children's refuge, and that man—just a boy—was Rama. But Rama could not possibly be a *player*, yet Carlos sensed that somehow, he was in the game.

Chapter 15

Carlos stepped from shack he had fashioned of sycamore branches and lumber scavenged from spike crates abandoned up on the Gulf-Colorado & Santa Fe railroad line. He cradled a cup of maté and listened to the wilderness. Above the rustle of quail and the drone of wild bees, he heard the faint music of voices from the golf course, but something had changed. Niña cocked her head toward the fifth tee. Carlos imagined she sensed it, too.

"Si, my friend, is a new sound, no? Not thee voices of thee usual Sunday fools. Perhaps it is as your Carlos has dreamed. By a miracle, our Rama…with the spirits of thee children, may be upon thee course again."

Carlos recalled the vision—the children's return "in the heart of a good man"—but the vision never revealed how that person might become a player in this game. It seemed an impossibility. Yes, the grace of God had brought Rama to Mesquite Creek, thought Carlos, but it would take another miracle to satisfy his vision.

Carlos muttered a simple calculation. His soft breath rippled the maté below his lips. It would take less than two hours for Lee and Boney to reach the sixteenth green—the place of transfer—the spot where he was sworn to usher Dickey and Glendora Stone's spirits to eternal peace. He had not trekked the fairways of Mesquite Creek in daylight since drifting into exile years ago, but if it were true, if Rama were in the game, Carlos knew he must take his place at the sixteenth green. If a miracle must occur there, Carlos guessed it would take all the magic, all the prayers he could muster.

Niña fidgeted at her tether. She whinnied hopefully, sensing a walk through the barranca and out onto the bright sunny course. Its fringe would be lush with new grass. Carlos touched his pony's cheek to settle her.

"No, my little one. Carlos must travel in secret. Is not a trip for my Niña."

The fifth hole called for a decent drive to fly beyond a broad oak that dominated the left edge of the fairway—a drive with draw enough to curl left and avoid running through the fairway. Boney, as anxious as Carla had predicted, had taken a few too many practice swings in anticipation of burying Lee once and for all. He knew he could close out this match in six more holes and hardly break a sweat. The extra swings had worn the fine edge off his stroke; the flaccid effort that followed denied his ball even a chance to flirt with the tree. It sailed instead into the rough on the right. The good news for Boney was that he was in grass not brush; the bad news was that his ball was in plain sight of everyone. There could be no tampering; whatever lie he had drawn in the shaggy grass was the lie he would have to play.

Mirage quickly slipped in behind the frustrated golfer, who still stared in disbelief after his drive. He nimbly picked the club from Boney's hands like a stick of high explosives before it could be used in an act of unsportsmanlike conduct.

Boney grumbled off a few expletive-laced phrases in the general direction of Carla, something about Lee delaying the game. Carla answered by threatening to invoke long-ignored rules against behavior unbefitting a gentleman. She waved a dog-eared copy of the *Rules of Golf* toward the angry competitor.

Mirage countered by dangling a Garcia Vega before Boney's angry mouth. "Smoke?" he asked, flipping his Zippo into action. Better, he reasoned, for those lips to tug on a fresh cigar than to spew invective and incur a loss-of-hole penalty. Boney took a long foul drag.

Lee Trujillo breathed easier now. "Better to work the ball around that tree with some loft," he said, thinking out loud for Rama's benefit. "Hand me the 3-wood."

There on the fifth tee's rustic stage, with what he thought was a chance to help salvage his father's payday, Rama felt important. He hoped Hank was just as proud, and quickly searched the gallery for his father's face, but when he found it, his old man's expression was more perplexed than pleased.

Rama pulled a frayed knit cover from the club and placed the shaft in Lee's hand. The golfer was startled by a tiny jolt, like the spark from a doorknob after crossing a woolen carpet. A breeze was blowing but no storms charged the sky. He shrugged off the shock and turned his attention to teeing the ball, but as he bent toward the ground he found himself disconnected from the continuity of events. He felt vacant and feared he was going to vomit.

Lee closed his eyes and took a deep breath to compose himself. As the late morning air flowed into his chest, he imagined he was a boy again, wading in the shallows of a lively creek. Red pebbles twinkled up through the crystal water in broken sunlight. Senior Trujillo held his son's hand firmly, keeping the boy fast against the brisk current. The man's weathered face smiled down at Lee from quick brown eyes shadowed by a battered Stetson. Soaring above his father's head, the orange cathedral crags of the Guadeloupe Mountains tore at the eternal blue sky.

Suddenly Lee felt the poison flush away with the memory of crystal waters and his father. The spark returned in its place. His fingers found a powerful grip. From his stance Lee saw his destiny far up the course: It was bright and secure, and held many championships. The shot he faced now was important and would receive his best effort, but its accomplishment as an extension of his ego had no value and consequently offered no burden. Lee was free.

The upcoming shot's line over the fairway and around the tree was so obvious, so illuminated with possibility, that he laughed involuntarily at his folly for so often seeing the game in such a dark, forbidding light.

Lee turned, coiled, and released with the simplicity of skipping a stone. Never had the crack of the persimmon seemed so resonant nor had the flight of a perfectly executed draw seemed so enthralling. Lee posed for an extra moment at the end of the swing like a bronzed Harry Vardon, not for vanity but for the simple lack of will to exist in any better position—like one great stone in the desert balanced impossibly upon another.

The oak tree and Boney's ball lay forty yards behind the bright patch of turf where Lee's ball finally came to rest. Lee followed it in a trance, without remembering to return his driver to the bag. Rama trotted along to catch up and to reclaim the club.

Boney took a long drag off his cigar as he watched Lee's performance with concern. He had played enough golf to understand the rich body language of the game. A player's pose, a twirled club, a smartly snatched tee, or a hastily followed tee shot could all send a warning to one's competitor.

"Looks like there's a little fight in the hombre yet, Mirage," said Boney. But he was not about to surrender his cocky confidence in response to another's single, fortuitous swing.

"Got to admit, it was about the best drive I ever saw on this hole," Mirage observed objectively. "Pretty damn good considering he just looked like he was about to pass out. So what do you say, Bones, 5-wood out of the grass?"

It was a wise club selection. The big golfer definitely wasn't giving an inch, and he needed every inch of that fairway wood to recover. Recover he did, brilliantly, with a bullet from the rough that somehow floated up to transform what appeared to be a low-flying error into a gorgeous, rising approach that stopped just short and right of the green.

Boney's shot had neutralized most of Lee's advantage. Although Lee was revitalized with the grace of his caddie's mysterious Gift, a solid approach onto the green and a very respectable two-putt were still not enough to win; instead, Boney's skillful chip and one-putt halved the hole. Lee was still down by three, but he hoped that making a good solid par against Boney's unorthodox scramble had turned back the tide of a tsunami, just as something had turned back the tide of misery swamping him only five minutes earlier.

Lee smiled at a foolish thought: it was as if his prayer for Kaopectate had been answered. He hoped Donaldo was as fortunate.

Chapter 16

A dust devil traced an erratic path toward the sixth tee, casting a storm of grit and debris into the faces of the golfers and gallery advancing from the fifth hole. The crowd stumbled from the vortex onto the tee, coughing as they beat the dust from their clothes. Boney fished for a lighter to re-ignite his cigar and calmly surveyed the hole ahead, as if unaffected by the whirlwinds.

Chandler Stone's design gave the players a little relief here if Mother Nature and her capricious winds approved. The short par four played into the prevailing breezes, and it posed many questions. Brisk gusts lingered in the dust devil's wake, challenging Boney to find the right answer. Mirage left the club selection to his boss and pondered the futility of removing the particles that now peppered his Abba-zaba.

Still anxious to distance himself from Lee—especially now that Lee had shown some new life—Boney reasoned he could lay down a low drive that, at best, would eat up most of the distance to the green and at worst, would leave him some kind of a short scrambling iron shot. If Boney had anything, it was confidence. Without protest from Mirage, but with considerable resistance from the roiling atmosphere, Boney drove mightily into the teeth of common sense.

There must have been several layers of air swirling above that fairway, each with a different velocity and direction. Boney's ball reflected that chaos with three distinct course corrections, the last of which sent his ball plummeting into the brush far left of the fairway.

"A little breezy for that club," quipped Mirage at his partner's poor effort and abysmal logic. He extracted the driver from Boney's grip with one hand and abandoned his soiled taffy to a waste can with the other.

Boney took the poor shot and his caddie's comment badly. "I'll be god damned if you loop for me again," Boney responded in disgust. "Why'd you let me pull that lousy driver?" But Boney knew that Mirage knew there was no stopping a Carlisle once he had made up his mind to be an imbecile.

Indecision gripped Lee as he watched the wobbling flight of Boney's drive. He knew better than to be greedy on this hole. Maybe a long iron would be a safer bet, but he didn't want to sacrifice too much distance. The hesitant voice of his rookie caddie interrupted his deliberations.

"Why don't you hit this one again?" Rama held out the 6-iron. "You sure hit it good yesterday."

Lee was surprised at the suggestion; he had expected Rama only to tote, but the stand-in caddie's advice made sense. A shorter club would be easier to hit, and he already had an advantage here. Hood it a little, keep it low, he thought.

Seconds later Lee and Rama were following a low draw that had cut efficiently through the wind, leaving Lee's ball safely in the fairway. The atmosphere—and Boney—blustered menacingly as they moved up the fairway. Even with all his creativity, there was no hope for Boney on this hole now. A few futile strokes later Boney conceded the hole, and Lee celebrated his first victory of the day. Boney was still up two with twelve to play.

Lee savored the applause rippling softly through the surrounding gallery as Rama approached to recover the putter. The boy wore the same shy smile Lee had seen on the practice tee yesterday. "Never would have played the hole like that," he declared with gratitude. "6-iron was the right call."

It was Rama's nature to stifle the peaks and valleys of emotional expression— his comfort zone resided firmly in the foothills. His beaming smile betrayed a ripening assurance.

"I'm trying to help, sir."

"And you are. I told you last evening you were a natural," Lee said, still slightly amazed he had followed the novice caddie's advice without debate, and increasingly aware he had undergone a miraculous remission from the poison pozole.

The rejuvenation of Lee Trujillo appeared complete as he walked purposefully to the seventh tee. A nascent smile lurked, with only another victorious hole away from bursting fully formed across his face. His intention to merely participate in the match to preserve Carla's credibility was blossoming into a joyful desire to compete. The severe, thirsty course now looked inviting. Mesquite Creek had dipped the veil that obscured her soft secrets. Lee surged, and by the tenth hole the tide had turned. The match was all square.

With the match at least halfway through and the sun high in the sky, the heat was getting to Carla Stone. She was fit for a woman in her late sixties, but she had not taken a break from the daily operation of the club for some time and fatigue was setting in.

The golf business had not always been this hard. In the past, as the wife of a revered golf professional, she had journeyed by train to many fine country clubs—even, on several occasions, to Augusta National. There, as a guest of Chandler's associate, Mr. Robert Tyre Jones, she found herself in the company

of the south's social elite. Confident and charming, and with the added impri-
matur of a personal rapport with Mr. Jones, Carla slid easily into the graces of
Augusta despite her upbringing as a poorly bred Texan. While Carlos Taddio
looked after Mesquite Creek, she and Chandler had spent magical afternoons
sipping sweet tea and juleps while making pleasant small talk with the privileged and watching a procession of golf's legends trek the exquisite fairways.

That was a long time ago, before Carlos had led the children out into
the electrical storm; before the lightning struck her dreams and her children
down. After Chandler vanished she wondered if she should sell the course
and find a more dignified profession, perhaps in the environs of Atlanta and
in the bosom of her fond Georgian friends. But without a declaration of death
to clear Chandler's name from the deed, she could not easily walk away from
Mesquite Creek. She grew bitter and determined to mine it for every nickel it
would yield, even if the beauty of Chandler's green track had to suffer.

The years had rolled along like the Gulf-Colorado & Santa Fe locomotives
rumbling in the distance. Chandler was gone, and Bobby Jones had fallen into
poor health. Carla's beauty that, had she been properly widowed, might have
attracted a well-connected suitor, slipped away under the strain of her struggles. Still, she harbored the notion of one day reclaiming a spot on Augusta's
grand veranda, but in her heart she knew that spot was taken.

For years, on holidays, she had received polite cards from some of her old
Augustan acquaintances. But one day, by chance, she had discovered the signatures were identical from year to year—the imprint of finely rendered stamps.
Sadly, she imagined her friends' personal secretaries wielding the stamps in
obligatory "Best Wishes" to those who had descended to the bottom of their
greetings lists. Eventually even that feeble connection to golf's high society
withered. The caste to which she aspired did not include, nor did it embrace,
mere survivors.

Riding shotgun in the heat of her matches was a far cry from fanning
herself in the shade of Georgian magnolias. There were no marshals in
matching green blazers to police her enterprise here, just one overworked
sixty-eight-year-old woman to pass rulings and to clamp lids on the pots that
boiled between some golfers' ears. Although Carla was unhappy with her
social position, she was confident in her authority at Mesquite Creek. And if
tensions on the course ever boiled over, she always had her pistol.

How unladylike, she thought.

With this match settling into a real competition, the grumbling about a
rematch had faded. Carla was confident the game would run out to at least
seven or eight more holes. At twelve minutes a hole, that was about another
ninety minutes' refreshment sale. But she wouldn't make a dime until Melyssa
returned.

She looked back toward the clubhouse, as anxious over lost revenue as she was in need of a good, cold drink. "Damn, I didn't say take Donaldo *home*… just drop him off," she grumbled. But she breathed easier when she heard the old Cushman sputtering back up the cart path. Carla surveyed the gallery assembling at the tenth tee—they would be thirsty, too, she hoped. Carla relaxed and turned to Hank, who sat on a bench resting his good leg.

"You're looking a little peak'ed there, Mr. Schwain. Are you thirsty or is Lee's improvement getting to you? Don't worry, this is golf…anything can happen," Carla assured Hank. "We've got plenty of cold drinks in the cart to get you back on your foot."

Carla blushed like a debutante at a coming-out party. "I'm sorry…on your feet."

Hank groaned, not at Carla's slip but at Lee's back-to-back birdie putts on holes seven and eight. It was a whole new match at the halfway point—dead even. It was entertaining, but so was a come-from-behind run of the wrong horse across a finish line. Here, suddenly, he was in danger of losing a bunch of money to a surging Mexican golfer who allegedly had been sick as a damn dog. Some game. He wondered if he had been hustled, but it would have taken a lot of balls to have played that charade in front of so many damn cowpokes. Most of them, Hank figured, probably carried shooting irons. Besides, he had heard those two guys puking in the brush and it sounded uncomfortably like the real McCoy. So how in hell, Hank wondered, had Lee got to looking so good and playing so well so fast? And how was it that even as Boney ripped the wrapping from a new brownie in consolation of another lost hole, that Rama, even burdened by Lee's bag, was grinning so broadly?

Boney was determined to recover the advantage he had somehow lost in the last several holes. Nine tough holes had left him with perspiration streaming from his scalp and stinging his eyes. Squinting, he groped for the towel hanging from his bag, forgetting the rag's recent history and blind to the deposits of mud and goose droppings still clinging to the cloth.

"Got to put the wheels back on the wagon now, Mirage," Boney said as he scribed several filthy smudges across his face.

"Think that war paint's gonna help with the wagon, Bones?" Mirage replied.

As much as he would have enjoyed watching Boney complete the round with a broad stripe of goose crap across his face while in the company of friends and fellow golfers, Mirage labored under a deep sense of duty to protect his man's dignity. He dabbed at the offending smudge with a relatively clean corner of the cloth and attempted to assist Boney by offering a word of golf wisdom regarding the wagon's failing wheels.

"Now listen." Mirage looked directly into Boney's eyes. "If you try to fix what really ain't broke you'll break what's already fixed then you'll really be in a fix…and you could go broke."

"Run that by me again, Aristotle?" Boney looked perplexed. He noticed Mirage gathering a breath to comply. "No don't. That's enough Yogi Berra for one day."

"Just trying to help."

Mirage's advice, though convoluted, was good, and Boney would have been wise to heed it. Instead, over the next five holes he simply tried too hard. The image of a robust man in sweat-drenched jockey colors, clenching a dead cigar in his teeth while taking ineffective slashes at a mocking little orb, was anything but pretty. He lost three of the next five holes but managed to scrape out two halves to save himself from handing Lee the whole enchilada after fourteen holes.

Standing at the fifteenth tee, Lee, the unlikely challenger from El Paso, led three up with four to play. If he won one more hole, the match would be his.

Boney's back was up against a formidable wall of self-doubt as he watched Lee tee up at the troublesome fifteenth hole. Not only had the tough bronze customer managed to heal himself; now he was even singing! Boney recognized the damned Doris Day tune: "Que Sera Sera." He hated it!

Rama felt differently. The tune took him back home and to thoughts of his mother's health. "Que sera sera," she would bravely reply when he asked about her spells. "Oh, it's nothing, honey, just a touch of vertigo." But he had noticed an unusual number of doctor's appointments scribbled on a chalkboard inside the kitchen cupboard and the Latin names for what were apparently ineffective drugs.

The tune had a different effect on Boney: It brought out the critic in him. He figured that if you had to listen to a girl's song on a man's golf course, at least make it a song from a voice with some substance, like Patsy Cline or Kitty Wells.

"Not that sappy damn Day broad," he muttered angrily. He was about to chastise Lee for his musical tastes when, to Boney's irritation, Mirage—who never had been known to sing—joined in on the chorus: *Whatever will be will be...*

—•—

The fifteenth was an abrupt dogleg that curved to the right, following the bank of the deep barranca separating it from the sixteenth tee's commanding butte. It was here the night before that Carlos had pulled Rama up into the saddle to avoid the "vipers" in the gloomy hollow as they rode to the sixteenth. The barranca looked sinister even in the middle of the day.

Lee choked off the humming and concentrated on his swing. His tee shot started out beautifully, with a shape echoing the curve of the dogleg, but it took an unexpectedly severe hop to the right, then bounced into the fringe of hostile vegetation clinging to the rim of the barranca. As Lee emerged from his follow-through he turned to his caddie. "Did you see how far she went in, amigo?"

"Only a little way, I think…just past that red boulder."

Boney's irritation with the song selection and his satisfaction at Lee's long overdue miss-hit prompted him to pull himself together and launch a solid, safe 4-wood that would have made Gene Sarazen proud. Mirage had to jog to catch up with the churning golfer.

The scorpion was startled by the dimpled white object that had rolled into its angular world. The creature never would have noticed had it been tucked under the small flat stone it usually favored as shelter against the sun and jay-birds, but a group of rampaging college boys had recently disturbed its peace and dislocated the stone. The scorpion was lucky not to have been crushed and had spent the last several hours scouring the dry soil away with its rear legs to reclaim its lair beneath the stone. It was settling in to take solace from future tormentors when Lee's golf ball arrived.

Instinctively the scorpion curled its tail in defense, but the ball neither retreated nor advanced. To the creature's dismay, the ball had come to rest directly upon the depression it had nearly completed as its new entry. In fear, the scorpion scooted backward under the cover of a dead sage sprig. Beneath hard cutaneous plates, its muscle fibers were programmed for reaction. Venom glands secreted their potent proteins to charged vesicles in the crooked stinger.

Its eyes and its defenses locked on the offending ball, and it waited for the next move.

———•———

"My mom likes that song, too," Rama said happily to Lee as they walked along the edge of the barranca.

"It's Spanish," said Lee, "she *should* like it."

He smiled as they continued along the fairway's ragged edge. Rolling thunder sounded from beyond the horizon, muffled like tympani beneath a quilt. "Maybe we will get an electrical storm today," Lee mused, looking at the darkening in the distance. "I was wondering after I first got that shock off you back there…lot of static today."

Lee passed the boulder and looked to where his ball had dribbled off the fairway. God help me if I've gone in there, he thought. Peering at the gnarled tangle of broken rock and spiny plants descending into the barranca, he felt a shiver. He wanted nothing to do with this damned place. Better off to take a drop, he figured.

Just as he turned to have Rama toss him a new ball, Lee caught the bright white of a golf ball wink up through the dead sage. The ball rested against a small flat rock, but the rock was not in his line. Hope flashed that he might still have a shot if it were his ball.

Lee gingerly stepped into the fringe, taking care not to break any twigs from adjacent brush for fear of incurring a penalty from the watchful Carla.

He reached carefully down to brush away a desiccated seedpod that obscured his mark when, with alien velocity, a bolt of poisonous lightning pierced the back of his hand.

Blinded by the sting's dazzling, painful incandescence, Lee staggered back into the fairway. The golf ball, dislodged by Lee's flailing exit rolled from the stone and disappeared forever into the barranca. With the threatening intruder and the confounding ball gone, the scorpion skittered happily back into its quarters below the rock.

As Lee lurched back from the scorpion's lair, the air above the fifteenth fairway hovered in silence like the mute moment in which an infant gathers its breath to cry following pain or injustice.

Chapter 17

"**K**eee..rryst!" Lee howled in pain, holding his stinging right hand against his chest. His eyes darted in panic. "A snake…something. By that rock!" Rama's heart raced. He glanced where Lee's ball had just disappeared but saw nothing. He recalled the first aid for snakebites he had learned in scouts, never thinking he would actually need it. Rama had always feared his scoutmaster's advice was suspect—that the woodcraft the unhealthy fellow plied was of no more value than fake Indian jewelry. But with no better answers at hand, he was prepared to fall back on it now.

He told Lee to lie back, to hold his hand up and stay calm. Rama's mind filled with memories of pocket knife incisions and venom-sucking.

"How does it look?" he asked Lee.

Lee pulled his left hand away, revealing a bright red spot in the center of a swelling dome of flesh.

"It's not a snake bite," Rama declared with certainty.

"Well, God damn, whatever it is, it feels like a hot poker."

Rama fetched the golf towel from Lee's bag with the intention of making a wet compress, but Lee's water bottle was empty. Rama waved at Carla for help. "Don't worry, we'll get you back to the clubhouse, Mr. Trujillo, she's probably got medicine there."

Lee thought that might be a good idea until Boney Carlisle walked over to see what the screeching was about. Compassion uncharacteristically crossed the big man's face as he noticed the ugly welt rising on Lee's right hand. "Damn it, Trujillo, are you okay?" But trailing Lee with only four holes to play, the benefits of Lee's misfortune bumped compassion aside in favor of less noble emotions.

"Better call it quits, eh compadre? You need a doctor…you need something cold on that hand." Boney looked over at Mirage, who stood watching the exchange in silence. "Mirage, you got any H_2O…or do you only keep orange soda in that bottle?"

Carlos Taddio was lamenting his decision to walk to the sixteenth green when the howls from the fifteenth fairway reached his ears. Navigating the hidden paths in the barranca to the green would have been much easier on Niña's back. The sound of someone in anguish raised the hairs on his neck. It didn't sound like the voice of a boy—of Rama—but he feared that somehow his vision was in jeopardy. Although his feet were tired, Carlos picked up the pace as the rock outcropping adjacent to his destination came into view.

Mirage produced a canteen of water. Boney poured a stream over Lee's burning hand, then offered his stricken competitor a drink. "They'll get you fixed up pronto. Pretty damn bad luck, huh? But maybe you can catch me another day." Boney offered a hand to prompt Lee's concession. "Let's call it a day—make it legal."

It might have been the water, or an invigorating rush of endorphins—perhaps only brute pride—but something motivated Lee to reject Boney's offer.

"Thanks for the aqua, Carlisle, but screw the concession," Lee replied with a grimace. The image of his supporters walking away losers made the vision of playing through this latest misery seem tolerable. Lee looked at the wound again; a scorpion's sting, he guessed. He wouldn't croak from the critter's poison, but he suspected he might die of shame if he gave Boney a year's bragging rights.

Lee got back to his feet and flexed his hand trying to get some mobility into the tightening tissue. He gasped at the pain. "So Rama, where is my ball?"

Rama said he had seen the ball disappear into the barranca.

"Boney, where you lying?" Lee asked.

"Round the bend there buddy, dead center," Boney replied, hoping to sway his competitor to his senses.

"Okay, I'll concede," Lee offered, gasping with the quickening pulse in his chest.

Boney smiled victoriously.

"Lee can't quit!" The brassy voice of Carla interrupted the golfers' deliberations like a bugle. "What's the matter here, Lee? You don't *ever* quit!"

Carla Stone was dismayed at the second major medical crisis of the day and sensed that now the match would have to wait. She had already noticed Lee panting, and she worried about his heart. She'd be damned if she would be responsible for another tragedy on her course—she could leave that terrible burden on Carlos's shoulders. Carla tried to block them out, but the young faces of Glendora and Dickey played through her mind.

"Not exactly in the pink, eh, Lee?" she asked warily. "You know I'll stir the Alamo up all over again if I call this off. But if you can't play, then…"

Lee stopped Carla short: "Only this hole…I'll concede only number fifteen. Shit, I'd have to take a drop anyway, but I'm not giving up the match." Lee clenched his jaw in misery and reached into his bag for a flask of Tequila. Pinning the flask against his belt buckle with the butt of his lame right hand, he unscrewed the cap with his left and tossed down a shot. He poured some liquor on the wound and watched it sizzle. Hopefully, he thought, the curative properties of the Mescal would stabilize his racing pulse and get him through the sixteenth—the toughest hole on the course.

"Come on, let's get moving while I still can. Where do we stand?"

"You're two up with three more to play going to sixteen," declared Carla.

Carla waved Melyssa to bring the cart over. They drove to the highest point along the fifteenth fairway. Carla stood on the running boards and announced Lee's concession of the fifteenth hole. By now everyone knew about the food poisoning, and now, with the additional misfortune, no one could fault Lee for quitting—certainly not one hole—and if anyone had a lick of humanity, not even for the entire match. As it was, rather than eliciting jeers of resistance to the news, Carla left her customers buzzing about the courage of the stricken golfer. Without complaint, the gallery followed the golfers and their caddies down the trail through the bottom of the barranca and up to the butte looming above sixteen's long, crooked fairway.

—•—

Hank watched Lee's concession hopefully. "That's one way to play this crazy game," he muttered under breath already strained by his man Boney's teetering on the edge of defeat. The odds looked as if they had shifted back into Boney's favor. He realized that with three holes left, and with Lee in medical trouble, Boney was in the driver's seat. Heading to the elevated tee on sixteen, it looked like God was on his side after all.

Hank did the math; he would have won more if Boney could have put Lee away with as large a margin as it appeared he might have earlier in the round before Lee's amazing demonstration of will. But still, with Boney inevitably drawing even and eclipsing his crippled competitor through the last three holes, Hank figured he would leave this crazy place about $1500, richer than when he first crunched down its driveway.

Hank was in need of a decent payday to recoup some of his expenses. He had been surprised when Doris suggested he and Rama spend some time together, the only proviso being that the dogs and the horses—the real money—would have to wait until Rama was back in her loving hands. He was relieved that the races in Ruidoso hadn't panned out, for he didn't relish the thought of taking Rama to the track against Doris's wishes or asking his boy to participate in an alibi. Luckily, this golfing wager was off her radar so he could make a few bucks without misleading anyone. It hardly mattered, thought Hank. There was always less to explain in the harvest of winning than in the famine of defeat.

—•—

The atmosphere was charged with anticipation as the golfers and their supporters climbed from the gloomy barranca up to the sixteenth tee perched on the crest of a butte. Below, the fairway swooped away in a green arc toward the distant hole. Rama thought about Chandler Stone and his doomed children, happily striking balls from that magic place out into the night. Today, the tee would host different emotions.

Lee fell behind as he trudged up the dusty path.

"Need some more water?" Rama asked the injured golfer.

"Keep it, amigo." Lee's voice was strained. "You might need it when you carry me off this evil course."

As he climbed the stone steps to the tee and looked across the upraised faces in the gallery below, he turned pale. His vision darkened. The climb and the poison had taken their toll. As Boney entered the tee box, Lee raised his swollen hand to Rama to demonstrate its uselessness. "Too bad we can't get Carla to let you take a few shots for me, amigo; this hand ain't good for shit."

Boney noticed the alarming inflation of Lee's hand and felt true sympathy. "Jesus, Lee, you don't have to go through with this. Screw Carla's match." He fished a brownie from his pocket and tore at the wrapper. "Or maybe we can get Carla to let your caddie take a few shots for you," he smiled mischievously.

But Lee's tolerance for Boney had been stretched too far, and he snapped at him to hurry up and drive. His thoughts were turning rapidly away from valor; the sooner they got this ordeal over, the better.

Boney tossed the last lump of his brownie into his mouth and obliged Lee with a quick setup and a solid crack at the ball, sending it 250 yards into a headwind. He was left with 320 yards to a flag standing invisibly on the backside of a blind green.

Now it was Lee's turn. He thanked God that the scorpion hadn't bitten him on the left hand—if it had, this match would already be over. He realized that if he used irons he could manage a single-handed swing without involving his hopeless right hand. Lee asked Rama for the 6-iron. The swing produced an amazing journey of 185 yards after some generous downhill roll. His ball lay far behind Boney's, but he had dodged the dangerous right rough where Carlos's ravens scavenged for lost balls. Although it was a good start, the yellow oak guarding the green still stood almost 400 yards away.

In a moment Lee was over his ball again. The fairway curved right and narrowed into a stripe as it climbed to the green—a diminishing target for an aggressive golfer determined to get into chipping range on his second shot. That would be an issue for Boney, but at Lee's distance the stricken golfer was free of such dangers. He simply had to strike the 6-iron again without fear of anything but stirring the poisons farther up his arm.

Boney felt confident in the likely outcome of the match and fired at the stripe. From there a simple wedge up onto the confounding green would ensure another lost hole for Lee. Boney's bulky shoulders turned back and dropped with a less-than-artistic but surprisingly effective swoop into the ball. Flying in complicity with its master's wishes, the ball landed directly in the stripe, not more than sixty yards short of the green's seductive false front.

Both men knew the green had a history and was not to be trifled with. If Boney had any complaint with his solidly struck second shot, it was that it might have been a tad too far to the left to pick apart the interlocking puzzle of perfectly placed shots Chandler had intended to par this hole. Piece number two should have been deep and right to fit properly. Nevertheless, Boney seemed satisfied with deep, and patted his pockets for a victory cigar.

Lee tried to gather his wavering resolve as he set up for his third shot. From his vantage below, the false front edge of the green formed a skyline above him. Two hundred yards away and uphill, the green seemed too far, too blind, and too futile to even attempt. The weary golfer heaved a long pained breath out into the afternoon, bearing the question of a million other golfers, even those playing without venom in their bloodstreams: "Why do I torture myself?"

As if he sensed Lee's doubt, Rama answered the unspoken question with the same answer that shimmers without substance in so many hopeful minds: "You can do it." Four words that offer a toehold for great expectations and unwarranted justification for poor judgment, a phrase in which reality lies blinded by the dazzle of unreasonable optimism.

Lee was less concerned with failure than he was in finding a soft place on his sister's couch in the near future with a cold compress on his ravaged right hand. Without thought or discussion he stepped in, took a couple of one-handed practice swings, and slapped the ball viciously in the general direction of the target oak—leaving himself wholly in the hands of fate.

Fate returned his confidence by arranging that the ball, which had been struck low and carelessly, did not plug into the hillside but found a hard patch of turf from which to rebound to a lie behind the jagged rocks along the green's north fringe.

Lee didn't bother to ask after the shot, simply turning to Rama with questioning eyes. A flicker of hope flared as Rama reported that the ball had bounced somewhere up over the top toward the green.

"That lucky SOB," groused Boney. Although he was too low on the fairway to see the outcome of Lee's shot, he had seen enough in the ball's fortuitous bounce up the slope to be irritated.

"Some people get all the breaks."

Mirage saw things differently: "Yeah Bones, some break eh…getting the shit stung out of you on top of food poisoning. You'd better quit worrying about Lee's luck and pay some attention to your third shot or Trujillo's liable to beat you one-handed."

Mirage hiked the bag up a little higher on his shoulder and headed up toward Boney's ball. "Don't forget, Bones; he'll be on the dance floor in four."

Boney panted like a hound as he passed his ball and climbed the mound beneath the oak to get a view of the flag's position. The two-tiered green was tucked between the tree and the rock pile. On his right, the upper tier narrowed and descended into a pinched section adjoining the lower tier nearly ten feet below. Today the flag was all the way back on the lower shelf.

Boney knew his shot from the fairway would be completely blind. He envisioned an arc drawn from his ball over the tree and down to the cup. The imaginary arc would have to be high enough to clear the oak's menacing branches and land softly enough to hold the tiny lower tier of the green in putting range of the hole. With a smidgen of good fortune, Boney hoped he might also catch the bank above the green and run down to the putting surface, or even land in the center of the green and ride the narrow section down to the pin for a possible birdie or an easy par.

It appeared to Boney that the best Lee could do would be a lob over the rocks to get on the critical lower section in four, but with the top of Lee's ball barely peeking from thick rough, that lob looked impossible. Bogey might be a good score for Lee in this situation, and that would ensure that the match would continue with Lee only one up with two to play—and growing weaker by the minute.

"Piece of cake, Mirage," huffed Boney, returning like Moses from the mountaintop. Boney plucked the smoldering cigar from his teeth and tossed it to the grass. "Sand wedge all the way, buddy boy."

Boney swung with confidence and in sync with a perfect mental image of the hole's topography. His vision, however, was flawed in its failure to adequately respect the tree. He listened in dismay as his ball worked its way through the oak's silver limbs like a great arboreal pachinko game. The ball eventually plunged to the shaggy grass beneath the uncooperative oak. Like Carlos had told Rama: This puzzle was Chandler's best work.

—•—

The anxious gallery had gathered on Lee's side of the green and crawled up onto the rock pile even before he found his ball in the rough. With so much gone wrong for Lee in this game, Rama felt as if it could get no worse. But it did. In dragging himself up the steep slope to the green, Lee expended the capacity of his constitution to fight the double poisonings—even with the buoyant spell of his charmed caddie. Before the startled eyes of Rama, the gallery, and an incredulous Carla Stone, Lee Trujillo crumpled to his knees.

Hank Schwain watched from the shade of the yellow oak. Nearby, Boney and Mirage huddled in contemplation of their recovery shot. This should finally close out the match, Hank hoped. He could cut his losses, or better yet get his money back by default. No matter, he was ready to get back on the highway, to the Gulf, perhaps, and a little R and R with his son.

"Guess he'll be throwin' in the towel now, huh?" Hank asked Boney.

"Buddy, he should have tossed the towel back about the time he started tossing his lunch," Boney chuckled and puffed on his Garcia Vega.

Mirage was disturbed at the price Lee was paying for honor. He brushed his hand across the flat bristles on his head and felt sympathetic perspiration. Like Hank, Mirage also wanted the match to be over—at least to ensure that Lee got some medical attention pronto.

"Don't suppose that kid of yours knows any first aid?" Mirage asked Hank.

Hank had to admit he didn't know. Years of gambling and estrangement from Doris had left him out of touch—broad, blank panels interrupted the diorama of his son's life. Had Rama taken first aid in school? Or in scouts? Did he go to camp last summer? Had he played baseball last year? Who were his friends? All blanks.

"Well, I'm not sure," Hank answered honestly. From across the green he watched his son stoop down beside Lee. Rama's mouth move in silence as the pair receded in an illusion of terrible distance.

Hank shook away the disturbing lapse, preparing to assist Lee himself. But Carla, in the company of a white-haired fellow who carried himself with the demeanor of a doctor, was already hurrying to Lee's side.

Hank hesitated and looked at Mirage. "So where do we stand?"

"We're down two holes, after fifteen," Mirage replied. "If Lee had won this hole, then we would be packing it in. He might be sick, but he'd a won."

"Well he ain't dead just yet," Boney said somberly, peeking up from a practice stance over his ball. "I'm taking my next shot unless Carla calls me off."

"What if Lee quits?" asked Hank.

"Then he loses all the marbles cause he quit the remaining two holes," replied Mirage. "Don't seem too fair, considering…"

Boney looked down the steep bank of the mound and out toward the flag. He had missed this green once and was determined not to double his misery. He began setting up for a dangerous chip to the tiny target. The barranca yawned just beyond—hungry for his ball.

"Hold up!" cried Mirage. "What are you doing there, boss?" Boney stopped in mid-chip and listened. "You're gonna be better off making the easy bump 'n run over to the upper level and taking your chances on a putt for par."

Boney looked at his gaunt caddie with disdain. "Since when did you get so cautious?" he replied. "Damned if them abyyzabbies ain't been shrinking your gonads and your brains, partner. Nobody ever makes that putt."

"Bones…the brownies haven't exactly worked wonders on your noggin, either. I'd give you only 50/50 that the chip you're cooking up even stops on the green, let alone near the hole. You'll still need another chip to get on. And then you'll be layin' five and still looking at putts."

Mirage continued, confident that his words were sinking into Boney's substantial head. "Now, if you direct your attention to poor old Lee laying on his ass over by the rocks—without a rat's chance of a shot at the flag—then why would you risk a bogey or worse when his chances for par are squat?" Mirage rested his case and waited for a verdict.

"Makes sense to me, Mirage."

Boney returned to his stance. "But since when has T. Carlisle been sensible?" Without further comment he foolishly put his wedge into action. The ball tried to fly up from the grassy slope but came out low and hot—caroming across the putting surface then down through a breach in the fringe trampled the night before by an inquisitive puma.

Boney seriously considered the hallowed act of club tossing. He visualized the pitching wedge swirling deep into the brush like a helicopter's rotor—not in an act of frustration, but in an effort to avoid having to return the club to the bag and confront the grinning face of Mirage Jimson. Boney imagined Mirage tamping fat charges of scorn into a muzzleloader, and he wasn't anxious to face the blast.

"Stellar shot, Bones." Mirage's hands spoke considerably more than his words as they yanked the club away with disdain. If Mirage's lean fingers had their way, they would never return the club to such reckless, bloated hands.

"T. Boney Carlisle, you son of a bitch. Who said you could chip while we've got a player down?" Carla Stone cursed Boney as she and the doctor hurried across the putting green to tend to Lee Trujillo.

It was with reluctance that Carla ever set foot on the green at number sixteen. Like a defect on one's body, the green's awful history was an undeniable part of her, a part she avoided in defense of her sanity. Losing both of your children in the same crazy instant was burden enough; being absent when it happened made it worse.

She could never have known that those good-bye hugs on the steps of the Pullman Porter were good-byes forever. And if she had, she would have strained against the corner of the window to see Glendora and Dickey a few seconds longer as their waving fell away into nothing. But that would have appeared a less-than-dignified show of silly emotion, so *Goings on About Town* received her attention as the train gathered eastbound inertia and Carlos Taddio shepherded her children away from the platform.

Three weeks later, the startling message of a "domestic emergency" was delivered to Carla on a silver tray as she sat beneath the magnolias. The carefully scribed note hinted at grave news and offered her the use of the chairman's office and his personal assistant to make any necessary arrangements. She tried to make a graceful exit, but the faces of the Daughters of the Confederacy—her tea mates that afternoon—watched quizzically as she rose from the white wicker table. Her china cup toppled. A saucer of divinity fell to the grass. Six sets of perfectly made-up eyes searched Carla's face for a clue to her breach of poise.

The lightning bolt on the sixteenth had robbed Carla of her motherhood and her destiny with the elite. She would never return to Augusta again, nor would a Daughter ever cross the threshold of Mesquite Creek's humble clubhouse. Two generous wreaths of flowers followed her back to the tragic double funeral, along with the Confederacy's written condolences.

———•———

Rama looked up expectantly as Carla and the doctor tended to Lee. Rama knew they had no remedy for Lee's misery now, other than a seat in Melyssa's cart and a bumpy ride back to the clubhouse.

"Suppose you'll be needing the Last Rites next?" Carla joked, trying to buoy Lee's spirits. "I think we're fresh out of clergy, but Doc Otnes can help." Lee did not respond with his usual humor, but climbed slowly to his feet. Carla abandoned the irreverent track and signaled for Melyssa to bring the cart around as the doctor examined the wound.

"Seen better days, have we, son? Let me see that hand."

Lee grimaced and raised his arm obediently.

"I have an anti-toxin in my bag back in the car. You'll need a shot right away. Put you right as rain."

Carla gave Lee a sincere pat on the shoulder. "That's it, Lee. There's no disgrace in losing like this. Call it quits and we'll get you out of here before anybody gets too upset." She was careful not to suggest a suspension of play 'til another day. This was not the Pro Tour; everyone had a day job, including the gallery. Acts of God, from twisters to scorpions, all had to take their place in Carla's schedule. There was no tomorrow.

"You are up two, with three to go, Lee, so a concession here loses the match by only one hole. That will soften the blow to those betting on the point spread."

The chugging of Melyssa's refreshment cart mingled with the murmuring of the anxious gallery as the vehicle strained up the hill to the green. Melyssa caught Rama's eye as he watched her set the brake. She returned a quick smile but chopped it off in response to the desolate mood hanging over the foursome. Lee took refuge in the cart with Doc Otnes, grateful for the end of this struggle and the simple pleasures of a padded vinyl bench. He would have to think twice about playing golf on the Sabbath again.

"All right, Carla; make it official. Tell them Trujillo's had enough," Lee sighed.

Carla didn't particularly want to see Boney win, but she was as anxious as Lee to get off the course—especially this damned hole. It was early enough in the afternoon that with a little luck some of the winners might still leave a portion of their booty behind in the grill room bar.

With reluctance Carla agreed: It was time to call the match. As she took final stock of the implications of her decision, one spectator hidden in the crowd by the rock outcropping along the green's upper reaches raised his eyes to the Texas sky. With one hand the old fellow held his incriminating hat at his side; in the other he fingered his crucifix while he prayed silently for a miracle that would square with his vision. He visualized Rama in the game, and he shivered in anticipation of the Stone children's impending ascendance.

Before Carla could gather a breath to make her announcement, Rama Schwain's determined voice interrupted the solemn proceedings: "Mr. Trujillo, did you see Boney hit his last shot? It rolled clear off the green. That was his fourth. You're just three right here by the green and you're ahead by two holes. You could win easy."

Lee looked at the boy with interest. Somehow his own indomitable heart had found another voice and was speaking to him through this accidental caddie. There was no question the boy was right.

"Rama. Rama," Lee smiled bravely. "Let me off the hook, eh. Don't you see those rocks? To clear them and stop on that little piece of green down below…shit, I'd need a money shot: a high lob with backspin. Out of this deep spinach? And with this hand?" Lee shook his head.

Lee paused, visualizing the shot, and then raised his bright red hand for Rama's inspection. "That shot would take some serious feel. And amigo…*feel* I ain't got."

"I know a better way," Rama said hastily.

Carla looked at Rama sternly. Time would run out soon for changing Lee's mind. Rama stepped out onto the upper level of the green to the point from which he had seen Carlos's putt roll last night.

"Don't try to clear the rocks; just chip it to here. Then a putt can win," he called back from the green with the assurance of one who had tested the proposed strategy. Not a soul gathered at the green could know, but Carlos Taddio had placed the pin himself to ensure that this putt might come to pass and that Rama would know it. The line to the hole lay etched with inevitability for the one who knew its secret.

"Chip it to here. You can do that, with your good hand," implored Rama.

"Yeah, but why bother?"

"Because from there you can putt it real close…I know it. I *promise* a two-putt. The least you'll do is tie Boney." Rama returned from the green and whispered to Lee. "There's a secret line to the hole. You can still easily make par and win. Then go with the doctor."

Lee didn't know about secret lines, but he did appreciate the logic of trying for a bogey and a tie once it was spelled out so clearly for his feverish mind. Rama was right; he could easily get that chip to the spot Rama described, and what the hell, he thought, maybe that putt would drop. Before he knew it, he was dragging himself from the cart. A couple more strokes wouldn't kill him.

"Okay, Rama, pull my sand wedge." Without another thought the quavering golfer dropped a one-handed wedge behind the ball. Like a fat grasshopper, the ball hopped up from the grass and clung to a landing spot right where Rama had intended. Lee winced with pain; there was no joy in the accomplishment. Even that soft little chip was one swing too many for that luckless day.

"Son of a bitch, he's still playin'," Boney grumbled. "The chicken shit didn't even try to fly those rocks…thinks a two-putt is gonna win? Crap, you'd think by now he'd respect my short game." Boney considered his ball somewhere down below the lower green. "But I'd be damned if I don't get up and down from there. Then our Mexican buddy is gonna have to one-putt if he wants to take this match."

Boney paused. "What was he thinking, Mirage?"

Mirage always considered the game in its most elemental terms: a test between himself and par played over, around, and through whatever obstacles nature presents, pure and simple—except perhaps for yesterday's god-awful grasshopper swarm. But after his years of wrangling with Boney and his buddies, golf had taken on the feel of dirty pool or craps with loaded dice. He didn't appreciate the change.

Mirage raised his head from cleaning the grooves in Boney's sand wedge. "Maybe he was just playin' smart." He slid the club into the bag and stretched his spindly frame before hiking down to find Boney's ball in the barranca. As he descended, the scent of distant rain and ripening alfalfa settled within Mirage's mind and with it flowered the memory of a sorely missed acquaintance, one whose words rang with a purity long missing at Mesquite Creek.

"Golf aeys just a *nahtural* act," Chandler Stone used to say when Mirage, in his lithe and limber thirties played with the enigmatic Scotsman, back when he could still reach straightened arms above his shoulders in an enviable backswing. Mirage recalled how Chandler could make a man, a boy, or a girl appreciate the rustic nature of the game and its odd tidal character: the ebb and flow of swing, confidence, and luck, from the favorable to the formidable. Under the inscrutable laws of chance, a golfer's fortunes were, as he often said, "wisped abouwt like wynd combing waves 'cross timothy fields." To Chandler's way of thinking, that was not a bad thing.

"Ye are the ayr itself eyn this endeavor," Chandler would say with sparkling eyes. "If ye dayn't enjoy blowin' round a bit, feynd yerself a nice parlor gaym."

Mirage chuckled at the memory of Chandler's description of golf's menacing nature and that the game was more than willing to "chop the pryde of mid-handicap roosters to shreyds whyst hurling bolts of bad luck, merciless irony, aynd injustice upon innocent fools."

Although the Dornoch man's game was not immune from big numbers, he always savored his rounds with a dignity that touched everyone he encountered. It had been too long since Chandler disappeared, lamented Mirage. There were many folks who insisted that Chandler must have died, likely by his own hand. His retreat from his beloved Carla, from golf, and his alleged withdrawal to the widow's watch were evidence of his breakdown following his children's deaths, they thought. A discreet suicide somewhere in the most remote depths of the barranca wasn't an unthinkable eventuality. Mirage never believed his old friend could fall that far from his noble view of life but realized he would probably never walk these fairways with Chandler Stone again. More than ever, he was thirsty for a cool drink of simple, honest golf and for the chance to savor his own efforts in silence save for the crunch of July turf below his spikes and the supportive song of a meadowlark.

But that game would have to wait.

Mirage nudged Boney, who appeared to be entranced by Lee's unexpected chip to the green. "Bones, better get over to your ball and see what you can do with it…pronto. Carla's liable to throw a slow-play penalty on us if you keep daydreaming."

Luckily for Boney, his ball, in jeopardy of tumbling into the tangled brush behind him, was still in play. After executing a skillful chip, a ripple of applause followed his ball's arrival on the green. Too far below to see the outcome, Boney guessed that it was good-shot applause rather than an in-the-hole response. As he clambered up the bank he saw the ball sitting within five feet of the flagstick, and he felt some vindication for the previous lapse in judgment.

"That'll give him something to shoot for," Boney huffed. He was on in five and looking at a bankable bogey six while Lee, who lay on the upper level in four with a long and convoluted path to the pin, was looking at a far less certain score.

But Lee *wasn't* looking. He had heard the gallery's reaction to Boney's masterful chip, but he didn't care. In fact, he had returned to the seat in the cart and propped his feet up on the dashboard, as close to prone as the little seat would allow. He held a Dixie cup of ice upon his useless hand. Carla looked at her contestant without a doubt in her mind: This match was over. She strode to the middle of the green with an imperial demeanor. She looked down the slope to Boney and waved him back up.

"Pick it up. We're through," she called. "Come on up."

The gallery came to life as scores of customers began to digest the implications of her command. Through with what, they wondered: another hole again, or the match?

Down on the lower green, Boney cursed the call and stooped over to pick up his ball.

Fifty feet away, Carlos Taddio raised his head cautiously from behind the rocks to see Boney's lie on the green. As Carla's decree echoed above number sixteen, his old but hopeful heart sank as it became apparent Rama would only get as close as a *caddie* could to being a player and fulfilling the vision. Rama stood beside Lee on the green's very fringe, but the leap to his participation and release of the Stone children's spirits was a gap too far. Carlos feared the walk back to his camp would be painful. Perhaps he had asked too much of his Lord.

"Don't touch it!" Mirage barked. "Better see what old lady Stone has in mind before you write off this hole."

In a few seconds Boney was panting breathlessly at the top of the green where Carla waited to explain her decision. A group of spectators began to gather at a respectful distance; Hank Schwain found himself swept along on a current of anticipation.

"What the…what do you mean by we're through?" Boney nearly gagged on the aborted expletive. "Remember, Lee said he'd play out this hole after he conceded the last one."

"That he did," Carla responded calmly. "But my judgment is that after playing so," she paused, "heroically, through these setbacks, Lee need not be penalized for an Act of God."

Boney protested: "Mrs. Stone, it's too damn bad Lee's hurtin', but he only got bit because he didn't keep his ball in the fairway. That's what golf is all about. That snake or scorpion, or whatever it was, was just an 'outside agency.' Lee's only paying the price for *inaccuracy*. I shouldn't be penalized by losing the advantage I earned by hitting that fairway." Boney rested his case; even Mirage seemed impressed. He offered his companion one of the few smiles he'd wrenched from his face the entire day.

"Mr. Carlisle, don't push your luck," Carla replied. She tapped her glasses firmly into place and with a long breath inflated her judicial stature to its fullest. "I'd like this match over just as much as you, but as far as I am concerned, Lee's got the right to replay the hole in better health. It's only fair; he granted you the last hole after getting bit, did he not?"

Boney nodded.

"I don't give a damn where you're both sitting on the green; I'm not granting anything." Carla extracted a little booklet, *The Rules of Golf*, from her pocket and pointed it at Boney like a pistol. Then she raised her voice to carry to the surrounding gallery: "The Committee has decided there will be a suspension of play, and that in lieu of the debilitating condition of one of the contestants…the equitable course is to replay this hole at a time to be determined and let the previous hole's concession stand."

The die was cast. Carla's concern focused straightaway upon the gallery's reaction. She had only to wait a few seconds before cries of protest rang from the potential mob. If she had called play off immediately after the scorpion's bite, it would have squared better with the spirit of the rules or the sympathy of the spectators; but now, with Boney's ball less than five feet from pay dirt, the decision to replay was proving hard for his supporters to swallow. Most worrisome to Carla were the angry voices of Lee's boosters beginning to tangle with Boney's. This could get ugly rapidly—Santa Anna and Travis came to mind.

A shiver of apprehension raced over Rama's skin. This was something new and dangerous: the heat rising from a hundred angry men. He wished he could throw down the miserable golf clubs and leave Mesquite Creek to those who played out their ugly vision of the game on it. It was hard to believe how beautiful it all was the night before.

Lee Trujillo stiffened in response to the commotion. His arm throbbed mightily, yet he guessed a quick show of support for Carla's ruling would dampen the rising tide of unrest—at least within his ranks. The words *spic* and *wetback* rose from the crowd. A half-empty beer can slammed violently against the fender of the Cushman. Melyssa cried out in fear.

Without warning, a pistol shot shattered the afternoon sky. The mob fell silent.

Carla stood at the edge of the green with one arm extended, aiming the smoking revolver straight into the sky. The other arm clutched the book of rules against her chest. A green sweater draped down from her shoulders.

"My God...she looks like the fucking Statue of Liberty," Mirage whispered.

Carla held her majestic pose as the bullet's report echoed from the crags above the clubhouse and back across the vacant fairways. Then her voice filled the void.

"Cut the crap," Carla bellowed with startling authority. "Let's be sporting. Which of you SOBs would play your best one-handed? We will replay the sixteenth hole tomorrow and continue the match from there." Carla was not going to try and reason with these animals, but in light of their discontent, she offered a welcome reparation: "For the remainder of the evening, and prior to tomorrow's replay, all drinks will be half-priced."

The crowd simmered in respect for Carla—or at least her weaponry—and for the moment seemed satisfied with the discount drinks and a replay. As a more civil mood settled over them, Carla tucked the warm pistol back into her handbag.

"Not very ladylike, eh?" she whispered to Lee. If things boiled again, she feared she had already played out her best hand. Then to her chagrin, Boney Carlisle took the floor.

"I protest that ruling, ma'am." The big man's voice followed the pistol's report with authority. "If you insist on not giving me this match, even considering Lee's intended withdrawal, then the least you can do is to resume play from right where it is now. Don't make me pick up a clearly superior chip. That's only fair."

Carla cursed Boney's intrusion, but it was a reasonable proposal. She cursed herself for the oversight. Maybe the mob would have bought his idea without her offering to give half her liquor away. Maybe she could still rescind her offer.

"The Committee has considered your proposal," she began formally, but weary of the magisterial image cut her prose short, "It's alright by me." She could eat a little crow if it cut her losses at the bar.

"Well it's not okay by me, amigos."

The feeble voice of Lee strained from the cart. "It's punishment enough I've had to play one-and-a-half holes with my hand like this, but if we're gonna play later, it sure as hell won't be tomorrow or anytime soon. I've got a gig in El Paso starting Tuesday morning, and I can't be up this way for another week."

"Christ, we can't wait a week," Boney complained, fully aware that a refreshed Lee Trujillo would cut him to ribbons.

"Carlisle, quiet down," Carla snapped. "Mr. Trujillo, I am so sorry but we must conclude this match tomorrow one way or another on the Committee's terms, or you'll have to concede. I also have a busy schedule as well."

Lee had had enough talk and was ready for whatever magic the doctor had back in his bag. "Screw it. This hand ain't gonna be much better tomorrow than it is today—might be worse. Alright, Mrs. Stone; I'll concede the match today and make you all happy after I get my fifth shot to match Boney, who's already layin' five…but with one condition."

Carla nodded. She appreciated Lee's desire to at least have a final shot but was surprised that he was willing to get up from the cart for another painful stroke. "And that would be?"

Carla and the gallery waited as Lee motioned Rama over to the cart. "Do you really believe in this putt?" he whispered.

Rama's eyes sparkled yes.

"Well, I can't say that I do, Rama. And confidence is half the battle, ain't it?" Lee slipped the club into Rama's hands. "Here, you take the shot for me, *brujo*."

Rama blushed. He didn't know golf's arcane rules, but he suspected playing for another was not one of them.

Carla watched the conference at the cart with diminishing patience; she was anxious for an answer. "And that condition would be?"

"That my caddie takes the stroke in my place." Lee held up his swollen hand for evidence of his handicap. "If my competitor agrees."

Boney nearly choked on the chance to accept Lee's offer before the crazy Mexican came to his senses or before Carla shot down the whole bizarre idea. The scorpion's venom was obviously working on Lee's brain as well as his right hand.

"You heard him, Carla, one more shot and we can forget about all this resume and replay shit. Hell, if he wants the boy to putt for him, it's okay by me." The magnanimity of Boney's gesture was betrayed by the daunting odds against a ninety-degree sixty-foot downhill double-breaker, even if stroked by Ben Hogan himself, actually finding the hole and winning the match.

Both competitors looked to Carla for a ruling. Oddly, they both were in agreement that Rama could take the putt. They only needed the Committee's blessing to make it legal. A smile flickered across Lee's face. What did he have to lose now? Boney stared at Carla with a prayer on his lips. How could he lose?

Carla was relieved that this unorthodox proposition to finish the match had come from the contestants—no one would have accepted it from her. The thought of avoiding a hundred or so money-losing shots of liquor was all the justification she needed to agree. Carla cleared her throat for the last time.

Carlos froze in his disheartened retreat from the rocks. Carla's intention rekindled hope in his chest. He fingered his beads and prayed that her greed wouldn't be an unworthy means to fulfilling his vision. The old greens keeper prepared to face Dickey's and Glendora's happy spirits once again and to bless their passage from this hallowed place to eternal bliss.

"It has been agreed that due to injury to one of the participants, and in the Committee's inability to find a timely date for a resumption of play, that the opportunity for a conclusive putt shall be granted on the sixteenth hole, and that the caddie of the injured player shall be assigned surrogate power to take the putt. This decision should have minimal impact upon the outcome of the entire match."

Carla was relieved that her decree went down well with the gallery; perhaps Lee's supporters had given up, too. Perhaps she should look into politics, she thought.

Boney nudged Mirage. "You catch all that? Baffle 'em with bullshit…works every time."

"You oughta know, Bones."

"Resume play, gentlemen," Carla declared with finality.

With nothing more than a wink and a simple admonition to make your old man proud, Lee handed the putter back to his caddie and waved him onto the green stage. Rama tried to remember what Carlos had said about not thinking too much, but aware that he had suddenly become the focal point for more than a hundred strangers in a strange place, it was impossible to think too little. A bashful boy could become paralyzed if he lingered upon the reality that had befallen him.

Rama briefly scanned the gallery for his father. Every second he searched, the crowd looked larger and less benign. He located Hank on the slope below the yellow oak and flashed his most courageous smile. But, strangely, his father didn't return any expression remotely resembling support—not a smile or a thumbs-up—just a stern face racked with anxiety over the putt's outcome.

Why now, Rama thought, when everything in his being screamed yes, did everything in his father's face signal no?

A spasm of stage fright set his hands to trembling, but as he visualized the line Carlos had scribed for him last night, the tremors were replaced with confidence out of all reasonable proportion. If Boney had any idea of the certainty whirling like a gyroscope inside his new opponent, he would never have agreed to Lee's final condition. Now, as if directed by another, Rama crouched behind the ball and sighted across the green like a veteran. All questions flew from his mind. He remembered only the roll toward the rock pile, then the unlikely swoop down into the chute. The only line he had to deliver in this drama was a firm putt toward the rocks—an act of faith conjured by Chandler Stone and Carlos Taddio to turn away the unbelievers.

The putter lay comfortably in Rama's fingers. He curled his grip into place and waited for the right moment to tap the first domino of this complex figure into action.

From the cart Melyssa giggled softly, "Good luck, Tarzan."

"Knock it in, amigo."

Rama imagined a whisper in his head—a young, confident voice—then the sound of his own heart counting off low numbers somewhere near the beginning of a life's long tally. When he could no longer distinguish the sound of the wind rustling in the yellow oak's branches from the whisperer's memory of ocean breezes hissing through the whins along some heavenly links, Rama and Dickey Stone let the putt go.

Like a skater tracing his own compulsory figures, Rama's putt lapsed the ideal line toward the very rocks where Carlos crouched, straying slightly as it banked into the narrow slope. It returned to ideal just in time to slide past Boney's ball by a fingernail, then curl rightward back toward the barranca. The barranca's influence pulled the ball on a track that dipped into the right edge of the cup and then through a hair-raising half-circuit of the rim before yielding to the same orbital mechanics that would soon spin tonight's moon above the jagged horizon. Thus spent, Rama's ball fell exhausted to the bottom of the cup.

Mirage exhaled a deep breath held in respect for the entire time Rama was above his ball. "For the love of god!" he cried to no one in particular.

"That was pure!"

Chapter 18

As the ball disappeared, Rama heard cheers from Lee's supporters, and groans of disappointment from those who only moments ago had accepted the contortion of the rules and welcomed Rama's putting for Lee as a hopeless endeavor. Within that conflicting chorus, Rama heard the angry voice of his father.

With his single line on the green stage thus spoken, Rama looked uncomfortably for an exit. Mirage walked out to fetch Boney's irrelevant ball from the green. He was surprised to find the face of the miraculous young golfer far less confident than the putt just delivered.

"Hell of a putt. Hell of a putt. Come on, Ace, let's go pick 'em up," Mirage smiled at Rama's bemused expression. "In case you don't know, you just won the blinkin' match for Trujillo. Damn it, Ace. I don't know what you've been drinking, but somebody should put it in a bottle."

Mirage pulled the flagstick, careful not to bring Rama's ball out with it. "It's all yours," he declared. "I've played here for years and never made a putt from up there. That lucky stroke's liable to set Boney back a notch, and it looks like it might have pissed off your pop, too."

Rama looked toward the oak. His father leaned heavily on his black iron-wood cane and glowered at the couple on the green. Neither Rama nor Mirage could know the gnarled logic that surged through Hank's mind—seeking sense in the twists of fate that had led him to losing $1500, at the hands of his own son. Mirage glanced at Hank, then dropped the flagstick into the hole with a clank. "It figures, Ace. Seems like in this game, whatever you do it's never good enough."

"Fucking unbelievable! Yesterday in the can he wins fifty cents, today, fifteen hundred," Boney cursed as he looked to Mirage for sympathy. But his usually reliable—if slightly cynical—caddie was still lingering out on the green with Rama. The losing golfer fumbled for a cigar, but he couldn't smoke away the fact that he had approved the surrogate putter. Boney had been outplayed, and he knew it. Even with the poisonous setbacks, the happy-go-lucky fellow from El Paso had bested him. The wisest move now was to preserve his dignity and to make a mental note never to play Lee Trujillo again—at least not for money.

Down on the green, Mirage offered his hand to Rama in congratulation and good-bye. "Now, if you catch up with him, tell Lee he did damn good. That hombre is gonna be big-time one day." Mirage and Rama looked up as the huffing old Cushman cart bore Lee, Doc Otnes, and Melyssa away.

"Probably making off with your winnings, kid," Mirage laughed.

Melyssa's black ponytail bounced on her shoulder as the cart disappeared. Rama's heart sank at the sight of her departure. "Oh no, I didn't give Lee back his putter," he cried.

"Keep it, Ace. You hit it better than him, from what I saw." Mirage turned up the slope to deal with Boney. "Gotta go cool down Carlisle. And it looks like your pop might need some chilling, too. Happy trails, Ace."

Mirage was right. Hank didn't appear to be enjoying this payday. Rama remembered the rolls of bills on the coffee table and his father's awkward dance for Doris after a lucky day at the track long ago. Rama was confused. He approached his father with humility, awaiting the complementary greeting, but no such words would arrive today.

"What the hell did you think you were doing?" Hank demanded.

Rama understood the question but not his father's tone. "They told me to putt it 'cause Lee was too sick," Rama explained. He pleaded for recognition: "I won, Dad...we won!"

"Like hell we won," Hank declared. "I was betting on the Brownie King over there."

Hank turned to follow the crowd back up the fairway toward home. Rama remained a few careful steps behind, struggling to suck back the wind that had just been knocked out of him with the realization he had just beat his own father. There would be no acknowledgment of his putting heroics. Once again, Rama's victories fell short.

From his first wobbling bicycle ride down the driveway to his claiming a blue ribbon for a model moon rocket at the science fair, it was always his mother who reveled in his successes. His father, it seemed, was always present for the failures. It was Hank's mortified face Rama had picked from the ballpark crowd when, as a fledgling pitcher, he had struggled helplessly through a nine-run inning in his first and only pitching performance.

And Hank had stood unavoidably at the front door as Rama returned home in defeat following a fumbled after-school date with the celestial Cynthia. It was love's first letdown. The long-imagined rendezvous had collapsed in awkward silence, the victim of his bashfulness and a mind bereft of worthy small talk in the presence of his consuming infatuation.

Rama could have imagined no greater humiliation than facing his father's sly questions in the face of such failure. For both their sakes, Rama longed for a victory under his dad's scrutiny. For a moment he thought his glory on the sixteenth hole was going to be it. But somehow, someone had put that pea under the wrong shell.

"You didn't bet on Lee?" Rama asked in amazement. He spoke carefully, out of respect for a volatile loser's temper. "You said you would this morning."

"Yeah, that was before that god-damned Mexican crawled in sick. Who'd have put money on him after that?" his father snapped. Hank pulled a small flask from his hip pocket and fortified himself. "Been better to have taken my chances against the Apache's ponies up in Ruidoso than to have stuck around this damned place and watched you roll in that lousy putt."

Hank saw pain replace pride in his son's shining eyes. "Christ, son," he offered, "I'm out way over a thousand bucks on this infernal game."

Like gold back to lead, Rama's victory had been transmuted to defeat by his father's decree. Rama felt a tingling in the corner of his eyes, but an ember of newly kindled confidence that had been burning in him since he first hit Lee's 6-iron the previous day evaporated any tears before they could drop.

"I told you, Dad, Boney would lose his advantage on…"

Hank cut Rama's defense short: "And I told you, nobody would bet on that spic after he showed up sick." Somewhere in Hank's angry mind, the Cathedral of St. Claude loomed and the statue of Mary peered blindly at him from its spire. "I ain't *that* reckless," he snapped. "But what difference would it have made if you knew?"

Rama swished Lee's putter across the grass at his feet to divert his eyes from his angry father.

"Then I would have missed."

⎯•⎯

"On purpose?"

Carla's voice cracked like a whip behind them. The matron of Mesquite Creek had wandered over to join the Schwains in the walk back to the club-house. She was in a good mood, glad to have resolved this match early. "No player on my course would ever get away with throwing a game—not if I knew about it," she laughed. "We'll leave that to the Black Sox."

But Carla looked disapprovingly toward Hank. "You should be glad for your boy. It was a one-in-a-million putt he made." She raised her eyes to Rama. "You didn't really think you had a chance to make that did you, Sweetheart?"

"Yes, I did…it wasn't just luck," Rama explained. "There's a secret to it."

"A secret?" Carla's eyes widened and she dropped her glasses down to look more carefully at the boy. "What are you talking about?"

Rama looked uneasy. For the moment curiosity began to replace betrayal in his father's eyes. Rama was reticent to reveal his late-night outing on Carla's course, but be wanted to explain while he had his audience's attention. "Well, if you aim up at the rocks like you were trying to knock it off the green, it will turn back toward the hole."

"It will?" asked Carla. "Come on, Honey, you've never even seen that green; how would you..."

"Sorry, ma'am," Rama interrupted Carla, then looked bashfully down at his putter. "But last night Carlos showed me the putt. I knew Lee could make it."

A darker look descended over Hank. "Damn it, Rama; you were out traipsing around last night? Doris would wring my neck if she knew I wasn't keeping a better eye on you."

Carla had turned very serious. "Did you say you saw Carlos?"

"Yes ma'am."

The colorful proprietor of Mesquite Creek turned a shade of pale. "What did your Carlos fellow look like?"

Rama described Carlos's flat-brimmed hat and silver braid, and his little horse, Niña. Carla was transfixed at the image Rama conjured.

"My God!" Carla gasped. "No one has seen Carlos around here..." she paused, "in many years."

"But he takes care of your greens."

"No, I've got hands to help now," Carla explained. "He used to care for the greens until Chandler disappeared, then..." Carla paused at an icy recollection. "I guess he felt unwelcome. We'd see him less and less until he drifted off for good."

"A few of the hands have said they thought they'd seen him late at night, like a ghost, but that's been a while now. I thought he had died or maybe found his way back to Argentina." Carla remembered the old gaucho and his attachment to her children. She remembered the day of the lightning. "What else did he tell you about the sixteenth besides the putt?"

Rama looked uneasy now. "He told me about the lightning."

The image of her lost children flashed through Carla's mind. The interminable trip back from Augusta to Mesquite Creek burdened by the relentless reality of her loss. Until she had returned and seen the small coffins with her own eyes, the deaths were nothing but an insane abstraction.

Rama saw the darkening memory flicker in Carla's face and without thinking, added: "Carlos says they are happy now."

"Golfing together in Dornoch. Yes I know."

Carla had heard Carlos's dreamy vision before. The image of the children playfully roaming the links abloom with heather was cold comfort in the grieving months following the fatal bolt yet, in time, offered her solace. But what comforted Carla consumed Chandler. He had embraced the lustrous vision of his precious links, the sparkling green, and the sharp salty breezes as his children's heaven. But he couldn't let it go. He had buried the twins near the rocks beside the sixteenth green, but eventually the fog from the firth enshrouded Chandler's sunny mental fairways and he was lost. He had retreated from her and all things in his diminished world that he might yet love.

For days on end Chandler would remain in the widow's watch, the special room he had built for the children. She had seen his face peering from between the louvers and could only imagine what he saw. One morning when she brought him his breakfast, he was gone. No note. No clue. No good-bye. For months she had chased down rumors of his whereabouts, but every trail came up cold. For years thereafter she remained torn between grief and her own reluctance to forever seek what might be impossibly hidden.

Carla knew she owed a lot to the old gaucho. Despite her bitterness, he had stepped into the void and carried her through her grief. And even before Chandler's collapse, as her husband's attention to the course evaporated with his spirit, Carlos had taken up the slack. Yet she never released him from his guilt at presiding over the twins' fates. In time, she had allowed him, like Chandler, to drift from his chosen home into the pitiless Texas plains, then finally into the night.

What was she to make of this, she thought: that this young stranger heralds Carlos's return and brings the old man's comforting vision to her again. Carla Stone softened noticeably; she even dabbed at troubling dampness in her eyes but quickly regained her professional demeanor. The thought of extracting her cut from the Sunday wagers replaced those old and painful memories.

"I'm not your churchy type, but maybe the Lord does work in mysterious ways. If you can make a putt like that, Rama, I guess I can believe that Carlos is alive…and that heaven is in Scotland."

"Just an unlucky, lousy putt as far as I'm concerned—nothing heavenly about it." Hank thumped his cane against the dry fairway turf, then raised it toward Rama. "Next time we're traveling, Chief," he said with authority, "you'll stay indoors at night. No putting, no ghosts, no heaven, and no golf. I don't know what all this crap is about; I only know that if you'd kept your nose out of this damn game I'd have been a damn sight richer."

"Mister Schwain, your boy was just doing what he was told, and damned if he didn't do it beautifully. I'd be proud of him for stepping up to that putt. It would have scared me to death." Carla patted Hank on the shoulder. "And if it makes you feel any better, if we'd have talked Lee into finishing the match on another day, or if he hadn't tangled with that scorpion, Lee would have won anyway."

Carla paused to peer into the future: "In fact, Lee's going to beat 'em all one day. I mean everybody, right to the top. And Boney…he only got as deep into this match as he did because of some lucky bounces and Lee's sister's lousy cooking.

"This is a crazy game, Mister Schwain, no matter how you look at it. Maybe you should stick with the ponies."

Hank scowled sarcastically, well aware that a portion of his loss was headed her way. "Thanks for the advice. I'll never lay a dime on golf again, and I'll be damned if Rama ever sets foot on a golf course, either."

There, in one stroke, Rama's aspirations to pursue the game were paralyzed; the Gift he unknowingly carried that might be destined to elevate the games of future golfers seemed doomed to remain trapped in an inaccessible vessel. Rama felt an emptiness expand in his core and he shuddered, unconscious of the threat to his destiny. At once he realized that he and his father had overstayed their welcome at Mesquite Creek. He longed for the road. Maybe the rumble of the highway would restore the connection with his father that had been torn by this strange detour.

—•—

The sky churned in turmoil over the southeastern horizon as the last of the gallery straggled into the clubhouse to claim their winnings or mourn their losses. Without words, Rama and Hank returned to their rooms to gather their belongings. Chandler's rusted old brassie lay across Rama's bed. He picked it up and the memory of the train whistle blowing through his first swing sounded in his mind. He wondered what he should do with the club. Carlos had given it to him, but with what authority? Rama decided to return it to Carla—she was as close to Chandler as he was likely to get.

He reached to sweep a few coins and a pocketknife off the dresser into his bag when he noticed the key Carlos had given him before dissolving with Niña into the darkness. The key to the crow's nest. His heart quickened; it was time to leave, but he had to have a look in the nest. Carlos had implied it was important.

Nervously, Rama entered the closet where he had discovered the door to the crow's nest. In a second the key was in the lock and the door was free from its jamb. He gave the door a tentative shove, and a flight of stairs revealed itself in the light falling from the broken louvers above. Behind him Rama heard the unmistakable pattern of his fathers crippled step.

"You 'bout ready to roll?" his father asked, poking his head into Rama's room.

Rama's heart skipped as he hollered back from the closet, "Yeah, Dad, be right out." He wasn't going to aggravate the old man anymore by delaying him now. The stairway to the crow's nest disappeared once again behind the door. Rama set the lock and dropped the key back into his pocket.

"Better do something 'bout these damned clubs, too," Hank said as Rama emerged from the closet. Hank rapped the old brassie and Lee's putter with his cane. "Had enough of this golf shit for a spell."

"Yes sir," Rama replied. "I'll give them back before we leave."

A minute later Rama stood on the veranda. The course beyond faded back into the hazy afternoon as patches of light breaking through the gathering clouds prowled its fairways. A group of golfers preparing to tee off chattered hopefully through beautiful sweeping practice swings that would likely never be duplicated in the forthcoming round. Hank Schwain had no further business in Carla's Stone's clubhouse. He had already returned to the dusty wagon and was cursing its stubborn hinge and a dozen grasshoppers trapped within.

Before joining his father at the car, Rama entered the grill room to return the clubs. He found Carla back in her role as gracious hostess, cordially serving the few winners who had settled in for barbecue and an afternoon beer. Outside, the gravel drive crunched with departing vehicles. Rama noticed Boney hunched over a drink and talking with a couple of friends. Boney spotted Rama and without hesitation raised his glass toward the boy and offered an exaggerated toast. He was remarkably jovial for a fellow recently relieved of a substantial sum.

"To our little Hogan," Boney called. "Should have known better than to let you putt."

Maybe the strange turn of events in the match squared with Boney's sense of justice. Perhaps Rama's unorthodox participation and his incredible putt canceled out Boney's own secret transgressions. Somehow, the portly golfer looked strangely at peace before a backdrop of illuminated liquor bottles. He seemed to be mending well from defeat. The cubes in Boney's raised glass rattled again as he amended his toast slightly:

"And kid…damned nice roll. I'll get you next time."

Somewhere in the crests of the clouds gathering above the humble clubhouse, the Gods of Golf checked the tally again: One mark in Boney's favor.

"Your daddy's already out the door, Sugar," Carla said, reverting naturally to the motherly voice she saved for paying customers. She noticed the two clubs. "You got something for me, Rama?"

"Yes ma'am. This is Lee's putter, and this is…"

"Chandler's old brassie," Carla gasped.

Rama handed her the club, and like a baton passed through time it linked Dickey and Glendora's lively fingers to her own. The weathered grip triggered memories like a forgotten scent.

"Where did you find this club, Sweetheart?" Carla asked in amazement.

"Carlos gave it to me up on the sixteenth tee last night," Rama replied.

"The sixteenth…my God, yes. That would be about right," Carla sighed, remembering how she scolded Chandler for returning with the children so late after the night lessons up on that forbidding butte. But the scolding had been futile in the face of a father's love and the glow of his adoring children. Carla looked over the aged persimmon and the tarnished shaft. She remembered it clearly: one of Bobby Jones's gifts to Chandler.

"Take good care of it, Son." Carla returned the club to Rama's reluctant grasp. "I think he would have wanted you to have it. You might try some naval jelly on that rust, though."

"Thanks, ma'am," Rama replied, although he was apprehensive about smuggling the banned golf club into his father's car. Then he held out the second club. "This is Lee's putter."

Without a word Carla pulled an envelope from her apron. "Lee ran out of here in a hurry with doctor Otnes and Donaldo. He said that if you brought in his club, to give you this." Rama and the tough proprietor of Mesquite Creek exchanged trinkets. Rama tucked the envelope into his shirt pocket; she held up the old Bulls-Eye putter for inspection. "This club's going to have a history," she predicted. "He'll be mighty pleased to have it back."

Carla patted Rama's head and stifled a motherly urge to straighten up his tousled brown hair. "Looks like your dad's getting impatient, Sugar." She nodded at the window overlooking the parking lot.

"Yeah," Rama agreed. He searched for an appreciative closing line. "The pie was real good."

"We try."

Rama swung the door open and emerged from the cool grill room into the warm afternoon. The contrast was shocking and slapped him into the realization that he might never visit this remote place again. To leave without a word to Melyssa or Lee or Carlos left him feeling empty. As Rama crossed the veranda's blistering floorboards, he remembered the key in his pocket and whirled around to face Carla again.

"Mom...I mean, ma'am," Rama blushed, "I forgot to give you this. It's the key to the crow's nest."

Carla looked puzzled. Chandler had built the widow's watch to serve as a tower for his airstrip—but he called it the crow's nest in homage to the curious dormitory atop Augusta National's clubhouse. As far as Carla knew, no one other than the kids had ever gone to the little hideaway—except perhaps Carlos. She had never paid it any mind and somewhere, long ago, had lost the key.

Rama pressed the brass key into her palm. "Wish I could have seen it," he said, then hurried down to the car, leaving Carla to ponder the improbable circumstances by which this key suddenly rested in her hand.

Carla watched a plume of exhaust boil from the rear of the Schwain's green station wagon. The crackling gravel followed the car up the drive and to the plains above. Rama and Hank Schwain returned to the road, richer by the presence of an ancient brassie beneath the back seat, an unopened envelope in Rama's shirt pocket, and a Gift residing deep in Rama's heart.

Standing alone on the veranda, Carla felt the tides that for so long had pulled her onto the rocks of remorse suddenly turn. The metallic squeal of Chandler's little bagpiper rang down from the roof as the winds changed. To Carla, the piper's tune that had cried so mournfully now sounded hopeful.

"I must get Carlos back," she said softly to herself. "That darned weathervane needs a little grease."

Chapter 19

When the Schwain's wagon stopped again, it was two hours east of Mesquite Creek. For 100 miles the scenery had remained as bleak as the silence between Hank and his son. The only sounds in the car, save for the drum of retreads on hot pavement, were those of radio evangelists, hillbilly musicians, and vibrant Mexican bands vying for attention beneath Hank's twiddling fingers. Rama watched the land stream by and worried that the ancient club he had smuggled aboard might be discovered. His father was in an especially unforgiving mood when it came to golf.

Soon, the road dropped to the flats along a sleepy brown river. Its Yoohoo-colored waters slid silently behind a thick apron of willow and blackberries. The road zigzagged through lush bottomland crops and cotton fields along the river before leaping across the sleepy waters on a rusted iron bridge. Before climbing the approach to the fragile structure, Hank pulled the wagon to a stop. The engine fell silent and the sounds of the road gave way to the hush of the river.

"If you gotta piss, now's the time," Hank announced as he stepped out to take aim at a field of pinto beans. The radiator creaked and Hank groaned as man and machine both found relief. Except for the caw of distant crows and the creaking contractions from the wagon's cooling system, it was peacefully quiet. The shade of a thorny locust tree flickered across the Ford's hood.

As the Schwains' ears adjusted to the still afternoon, the distant drone of an engine rose slowly into their awareness. Hank recognized the rich harmonic overtones of a radial aircraft engine. Instead of returning to the car's sticky vinyl seat, he stood attentive and unmoving, locked onto the approaching plane's sonic signature.

The sound swelled suddenly as an agile green airplane emerged from behind a distant windbreak, then dropped down toward the fields, skipping across the crops like a huge dragonfly. When the next windrow threatened, the engine wailed as the pilot asked for deliverance. His wish was granted as the craft pulled at the heavy afternoon sky, climbing steeply—just high enough to clear the windrow's waving leaves—before planting a wingtip in the air and pivoting down in a daredevil swoop to resume work over the fields.

Hank and Rama watched as the plane swooped back down, leveling out into another pass across the field. The plane's wheels skipped just above the cotton plants' brown tips, carving eddies in the "dust" cloud billowing down on the crops. Hank stood transfixed as the pilot danced a cheek-to-cheek tango with the field's flat tops and the windrows' highest branches.

The art in this gravity-defying choreography was not lost on Hank. He watched the rise, the pivot, the swoop, and the rise again—pass after pass—as the duster did its work. Like the sensation of phantom hands to an amputee, Hank's hands and feet worked the flaps, the rudder, and the throttle in sympathy with the dancing aircraft, but the pulse to action never left his brain for his grounded limbs. His attention slipped from the grandstanding crop duster back to a dusty afternoon in Othello sixteen years earlier when he pondered his draft notice as he shuffled back from the mailbox—his aeronautic dreams in doubt and his destiny fixed. One would destroy the other in the black skies above Normandy's sleeping farmlands.

Now, under the intoxicating influence of high-octane exhaust and the sweeping acrobatics of the busy little plane, Hank recalled the lure of the old *Learn to Fly Them* advertisement that had directed him toward the promise of a life skimming like a swallow across shining green fields—a promise that eventually led him to tragedy.

—•—

The crop duster dropped into one final pass. Its course ran in a line parallel with the boy and his spellbound father. From the vantage point of the raised roadbed, the plane flew at eye level toward Hank and Rama. They stood bound together in fascination as they watched the plane hurtle their way. In seconds its wingtips would pass within feet of the lucky spectators. Hank stood his ground even though the approaching plumes were swirling with poison.

To hell with the chemistry, thought Hank; he wasn't about to turn away for fear of a little insecticide. As the plane raced by them—its fuselage not more than forty feet away—Hank could see the bright sparkle from instruments in the sunlit cockpit. For an instant the pilot's and Hank's eyes met. The pilot's right hand flew up in a quick salute beneath the brim of an oily baseball cap. A white speck of tooth in the grimy face telegraphed a grin—a satisfied mind.

The plane screamed as it swooped up and over the farthest windrow. Its whine dissolved into a chorus of insect chatter and the rustling of bottomland foliage in the duster's slipstream. The thought of golf and his recent losses fled from Hank's mind.

"I was gonna do that…"

Hank exhaled a breath held in wonder at the passing plane. He hadn't watched a duster work a tight field in years. The tang of the settling dust tasted like strange medicine as he regained his breath: "...the war got in the way," he sighed.

Hank gathered himself from the old memory to ensure his precarious footing in the real world. His dreams hung like apparitions, like the insecticides settling on the fields before him—vulnerable to stray winds, but resistant. There in the locust tree's thorny shadows, with the image of the crop duster seared into his mind, Hank's forgotten aspirations returned to focus again and struggled against being locked away once more behind fearful excuses and the false promises of chance.

"Dad, you still can." Rama intruded upon Hank's musings with a hopeful voice still charged from his improbable victory.

——•·—

Rama preferred to think of his father as a pilot. The stories about gliding trials in Missouri and the horrific invasion night flight were rare, but they were all the legend a young boy needed to provide the missing strokes in the portrait of a heroic father. As far as Rama was concerned, his father still soared.

"Yeah, yeah," Hank scoffed. "It's not in the cards anymore."

Hank Schwain cringed at his own weary acceptance that his dreams were now only of paydays or of crumbs falling from the tables of the unlucky.

"No, Chief, it's too damned dangerous...ain't got the time or the money for that crap anyway..." said Hank. He turned his head back from the sky above the fields and looked directly at his shy son, "especially the money!"

Rama felt a chill; it was going to be a long ride back to Memphis. A vacation on the Gulf's white beaches was probably out of the question now.

Rama didn't know how much money flying took, nor did he understand his father's rationale for remaining grounded. But it seemed the dangers—the risks of careening through the air like the pilot who just buzzed them—were right up a gambler's alley, and he said so.

Hank became irritated at defending his choices. "Christ knows there's a difference between taking chances with a few bucks and putting your own damn ass on the line," Hank declared. "How'd you and your mom like it if I went out and killed myself flying around for a few thrills?"

Rama fidgeted with the envelope in his shirt pocket in lieu of a reply while Hank grumbled on: "For all we know that hot shot has already run his little coffin up a tree over yonder. Could be a damn fool...seems like there's plenty of them in these parts."

"Seems like he's smart...if he's getting paid to have fun."

In his heart Hank could only agree with Rama, but he nearly choked on his own sarcasm. "Fun? Shit, he's just working, Chief. He's ripping up his eardrums. He's suckin' down all that poison shit…and hanging his butt out on the line. I don't think that sounds like fun."

Hank was suddenly anxious to get moving. He hadn't convinced himself, let alone Rama, of the pilot's folly. A change of subject and some fresh air were in order. Playfully, he tapped a finger against Rama's shirt pocket.

"What you fiddling with there, a love letter from that cart girl?" Hank laughed. "Boy, you're something for an eleven-year-old."

Rama smiled innocently. He hadn't looked at the envelope yet, but now was as good a time as any. He pulled it free.

"No, Dad," Rama protested proudly, "it's from Lee."

The twinkle only just returning to Hank's eyes quickly twinkled out. "The Mexican guy, the golfer?" Hank asked.

Rama didn't answer but in happy anticipation of its contents, ripped the end from the thick envelope. He wondered what Lee would have sent him. The question was answered in a note written on a Mesquite Creek note pad folded around a sheaf of fifty-dollar bills. Rama's eyes widened at the sight of the money.

So did Hank's.

In reaction to the flash of green, Hank plucked the bills from Rama's hands like a crow plundering a swallow's nest. "What in hell's name is this?" Hank asked in the suspicious voice of one probing a bluffer's intentions. "Your cut?"

Incredulous at the thought of his son receiving so much money, Hank could not fathom its path to Rama's pocket beyond terms he understood: deals, plots, and payoffs. Sadly, he assigned his own son's innocent reception of this largess to such motives. Hank indignantly began counting the bills—muttering the numbers to himself as Rama unfolded the note that accompanied the cash. It was written in perfect girlish script. Lee must have dictated the letter to Melyssa, Rama thought as he read the note to himself:

Caddie,

You saved my game and my 6-iron, and now you have returned my old Bulls-Eye. Melyssa says your father bet for Boney. I would not have asked you to putt against your dad if I had known that.

This should cover some of his losses. It's all I can afford. If you ever visit El Paso you can find me at the Sunset Hills. Maybe I can give you a lesson.

Lee Trujillo

The generous sentiments in Lee's note were swept away by an angry curse as Hank completed his tally: "Fifty percent…son of a bitch, half my losses. This is your cut? You two split my money?"

Hank's anger was rising fast. "Right down the middle…damn good pay for one putt, Chief." Hank was certain he had been cheated. "Is that what you and that spic were cooking up out there on the damned course?" Hank slammed his right hand down hard upon the hood of the wagon just inches from his frightened son. A flock of starlings bolted from the bushes into the distance.

"No Dad, I wouldn't…"

"Damn it. It's bad enough you played against me. Don't lie."

"I didn't know about any money. I thought you were betting on Lee, remember?"

Hank growled. He overlooked Ram's point. "You tell me, if I hadn't mentioned the envelope, who would have that money now?" Hank asked in a trick of logic lifted directly from the used car lot. But Rama was no bimbo drooling over a convertible.

"Why would I keep it here," Rama tapped his shirt pocket, "if I was hiding something?"

"God damn it, don't get smart with me," Hank shouted as he slammed another fist onto the wagon's hood—he could only see red for all the green. The thought of hundreds of his dollars languishing in his son's pocket short-circuited his reason and his fatherly instincts. In a blind instant, rather than giving his son the benefit of the doubt, Hank struck Rama across the temple—a blow driven by regret over squandered money, by years of frustration at his own shortcomings, and by jealousy at Rama's courage under fire.

Rama staggered away in surprise and pain. The blow hurt him at the heart as much as at the surface, and he struggled to hide the sobs that were building like spasms in his chest. But he held his tears in check and ventured a defiant glance back at Hank. There would be no more blows. Through vision distorted by unshed tears, his father looked weak and deflated. And like the trick of a feverish mind, Hank receded to a fearsome distance.

Standing at the edge of a highway in the gaping emptiness of eastern Texas, Rama felt abandoned and homesick.

Hank blushed with remorse at his cowardly blow. Maybe there were times to strike a child, he thought, but he wasn't clear if catching your son in a hustle was one. "Just trying to wise you up, Chief," Hank offered in utter futility.

Rama had no intention of responding. He feared the words that might come from his taut throat—words that might bring him to tears or worse. Instead, he thrust Lee's note into his father's bewildered face.

Hank held Lee's message at arm's length as he read.

"Oh Christ," he whispered.

In a moment he dropped both elbows on the hood of the wagon and ran his hands over the back of his head before standing up again to pat his son's shoulder in apology. But his blow could not be withdrawn or the words expunged; he felt the sickening sensation of the irretrievable, like watching car keys dance on the metal grate of a storm drain in the instant before they disappear into the void.

A cricket chirped prematurely somewhere deep in the brush by the river. Up on the bridge, loose decking clattered alarmingly under the tires of an approaching pickup truck. In a few seconds the truck hurtled past. Hank and Rama both stood stiffly at the grill of the green station wagon—suspended without words or direction to proceed from this awful moment. This was not what Hank envisioned for a father-son adventure. He slumped at the thought of Doris's reaction and tentatively tried to pat his son on the shoulder again, but Rama moved nervously away.

"Jesus, I am sorry, Son. Come on…let's head 'em up. We can still make a run for the Gulf—maybe Galveston. We got the money for a little fishing charter, what do you think? We'll get us a good seafood dinner…some crab cakes." Hank struggled with renewed vigor to put the awful events of the last few hours behind them.

Hank battled his sticky door hinge again, taking care not to swear. "In a couple more years, Chief, this rig will be yours." He almost chuckled at the thought of his son wrestling with the door.

A quip about maybe getting around to lubricating the door before his son was old enough to drive formed in Rama's head, but his mistrust of Hank was still reverberating. He didn't venture the joke, and the humor withered in his churning mind. The bond of confidence had been broken.

Without another word, Rama settled back into the car and pressed his face against the side window. He gazed blankly across the bottomlands while his mind turned to memories of sermons on forgiveness Father Rulon had delivered back when Rama regularly accompanied his mother to church. But how could he muster such lofty emotions now when so hurt? Perhaps that was one of the holy mysteries the wise fellow had hinted at so cryptically.

In a moment the station wagon was rumbling noisily across the old bridge as a light sprinkle of rust settled on the brown waters below. The two passengers headed south in silence, preceded by a green hood with imprints of two elbows and one fist etched on its dusty paint.

Chapter 20

Carlos Taddio returned to his camp in the barranca in fatigue and confusion. He had been drawn to the unlikely events on the sixteenth green by the convergence of his vision and the presence of Rama in today's game. He had envisioned that with Rama in play, the children's souls were poised to leap heavenward. Somehow in that moment he was bound to work the instrument of their ascension where their airy hands could not.

This was not the fancy of the herb or the mescal. He accepted in faith that it was his lot to so serve the Stone children but feared that he might fail at such an inscrutable task and plunge the twins into some dark purgatory. For a thousand fretful nights Carlos had brooded upon the weight of his vision and the nature of the service he was bound to perform. With the stars winking through the thorny branches above his shack, he had recalled the children left at the jagged mercy of the lightning. He owed them so much, yet they never came to haunt him with blame, asking only for assurance that their mother and father be delivered from grief. This afternoon, Carlos feared he had failed them.

He had come to the sixteenth green as he had always believed was his calling. After witnessing Rama's single stroke as a player, a miracle in its own right, he was spent. As Rama's putt spiraled home Carlos expected the lightening of a spiritual load, but no burden was lifted. No joy had visited him. There was no sign that Carla and Chandler's children had finally found peace. Shrouded in melancholy, he had walked out onto the damned green after Rama, Lee, and the entire gallery had departed. As if eleven years had never passed, and as if the bridge between life and death were crossed like friendly stones across a shallow brook, Dickey and his sister, Glendora, stepped from the cover of the barranca and joined their old friend.

"Don't be sad, Carlos." Dickey smiled in the face of eternity as easily as he had smiled at his sister's silly jokes.

Carlos's eyes moistened at the sight of the children. "Forgive me. Carlos has failed you again…first with thee lightning, and now, you are trapped in this world. Rama will never come this way again."

Carlos tried to make eye contact with the children's vaporous forms, but they already were fading as Rama was making his way back to Hank's Ford Wagon. Dickey's voice remained clear. "No, Carlos, you have never failed. I chose to remain with Rama. He has held us in his goodness for eleven years, but it is now our duty to protect him. I see trouble. He needs my spirit."

Carlos was confused. "Is it not true that you may only return to peace through Rama on this very green...and at thee time of thee locusts? Or is Carlos a loco fool?"

Dickey's smile was apparent even though growing diffuse. Carlos could make out the image of the young man's sister, Glendora, pulling him back into their dimension as he spoke. "You are not crazy. Yes, we must return. But Carlos, you taught us the world is full of mystery...that all is possible. You must believe in our return. I cannot tell you how, but somehow you must work the magic to bring us home...to paradise. Remember, Carlos, the locusts will swarm again in eight years."

Carlos was speechless as the twins' forms faded. A question caught in his throat.

"Carlos, you know how," answered Dickey. "Your power is in your under-standing. It is in your art."

Dickey's last words echoed in Carlos's mind. Now, with the dream receding, he realized it hadn't been a premonition. There was no certainty in the future or in Rama's return, but Dickey's last words were a gift, a riddle by which he might work the machinery of fate.

His art, Dickey had said. It was not Carlos's nature to be skeptical, but the idea that he might paint the children back into heaven was a stretch even for one as much a creature of magic as he.

Carlos stepped into his shack for the last time. The jagged shadows of firethorn and mesquite played across his hidden world like patterns in an un-finished composition. A bed hewn from sycamore branches, several wooden crates, a clay basin, a caboose stove, and a slab of yellow pine scavenged from an August twister, were his only furnishings. A humble collection of cooking utensils and the tools of an abandoned craft lay undisturbed on the pine slab.

In the tradition of the Taddio family, Carlos was an artist—a painter—but his brushes had long ago dried. He was not the only Taddio to be so gifted; his sister was a portraitist in São Paulo. One of his brothers—a fisherman by ne-cessity—had developed his skills to the point that he would soon leave the icy southern seas for a safer trade behind the easel, or so said his last letter. Long ago Carlos had left Argentina to hone his skills in the studios of San Francis-co, but his quest never got beyond the cattle ranges of Texas. Instead, he met Chandler Stone, and his art was channeled to the sculpting of Mesquite Creek's beguiling course.

Except for the rendering of dimples on the great steel sphere that stood along the highway, Carlo's art had been confined to private painting in the crow's nest above the clubhouse. But that sanctuary was vulnerable. After lightning had ravaged the Stone family, he had drifted from Carla's confidence and the comforts of the canvas, and out into the wilderness.

These would be his last hours in exile.

Carlos considered the tools laying dormant on the pine slab: a china palette smudged in a vortex of whirling hues; jars; brushes; and a forlorn collection of oil paints in elemental colors. His brushes remained where he had last touched them on the day the spark left his soul.

But with Rama's departure and the vision of Dickey still vivid in his mind, he felt the spark returning. Art was always an act of faith; painting begged belief in strokes untaken, in thoughts unresolved. This was territory in which Carlos was familiar. Beyond maintaining the greens of Mesquite Creek, Carlos realized he had a larger task. He would begin today in faith that a mere painter would find a way to chart Rama's return, to prepare the children's path to heaven, and, he prayed, to ease Carla and Chandler Stone's grief.

Like pulling a shimmering spectrum from an onyx palette, it would be Carlos Taddio's greatest creation.

A wooden easel supported a canvas held taut with nails borrowed years earlier from Niña's shoes. The old canvas hosted the incomplete image of a man standing alone before the featureless underpainting of a turbulent ocean. It wouldn't be long now, thought Carlos. One day the glimmer and hue of troubled waters and the bloom of wildflowers along the seaside cliffs would sparkle from the painting, but now the only colorful strokes were those of a brilliant red scarf billowing at the man's neck.

His brushes stood brittle in jars blued by the brutal sun, his paint caps welded to their tubes in neglect, but he knew the hand that had begun this composition would soon return to re-animate the lifeless tools. He sensed that the bold splash of crimson would become the fulcrum about which new shades would balance to form a tribute to the figure emerging from the nascent strokes of this work. Carlos shivered in anticipation; until yesterday and the arrival of the locusts, the completion of the painting of his lost patron, Chandler Stone, had been unthinkable.

Niña fussed as Carlos pumped the stove to life and dropped a kettle on the flame. As its plume scented his hidden place with an earthy aroma, the spark of inspiration returned to the old gaucho. He plucked the green glass paperweight from his papers and pulled a blank sheet free, sending earwigs scurrying for cover. Before the maté was done, Carlos had sketched the lines of a new piece. Two figures emerged from the surface of the yellowing paper: a man and a teenage boy seated in the front seat of a large automobile. Carlos considered the color. It would be a midnight blue...a convertible.

Awake now, Carlos understood the logic of the composition materializing in these scarce lines: the image of arrival must be created before the painting of farewell, so long stalled upon the rigid canvas, could be completed.

Carlos set the sketch aside and poured his maté. The warm liquid brought a smile to his wrinkled face—only Niña saw the glint of gold.

"It is time, Niña, for Carlos to take up thee brush again, no?"

Niña whinnied on cue like a horse from a matinee western.

The old gaucho began collecting his paints and the palette to pack away in Niña's saddlebags. He moved confidently through the spiritual landscape that lay before him as clearly as the confounding breaks of Chandler's greens, confident that Rama would return again and that this time he would be ready.

Carlos pulled the straps of the bags tight. He rolled the woolen blankets from his cot and tied them behind the saddle. Running his hand along Niña's forelocks, he paused to let his pony smell his hand. She relaxed at her own scent. The old man's eyes roamed the empty lean-to; the straw roof still had another season in it, but it no longer mattered. He placed his left boot in the stirrup and nimbly settled into the saddle.

"Let us go, Niña...it is too lonely here, no?" Carlos Taddio clicked his tongue twice.

Carla was relieved that the remainder of the afternoon's business was light. About a dozen groups had teed off after the match, and only one was going to squeeze in the whole eighteen. After those players made the turn, she would have some precious peace. For once she was happy to trade revenue for rest. She had sent the kitchen help home for the day, and as soon as she could politely budge Boney from his bar stool, she would close down the grill room. The finishing golfers would have to be content to watch the sunset from the veranda with nothing more potent than cold soda from the vending machine.

Late-afternoon sun penetrated into the grotto of the grill room bar; its orange light cast long shadows across the Formica tabletops and illuminated the glassware like cheap jewels. Carla purposefully filled saltshakers and replenished napkin racks on a route that took her by Boney Carlisle.

"Calling it a day here pretty quick, Carlisle. This'll have to be last call," she said diplomatically.

"It's a hell of a racket," Boney grumbled. "First you charge me to play, you set up the pins like the damn Masters, then you get that ringer kid to putt for Lee...and then you take my money!" A flicker of a grin belied the sincerity of his accusation. "And now you won't even let me drink off my sorrow."

"Oh, I think you've done a fine job of that," Carla replied. "You know you could have changed your mind about letting Rama take that putt. Hand me those shakers, hon."

"Hell, Carla, what were the odds? It was just a lucky, lousy break." Boney tossed back his beer with an impressive stroke and slid the shakers Carla's way. "Got to drive," he said with a mighty belch, as he made the transition from bar stool to teetering high on his spikes in perfect balance—a fact that comforted

Carla considerably. He started for the door, then stopped. A question had been nagging him all afternoon.

"You ain't leaving those pins like they are, I hope?" Boney asked. "It's like damned Oakmont out there. You're likely to run off your business if you keep this hellhole too tough."

Carla raised a gray eyebrow. She didn't pay as much attention to pin placements or turf management as she should, and she knew it. A couple of hired hands kept things alive; as far as she knew, they moved the pins to keep traffic from wearing bulls' eyes in her greens, but strategy was out of the question.

"What's different about them...they're the same as yesterday, aren't they?" Carla asked. "The boys never touched them that I know of."

"They sure as hell weren't the same as the day before when the locusts came through. I'd never forget that. I won a few bob that day," Boney insisted. "Didn't you notice? They were tucked in all sorts of crazy corners and a couple damn near on the fringe."

Boney thought for a second. "It was like old Carlos and Chandler used to set 'em up back in the days when they'd get a wild hair up their..." Boney's ruddy face heated up in embarrassment. "Well, you know."

"Sure, Carlisle, I know," said Carla. "Up their asses." She smiled. "Boney, we'll make this place into a pitch and putt if it keeps you and your friends coming back."

Carla laughed, glad to move away from the past. She watched as Boney made his way out to collect his clubs; then she continued with her chores. But the reference to Carlos and the pin placements troubled her. She knew Boney well and knew he would not have mentioned it if something hadn't been odd.

Carla recalled the afternoons when Carlos and Chandler, tipped far back on the rockers out on the veranda, talked golf. They would compare notes on courses they had seen and on books they had read. And Boney was right; they did talk about the devilish greens out at Oakmont. On some mornings, Carlos and Chandler would stalk out onto the course with drill and bucket to add a touch of the devil's own mischief. Some mornings the kids would tag along. Carla remembered their voices drifting back through the crisp air.

The quiet of the grill room suddenly cast a pall of melancholy upon what had been a strange but lucrative day. She wished the last foursome was clattering in for a beer. She didn't want to be alone. Carla reached into her pocket for a handkerchief. It was okay, she thought, nobody could see her cry now. But rather than a hankie, her hand found the brass key Rama had given her. "The key to the crow's nest," he had said.

Other than Boney loading his clubs into his trunk, there wasn't much to distract her at the moment. Might as well give it a try, she thought. She hurried out into the late sunlight and up along the clubhouse to the stairs. She remembered that the children's secret passage to the crow's nest originated from the closet in one of the tourist rooms. In a moment she stood before the little door.

"The boy was right; how in the world…" Carla whispered as the lock yielded easily.

The light from the louvers illuminated the stairs up into the widow's watch. Instinctively, she called hello to the silent space above. She felt no misgivings as she ascended the dusty stairs. The room, although long abandoned, was warm with bright sunlight shining through hazy windows. Carla gasped as she reached the top of the stairs. What she had once thought her children's secret playhouse was alive with dusty but carefully assembled memories. Along the wall directly before her were photos of Chandler and some of his old mates. She recalled some of their names—a few had even visited Mesquite Creek. The images were from golf tournaments played in days prior to Chandler's arrival in Texas, from tournaments on courses like Dundonald, Prestwick, Machrihanish, and Dornoch. Carla brushed a spider's web from an image of Chandler.

The adjoining wall served as the final resting-place for her family's golfing equipment: balls, shoes, a battered shag bag, and three sets of clubs—one of hickory and two with shiny metal shafts. Carla recognized the metal sets immediately; their shortened shafts gave them away. She carefully lifted a 7-iron from her daughter's set. Her fingers gently brushed across the soft leather grips where Glendora's confident fingers had last rested. Carla closed her eyes and their hands bridged the gap of eternity, touching for a moment. She was not saddened by the encounter. In fact, as she stood alone in this bright room, her daughter's humor cheered her.

She returned the club and picked her son's putter from its rack. She could trace the wear from strong fingers that had once handled the club for hours. Dickey had been a putting fool, she remembered. He would putt around the house: on carpet, on hardwood, on tile. It did not matter where; he was certain that practice would someday serve him well. Carla shuddered as she noticed the blue-and-garnet discoloration that extreme heat had burnished into the putter's metal shaft, and she whispered a mother's prayer as she returned his tempered club to its rest.

The room's meticulous display mystified Carla, yet she was grateful beyond anyone's knowing for its preservation and for its curator. She hadn't known how much she needed the touch of these things, but someone did. Perhaps this was what Carlos did on those evenings when she had seen amber light escape the louvers of the crow's nest for a starry sky?

She wondered if this collection was intended for her.

Carla turned to the third wall and was greeted by her own young face smiling back from photographs she didn't remember having been taken. She and Chandler, heads happily tipped together, singing in a boisterous pub somewhere in Scotland. She and Chandler, feet together on a shovel, celebrating the groundbreaking for Mesquite Creek. She and the children, smiling above a sand castle on the strand at Corpus Christi.

Carla would have wept, but another photo brought a smile. A beaming Carla was framed by the broad shoulders of Mr. Robert Tyre Jones and his friend Chandler. The camera trapped Bobby's boyish smile forever in genuine laughter just above Carla's glowing face. Behind the three, the images of forgotten ladies lurked out of focus.

"What a day," Carla sighed. The memories were still vivid.

Then she noticed an elegant bonnet hanging on a hook nearby. Its wide brim had once graciously shielded a lady from the Georgia sun. A dried magnolia blossom was still tucked beneath its soft green ribbon. She reached to brush dust from the familiar old hat but stopped at the whine of a starter and the laboring growl of an automobile down below. Boney was finally getting on his way. She took a deep breath; she should be getting along, too.

Carla made a mental note: if she ever caught up with Carlos again, she would have to thank him. All these memories suspended just above her head while she bulled joylessly through so many busy years in the clubhouse below…how could she have let so much life pass by?

She turned to go, and as she did another astonishing gift from the old gaucho greeted her from its place in a shaft of light. It was a large oil painting of Dickey and Glendora. She lost her breath at the sight and nearly stumbled as she approached the mesmerizing work. Alive in color and atmosphere, it was a mural of the children at play along brilliant emerald links. The painting danced lightly across the bare pine boards over which it was painted. Carla couldn't help herself; she reached out to touch the brushstrokes that captured her lost children.

How could she have known? Artistic talent was one of the secrets Carlos had brought from Argentina. He had idly fussed with miniature paintings on small scraps of board—offhanded expressions not unlike a whittler's musings—but no one knew he had ventured beyond such trifles. His masterly hand had captured his subject's joyous spirits. Ambers and reds highlighted Glendora's tossed, tangled hair. Restrained strokes preserved the delicacy of young skin blushed by crisp salty air from the sea sparkling beyond. Minute jewels of blue escaped eyes twinkling with laughter.

The faces were not directed to the viewer but were focused on their own pursuits across the links. Dickey triumphantly held an iron that, an instant earlier, had propelled a ball toward a tiny yellow flag snapping brightly in the background. He had just glanced back to his sister in pride when the brush captured him. It was her turn to swing, but her club rested on the soft grass. Carlos had caught Glendora reaching for the shaft with her left hand while her right held a fistful of purple blossoms. The happy girl would soon have to choose between pleasures.

Carla hardly breathed. The image of the children spread so generously across the boards was nearly life-size and unconfined by a frame. She thought she heard the surf and smelled the heather above the tang of salt spray.

The painting pulled at her for several minutes, then gently it revealed another image deep in middle ground. A tiny figure, partially obscured by a tuft of fog, floated above the yellows of a distant broom thicket. Unlike the children so involved in their green world, the man was looking out to sea as he receded into feathery gray brushstrokes. His right hand was raised in a sign of farewell, like Jesus in the Ascension.

Carla looked closely. The figure was too small to reveal a likeness, but a splash of crimson like the red scarf Chandler so often wore confirmed his identity. The beautiful vision of their links heaven had only been strange words on Carlos's lips in those first painful years. The thoughts had been intended to comfort the children's grieving mother, but now as Carla was swallowed into the painting, the vision was burned into her mind. Yet there was something unfinished—disturbing—in the grays of Chandler's image. Maybe the painting was a clue. She placed her tired hand upon the banister post to brace herself, and alone in the crow's nest she wept healing tears.

———•———

Voices in the clubhouse below startled her back from the painting's spell. With one hand she blotted up any makeup softened by her tears, and with the other she guided herself down the stairs. In seconds she was strolling, all business again, into the clubhouse to greet the final forgotten foursome. The golfers eyed the Bavarian Beer sign thirstily.

"Sorry fellas, we're shut down now," she apologized. "Even bartenders gotta have a day of rest now and again. There's plenty of cold soda in the machine out there," she said with a nod to the porch.

Any other day she would have accommodated the golfers, but this afternoon was an exception. She hurried them along by switching off a few lights and reaching for her key chain. The golfers considered the soda for an instant, but seemed resigned to calling it a day without further celebration. Carla watched them trod heavily down the steps toward their cars.

She had turned to fasten the locks when one of the men called back to her. "Ma'am, better make sure that odd-ball don't tear up your greens or nothin."

Carla looked puzzled. "Beg your pardon?"

"That old-timer, on the horse," the man explained as he pointed down the last fairway. "We saw him as we was finishing up on seventeen. Funny old guy…riding up out of the barranca—like he owned the place."

"You allow horses on this course?" the man asked, looking up at the wiry proprietress of Mesquite Creek who now stood on the edge of the porch above him.

Carla Stone didn't answer; her attention was directed far up the fairway to the tiny silhouette of a rider in the distance. The question eventually worked its way into her consciousness, and she replied absently through a soft smile.

"Only on special occasions, Honey."

———•———

Three hours east of Mesquite Creek—even as the gulf between Carlos and Carla closed in the wake of Rama's inexplicable visit—the gap separating Rama and his father widened.

The station wagon's radio provided relief from the awful silence surrounding the two travelers. An hour had passed since Hank had struck his son. By the time the junction for the Gulf Coast and its attractions arrived, Lee's money was tucked deeply into Hank's pocket and his affront to his boy had been tucked deeply into Rama's consciousness. A right turn would extend their trip together; a left turn would return them home and to a continuation of their estrangement. Without a word, Hank cranked the wheel counterclockwise.

Miles passed, and with Jimmy Webb's "Wichita Lineman" peeling from the radio like a lonely bell, Hank pulled two 50-dollar bills from his pocket and slid them across the seat to Rama—his reward for a brave performance on the golf course. It was a mute attempt at an apology to a boy with a bruise still blooming upon his temple. In time they would speak again, but always with reserve and always with a wary eye on this day.

Eventually, Rama folded the bills into his shirt pocket. Mom could use the money, he guessed.

The car moved eastward and the landscape softened into hill country. A few more miles rolled by, and as dusk signaled the search for a motel, a fine, well-conditioned golf course came into view on the left. Rama could see several twosomes scattered about lush green mounds. He wished he could have stopped his father's car and joined the players in their peaceful stroll over the warm evening's final holes in the warm evening. But Rama turned his head away and pondered a colonnade of grain elevators looming on the horizon.

He would pay no attention to the game of golf or hear Dickey Stone whisper in his ear for another eight years.

Chapter 21

A humble Renault Dauphine wound its way up the drive to Bluff Meade Country Club like a minnow struggling upstream. The Cadillacs and Lincolns descending the drive left little but the shoulder for the diminutive embarrassment intruding into their pond. It was Sunday afternoon, and the members were deserting their club in droves—the memories of their tennis, their golf, or the taste of their early suppers already fading as they slid behind leather and walnut dashboards for home.

As it arrived at the clubhouse, the Renault did not enter the drive that swept majestically before the grand columned entrance. It bypassed the eager hands of the parking valet and turned instead into the service entrance, where it rattled to a stop beside the worn Chevrolets and Fords driven by the help. Golf operations were winding down for the day, and to the eye of the Renault's driver, the pristine golf course looked ideally under-populated.

"Nearly deserted…perfect," he sighed with anticipation.

Ivar Guidance was a man of means and could have driven in considerably more style. He could afford Britain's or Italy's finest automotive offerings but was more concerned with arriving at the club in anonymity rather than in style. He wouldn't be recognized in such an uncharacteristically cheap car.

Ivar unfolded his long legs from beneath the instrument panel and pivoted in the seat in order to slip off handmade Italian loafers in favor of custom golfing shoes. When properly shod, he chased a wrinkle from his tailored slacks and stood beside the car, stretching as he surveyed the premises. His willowy frame responded with a salute of loudly protesting joints.

Twenty years earlier, according to his driver's license, he was six-foot seven, but time takes its toll. Even now, stretching beside the tiny car, he looked impressively straight and fit for a seventy-one-year-old. With a generous shock of white hair crowning a face chiseled into a thoughtful expression, Ivar might have been perfectly cast as a kindly cross between Robert Frost and Abraham Lincoln, should the part for a poet-president ever be scripted. Perhaps it was his appearance, or perhaps it was an endless streak of good fortune broken only by the loss of his wife, Rebecca, but life offered up its best to Ivar, and he always returned the favor. Success hung as comfortably upon the gracious gentleman as did his tailored clothes. Although his automobile and his preference for the service entrance belied it, no one, especially the club's gentry, would have expected an esteemed member to make such an unprepossessing entrance— which was exactly the cover Ivar had sought to conceal today's practice.

He smiled as he opened the trunk and extracted an old black leather golf bag and pull-cart. In a moment Ivar was happily strolling toward the caddie shack, accompanied by the clicking of Italian spikes.

Five paces from the car he remembered his keys. Preferring not to carry any extraneous items when he golfed, Ivar tossed the key ring back through the driver's open window with the grace of a point guard. With the peace of one who believed in people's better nature, he turned back to the course and today's business.

Ivar hoped his swing would be as smooth as his key toss, but he knew better. Golf's evasive techniques, its befuddling physics, and its frustrating resistance to the most earnest efforts at improvement were three of the glaring exceptions to the benevolence with which life usually served him. The fourth was Ivar's nemesis, Mr. Wallace Byrne. Mr. Byrne was also known by those who were unhappily acquainted with him as Wedgy. It was the specter of Wedgy that brought Ivar to the club this evening.

Contrary to the commonly held association of his nickname with a prank involving undergarments, Mr. Byrne's moniker was derived from his adept but misplaced skill with golf clubs, particularly the highly lofted "scoring" clubs known as wedges. Wedgy, and his scoring skills, were a continuing problem for Ivar Guidance, a problem made more acute with the recent arrival of a postcard addressed to the Bluff Meade Men's Club from Mr. Wallace Byrne.

Wedgy Byrne had once been a self-described venture capitalist and a member of Bluff Meade. He had been an outstanding golfer and held in good standing for years, but, in time, a tendency to cheat on the course and to invest a shade too adventurously with others' capital forced him permanently from the club's roster and nearly into federal prison.

Fortunately for the financial community of Memphis, Wedgy's career in business was over. Unfortunately for the more sport-oriented types at Bluff Meade, Wedgy's departure dealt a larger blow to the club's golf fortunes than it did to boosting the club's reputation as a haven for honorable gentlemen. The fact was that Wedgy was the best member-golfer who ever signed in on a Bluff Meade tee sheet. A business hustler by nature, the excommunicated Wedgy Byrne easily retooled his modus operandi and found an acceptable life in hustling lesser golfers.

Wedgy had forged a living with his game and had adopted a mobile lifestyle to avoid lingering too long on other hustlers' turf. Once a year he would come back through Memphis to lift a few bob from the hard-working, hard-golfing fellows down at the municipal links and, more importantly, to take down the best players Bluff Meade Country Club had to offer. He sought this annual match not as much for money as for a chance to look straight into the bewildered, defeated face of Bluff Meade's best player to savor his pain and to lie, "Nice round, Jeeves!"

—•—

The postcard from Wallace Byrne had found its way onto the bulletin board down in the men's locker room. Hanging askew on a thumbtack, the simple little note scribbled on the back of a Dairy Land USA postcard tossed an irresistible challenge down to Bluff Meade's gentlemen golfers:

Howdy Bluffers:

Anybody up for a friendly little match?
By now somebody in BM should be able to
finally give this old boy a decent game.
I'm not getting any younger you know.
Maybe one of you duffers can catch me this year…
but I doubt it. I'll be in town on Saturday, July 15th
looking for a match on Sunday, if you'll let me on the course.
What do you say?

Your dearly departed,

Wallace Byrne

Only pride and the fact that the annual challenge from Wedgy had become an unofficial but established Bluff Meade tradition prevented the postcard from taking its place in the trash can. The event was not listed in the club calendar or on the tournament schedule. There were even members who were unaware of the match and who would never have approved of it had they known that many of their golf-stricken peers scrambled to accommodate the egomaniacal whim of a deflowered member while squandering foolish bets and perfectly good tee times on his behalf.

But plenty of others relished the yearly arrival of Wedgy, and they would be on hand come hell or high water on July 16.

Ivar Guidance liked a challenge at roughly the same level that he disliked Wedgy. He had originally recommended a sparkling Mr. Byrne to the membership committee, and now, bearing the weight of the disgrace wrought by his nominee, felt compelled to right old wrongs. On this Sunday afternoon, as Ivar took to the deserted course, the thought of trampling Wedgy's overdeveloped pride seemed almost a responsibility, but like his nemesis, he, too, was not getting any younger. If he were ever to smile victoriously into Wedgy's defeated eyes, some serious practice was in order.

But beating Wedgy Byrne was a long shot, a conundrum all tied up in the two glaring exceptions to Ivar's orderly life: To deal with who plagued him most he had to master what plagued him most; and what plagued him most was golf.

Ivar looked at the game rationally and mathematically even though he knew intuition was often preferable. He perceived the peak of one's performance as a graph: When the upward curve of skill met the declining curve of physical potential one should be at his best, he reckoned. Trouble was, these lines tended to converge somewhere around thirty years. The trick was to keep pushing the skill line up while holding the physical potential line back from its inevitable plunge toward the abyss.

At seventy-one, Ivar knew his curves had begun to diverge years ago. But in his view, which combined the natural optimism of his personality and the blind hopefulness of his golfing nature, he felt that spikes in the two curves could bring dramatic but short-lived peaks in performance.

This afternoon would be a fine day to file away at the spikes, thought Ivar, as he approached the caddie shack.

Several teenage boys, energetically wrapping up their activities for the day, buzzed around the premises—oblivious to Ivar's approach. Competition to out-hustle their contemporaries for tips and the extra bag had fueled their hyperactivity and had worked the athletic young men into a ripe, skunky sweat. Charlie Vestal, one of the rumpled, damp young dynamos, recognized Ivar's distinguished stride and snow-capped head. Charlie regularly caddied for Ivar and considered the lucrative association a sure thing—his own personal account.

"Mister Guidance, sir," he called, hoping to snag the wealthy member's attention. "Let me help you with your bag, sir."

The boy approached, and Ivar chuckled quietly at the youngster's vain attempts to maintain his dignity while tidying up a half-tucked shirt and attempting to plaster down an unruly haircut. As the young man got within range, so to speak, Ivar mused that on such a humid day perhaps the youngster should have directed his grooming energies more to the glandular and less to the lay of his locks. Ivar kept his thoughts to himself and tried instead to smell the roses.

"Will you be needing a caddie?" asked Charlie.

"Hold it there…" Ivar's charismatic nature carried with it an authority that stopped the eager caddie in his tracks, just slightly downwind. He smiled a broad, Lincolnesque smile at the frozen boy.

"Charlie Vestal," said Ivar recognizing the young man. "Back for the summer, are we? How did law school treat you?"

"Fine, Mr. Guidance. I start junior year this fall."

"Excellent, always room for an honest lawyer," Ivar quipped. "But no, Charles, no thanks. I'll just be walking out alone."

"Well, I'll get those clubs up to the starter for you then," the young man pressed, anxious to salvage any chance for a tip.

"Tell you what, Charles," instructed Ivar, thinking both of his need for invisibility and the boy's need for cash. "You just wheel this little rig on down to number three and leave it parked by the ball washer, then get on back to work. I'll head over there just as soon as I'm ready."

Ivar said nothing about a tip or made no motion toward his billfold but looked into the expectant eyes of the future lawyer for a flicker of trust. "Go on, don't wait for me," said Ivar. "If you promise not to tell anyone I've been sneaking in a little practice, there will be five dollars in it for you."

The caddie brightened at the proposition and looked suddenly less rumpled. "Oh yes, very good, sir. I won't say a word," Charlie replied. He drew a breath to speak, then, after balking theatrically to give Ivar a moment to produce the tip, grabbed Ivar's cart and started for the fairway. Talk is cheap, thought Charlie, wondering how he would get his five bucks if old man Guidance began alone and finished after everybody had gone home.

After Charlie had taken a dozen steps, Ivar called after him. "Oh, I beg your pardon, Charles. Your tip…of course! My wallet is in the bag. Help yourself to a Ben Franklin when you get down to number three, then toss the wallet back in the bag. I'll be along soon enough."

Ivar watched the boy disappear beyond the crest of the fairway and into what Ivar hoped was the company of folks who knew that trust was a two-way street.

Fifteen minutes later, Ivar arrived on tee three and fetched a ball from his bag. Luckily, the trusting, white-haired gentleman didn't glance in his wallet or he might have discovered that Charlie Vestal had doubled the tip under the assumption that the rich guy would never miss another five bucks. Such a discovery might have spoiled a beautiful practice round.

Ivar teed up a fresh balata. He was oblivious to the petty crime but acutely aware of the familiar shady fairways striped with lengthening shadows. In any light he knew the course's features intimately: its subtle topography, the turf's textures, the bounces, the rolls, the risks, and the rewards. If only he could master the swing—two seconds of action that trumped all the treachery a course might raise in defense of par.

On such a fine peaceful evening, it hardly mattered that he master anything. The pleasures of the course and the company of its crickets chirping softly in anticipation of the night were sufficient. Yet the image of Wedgy Byrne intruded into Ivar's pastoral reverie often enough to remind him that there was purpose on these links as well.

Obligingly, Ivar practiced with focus and unwavering concentration until he arrived at his lucky hole: number seven—a dogleg left par five that twisted around a low hill and eventually down to a small green backed by a grove of trees, a creek, and Crutchfield Lane. Such was Ivar's history of good fortune on this hole that he almost expected good things to happen. On in three with a putt for birdie was good; on in two with a chance at eagle was fantastic. This evening Ivar landed his approach just off the green in three. He found the ball laying several feet down the thick, grassy slope that descended to the creek. He faced two strokes—what golfers call an up and down—for par.

Not bad, he thought, although he recalled several years earlier on a particularly magic Sunday morning that, with the help of an astounding 3-iron to the pin in two, the hole had yielded a double-eagle, the rarest shot in golf: two strokes on a par five. All the luck in the world might never bring such a shot around again. He had taken some ribbing from his fellow golfers when he turned in that card. Any score is possible when one plays alone, they had scoffed predictably, though never really doubting Ivar's integrity or his amazing feat. The white-haired gentleman wished he had asked his only witness—a boy on a bicycle—to climb down from Crutchfield Lane to sign the scorecard on that magic day.

"No such luck today," Ivar sighed as he carried his sand wedge and his putter down to his ball. He stood on the slope to size up his chances for a birdie chip-in. It wasn't out of the question, he thought. He laid the putter on the grass and settled into a chipping stance. After a moment's visualization, a creative flop sent the ball floating high and straight for the cup. The ball spun enough to grab the green's afternoon shadow and stop less than three feet from the hole. An easy par loomed large, causing Ivar's concentration to evaporate into complacency. He would need a birdie here if he were to best Wedgy.

With the irritating thought of Wedgy's ruddy face in mind, Ivar dropped the wedge and picked up the putter, then trotted out onto the green. Sure enough, the putt dropped and Ivar happily retreated from the kindly green, tossing the putter back into his bag before rolling on to the next hole.

As dusk approached, he experimented, fiddled, and tweaked the variables constituting a reliable swing until the light failed him. He tried draws, fades, cuts, and knockdowns. He worked his way through his playbook yet could never bring himself to intentionally hit into a bunker, so the sand wedge remained untested and its absence from the bag unnoticed. Ivar dropped ball after ball in the deserted fairways. He was in no hurry to return to an empty mansion.

—•—

The long days of June seemed to stretch to new lengths for the teenage boy piloting the shiny blue Oldsmobile onto Crutchfield Lane. Doris Schwain's Super 88 stirred ponderously at the command of Rama's right foot. An automatic transmission dampened his youthful intention to liven up the taffy-like passage of a lethargic afternoon with a burst of acceleration and, he hoped, the rewarding screech of Goodyears.

It had been a slow day. In fact, Rama felt as if all the days this June had been grinding along at a tempo several beats behind those of previous summers. The photographs of his high-school graduation had shown up in the mail only two days earlier, and already the images seemed dated and distant. He wondered if graduation was some sort of barrier beyond which carefree summers ceased to exist, or was it just *his* summer that was different?

There was more to do around the house now that his dad was absent. The lawn and his mother's garden begged for attention, but to a young man intent on matters more daring, hours spent in the service of plants were torturous.

And then there was the troubling question of his education. What was taking Trent Institute so long to process his registration? He could not languish forever in this limbo between boyhood and whatever "hood" followed. He could not remain vulnerable to the draft and a war that chewed like cancer at the flesh of boys unprotected by student deferments. Soon he would have to commit to a student's life somewhere—anywhere—assuming his parents still had the funds.

Doris knew her son was temporarily trapped in the horse latitudes of a young life, and she saw how its tedium tired him. Earlier that evening she had slid the car keys across the table. "You've done enough today, Rama. Go have some fun with your friends…I'll finish up." A sunny smile shone impossibly from her drawn face. Life for her son would only get more challenging, she feared, at the thought of her decline. She sighed with regret that she was stealing valuable time from the irretrievable days of a nineteen-year-old's life. No, she would indeed finish up, even if it left her exhausted and sound asleep with Chester, Matt Dillon, and Miss Kitty flashing across the television screen.

"I'll leave the porch light on," she said. She produced a ten-dollar bill and tucked it into Rama's palm. "Bring home a bottle of syrup…I'll make pancakes in the morning. You can keep the change."

She flicked the backs of her hands at him: "Scoot," she commanded as if he were still a child.

The Oldsmobile roared gratefully as it began its rush into Crutchfield Lane's cool descending curves. No doubt, this summer was different. It used to be that he could get on the pay phone at Hibbit's Drugstore and jingle up some buddies for a cruise down Church Street or roll a few frames over at Melrose Lanes. Once, just by showing up in the parking lot at Ringler's Drive-In, he could simply bump into friends and allow the night to dictate its own adventurous course.

But the black pavement, the sticky white picnic tables, and the red cinder-block walls gleaming beneath Ringler's sputtering vapor lamps dazzled less brightly now than they had in his senior year. The drive-in competed now with fiancées, fraternities, and fortunes for his friends' attention. Tonight it seemed lifeless. In the fall, today's juniors would assemble by some migratory instinct and rule the Ringler's lot for their year. Their cars, their bright clothes, their shining hair, and the cherry red of plastic ice-cream spoons would all sparkle beneath the flattering light of new mercury lamps.

The Olds' V8 rumbled just beyond Rama's tennis sneakers. Hopefully, his friends would be home tonight. Too often in these post-graduation days the voices at the other end of his hopeful phone calls were parents or younger siblings—just as lost at the absence of their sons or brothers as was the caller searching for a friend.

—•—

With cold lime soda sizzling on his tongue and the fragrant summer evening streaming through cocked quarter windows, the day's tedium washed from Rama's mind. The sway of the car through the familiar curves reminded him of coasting down the same pavement as a kid. Some things didn't change: the hedge, the creek, and the lush green golf course. Even the memory of the golfer, like an angel in glowing white on that distant Sunday morning, resisted time's dissolution. It was as if something important had happened on that day: a glimpse into a future just beyond perception. Rama felt the urge to stop and peer through the gap in the hedge again, in case he might see what he had missed years ago.

Four white sidewalls eased to a stop where he had once skidded on two bicycle tires. The foliage above the creek's bank was heavier now. The gap was almost closed, but he could still see the impeccably manicured fairway that curved east to the low hill over which the angel golfer had once come to shoot his double-eagle. Except for that ghostly figure, Rama could superimpose the image of that morning over this evening's scene with perfection. But something was out of place.

From the bank just below the surface of the green, the glint of silver winked from the rich green grass. It was too late in the afternoon for the sparkle of dew. A careless golfer had abandoned a club beside the green.

"What the hell," Rama murmured to himself. He would fetch the club. For a lifetime he had only lain eyes on this course and its majestic clubhouse; now he had an excuse to enter its hallowed grounds. If anyone asked, he wouldn't be trespassing just returning a lost club—an honest intention and a good excuse for breaking his father's ancient decree against the game.

Rounded stones poking above the creek's feeble summer flow provided a path to the flanks of the seventh green. It had been eight years since he had prowled Mesquite Creek's rugged fairways and been forbidden from golf by an angry, confused father. Now just placing his feet upon the great expanse of Bluff Meade's emerald turf stirred a forgotten spirit inside him. He shivered at the cool water and at the memory that a game played in such tranquility could yield such painful consequences.

The heady odor of geraniums blended with the comforting scent of mowed bluegrass banished his dark thoughts. Rama stooped to pick up the club. He carefully handled the leather grip and the shining shaft. With the club resting gently in his fingers, he surveyed the same line across the green as had the club's owner just an hour before. He imagined a phantom ball gliding along a gentle arc toward the pin. The black-and-white checkered flag fidgeted at the end of its staff while the imaginary ball silently disappeared into the cup like it had eight years earlier.

Eight years, he thought. He had been robbed.

Above the stillness of the green and the trickling creek, an angry voice startled him. "Damn it, Dad!"

It was his own voice.

Chapter 22

Rama shivered as his words trailed off into the dusk, fearful that his voice might betray his presence on this most private turf. Silently, he retraced his steps across the creek, steadying himself on its stones with the lost club before stopping to inspect his find. Even a newcomer to the club making arts would have appreciated the golf club's fine forged head, the precise Gothic *S* etched into its sole, and the supple leather grip that crowned its shining shaft. Rama felt like a thief; there would be no keeping this prize. Most likely someone was already missing it. He laid the club on the back seat in lieu of tossing it to the Oldsmobile's gritty floor.

His key was already in the ignition when he noticed a thin gold band girding the club's shaft just below the grip. He raised the club and read its curious inscription:

Dum Spiro Spero.
Love, Rebecca

Funny, thought Rama as his mother's car roared to life; he had expected the owner's phone number. He continued along Crutchfield to a modest green-and-white sign: Bluff Meade Country Club—Members Only. For the first time after years of admiring the club from a respectful distance, Rama ventured onto its storied grounds. The Oldsmobile passed into the generous shade of the great magnolias that lined the drive up to Bluff Meade's clubhouse. He was in good company, Rama recalled. Even President Eisenhower had ascended this very drive...or so it had been said.

Rama navigated the circular driveway to the club's entrance. He slowed but did not stop—the great doors at the portico seemed too formal an entry for such an uncertain stranger on such a simple mission. Even vacant in the gathering dusk, the grand building appeared more than worthy of Ike's presence; perhaps one of the more modest service buildings nearby would be a more likely locale for the Lost and Found.

Rama pulled the '88 into an adjoining lot and eased into a space beside an impoverished Renault Dauphine. He hopped out, locking the car as his mother had always insisted, but as he walked past the Renault he noticed its windows were down and its keys lay on the seat.

Guess they're not worried about crooks, thought Rama, unaware that the thieves at Bluff Meade committed their crimes *upon* the golf course.

He followed a flagstone walk past the first tee, the eighteenth green, a pro shop, and a perfectly manicured putting area. Geraniums blazed blood-red in the failing light. Rama peeked into the shop but it was deserted; its racks of expensive clubs and clothing illuminated only by the glow of a cigarette machine and a neon ring around the wall clock. A basket of bright yellow range balls stood abandoned on the counter. He called for assistance, but his cries died in the stillness—muffled in the fabric of fine golf attire.

Rama considered leaving the lost club there, but the sound of automobiles roaring to life out in the parking lot distracted him. He stepped out to the walk and watched several boys from the cart barn speed down the drive and into the night; only the Olds and the Renault remained in the lot. As the boys disappeared beneath the Magnolia's canopy, a flash startled Rama from behind. He turned to find the floodlights of Bluff Meade's practice range sputtering to life, and below them a tall, white-haired man was already hammering balls into the gloom.

Rama reckoned the white-haired fellow to be a senior employee getting in a little complimentary after-hours practice—he probably ran the pro shop and he probably owned the Renault. Judging from his car, the fellow could use all the perks he could get. Rama approached the range cautiously, uncertain of the etiquette in such a formal place, but this appeared to be his only chance to hand off the club tonight.

—•—

Ivar Guidance's swing had come and gone during his late-afternoon practice session. Unfortunately for the hopeful old gentleman, his swing was more gone than come. He had trudged from the eighteenth green with his tempo and his confidence in tatters. Ivar knew one thing: He would not go home and to bed with visions of those atrocious swings in his head. He had sent the club pro away with a decent tip and was free to stay on the range in search of a few good shots he could sleep on.

Ivar was still smarting from yet another exasperating shank when he noticed the young man approaching. He felt a tinge of embarrassment; usually he didn't mind spectators, and he might have ignored the young fellow had it not been getting late and had the young interloper not been carrying what appeared to be a sand wedge.

He tried to ignore Rama as he raked another ball into place and swung again. His posture following the swing collapsed from a Ben Hogan-like pose after watching another very un-Hogan-like pop-up slice sail high over the right screen. Maybe he didn't like spectators after all, thought the frustrated golfer as he followed the abysmal shot into the dark. He knew better: blame for a bad swing couldn't be so easily assigned.

"If you're looking for balls, my friend," Ivar said with a whiff of impatience, "I left a bucket on the counter back in the shop. Go ahead, they're on me. Misery loves company you know, and I could use the company up here about now."

Rama was surprised at the unexpected invitation to hit balls on the very golf course he had held in such lofty fascination since he was a child. Now, he wished he really were a golfer. The handful of lucky shots he had hit years ago at Mesquite Creek hadn't given him that cachet; otherwise, he might have accepted the fellow's offer.

"Thanks, but I can't play. I was just looking for the Lost and Found. I found this club down by the creek."

Ivar propped his driver back against the bench and considered the young fellow. "Come on, son; you can't be any worse than me. Let's have a look at what you've got."

This young fellow dressed in blue jeans, a Penny's madras shirt, and Buster Brown penny loafers was not likely a member's son, thought Ivar. Regardless, a welcoming and genuine smile spread beneath white locks tussled by his recent struggles with the damnable driver.

Any notions of fabricating a fable to disguise his trespassing along the creek vanished from Rama's mind.

"I was just driving by and I saw the..." Rama started to explain.

"Driving by? You must have been down along number seven," said Ivar. The floodlights illuminated the old gentleman with a shaggy halo. "A few folks stop there now and again just to have a look," he continued. "It is a gorgeous view down through those shrubs, eh?"

Ivar considered telling his favorite golf story, but wondered if the young man would appreciate the tale of his Sunday morning double-eagle on that very hole. He held his tongue.

Rama felt as if the gentleman on the range was toying with him, as if the old fellow knew how special that hole really was, as if he, too, had once coasted along Crutchfield Lane on a bike and stopped to savor the view, only to witness a miracle.

"Yes, sir," Rama replied, "but I never crossed the creek 'til today when I saw this club." Rama raised the wedge higher.

"Well, if you're about to apologize for trespassing, don't," said Ivar. "You've obviously gone to a lot of trouble. This will make someone very happy, I'm sure."

Ivar was anxious to resume practice; he pointed toward his golf bag with the butt of his driver. "Just slip that club into my bag there, and I'll take care of it tomorrow."

Rama did as instructed, unknowingly returning the sand wedge to the very spot it had occupied earlier in the afternoon. He turned to go, but hesitated for the right parting line. Ivar noticed Rama pause and considered the possibility that the kid sought a reward, yet he sensed that gratuity was not the young fellow's motivation.

"Don't suppose you could take a quick look at my back swing?" Ivar asked. "Just a couple of strokes—don't mean to keep you from your evening plans."

Rama nodded.

"For starters, just stand straight behind me here and see where in heaven's name this club head is going. Keep an eye on my elbows, too—you know, the old chicken wing."

"Sir, I don't know if I can help you that much, I'm not really a golfer." Rama feared he was getting in over his head.

"Fiddlesticks…you've got this game written all over you, son. You probably just don't play enough."

"No sir, I don't. Not nearly enough," agreed Rama. He feared the weight of that understatement verged on the borders of a lie. "But I'll watch you…can't hurt, I suppose."

The white-haired gentleman extended a long, graceful arm. "I appreciate it, son. My name is Ivar Guidance…and you would be?"

"Rama Schwain." Rama returned the golfer's solid handshake. Ivar's hand felt warm, as if he still radiated heat from this afternoon's sun or from the collected warmth of a thousand rounds upon sunny links.

"Rama, huh?" repeated Ivar as the name lodged securely in his memory. A faintly quizzical look blossomed as he pondered the name. The floodlight dancing across the terrain of Ivar's wise face exaggerated the expression. "An interesting name…is that your given name or a nickname?"

"Um, it's the only name I've ever had…given, I guess."

Ivar smiled, content to get back to swing analysis. "What do you say, Rama? Take a few peeks at this disaster unjustly called a golf swing and you'll be on your way."

Ivar took up the driver, carefully layering his long fingers into what the instructors called a powerful grip. His tailored trousers and silk shirt hung elegantly as he settled into a relaxed stance over the ball. "Now up to here, Rama, everything feels about right," Ivar announced at mid-takeaway. The swing continued to the top, but from there it tumbled awkwardly down, scribing a complex path to the ball—clearly the wrong path to mastering Wedgy Byrne.

Ivar completed the swing, and the ball, like the previous dozen, recoiled from the face of his club with the buzz of a poisonous insect as it followed its predecessors into the range's right-hand screen or beyond.

"And from there…" Ivar turned back to face his analyst, "as you can see, everything turns to Poupon. Pardon my French." The white-haired gentleman looked hopefully at Rama Schwain.

Rama remembered what little golf he had seen—the match at Mesquite Creek eight years ago. He inventoried the swings he had watched then: Lee's compact, powerful swing and even the unlikely grace that Boney had produced with his ponderous limbs. Rama could not define what was common in them, other than the ball's apparent cooperation with the golfer's intent.

"Could you hit a few more, sir?" Rama asked with uncertainty. "Maybe I can spot something."

"No more 'sirs' if you please...just call me Ivar." The gentleman golfer stooped down and teed up again and again, but with every swing he seemed to widen a disconnect between his desire and the results. Ivar Guidance was a patient, positive man, yet here on this fine summer evening he was being cruelly tested.

Rama shivered inexplicably as an old spirit stirred at these matters of golf, and without Rama's knowledge, intervened to stop the flow of logic that was taking Rama and his new acquaintance nowhere. Rama couldn't put his finger on the mechanics of Ivar's swing-faults, but he sensed it was motivated by a force contrary to Ivar's nature.

"Hold on a second, sir...I mean Ivar."

Rama recalled Carlos Taddio's description of Chandler Stone's night lessons and his children's joyous shots into the Texas moonlight. And he remembered his own swing on the promontory tee as a train howled in sync with his very first blow. What could he take from *that* night for *this* man in such need of an answer?

"Could you tee up another ball then relax a minute," Rama instructed with an authority he had overlooked in himself. "I have an idea."

Ivar was a trusting soul. He stood poised again over the ball, wondering what the strangely named young man was thinking. But at Rama's suggestion, his eyes slipped closed and the sound of sprinklers whispering softly somewhere out on the course flowed into the reaches of his consciousness, replacing the distressing image of shanks and low, buzzing slices. For a few blessed moments, even Wedgy Byrne's cackling face vanished from his mind.

When Ivar opened his eyes, Rama was hunting in the range keeper's shack for the breakers to the range lights.

"Do you mind sir, if I cut the lights...it's a trick I saw in Texas."

Ivar nodded, and Rama threw the range into darkness.

Ivar did not flinch, but Rama did.

A tingling sensation like the shivering at a spider's touch coursed through Rama's limbs. Static from the light switch, he thought, but his hand was already beyond the reach of any electrical fields. Rama had felt the spark before—the signature of a spirit that he did not clearly perceive or understand. Like a dormant seed, the spirit had languished through Rama's exile for the chance to charms its host and his fortunate golfing companions. Since Lee

Trujillo had staggered from Mesquite Creek's sixteenth green eight years earlier, there had been no beneficiary of such charms—until Ivar Guidance.

Rama approached Ivar's place at the darkened practice tee. In the feeble light shining from the pro shop's windows, Rama could see that Ivar was smiling—obviously receptive to a different approach.

"Okay, now try it in the dark," said Rama.

Ivar laughed heartily at the unusual suggestion. "Well, why not? It's not me that's got something better to do tonight. Night lessons it is, Maestro."

Ivar stood motionless at the tee, waiting further instruction. "Alright, what now?"

"Hit the crap out of it, sir."

"With all due respect, young lad, our esteemed club pro, Mr. William Kurtez, has instructed me to never to take a swing without aiming for a target," explained Ivar with a sarcasm betraying his respect for the pro.

"But come to think of it," Ivar laughed, "Kurt never had me swinging in the dark either. So how am I…"

"Going to aim?"

"Exactly."

"Aim for what you pictured when you put your clubs in the car this afternoon," offered Rama. "You don't need any lights to shoot for that."

Ivar prepared to speak again, but there was no questioning the eloquence of such logic. He chuckled at the Zen-like notion and steadied himself over the faint white shape at his feet. From that moment he drew the club back into a new dimension. The same delight that made him chuckle now powered the club downward into a solid, respectable collision with a ball he could scarcely see.

Ivar hadn't heard the "thwock" of the sweet spot in a long time, but he heard it now. When he looked up, he saw nothing; the ball had already disappeared far into the dark center of the range.

"Ho, ho!" Ivar hooted. "Learned that out in the Lone Star State, did you, Rama? I've always heard the players out there could shoot the lights out." Ivar laughed heartily. "Now tell me, how did that swing look? It certainly felt right."

Rama was enjoying the night lesson as much as Ivar now and laughed at the question. "I don't know. I can't see that well in the dark, either. But yes sir, it *sounded* good."

"Sound—that's half the battle, eh coach?" replied Ivar. He turned back and fished another ball from the cluster that remained at his feet. In a moment the ball was upon the tee and Ivar was swinging freely again, like a child with the strength of a man.

—•—

As a boy Ivar had picked up his first hickory club without intention of competing or ever achieving a two-digit stroke count. He swung for the first times with the expectation that the ball would simply soar at the end of a natural swing—like throwing a stone. He trusted that the reality of its flight would compare with his vision...and of course it didn't.

Older players, having already experienced the futility of aggravation, had instructed the young Ivar: Just have fun. Still, he flailed mightily with his hickory sticks, not understanding that their admonition was ultimately the root of success. Unfortunately, the fragile parchment that bears such simple and true lessons burns easily in the fires of pride and impatience. Ivar had grown into a wise and gentle man; he had learned to expect less from the game and had thus avoided its flames. But recently the specter of Wedgy Byrne walking victoriously from the eighteenth green on the sixteenth of July had rekindled the selfish fire.

Ivar was destined for failure until Rama's arrival.

Until Rama appeared, the lesson that begets mastery of the game was in danger of immolation in Ivar's heart. And like it had for a million discouraged golfers before him, the lesson's simple wisdom would be consumed. But tonight, beneath the darkened range lamps and under the influence of the buoyant, peaceful spirit that flowed through Rama, the flames of conceit beginning to burn within Ivar were extinguished. The fine carefree swing with which he had flirted earlier returned, and the range basket emptied into a succession of fine, invisible arcs in the night.

Rama took a seat on a bench behind the practice tee and with his eyes closed listened to the hum of Ivar's shots hurtling away. The low diesel rumble of a tug down on the Mississippi contributed a comforting bass line to the evening's chorus of whispering sprinklers and the drone of distant automobiles. His thoughts drifted to his mother, and he wondered if she had the energy to make it through a full episode of *Gunsmoke*.

Chapter 23

Only a few days earlier, Rama had listened as the doctor told his mother that had she not been a stronger woman, the sclerosis might have claimed her already. But Doris had been quick to correct the doctor and had explained that she couldn't claim credit for her durability; it was the will and the remarkable strength she received from her charmed son that had bolstered her beyond any actuarial tables.

Rama had written off the magic she had always ascribed to him as another in an endless stream of endearments from a loving mother. But it couldn't be denied. Even though the trauma of her separation from Hank years earlier had taken its emotional and financial toll, Doris somehow held remarkably fast against the oppressive disorder. But lately it was undeniable; she was losing her grip.

Rama listened to the swoosh of Ivar's club and hoped his mother was getting a good night's rest, even if it was in the televised glow of Miss Kitty's Saloon. Only now that he had graduated from high school and contemplated his place in the world did he begin to appreciate what Doris must have gone through. It must not have been easy raising a boy alone. He now realized that his mother could have pressed for a divorce to secure alimony and child support to make things easier—God knows his father's bad habits had given her reason enough—but she held out faith in Hank's return from his demons and had only asked for a separation to work things out.

Sometimes Rama wished that she had written his father off as a loss and moved on. There were a lot of nice men out there, and she was still a pretty woman—just a bit ill.

As Ivar neared the bottom of the basket, Rama smiled at the thought of his mother's courage. She had soldiered on at an undemanding job in a grocery store, knowing that if she sipped slowly at a modest annuity her mother had left behind, she could cover life's most basic expenses while diverting a trickle into the tuition fund Rama would one day need for college.

Rama appreciated his mother's optimism, but his parents' separation had its price—adding irretrievable, fatherless years to his boyhood. Rama remembered that Hank had come by the house far less frequently after their trip through Texas, and he learned that his dad's contributions to the household expenses had become sporadic. Hank always assured Doris that used car sales at Big Muddy's AutoTorium were just a little slow—only temporary—and that they'd pick up. He promised he would never let the family fall on hard times, and next to putting food on the table and keeping a roof over their heads, Rama's college fund always came first.

Rama's eyes drifted from following Ivar's balls into the dark to picturing the vaporous image of his future. Each was equally hard to fix upon. He had, at one time, appeared headed to Trent Institute of Landscape Design's North Carolina campus. He had returned a pre-registration kit with a check from his father for the deposit, but he had heard nothing since and was beginning to have some doubts. He would soon have to languish in a community college or face Robert McNamara's fearsome alternative.

Before Rama's thoughts ran further down that jungle trail, the happy voice of Ivar Guidance roused him.

"I don't believe you're watching," Ivar exclaimed in astonishment. "The student is hitting his best shots in weeks—no, months—and I swear, the teacher is dozing!"

Ivar grinned in contentment at the enormity of the improvement wrought by his brief encounter with Rama. "I have never heard of that lights-out trick, but darned if it didn't help." Ivar was laughing now and would feel good the rest of the evening. He wished he could share this story with his dear Rebecca.

"That's enough for one night," he said. "Come on, let's turn the range over to the Rain Birds."

The two rambled back to their cars as the caretakers buttoned up Bluff Meade behind them. Ivar felt like he owed Rama something for his time and for the effectiveness of the night lesson, but he sensed that, for once, here was a young man who was not greedy—nor was he particularly talkative.

"Anything else bring you up here besides that lost club?" Ivar asked. "Sure seems like dull doings for a weekend."

"No, I've just always been kind of curious about the place…a good excuse to come up," Rama replied.

"Well, maybe you and your father should drop by for a round of golf one day—as my guests."

Rama didn't reply. His silence betrayed the fact that he was intrigued by the suggestion, but he knew such an event was impossible; even if his father had been around or approved of golf, neither of them knew how to play.

Ivar noticed Rama's expression and feared he might have struck a sensitive nerve in a world of broken marriages. "But, I beg your pardon if that's not possible…"

"No sir, it's alright. Sure, maybe sometime." Rama would love to have taken Ivar up on the offer, but his father's loathing for the game was only one of the obstacles to a father-son appearance at Bluff Meade. "Maybe…"

"Well, I sincerely hope so." Ivar sensed a current of longing that seemed to run contrary to the encouraging spirit the young man brought to the range. The old gentleman could see something out of kilter in his new acquaintance's world; he suspected it was Rama's father. He dared not pry but could not resist the blush of compassion.

"If you don't mind me saying…some people run into a little more fortune than others, Rama. I've been one of the lucky ones. Trust me. Things will look up for your family again." Ivar paused and considered his words carefully. "And I'm sure your father has high hopes for you."

Rama felt uncomfortable with the stranger's insight. "It's not like we're in trouble or anything. Heck, I'm driving an '88."

Ivar laughed in appreciation of the young man's spirit as much as for his automotive wit. "No, I guess that's not too bad, son," said Ivar. Then slapping his lanky hand against the fender of the Renault like an oil drum, he added, "Want to trade?"

After they had wrung the humor from their automobiles, Ivar turned serious.

"Don't suppose you need a little work, do you, Rama? Just for the summer perhaps?" Ivar didn't wait for an answer, but handed Rama a business card from Guidance Industries.

"If you are interested call my office, or any time you see the old Dauphine here in the lot, just show this card at the clubhouse—they'll fetch me."

"Thanks mister…*Guidance*," Rama repeated the name imprinted on the card, then tucked his ticket to Bluff Meade Country Club into his pocket. He slid into the Oldsmobile and fired the engine to leave, but several of Ivar's words nagged at him and he pulled alongside Ivar's car.

"Mr. Guidance," Rama began self-consciously, "How come…I mean, you said my dad has hope for…me?"

"Well, yes, that's why I asked about your given name," Ivar replied. "Your father must have especially high regard for you—he named you after God."

"God?" Rama blushed at his ignorance. "Oh…right."

Rather than pursue such a revelation, Rama sheepishly raised his hand good-bye and turned the Oldsmobile down the drive.

Ivar whistled a Duke Ellington melody as he kicked off his spikes and stowed his golf bag in the Dauphine's trunk. The tiny bulb cast a faint glow upon the well-maintained set of Ben Hogan Apexes.

"Oh yes, better pull that wedge out before I forget to report it," Ivar murmured. He pawed through the bag but there was no extra club—no lost wedge. He counted his clubs: fourteen, the same legal number he always carried. Odd, he thought; he had seen Rama bring a club up to the range, and he swore the young man had put it in the bag. Must have left it on the bench, he thought and hurried back up to the range.

Ivar stood alone on the darkened tee. Overhead the Milky Way spilled across the heavens with more clarity than he could ever recall. He gazed deeply through the ink into which the galaxies were embedded, hoping a falling star would whisk a silent, lucky trail across his vision.

No stars fell, but the bells at the old Union Station far across town began chiming: ten o'clock. Almost at once a spray of cold water shot across his chest and startled him back to earth. The sprinklers on the range had come to life— the Rain Birds were right on schedule.

Ivar chuckled at the timing and the wonder of his disappearing slice. He laughed out loud at the seltzer-bottle slapstick of the sprinklers. Surely this was the punch line to some cosmic joke, but he was still puzzled at the vanishing club trick.

Ivar stepped clear of the sprinklers and nearly stumbled over the bench in the dark. A small slip of white paper rested where Rama had been seated. Ivar poked the annoying litter into his pocket and returned to his car. Later, with the dome light on and the heater running to dry him out, Ivar policed his pockets for extraneous tees, ball markers, and his divot tool. He extracted the piece of paper and glanced at it. It was a receipt from Hibbit's Pharmacy for $120. Ivar didn't recognize the six-syllable prescription, but it was obviously an important medication. The name attached to the prescription did ring a bell: Mrs. Hank Schwain.

Rama's mother, Ivar guessed. Seriously ill…a run of bad luck indeed!

The white-haired gentleman resumed whistling and eased the Renault from the parking lot. He hoped the young man would follow up with him; having trouble with both parents was more than any youngster should bear alone, but it was not Ivar's call to make. As he drove into the night, his mind wandered from Rama to those exquisite strokes on the range and to the thought of a warm shower.

———•———

Rama rolled the '88 into the lot at Ringler's Drive-In and ordered a Coca-Cola from a carhop. He watched the perfect wiggle in the girl's tight turquoise capris as she came and went with his order, but she was all that interested him on this night; he recognized no one else. Only two months since graduation's great expectations, his friends in the class of '67 had vanished. In the presence of Ringler's new crop of kids, Rama suddenly felt old and unwelcome—as if he were twenty-three or so. He didn't even bother to finish his Coke but piloted the Olds to his old stand-by, Melrose Lanes.

Ten o'clock used to be prime time for ten pins. In summers past, even Sunday nights at Melrose held out the promise of a few frames with friends. Rama had fearfully respected his father's moratorium on golf, but there had never been a reason he couldn't bowl. Tonight he was less interested in rolling turkeys than he was anxious to tell someone about actually getting up onto the range at Bluff Meade—about cutting out the lights, the old fellow's business card…it was great grist for the bullshit mill. But Rama discovered that his friends had strayed from Melrose as well. There would be no strikes and no two hundreds tonight. He poked up an old Del Shannon song from the radio buttons and headed for home.

His mother offered no greeting as he closed the front door behind him. The twang of Festus's voice made the dim living room feel like a hillbilly cabin. Doris Schwain lay very still on the couch; a copy of the *New Yorker* lay across her chest and a half-empty glass of orange juice stood abandoned on the coffee table.

Alarmed at her deep repose, Rama leaned closer; he noticed her chest rise and fall slightly under the pages of the magazine and he relaxed. With the turn of a knob, Festus was sucked back into the TV screen's blank void. Rama slid a blanket of granny squares up to his weary mother's chin and tiptoed to bed.

Before dousing his own lights, he pulled Ivar Guidance's calling card from his shirt pocket and tossed it on his bedside table. In the dark of his room, Rama Schwain turned down his summer sheets, wondering where and with whom his friends were spending their Sunday night.

As he imagined rollicking good times out there somewhere, the business card from Guidance Industries lay in the darkness beside him like a ticket to the future.

Chapter 24

In the frozen moment that the carton slipped from Doris Schwain's shaky hand, it seemed entirely possible that the six bottles suspended above the floor could still be snatched from their fates. With her mind racing far ahead of her reluctant reflexes, the accident seemed like a dream of deficiency—if only she could have gotten up to speed. But it was no dream, the Luva'Lime soda shattered on the unforgiving tiles of Worley's Market—the third such incident in the last two days.

"My heavens, are you alright?" the tidy little lady waiting for Doris to check her groceries asked in alarm. The timbre of shattering glass and the pop of pressurized soda had sounded dangerous. "You're not wounded or anything are you, Dear?"

Doris was shaken by her failure and struggled against a gnawing fatigue as she attempted to compose herself in the face of this setback. "No, I'm fine, thank you," she said. "I am just getting so terribly clumsy. Let me get you another carton."

"No no, Sugar, you look like you've got your hands full."

Doris sighed heavily and rang for a bagger to remove the abstract pattern of glass and green soda from Worley's white floor. It was going to be another rough day, she thought. She was dabbing ineffectively at the puddle with a towel when one of the boys showed up bearing a mop and a dustpan. The teenage boy looked simultaneously bored and exasperated at the prospect of cleaning up another of her messes again. He said nothing as he slammed the mop around.

Cringing with self-consciousness under the weight of his oppressor's scrutiny, the boy made fleeting, sullen eye contact from beneath a greasy attempt at a Beatle haircut. He wore dirty black slacks and the obligatory white shirt, a garment that in its heyday might have seen an iron but had now collapsed into a sad bag of wrinkles. The limp white collar was crowned with a Worley-issued bow tie, which could have been the source of his bad attitude. The Beatles would never have approved, and he knew it.

In the time it took the lady to retrieve another six-pack of pop, the young man had more or less completed his task. Doris apologized for the inconvenience and soon the woman was on her way. By the end of the day, so was Doris—for good.

She had been forced back to work since Hank's assistance had become less than reliable. Now with her strength declining steadily, she was being forced out of that, too. She would have to find another job that didn't require standing and lifting heavy groceries. She would have to do something to supplement her tiny annuity; she certainly didn't want to lose the house.

Doris couldn't live with Hank's demons, but she was having a hard time living without him. She couldn't completely slam the door on the man who had given her so many happy, hopeful days and who shared the blood of her son. Their separation had already lasted nine years, and she had paid a high price for her restraint. Voluntary contributions to her and Rama's welfare were becoming less frequent as his fortunes followed a similar trajectory to his tragic flight into St. Claude's spire, but at least he hadn't taken anything from the equation—until last Friday, when Hank had pulled up to the house after earning another goose egg at Big Muddy's AutoTorium.

Following a brief civil exchange concerning her health and Rama's activities, Hank had walked to what had once been *their* bedroom and retrieved two dusty hunting rifles from the closet. The rifles were destined for pawn.

"Don't worry, Doris, I'll be getting 'em back in a few days." Hank had tried to soft-pedal the fact that he had finally sunk to the liquidation of his belongings. "Just nobody's buyin' cars these days," he had said in reply to Doris's concern for his financial health. She could have cared less about the rifles; in fact, she was glad to be rid of them, but Hank's desperation was unsettling. She had hoped to speak with him then, but before she had gathered her thoughts, he had pulled the old green station wagon's door shut with a rusty blast and was gone. Doris remembered walking slowly back to the silence of her home, and wondering what it would be next.

Mr. Worley was understanding of her intention to quit and let her off without a fuss. She had been a faithful employee and a favorite of many customers, but he didn't relish the idea of watching more valuable inventory slip out of her unreliable hands. Sooner or later her health would become an issue. It looked like sooner had come.

As Doris walked unsteadily to Worley's parking lot, she considered her options. Maybe it was time to give up on Hank's potential for recovery and press for a divorce and some security. The state of Tennessee would probably help Hank remember his financial responsibilities. In the meantime, it was clear that she could no longer afford the luxury of picking up her son's tab for living expenses before he left for landscape design studies at Trent Institute— assuming the admissions people ever returned his registration papers. Rama would have to find a job and she would have to consider a boarder.

Doris drove home from her last day at Worley's as circuitously as possible. She purposely passed through the little village of Melrose and an avenue of memories. The narrow street was lined with shops and businesses still holding fast against the sprawl of a neighboring metropolis. Melrose Avenue was still lined with tulip poplars; their syrupy scent blew through Doris's car as she passed, reminding her of shopping with her mother when the shops were new and the trees were saplings. Passing slowly, she could see displays of colorful new clothes—whimsical at best, tasteless at worst—begging for attention in the same windows that had once displayed fashions for swingers and bobby-soxers. Now, like it or not, Carnaby Street and A-Go-Go had found their way to Melrose.

"Mercy, I could never wear that," she spoke to the empty seat beside her.

Doris had to admit that no matter how outlandish the style, the displays along Melrose had always cheered her. She wouldn't likely be wearing the mod gear on display this summer—her sense of style had receded far from that adventurousness—but she wasn't sure her spirit had. She imagined that if she could still stroll in the evenings along this boulevard as she once had with a younger, less embittered husband and with the tang of after-dinner brandy still sharp on their tongues, she might yet yield to the tableau carefully constructed in the shop windows. With her hand resting securely in the hand of a man not consumed by the fevered quest for a payday, she might yet find the daring to try on something new.

Doris smiled at the thought of those walks with Hank after he had been medically discharged and they had settled in Memphis to be near her mother. The war and the glider disaster on D-Day were behind them. Hank appeared only to require healing of the flesh. How grateful she would be now for an older Hank to take this empty place at her side and walk these evenings along Melrose again. She would willingly grant him his age, and his infirmity, but she could not grant him the weakness in his will. Her resignation to that decision, and to the dropping of new burdens on Rama, wiped the go-go smile away.

———•—•———

"I've been needing a job anyway, Mom," Rama said brightly over a cup of breakfast coffee. "Everybody's going off to somewhere else. If I don't have something to do around here, at least until Trent Institute comes through, I'll die out of boredom."

The blueberry pancakes that followed were good, but she needn't have bothered with her son's favorite breakfast just to soften him up for the room-and-board concept. He already knew change was in the air and would do whatever he could to help. Rama craved something more substantial than retracing his own steps through a directionless summer. Keeping his mother's garden was no longer viable employment; he needed a real job.

"But if you need help with…things, Mom, I could hold off on school for a while. Of course, Trent hasn't accepted me yet."

Doris's eyes glistened as she listened to her son's generous offer, but it was out of the question. Remaining out of school much longer would put him at risk for getting mixed up in that unfathomable conflict over in Laos or wherever it was. The thought of her child imperiled in that sickening struggle twisted her thoughts from breakfast to black consequences. If being a student was all that protected Rama from being drafted into those dark jungles, and if her health was all that kept him from school, then maybe he would be better off if she just surrendered to whatever was feasting on her vitality.

Luckily, the Caddie's Gift did not include mind reading or Rama would have been crushed at his mother's musings; as it was, he noticed only the dampness in her eyes. He slid his arm across the breakfast table to pat the back of her hand.

"Hey Mom, if I get a good job, maybe I'll get you a color TV. Just a little one," he assured her. "They broadcast *Gunsmoke* in color, don't they?"

"Now Rama," his mother said, "don't get carried away."

With two more pancakes awaiting his attention, Rama's mind raced ahead to consider his options. His best friend Pal Blackgrave's father was hiring roofing crews for new developments over in Arkansas, and there was that recent opening at Worley's Food Mart, but he couldn't imagine taking his mother's old job. Then he remembered Ivar's offer.

"Mom, there is this guy I met up at the country club. He said he might have some work for me. He's a rich guy…but he drives a junker. Cool, huh?"

"Do you recall his name, Honey?"

"Yeah," said Rama, "well his first name anyway. It was Ivar…something. His last name is on a card he gave me. He said I can call him or drop by the golf course, whenever. He's probably there now. Says he's on the course a lot lately… getting ready for a big game."

Doris stopped Rama with a look reserved for serious commands. "Forget the dishes, Sweetheart. I'm not too tired to scrub a few plates. Take the car and catch up with your friend Ivar before someone else does," she declared. "It sounds like a good opportunity." She fetched the car keys from her purse and dropped then on the end of the counter.

"Thanks, Mom, but you keep the car. I'll ride my bike down there."

"Your bike? Does it still work?" Doris broke into a wistful laugh as a memory flashed through her mind: her four-year-old boy in blue shorts and a striped jersey teetering on the brink of a two-wheeled disaster as he coasted down their driveway and into the empty street—his first successful ride on his first real bicycle.

She had worried that day about the consequences of a fall. She imagined his sandal straps getting fouled in the sprocket, but Rama had surprised her with a scrape-free ride and a soft landing.

Doris recalled how Rama's blue eyes blazed from beneath a yellow shock of untended summer hair: "I did it, Momma…I *rided.*" It was a perfect cherished moment, one of the few parents receive even though they arrange their very lives to ensure such happy moments. If only Hank had been there, recalled Doris. Somehow he always missed Rama's big days.

"Rama, you haven't been on that bike in years. Do you think you still know how to ride?" Doris laughed again; the pancakes had given her strength. She watched from the front door as her tall nineteen-year-old wheeled the forgotten Schwinn Phantom from the garage and brushed a puff of dust from its seat. He pumped the flaccid tires back to life and fiddled with something in the spokes. She watched as Rama extracted a mangled playing card still secured against the spokes by a bleached clothespin. He held up the card and called over to her, forgetting the secrecy with which he had once guarded its origin.

"It's a playing card…a nudie one."

Doris felt a cold breeze well up unexpectedly. No doubt the card was a relic of one of Hank's frequent poker parties. She hadn't known her boy had also profited from the men's little get-togethers.

Doris shivered in the cool morning as she watched her son fuss with the bicycle. She thought about her and Hank's obligation to launch Rama into the future and how near the time had drawn for lift-off. She wondered if Hank shared her vision. She feared that in empathy she had grown far too lax in her demands or her expectations from him. Doris made a mental note to arrange a meeting with Hank soon to account for Rama's tuition, and although reluctant to press another financial issue, she had to confirm his good stewardship.

As Rama climbed aboard the bike and wheeled out onto the street, she silently wished him good luck and another soft landing.

—•—

Wedgy Byrne hadn't been so lucky that day up in Columbus, Ohio. A soft landing would not have adequately characterized the impact of his unexpected arrival at the bottom of his game. The fact was, he had played respectably. It was his judge of character that had failed him.

Thinking about it now, with the green farmland of Ohio racing past his southbound windows, there was no way any damned dentist in Columbus fucking-Ohio could have been so good—or so lucky—as to have birdied those last three holes, especially when the press was on and the stakes had risen so high. Six hundred dollars made most local yokels turn rigid or spastic, but not old Doc Grossenbacher.

Wedgy fished a Pabst out of the ice water sloshing in the cooler on the floor beside him, and deftly handled the church key with a sunburned right hand. He took a long drink. "And when in hell's name is a dentist gonna have the time to master this lousy game," he cursed. "If that son of a bitch really is a fucking dentist, then there's a lot of folks running around Columbus with rotten teeth."

As Wedgy savored the cold beer on a hot drive south, he cursed his miscalculations. Who'd have imagined that pars at the closing holes wouldn't have done the trick against a damned dentist who had scored so poorly on the front?

"God damn," he cursed when the picture fell into place; "I'm meant to be the hustler."

It wasn't like he hadn't been warned. Others in his trade had reminded him that Ohio was about the hardest place to escape with much money. Don Angelo, his one-time playing partner and nearly famous impresario of a forgettable trick shot exhibition back in the late fifties, was very firm on the subject. Don had retired to the operation of a crab-grass driving range somewhere out in Oregon after receiving one too many violent blows to the head during his driver-on-a-rope routine. Yet Angelo still had a lick of sense and had confided in Wedgy that he, too, had lost at the hands of far too many so-called Ohio farmers.

Better late than never, perhaps, but Wedgy recalled Angelo's advice: "Those folks are smart but they don't look it. Hell, even the worst damn player in Ohio is probably about a nine handicap, but that SOB will claim he's a *twenty*." Then with veracity only a hustler could claim—and with no fear of the Golden Bear himself—Angelo would summarize his take on the Buckeye State's golf community: "Lucky cheatin' bastards."

Wedgy Byrne was sure he wasn't going down his buddy Don's hopeless road. Somewhere out on the dry side of the Cascades Mountains, Mr. Angelo was still fruitlessly scuffing the range's parched turf with a wheezing mower and counting up the day's take on five fingers. To Wedgy Byrne, today's debacle was just a little blip on the radar screen…a wake-up call for awareness of his own shortcomings.

He may have had his setbacks with the good folks of Columbus, but he still had a lot of good competitive golf in him and was looking forward to the Bluff Meade match. There'd be no fictitious dentists lying in the weeds there. Wedgy knew every player and every handicap. In that fish-in-a-barrel scenario, his fortunes could only get better. But even as he licked his chops at visions of easy winnings, he noticed an alarming wisp of steam escaping from his Coupe de Ville. Ohio was too fond of Mr. Wallace Byrne to let him, or his car, go without one last fight.

"Somebody's gonna pay," Wedgy bellowed as he coasted the overheated Cadillac to a stop along the country lane. His fortunes would have to wait for the near future.

In a field beside Wedgy's hissing automobile, several wide-eyed dairy cattle wandered over congenially to visit their new friend struggling with his hood's latch. Wedgy was in no mood for inquisitive bovine company and spurned the animals' languid approach.

"Stupid, slobbering, shit bags…shoo!"

It takes some doing to rankle carefree grazing animals that literally walk in fields of clover, but even these placid beasts had better things to do with their afternoon than take insults from the ill-tempered character across their fence. Taking great offense, the cattle retreated a few steps, then turned their tails to Wedgy, and in his honor added a considerable contribution to the fertility of the rich mid-western soil.

Chapter 25

It was difficult for Rama to imagine that after years of coasting down Crutchfield Lane he had never dared pedal up to Bluff Meade. With the insight of his advanced age, he now realized he had been intimidated by the grand building's very oeuvre. Today, with Ivar's card in his pocket, he was equipped to confront any reproach the members of the stately club might cast his way.

He had dressed well for the adventure, sporting khaki slacks and a sport shirt that, in his mind, would comply with most dress codes. But Rama felt increasingly out of place as he circled through the horseshoe drive and up to the great entrance. He dismounted and looked for a suitable place to park his bike, but the grand entrance offered only a quartet of white columns and two great stone urns from which swirls of wisteria rose to the portico's paneled ceiling. Rama unraveled the chain from around the seat's post and was mentally gauging the circumference of one of the columns when he was startled by a voice.

"Excuse me. May I be of service?" A stout, middle-aged man in a blue blazer with brass buttons and modest epaulets had materialized on the porch.

"I'd like to park my bike but I don't think I can lock it," replied Rama, presenting the chain's obvious shortcomings.

"I am *so very* sorry, but you cannot park your bicycle here," the blue man said with contempt. "And you needn't lock it even if you could," he sniffed. "Who would take that relic here? Do you have an appointment…at the caddy shack perhaps?"

"Yes, I have an appointment…right here at *this* shack!" Rama had expected a snooty doorman and wasn't disappointed. If the disagreeable fellow was going to call his Schwinn Phantom a relic, then he was going to cast his own aspersions. Rama was shy, but he wasn't a pushover.

The blue man was gathering himself to order the teenage bicyclist off the premises when Rama thrust a calling card beneath his elevated nose.

"Mr. Guidance asked me to have him paged," Rama said, adding with a wink, "upon my arrival."

At the invocation of the name Guidance, the blue man straightened to a formal posture and politely returned the card to Rama, asking deferentially, "And your name, sir?"

Rama obliged, adding a roman numeral behind his name for effect.

"Mr. Schwain, please," the blue man said with a slight bow as he opened the doors to the temple. "Welcome to Bluff Meade."

Rama could see cascades of tapestry and cut glass inside but hesitated before entering. The blue man, a master in the arts of both obtrusion and service, instantly assured him: "I shall bring your bicycle around whenever you desire to leave, sir. Perhaps we might shine it up for you a bit?"

Soon Rama was settled deeply in an armchair overlooking the golf course with the full resources of Bluff Meade's staff at his disposal. An impeccably dressed hostess explained that Mr. Guidance had teed off one hour and twenty-five minutes earlier but would be alerted of your arrival when he made the turn.

"And if there is anything else we can do—brunch perhaps—do not hesitate to ask," the hostess said earnestly before fading into the tapestries.

"Thanks," Rama replied, wishing he had thought to ask her what a *turn* was.

It was still early for lunch, but after a few minutes the offer of the kitchen's resources was too much to ignore, so he ordered a cheeseburger and a milk shake. It seemed the safe selection in light of so many entrées beyond his vocabulary. Even with his marginal appetite, Bluff Meade's prime beef hamburger blew the socks so far off Ringler's uninspired version that Rama feared he had been spoiled for life.

As he ate, Rama watched the action on the tenth tee. A parade of perfectly attired—if not perfectly fit—members of Bluff Meade's golfing clan popped, foozled, sliced, and slew hapless golf balls into the least-playable regions of the tree-lined fairway. In some cases, their efforts produced no forward progress whatsoever. It was with some comfort that Rama came to realize that superior golfing skills were not a birthright of the wealthy. He had seen more impressive swings generated by the calloused hands of dusty hombres out in Mesquite Creek, Texas.

But he enjoyed the show. A gaggle of old women passed, each taking stiff, studied swings that yielded only minor gains in real estate. The ladies seemed unconcerned with their weakness as long as they had sisters in failure. Then a couple passed, the husband coaching his wife in exasperation unwarranted by any significant divide between the meager golf skills of his long-suffering "student" and his own dismal technique. Occasionally, decent players would step to the tee box. They would quickly tee, waggle, and strike, then promptly follow after their tidy tight fades around the dogleg below. There were only a few such players but enough to remind Rama that the club was not entirely populated by the inept.

Soon Rama recognized the tall figure of Ivar Guidance, whose white hair flared from beneath a simple straw hat. He had no caddy, although his playing partner did. Ivar looked to be laboring as he made his way up the steep ninth fairway pulling his clubs on an aged cart.

Rama hurried off to catch Mr. Guidance before the breathless old gent needlessly headed up to the clubhouse to answer his page. "Hello sir," Rama called. "Don't mean to interrupt your game. Should I come by another time?"

A broad smile brushed the blues from Ivar's tired face. "Nonsense," he replied as he spotted Rama. "You couldn't have timed your arrival any better. This thief is robbing me blind; maybe you can bring me some luck."

Rama fell in with Ivar and his group as they made their way to the next tee. Ivar slapped Rama's shoulder in greeting and introduced his playing partner with a sweeping gesture: "Meet the bandit, Mr. Dustin Pepper...a.k.a. Pep, king of the Luva'Lime soft drink empire."

"And Pep, this young fellow is Mr. Rama Schwinn...Schwain. I told him to drop by if he ever needed some work. It's very fortuitous that he arrived now. I can use some help immediately, since you have stolen my regular caddie."

Mr. Dustin Pepper was a perfect complement to Ivar: short and compact with the fast, jerky movement of a squirrel. And he was a southpaw. He shot a gloved hand out to greet Rama in a flash of white lambskin so swift that it took Rama a moment to respond. "Any friend of Ivar's..." Pep grinned. "And this is Charlie Vestal, my caddie."

Rama nodded at Charlie, who flashed a suspicious smile. Rama felt that he had strayed onto uncertain ground.

Ivar quickly firmed up Rama's footing. "Have you ever caddied?" he asked.

"Well, part of a game...once."

"Perfect," beamed Ivar. "You won't plague me with hopeless old ideas."

Ivar released the bag from his pull cart and held the shoulder strap open for Rama. "Just throw this sling up over your shoulder and we'll make a proper caddie out of you."

Rama looked at Charlie and how he held the bag off his shoulder like a fat quiver. Without hesitation he hoisted the bag and hiked it around until the strap settled into place. Ivar's Ben Hogans clattered with the effort as the group headed for the tenth tee.

"Good luck to you, you poor SOB," cackled Pep. "Glad to have you on board. Your boss here has been killing himself dragging that antique trolley of his up and down these blinkin' hills."

Ivar got quickly down to business as the group moved to the tee. He addressed Rama in a hushed voice. "Well my boy, that cursed foozle/slice cropped up again—you know, the one we fixed the other night. I am getting behind on every hole and am pressing too hard to score and that's just making things worse."

"Are you playing for much money?" Rama asked.

"Ten dollar Nassau."

"Doesn't sound like much," Rama bluffed, unaware of the bet's definition.

"No, but when we get down toward the end and old Pep starts getting creative, Lord knows how big that little bet might get. But it's not about the money."

"What is it about?"

"Satisfaction," Ivar said without hesitation. "I can lose whatever Pep wants to bet, but honestly, if I feel satisfied that I am playing well—or at least getting better—then I'll even have fun *losing*." Ivar chuckled, "Of course, Jack Nicklaus might not approve of that philosophy."

"Too bad you can't just turn out the lights like the other night," said Rama. "Maybe you can swing with your eyes closed?"

Ivar looked at Rama in alarm. He thought about Abraham, coaxing his son up onto the altar. "Whoa, let us not get too revolutionary, Rama."

Rama watched Pep and Charlie preparing to tackle the back nine. They looked intent on continuing what must have been a good front nine. Pep teed up with little fanfare and smacked a nice easy 3-wood down the center—good, but not perfect. It moved just enough to shy slightly away from the turn of the dogleg and threatened to carry across the fairway. When the ball came to a stop, Pep faced a challenging second shot that would have to move tightly along the tree line on the left side and then curl right to approach the green—a difficult shot for a left-hander from a confined fairway.

When Ivar stepped to the tee, he deferred to his caddie. Without a moment's hesitation Rama pulled the 4-wood and mustered what he hoped was a reassuring voice: "Here you go, sir, one club less than Mr. Pepper. You have an advantage, so you don't have to try too hard. If you are a little short here it can't hurt, huh?"

Rama's voice softened with a hint of uncertainty. He had deduced the club selection by keeping a careful eye on the numbered head cover that Charlie slipped over Pep's club, hoping that was adequate grounds for his reasoning.

"Rama, I thought you didn't know anything about golf...that you weren't really a caddie?"

"No sir," whispered Rama, "I don't. I'm not...but doesn't the four just make common sense?"

Ivar laughed. "I suppose it does, Rama, I suppose it does. And by the way... don't call me sir." Ivar's greatest advantage—his trusting nature—was soon to be harnessed to Rama's good sense and the beneficial spirit of the Caddie's Gift. And he soon realized he had found his caddie.

When Rama handed Ivar his 4-wood, something transcended all sense. The white-haired gentleman noticed how the midday sun encouraged warm burgundy hues to rise from within the club's rich persimmon grain. The tight black windings on the hosel seemed coiled like a snake in contrast to the shaft's smooth steel. As the beautiful old club passed between them, it linked the golfer and his caddie with the spirit of Dickey Stone.

A rattling of clubs broke the spell. Pep had been considering the locale of his distant ball and was growing anxious to be off. Apparently his clubs desperately needed repositioning in his bag. Ivar got the hint and stepped toward the tee markers.

Rama politely restrained Ivar's left arm and offered a final suggestion. "Maybe just close your eyes in a practice stroke," whispered Rama, "and imagine your very best…"

—•—

The rumble of distant, unexpected thunder distracted Ivar for a second. He was unaware that any bad weather was in the offing, but his mind quickly returned to the upcoming shot, settling on success like a petal.

My very best, thought Ivar.

His eyes closed and his one-and-only double eagle soared again through years of memory. The child on the bicycle signaled "in the hole" with his hands. Fortified with this image and freed to maneuver on the fairways of his imagination, Ivar could not lose.

He opened his eyes. The grace and confidence that in countless games had briefly visited him only to flit away had come again. But with the welcoming presence of his new caddie, this time it lingered until the last putt had rattled to the bottom of the eighteenth cup.

With Rama on the bag, Ivar's golf had settled into its rightful place in the roster of his endeavors. It was only a game, and as grand a game as it was, it weighed in as trivial on the scale of life's values. With his game thus devalued, its playing had become more precious. Stripped of its significance, Ivar's golf had become play again, his swing free and natural. He played for the simple satisfaction of a good loud *whoosh* and for the basic joy of lofting an object high into the empty sky. Concern for a shot's outcome never bedeviled him in mid-stroke, nor did hazards ever threaten to shrink his fairways beyond proportion.

In the charmed eyes of Ivar Guidance, the essential vision of the ball soaring, bounding, and rolling into the hole readily took up residence where doubt and images of shanks, miss hits, and lip-outs had previously resided.

"What've you been drinking, Ivar?" gasped Pep as he had watched his friendly old adversary send a glorious 8-iron approach curling gently over the branches of a live oak before falling softly to the receptive arms of the fifteenth green. There, in the middle of Ivar's resurrection, it was evident to Pep that something was up and that two-thirds of his Nassau were in jeopardy.

Dustin "Pep" Pepper had made a living out of promoting refreshment and promising rejuvenation. He had created Luva'Lime Soda as a restorative soft drink that, his advertisements claimed, could bring the type of resurgence that his friend, Ivar, was enjoying. His drinking question was anything but rhetorical; Pep would not pass off Ivar's change of fortune as a fluke or a change in luck.

He had carefully watched the caddie accompanying Ivar through this remarkable transformation. The young man was quiet and polite, even a little awkward in his apparent unfamiliarity with the handling of the flag, the bag, and his shadow on the green. Probably new to this game, thought Pep. Maybe there was some chemistry—some magic—conjured by the unique interaction of their personalities. Anybody in sports could attest that the search for the right mixture was the Holy Grail in team construction. In the two-man golfing team methodically knocking in pars before Pep's astonished eyes, some sort of chemistry was at work. He wanted to know more—a formula, perhaps. Pep wondered if Rama's effect might be as pronounced on his own game. The thought brought him to Charlie Vestal.

Sooner or later Charlie would have to understand that golfers are a fickle lot and that a caddie's job security could pop out of existence like a quivering soap bubble. Pep would have to be diplomatic; it wouldn't do to have a future lawyer pissed off at him. But like Ivar, he might be ready to try this unusual new caddie for a game or two.

Over the last three holes Pep tested Ivar and Rama by repeatedly pressing the bet. Ivar responded with a bold carry across the sixteenth's threatening ravine in lieu of his traditional lay-up. He played a critical fade into a tightly tucked pin on the seventeenth's shallow green and then sunk a masterful twelve-foot putt down a slippery green into the final cup. To Pep, the tenacity of the spell clinging to Ivar had been revealed. On most days the execution of those critical shots would have proven too vulnerable to pressure, but today Ivar rose to each occasion.

Soon handshakes and scorecards were exchanged and the four yielded the last green to another group. Pep slapped his old partner on the back in congratulations. "I got you down for a thirty-four on the back, you petrified old codger," he said. "My God, Ives, if you had played that well on the front, you would have shot below your age."

Ivar was strangely quiet for a man who had just played nine holes below par for the first time in his life. The same serenity that worked in his favor on the course now robbed Ivar of a rare opportunity to cash in on a bonanza of bragging rights. "But Pep, look at *you*! You just broke eighty...can't say that I remember you shooting that well in at least a geologic era." Ivar's eyes twinkled at their brightest.

"No, I am as amazed as you, Pep. It just seemed so easy...I don't know what happened," Ivar said.

"I think your caddie here is what happened," Pep slapped Rama's shoulder jovially. "You got some kind of magic brewing, that's for sure. Wish I could bottle that."

"Hey how about a bite?" asked Pep. "Getting one's ass whipped makes a man mighty hungry."

Charlie Vestal understood that a lunch offer that didn't include him was his cue to leave. "Same time next week, Mr. Pepper?" he asked.

"Well, let's see how it goes," said Pep. "I'll let you know."

"Of course," replied Charlie with practiced courtesy in the face of a kiss-off. After a nod, he quickly disappeared along the flagstone walk to try for one more afternoon bag. In a few more minutes he would be on the course again and the story of Ivar's lucky back nine and the new caddie would begin circulating among the club membership.

After Rama had retrieved Ivar's old pull cart and strapped the bag back in place, he was stopped by a valet and asked to meet Mr. Guidance and Mr. Pepper on the patio for lunch. He accepted graciously but with some trepidation, knowing that Charlie had been dismissed. Rama soon found Pep and Ivar huddled over their scorecard at a table in the shade of a bright yellow umbrella. A little pile of cash accompanied their scorecard and three frosty glasses of Luva'Lime Soda. Ivar would have preferred a beer had he been with anyone but the Luva'Lime King.

"There you are. Please have a seat, my boy," said Ivar. "Now first things first." He took thirty dollars from the pile and turned it over to Rama. "Hope this is adequate. Looks like we *both* made money today." Ivar cast a sly grin at Pep.

Rama looked grateful. He hadn't even thought about a tip. "You played great sir...Mr. Guidance."

"Call me Ivar, remember?"

Pep immediately turned his attention to Rama. "How's the soda, son? Sweet enough? Too tart...what do you think?" Dustin Pepper took his soda creation seriously. He didn't often get a chance to sample a new acquaintance's opinion, and most certainly not that of a young acquaintance.

"It's good...especially real cold like this," said Rama, fingering the frosty glass to conceal a white lie. He really thought the aftertaste too earthy.

"Yes, son, it's the first time anyone's put ginseng in soda pop. Discovered it out in the South Pacific during the war. Gives you a real lift."

Pep recalled that Rama had come looking for work and without further small talk staked his claim on a little of Rama's time—and hopefully some of the magic—before Ivar could protest.

"Rama, I have decided that golf might be considerably more enjoyable with you on my bag, unless of course you have a scheduling conflict with old man Guidance. I'll pay you twenty-five dollars a round plus ten percent of any wagers I collect. Of course, if I lose too much, the percentage thing is off, but you'll always get your fee."

Rama was enticed by the thought of a percentage of Pep's winnings, even though he wasn't sure if Pep ever won. But Ivar had originally offered him employment, and Rama felt an obligation to him. He glanced at the old gentleman.

Ivar read Rama's face accurately. "Say yes, my boy. There have been times when that offer would have been stellar," said Ivar. "Even in his game's current state of decline, our friend Mr. Pepper finds enough foolhardy old farts to humor him with a round. He still manages a few wins and probably makes a few dollars, though the sandbagger won't admit it. Better take what you can get, Rama."

Ivar enjoyed the look of indignation spreading across Pep's round face. Like any two old friends whose relationship was built around competition, their barbs had ascended into art.

"And Rama, make sure old Doc Pepper here drinks his ginseng before he tries to keep up with the seniors."

"All right, Ives," growled Pep. "One more Doc Pepper out of you and I'm not signing your card. That thirty-four just never happened."

Calling Pep by the name of a competitive and unfortunately named soft drink was a low blow. Satisfied that his needle had found its mark, Ivar paused for a sip of soda and turned his attention back to Rama. "I had hoped that we could have found you a little job as keeper of the range or some such thing, but after today's game, I'd be crazy if I didn't ask you to caddie for me as well. So how does this sound: thirty dollars a round, period. And you must promise to keep the sixteenth of July open. I'll need you that day, for sure." Ivar extended his hand to close the deal. Rama shook it.

Before Ivar's and Pep's luncheon arrived, Rama excused himself from eating a second meal. He left the table with all parties happy. The two fading golfers looked forward to new life on the links, and he had secured enough work to make a difference at home. But another young man making the turn with his second bag of the day noticed Rama leaving the patio and the lunch that had eluded him for three years.

"Lucky prick," muttered Charlie Vestal.

Rama couldn't wait to share the good news with his mother. As he wove his way between the patio tables, Pep and Ivar fell back into conversation. Before Rama disappeared, his keen young ears picked up a snippet of his two new employers' dialogue:

"…and what about Wallace Byrne?"

"…won't know what hit him."

Chapter 26

"**F**east or famine, eh boys?" Hank Schwain smirked as he slid another stack of poker chips to his corner. The table's green felt glistened where it had been repeatedly brushed in his direction.

Hank was having quite a night. He needed it. By his reckoning he had been having a lousy month, no thanks to Doris. She had called two weeks earlier to review the status of Rama's college account, which, thanks to her timidity—or was it trust?—had remained in his hands. He shouldn't have been surprised when she phoned; the call to account was inevitable. After pushing the meeting as far back as his excuses would allow, he now had two weeks to raise the $10,000 he had "borrowed" from the account. Between used car commissions, the racetrack, and Calcutta Finance, he would have to find a way to produce the money. Even Doris had her limits.

Lately auto sales had been flat and Calcutta was, at best, an unhealthy means of financing his son's education. That left Hank with the track. To his relief the horses, God love them, had recently been running his way. Six thousand dollars were safely stashed in a tackle box in his apartment, and now the cards were landing in his favor, too. A lucky night like he was enjoying now certainly wouldn't hurt.

From the looks of the table, he might just have enough to cover the rubber check he had put down as deposit on Rama's tuition. From the moment he sent that check, Hank knew he was on borrowed time. In his heart he knew that gambling with Rama's future was beyond the pale, but like a million other gamblers, he always believed in his impending good fortune. Tonight at the Big Star's poker table it had arrived. But a lucky streak piled like chips on a compulsion to gamble does not necessarily make a good poker player. In fact, it often makes a foolish player—one ripe for prey at the hands of more perceptive judges of character at the table or sinister sore losers away from the table.

To his dubious credit, Hank wasn't a bad judge of horseflesh and had started the lucky evening in his element at Volunteer State Studs—better known as The Stables. The Stables housed a four-furlong track and, under the guise of a thoroughbred training facility, hosted west Tennessee's most active illegal racing operation. Hank had pulled down decent winnings on a couple of early races, but his good fortune had not gone unnoticed. When he retired to the Paddock Room for some refreshment, an over-groomed fellow in a silk suit took a place beside him at the bar overlooking the track. The man sipped a beer and penciled in some notes on a rumpled racing form.

"How are they running for you, my friend?"

Hank, looked at the man warily, but the fellow seemed harmless except for the sharp crease in his suit and the scent of excess Brylcreem. "Doing okay."

Together they watched the horses promenade and then run another race. Hank's luck held fast with a win on a twelve-to-one three-year-old. He scooted his chair back from the bar, rose to his feet with the help of his cane, and nodded to his neighbor. "Good luck to you, bud; gotta call her quits while I'm ahead."

The man didn't get up from his seat but stopped Hank before he headed to the cashier. "Hey, if you're looking to keep your roll going, give this a whirl." He produced a business card that read Big Star Bingo Parlor in bright red letters over a metallic gold star. There was no address and no phone number.

Hank looked at the man quizzically.

"Full service casino: slots, roulette, full bar…the works," the man said quietly. "You're invited; just show the card at the door."

Hank considered the offer and the glitzy card.

"Best odds you'll ever see on the slots. The Big Star doesn't have to share the take with the state." The man winked. "Got too damn much government as it is, don't you think?"

Like any lucky customer of the Stables, Hank was inclined to agree. He took the card and pulled a pencil from his pocket to add an address. "Where'd you say the place was?"

The man in the suit scribbled the address on Hank's racing form. "Gotta keep those cards clean," he smiled.

———•———

Hank snapped his fingers at the dealer with finality. "The feast is over, boys, sorry. Catch me next time. Got a sick wife…bills to pay. I'm out." He abruptly lurched from his seat, nearly toppling a couple of cocktails. Had he been a little less tipsy, he might have found a more diplomatic way of bowing out with most of the table's money in his corner.

As the cashier tallied the chips, Hank felt the eyes of the losers pierce him with loathing for his luck and his clumsy, unsporting exit. He cringed, imagining that the most perceptive of the players might have taken offense at his cynical use of Doris's health as a foil to bail out with their money—or worse, might sense that he hadn't spent a dime on her medical bills. His eyes flitted impatiently from the cashier's bright dangling earrings to her cleavage and to the substantial pile of bills she methodically counted into his anxious palm.

As Hank finally stepped into the yellow glow of the bug lights on Big Star's porch, he was greeted by a cicada chorus singing in the humid night. Somewhere nearby, the waters of the Mississippi slipped through the dark. The air reeked of its muddy banks.

Hank's two-door Riviera was parked in a trampled lawn that served as a parking lot. Streamers of Spanish moss hung nearly to the hoods of the cars parked askew in the grass. He fiddled with his key chain, hoping to speed his departure. The ground felt comforting under his shoes and cane as he approached his car. In the instant between thinking he had heard feet on the grass behind him and realizing the danger in it, four strong arms had immobilized and deposited him into the trunk of a black Cadillac.

The last things Hank recalled before passing out in the pitch-dark trunk were awful memories of his boy, Rama, recoiling from a blow delivered in greed by a suspicious father's hand. Then, in his last conscious moment, his mind, reeling with carbon monoxide, recalled the frantic voice of his co-pilot to "get her down fast" as the stone face of the Holy Mother loomed in the dark.

On this night, like the terrible night of the D-Day glider assault, Hank would awaken to a new morning and a tangled knot of trouble.

—•—

The whine of an aircraft engine swelled up through his poison dreams and roared into his consciousness. He squinted up into a cloudy morning to spot the plane. The engine grew louder as the belly of a twin engine Beechcraft sailed not more than thirty feet above. Its slipstream fluttered across his upturned face. Although bruised, nauseated, and hung over, he was lucky to be alive—or perhaps he had awakened into some kind of aviation purgatory.

He propped himself up on one arm and watched as the plane crabbed slightly in the south winds and lowered itself softly onto the tarmac. Its engines faded as it taxied to the far reaches of the runway and disappeared behind some small hangars.

Hank's head throbbed from cheap liquor, exhaust, and the drubbing he must have taken somewhere between the Big Star and this field of weeds lying beneath the approach to Aero Meadows Air Park. Hank pawed at his jacket and his pants to take stock of his possessions: keys, wallet, and money—all gone. They'd even taken back their damn business card, but to his amazement hadn't stolen his cane. For a moment he almost felt grateful for the muggers' compassion.

Hank rose to his feet and attempted to slap the wrinkles and grime from his clothes. He remembered better days and recalled dancing on the couch while his incredulous wife watched him drop rolls of bills onto their coffee table. The glorious image vaporized in the discomfort of the wretched moment.

Hank almost wished a water moccasin had put him out of his misery as he lay in the grass that night. But that notion vanished as another plane approached. The drone of its pistons and the slashing of its prop through the damp morning air weren't as steady or as finely tuned as the previous aircraft's. The noisy little plane, a bright red Piper Pawnee, had seen better days, too. As the plane plunged toward Aero Meadows's cracked runway, Hank recognized it as a cousin to the aircraft the duster companies back in Yakima used to fly. In true duster style, the Pawnee flattened out just before disaster and salvaged a decent landing. The craft taxied to a stop just before a split rail fence that separated Aero Meadows's parking lot from its flight line. Hank could read the words *Glider Rides* in white letters over chipped red paint.

A soft breeze and a few drops of rain blew in from the south as Hank staggered from the weeds in hopes of finding a way back to town. He limped down the runway and approached the open door of the Pawnee's hangar. Then, sucking up his dignity, he stepped inside.

Two men sat at a picnic table just inside the wide doorway. One man fiddled intently with a carburetor linkage. As he worked, his oily hands supplied his lips with a steady stream of sunflower seeds. The mechanic fired the husks back out the hangar door without looking. The other fellow, the pilot of the Pawnee, had his feet propped up on a crate as he leisurely sipped coffee from a stained mug and flipped through the pages of a *Playboy*. The mechanic sensed Hank's presence first, looking up quickly to consider the intruder with suspicion.

"Who the hell are you?" he said defensively. "Didn't hear you drive up. Suppose you're looking for a ride."

"Well, yeah I am…I had a little trouble."

"Last flight for the day is already underway," the mechanic interrupted. "Some weather's comin' through…gonna ground us for a couple days."

"Oh…no, I wasn't thinking about a plane ride," Hank replied.

The mechanic lowered his mug and glared at Hank. "*Gliders,* not planes." He noticed the disheveled intruder wince at the *G* word. "Damn, mister. You've been sleepin' out? What the hell are you doin' this far from the railroad?"

Hank didn't think haggling for a lift was going to be easy, especially without any money, but this was ridiculous.

"Well I'm no hobo, but I sure as hell feel like a bum right about now," replied Hank. "Some thugs waylaid me last night, took every god-damned thing off me. Stole my car, too. I'm just trying to get a lift back into town. Christ, I'd take a taxi except those bastards didn't leave me a dime."

The mechanic's interest piqued at a good story…or anything to relieve the boredom of a gray morning. "Sounds about right, Bub," said the pilot. "Seems like a lot of folks get dropped off out around this neck of the woods, but most of 'em ain't too lively, if you know what I'm sayin'. There's some seedy shit goes on in some of them roadhouses hereabouts." The mechanic took a well-timed sip from his mug. "If you're foolish enough to go in 'em."

"Christ," Hank groaned.

The tow pilot had seen enough of his partner's inhospitable behavior. "Here, buster, have a shot of java," the pilot offered. "Sure, you can have a ride, but you're gonna have to wait. Nobody's goin' back into town for a spell, yet. Might as well have a seat."

Hank cleared a spot to sit among the maintenance bulletins, news-papers, and *Playboys*, then gratefully drank the tepid coffee. He looked out through the hangar door to an overcast sky, thankful that his companions were now content to sit quietly. But the silence soon ended with the crackle of a walkie-talkie.

"That's Miss Gold! Better get out there," announced the mechanic.

Hank looked up from his coffee as the two men rose with a duet of flatu-lence and hurried out onto the tarmac. A distant glider silently worked its way downwind over the tangled forest bordering the airfield. She wobbled through a tight turn off the approach, lined up with the runway, and then settled like a lazy dragonfly several feet left of the broad white center stripe.

"Missed her line again," exclaimed the mechanic. He turned to Hank. "Well, Itchy, there's your ride...if you're lucky. She'll be goin' home directly unless she's plannin' on hangin' out with us honkies. C'mon, give us a hand."

The three men trotted out to the glider to walk it back to its tie-downs. As they approached, the canopy opened and a set of substantial brown arms grabbed at the edges of the fuselage and helped an equally substantial woman to her feet. A bright smile gleamed in contrast to the rich chestnut hues of the glider pilot's skin.

"God almighty, it was getting mighty rough up there," the woman said as she exhaled a prodigious breath. She balanced herself as she prepared to step down from the cockpit. "Come on, mister," she said to Hank, offering her arm. "How about a hand?"

Hank steadied her as she stepped down. He realized he had never touched a black woman before.

"Sorry, Marcile," said the pilot, "that turbulence was just outta nowhere. We'd a been better off sitting out that bumpy spell."

Marcile smiled broadly. "Tell you what, you get me killed out here and you be the one to tell my fans. Those crazy folks are liable to lynch you." She laughed at some dark irony. "Bumpy? Oh, yeah. But still some damn good fun."

"Put it down pretty straight too, huh?" She nudged Hank playfully with her shoulder for affirmation.

"Like an arrow," agreed Hank absently.

—•—

As glider pilots go, Marcile commanded uncommon attention. And attention was stock and trade in her business—Rhythm and Blues. Hank never had paid much attention to the radio and didn't give a damn for celebrity, so he wouldn't have known he was in the presence of Marcile Gold, a one-hit-wonderess arguably renowned for her hit record "Blue Light Voodoo". But despite her show-stopping charisma and the spicy scent of last night's perfume still clinging to her black curls, Hank's interest had strayed to the little glider.

He traced his hand along the wing's aluminum skin and gently tried the action of the elevator in reprise of a preflight inspection learned years before—in the insufferable humidity of Sedalia, Missouri's glider training fields and on the foggy makeshift airstrips of southern England in preparation for the suicidal hop into Normandy. Marcile was surprised at the crippled fellow's interest in the glider, but she couldn't have guessed that this was the first time he had touched such an aircraft since the last one disintegrated beneath him.

"Got a husband who oughta learn to handle a woman like that," Marcile quipped.

Hank blushed. "Well, she's a mighty fine bird," he said. "Haven't touched one of these since the war."

"Which one, Honey? We've had quite a few."

The group rolled the glider back to its slip and secured its tethers. The mechanic gave the craft a little pat on the tail for good luck. "Sorry to tell you, Marcile, but that'll probably be your last flight in the Schweitzer. Better give her a kiss for bringing your famous ass down in one piece again."

"Famous…God, you are full of shit," said Marcile. "What are you talkin' about? A couple dozen drunks droolin' over my butt don't exactly make me famous."

"Hell, Lady Voodoo, I wish a few folks was drooling over me. No, I'm trying to tell you that this little glider right here is going on the block…selling it before the fourth of July, I hope," answered the mechanic. "We're bringing in a new sailplane and a new trainer. This baby will be gone by the time you get back from Tim Buck Tooth or wherever it is your tour is taking you."

Marcile seemed genuinely shocked. "And you're not gonna give me a crack at her? Shit, if business was better you know I'd buy her in a heartbeat. How much you askin'?"

"More than you got, Marcile," said the pilot, "unless you get your ass back on the hit parade."

Marcile traded a few more barbs with the men as they walked back to the hangar. Their simple world of machinery and meteorology had long been her refuge from the racket and artifice of the music business. She had learned to fly with these men, and their mutual respect for aviation had reached across a chasm that might have stopped people so outwardly diverse. She expected their aircraft to be safe, and they expected her to bring it back in one piece and maybe actually land it on the stripe one day.

Marcile gathered up her handbag and wished her flying friends well. Before she left she tossed their girlie magazines in the trash, knowing they'd be back out before she'd gone far down the road. She said she'd be looking forward to going up on a check ride in the new craft when she got back from the Tab Tabby Oldies Revue—assuming Tab put his money where his fast-talking mouth was.

Hank seized the opportunity to ask for a lift as Marcile started out the door. Before he got far into his pitch and his intention to pay her back, Marcile stopped him. "Save your breath, the ride's on me," she said. "But let me guess: You tangled with the Big Star."

Hank groaned, "Christ, if it's that obvious, how dumb am I?"

"Drunken-sailor dumb, I'd say." Marcile laughed with a voice that could easily fill a rowdy roadhouse. "What'd you say your name was again, Honey?"

When Hank replied she cast her eyes heavenward for deliverance from anyone named Hank. "Shit, Hank, they've ripped me and my band off, too," she laughed. "But at least I stayed out of their god-damned trunk."

The partners at the picnic table nearly choked on their coffee and sunflower seeds. Hank didn't mind their laughter; he was on his way home.

He followed his savior through the hangar door but stopped to give the glider a last look before disappearing around the corner. A gentle rain had begun to fall and ran in delicate rivulets from the wings' trailing edges. Lift from an accompanying breeze caused the craft to flutter slightly, alternately tightening and relaxing the tie-down lines as if they were restraining a live thing. The wings creaked under their restraints in a soft metal voice that asked the disheveled man leaning on his cane if it wasn't about time to try for the sky again.

Since the terrible events over Normandy, Hank had suffered in guilt that his dream to fly had proved only to be a means to deliver thirteen soldiers to the grave at St. Claude. The possibility of ever flying again turned on closing the wound those deaths had torn in his spirit. But possibility rings of chance, and chance had failed him for too long, even when his luck was as good as it had been at the card table last night. Yet there were signs that things were different this morning: Today, at his lowest ebb, the opportunity to follow that dream might have finally come again: an aircraft flown directly from the sky by a one-hit wonder. It waited on the tarmac, dripping in the soft rain—impractical, inopportune, and unaffordable.

Hank turned back to the men settling into their places at the picnic table. They looked up, still smiling from Marcile's wisecrack and surprised that a man so in need of a ride was still lingering in their door. Marcile's Thunderbird revved a few times to remind Hank that she, too, was waiting.

"So…what are you asking for her?" Hank asked.

"The Schweitzer? Oh round six grand or so," replied the pilot. "Deal of a lifetime, Bub."

"Why?" asked the mechanic.

"Oh, just dreaming." Hank said, hurrying from the hangar.

—•—

Marcile Gold hadn't sung a note, but it may have been one of her best performances—a sermon delivered not from a roadhouse stage but from behind the wheel of her T-Bird as she and Hank sped back into town. Her captive audience never stood a chance against her powers of persuasion. Marcile believed a Rhythm 'n Blues singer and a preacher performed nearly identical arts. Whether singing to the profane or preaching to the reverent, the task was to deliver the flock from the cool hands of apathy to the hot bosom of belief. There was a lot of preacher in Marcile. She could grab the attention of folks hidden in the darkest corners of a smoky room and bring them into the spirit of a song.

As a child, Marcile injured her knee in a jump-roping accident. Her parents had seen to it that she got good medical attention, but having seen the miracles performed every Sunday on Reverend Roberts televised faith-healing service, she had been impatient with the slow pace of the doctor's medicine. She turned to the holy man for a cure and for the drama that electrified his flock as the healed threw off their crutches and rose from their wheelchairs. The reverend instructed his infirmed viewers at home that they, too, could receive healing if they just placed their lame parts against the TV screen.

Marcile pulled her daddy's easy chair up to the television so she could sit high enough on its arm to extend her knee against the screen. She teetered on the slippery perch, risking further injury and ridicule from her sisters for expecting a miracle to flow from the earnest white face flickering from Tulsa and out through the TV tube. But by the next day she had removed her bandages and was inspired to join the choir. Marcile was a believer, if not in the actions of God, certainly in the value of good showmanship.

Marcile glanced at her passenger. She had no good reason to have a lick of concern for this rumpled honky who had been foolish enough to get himself rolled. But stuck in the car with the defroster struggling against the damp morning, she warmed to him. As he scratched at a mosquito bite on the back of his hand, she noticed that he wore a wedding ring

"Skeeters must have been bad last night, eh?" Marcile observed. "You know you're a mighty lucky fella. I'm surprised they didn't chop your finger off for that little trinket." Marcile raised her ring finger from the wheel to acknowledge Hank's wedding ring. "How long you been hitched?"

Hank looked at the gold band still miraculously encircling his finger. Doris had never asked for a divorce—a rare stroke of good financial luck, he thought. He marveled that she had always found the patience to wait for the wheel of fortune to turn his way again.

"Twenty-two years."

"Twenty-two! Then what's a married man doing getting mixed up with the Big Star?" she nearly shouted but soon settled into pursuit of more elemental questions: Where was his wife; how did they meet; why were they separated; and why were a few lousy bucks so damn important that he would find himself in the Big Star?

Each of Hank's answers was grist for a mill of oration that turned slowly from quiet empathy into a steering-wheel-thumping sermon that ground a decade of Hank's excuses and self-pity into weightless powder.

She never mentioned God, the Devil, or damnation but leaned instead on home, hope, and love for her message. Hank hung on every word as she moved on the white leather seat to the rhythm of her phrasing. Her hair swung, her shoulders dipped, and her hands churned the air above the dashboard. Hank imagined sparks shooting from the generous stones in her rings. The performance was intended for him, no doubt, but Hank could sense that in her most eloquent passages she was preaching to herself as well.

Eventually Marcile descended from the reaches of rhetoric. Hank nearly gave her a hearty amen but offered instead that he and Doris's faithfulness was never an issue: "It was things that got between us—money, mainly."

"Well, sugar. Things can always be negotiated…or even ignored," Marcile replied, "so there's always hope. Why else would you still be wearing that ring?"

Hank wished those words to be true, but some things he had taken could not be so easily replaced or renegotiated. There was no undoing of his wife's lonely celebrations at their son's steps through childhood, or at Rama's longing for his attention. Hank had borrowed as heavily from Doris's right to have an involved husband as he had from their savings accounts. At least the winnings lying in his tackle box would soon restore some of that inequity, but it could do nothing to restore his tarnished image. He couldn't claim any respect for the replacement of assets that should never have been touched in the first place.

Hank's creased brow prompted a question from his driver: "How long since you and your lady been out to a nice dinner?"

Hank couldn't remember. In a moment he motioned to Marcile to slow down as his apartment approached.

Marcile slapped her hand on the wheel. "Well, she does *eat* doesn't she? Surprise her. Bring over some dinner—Chinese. Everybody loves Chinese food, don't they? Do it tonight, Cupid."

As they pulled up to the curb, Hank offered to make Marcile breakfast in lieu of cash. She declined but countered with an invitation to take him up for a glider ride. "Offer's only good on Monday mornings…early, when the air is still and I'm off work," she said.

Hank had never spoken a word about flying but wondered if his passion was that obvious. As he flung the door open, Marcile Gold regally offered her hand with a calling card pinched between two fingers. For one confused moment Hank couldn't decide if he should take the card, shake the hand, or kiss the ring. He opted for the card.

With Marcile's Thunderbird roaring into the asphalt yonder, Hank lingered on the empty sidewalk as he realized he had no keys to his apartment. He glanced at the card: *Marcile Gold: Rhythm and Blue Light Voodoo.* On the flip side she had written the phone number for Aero Meadows.

Hank tucked the card into his pocket and faced the prospect of breaking into his place. Feeling as desperate as a thief and as lonely as a hobo, he bundled his jacket into a wad and placed it against the bedroom window. The glass gave way easily under a stiff elbow. He reached in to unfasten the lock so he could raise the frame and crawl in over the sill, but the window was already unlocked.

Hank fumed at what would be another uncomfortable chat with the landlord. He tossed his jacket on the bed and headed to the bathroom. With a good hot shower foremost in his mind Hank threw open the curtain, surprising a couple of cockroaches. The primal insects looked at the creature looming above them and by some sense detected his foul mood, determining that an immediate dash down the drain would be in their best interests. Hank followed their descent with a torrent of hot water and Draino.

"Had enough god-damned bugs for one day."

Chapter 27

Something odd was in the air at Bluff Meade Country Club. Men of sound mind and good judgment—the golfing cognoscenti who knew the game and should have known better—found themselves falling like ten-pins at the hands of two golfers whom they knew were their inferiors.

Through the end of June and into the opening days of July a parade of disgruntled golfers had stalked away from the eighteenth green to pony up their losses and proclaim their excuses for losing to two gentlemen who, by all previous records, had less-than-exceptional games. The sources of the losers' despair were the remarkably rejuvenated Ivar Guidance and Dustin "Pep" Pepper.

Some noticed that lately the duo no longer appeared on the course together—the Clark Kent and Superman of Bluff Meade. Others pointed out that they couldn't because they both now used the same caddie, a new face at Bluff Meade: Rama Schwain.

Charlie Vestal had seen the transformation in Ivar's game first-hand. Even before he realized that Ivar's performance with Rama on his bag was not just a fluke, he had complained of Ivar's and Pep's eagerness to let their trusty, well-compensated caddies go on the basis of nothing more than a single game that had turned from terrible to sublime in just nine holes.

"Eight-over to two-under…just like that," Charlie had said, snapping his fingers in reference to Ivar's first outing with Rama. "And this Rama kid doesn't know shit about golf. Ivar just got lucky."

Luckily for Ivar and Pep, the story was just the word of a caddie who was soon off to law school. And who would trust a future lawyer, anyway? But if more golfers at Bluff Meade or its reciprocal clubs had listened, fewer would have fallen victim to the Guidance-Pepper juggernaut.

Fortunately for Rama, there were many who didn't give a damn whether Rama knew a solitary thing about golf—they only wanted in on the magic. The game of golf already made a complete mockery of logic, so why should a touch of the fantastic be so hard to accept? It was such sound thinking that soon lifted Rama into demand at Bluff Meade and installed him as a reluctant engine of a small industry.

But one young caddie can serve only so many golfers. Rama's services had become the object of Bluff Meade locker-room bidding. Supply and demand sent his fees rising like a fever, but he had never asked for more and could only smile when his fair market value for the day was posted. Even though Rama wasn't privy to the behind-the-scenes wrangling, he made it known that he would never be available at any fee should Ivar or Pep desire his services that day. He had loyalty and magic in equal measure.

Rama's effect pulled scores down toward par or better with a reliable, improbable gravity. It spawned new stakes out of necessity to those wagering against his fortunate player. At Bluff Meade, a golfer playing against Rama's man invariably would ask to be spotted a "Rama"—a six-stroke cushion in addition to any other handicap adjustments.

From Rama's point of view nothing unusual was afoot. He knew nothing about the Caddie's Gift or the spirit of Dickey Stone. In fact, he hardly remembered that years ago Carlos, the nocturnal groundskeeper at Mesquite Creek, Texas, had mistaken him for Dickey's ghost. Here, in the watershed of Bluff Meade's wealthy, golf-crazed membership, Rama had simply found his thing. He gladly accepted the generous tips that rained down while feeling fortunate to be in a position to watch people enjoying a game that for so many so often was a struggle.

Beyond their locker room, the players at Bluff Meade stayed mum about the Rama Schwain phenomenon. To a man they all instinctively understood the value of their little secret. When competing against neighboring clubs, the impact of their ace caddie had far more wagering value when held face down—to say nothing of his power as a sales tool for members seeking to ensure that a prospective client's golfing outing would leave the happy fellow giddy with accomplishment and in a receptive mood. Downstairs in the brandy light of the Bunker Bar, contracts, POs, and letters-of-intent were signed by a stream of CFOs, CEOs, and VIPs still drunken by their lives' best rounds at Bluff Meade's felicitous course.

Rama remained oblivious for a while. But working in a game that was usually all too eager to deliver bad fortune, it seemed to him that he was present at far too many exceptional games. He began to wonder if he were, as his players implied, part of the process. He wondered if anyone else beyond the tight-lipped players reaping the benefits of his alleged magic even noticed?

—•—

"Well, I'll be gone to hell…what is *with* this kid?" Roland Bandon III scooted forward to focus on the ledgers spread across his desk. The accountant for William Wilson Manufacturing by day, handicapping committee chairman for Bluff Meade by night, was burning the midnight oil.

When he eventually closed the books, he knew he would walk away with all scores posted and with all his members' handicaps in order. He worked with some urgency: the low golfer was to be announced tomorrow as defender of Bluff Meade's honor against Wedgy Byrne.

Twenty-five pounds of complex steel instrumentation rested heavily on his desk in service of his efforts. Roland had been attempting to streamline the calculation of handicaps with the help of a Royal computing machine in order to focus on what he loved best: the regimented beauty of scribing well-kept stats. His passion lifted Roland above the tedium of his trade.

The cumbersome machine clattered like a dozen busy typewriters at every pull of its lever. Although the noisy Royal and its display wheels beat longhand, Roland imagined how sweet the work would be if he had access to one of the big computers like the boys down at Cape Canaveral had. Hundreds of calculations a second, he had heard. It seemed mind-boggling.

There in the office overlooking the darkened putting green and beneath the glow of a Ringling Brothers commemorative lamp, he had made an interesting discovery: a statistical connection that anyone less scrupulous might have missed and certainly one that the players down in the locker-room had hoped to keep to themselves. There, hidden in the pristine columns of his own handiwork and in the slovenly daily log submitted by caddie master Turks, was a link between the remarkable decline in several members' handicaps and the employment of one particular caddie.

"I'll be darned," Roland gasped. He was not too boggled to notice the consistent decline in the handicap numbers whirling into place for a particular duo of golfers. The fact that a caddie named Rama Schwain was present at all the best games posted by Mr. Guidance *and* Mr. Pepper both troubled and fascinated him. Was anybody such a good caddie that he could improve a player's game so profoundly? These numbers could just have well been written in hot pink for the way they glowed in their improbability from the orderly pages of his ledger.

Could this be right? Roland did not relish the idea of someone making a mockery of his carefully run handicapping system. If there were vanity or sandbagging action in play here, Roland's numerical bloodhounds would sniff it out. But if these odd numbers were on the level, Ivar Guidance had suddenly become, statistically, the best golfer at Bluff Meade. If Roland was not mistaken, that qualified old Ives for the dubious honor of having to face the disagreeable Mr. Wedgy Byrne in next week's unofficial but highly anticipated match. Roland knew that a lot of money would be booked on this match and that the negotiation for odds had to start with honest handicaps. After that, wherever folks' haggling took them was their business, but at least the statistical cup would have passed from his hands.

Roland scooted in his chair for a closer check. He didn't want to make an error now, for in a sense Ivar's fate was in his hands. But the numbers checked out. Roland sat back, stretched his arms behind his head, and peered out to the dark course. He remembered doing the handicaps back when Wedgy Byrne was a member. The distasteful fellow's numbers had always been impressive, but news was that life this year had been rough on old Wedgy. Roland knew that if Wedgy's feet were not held to the fire, the hustler would claim nothing short of a miraculous convergence of blood poisoning, shingles, and paralysis as an explanation for his disintegrating game and lobby for handicap strokes he didn't deserve. Business as usual for Wedgy Byrne.

If Wedgy could be held accountable for his *real* game, and if Ivar produced a game under match pressure like he had been posting so regularly of late, then Bluff Meade might have a chance come July 16.

Roland poured a glass of claret and stepped to the window. As he let the wine warm him, he watched an owl glide through the night above the putting green. A smile in appreciation of that occurrence's improbability warmed him as much as the drink. What would Wedgy be shooting these days? He used to be scratch, thought Roland. A few discreet calls to some of the clubs up in Wedgy's Ohio stomping grounds were in order. Confirming the elusive Mr. Byrne's actual handicap would be difficult—and pinning him to it even harder—but Roland had to give Bluff Meade some bargaining power.

Roland muttered to himself as he switched off his circus lamp: "Hope you know what you're doing, Ives…better book this Rama fellow for your little battle." The statistics were proof enough; Ivar Guidance might be a decent bet, thought Roland, as long as Rama was on his bag.

But he wasn't a gambling man.

Chapter 28

Doris sat on the steps of her front porch and listened to the crickets' summer song. On this July evening, with her weary world filling gradually with dusk's soft shadows and insects' gentle chirping, she confirmed that this world was still a wonderful place. She had tended to the needs of her flowers, had even managed to pull a few weeds, and now felt the special contentment of a gardener, but it had taken a lot out of her.

Rama, who seemed to be in demand up at the golf course, still found time to keep the lawn mowed and even managed to trim the drive and walks. But tending the roses and pinching off the old rhododendron blooms had somehow escaped him, so this afternoon she had given it a go. Her "condition," as she referred to it now, left her dizzy and without stamina after only a few minutes' work. To make matters worse, she had been plagued recently by episodes of tunnel vision and had suffered painful headaches.

With gardening gloves folded neatly across her lap, she listened with her eyes closed. Above the song of the insects and the occasional laboring of a car up Crutchfield Hill, she heard a new sound: an unfamiliar engine, an unfamiliar exhaust note. The new car on her block was an old car—a red and black Rambler Ambassador—and it sounded sick. To her amazement the car turned right and pulled boldly into her driveway.

Doris mentally rehearsed her "thanks but no thanks" speech for the anticipated salesman, but as the door of the Rambler swung open she realized she had rehearsed in vain. It was Hank. Relieved of the prospect of another withering Encyclopedia Britannica or vinyl siding sales pitch, Doris smiled at his unexpected arrival the way she once smiled when his arrivals were regular early-evening occurrences and her body was filled with life.

Doris was surprised at her reaction. She wondered what had become of Hank's beloved Riviera—not that she missed it. She had always thought of that car as an emblem of his infatuation with easy money, and she resented it. The Riviera never fit well in their driveway.

"Well, if it isn't the Rambler gambler," she joked as Hank emerged from the car juggling his cane and a bag of take-out food. "You finally scuttled the submarine, did you?"

Hank smiled minimally. "The Riviera? Not exactly; she's gone on to a better place...I hope. Got a deal on this one. Couldn't say no."

He limped around the front of the car, his cane clicking on the walk. "You're keeping it real nice out here," he said, glancing around the front yard.

"Mostly Rama's doing. I do what I can between my spells," Doris replied. She pulled the scarf from her head and tamped her strawberry hair into place behind her ears. "What have you got in that bag? Did you bring me a surprise?" She smiled at the thought of a younger Hank once so fond of making a performance out of surprises—especially winnings. She recalled the rolls of bills dropping dramatically onto the coffee table back in the days before she thought much about the cost of losing.

"Just a little dinner, that's all," Hank said. "Can't remember if you like Chinese. You hungry?"

"Starved."

With legs dangling over the edge of the porch, the two shared their first meal together in years, not counting a few strained appearances as a couple for Rama's birthdays. Sitting on the front porch seemed natural, and words came easily to Doris. She confessed her health had been steadily declining but had recently received a promising call from one of the fellows at the golf course where Rama caddied. Hank raised his eyes at the mention of his son's employment in golf. His old decree against the game still lurked in his memory. Doris continued, saying that the fellow had heard about her illness and was checking with some doctor friends down in Atlanta to see if she might get a second opinion.

"You can just imagine how those people at the club must drop names," Doris sighed. "Probably just talk...I'm still waiting to hear more from him."

"Damn," Hank muttered, his mood darkened by jealousy at the clout of the wealthy.

Doris raised her eyes at Hank's negative reaction.

"No, that's great...that's good," Hank searched for better footing. "It's just that if anyone should be looking out for a better doctor, it's me. You're still my wife." Hank shivered at a statement that resembled a vow.

"Look, Doris, I know this gambling has nearly killed me...or us, I suppose. I've always dreamed that we'd have a little cash to throw around, you know. Look how short I've come up...how much I've let you and Rama down."

Doris blushed at Hank's confession. Perhaps a moment of correction had finally arrived. She had long believed, against advice from some friends who counseled her to "divorce the loser," that her husband would find a route back from his bleak memories. She could only guess how, or why, or when. There on the front porch, the turning toward something better hung like a spirit between them.

Hank's eyes prowled the porch's cracked red bricks, then rose to meet hers. Doris's warm, friendly face still delighted him, even through its weariness. He fumbled through the take-out bag and presented her with a pair of fortune cookies.

She picked the nearer one and cracked it open. *Nothing is as you imagine*, she read, smiling back at Hank.

Like a kid learning his way around his first girlfriend, Hank cautiously touched the hair pulled tightly back from his estranged wife's temples. "You know I didn't just come by to bring your dinner. I came to make it clear I'm through with the racetrack and the craps—all of it," he said with conviction. His eyes dropped to the remaining cookie. "I've been so damn sidetracked since…"

"The war?" asked Doris softly.

"It's been a long time now, Hank," she said, aware that his dreams of soaring— dashed in the crash at St. Claude—were the key to his recovery. As a young wife she had never known how deep the pain of that event had cut. It was a pain she couldn't love away or their child couldn't giggle away. And it was certainly not one he could gamble away. Perhaps he could only fly it away.

"No, Hank, it's never too late to get back on track." She looked at him with singular understanding. "I know what you've dreamed of since we were kids, Hank Schwain, and it's not money. I remember you telling your dad to pull the truck off the road just to watch those crop dusters." Doris smiled at the memory. "Made us late on more than one trip to the movies. Do you remember? We missed the newsreel, and the cartoons…even a couple of features for those daredevils.

"Hank, Honey, I can't rely on a haunted man. You've got to find a place to put those boys' ghosts to rest, and you'll never find it while you're grounded." Her voice trailed off; the emotions and the gardening were almost too much for one evening. Her frail hand traced a flight path in the air before her.

"You'll have to…"

"Fly?" Hank almost choked on the word so propitiously spoken only a day after his encounter with Marcile and the glider. "Doris, flying is a rich man's game."

"Oh come now, Hank, you can afford a few lessons if you've given up gambling," Doris insisted. "You've got to try."

She was realistic enough to know that a long-shot three-year-old or a couple of friendly poker hands might prove too tempting, but if Hank didn't at least make a run for something better, the void of the untried would pull him back to his weakest place. She knew there was no room for her there.

Doris leaned her brow against Hank's shoulder. She had forgotten how solid her husband still was. "Go on, Hank. What you *can't* afford is to remain miserable."

For an instant, she let the crickets' chorus flood back into her mind. She recalled how as a teenager she had pictured herself at the side of a heroic aviator. A shy smile illuminated her drawn face.

Hank was glad to see Doris in an amiable mood. Marcile Gold was right: A dinner, even if only Chinese take-out, helps untie the knots that bind up potentially troublesome conversations. He was surprised at Doris's welcoming spirit and her encouragement of the pursuit of his passion. It was funny she mentioned it, he thought, since it was only yesterday his interest in flight had been rekindled by the sight of Marcile's glider settling down from the sky. The revelation that the glider was for sale—on the cheap—had plagued him. He had imagined buying it with the money earmarked for return to Rama's education fund, but to his credit, the reckless thought had passed last night with his resolve to straighten out his pretzel life today.

No, Hank hadn't planned it when he came to visit, but with her encouraging attitude toward his taking to the air, the window on an opportunity to fund the glider without touching Rama's account might have opened. He remembered a small inheritance she had received from her mother; perhaps she might have the wherewithal to put her money where her mouth was and loan him the cash the pilot and the mechanic were asking for their bird. He knew owning a powered plane was out of the question and the glider might be the only aircraft he could ever afford. Like Chinese food's temporary effect on the appetite, Hank feared the window on his opportunity might close quickly. He had to ask. If she said no, he would forget he ever saw the little aircraft. The money in his tackle box would go immediately back into Rama's tuition account; no harm done.

He never would have suggested she loan him another dime, but here was an "investment" he could propose that wasn't about risk or loss or unrealistic returns. It was about ideals and aspirations. Doris had made such a fine case in favor of his return to the air that maybe purchasing the glider wasn't out of the question.

"You ever heard "Blue Light Voodoo"? Hank asked, still holding the unopened fortune cookie in his palm. "You know, kind of a swampy song like Screamin' Jay Hawkins would do, but it's by a woman, Marcile Gold. It was a hit a few years back. Well, damned if I didn't meet her, and damned if she doesn't fly…I mean glide."

Hank described how Marcile relied on Monday morning flights to clear a weekend's worth of gigs out of her nearly famous head. He explained that the glider was on the market and was cheap—only about $6,000—and that it was in danger of being snapped up by bargain-hunting airplane nuts once the news got out.

But Hank might have saved his breath. Although Doris saw passion and hope flickering again in his eyes, there was only one investment left in her and that was her son's education at Trent Institute.

"Hank, Hank. I hope my encouragement counts for something," began Doris, wedged between her husband and her son's future. "I know in a few weeks you'll be paying the balance of Rama's tuition. I know it's been hard, and I so appreciate your help, but we both know Rama will need more support. Times are tough, and I fear we will have to fall back on what's left in my mother's old account for other purposes. I just can't spread that money too thin."

Hank grimaced at the word *balance*. Up 'til now he had only floated a bad check for the initial payment to Trent Institute. He thought he heard a hint of suspicion in Doris's reasonable refusal. "Oh, of course not," he swallowed. "Nothing ventured, nothing gained." He realized that although she might embrace his personal revival, touching money earmarked for Rama was beyond her tolerance. He silently vowed to return the cash to his son's account tomorrow and to cover the rubber check. He would forget the glider like a bad habit. Hank struggled to hide his disappointment but was soon warmed by his wife's welcoming invitation to come home for a few days, "just to see if we can still stand each other."

Hank eagerly agreed. "I'd lay good odds on it."

Doris winced at Hank's choice of words but moved quickly to the happy pursuit of plans for a new start together. After fifteen minutes of encouraging conversation, Hank remembered the fortune cookie. He cracked it open and drew out a tiny paper message from Son Yung Ltd.

Change comes from the North, he read aloud, shrugging his shoulders at the cryptic prophesy. "Well, for once I got a fortune that really sounds like one."

—•—

The next morning, armed with his tackle box, an extra dose of Maxwell House, and good intentions, Hank eased the Rambler into traffic on a heading to begin repairing the chasm that gambling had eroded in the fabric and finances of his family. His destination, the Automobile Retailers' Credit Union—the repository of Rama's college fund—was a friendly branch that would welcome him and his deposit, even after such a long absence. There was no reason for Hank to balk, yet his route to the bank was unusually circuitous. No need to hurry, he thought.

The morning was still blessed with the scent of last night's blooming jasmine. Sweet air streamed generously through the Rambler's quarter windows as Buck Owens's Telecaster blew hot electric gusts from the radio grill.

Hank sang along with Buck, broadcasting the virtues of acting naturally as the car left the Melrose shopping district and headed east. After five miles, the roadside oddity of the Kings Kreek Golf Center's ghastly crown-shaped pro shop slipped by, but Hank hardly noticed. He was as happy as he had been in years. His wife had warmed up to him, and he had resolved to put the ponies in the past. The bank could wait another hour in favor of the simple pleasure of driving through a sunrise with an earful of music and a brain full of caffeine. Only the news and its routine reports of casualties in the Asian jungles had the power to snap Hank from his trance.

Distracted from the tug of pavement unfurling ahead, Hank remembered his business back in town and slowed the Rambler. He patted the seat beside him to locate his cigarettes. A smoke seemed like a good antidote to the bad news from LBJ's uncertain crusade to stop a string of southeast Asian nations from falling like dominoes into the Red empire. Hank shivered at the imbeciles at the helm in Washington. There were horrors aplenty awaiting our troops in Vietnam, but at least the brass weren't sending boys from the Gulf of Tonkin on gliders during the black of night. Hank shivered at the thought as he found his smokes.

The pack of Pall Malls came up empty. Hank grumbled softly and put his foot back on the accelerator, remembering a store another mile or so up the road, somewhere past the lane out to Aero Meadows. Soon the marquee for Reel Foot's Live Bait and Bite Shop approached. The hand-painted sign promoted *Leeches and donuts – all fresh daily*. Nice to know the bloodsuckers were fresh, thought Hank, but his main concern was that Reel Foot's tobacco selection was as ample as was its collection of smut.

Hank snatched a coffee to go and a carton for good measure, then headed past the magazine racks toward a bored Indian fellow brooding over his cash register. A man, having just deployed the full glory of August's *Playboy* centerfold, stepped back to better focus upon the girl's impossibly perfect delights. He crashed directly into Hank, sending half the coffee to the floor.

"Whoa there, buddy," barked the man without apology. "Ever seen tits like these?"

Hank looked at the liquid sloshing precariously in his cup and then back at the man who, without a trace of remorse or embarrassment, still held up the magazine for Hank's scrutiny. Before Hank could weigh his opinion on the girl's glories or the man's rudeness, the fellow broke into a cracked smile.

"Son of a bitch…small world," said the man. "You're the fella come dragging in from the brush over at Aero the other day…am I right? Shit, sorry 'bout the java."

Hank should have recognized him earlier; it was the pilot from Aero Meadows. Hank couldn't help but warm to the audacious character. "Yeah, that was me. No, never seen anything like *them*," Hank replied, his eyes momentarily captive to the playmate's perfect nipples.

"Well damn, let old Injun Joe worry about that puddle…I'll fix you up with a new cup," offered the pilot.

Hank paid for his cigarettes and took a seat at a Formica table in the snack bar, right beside a large glass bait tank. The pilot returned with his magazine, two Styrofoam cups of coffee, a bag of sunflower seeds, and several donuts balanced perilously atop the cups.

"Small god-damned world, eh my friend?" reiterated the pilot. He skillfully kicked a chair into position with one foot and settled at the table. "Breakfast is on me."

Hank wasn't going to argue over an allegedly fresh donut. He helped himself and casually dunked it in his coffee under the scrutiny of ominous black creatures clinging to the glass beside him.

"Never seen you before, and now twice in one week. If you're one of those FAA boys…well, we're all legal."

Hank chuckled at the thought of being mistaken for a Fed. "No, just coincidence, I guess."

The pilot looked for deception in Hank's face but found none. "The last thing we need is trouble at Aero Meadows, that's for sure," said the pilot. "Matter of fact, we could use a lot less trouble."

Hank tried to imagine how much trouble it could be lolling around their hangar, sipping coffee, and ogling girlie magazines when not soaring into the west Tennessee sky. He turned an unsympathetic ear to the pilot's complaints.

"Damn county is jacking up the lease, and the Feds are demanding we resurface the runway. Can you believe it…right after we ordered a couple of new craft? The fuckers think we're made outta money. To make matters worse, we got Marcile's glider on the market to raise a little cash, and it ain't exactly flyin' off the shelves."

The pilot turned back to his girls and his coffee for several silent minutes, then glanced at his wristwatch and jumped abruptly to his feet: "Nice talkin' to you, mister…"

Hank met the pilot's jangled eyes. "Hank Schwain."

"Well, Hank, I gotta vamoose. Got a guy comin' over to have a look at the glider in half an hour." The pilot rolled the *Playboy* into a cylinder and tapped his forehead in farewell.

The leech tank gurgled as Hank's thoughts returned to business at the bank, but the quiet didn't last long; the screen snapped open and the pilot poked his head back into the bait shop.

"Ain't got jumper cables in that Rambler do you, buddy?"

—•—

The pilot was still swearing at the shortcomings of his truck as he and Hank rolled into the parking lot behind Aero Meadows's hangar. His pickup had proven immune to the jump-start and would require more serious repairs. It was with uncharacteristic gratitude that the pilot had accepted Hank's offer to drive him to the hangar.

Hank had been happy to help. His appointment at the bank could wait. But forty-five minutes passed before the prospective buyer turned up the drive. After no more than a simple walk-around, the man turned up his nose at the aircraft.

"Inferior maintenance," cited the buyer as he made his retreat under the angry pilot's eyes.

"Inferior fucking maintenance?" grumbled the pilot as his only prospect pulled out of the parking lot. "And he wipes his ass with a silk hankie, no doubt. Christ, the jerk-off doesn't know the difference between a little weathering and poor working order." The pilot ripped open a new bag of sunflower seeds and popped a dozen into his mouth. He noticed Hank, still lingering out on the tarmac.

He turned to his mechanic. "You'd better hop in that gimp's Rambler and get on back to Reel Foot's. Maybe you can get that piece-of-shit truck started."

The mechanic looked up from a tangle of wires in a disassembled radio receiver and pointed a soldering iron out the hangar door toward Hank. "What about him? He looked downright mesmerized out here the other morning; he even asked about the price...remember?"

The pilot scoffed at the mechanic's implication, "What? Him? Buy the glider? I doubt that fool's got a pot to piss in."

"That fool," observed the mechanic, "is a gambler. That's why he got dumped on our doorstep. You never know what resources a gambler's got." The mechanic rubbed his thumb and forefinger together to suggest cash. "The tow's all set up; might as well put it to good use. Offer the sucker a little ride... you never know."

The pilot was skeptical and reticent to waste perfectly good fuel on a speculative flight, but his mechanic had a point. "Five bucks says you're full of shit." He spit a wad of husks to the cement floor.

The mechanic smiled. "You're on. Five bucks says he creams his jeans the minute we get him off the ground."

—•—

The pilot scuffed his boots on the tarmac to avoid startling Hank who appeared to be entranced at the gathering of light aircraft and gliders that populated Aero Meadows's flight line.

"Don't get any on ya, Bub," the pilot laughed.

Hank turned back from his daydream. "Ready to go put that rig back on the road, eh? Maybe I can get you into a decent truck for a good price. It's what I do." Hank fished for a business card.

"Thanks, but my mechanic says he can fire it back up, no sweat."

The pilot looked into the sky. The sun had already sizzled away most of the morning's low clouds. The most tenacious of the flock fought back with a fiery orange glow but were destined for evaporation into a blue canopy. "Damn nice weather," he declared. When his prey looked skyward in agreement, the pilot knew he had him. "You ever thought about flying?"

"Who hasn't," replied Hank.

"How about I take you up for a little scoot around what's left of them clouds. Call it good for giving me a lift…if you got a few spare minutes, of course." The pilot smiled, "What do you say?"

The pilot watched as Hank's face beamed in astonishment like a man who had just rolled his fourth straight craps. Maybe the mechanic is on to something, thought the pilot. Without waiting for Hank's reply, he flashed a thumbs-up to the mechanic.

Before Hank could register any fear, doubt, or common sense, he found himself standing beside the open glider as the pilot double-checked the tow-line and raced through a pre-flight. The prop wash of the tow plane blew the sharp scent of burning oil and exhaust into Hank's lungs, and he began to feel nauseated. He remembered the sickening anticipation he had felt as a kid waiting in line for the roller coaster down in Portland Meadows. With as many of his friends as could be fit into the back of his dad's truck, they had traveled to the amusement park down by the Columbia River for their first taste of flight. Ten years later he would feel the anticipation again as he rose in the darkness above the English Channel, tethered behind a C-47.

Suddenly Hank feared he had lost his appetite for such sensations. Maybe it was Reel Foot's lousy donuts…or the leeches.

"Okay, Bud, in you go," yelled the pilot above the roar of the plane. Without protest, Hank took his place in the forward seat. At the pilot's command, Hank pulled the canopy down. The roar of the tow plane—and his apprehension—were muffled by the Plexiglas. The pilot reached forward to secure the canopy and help Hank with his harness; then on the pilot's thumbs-up, the tow plane gently pulled the slack from the line until the glider rose with a lurch onto its single wheel like a ballerina on point. The sound of the wheel bumping down the rugged tarmac grew alarming as the speed increased. Hank feared that the light aluminum structure would simply rattle itself apart, but then the sound stopped as if by a switch. They were aloft.

Every trace of doubt or fear vanished at his long-delayed return to the air. Hank watched as neighboring outbuildings, a junkyard, and a stand of oaks fell away. He chuckled silently as a chevron of geese passed beneath him. Not a word was spoken as the mechanic towed the pilot and his charge three thousand feet above the Mississippi floodplain.

"Hang on, Bud; we're cutting loose." With no further warning, the pilot pulled up the nose. In an instant the shocking pop of the towline release sounded through the airframe just below Hank's feet. Safely disengaged, the pilot immediately rolled the glider in a hard left bank to escape the lethal cable. The turn gave Hank a thrill that threatened to win five bucks for the mechanic.

"Fun, eh?" the pilot barked.

Hank answered in the affirmative, but no words escaped his mouth. The pilot settled into a straight and level course with the craft's nose pointed down the Mississippi like a barge for Baton Rouge. With the bright morning sun, Hank could enjoy the view far down the river. On the horizon he could see great cloud constructions boiling in the golden light somewhere over Arkansas. Locally, a few soft puffs hovered over the environs of Aero Meadows. Hank imagined flying to them—through them—but the pilot had no such intentions or powers.

The southern horizon suddenly tipped forty-five degrees to the east as the pilot worked the craft into another hard left. He let the glider rotate through 180 degrees before he slapped the stick to arrest the turn. Looking back upriver, Hank saw a stately parade of barges stretched to the horizon. He pressed his face to the Plexiglas and could make out the crazy crown landmark of the Kings Kreek Golf Center. Beyond that, the sunny airstrip of Aero Meadows promised a landing safe from threatening church spires or blinding darkness.

"Your turn, Bub. We got a few more minutes under us…take her."

The pilot slapped both hands on Hank's shoulders to prove he was off the stick, then sat back to see what his guest would do, confident that two thousand feet of elevation gave him plenty of room to correct any errors this unproven pilot might make.

Hank froze—his right hand suspended an inch above the controls. The vacant stick reached toward him like an accusing finger: "For one once so impassioned at the thought of flying, you should know what to do now," it scolded. But he didn't know; he only pictured the doomed glider over the dark Normandy farmlands and the last tragic moments when he had clung so futilely to its controls. Hank balked, fearful that gripping the stick here over the sunlit Tennessee countryside could somehow plunge him back into the horror of that night. The pilot fidgeted behind him. The glider had begun to execute its own gradual bank to the east, away from the airstrip below.

"Christ, Bub, what are you gonna do, fly her with your fucking mind? How 'bout a left turn…now!"

Hank's mind filled with memories of the paltry instruction he had received in the days before the invasion—lessons learned on trainers beneath camouflaged tents—as the glider squad awaited word from Ike to go. The pilot's voice ringing in his ears spurred Hank into action. Sketchy as his knowledge was, he immediately grasped the stick and dropped his feet to the pedals and lunged into the semblance of a left bank—a rather tight left bank.

"Fucking A," cried the pilot. "Center the stick."

Hank remembered: The stick always had to go back to center unless he was aiming for a nice compact death spiral. In a moment he leveled out, westbound now, but his rudder was askew and the glider crabbed noisily. Its aluminum skin ruffled as if it might throw out its rivets like water off a shaking dog. Before another set of expletives could escape the pilot's lips, Hank quickly corrected that mistake as his feet and his hands fell into sync.

The pilot and Hank both heaved breaths of relief. "A little rusty, eh?" laughed the pilot nervously. "I'll take her back in another minute. Why don't you try a right turn? Maybe a tad cleaner this time."

Hank felt sweat accumulating between his palms and the stick. He worked his fingers to relax. "Easy does it every time, Schwain. Only take the medicine in small doses," implored the flight instructor when Private First Class Hank Schwain had jerked too aggressively at the mock stick on the trainer. Now, twenty-four years later, Hank got it right. He eased Aero Meadows's glider into the requested turn. The green horizon began to rotate counter-clockwise about the nose, as if the planet, not the glider, were responding to his command. Hank listened to the sound of the air streaming over the wings, and he worked the pedals to quiet their passage through the dense morning atmosphere. For a moment he was really flying.

"Now we're talking. Now we're talking," murmured the pilot.

Hank relaxed and enjoyed the fruits of his labor. As the landscape below approached, its details came into resolution and his sense of motion above it came together to form flight's most satisfying sensation: the dreamy suspension of gravity while soaring bird-like just above familiar landscapes.

A large barn passed below, its weathered metal roof painted with a Bull of the Woods tobacco advertisement. The shadow of a large oak cast a looming blue shadow across the ad. Through a break in the foliage, Hank could see a tire swing dangling over a worn patch of grass. A pickup truck idled in the driveway beside the neighboring house; its smoky exhaust plume floated into the morning. The truck's driver stood by the open cab and smoked as two children burst from the house's back door. An Irish setter trailed at their heels.

The last thing Hank noticed before they all passed from the corner of his window was one of the children pointing up at the aircraft slipping silently through the morning sky two hundred feet above them. Hank imagined pulling the nose up and racing back around to the farmhouse. He would drop, then skim the cornfields like a flat stone across a glassy lake. Then, while the children cheered, he would pull up to kiss the highest leaf at the peak of their oak tree. Of course, such antics would require power. The steady rush of air across his canopy reminded Hank of his inevitable race toward the ground. His heart skipped several beats in fear.

"Okay, yes…very nice," Hank said, trying to conceal an upwelling of panic that the pilot might actually expect him to land the craft. "She's all yours." He had finally tasted real flight, and it was sweet. For now that was sufficient.

The pilot laughed. "I had no intention of you landing. I was only wondering if I would have to wrestle the stick back from you. Now, just enjoy the ride, Bub."

Hank relaxed and watched the treetops straining to meet the belly of the passing glider. An explosion of starlings burst from the tallest tree just fifty feet beneath them, and for the first time he watched from above as birds scrambled to reunite with their shadows. As the starlings returned to their perches, Hank and his pilot settled back onto the beaten tarmac of Aero Meadows.

Hank sat breathlessly beneath the Plexiglas, waiting for the pilot to open the canopy and help him unfasten his harness. The cunning fellow wasted no time in accommodating his smitten prospect. "By the way, did I mention my partner is willing to make you a deal on this little bird? You'll never get a Schweitzer this cheap."

The mechanic quickly repositioned the tow plane for another flight, then caught up with Hank and the pilot as they walked back to the hangar. A broad smile broke across his face as Hank inquired about the glider's price. The mechanic winked at the pilot; the five-buck bet would cover this evening's beer. Hank hadn't noticed before, but half of the fellow's front tooth had been broken away in an accident with a torque wrench. The gap lent a pirate-like nuance to his otherwise greasy features.

"The price, eh? Hell, I thought you were just blowin' smoke out your ass the other day when you asked about her," said the mechanic, exposing his teeth. "If I recall, you had just collected yourself from—what'll we call it?—a low point that day. Didn't think you'd ever be back around here."

"I sort of land on my feet sometimes."

"Well, hell yes, she's still on the block," the mechanic cried. "If you're actually comin' around to make an offer on Marcile's little bird, then I've got to hand it to you. You've sure got some fertile resources. It didn't look like you could afford a quarter for a crapper last time you crawled in here."

"Things change. Shit, haven't you ever had a bad night?" smiled Hank. "You were asking six thousand, if I recall."

"Sixty-five…not including licensing and all the FAA crap."

Hank thought about the cash destined for the bank that morning; it wasn't really his, but this was the chance of a lifetime. He hadn't planned on coming back to Aero Meadows. This opportunity was fate. It wasn't his doing. He was off the hook. Six grand was all he had in that tackle box, so the least he could do was whittle something off this price—for Rama, he thought with twisted logic.

"I'll give you 4,500," offered Hank.

The mechanic thought about the offer. The sailplane aficionados that he had thought would swarm around his offering hadn't materialized. The anxious vet standing before him was looking more like a gift horse every minute, but dropping two grand was asking a lot. "Ain't *that* desperate, don't care what lies our damn pilot here's been tellin' you. I'll take five-five."

"Shit, I can go five thousand. Tops." Hank couldn't give in so easily.

"Where you planning on hangarin' her?" asked the mechanic.

"Uh, don't know for sure." Hank hadn't really thought that through, but Aero Meadows seemed all right, maybe a little out of the way.

"Well, you're gonna have to keep her somewhere. I guarantee it's gonna be substantial. And don't forget transport costs out of here. Tell you what, I'll go your five thou' if you sign on for one year to keep her right where she's sitting now."

"What's the fee for that?" asked Hank.

"Bout' forty-one dollars and sixty-six cents per month," replied the mechanic—momentarily a math wizard.

"What's that come to?" Hank started figuring in his head.

"Look at it this way. You pay five thousand and I'll give you three days to get her out of here—carry her out in pieces if that's what it'll take—or you pay 5,500 including a year's free room and board for our little Miss Gold," concluded the mechanic. "Cash of course."

Hank looked at the mechanic with respect learned out on Big Muddy's car lot. "Kind of 'heads I win tails you lose,' eh?"

"Well, I'll throw in a couple of tows: under three thousand feet, in good weather." The mechanic held out a soiled palm to seal the deal.

Hank stalled before accepting; he could still save a few bucks of Rama's cash if he played his last card. "Cash, huh?" groaned Hank. "I'd have to have a discount—say five percent—for a cash purchase. It's not easy coming up with money like that on an impulse." Hank raised his hand to conclude the negotiations.

The mechanic hesitated at Hank's proposal; he wasn't going to make it easy on a used car salesman. "Fine, I'll give you your five—that'd be two hundred fifty bucks off—but only if you bring cash here by noon today."

The mechanic grinned and slapped the picnic table. "Maybe Calcutta Finance can help you raise that cash, eh? Probably be a little steeper than five percent."

Hank was poker faced; his ace in the hole remained in the tackle box out in his car. "Cash today. Okay, and I'll need a long look at her maintenance log just to be safe," Hank bluffed.

"Done. See you by lunch time," said the mechanic, concluding the deal in an oily handshake.

Hank quickly left the two men at the picnic table and hobbled briskly to the Rambler. In a moment he had extracted most of the contents of his tackle box. Less than a thousand remained for Rama's college fund. That wouldn't even cover the bad check he'd written for Rama's tuition deposit, and it certainly wouldn't look good if Doris insisted on a meeting to review the account.

Jesus, thought Hank, he'd better have a hot streak at work, maybe move a few big-ticket cars if he were to keep Doris, Rama, and Trent Institute happy.

Hank headed back into the hangar less than five minutes after he had departed. To the dismay of the mechanic, Hank counted $5,225 onto Miss August's airbrushed chest. "Five percent cash discount from the 5,500 is 275, I believe," said Hank. "Got that log yet?"

The mechanic picked up the tightly wrapped bundles of fifties. "I should have known," he grumbled and kissed his discount goodbye. "Schwain, you got yourself an aircraft."

"Got my *son* an aircraft," Hank replied as he instructed the mechanic to list Rama Schwain as owner on the bill of sale. Hank had no intention of sharing the existence of this extravagance with his family until he had met his other obligations, but in the meantime, leaving the aircraft in Rama's name got him off of guilt's hooks by ensuring that Rama had an asset to offset his missing tuition should push ever come to shove.

"It's a lucky kid gets his own Miss Gold," scoffed the mechanic.

"Call her *Little Crow*," replied Hank. "I'm naming her after a guy I knew during the war. He'd appreciate it."

Hank thought about Rama for the rest of the day. It was high time to meet for a father-son chat…over burgers down at Ringlers. He worried how much tolerance his "lucky" kid would have for a delay to his education, should his father's fortunes on the car lot fall flat. And he wondered what Rama would think about the possibility of sharing the house with his old man again.

Chapter 29

"**D**on't die, you cocksuckin' Caddy," rasped Wedgy Byrne through parched vocal cords. "We've got business ahead." The old golf hustler had already nursed his steaming '59 Coupe de Ville south down Highway 61 and along the Mississippi levee, about fifty miles shy of his destination: Memphis, Tennessee. Now, with his car critically overheating, he was still an hour from the "home of the blues" and was rapidly acquiring a case of that town's namesake emotion. With his throat drying into jerky he even *sounded* like a blues man, a simile Wedgy would not have found particularly humorous.

He would, in fact, have found nothing funny at that point. He had already expended what cooling potential remained in his car's circulatory system and had depleted what little cool remained in himself by running the heater for an hour at full tilt on a hot July afternoon, but even that hadn't saved his car.

The grand old Caddy was dying, and Wedgy was wilting.

Without another thought he pulled the steaming car up a dirt rut to the crest of the levee and rolled gratefully to a stop. Wedgy switched the laboring engine to silence and staggered from the car. From atop the levee the view down the river was picturesque. Wedgy paused to consider his options. He figured he could pry the cap off a bottle of Busch and watch barges trace the crooked channel beneath the murky water while his damned car cooled, or he could release the emergency brake and turn one of Detroit's finest into a navigational hazard—and a claim on his insurance. Surely some unsuspecting agent would buy the story of his vehicle having been stolen at gunpoint and would compensate him generously. After all, it was a prestige car.

That option collapsed when Wedgy recalled he hadn't renewed his insurance out of disdain for those whom he reckoned were the hustling bastards in the liability racket who robbed gullible rubes of their hard-earned money. Without coverage, he was back to option one. It was cool-down-and-pry time. Wedgy flipped open the lid on his ice chest and groaned at the discouraging sight: he was out of beer.

The sweltering golf hustler cursed as he slammed down the lid and threw open the caddy's hood; it would be a long miserable wait for the huge V8 to simmer down on this molten afternoon. He knew the meager pool of cold water in the ice chest wouldn't go far toward cooling down the thirsty Cadillac. The river offered the only solution.

"Christ she's low," he muttered as he considered the muddy water sliding silently by far down the levee's steep bank. Wedgy could see that the thick brush and threatening nettles wouldn't make it any easier for a sixty-seven year-old road-weary traveler to clamber down to the river's edge and back with water to satiate his feverish car.

"Shit, this is no damn way for a golf professional to travel."

But travel and its discomforts were unavoidable for low-rolling hustlers like Wedgy Byrne. He, like the others who relied upon the bad judgment of poor golfers and the greens of summer for their livelihood, had to be prepared to move when their prey came to their senses or when the first chilly gusts blew down from Canada. It seemed improbable, he thought as a robust cloud of steam escaped his radiator, but by the end of next month in the north country it would already be nearing time to bail out…to let someone else hold the frosty fort.

Wedgy imagined farmers struggling with late crops and early frosts—exposed, rooted, and without options—stuck with whatever kind of hell Mother Nature whirled up. Not my cup of tea, he thought. Even children know when to pack up their lemonade stands.

Like the wise creatures that instinctively lower their latitudes as summer wanes, Wedgy was already on his way to warmer climes and a fling with the cash cows waiting just a little farther south—particularly the herd at Bluff Meade Country Club. That is, if his car cooperated.

—•—

Wedgy rummaged through the Cadillac for a container but could only find a milkshake cup, the remnant of far too many meals at the Krystal. It would have to do. An hour later, after innumerable trips down to the river, he finally topped off the radiator.

"Shit, shoulda kept the Kentucky chicken bucket," swore the sopping hustler. Indeed, a twelve-piece Sunday Supper bucket might have kept his visits to the river bank in single digits—a number far lower than his handicap had been lately. He leaned against the trunk to catch his breath, confident that the Cadillac would at least get into town before she blew again. Brown water sloshed from the cup onto the car's bright red paint, but Wedgy didn't care anymore. He figured he'd had enough, and although he might miss the fins, the old '59 was destined for a new home as soon as he got to Memphis—assuming he could find a sucker.

Watered but sizzling, the old car still needed to rest and so did Wedgy. "Take her easy you old bitch," he gasped. "This might be our last ride…there's no hurry."

After Wedgy regained his breath, he thought this unscheduled stop might be as good a time as any to get in some practice for the match tomorrow just in case old Ivar had somehow sharpened up his pitiful game. He threw open the trunk and pulled out an 8-iron and a threadbare shag bag bloated with range balls stolen from a smudge of a driving range somewhere back in Wisconsin. He walked a few paces over to the crest of the levee and dropped the battered balls to the dandelion turf.

Wedgy mimed a few stiff swings and prepared to sacrifice a sampling of the cheese heads' balls to the Father-of-Waters.

"Practice makes perfect," he mused—still in no hurry.

As he fussed with a sweaty grip he admired the serene riverscape stretching before him. But he admired even more the way the Cadillac designers had faired the '59's taillights into the fins. Classic, he thought, a pity to lose her. Alone on the crest of the levee, Wedgy saluted great automotive beauty by raising the milkshake cup and pouring a stream of murky water down his neck.

Gasping with relief, Wedgy's attention was captured by an object floating just upstream: it was a fifty-five-gallon drum bobbing imperceptibly in his direction on the brown current. A perfect target, he thought, right up there with a range cart. He raked a ball into a reasonable lie at his feet and considered the shot.

"About 135," he muttered, "take a little something off it."

With one more glance at the drum and one more tweak of his grip, he executed a fine three-quarter swing—lazy but purposeful. The ball found a satisfying arc above the river and splashed down, not more than three yards to the left of the drum.

"Oh, you are heaven sent," Wedgy barked into the stillness atop the levee, referring more to himself than to the appearance of such a fortuitous target. Happily, he coaxed another ball into place and swung again.

In the next few minutes, as he fired golf balls from his makeshift tee into the drink, Wedgy Byrne had more fun golfing than he'd had in years. As the drum continued its slow advance past his place atop the levee, the distance shrank to eighty yards, then grew as the target drifted downstream. Wedgy stayed with the 8-iron and manufactured shots to accommodate the ever-changing distance and a persistent crosswind from Arkansas. He would have worked up to longer clubs, but something strange cut his practice session short.

About two-thirds of the way through the bag, an unintentionally low stinger happened to strike the drum's eastern flank in an improbably sweet spot. Suspended in the water, the drum reverberated with an amazing sound: a wondrous warped set of overtones that rang as if they were struck from a huge, holy gong.

A chord of converging, divinely harmonious tones rose like the impossible music of a secret bronze instrument played by monks solely to herald God's arrival—a music that might have rung more appropriately from a Himalayan ashram than from the lazy brown ripples of the Mississippi River.

On the edge of its lapping waters, a murder of crows raised black heads in unison and bolted from the carcass of a rotting deer and flew directly from the alarming sound in the river. Wedgy's hair stood up through the dampness on his neck as he watched an incredible pattern of shock waves propagate through the opaque water.

"Bingo," he replied with reverence.

Then dumb with the strange moment, the weary golf hustler absent-mindedly took a hearty swig from the filthy river water remaining in the Krystal cup. "Jesus," he cried with a sudden loss of reverence as he tossed the cup to the ground, viciously spitting away the foul waters. It *had* been the most fun he'd had golfing in some time.

Upriver, a southbound barge pilot responded to the drum's majestic sound with a tug at six days' whiskers and a perplexed look into his radar screen.

"What the hell?" he cursed. "There ain't a craft down that-a-way." But just to be safe, he pulled the lanyard and answered the mysterious sound in the river with two long, mournful blasts on his air horn.

Wedgy's face was still locked in a grimace from the evil flavor when the barge returned its call. The crows circled overhead, and Wedgy shivered with apprehension in the heat. Suddenly he felt lonely and exposed, as if he were trespassing up there on the levee. Without another thought he tossed his clubs back into the trunk.

"Enough practice for one day," he whispered and ignited the reluctant Cadillac for one last drive down to Memphis. Before Wedgy had bounced down the ruts and back onto highway 61 toward his date with Ivar Guidance, the crows had returned to the carcass and the Mississippi's lapping waters had muffled to silence the music of his arrival in Tennessee.

Chapter 30

Earlier that morning, before Wedgy had found his way up the levee and drawn a bead on that resonant drum, Rama had driven to Ringler's drive-in to meet his father for lunch. In a rare phone call, Hank had proposed to buy him lunch for old times' sake.

Rama had been surprised to hear his father's voice. The metallic showroom PA in the background revealed that Hank was calling from Big Muddy's AutoTorium. Rama reluctantly accepted, guessing that if lunch warranted a call from Big Muddy's, it must be important. They agreed to meet at noon.

But now Rama was worried. The clock on Ringler's wall read *Frosty Man, Frosty: 12:20pm*. He ordered a chocolate milkshake to while away the time; he was nervous as he always was when meeting his father. Another glance at the clock reminded him that he had a bag with Dustin "Pep" Pepper at 2:30, and the caddie master at Bluff Meade wouldn't tolerate tardiness for any caddying assignment, especially this one. The shake arrived and Rama quickly sucked down a treat that deserved more leisurely attention.

The last time he had caddied for Pep, the golfer had been particularly insistent that Rama be available for today's match. Pep said he would have an important client in tow, and he implied that Rama and the fellow should strike up a productive golfing relationship. So be it, you didn't say no to Pep, but you were paid generously to say yes.

Rama watched the traffic pass, but he never noticed his father pull into the lot; he had been looking for a Riviera, but no Riviera arrived.

"Who you lookin' for out there?" The laughing voice startled Rama from behind. He jerked his head from the window to see his father standing at their booth.

"How'd you get here?"

"Drove in just like you," replied Hank. He offered his hand; Rama had expected at least a hearty pat on the back. "Surprised you, huh? Those are my new wheels." Hank pointed out a used red and black Rambler wagon parked near the door.

"Don't ask," added Hank before Rama could muster the obvious question. "How you doing? Hear you been golfing up a storm."

"No, I haven't," Rama replied solemnly—acutely aware of his father's ancient decree against the game. "I've been looping...I mean caddying, for some of the gentlemen up at Bluff Meade Country Club." Rama felt a surge of pride as he described his work. If he had sensed any verbal resistance Rama was ready to defend himself and the game, but Hank seemed accepting enough.

"And how have you been, Dad?" Rama was anxious to turn the attention from himself.

"Well damned good, all things considered," Hank replied uneasily. He longed to share his excitement at the purchase of the Little Crow, but he was reticent at the reaction to such a revelation; the news might reach Rama's mother before she had been properly prepared.

"Biz has been a little slow at the lot, but hey, don't worry, I'm not too broke to buy your lunch."

Hank pulled a vinyl-covered menu from behind the napkin rack and slid it across the table to Rama. "Order up, just keep it under a buck." A gold tooth gleamed from Hank's smile.

The two laughed, eager for relief from an awkward encounter. Innocuous conversation bloomed in the soothing environment of steaming chili and cheeseburger platters, but eventually Hank turned the talk back to business.

"Just like old times, huh Chief?" he began. "You know, your mother and I have been talking a lot lately—better late than never—and we're gonna get back together." Hank watched his son's face for a sign of hostility, but Rama seemed unfazed.

"Anyway, I just wanted to be the first to tell you. Of course your mom insists that I leave the..." Hank searched for a comfortable word: "the *gaming* behind."

"If you mean gambling, that would be good, Dad," said Rama without a trace of patronage. "I'm glad Mom won't have to be alone when I head off to school; she's gonna need some help with the garden."

Hank relaxed and drew a long noisy slurp from his straw. He had expected at least a little resistance from Rama. It had been more than two years since Hank had left home, and it had been eight since he had struck his son in that terrible misunderstanding on the road from Mesquite Creek. He feared that Rama, now nineteen and the only man at the Schwain house, might have taken on a more alpha role.

"Well, don't tell Mom, Dad, but I'm looking forward to moving out and getting into school at Trent, especially if you're taking good care of her." Rama looked at his father with a directness that defied his usual shyness. "She's been pretty sick, you know."

"You can count on your old man. I got my feet back on the ground...you can tell by the damned Rambler, right?" Hank hoped to share a laugh over that line, but Rama didn't reply. Hank's eyes dropped to his french fries, and he squirmed uncomfortably with his son's commitment to attending Trent Institute. He had hoped that he might gently persuade Rama to postpone school, but his son's resolve crushed any such thought.

"Yeah, you can count on me, son." Hank's smile returned, but his heart sank at the realization that if Rama were to attend school this autumn, the tuition account from which he had secretly dipped would have to be replenished sooner, not later. Buying the Little Crow hadn't helped.

"So what about that caddying job…any money in it?"

"It's the best job I can get around here these days," said Rama. "And sometimes they tip pretty nice. A few of the other caddies are pissed because I've gotten sort of popular."

Hank smiled at the idea of his son's notoriety, but was puzzled: Wasn't a caddie a caddie? "No offense, but what do you do that's different? Don't you just haul clubs around?"

"Dad, they like me 'cause they win. Better yet, they beat their own best scores sometimes, and that seems to make them happiest," explained Rama. "It's worth a lot to them." Rama considered the alternative to watching men succeed so regularly—he had seen that, too—and he shivered at the thought.

"I'm making enough to help Mom out a little, and I'm pickin' up some pointers from the guys I'm looping for. Guess I lied a little when I said I didn't play. Every once in a while I play a few balls up around the corner holes in the afternoon," Rama explained. "With Jimmy Jim, a Cherokee guy who tends the flower beds. He gives me some real good lessons. The guys at the club say he almost made the big time before the war. Crap, he can putt the lights out."

Hank remembered the putt Rama had rolled in on number sixteen way back when at that rugged little course in Texas. He couldn't recall the name. "Well, you're quite the putter, if I recall rightly. That was a hell of a putt you made down there in Texas…guess you got a gift for it, huh?"

A chill swept Hank as he blundered into the dark memory of that day. He remembered the money he lost when his son sunk that unlikely putt, and he recalled the blinding anger.

"Oh, that…thanks." Rama replied uneasily. Like his father, he wanted to move quickly from that memory. But the compliment, like brandy, felt deep and warm as if spoken from the green's fringe by a proud father while his son's magic golf ball still rattled in the cup.

"Yeah, a gift. That's what Pep and Ives call it sometimes," Rama said.

"Who is Ives?"

"Oh, I carry his bag the most. He's a real nice old businessman. He says he's never played so well, and he's in his seventies. Hasn't lost a match since I've been caddying for him, maybe about twenty times now. I think if he was younger, he might make some money at it…as if he needed any more. He's rich."

Hank perked up. Even though he hoped to leave gambling in his past, he would always be intrigued by wealth. "The fellow who's never lost with you... what did you say his name was again?"

"That's Ivar...we call him Ives. Mister Ivar Guidance. He's a tall, skinny guy with white hair, kind of like Andy Warhol's."

Rama checked the clock and said he had to hustle off to get ready to caddie for a game with Dustin Pepper and some big wheel from a supermarket. He explained that Pep was the creator of Luva'Lime Soda. Rama thanked his father for lunch and congratulated him on trying to work things out with Doris. As he climbed behind the '88's wheel he suggested lunch again, maybe with no agenda other than small talk and a good appetite. Hank didn't respond.

As Rama pulled the Oldsmobile out of the lot he noticed his father was laboring over the Rambler's steering wheel like it was a capstan, trying to maneuver the less-than-nimble wagon out of its narrow slot.

"I like the car, Dad...better than the Riviera. It suits you," he hollered across the parking lot.

Hank cast a bemused expression his son's way. The Rambler and the Oldsmobile both turned in opposite directions as they left Ringler's lot—Rama to his precisely appointed tee time at Bluff Meade, and Hank to an accidental encounter with a man in serious need of a prestige car.

Chapter 31

"**B**iggest piece of shit I've ever owned," cursed Wedgy in reply to the tow-truck driver's gush of admiration for the blazing red '59 Cadillac. "Come on mister…you can't help but like them *fins*," the driver observed.

"Fuck the fins! This bitch has been steamin' around the country like a locomotive. Took half the damn Mississippi to cool her down, and that was only an hour ago." Wedgy's stomach turned at the thought of his brief sampling from the Father of Waters.

"A fifty-niner…yeah, bet ol' Elvis got a whole stable of 'em." The driver's deep admiration for the King of Rock 'n Roll's automotive excesses drooled from his lips like tobacco juice.

"Well, maybe the King can hitch up this one, too, 'cause it's stayin' in Memphis soon as I can unload it."

Wedgy pressed his ruddy nose to the tow truck's passenger window. He didn't relish the idea of pulling into the Bluff Meade Country Club tomorrow with anything less than a *prestige* car. The old Caddy had served his purposes well, but eight years and 200,000 miles of chasing foolhardy golfers around the country had pretty much worn the prestige right out of the engine. He had to face a divorce from her now and had to make sure *someone else* paid the alimony.

Wedgy watched the bottomland roll relentlessly by. "Where in hell are you headed, pal…Natchez? Christ, we've been driving long enough." Visions of the tow bill were beginning to cloud his focus from the critical used-car haggling awaiting somewhere down the road.

"This fucking tow's gonna cost me a fortune," growled Wedgy.

"Well sir, it ain't that bad. Lookie here: you got your twenty-five buck hook-up, and your minimum mileage fee, and your…"

"Spare me!" Wedgy silenced the driver in mid-disclosure. "Whatever it is, it'll be too damned much. How much farther to the *nearest* Cadillac dealer?"

"Well sir, that would be smack dab downtown. See those buildings yonder?"

"Oh, Jesus," yelped Wedgy at the gray shapes stalking a distant horizon. "Let's say we keep our eyes peeled for a halfway-reputable used car lot...and soon. Hell, I probably couldn't make much of a deal with those greedy assholes in town anyway."

The driver nodded in agreement. "Well sir, we do got Big Muddy's Auto-Torium comin' up here directly. Probably get you a sweet deal in there."

To Wedgy's relief, the tow truck soon braked and lurched toward the AutoTorium parking lot. He glanced at the sign and sure enough: Big Muddy's.

Crooked lines of used—very used—cars were arranged in rows along the highway, with hoods open to reveal engines best left under wraps. Strings of pennants in primary colors flapped on a breeze that smelled like the car lot's namesake. Missing pennants made the festive strings look more like smiles punctuated by bad teeth than invitations to stop and browse.

Once-bobbing balloons lay dead—strangled, then left to hang from radio antennae. Irresistible two-word phrases in praise of each car's supposed attributes were scrawled in Ivory soap on the windshields. The words *Runs Goood, Lowww Miles, Red Hot!!* were melting onto the unwanted cars' hoods like lipstick from a drunken streetwalker.

"Well...here we be," sang the driver.

"*Here we be...*" echoed Wedgy apprehensively as the tow truck clattered to a halt. Indeed, this was no way for a golf professional to travel.

In that moment Wedgy realized three significant facts: His driver had taken "halfway reputable" literally; he would have one hell of a time finding any prestige on this lot; and the god-damned tow truck driver sounded exactly like Gomer Pyle.

"What the hell, just drop her off here," instructed Wedgy. He figured he would easily take these yahoos for a ride and would soon be on his way.

Wedgy sorted through his wallet for the appropriate bills to cover the tow and a little something else for Gomer. Suddenly the Cadillac's front end came loose from its cradle and dropped about three feet to the ground. The front bumper bottomed out with a crash, tossing Wedgy back against a Dodge Satellite in horror.

"Goll-lee!" exclaimed the driver.

"Are you shitting me?" cried Wedgy. He tucked Gomer's tip back into his billfold.

The noisy arrival of the tow truck and the sickly Cadillac attracted the attention of a couple of salesmen lingering in the shade of the showroom entrance. The older of the two leapt into action and blocked the young gun's path to the lot with the deployment of a stout black cane.

"Pecking order, my boy, pecking order," Hank Schwain declared firmly. He flashed a welcoming smile as he limped out onto the lot, anxious at the prospect of a new customer.

"Somebody looking for a good *pre-owned* car today?" he asked as he approached the exasperated fellow standing beside the '59 Cadillac. Hank switched the cane from his right hand to his left and extended his palm in one well-practiced motion.

—•—

Hank hoped this might be the sale he was looking for. A Cadillac driver was not likely to step too far down the ladder of pretension. Indeed, Hank was hungry for this sale, but he may not have been hungry enough to deal with the likes of Wallace "Wedgy" Byrne.

Without hesitation Wedgy went to work, instinctively feigning a look of concern for the salesman's handicap.

"You a vet? That's a three-letter word for *hero* in my book." He grasped Hank's hand and shook it carefully. The grip, the resistance, the recoil in the arm's stroke all communicated information vital to Wedgy's car-buying strategy. The golf hustler's antennae reported that the car salesman didn't feel confident enough to trust his own judgment if faced with sufficiently artful bullshit.

"Well, God bless you," gushed Wedgy. "No, I'm not looking for a car, just a little repair. Ain't never gonna trade away one of the King's own Caddies. Howdy friend...Wallace is the name."

Hank was staggered slightly but regained his footing. "Never knew old Elvis to drive a *red* one," replied Hank. "He mostly favored black."

"That he did, that he did," said Wedgy, buying an instant to think, "except for the present he bought for his buddy Red. I think it was on Red's twenty-second birthday to be exact."

"Oh, *that* car. Might have forgotten about it," Hank lied. "No doubt about it, in this town a fella's got to know his Caddies...and I'm not talking golf," Hank laughed.

"No, Wallace, if you've got a Presley ride there—Red's or not—I guess you'd best keep fixing her up, 'cause the trouble is..." Hank paused to deliver his trump: "we won't lay as much as a pair of pliers on a collector car in this shop—too much liability if you know what I'm saying. Now, if you can hook back up with old Gomer there, you'll probably find someone be happy to work on it down the road." Hank smiled graciously. "By the way, the name's Hank Schwain."

Wedgy looked up as the stars and bars on the tow truck disappeared out onto the highway in a swirl of red dust. He didn't even try to act surprised except at his own error in judgment. He turned back to Hank and smiled bravely as only those firmly ascribing to the win-one-lose-one theory of cosmic balance might. Today Big Muddy, tomorrow Bluff Meade, he thought; it would all even out once he got back on the road.

"Shit, Hank, don't tell me these rattletraps don't have a little *story* or two behind them." Wedgy smiled sarcastically in temporary defeat. He threw the Caddy's door open for Hank's inspection. "Interior is good as new. All original miles…never spun the meter back, honest," Wedgy said as he stepped aside.

Hank peered at the dashboard and withdrew his head from the car. "Two hundred and three thousand miles? Shit, Wallace, you *shoulda* turned her back."

Having lost the essential hustle, Wedgy had to settle with badgering Hank over a price on the best- looking Lincoln Continental convertible he could find—best being a highly subjective word in this case, for there were no Cadillacs. The Lincoln wasn't all that bad; it featured a repainted midnight-blue exterior, suicide doors, a baby blue vinyl interior, and a Continental kit—very Beale Street.

Hank could barely hide his pleasure at the deal. Always make the customer feel like they are getting the better of you was the old saw, but when a customer had already stumbled as bad as this one, it was pretty hard to instill that feeling. There was little Wedgy could have done to come out ahead. Big Muddy had acquired the Lincoln at an auction from a desperate women who had "earned" the car while in the employ of—in Muddy's words—"one of our town's nastiest celebrities."

After a hasty little shake-down spin, Wedgy pulled the blue Lincoln up beside the Cadillac. Hank limped around the back, feeling charitable after calculating his commission on the Lincoln. "Let me help load up your gear there, Wally."

Wedgy threw open the trunk and grabbed his golf clubs before Hank could put any strange luck on them.

"Hey, my boy is a golfer," Hank exclaimed when he saw Wedgy's handsome leather bag and a trio of plaid head covers. "Well, I guess more of a caddie really."

"Sure, everybody's a golfer nowadays," scoffed Wedgy, still peeved at his extraordinarily clean clock. "Where does he loop…I mean work?"

"Up at Bluff Meade, a fancy ass country club."

"Well now, isn't this a small world? I'm headed there now to get in some practice; got a game tomorrow—a big money game."

Hank brightened with rising curiosity. "What's *big?*"

"I don't know, six or seven thousand to the winner," replied Wedgy. He noticed interest flare in the car salesman's eyes. "But that's nothing compared to all the side bets those rich jerks will lay down. I'd like to get my hands on some of that action. Yeah, it can get pretty *big*," Wedgy replied, dropping Hank's three-letter word like a ripe fruit.

"Shit, a guy playing smart and decent can make more than most of those professionals some days. I expect I'll make out pretty good tomorrow. Just between you and me, I'm going up against a fellow who doesn't stand a chance; the fool is playing me out of pride or some such bullshit. I got his goat real bad—always have—and that works in my favor," explained Wedgy, careful not to disclose his own deteriorating skills. "You know, this game's like poker: You get up against a sucker and the odds all go your way."

Wedgy looked at the salesman who stood transfixed at the car's open trunk. "Are you a gambling man, Hank?"

Hank felt a moistening in his palms and the craving for a cigarette. "Not really," he said avoiding the conviction of a solid no.

Wedgy didn't believe Hank, just as Hank hadn't believed Wedgy's Elvis story. The golf hustler in Wedgy knew Hank needed only a little nudge to jump into the pot up at Bluff Meade, and the more money that gets pumped into that pot the better.

"Well, Hank, if you *were* a gambler," Wedgy winked, "the starter up at Bluff Meade could take your bet. You'd have to get there a while before tee time—by about ten o'clock I'd say—or you could get your ass over to the Big Star Bingo Parlor, if you know where that is. Got a little arrangement with them. You could book a friendly little wager there."

Hank cleared a lump from his throat. "Just ask for the starter, huh?" He surely wasn't going near the Big Star again.

Wedgy fetched the remaining items from the Cadillac and patted the hood. "You know, Hank, Elvis *would* have looked good in this car," he laughed. "And I am gonna miss those tailfins, honest." He slid across the blue seats and fingered the ivory skull keychain dangling from the Lincoln's ignition.

Hank was torn with temptation and was anxious for Wedgy to fire up the god-damned Lincoln and blow out of his lot. He thought about Doris and his pledge, which was rapidly dissolving like footing on a sandy beach. If the wash back to the sea didn't stop real soon, he would stumble.

He prayed the old Lincoln's engine would start.

Hank stepped back from the car, anticipating its departure. He gave the sucker at the wheel—who now had him firmly on the hook—a little farewell salute, but his voice betrayed him. "So who's the guy you're so damn sure you're going to whip...in case a fellow might want to bet *against* you?"

"Bet for Ives to win...you'd be crazy," snapped Wedgy. He ignited the engine and all 430 cubic inches roared in a glorious waste of energy. A couple of limp balloons stirred at their moorings.

Hank grinned at Wedgy, then raised his voice above the Lincoln's tuneless growl. "Did you say, Ives?"

"Yes, good old Ivar Guidance," shouted Wedgy. "I told you, the old goat is a long shot. If you're gonna throw money away, why don't you just toss me back a little something on *this* screw job?"

Wedgy patted the Lincoln's dashboard, then cranked the wheel to the highway and thundered off without another word.

Hank stood by Wedgy's Cadillac, confused at the confluence of events that had brought this much-needed sale and that odd name—Ivar Guidance—his way again. He recalled the conversation with his son at lunch. Hadn't Rama said that his man Ivar never lost? And hadn't this Wallace fellow just said Ivar never won? There was a disconnect, and maybe there was opportunity in it. Hank's mind labored in logic: If this golfer only blew through town once a year, but Rama spent several mornings a week caddying for Ivar, whose take on Mr. Guidance's chances was he to believe?

Whatever the Gift Rama had mentioned was all about, "never losing" meant one thing to Hank: With Rama on this Ivar fellow's bag in a big dollar match against an unsuspecting and, from all appearances, an unimpressive opponent, Hank felt certain he was staring an unusually lucrative sure thing square in the face—a sure enough thing to pull him temporarily from his resolution to reform.

Hank's logic churned on: Without risk, this opportunity wasn't even a gamble. As in a gambler's wildest dream, he had inside information on the would-be winner and the obvious loser. If what Wallace had said about Ivar's hopeless record against him were true, the odds for an Ivar victory were bound to be astronomical. Nobody would take them, but therein was the opportunity.

"Damn, that would be a good bet," Hank whispered. He leaned back against the Cadillac. "That Wally fella' don't know what's gonna hit him."

As Hank watched the Lincoln disappear toward town, he weighed the odds: Even with a conservative book in Wedgy's favor, it would make for a nice payday to anyone savvy enough to risk a little something on that Guidance fellow.

With frustration at his own poverty, Hank imagined what a $5,000 bet might return. At only four-to-one odds he could cover the Little Crow and the bad check to Trent, plus he'd have more than enough to take Doris out to Gulfport for a little fling and maybe still pay back the secret IOUs to his son's account.

Hank considered the alternative: the grim reality of explaining to Doris the absence of thousands of dollars and the real reason for the forthcoming nasty-gram from Trent Institute's admissions department. With the Rama-Ivar team in his corner, this one last bet would hardly be a gamble at all…if he only had the do-re-mi.

Hank pictured the empty tackle box. The damned glider had sailed into his life a day early and had cleaned him out; he was Schweitzer-rich and penny-poor—too poor for this investment. Then Hank remembered something in his wallet. He fanned through several tired old business cards until the golden ink of one gleamed from his fingers.

He held the card at arm's length and focused on its promising message asthe colored pennants flapped in alarm above Big Muddy's AutoTorium: *Cash In a Flash Calcutta Finance and Pawn.*

Hank tucked Calcutta's card into his shirt pocket for future reference, then went inside to brag on stealing one of the King's very own Caddies from an unsuspecting rube.

Chapter 32

The sound of Hawaiian guitars from Bluff Meade's Pago-Pago Room moved through Dustin "Pep" Pepper's mind like syrup as he stared into the blank tiles above the urinal. Pep was thankful for a moment's relief from the endless self-analysis of his dinner partner's poor golfing performance. He cursed himself now for putting pleasure before business on the golf course that afternoon and for beating Wessel Waddley. There had been considerable diplomatically concealed pleasure in taking thirty-six dollars from Wessel, but now, an hour into dinner with the unhappy loser, Pep wondered how a successful businessman such as Wessel—the founder of Waddley's Food Parade—could fall into such an irritating vortex of complaint at the loss of a few lousy bucks in a friendly little skins game.

Pep should have known not to get tangled in the psychodrama that was Wessel's golf. Such entanglements were bad business for Pep, who was court-ing Waddley's valuable soft drink contract. He knew that in business there were three things you did not do: buy high and sell low, go to bed with an em-ployee, and beat a client at golf. Even in a friendly match, the clash of perceived ability against actual skill or the friction of results against expectation could drag a person down to an honest but unwelcome appraisal of himself. And it could lower either party's tolerance of the other to the flashpoint.

In a competitive match, inflated pride and deflated performance could strike sparks of temper from the vain golfer like flint against steel. Wessel was such a golfer: His game existed in his mouth and in his mind. Pep could have—should have—throttled back and given Wessel a half-dozen strokes and would still have beaten the grocery mogul, but by a more honorable margin. Pep cursed himself now for overestimating his opponent and arming himself with what turned out to be far too much firepower. He had played with Rama on his bag. In retrospect he realized that fortifying his game with the benefit of the amazing caddie's magic was simply unwarranted by Wessel's skills.

Pep had played with unshakeable confidence and with the uncanny ability to turn imagined shots into glowing white tracers to the pin. As a result, the game had not been the image of tight competition or gracious sport. In fact, Pep had approached his life's best round, but now, from the perspective of the Pago-Pago lavatory, he regretted he had not reserved his stellar game for another day. A great game could wait; Wessel's good will might not.

Pep had been carried away with his score. He should have resisted the temptation to silence Wessel's irritating excuses, worthless swing analysis, and tales of unjust greenside tragedies, but chose instead to hammer the voice into silence with a lopsided score rather than wait for it to quiet in fatigue at its own banality. Pep had become more concerned with kicking ass than kissing it, but this had been an unfortunate choice considering the ass in question was attached to the man who could put more cases of Luva'Lime Soda on the shelves than any other single human being.

Considering the 285 markets that Wessel owned, a pulled putt here, a deliberate under-club there, or the casual granting of a four-foot gimme in Wessel's behalf might have gone a long, lucrative way.

But Pep also had his reasons for being so unforgiving. Wessel had already let it be known that on his soda shelves—all 3,900 linear feet of them—it came down to Dustin Pepper versus Doctor Pepper. Although Pep had already given Wessel his rock-bottom wholesale price for Luva'Lime, as they took to the first tee Wessel announced he expected better. At that point Pep had seen red; he would rather inflame Wessel's hemorrhoidal ego with a sound thrashing on the links than grant him one more penny on the dollar. Even before his extraordinary round began to unfold, Pep had made up his mind: If WW wanted to win this game, he was going to have to earn it—screw business protocol.

Despite his embarrassment, Wessel could have picked up anywhere during the three-day golf outing-cum-business-trip to Memphis. He could have retreated to his estate in the Ozarks and chipped personalized golf balls around his own three-hole course or buzzed out to Pine Valley for some real golf, but he hadn't. He could have ordered the Doctor Pepper jobbers to go ahead and stock his shelves, but he hadn't. Even with the life and the luck long gone from his golf game, he stubbornly refused to admit weakness to Dustin Pepper or cough up a sales order. Instead, Wessel stayed in town for another free dinner at the Pago-Pago and demanded a rematch in the morning. He had even named the terms: a fifty-dollar Nassau—fifty for the winner of the front, fifty for the back, and fifty for the lowest total score.

If Pep had been Isaac Newton, the famous apple might have left no mark on physics except for a bruised forehead on a forgotten mathematician. The obvious had streamed by Pep for three days now. Why not do what all the other pragmatic businessmen from Bluff Meade had been doing most of the summer with their clients: turn Wessel loose on the course with Rama Schwain. If it was magic Wessel was seeking, he would likely find it with the charmed caddie in his corner, and Pep could swing away in competition without truncating his efforts. If he lost…well he could handle his hat being handed to him as long as it was served with a plump purchase order for Luva'Lime Soda.

As Pep wrung his hands under the blow dryer, he could almost hear the clinking of thousands of distinctive green bottles moving from the shelves of Waddley's Food Parade into thirsty customers' shopping carts.

Pep re-entered the Pago-Pago dining room with new empathy for his golfing foil, who sat alone at their table with his nose hovering above a brandy snifter. Pep approached Wessel carefully. "I've been thinking," he began cheerily. "I accept your challenge. We can still get one more round in before you fly out tomorrow afternoon." Pep paused for dramatic effect: "Let's play for a hundred-buck Nassau…and you take my caddie, Rama Schwain. I'm not giving an inch, but I think your luck is about to change."

Wessel lifted his nose from the brandy and smiled broadly. "Now you're talking, Dusty."

Later that night, as Dustin Pepper lay trapped in a dark dream of Dr. Pepper bottles marching like brooms in *Fantasia,* he woke suddenly to the memory of a grievous conflict on Bluff Meade's calendar: Tomorrow was Ivar's match against Wedgy. He shot up straight in bed. Rama was spoken for!

From the very day that the charmed caddie had stumbled into their midst, Pep and Ivar had agreed that if a conflict ever arose, Ivar had first rights to the young man's services. Now the conflict soared like a skyrocket: winning a huge soft drink contract versus defeating Wedgy, the scourge of Bluff Meade. It came down to soda versus honor.

Pep realized that for his friend Ivar giving up Rama tomorrow would be like tossing in the towel to Wedgy Byrne. He couldn't ask anyone to do that, but he reckoned maybe someone else could.

—•—

Roland Bandon, chairman of the Bluff Meade Rules and Handicapping Committee, was awakened at 5:15 the next morning by the phone's insistent jangle. He stabbed at the device and fumbled with the bedside light. Once energized, the lamp illuminated a pantheon of circus heroes parading ceaselessly around its shade: *Commemorating A Century of Circus Performance.* The voice on the line explained the necessity of reassigning Rama Schwain from his engagement with Ivar Guidance today to another match.

Roland grumbled: "Damn it, Pepper, didn't you look out your window before you called? It's daaarrrk. Sane folks are asleeep. And what the hell…bust up Ivar and his caddie? On what grounds?"

Pep had already consulted the fine print of the etiquette section of the Bluff Meade Member Bylaws. He made a case for Roland's excusing Rama from duty with Ivar on the basis that Rama's services had been requested by a guest, and that the book clearly stated:

> *As a matter of gracious etiquette and good sportsmanship, members shall yield all services and special privileges as much as is reasonable to meet the wishes of their guest – including caddie preference.*

"Are you paying attention, Roland?"

Roland sighed mightily into the phone. "Jesus, Pep. When I took this job they never said I'd have to come between a caddie and his employer, especially not on the day of a major event. I'm not an enforcer, Pep, I just do the numbers. That so-called rule you're jabbering about sounds like the bullshit old man Meade might have come up with."

"Oh it is…I got it right here in black and white," replied Pep. "But them's the rules. And I've got an important guest who wants Rama on his bag today."

"Why the blazes do you care anyway…are you working for Wedgy?" asked Roland suspiciously.

"My God no, it's for…" Pep paused, wondering how he could easily explain Rama's effect on players and his own need to bolster the game of a prospective customer. "Have you've ever been to a Waddley's Food Parade? Well my guest owns 'em all, and he wants Rama Schwain on his bag.

"Look, Roland, I'm invoking the rule. I just need you to tell Ivar…to make it official."

Pep emphasized the urgency of the request with a confidential offer of a sizeable contribution to the Rules Committee's coffers, with dispensation of the funds to be at Roland's personal discretion.

Mrs. Bandon stirred under the blankets beside her husband and Roland choked his voice back to a harsh whisper. "That would be a hell of a dirty trick to play on Guidance. I've got the numbers…Ivar has earned this shot at Wedgy."

"Earned? Like hell," Pep nearly spat into the phone. "If it weren't for Rama…"

"I know, I know," interrupted Roland as his mind's spreadsheet rolled out before him, "Ivar would be playing to about 8.5 strokes higher than he is right now. Remember? I've done the numbers."

Pep jumped at his opening. "Exactly! To be fair, Ivar shouldn't even be in this match. He's playing way over his head. The Lord giveth and the Lord taketh away, eh Roland?" Pep said with finality.

Roland's wife pulled herself up onto one arm and cast a sinister frown at her inconsiderate husband.

"Pepper, get yourself some sleep," Roland said abruptly.

"Hold on, hold on, Bandon. I'll throw in a new IBM All-Electric Calculator and two seats on the Ringling Brothers Circus train back down to Florida this fall. Come on, Roland, Ivar will do all right on his own. You know as well as me that Wedgy isn't the ace he used to be."

Roland pictured the countryside sailing past from inside the Ringling Brothers train—the atmosphere in the cars alive with foreign tongues and exotic odors. He imagined chit-chatting with the trapeze masters; then, as one of the chosen few, he would wave at the uplifted faces of children gathered along the tracks. Roland exhaled a long breath and directed a breathless whisper at the handset poised just above the hook.

"I'll see what I can do."

Roland lay back down, but his sleep was ruined.

Hank Schwain had tried a couple of shots of Old Crow and an hour of Johnny Carson, but he couldn't make the lure of Ivar Guidance's chances against the unsuspecting competitor go away. Skitch Henderson played but Hank didn't listen; he heard only the counting out of his winnings on a $6,000 bet. His ears were deaf to his own recently spoken intentions to leave it all behind and to old warnings against gambling on the most fickle of all games. The conflicting words of Wallace Byrne: "I'm a sure thing," and his son's confident statement: "Ivar never loses with me on his bag" echoed with implicit opportunity in Hank's mind. He abandoned his feeble resistance to gambling's siren and resolved to take the plunge tomorrow with Ivar and Rama. In the morning he would still have time to secure a loan at Calcutta Finance. It was such a sure bet that he could afford Calcutta's fees and still come out way ahead. Thus relieved, Hank collapsed into the sleep of a junkie.

Lew Raybon, the financier, tooth, and temper behind Calcutta Finance, was literally an evil bastard. As the mysterious cause behind several serious "accidents" and being the son of a streetwalker, he had staked fair claim to his reputation. Lew was a big man—broad but not fat—and as quick on his feet as he was with his wits. Unlike Howlin' Wolf, Lew was built for comfort *and* for speed. There was considerable menace in that combination.

It was ironic that those sketchy individuals who sought out Lew for relief from late-night cash flow crises considered *him* the extreme credit risk, yet without Lew's ready cash resources, many an engagement ring would have gone fingerless and many a car on Big Muddy's lot might never have been purchased. By the same token, many cheap diamonds were in his pawn, and many crappy cars on Big Muddy's lot were on consignment to recover funds on Calcutta's behalf. Through this symbiotic relationship, Hank Schwain was well acquainted with Lew. By essentially selling cars for him, Hank had come to know and use Calcutta's services on occasion. He needed them now.

The parking whiskers on Hank's car sounded off as he pulled up to the curb outside Lew's cheerless storefront. The words *Calcutta Finance – Cash In a Flash* were rendered in gold vinyl letters across the glass door. Emerging from the car, Hank nearly stumbled on a weed that was making a concerted effort to push the slabs of the sidewalk apart. "They should give this whole damn street a good spraying," he grumbled.

Inside, the lobby's simulated wood paneling was even less inviting, and it, too, could have used a spraying. Four brittle chairs, several old issues of *Argosy*, and an empty Lion's Club gum-ball machine shared the waiting room with a chain-smoking receptionist. Seated behind a cracked glass-brick wall, the girl idly touched up her satanic fingernails.

"You'd think the Lions would come in here to fill their damn gum-ball machine." Hank hoped to brighten the desolate room with some small talk. He peered over the glass bricks at the girl's nails, but the scent of her polish remover on top of his Spam and eggs breakfast nearly got the better of him.

"Why would Lions want gum balls?" the girl asked, oblivious to the empty glass globe on its snappy red pedestal.

"You know, they raise money for blind kids."

"Gum. Lions. Blind children. Are you crazy, mister?" she asked. "Maybe you need some java…still might be some in the thermos." Without looking up she waved one hand toward the lounge.

Lew appeared happy to meet Hank again. In better days Hank had sold a serious number of Calcutta's cars. Lew remembered that Hank had taken out a few small loans in the past but quickly paid them off at the discount rate of only 30-percent interest. Lew knew his customers well, and he knew Hank was generally a two-bit gambler who had a little problem with the horses and borrowed to bet on a particularly inviting race or to keep the mortgage company at bay. But now he was looking at some real money—more than double anything he had ever borrowed. It was not in anyone's interest to lend or borrow beyond one's comfort zone—not that Lew was shy about making one uncomfortable—but it could lead to trouble. Despite his reputation, Lew believed violence was always a distasteful last resort; he would much rather be reasonable, fatherly even.

"Six fucking grand! Give me one reason why I shouldn't say no dice and kick your ass out of my office. Maybe the credit union could help you out." Lew inhaled a menthol cigarette and blew two powerful streams from his nostrils like a bull on a frosty morning. Hank hardly noticed the bovine display. He was distracted by the contents of a highball glass on Lew's desk. The glass held a fine collection of kitschy ballpoint pens, the kind of souvenir pens in which a transparent barrel reveals a tiny tableau suspended in a liquid so it may move down the barrel to reveal a visual gag. In the case of Lew's collection, articles of clothing slipped away from the naked bodies of luridly drawn females. As Lew spoke, Hank plucked one of the pens from the glass and was momentarily mesmerized by the cheap thrill of a southern belle dropping her ruffled gown to reveal prodigious breasts and impossibly pink nipples in a rigid little striptease.

"For Christ sakes, Schwain. Are you listening? I'll be damned if I'm lending a dime to a pervert." Lew was clearly irritated. "Put the damn pen away; this is serious business."

Hank blushed as he dropped the *Belle of the South* back into the glass with her fellow floozies.

"Now, I'm gonna tell you, Schwain…as a friend. You start borrowing for bets…next thing you'll be circling the crapper. I'm not going down the shit hole with you…you dig? Gamble with your money—fine—but if you gamble with my money, then I'm sharing your risk…and I don't gamble. I'm a businessman. There's already enough danger in lending to losers."

Hank cringed at the lecture. The loser reference was a hard pill to swallow, but what was he going to do, get in Lew's acne-pocked face?

"Thanks Lew, but it's not for gambling, it's to cover an investment. I had a chance for a sweet deal on a classic airplane. The guy selling it was desperate, sold it for cheap just to get the cash. I lifted the dough out of my wife's account to get the deal done, but if I don't get it back in there quick…"

"You'll get caught with your hand in momma's cookie jar."

Hank sensed Lew was unmoved. "Look, Lew, this aircraft is going to rack up some serious appreciation. If you want to write it up as collateral…"

Lew frowned. "Collateral! I want nothing to do with selling anything to anybody to cover your debts. And I don't give a shit about airplanes. Fuck me, Schwain, but I'll do this: I'll nick you 20 percent per month on the outstanding balance. I'll call the loan at any time after the first thirty days if I get nervous about your…*reliability*."

"Well a little notice would be…"

"At *any* time." Lew's teeth made a brief appearance. "Those are my terms…you dig?"

Hank cringed at the enormous interest. He could walk away with no harm done, except to his stature in Lew's steely eyes, but he held his ground. The interest was just the cost of doing business; in this case, the business was getting a slice of the pie Ivar Guidance and Rama would soon be cooking up. What the hell, thought Hank, I'll be paying the money back in a couple of days anyway.

"Yeah, I dig."

Lew pulled a loan agreement from his desk and slid it across to Hank who gave the document a quick glance and signed his name. He scooted it back to Lew.

"Did you bring a briefcase, Schwain?" asked Lew after he separated the carbon copy from the contract. "You're gonna need something. We only deal in cash transactions here at Calcutta. Small denominations. You might need a sack.

"Don't worry; little Sheila in there'll fetch us something." Lew pushed an intercom button and called for a bag. While they waited, Hank casually asked what the bottom line would be if a guy's plans all went bad and he went bust with an outstanding debt on Calcutta's books.

Lew frowned. "Like I said, I don't want to mess with selling no airplane. But if its value comes up short we'll send an appraiser over to see what else you've got." A devilish grin came across Lew's wide face. "And there's always your house, isn't there?" Lew turned to his wall safe and in a moment swiveled back around to stack six tidy bundles of fifty twenties on the desk before Hank.

"What do you mean, my house?" asked Hank trying not to stare at the cash.

"You know, Schwain…" said Lew, rolling his copy of the contract into a cylinder, "you really should take the time to read the fine print on these things. Shame on you." He playfully rapped the back of Hank's hand with the contract.

The door to Lew's office opened and Sheila flowed in, a rumpled paper sack dangling from her outstretched hand as if it were roadkill. "It's all I could come up with," she apologized as she offered the Colonel Sander's Chicken sack to Hank. Without a word he dropped the bundles into the bottom of the greasy sack and nodded to Lew and Sheila.

"Now don't go cracking up my plane, you hear, Schwain?" A wide smile allowed a glint of gold to escape from one of the loan shark's teeth. Hank hadn't noticed it before.

"I'll see you in thirty days," Lew declared ominously. The smile collapsed as suddenly as it had formed. "Or less!"

Charged with the adrenalines of risk and anticipation, Hank nearly pulled the Rambler's door off its hinges as he rushed to put Calcutta behind him. The clock on the dashboard read 9:35. If the timepiece was reasonably accurate, he still had time to get over to Bluff Meade, find the starter who Wedgy had said could take his bet. The Rambler roared across town under Hank's anxious foot. He was less concerned about the dangers of the traffic or even Lew Raybon than he was about being seen by his son.

Hank was entering Rama's turf on a mission to do what he had vowed not to do again. If they crossed paths, what was he to say? What else might have brought him to Bluff Meade on the very day of the Wedgy-Ivar match other than gambling? He would have to keep his eyes open and his excuses believable until he had made that bet; then he could make himself scarce.

Hank found a suitably obscure parking spot in the deepest corner of the employee's lot, behind a battered old Renault. He paused between the two automobiles and lit up a cigarette. Raising his head to exhale a wisp of smoke, he noticed the late morning clouds preparing to yield to a glorious day.

Chapter 33

Rama rose early, already nervous with anticipation of the day's crucial contest against Wedgy. For the last month Ivar had spoken of his old golfing nemesis in a curious mixture of admonition and admiration. Their times together had bridged Wallace Byrne's transformation from clever businessman and fine golfer to devious opportunist and golf hustler. Along the way there had been good times, mutual respect, and a few knock-down-drag-out golf matches. Today would be no exception. But never before had Ivar carried the torch for his companions at Bluff Meade, and never before had so much money been invested in his success.

Rama dressed quickly and fixed himself breakfast. He moved carefully to avoid clattering dishes or banging lids that might disturb his mother; she needed all the sleep she could get these days. The front door latch fell softly into place behind him as he stepped out onto the front porch. A swath of thin cloud stretched artfully across the brightening sky. A hint of morning fire torched the clouds' lower flanks in dazzling contrast to the stubborn strokes of night.

Rama wheeled his bike from the garage. He was more than happy to ride to Bluff Meade on such a beautiful morning, and it was just as well: His mother needed the car to meet doctor Myer, the neurologist Ivar had recommended. As he pedaled the Schwinn Phantom out onto the street, Rama imagined that he and Ivar would dispatch Wedgy once and for all into Bluff Meade's history book about the same time Doris would be taking a new step toward recovery. It would be a glorious day indeed.

Halfway to Bluff Meade, Rama dropped into the cool shadows down along the creek, but in his excitement felt only warmth. A shortcut through the magnolias put him on a path that skirted the tenth fairway. It was a beautiful ride, with the splendid emerald course falling away on his right and the grand old clubhouse looming on his left.

As Rama flew up the path he could see a few dew-sweepers getting in a game before the gallery for the Guidance-Byrne match would spoil their solitude. Even though it was a couple of hours before tee time, an unusually large number of folks milled around the putting green and the starters' hut. It felt like a carnival. Rama rang the bell on his bicycle to clear a path through the throng as he coasted down to the caddie shack.

He flicked down the kickstand and entered the knotty-pine refuge. Two unrelated sofas and several overstuffed chairs populated the room along with four currently unemployed teenage boys and a scuffed pool table. In one corner a television flickered with a Japanese horror movie; in the other an institutional percolator filled the room with the scent of bad coffee. Two boxes of donuts lay open beside the coffee service, the pastries in disarray like Tokyo after the rampage of a radiological mutant. Rama searched for a raspberry Bismarck, poured a cup, and plopped down in one of the easy chairs.

The other caddies offered a few feeble words of greeting, then quickly returned to their 8-ball. They had never warmly embraced the new caddie who had so quickly risen in demand. Had it not been for the careful management of the caddie corps by caddie master Agunstus Tirk, jealousy might have flamed into hostility. Thanks to "Tirks" everyone got his share of bags; tips had risen, too, on the tide of Rama's higher value.

"Gonna be a beauty today, Tirks," Rama called across the room, waving his Bismarck toward the wide windows that faced the first tee. "Did you see that sunrise?"

The caddie master raised his eyes from the morning paper. "Yeah, great, Rama. Too bad you're here so damn early."

Rama blew across the steaming surface of his coffee. "Well, I thought Ivar might want to do some extra drills, it's a big match."

"That he might," Tirks said. "In fact, I think he's already up on the practice tee."

Rama jumped to his feet to head up to the range, but the caddie master gestured to slow down. "Hold on, you don't need to go anywhere just yet, Schwain. You're not on Guidance's bag today. You've got a guest." As Rama watched in disbelief, the caddie master ran his finger down a copy of the morning's tee sheet: "Mr. Waddley—Wessel Waddley—he's your man…in a twosome with Dustin Pepper at 11:50. I hear Waddley stinks."

Rama was shocked. After so many stories he had looked forward to meeting this Wedgy character, but, more important, he knew how badly Ivar wanted to win this match. Rama wanted to add that special magic he, too, now had come to believe was real. "Crap, Tirksie," Rama whined. "What gives?"

Tirks gave up on the morning paper and refilled an Arnie's Army souvenir coffee mug upon which the figure of Arnold Palmer lurching through his follow-through was still recognizable beneath layers of coffee stains. The caddie master looked out at the crowd gathering beneath the flaming clouds. "Old man Guidance came in here himself and made the switch an hour ago. He said something about yielding to the guest's preference rule. I guess his guest, that Waddley fella, really wants *you*."

Rama was anxious to ask Ivar about being replaced, but he had too much respect for the old gentleman golfer to second-guess him. "Was Ivar pissed off or anything?"

"Pissed? Ivar Guidance? Naw," replied Tirks. "If he should be pissed at anyone, it should be at Roland. That circus freak called him at five in the morning and read him the guest rule. But you know Ives; he's cool. He said it was only fair that someone else should get a chance at a great game." The caddie master had long ago joined the ranks of the folks who rightfully held Ivar in high esteem.

"That's Ivar. He's something else, isn't he? Just hope he can handle that Byrne creep without you," said Tirks with a wink. "I'm gonna send Guidance out with Charlie Vestal...maybe mend a few fences between them. And shit, Ivar might need a lawyer against Wedgy Byrne." Tirks snickered as he returned to his paper.

Rama dropped into his chair and looked back along the walkway toward the starter's hut. A group of people—silhouettes against a brightening sky—clustered around the hut like ghosts in the morning's haze. Suddenly, for a moment the form of a man with a cane emerged from the milling crowd.

Rama bolted forward. The figure appeared to be his father. Rama peered through the windows with uncertainty. At that instant a heavy blob of raspberry jam fell from the bismarck and landed on his clean white slacks.

"Shhhit," cursed Rama. He grabbed at a stack of napkins and swiped at the red stain. When he looked back up toward the starter, the figure was gone. Rama stepped out the door and gazed into the crowd. Nothing. He shrugged off the incident as nerves.

"When did you say Waddley was teeing off, Tirksie?" Rama asked as he stepped back into the room. If he couldn't be in the match, at least he might watch Ivar and Wedgy tee it up. Maybe he could give his friend some encouragement before moving on to Waddley's bag.

"I got you down for 11:50. Put about three holes between you and all that commotion around Ivar's match," replied Tirks. "Pep's idea, that was."

Rama figured he had some time to kill, so he slipped a quarter under the rail of the pool table and waited for the next game to come around. Fifteen minutes of waiting and three minutes of pool later, he was back at the door, anxious for something to happen.

"Hey Tirksie, I'm taking a stroll if anyone needs me." The thought of his father still troubled him. Rama stepped out to mingle with the crowd, but he didn't get far before he spotted Pep and his guest coming down the walk about the same time they spotted him.

"Hey there, Rama," called Pep before Rama could dodge away. Pep looked at his companion. "Wes, there's your boy...your salvation. Rama Schwain."

Pep made the introductions, billing Rama as: "the best thing to happen to Bluff Meade since they plowed under the Bermuda." As it turned out, Wessel Waddley was looking for far more than a casual game; he wanted to work on his distances, his club selection strategy, his mechanics, and his course management philosophy—quite a load for a new caddie. It was a perfectly reasonable request for a man planning the game of his life, but to Rama's chagrin, it consumed the rest of the morning. Rama realized he wouldn't have time to wish Ivar well or watch him tee off, or to ask him about the rule that had stripped them both of the chance to tackle Wedgy together.

—•—

Up on the range Ivar Guidance flinched as a familiar voice startled him in mid-swing. "Where was that fucking textbook swing way back when? Shame on you, Ives…you've been working on your game."

Ivar looked up from the practice tee to see a smiling Wedgy Byrne settling into a spot on range. Without waiting for Wedgy to claim the conversational high ground, Ivar approached his smug, redheaded adversary and extended his arm. Ivar's silk shirt hung serenely from his relaxed frame.

"Wallace! It's a crying shame that for all this work, the only reward I ever get around here, is a game with you," replied Ivar with a grin. "You're looking better, Wallace."

"Better?" Wedgy exclaimed as he returned Ivar's handshake, "You mean I've looked worse?"

"Wallace, we've all seen better days," Ivar winked.

"Guidance, I don't think you can claim better days," replied Wedgy. "From what I hear, you've been playing your best lately. What's happened to all the other Bluff Meade players to make *you* top dog? Did they take up tennis?"

Wedgy coaxed a couple of balls from the pyramid carefully stacked at his tee and tapped them into place on the turf with a pitching wedge. He flicked his cigarette to the ground and tucked the wedge behind his back to loosen up.

"So you finally earned a crack at me, eh Ives?" said Wedgy between twists. "Damn, I can't believe you fellas actually choose the poor bastard that's gotta spar with me based on something as logical as scoring average. Shit, I always thought you and the boys tore the guts out of a goat or some such voodoo."

Ivar laughed easily at Wedgy's joke, relieved that the scrappy fellow was no less crude than he remembered. "I've had some good fortune, even had a few night lessons, and that has made all the difference," explained Ivar. He kept any hint of Rama Schwain's mysterious contribution to himself. "I guess they had to choose me, but I'll pass your goat entrails idea on to the Greens Committee."

"Much obliged," Wedgy laughed, setting off a brief round of smokers hack.

Ivar chuckled at the thought of those stuffy old souls in the Greens Committee even acknowledging the existence of their fallen angel, let alone appreciating his humor. He remembered what he liked about Wedgy: The man made no pretense to be anything other than exactly what he had become—an itinerant golf hustler. There was an endearing trace of integrity in Wedgy's acceptance of his fate. Wallace Byrne was an increasingly rare but irritating bird, like a lone surviving passenger pigeon that lives just to crap on your car.

Ivar finished working his way through his clubs in silence, ending with some tasty little half wedges to the fifty-yard flag. Ivar had been quiet, but his clubs had spoken eloquently. He handed the last wedge to Charlie Vestal before moving on. His sullen substitute caddie for the day appeared less than thrilled by the reunion with his old boss.

"See you down at the slaughter, Wallace," Ivar quipped before strolling down to the first tee with a languid stride—the gait of a confident man.

Wedgy watched Ivar and Charlie walk away, content to leave them the last word. He looked at his caddie and then at the cluster of balls Ivar had lobbed expertly to the flag. The boy's face strained to contain a smug teenage smile.

"Whose side are you on?" Wedgy grumbled at his caddie. He realized that yanking on the teats of his "little cash cow" might not be so easy this time around. Ivar had miraculously improved. He would have to keep his eyes open for any advantage.

"Hey kid, is it just me…but that Charlie and Ivar don't look all that close?"

"Well sir, the truth is Charlie used to caddy for Ivar until Ivar hired the new guy, Rama."

"I'll be damned," said Wedgy, "Ivar dumped him, huh?"

—•—

While the crowds assembled on the first tee, Rama was dutifully helping Wessel prepare for his big day. They were working on correcting Wessel's odd alignment when they heard the booming voice of Roland Bandon announce the beginning of the match at number one. The rules chairman sounded for all the world like he belonged under the Big Top. A little too dramatic for a golf match, thought Rama.

"Ladies and gentlemen," sang the would-be ringmaster. "On the tee, from somewhere up the road: Mister Wallace Byrne."

In a moment Rama heard the appreciative applause for Wedgy's first drive—a good one, apparently. In another minute the crowd erupted in applause and cheers as another drive—an even better one—boomed down the fairway. Might have had some extra kick or a little draw, thought Rama. Whatever it was, it sounded like a fine beginning for Ivar Guidance. Rama hoped the night lessons stuck and that Ivar's luck would hold fast.

To elude his son, Hank Schwain had watched both drives from behind an oak tree, but to his dismay, Rama was nowhere near the first tee. Hank had hoped to see for himself what sort of magical advantage his son would actually bring to a golfer, but he couldn't attribute Ivar's first drive to anyone or any magic. Without Rama, how long could this old white-haired fellow stand against the notorious Mr. Byrne?

A rising fear clutched at Hank's throat: Had he been hustled? Hank had come to the course to place his bet on Rama's man Ivar, but now, with Rama missing and the certainty of Ivar's victory less than the slam-dunk he had gambled on, he might be in for a long nerve-wracking walk spoiled.

—•—

The comforting sound of voices and laughter quickly faded from Rama's ears as the gallery moved down to watch Wedgy take his second shot. Rama turned his attention back to the science of Wessel's golf, not knowing that somewhere in the crowd his father struggled to conceal his incriminating limp.

Despite the gulf between them, Hank and Rama both shared a wish that Ivar's luck held fast, but Ivar wasn't yet in need of luck. His beautifully placed drive was followed by a fine towering second shot that just cleared the false front of the green and rolled benevolently to within sixteen feet of the flag. Wedgy miss-hit his approach and could not get up-and-down in two, leaving an easy two-putt for Ivar to take a one stroke lead.

After scoring his five, Wedgy tossed his putter to his caddie with a velocity that left no doubt as to his disgust. Ivar simply floated off the green toward the second tee. Wedgy caught up with his competitor as Ivar considered the straightforward par four and the menacing oak tree that ruled its landing zone. His voice chopped into Ivar's vision of a ball curving safely from left to right and settling beyond the limbs' reaches. "Hey Ives, if you're gonna play like that, then you've got no excuse for not throwing down a few bob—just between us—to make it interesting. You do believe in yourself, right, or was that last hole just some of that goat gut magic?"

Ivar had expected nothing less than a running commentary peppered with Wedgy's carefully placed jabs to his confidence. Ivar calmly inserted his tee into the soft green turf, ignoring Wedgy as he stepped back to visualize his shot. He felt the first real heat from the morning sun. As a lingering haze gave up the ghost, his beautifully struck ball followed his mental rehearsal and came to rest beyond the oak's clutches.

"Never a doubt, Wedge. Never a doubt. Just watch out for that darned tree," Ivar advised with a smirk while brushing back a lock of white that had become dislodged during his swing.

Wedgy found the tree to be more of a mental hazard than a physical one. In trying to avoid it, he managed to avoid the fairway as well. When the damages were totaled, he had lost another hole and another stroke to Ivar. Hanging purposefully back behind the gallery's greenside ranks, Hank kept a tally of the golfers' stroke differential. So far so good; maybe he could enjoy this match after all, he thought as he limped to the next hole.

At number three, Ivar's supporters were disappointed as a blind shot and dumb luck alternately took their tolls. With honors, Ivar had faced a 180-yard carry high over a hollow from whose fertile bottom sprung a thicket of alder. The weed-like trees had been left to grow, either by groundskeeper malaise or greens committee malevolence, but regardless of reason, a once-respectable carry had been converted into a blind, hair-raising moon shot. To retain any chance at hitting and holding the small green beyond, the shot had to be hit high and mightily above the tree tops.

Ivar's tee shot looked good. He listened for the discouraging slap of his ball against the leaves but heard nothing; he guessed he was in good shape. The same was not true for Wedgy. As his shot rattled like a pachinko ball down through the unforgiving branches, his spirits descended as well.

The golfers and caddies walked single file along the narrow trail that passed through the hollow and back up to the elevated green. Wedgy grumbled as they walked. "Remember when this used to be fair, Ives? Why not tell those bastards in your club to trim the fucking trees before you need a mortar to play their damned hole?"

But Wedgy's mood lifted considerably as they emerged. His ball had somehow found one last bounce out of the hazard and had come to rest on the upslope to the green. He still had a tough shot to a pin whose flag he couldn't even see, but at least he was spared taking a drop. Ivar wasn't so lucky. He had overshot the green by a dozen feet and lay in thick grass on a steep bank above the putting surface—not an easy chip, but still a preferred shot over what Wedgy faced.

The uncertainty that places sports apart from scripted, rehearsed entertainment came immediately to bear upon the outcome of the hole. Unpredictably, Wedgy made par and Ivar bogeyed.

Now his spirits soared. "What trees, Ivar?" he sang as he slapped his opponent on the back. Through the fine fabric of Ivar's silk shirt, Wedgy felt the lean muscle across Ivar's shoulder; the old fellow's bones weren't far below the surface. Wedgy remembered how much they used to enjoy playing golf together when the muscle was a little more generously distributed. Ivar's trust and honesty had always freed Wedgy's doubtful mind from second-guessing his opponent's score, or watching out for the foot wedge, or for covert "manufactured" lies that in games with less-honorable players were always a worry and an unwelcome distraction. Wedgy smiled at the thought of simpler, honest times.

Ivar looked blankly at his opponent, mistaking Wedgy's nostalgic smile for gamesmanship. They both knew that on this hole Wedgy had enjoyed an equal share of luck and skill; there was nothing further to claim or defend. For the next three holes they played quietly and nearly identically—each taking a bogey six on the twisting, maddeningly tilted fourth; each a bogey via a splashdown, drop, and similar up-and-downs on the pond-sided fifth. On number six, the easiest, straightest par four on the course, both players managed a complacent par. With six holes behind them, Ivar still stood one stroke ahead of Wedgy Byrne.

For the aficionados of competitive golf, a match that already featured seven bogeys between the two players left a lot to be desired. The crowds' dark murmuring was not lost on Wedgy or Ivar. Whatever kind of truce they had wordlessly written on the third hole would have to be ripped apart and forgotten. This match was not about understanding. This match was about bragging rights for twelve long months, and it was about other people's money.

Indeed, Hank Schwain, in particular, was beginning to feel uneasy over his investment. Years ago he had cursed Rama's contribution to a golf match at Mesquite Creek; now he prayed for it with wasted breath as Ivar and Wedgy stood on the seventh tee.

"Used to be your lucky hole if I recall?" Wedgy addressed Ivar with the intention of defusing any damaging déjà vu on the abrupt left dogleg hole that had once—if he believed Ivar—hosted the old fellow's legendary but unwitnessed double-eagle. Wedgy still had the honors from his unlikely par on number three and scanned the tee box for the perfect spot to plant his peg. "And it might take a repeat of that albatross to beat me today, Ives."

Ivar Guidance was impressed that Wedgy remembered that shot and was alarmed that Wedgy even took the same line that Ivar's own drive had taken on that sunny Sunday morning so many years back. Wedgy's deep driving hook soared toward the flanks of the hill inside the dogleg. The reward of a shot in that direction was a chance at reaching the green in two or ensnarement in the deep rough that flourished on the hillside's sunny slope.

Ivar knew in his heart that his drive that day had been accidental and that his second shot had been nothing short of miraculous. He could not see the outcome of Wedgy's drive over the hill, and he wondered if he should follow. He also knew that Wedgy, like Arnie, could extricate himself from impossible misfortunes. He wouldn't put it past Wedgy to attempt to lure him into a trap, but Ivar remained content to wait another two swings to reach the green and perhaps a lifetime for another double-eagle. His drive flew conservatively down the fairway.

Arnie's scrambling spirit may have been back on the hammock in Latrobe that day—at least it wasn't lending its services to Wedgy on this hole. Wedgy's attempt at capitalizing on his proximity to the hole literally blew up in his face. Only by a remarkable third shot was he able to get within a hundred yards of the green. Ivar's wise play resulted in a routine third shot onto the green with a long, but makeable, 30-foot putt for birdie.

Wedgy made a mockery of Ivar's lucky hole by miraculously getting up and down again for a par after Ivar had unluckily missed his birdie putt. Ivar was briefly unsettled by the injustice of Wedgy wringing good fortune from thin air—even on "his" hole. Ivar knew better than to fall into the trap of declaring oneself the victim of inequitably distributed bounces; that was the precursor to predicting your defeat and the inevitable fulfillment of a losing prophesy. But knowing better didn't prevent Ivar from falling into a mental trap on number eight where, after Wedgy carded a beatable bogey five, he responded with a disheartening six. Hank Schwain watched uncomfortably as the match and his intestines were now tied up.

Wedgy took the sloppy hole in stride and lit up a Pall Mall. A little nicotine fortification was in order as they faced a steep return to the hilltop clubhouse and the ninth green. "Come on Ives, let's make this one interesting. Fifty bucks for the hole, double for the closest to the pin." Wedgy drew a few long puffs. "What do you say?"

Wedgy taunted Ivar by offering a cigarette to his notoriously non-smoking competitor. Ivar steadied Wedgy's outstretched hand and pulled four cigarettes from the six remaining in the pack. Under Wedgy's startled gape, Ivar dropped three in his shirt pocket and tucked one behind his ear. "For later…thanks. Sure, I'll take the bet," said Ivar with a grin.

With the thought of only two smokes left to see him through the match, Wedgy missed the green in regulation and lost fifty bucks. Then, the victim of a long par putt by Ivar, he lost the hole for another fifty dollars and a one-stroke, four-smoke deficit at the turn.

With his man Ivar ahead again—even if only slightly—at the halfway point, Hank breathed a little easier. The unlikely swings in the game already had convinced Hank that Wedgy was not as dominant as he had claimed at the used-car lot yesterday. But with Rama out of the equation, neither was Ivar's victory as certain as Rama's claim to the old fellow's invincibility had suggested. The uncertainty surrounding his wager left Hank in a repentant mood. As he struggled to remain hidden in the gallery milling toward the tenth tee, he swore that this bet was a forgivable lapse in willpower never to be repeated again. He vowed that once he had put this aberration behind him he would never hang his fortunes from such a tenuous thread as a so-called sporting event between two athletes as long-in-the-tooth and short-in-skill as these two unpredictable geezers.

Chapter 34

Ivar stood breathless at the tenth tee. Somehow the climb up from the ninth green had seemed steeper than usual. He lingered to compose himself before he gripped the club and attempted a drive down the troublesome right-doglegged fairway. His breath and his spirit were soon restored as the ball settled into a small, elusive patch in the leg that offered the only clear line to the green. He was as grateful for the good shot as he was for the descending walk down the tenth's fairway.

Cocky again, Ivar started from the tee box but stopped Wedgy in passing. He pulled the sweaty Pall Mall from behind his ear and tucked it in Wedgy's shirt pocket. "Guess I didn't need it after all. My nerves are fine."

To Ivar's delight, Wedgy tossed the damp cigarette to the turf. Perfect, he thought; anything to keep the old hustler off-kilter.

"Forget it, Ives. You're gonna need all the bad habits you can get before this game is done," Wedgy growled. Then in irritation he took his stance carelessly and proceeded to miss the sweet spot on both the club and the fairway, eventually managing only a par four while Ivar finally converted a birdie three to gain another stroke.

Hank, observing that Ivar was now back up by two strokes, felt less urgency in his recent rush to repentance.

On the next hole, a par three to an elevated green, Wedgy demanded a chance to win his hundred dollars back. Ivar gamely took the bet. Both shots appeared headed toward the flagstick as they disappeared behind the green's high front apron, but any outcome was possible: tap-ins, stymies, even a rare double ace. As they crested the apron, Wedgy and Ivar could see both balls on the green. Ivar's next putt would miss and Wedgy's would not, which dropped Ivar's lead back to one.

Nothing changed on holes twelve and thirteen, and soon the golfers overlooked the fourteenth. It was a par three, Bluff Meade's tribute to Pebble Beach's scenic seaside seventh—the same elevated tee and encircling bunkers. Meade Creek sat in for Monterey Bay, wrapping itself menacingly around the back of the green. And on this July day, the atmosphere stirring in response to a tropical storm's bluster in the gulf more than two hundred miles to the southeast, even provided a facsimile of the Pacific's on-shore wind.

The flag was tucked tight into the right rear quadrant of the green, not more than ten feet from a wickedly sloped bank that offered no more chance of stopping a ball rolling toward the creek than did its owner's prayer. Even the drop area behind a hungry bunker on the front right side offered little guarantee of a bogey. A round could swing widely to or from victory solely on the quality of the tee shot at this devilish little hole.

Ivar had a hunch that on a hole as tantalizing as this one, Wedgy couldn't resist a side bet or any other breed of mind game. He hoped to take the initiative from his competitor, who still remained flustered at gaining only one stroke back in the last three holes.

"The silence here is deafening, Wallace," said Ivar, strategically interrupting Wedgy's survey of the landscape. "If you are not proposing a wager here, then I am. One hundred dollars for the hole outright and another for closest-to-the-pin. I'll even give you the honors."

Ivar watched Wedgy's response with concern that, by throwing down two hundred dollars, he risked putting Wedgy back into his element. But even without his magical caddie, Ivar felt confident that winning here could prove pivotal.

Wedgy looked at Ivar like the conservative old fellow was off his feed—first the cigarettes and now this bet. "You wouldn't believe it, Guidance, but I didn't come here to take *all* your money. But if you're offering, how can I say no…it just wouldn't be sporting."

Wedgy wasted no time in pulling a pitching wedge and jabbing a tee into the fourteenth's aerial tee box. He could draw even and begin Ivar's inevitable slide to defeat if he poured on a little heat now.

Wedgy imagined the drum bobbing down the Mississippi and the unhurried swings behind those fine shots at the top of the levee. He recalled the happy anticipation that led him to this hole again and again on fine blue-sky afternoons in the years before he had allowed the line between shrewd and shady business to smear. The shock of his ejection from Bluff Meade had hurt then, and still hurt today, but the blow had broken a chain of dangerous affiliations that could have led him to a fate far worse than being condemned, as he was now, to a perpetual golf outing.

The Members' Ethics Council may have saved Wedgy from himself when they bounced him from the club, but they robbed him of happy circuits of Bluff Meade's peaceful track and of regular visits to this alluring hole. He missed the days when nothing rode on an attempt to cozy a ball in to this Pebble-like pin except the mere satisfaction of watching the white spot suddenly flash against the green at a point well within a birdie's reach.

Back on this tee again for the first time in a year, he hoped to make the most of the visit, but the harrowing proximity of the flag to the creek stared at him like an inhospitable blackjack dealer. He backed away from a risky cut that might curl in from left to right, choosing instead to shoot straight at the middle of the green. Playing the odds seemed wise, even if a tad less dramatic. His ball drifted left and found the green, about fifteen feet from the pin.

"What was that, Wallace…a little hook creep into your shot? Or were you actually playing safe?"

"The Pacific's a little blustery today," joked Wedgy. "But take a shot at it. Fade something in tight…be my guest." He bowed as if to graciously offer Ivar the chance to blow his whole game into the creek.

Ivar endured Wedgy's little pantomime and followed the hustler's shot onto the green using a slightly open pitching wedge propelled by an aggressive swing. It may have been as high and as risky a shot as he ever hit, but the shape served him well. Without fear of the ball sliding away after such a vertical descent, Ivar felt free to shoot straight at the flag. To Wedgy's chagrin, and to the tune of another hundred dollars, the ball came to an immediate stop on the narrow slip of green between the flag and the fringe.

"Crap…another birdie," Wedgy muttered. He had a birdie putt as well, but much too long for his liking. Wedgy made par against Ivar's one-putt birdie and begrudgingly gave up his second hundred dollars and another stroke. With four holes to play he was now down two strokes again, but Ivar was right: Wedgy Byrne was coming into his element.

Wedgy bristled at the prospect of losing another buck and responded by pressing the bet, double or nothing, onto the next hole. He was down but certainly not out. The wager was now creeping into the outskirts of serious money by Wedgy's standards, and he found it energizing. He guessed that Ivar would accept the press coming off a birdie, and indeed Ivar did. With the bait thus taken, Wedgy smiled as though the match was in the bag, but his seemed to be the only smile in evidence around the fifteenth tee box. He glanced at Charlie, who stood uncomfortably beside Ivar. Wedgy had noticed the caddie's continued icy attitude toward his employer. The young man had remained impassive at Ivar's fine performance through fourteen holes. Even Ivar's last birdie was met with little more than an open hand to receive the putter.

"Who needs Rama?" was all Charlie said in congratulation.

Wedgy made a mental note: Might be wise to cheer that boy up.

After watching Ivar's drive buzz like a hornet off into the rough, Wedgy knew the double-or-nothing bet had rattled him, and finally he had a good chance to make some hay. Wedgy crafted a hooking drive that drew him into great shape beyond the crook of the fairway, almost a hundred yards closer to pay dirt than the white-haired combatant who languished hopelessly behind. Finding the green took one shot too many for Ivar; he lost four hundred dollars, a stroke, and a measure of his usually tenacious optimism. With three holes to play, his lead was back down to one.

———•——

Dustin Pepper couldn't even remember his score, nor did he care as he and Wessel Waddley walked toward the twelfth tee. They had followed the Guidance/Byrne match by four holes and well within earshot of the drama unfolding ahead. Pep was feeling some remorse for engineering Rama's assignment to his business prospect's bag and hoped his friend Ivar was holding his own without the magic caddie.

For all the good Rama was doing for Wessel's game, Pep wondered if he had expected one too many miracles from the caddie. There was no denying that since encountering young Schwain, Pep and Ivar's recent low-seventies rounds were well within any definition of a miracle, but Wessel's lackluster trudge around the course today was anything but miraculous. To Dustin Pepper's dismay, the much-ballyhooed Rama looked like nothing more than a run-of-the-mill rookie caddie.

Pep couldn't know that a phantom glimpse of Rama's father had distracted the caddie with thoughts of the ill that his old man's presence in this high-rolling place might portend. The Caddie's Gift was too insubstantial to stand against both its host's and his player's doubts, nor could its powers be summoned at will for profit or soda pop sales. To Pep, it simply appeared that Rama's string had finally run out.

Lousy damn timing, Pep cursed to himself. Since he was this close to the end of his would-be customer's visit, and since the vision of Wessel's sparkling game seemed tarnished, Pep figured there was nothing left to lose now by venturing a little business. After Wessel had blessedly hit a decent drive up the thirteenth's wide swath, Pep pounced.

"Nice. Nice. That'll play. Your drives, my irons…now wouldn't that make a team," he gushed. Pep swallowed hard, attempting the casual segue: "Like Luva'Lime Soda and Waddley's Food Parade…and discriminating soft drink lovers. At five dollars a case to you, everybody'd be a winner."

Silence cloaked the tee box. Pep felt like he just blundered into a marketing 101 class without his trousers. He fiddled with the grip on his driver, then tossed off a volley of damage control: "That's a penny a bottle more profit in your pocket, Wes. Just seems like the right thing to do today. What the hell! Guess I'm in a generous mood."

"God almighty, Pepper. Rama and I are working on a game here."

Wessel absorbed Pep's little sales pitch like an amoeba. The poker face had been replaced by furrows of golfing concentration below which his eyes, locked in a withering glance, appeared to discard Pep's offer while scolding his host for a breach of sales etiquette.

Defeated, Pep took a stance with considerably better footing and foozled a drive that threatened every crawling creature in seventy-five discouraging yards. Before turning to the trio feigning inattention back at the tee, Pep raised a grimace to the sky. "Faah…uck!" He mouthed the words in angry silence, especially for the Gods of Golf.

Wessel Waddley had been grinding so hard on his own game that he might have missed his host's miserable drive; at least that is what Pep hoped. Why else, Pep figured, would a reasonably decent man follow such an embarrassing shot with such a cruel statement: "Pep, I care about my customers, and they aren't buying your ginseng nonsense…tastes too much like dirt. I don't care about the penny."

Pep stared at his pathetic position just beyond the Ladies' tees with Wessel's ginseng comment ringing in his mind. He took the formula of his beverage very seriously, but in offense at the dirt reference and in disgust at his horrific stroke he had overlooked Wessel's softening on the price. He had just been tossed the keys to the soda kingdom and in frustration had nearly dropped them through a storm grate.

—•—

The scent of cypress, shrimp, and palmetto blew in on a stiff south wind. For a moment the sixteenth tee smelled like Gulfport's salty strand. Wedgy and Ivar could see the tops of willows waving from the ravine that bisected the fairway. The hazard cursed what otherwise would be an enjoyable test of par-five golf. Placed a little farther forward or backward, it might have permitted the C student to pass easily. Such was not the case. The unplayable ravine lay at a distance so strategically crucial that he who had hit a stout drive would be tempted to carry it on his second shot and earn a chance at a four. The weak or conservative player faced no such temptation, and even though forced to lay up his second, could still reach the green with a chance for a five, but only if his third shot across the ravine was at the leading edge of his ability. If the wind was in the player's face, all bets at success in either strategy were off.

On this day the insistent stream of northbound air was particularly troublesome to a ball that, one way or another, would have to cross the abyss. Wedgy and Ivar found themselves side by side, considering the hole's difficulties and the rising wind.

"You know, Ben Hogan called this hole the…"

"I know: The hardest par four and the easiest par five he ever saw," replied Wedgy with words stolen right from Ivar's mouth. "Damn it, Ives, we've played here before, remember…you break out the same quote every time. But the Hawk was right about the hardest part," continued Wedgy, "I'll give him that. But it's the five that's difficult. The four is downright impossible." He slapped Ivar on the back. "Unless you've got some real incentive to carry that jungle. Say another fifty if safely across in two, regardless of the hole's outcome."

Ivar hesitated.

"Come on you cheap old goat, you've got money to burn," insisted Wedgy. "I need the dough…got upkeep on that piece of shit Lincoln some hillbilly swindled me into."

"Alright, Wallace," Ivar said, "but put it in the gorge and you pay, too, no matter where I hit it."

Wedgy imagined claiming on both ends of that bet and instantly accepted Ivar's amendment.

Wedgy pulled his persimmon Walter Hagen and took several nervous tugs on a cigarette. He tried to fashion a smoke ring as he exhaled—a true sign of nonchalance—but the tropical breeze twisted the character into an infinity symbol, then a Mobius band, and then into chaos as he tossed the cigarette to the turf.

Wedgy's nicotine swing was sound, but just a smidgen off the screws. Frozen in his finish pose, he followed the ball, trying to calculate its disappointing carry. Ivar slipped silently behind his competitor. "I think I've got a slide rule in my bag there, Wallace," he whispered. "Might help you with the math."

Wedgy picked his tee from the grass. As he peered down the fairway lost in strategic thought, he absent-mindedly raised the soiled peg to his lips and attempted a toke.

Ivar had no intention of risking his first two shots. A 3-wood and a 7-iron later, his ball lay as planned: safely on the front bank of the ravine. Wedgy arrived at his ball and cursed the twenty critical yards his drive did not roll. Those twenty yards would have moved an attempt at flying the ravine on his second shot from the realms of utterly foolish to merely risky. He checked his yardage; he even had his caddie pace the distance to the ravine's front bank as he lingered over his decision. A 9-iron would place him next to Ivar, a 2-iron would land him beyond the gorge and firmly in the chips.

Ivar broke the silence shrouding Wedgy's deliberations. "It's your money, Wallace. But it shouldn't take Warner Von Braun to tell you it's a lay-up in this breeze."

Wedgy looked back at his tormentor, clearly irritated by the suggestion to play it safe. "Ives, those eggheads down in Huntsville have blowed up their fair share of rockets, too, ya know."

Ivar chuckled, uncertain if Wedgy was referring to the fallibility of the well-calculated shot or the looming disaster of a high-altitude rocket shot. Wedgy may have had doubt at his own intentions as well—enough doubt, as it turned out, to rob his swing of the commitment needed to send his ball screaming to safety 230 yards up the fairway. Instead, the ball became an instant artifact, buried somewhere in the face of the ravine's far bank for the scrutiny of future archaeologists puzzling over the collection of odd, dimpled fossils.

An evil swarm of thoughts swirled in Wedgy's head. Had he not been a "professional" he would have allowed obscene references to the ball, to Hogan, to Von Braun, even to Ivar Guidance to escape his lips, but instead only the thunderous thump of a 2-iron sunk deeply into Mother Earth resounded across the sixteenth fairway.

A ripple fluttered through the gallery. Hank Schwain released a deep breath of relief.

With no fanfare whatsoever, Ivar simply knocked his third shot across the hazard and up near the green with a safe 4-wood. As Wedgy dropped a new ball behind the ravine and prepared to play his fourth shot, Ivar asked in his most civil tone: "Excuse me, Wallace, but if you hit it in there again, do you owe me *another* fifty?"

Wedgy had forgotten Ivar's amendment to the ravine bet, and facing his fourth shot was a lousy time to remember. He was rattled but managed to fly his ball within thirty feet of the green. His subsequent up and down for a six was not good enough to catch Ivar's two-putt for a five.

The two golfers with caddies in tow vacated the sixteenth green. Ivar imagined the satisfaction in shaking Wedgy's losing hand two greens ahead. Wedgy envisioned a far wider image: one encompassing his world—vulnerable and insubstantial, a hustling existence balanced in recent years on a tenuous foundation of wit and skill that was clearly diminishing. He was sixty-seven years old, for God's sake. More than ever his wits were crucial, yet here he was on a course he knew well with an honest and usually inferior golfer, and he was still being outplayed. But worse, he was being outsmarted.

Walking to the seventeenth, down by two strokes, Wedgy concluded that he needed a new attitude, a new profession, or just some dumb luck. He fished for another cigarette, but the deficit resulting from Ivar's theft left him smokeless when he most needed relief. Pride did not permit him to beg one of his own Pall Malls back from his opponent. Instead, he picked up his pace to draw within earshot of Ivar's caddie, who lagged far behind his boss.

"Charles...you got a fag?"

The caddie/would-be-lawyer turned back to face Wedgy. "Whatever you need, Mr. Byrne."

Wedgy waved his own caddie on, then tipped his head close to Charlie to ignite a Winston against the growing winds. For a moment the two stood alone on the tree-lined path to the seventeenth tee. They lingered long enough to strike up a light and a deal.

Pep Pepper had tried everything else to make his sale, but he had never considered the obvious: Wessel Waddley just didn't like the taste of Luva'Lime's secret ingredient. Plenty of other folks said they did, but if a hint of ginseng was all that stood between him and a good run at Dr. Pepper, then the Chinese could keep their damned herb.

When they arrived at the fourteenth tee, Pep stepped to Rama's side as Wessel busied himself with several cycles at the ball washer. "Can you believe it? That son of a bitch got three days of free golf," Pep whispered, "and a penny a bottle concession out of me before the bullshit artist even mentions that he's got a problem with the flavor. Flavor...*that* I can fix. No matter how bad Wes plays now I think I've got a deal."

Pep patted Rama on the shoulder. "Don't you worry; you've done all you can. Jesus couldn't fix that poor bastard's game. Maybe that magic of yours will come back around another day."

Pep faced Wessel with a grand smile. "Number fourteen. Now this little number is Bluff Meade's answer to Pebble's number seven. Pretty, huh? You know I was thinking I might be getting a little tired of that flavor myself," he chimed.

—•—

Ivar and Wedgy stepped to the seventeenth tee. The hole was a knock-off of Alister Mackenzie's twelfth at Augusta, except it was a par four. It featured a shallow, fast green that drained putts and short approach shots over a rounded apron and into Meade Creek. Unlike the original, Bluff Meade added an extra 200 yards to turn the renowned par three design into a short, but treacherous four. Wedges were king on this tricky 355-yard hole; both Ivar and Wedgy knew who had the obvious advantage.

Ivar expected another side bet, but Wedgy Byrne stood silent, secretly considering the pros and cons of insurance sales should this hole fail him, too. A muzzled Wedgy was fine by Ivar, and he effortlessly launched a 240-yard drive up the middle. As he stepped from the tee box, a break in the cedars along the fairway allowed him a glimpse of the Pepper group up on the fourteenth tee. He recognized Pep, and he wondered how Pep's guest Mr. Waddley was doing with Rama on his bag.

Wedgy returned from his dreams of the insurance world long enough to answer Ivar's respectable tee shot with a stratospheric missile that finished fifteen yards beyond Ivar's ball. For Wedgy, the pin was now just a full sand wedge away.

Hank Schwain was not impressed. He had just about reached his fill of golf. Limping seventeen holes, even with the assistance of a cane, was wearing him down. If it hadn't been for the buoying effect of his man Ivar's lucrative two-stroke lead, Hank might really be dragging. He looked forward to a stiff

Old Crow and what now appeared to be a $12,000 payoff. Pausing to catch his breath, his eyes were drawn to four figures up on the fourteenth tee. One was familiar.

"I'll be damned," he whispered as he recognized his son. For the first time that day, Hank smiled. "Guess we didn't need you after all, Chief." Hank stepped behind another spectator lest his son spot him. He had already had enough close calls for one day.

As Wedgy caught up with the others on the seventeenth tee, Hank was already looking forward to settling his debt to Lew Raybon and returning the "borrowed" cash to Rama's account. He would close the book on gambling forever and surprise Doris with a night out—something a little more glamorous than Chinese take-out. Hank anxiously awaited Ivar's next shot as cedar boughs swayed in the fragrant south wind.

———•———

"Pep, maybe we can talk about it…later." Ginseng was clearly not foremost in Wessel's mind as he looked down at the beautiful little par three. His eyes shifted to Rama's. "This game's not out of reach, eh boy?"

"No sir, five holes counting this. A par would get you back on track nicely. Play bogey golf on in and you've got your 89." As lackluster a round as he had been having, Wessel had the smarts to keep his expectations realistic. He had told Rama that an 86 was his career best, but anytime he broke 90 he figured he was really playing golf.

Rama watched as Wessel pulled a pitching wedge from the bag and teed up. The hole was playing to about 110 yards—so inviting and so dangerous. Rama bit at his thumbnail, worried that Wessel might waste this great opportunity now. It was too windy. It was the wrong club.

"Excuse me Mr. Waddley. Take one more club…please."

Wessel relaxed and stood with the club-head resting on his shoe like he'd seen in an old photo of Bobby Jones. He clearly visualized sticking the green, but now this interruption.

"It's the wind. Trust me, sir. Take a 9-iron…you won't overshoot." Rama pulled the club and waited for Wessel to make the final decision. Wessel looked back down at the green and then up at the clouds racing northward. He looked into Rama's eyes for assurance, and in that moment felt a rush of embarrassment at his vanity and a rush of adrenalin at the hole's prospects. He traded clubs without question.

"Thank you, sir. No hurry…just start all over," said Rama.

———•———

Down on the seventeenth fairway, Ivar settled in over his ball. From his point of view, the slippery little green was foreshortened into nothing; all he could see was the apron rolling down from the green. His approach shot had to be high and within about three yards plus or minus of the 125 yards he figured was perfect.

Ivar pulled his pitching wedge. "Hit down to fly high." The words of every instructor or author he had ever consulted floated up from his memory. If that concept was ever critical, it was now. He set up with the ball back slightly and rehearsed the important early cocking of the wrist and the steep angle of attack. His confidence soared: He was on great turf and the wind was at his back.

———•———

Pep winked at Rama as the caddie stepped back out of Wessel's sight. Together they watched as the awkward little man strove to match a real swing to the vision of a perfect, graceful swing stored somewhere in the convolutions of his grocery wizard's mind. Rama had reminded him that he had plenty of time, and Wessel had listened. He allowed his body to coil and release without hurry or hesitation. His eyes found the ball in mid-flight.

"Beautiful," whispered Pep.

Together the two golfers and their caddies followed the ball against the gray clouds far above the green. It seemed bound to carry forever, but the air from the Gulf had its own destiny and the ball would yield. Robbed of its lift, it plummeted to the green and expended its momentum on two small bounces and a six-foot roll against the quivering flagstick. It hung there for an instant, flirting with destiny, then disappeared. Both golfers and their caddies howled at the unlikely ace.

———•———

The quartet of ecstatic voices cheering at Wessel's hole-in-one reached down to the seventeenth fairway in the top of Ivar's carefully planned downward attack. The distraction caused his swing to bottom out one-half inch farther behind the ball than intended. Although only slightly miss-hit, the shot still looked good. But when plugged into golf's diabolical equations, the miscue resulted in a number just less than needed—two yards less, to be exact. The ball hit the front edge of the green but couldn't hold and began an inexorable slide back down the heartbreaking slope into Bluff Meade's own Ray's River Styx.

Hank watched in shock as his man's fortunes rolled into the drink. He raised his eyes and peered in curiosity up through the dancing cedars to the joyous celebration on the fourteenth tee. His mind darkened at the thought that his son's misplaced gift and perhaps even Rama's gleeful young voice had interceded in Ivar's most crucial stroke and against what could have been the Schwain's greatest payday yet.

He could see Rama jumping in delight at some stranger's success. In a per-version of justice, the son was celebrating the father's loss again. Hank turned to a fellow who also had some money on Ivar: "What happened up there?"

The fellow looked at Hank as if he really had asked if the Pope was Cath-olic. "Buddy…they only holler like that for a hole-in-one. Some bloody timing, huh?"

Bloody. The word reminded Hank of his arrangement with Calcutta Finance. He felt a surge of panic constrict his breath. The fairway around him began to rotate. The ace so certainly attributable to Rama had spun Hank's head with the cosmic implications of its impossible timing. Fate's careening Tilt-o-Whirl had revved up and now threatened to toss him out into the House-of-Horrors. Hank told himself to relax, the game wasn't over. He steadied himself with his cane and waited for Wedgy's shot, wishing that this Byrne character had never showed up at Big Muddy's and that he had never uttered a word about golf. He wished he had sold him an even more hopeless automobile than the blue Lincoln. He wished Wedgy ill—at least two strokes of ill.

Ivar Guidance was still standing in the fairway talking to Charlie, who strained to make out the action up on the fourteenth tee.

"I'll be go-to-hell," said Charlie, "That's Pepper on the tee now. It must have been his pal Waddle that made the ace." Charlie's mind skipped across the assignment sheet. "That's Rama's guy. Jesus, it figures," he frowned.

Ivar's heart glowed at Rama's and his friend Pep's good fortune. He hoped Wessel's ace might put the Luva'Lime contract in the bag once and for all.

Even from his place in the trees, Hank could easily make out the broad smile growing inexplicably across Ivar's face. "Damn it," Hank swore out loud, "What's he so god-damned happy about? He's in the fucking drink!"

Wedgy looked back toward the gallery, peeved at the distraction to his pre-shot routine. He recognized the angry source of the disturbance and hissed under his breath, "Shit…it's the damn hick from Big Muddy's." He would like to have conducted a little discussion about the blue Lincoln's shortcomings then and there, but instead he remembered the fact that this was also the lucky bastard he had introduced to this match and to whom he had pitched its likely lucrative outcome. He had even given the poor crippled SOB the scoop on Ivar's pitiful competitive record.

"No wonder he's pissed," muttered Wedgy in misunderstanding. "I promised him an ass whipping and I'm still two strokes behind." But, Wedgy wondered, just how much money could a hillbilly used-car salesman have plunked down to get so worked up?

Motivation, magic, and the muse all come from mysterious places. As Wedgy contemplated a hundred-yard wedge shot to a shallow domed green, the three graces arrived via a mistaken sense of responsibility to a used-car salesman. Rightly or wrongly moved, Wedgy bore down. Ivar was wet, and Wedgy knew that if he could hit this one stiff, he could pull even or better.

Unlike Ivar's shot, nothing interfered with Wedgy's attempt—not his ego, not his tired arms, and not a neighboring ace. His swooping sand wedge came down solidly with a little cut action at the bottom to hold off the winds he guessed were leaking through the boughs up along the right flank. The ball landed softly and held the green easily within twelve feet of the hole. His caddie jogged to catch up as the energized old hustler strode to the green.

The muse did not grant Wedgy his one-putt; he had to settle for par, but that was sufficient to close the gap with Ivar after the old gentleman had failed to get up and down from a drop beside the creek. With the match tied and the last tee box coming up fast, a misplaced appreciation for Wedgy's skills welled up within Ivar's caddie.

"Holy hell, nice shot!" Charlie exclaimed, blind to any implications his compliment might raise regarding his allegiance to Ivar. "Cut it against the wind…and under all this pressure. Wow!"

Charlie's sudden enthusiasm eclipsed his attention to Ivar's game and transgressed his principal duty: to help his player navigate golf's mental landscape. Knowledge of club and course were fine, but understanding when to contain the highs and recover from the lows were the essential skills—or in the words of his would-be mentor and Bluff Meade's assistant pro Billy Kurtez: "Sooth their nerves. Coddle their confidence. And keep the damn fools' eyes off the cart girl."

Mr. Kurtez's nerves would hardly have been soothed had he witnessed his student's traitorous admiration for his opponent's most important shot. To be an asset, not just a shoulder beneath a leather sling, Charlie would have to understand his man's humanity, a skill that might not bode well for a future in the legal trades.

Ivar may have been happy that Rama's man had scored an ace—a magnanimous expression given the unfortunate consequences—but he was only human and he wasn't happy with the double-bogey or the tie in which he now felt trapped. With the game on the line he certainly didn't need to hear praise for what he wished to forget.

"Yes, Charles, I saw," said Ivar. "You don't suppose they call him *Wedgy* for his *putting*, do you?"

Charlie avoided Ivar's rare, cynical glance and hurried to keep up with Ivar's deliberate stride to the final tee.

Wedgy met Ivar's somber eyes with a carefully calculated wink as his opponent arrived at the tee. "Kind of feels like the fucking US Open up here with the pressure and all, eh Ives?"

For all the gamesmanship behind the comment, it was true: The match was down to one hole with no margin for error. The gallery's murmur of anticipation was louder and more insistent than in the seventeen preceding holes. For the spectators invested comfortably in the match, it was good

nail-biting theatre; for those in over their heads, like the man nervously jabbing at the earth with his cane, it was a looming existential crisis.

Wedgy peered up the final fairway. The hole was not long, but defended
against the rampaging golfer with a pinched fairway that tilted toward a stand
of weeping cedars. The first shot could easily miss or carom off into an ever-
green jail.

The narrow ribbon of fairway rose continually until it reached a confounding three-tiered green just below the clubhouse patio. The smart caddie
always checked the hole's location before starting his round, since from below
the green the flagstick's lower regions were invisible and its location could only
be surmised—a foolhardy and unnecessary gamble.

Foolhardy also described Hank's rueful opinion of the round in light of
the previous hole's two-stroke swing against him and his man, Ivar. As the
cocky, rejuvenated Mr. Byrne stepped to the tee, Hank wished to be employed
in some less risky activity, like hosing dust off cars lined hopefully along Big
Muddy's lot or convincing a teenage boy alight with first-car fire that he was
making a wise decision as he peered under the hood of a sexy but exhausted
GTO.

Hank had no choice but to endure, like watching a horse with an evening's
winnings parlayed upon its back hopelessly finish a race after stumbling out
of the gate. As if he were a greenhorn in the wagering world, Hank Schwain
crossed his fingers and could only watch.

Wedgy stepped into place between the tee markers, a ragged cloud of
tobacco smoke tangling about his head. Before taking his grip, he flicked his
spent cigarette toward a trash basket beside the ball washer. The butt flew fifteen feet, then plunged expertly into the target.

One in a hundred, thought Hank, intuitively figuring the odds.

With pay dirt just 380 yards away, Wedgy played it smart. He drew the
3-wood and slashed a reasonable drive. Although the ball first appeared destined for the cedar grove, the swirling winds arrested its fade and the ball fell
safely to the fairway. Relieved, Wedgy vacated the tee box, passing deliberately
beside Charlie.

"So you liked that wedge back yonder, huh?" Wedgy whispered, as Ivar
took the tee. "Appreciate your support, kid…it's worth a lot."

Still feeling the sting of the last hole, Ivar composed himself with dignity.
Swinging boldly with driver and with resolve to put Wedgy's curse to rest, he
propelled his ball a good twenty yards beyond his opponent's. But before it
bounded to rest, the rightward tilt of the fairway kicked it to the fringe of the
cedars. From there, Ivar's path to the flag was possibly in jeopardy.

Wedgy wasted no time in getting to his lie in the short firm turf. He knew
exactly how far forward in the complex green the flagstick stood and was happy to use his sand wedge to fly the ball onto the blind surface.

"Nice call on that 8-iron," Wedgy proclaimed deceivingly to his clueless caddie as he rammed the pitching wedge back into his bag.

—•—

The cedars' windblown boughs intruded in and out of Ivar's line of play. He rubbed his hands through his white locks and realized foliage was only half his problem; he had also forgotten to check the pin position that morning from the clubhouse.

"I never even peeked at the green this morning, Charles," Ivar admitted with a tinge of embarrassment, "Which level are we on up there…how far you reckon?"

Charlie's response to the realization that he also had not checked that which was any Bluff Meade caddie's business to know should have been an honest admission, but instead he had other intentions. "Shoot for the middle…Wedgy hit an 8-iron right in there."

Ivar, who was preoccupied with his ball's awkward lie, seemed satisfied with Charlie's assessment. He deducted the distance between himself and Wedgy's alleged iron and determined that a 9-iron would find the middle tier, but as the jittery young men laboring in his office's fledgling computer department were fond of saying, "shit in shit out," and unfortunately the output from his club selection equation was similarly tainted. The 9-iron, timed perfectly to fly through the waving cedar boughs, was struck skillfully but the ball flew unexpectedly to the back of the devilish green.

"Looks like it might be nice," declared Charlie.

Ivar didn't reply but stood poised with the 9-iron in his hand. The delicious sensation of a purely struck short iron mingled with the fearful suspicion that he had over-flown the green. Only a walk up the ascending fairway would confirm or deny his fears.

Out of breath and out of luck, Ivar found his ball perched on the farthest end of the green, three distinct tiers above the flagstick. Both he and Wedgy lay on the green seventy-five strokes into the match. The difference would come down to the final putts. Ivar faced seventy feet, two steep plunges, and one careening right break for a hugely implausible birdie. Wedgy lay pin-high and only fourteen feet from the pin—his reward for doing his homework and for a few well-chosen words with Charlie Vestal.

Frustration and breathlessness gripped both Hank Schwain and Ivar Guidance as they recuperated from the ascent up the final fairway. Four holes behind, the Caddie's Gift had blossomed again and its magic flowed from Rama through Wessel Waddley. Wessel played golf with a joy that had eluded him since he had been a kid and with his younger brother Donald had stolen onto the secluded middle holes of a snooty private track near their home. They had played free, hushed golf at first light, leaving tracks on the dewy greens to befuddle and amuse the morning greens keeper.

When a putt rolled in for a birdie, Donald would scribe Bird in the dew alongside the hole. Soon they found themselves rolling balls backward from the hole and assigning Bird and Eagle to what appeared to be heroic putts on the damp greens. Their humor echoed the abandon with which they played in those carefree days.

In time the grocery business laced a tight corset around Wessel's swing. His brother became an orthodontist and their golf games went to hell. The ace on number fourteen might not deliver Wessel's game forever from the flames, but with the holy grail safely bagged and with the curious good nature of Rama Schwain somehow loosening the laces, he was well on his way to an 83 and the most fun he had enjoyed since he learned to operate a cash register.

When Wessel's birdie putt rolled convincingly into the center of the fifteenth cup, any lingering sense of unworthiness in the company of golfers vanished. A stamp of credibility as a deserved member of the club descended on him. One of his first duties, as such, was to reward his patient companion, Pep. Without extending the negotiating ruse any further, Wessel announced his intention to award the Food Parade contract for an improved Luva'Lime Soda to Dustin Pepper. Toasting the decision with beer from the refreshment cart, Wessel even suggested that a special soda with essence of ginseng might also have a place on Waddley's shelves. Such was the power of the Caddie's Gift.

The hollow clunk of their beer cans together resonated only an instant, but the happy sound of their voices drifted as far as the hush that had fallen over the eighteenth green.

Chapter 35

On the deck just above the eighteenth green a trio of patio umbrellas tugged at their stands as a balmy gust blew up from the fairway. Ivar and Wedgy were distracted from their focus on the round's decisive putts when two of the umbrellas took briefly to the air then plunged back to the patio in a commotion of colorful canvas and bamboo. Hank could not help but follow their awkward descent. As the umbrellas' brittle stays cracked upon impact he shuddered, then turned quickly back to the green to face Ivar's and his fate.

From the green's upper tier, Ivar's chances of winning looked slim, but trading two putts with Wedgy would at least assure him of extra holes and another chance at regaining the command he seemed to possess before the incredible distraction of Wessel's hole-in-one. Two putts were not out of the question, but from Ivar's daunting locale, neither was a losing three-putt.

Charlie struggled to cover his suspicious tracks after his misleading call on the pin placement. He paced off Ivar's putt and whispered topographic nothings in his man's ear. Satisfied that he had done all that appeared he should do for Ivar, Charlie trod resolutely down to tend the flag. As he arrived he cast a discreet glance at Wedgy, confirming that Ivar's two-putt was not the spurned caddie's highest interest.

Ivar waited for Charlie to gather the restless flag and steady the stick. He actually loved difficult putts more than any other part of the game. The expectations of a long winding roll were less oppressive than any unforgiving four-footer. The ball didn't have to find the cup to be a success, it merely had to get close. After meticulously planning such a complex roll, Ivar eagerly anticipated pulling the handle and watching the fruit of his mental calculus fall into a jackpot line.

With a lingering breath Ivar passed his rational efforts and—although he couldn't know it—Hank Schwain's fortune over to snickering fate. He launched the ball confidently across the upper tier with just enough momentum to propel it to the crest from where it would plunge down and across the second tier at an angle and velocity sufficient to carry it to within comfortable proximity of the hole. At least that was the plan.

Charlie, Ivar, Wedgy, Hank, and two hundred others held their collective breath as the ball rolled with purpose along an invisible track laid gracefully across the green by the ghostly hand of Isaac Newton. As the distance between the ball and its destination shortened, the line transformed from the possible to the probable to the inevitable. All eyes were transfixed as the ball correctly found each waypoint on Ivar's mental course and tumbled into the final curve, breaking perfectly, briskly toward the flagstick.

The magic of the ball's attraction to the hole transfixed Charlie, who, in his heart, longed to watch the ball complete its rendezvous with the cup, although he had other plans. He never really expected that the lucrative opportunity for an "accidental interference" with one of Ivar's putts would ever come, certainly not at such a critical moment or at the end of such a brilliant effort as this. Yet here it was: His chance to earn, as Wedgy proposed, "double whatever old Ives was gonna tip you." With the ball only an instant away, Charlie tugged dramatically at the flag, but the stick appeared to remain stuck in the cup. In truth it was held by nothing more substantial than the guile of a traitorous caddie.

Two sounds would ring in Charlie's ear from that hypnotic moment forward: the urgent voice of Ivar Guidance pleading "PULL IT" and the sickening clank of the ball against the metal flagstick.

Pull it Charlie did, a microsecond after Ivar's ball struck the stick. The ball came to rest three easy feet away, but the collision with the tended flagstick would cost him an unexpected and unforgivable two-stroke penalty, as Wedgy was quick to point out.

Suddenly, and fatally, Ivar lay five on the green with Wedgy laying only two. The match was over. The putts would have to be holed out, but the milk was spilt and the crying began in earnest. This was not an ending conducive to civility within the ranks of the gallery. Wedgy struggled to screw his face into a sympathetic expression as he apologized for the rule's brutality. "I know, I know...two strokes, a lousy damn rule," he sighed.

Wedgy choked back his jubilation. He'd take a win any way he could get one—it was what he did—but he never really believed Charlie, after misleading Ivar on his club selection into the final green, would have the guts or the opportunity to fake the flagstick faux pas. One hundred dollars well spent, thought Wedgy. In a spasm of morbid cynicism, he wondered whether Ivar would still pay his caddie a tip after such a blunder and whether Charlie would have the gall to accept another gratuity. Wedgy kept his distance from the discredited caddie as angry voices citing foul shot through the crowd like lightning bolts. Playoffs, do-overs, and replays were all tossed up as salves for the spectators' displeasure.

The scene at number eighteen might have grown ugly had Rules Chairman Mr. Roland Bandon not waded bravely into the fray. The booming voice of the would-be ringmaster proved especially compelling under these circumstances. He demanded attention, and receiving it for a moment recited Rule Number 17-3's provisions for assessing a penalty in the event of a putt accidentally striking a flagstick that had been asked by the offending golfer to be removed or tended. This severe penalty was not his doing, Roland explained, but was an edict from the Royal and Ancients of St. Andrews, Scotland. He spoke with authority and force, taking great breaths between passages like Dizzy Gillespie. For the stentorian majesty he brought to his decree, he might just as well have been introducing the awesome spectacle of the human cannonball rather than stamping the seal of approval on Wedgy and Charlie's scam.

The losing gallery's thirst for a replay or for Charlie's blood slackened slightly after Roland's ruling, but it was not until Ivar—the victim himself—stepped to the defense of the rules and the protection of his caddie that grudging acceptance finally settled over the scene. Ivar Guidance's long left arm clamped the embattled young man to his side as a demonstration of good will. Ivar felt the guilty caddie tremble under his touch as he cleared his throat to speak.

"You all know this game is about judgment as much as skill," he began. "I asked Charles to tend that stick. I could have asked him to pull it, but I took my chance with the flagstick in so I could judge the putt a bit better. Darned if I didn't leave myself open to just such an accident. It happens…we've all seen sticks stuck in the cup before." Ivar surveyed the faces of his many friends in the gallery. "Have we not?"

It hurt Ivar to lose, especially by two strokes of extraordinarily bad luck on the final two holes. He understood that against Wedgy he would always need more cushion than two strokes. He could blame no one but himself for not earning that margin, yet in his heart he knew that he had played his best. Except for those misfortunes he had defeated his old nemesis. Above all Ivar knew that Wedgy knew, and that was the real trophy from this game. As he and Wedgy finished off their putts, Ivar hoped that no one had placed too much money on his insufficient efforts.

Ivar extended his hand to Wallace Byrne in congratulations. At the winner's touch he suddenly felt the weight of the loss and was fatigued beyond any previous game's rigors. He knew this had been his last crack at Wedgy.

"Christ, you're goin' easy on that fuck-up caddie of yours, Ives," Wedgy said as Charlie bolted for the caddie shack. Wedgy raised a facetious voice in pursuit of the retreating young man: "I'd have kicked your stupid ass if you were working for me, Vestal."

Wedgy turned back to his victim: "Maybe next year eh, Ives?"

Ivar had nothing more to say regarding his or Charlie's performance. He just smiled like a champion although he felt like hell.

For a few moments, even Wedgy felt bad after his dubious victory. Oddly, he took some comfort in the good fortune he imagined this victory had brought to that crippled car salesman. The poor fellow must have thought he was a goner back on seventeen with Ivar up by two strokes. But odder still was the fact that this very fellow was struggling up the grassy slope toward the parking lot when the payoff would be down the flagstone path at the starter's hutch.

—•—

Hank Schwain cursed whatever it was he had eaten for breakfast as he put as much distance between himself and the damned golf course as his bad leg would allow. The wrenching loss and the sickening good nature in Ivar Guidance's reaction to his defeat had turned his stomach.

In the course of a few hours, his emotions had careened from buoyant anticipation at finally settling all his debts to reeling at the realization that he had now added a new unsympathetic creditor to his discouraging portfolio. He was condemned to meet Doris in two days for an accounting of Rama's education fund, much of which was now irreplaceably absent. Hank's heart sunk even further as he recalled that he had intended to send up his wife for a ride in the Little Crow before they went to dinner. Soaring would be a special surprise, but with his finances in shambles the glider was just another lie he couldn't bear or afford.

Hank steadied himself against the Rambler's stubby tailfins and gasped for air. Where was the feeling of renewal he had felt just a few days ago? He knew the answer lay in his own damning compulsions. He looked to the sky in despair, only to be struck in the face by the first fat droplets of an impending rainstorm.

"This was a sure thing! God damn it, Rama!" Hank cried as the water stung his eyes.

Members of the gallery filtering back through the parking lot were puzzled at the sight of a man cursing crazily at the sky. Hank shivered at the rain and at his own stupidity. He knew he should have realized by now that nothing was sure, especially in golf. In his despondency Hank viewed his life with the same hopeless perspective that many an ex-golfer regarded the damnable game: Why bother trying when you are destined to fall short over and over again?

Hank slammed the Rambler into reverse and swung out into the parking lot. Somewhere on the course behind him, his son was still working the Pepper/Waddley game. Somewhere, Rama was guiding another man to his finest moment. Somewhere, Rama was building what had always remained beyond Hank's horizon.

From his position down amongst the weeping cedars that lined the sixteenth fairway, Rama caught a glimpse of a red Rambler wagon hurtling along the drive toward Crutchfield Lane. Wessel Waddley, the newest member of the hole-in-one-club, looked at his distracted young caddie curiously. He noticed a shiver of anxiety raise the hair on Rama's neck.

—•—

A sudden rain ran Doris Schwain in from her garden, just in time to hear her telephone ring. The voice on the phone introduced himself as Doctor Myers, a friend of Ivar Guidance. Doris did not make the connection until the doctor explained he played golf with Mr. Guidance on occasion at the Bluff Meade Country Club. In fact, he had met her son, Rama, "a delightful and charming young man."

"Oh yes, yes!" Doris answered breathlessly, "Rama said Mr. Guidance might have an acquaintance in the medical world, that you might call."

The doctor apologized for phoning so late on a Sunday afternoon, then explained that he was a specialist in neurology. He would be pleased to find a slot in his schedule for a preliminary evaluation of her condition.

"That is a most generous offer, Doctor Myers, but I just have…a sclerosis, I think they call it. They tell me there's nothing anyone can do," explained Doris. "I wouldn't want to interfere with your valuable schedule."

"They might be making an unfortunate assumption," cautioned the doctor. "Have you ever had a head injury, Mrs. Schwain?"

Doris combed her memory. She blushed as she remembered scrambling up a rocky eastern Washington draw with a handsome young Hank Schwain for an afternoon in their secret spot. She had fallen one evening as they hurried down to avoid the scandal of returning home suspiciously late.

"I took a little spill once, nothing really," she said.

"Did you see a doctor about it?"

"Oh no. It was really nothing," she said. Doris neglected to say that Hank had dressed the wound and that the two young lovers had both agreed, for lack of a plausible alibi, to keep the accident secret.

"Mrs. Schwain, you deserve a second opinion," insisted the doctor. He explained that there would be no charge. "Would next Wednesday at ten in the morning work for you?"

"Well, it is your time, doctor, but if you think it is worthwhile, let me jot down the address."

Doris felt encouraged as she settled down on the sofa to await the end of the rain. It looked like a short-lived storm. Doctor Myers seemed a smart fellow, but she wouldn't get her hopes up. Still, this would be some nice news to share with Hank when he came by on Wednesday to discuss Rama's college finances and to take her out for dinner and a surprise.

Two dates in a week. Doris smiled at her good fortune and her husband's improvement. Things were looking up, she thought as she tossed her gardening gloves onto the coffee table. The sound of rain splattering on the front walk carried her off to sleep long before she could return to the garden.

Doris slept through her son's return. Rama had leaned the bike against the garage and shot up the front stairs, skipping three risers and his mother's gardening tools in each step. He had earned eighty-three dollars—the best tip he had ever received—as a special reward from Wessel for helping the grocer shoot his life's best score and an ace in the same round.

The jubilant golfer had gratefully counted the bills—a dollar a stroke—into Rama's hand, saying, "I know good food and I know good business…don't think I don't know magic when I see it."

Rama wanted to share the news, but it would have to wait for Doris. He opened a paper sack he had brought down from the course and extracted one of Bluff Meade's royal hamburgers and a book Ivar Guidance had loaned him: *Bernard Darwin on Golf*. Highbrow reading from some old English writer, Rama figured, but if Ivar said it was worth his attention, so be it. The sound of his mother's breathing told him that his tales of today's remarkable round might have to wait 'til tomorrow. Rama settled down with the book, still plagued by the image of his father at the starter shack and the Rambler racing down the drive. That tale would remain his own little secret.

—•—

In the warm glow of the Bunker Lounge, deep in the bosom of Bluff Meade's clubhouse, booze flowed like blood from hearts broken at the bitterness of Ivar's loss. Wedgy slipped quietly into the room, aware that violating the sanctity of the members' most sacred spot might be pushing his welcome. The wiser course would have been to lay low until the initial shock of his victory had subsided or until the least forgiving members had either gone home or drunk too much to care. But he could only contain himself so long. The essential prize here was the dung he would leave on the members' noses after a good rubbing into his "victory"…the more noses the better.

As expected, he received a reasonable helping of baleful looks and muttered expletives—that was part of the fun. But the mood in the room was far too congenial for his liking. Wedgy didn't realize it then, but the pact between Pep and Wessel and the rare occasion of an ace—the first in twenty-seven months and two days, according to Roland Bandon's meticulous records—had lifted the mood in the room above Ivar's defeat. Wedgy gratefully acknowledged a few obscenities as he made his way across the lounge to settle at the bar for the one day of the year the members would tolerate his presence in their inner sanctum.

"What gives? Feels like a bloody birthday party in here. Double Black Label…three cubes." Wedgy reached for his money clip.

"Oh no, Mr. Byrne," insisted the bartender, "Mr. Waddley is picking up the tab this afternoon. Made ace on number fourteen."

The bartender anticipated Wedgy's next question. "That's him with Dustin Pepper. You remember Pep?"

"Sure, the Ginseng King. Always got along with him," replied Wedgy. "He never wanted anything out of anybody except to sell 'em that damned soda pop."

The Scotch arrived and Wedgy pulled a couple of extra dollars from his pocket. He lofted the bills down on the bar with a grin: "For remembering my name…"

Wedgy turned from the bar, twirling the cubes in a vortex as he headed toward the epicenter of all the goodwill.

———•———

"How damn far have I fallen, that one of my few friends around here didn't even watch today's little skirmish with Ives?" Wedgy smiled and extended his arm to demand Dustin Pepper's handshake.

Wedgy's sudden appearance had startled Pep from his effusive chatter with Wessel Waddley. Not Wedgy…not now, thought Pep as he imagined a list of transgressions the troublesome Mr. Byrne might commit that could endanger his newly born relationship with Wessel. Pep feared Wedgy to be a threat to any honest, mutually beneficial business relationship. He shook Wedgy's hand without enthusiasm.

"Wallace, it's been another year, my God. How long are you going to keep at this vendetta?" He did not introduce Wessel.

"Long as I can keep walking away with all the chips," replied Wedgy. "Ives made it a little difficult this time around. Must be losing my touch. Luckily I was the beneficiary of a technical ruling."

Wedgy turned to Pep's companion and raised his glass: "To your ace, sir. I heard all the commotion…never got your name."

Pep intervened in the potentially dangerous discourse between his fresh new partner and his tawdry old acquaintance. "Wessel," he said, "meet Wallace Byron."

"Byrne…like a fire," corrected Wedgy, disappointed at his old friend's memory. "At least the bartender got my name right. Just call me Wedgy…like the club but with a *Y*." Wedgy chuckled at the speed with which the scotch had lubricated his wit.

A few hole-in-one cocktails had lubricated Wessel as well. He shook Wedgy's hand vigorously and introduced himself. "Wessel Waddley…like a duck, but with a *Y*."

Wedgy took a liking to the King of the Food Parade. The two fellows fell into the comfortable palaver of old friends. An ace, a lifetime round, and five years of golf hustling history gave them plenty to palaver over.

Pep sat by like an anxious hen at her eggs, but he had nothing to worry about; Wedgy was well behaved. In fact, Pep was becoming so bored with the whirlwind of self-congratulation in the air that he moved to release a little of Wedgy's wind.

"What's with the razor-thin advantage this year, Wallace? Against a seventy-two-year-old, no less," needled Pep. "I heard Ivar had you beaten until a slip-up on seventeen."

"Well, Dustin, that's golf, isn't it? Anybody can have a bad day."

Pep stayed on the offensive. "I heard old Ivar just about rolled in a sixty-footer to win. Except for a stuck flagstick, he might be strutting around here now."

"Ivar doesn't strut," Wedgy said sarcastically. "He just loses."

Pep bristled at Wedgy's remark. He felt some remorse at the selfish manipulation of both the Guest Rule and Roland Bandon's little circus fantasy that had robbed Ivar of his special caddie when he needed him most. The specter of Wedgy growing cockier as the evening wore on picked like a fingernail at the veneer of Pep's tolerance.

"You were just damn lucky, Byrnes," Pep said flatly. "Ivar's been shooting under your score the last couple of months, ever since he took on a new caddie. You were lucky Rama wasn't there today."

Wedgy laughed at Pep's claim. "I know how Ivar plays here; no caddie is gonna make that much difference."

"Believe me, this one does."

"Well, if he's that great a caddie," Wedgy observed, "then where in hell was he on Ivar's biggest day?"

Pep hesitated, not wishing to bring Wessel into this discussion. "He was caddying for...a guest. I figured a guest at Bluff Meade should always have the best."

Wessel looked at Pep in astonishment, uncertain whether to be thankful for Pep's obvious interference on his behalf with a caddie assignment that might have cost an old friend dearly. "You mean Rama is Ivar's caddie?"

"Well yes, mostly. He is in some demand here."

Wedgy listened to Pep and Wessel, realizing there was truth in Pep's claims for Ivar's recent scores and in the influence of that oddly named caddie. Maybe he did dodge a bullet today. "What scores has old Ives been shooting here lately?" asked Wedgy.

"Seventies...low to mid."

"Wessel, what did you shoot today?"

"Eighty-three, best ever," replied Wessel proudly. "Oh, and don't forget the hole-in-one."

Wedgy didn't. He imagined a caddie heeling golfers like some magic pill: "Take one, knock ten strokes off your game and call me in the morning." Ten strokes, he thought; how many years would that put back on his game? How many more dollars?

"What did you say his name was again?" asked Wedgy.

"Rama Schwain."

"Boy, that name sounds familiar," said Wedgy. His mind nearly made its way back to Big Muddy's and the conversation with the used car salesman. "Didn't Ivar pitch a fit when he lost his caddie…this Rama guy?"

"No, he was quite gracious according to the caddie master," replied Pep. "But you know, that's Ivar."

"Yep, he's some kind of gentleman," Wedgy replied sincerely. The thought of Ivar standing up in defense of Charlie's inexcusable blunder on what could have been the winning putt remained vivid. And so, too, did the name of Wessel's amazing caddie, Rama.

Wedgy tipped back the remainder of his scotch, momentarily lost in thought: Ivar was a fool for giving up his caddie. If the kid was anywhere near as magical as Pep said, he'd have taken him off Ivar's hands in a heartbeat. Wedgy smiled as a new possibility came into focus. "Come to think of it, maybe I still could."

Then, with the dawning of a crucial idea the trio of ice cubes welded precariously together in the bottom of Wedgy's glass separated, releasing an embarrassing torrent of chilled Black Label down his chin and into his lap.

"Son of a bitch," he gasped as several members at the bar laughed at his misfortune. For a moment the exchange rate of his boasting capital fell through the floor.

The door to the caddie shack burst open, startling several of the young loopers who had been quietly whiling away the afternoon in hopes of picking up a late walk-on bag. Charlie kicked the door shut and leaned his back against it as if to hold back an intruder. All faces had risen from their pool games and girlie magazines to their colleague's angry entrance. With eyes trained to read the invisible topography of a tightly mowed green at high noon or to detect clues of psychological unraveling in a golfer's step, they watched Charlie take two long slow breaths, then erupt.

"Christ, on a fucking crutch, what's goin' on around here? They nearly crucified me," Charlie cursed viciously. "Damn Guidance loses his grip on seventeen, then leaves himself a nightmare putt on eighteen and they're all on my ass for interference on a sixty-footer. As if it had a chance."

No one had asked, but Charlie was determined to build his case first—like any good lawyer—before other arguments were aired. "Some asshole jammed that stick in cockeyed before we got to the green. Check the log, Tirks…bust their chops. I couldn't get the damn stick out. Even if I could, that damn ball was going too fast, probably twenty feet past the hole if it didn't run out of green first. Hell, I felt it when it hit, there was no way it was going in the hole—stick or no stick—that interference wouldn't have changed anything."

One of the pool players was unconvinced. "Except for the two-stroke penalty. How does that *not* make a difference, Vestal? And what do you mean you felt it?"

"He means he felt it cause he left the damn pin in," said another player.

"Like I said, the damn bitch was stuck," insisted Charlie. "Guidance was a goner anyway. He'd have needed two strokes just to get back to where his ball ended up after hitting the stick. Same outcome…case closed."

"Ives could've used a little touch of the Rama out there, Charlie," suggested a voice from behind a *Sports Illustrated*. A volley of laughter filled the room.

"Now that's funny…ha ha. 'A little touch of the Rama,'" Charlie practically spit the words. He and Ivar had been doing fine until a little touch of the Rama came ringing down from the fourteenth tee and derailed Ivar's swing. And until Wedgy waved the promise of $100 in his greedy face.

Charlie stepped away from the door to search for a Yoohoo in the soft-drink cooler. "By the way, where is our pal Rama?"

"Rode his bike home already. Guess his mom is sick," replied one of the boys.

"Well good, cause I got a bone to pick." Charlie tried to wash his guilt away with the chocolate drink but found no relief. "That Rama's got some touch all right. How many times have you guys been sitting in here waiting for some cheapo bag to happen along while Rama's been down there looping for the A-team? Do you guys know the members bid for Rama down in the locker room? Christ, that's not touch, that's robbery.

"Sure, he's a lucky shit," said Charlie, acknowledging Rama's impressive impact, "but his luck will change. In the meantime he's making us look bad. He's costing you guys money."

The faces, which had been chiding him for his stuck pin explanation, now looked at him with interest. "Seriously, boys. If you haven't lost a bag or two or been stuck with a loser's chintzy tip thanks to Rama, raise your hand." Charlie was strutting around the lounge now like a prosecutor who had just found the defendant's fingerprints on the murder weapon. He paused but no hands went up.

"I rest my case," said Charlie. "So, let's do ourselves a favor. Let's vote him out of the shack," concluded the prosecution. "We'll all do better without Rama snagging off more than his share of the winner's tips. The vote will be democratic…nobody has to be the bad guy."

One of the pool players spoke up. "Charlie, where does it say we can vote a caddie out of here? Shit, all our jobs could be in jeopardy."

"Well, where does it say we can't?" countered Charlie. "Besides, it doesn't matter; Rama Schwain ain't the type to put up a fight on this anyway. If we say he goes…he'll go. He's a pussy."

Charlie rummaged through the caddie master's desk and found a few sheets of Bluff Meade letterhead. With a channel for his anger at losing Ivar's business and a dense smokescreen for today's crime, he was feeling eloquent. He quickly crafted a statement outlining the caddies' objections to Rama's "interference in the equitable process of caddie selection" and to his "blatant ignorance of the strictures of seniority" and to his "collusion in suspicious circumstances leading to mathematically improbable scores."

The paper was circulated. After considerable praise for its convincing language, the petition, as Charlie tagged it, was grudgingly signed by all the caddies present and posted on the bulletin board for consideration by those absent.

Charlie rummaged through the remains of the hardened donuts and found one twist that still had a flicker of life left in its braid. He walked back to the window and looked up the walkway toward the ninth and eighteenth holes. The crowd had thinned and would soon be gone except for those who had descended to the Bunker Lounge. With Wedgy's secret gratuity tucked in his pocket and the gears of democracy grinding in his favor, Charlie looked pleased. His imagination drifted forward. Tomorrow he would volunteer for Youth for Nixon; a job in the presidential campaign might jump-start a career in politics.

Charlie Vestal turned back from the window to congratulate his constituency. "Good job, guys. It was about time we put an end to Rama's magic bullshit and got this place back to reality," he declared in a puff of powdered sugar.

Chapter 36

Rama woke to a bright day and leapt from his bed to assess the weather for his round with Ivar Guidance. A trio of hummingbirds darted in and out of the morning's sunbeams as they jockeyed for honeysuckle blossoms. Definitely a good day for golf, he thought, never guessing that a day beginning so beautifully could possibly contain a sad ending.

He heard the sound of water running in the kitchen and the happy clatter of his mother preparing breakfast. She hummed a popular song while stirring up a batch of pancake batter. Rama smiled as the melody rose from her chest to his bedroom. By the tone of her voice, he gathered she must have had a good night's rest. He paused and savored her song, the ringing of the wooden spoon against the glass bowl, and the soft music of the water. The timbre of running water still soothed him as it had years ago. As a child he would lie in bed and relish the comforting sound. Whether it came from the kitchen or from his parents' bathroom didn't matter; the sound had always promised that his folks were about and that he was secure. Conscious even then of his limited turn at such innocence, he would listen to the music in the pipes and wish it would play forever.

Rama dressed quickly, as he had done a thousand times before in anticipation of his mother's generous breakfast, but on this day little else would remain the same. Before he darted from his old bedroom, a memory prompted him to peek under the bed one last time. Rama half-imagined that an old favorite fire truck might still be parked where he'd left it after a blaze of adventure a dozen years ago. Of course, the truck was gone—sold at a church bazaar or stored away for a future grandson. But he found an even older relic: an old golf club. God knows how Doris had missed it after years of hunting dust bunnies. It was the old club Carlos Taddio had given him on that dreamlike night at Mesquite Creek—the persimmon brassie Chandler Stone and his children had swung in the night lessons years before Rama had ventured to their magical tee.

Rama recovered the club and raised it to the light. The exposure of years in the elements up on that Texas butte and then eight years beneath his bed had taken its toll. The grip was brittle, but the club still felt young and vibrant in his hands.

"Need to soften it up a bit," he mused to a room of memories and childish treasures. Those objects had accepted their abandonment years ago and watched now as Rama took up the forgotten club again. It seemed only an instant since he had returned from his Texas trip, brokenhearted by the wound his father had inflicted upon him. They watched blankly as the boy slid the useless, banned club from beneath his bed.

Rama waggled the old brassie and wondered how he could have ignored it for so long. Standing in the middle of his bedroom, he made a few low half-swings, just fast enough to hear the rush of air around the rusty shaft. He swung with knowledge and purpose, churning the bedroom's atmosphere to the delight of his mute audience. It had been a child who stowed the club away, but it was a man who brought the brassie back into the light.

Rama resolved that he would take the club back to the pro shop at Bluff Meade after breakfast and order a new grip before checking in with the caddie master for the afternoon match with Ivar. Later he would be meeting Cherokee "Jimmy" Jim, the grounds keeper at Bluff Meade, for a little practice on the secret course they had fashioned far beyond the practice range. Jim was a respectable player and had once been a regular at Monday morning qualifiers where he had come within single digits of becoming a tour player.

Rama and Jimmy Jim had mowed several acres of the expansion area Bluff Meade's director's had optimistically set aside to accommodate a future US Open. They had created two fairways with four ad-hoc greens and twice as many tees. For weeks, under the tutelage of Jimmy Jim, Rama had been working at his game on the improvised track. The combination of watching a few fine players' techniques from his vantage as a caddie plus his sessions with Jimmy Jim had polished his talents into a game that, although never tournament tested, looked good to Jimmy.

"You'd likely beat the bejeezus out of the hacks at this club, and you're playing with *fish sticks*," Jimmy had said.

Fish sticks, Jimmy explained, were golf clubs the grounds crew regularly dredged from Bluff Meade's water hazards and then tossed into a jumble in the maintenance shed. Although most folks avoided the heap of bad karma as if the devil lurked in the tangle of rusted shafts, Rama and Jimmy Jim often rummaged for the rare gem, eventually completing two decent sets.

— • —

Rama strode confidently into Doris's kitchen wielding the old club like a cane as he faced pancakes and a hopeful day. Like Bing Crosby at his Clam Bake, life was sweet.

"You sound good today, Mom."

Doris smiled at Rama from behind the counter, thankful for the compliment. "And you look mighty sporting, Mr. Snead," she replied. But as she spoke she felt a current of change sweep through her sunny kitchen. The tempo of her spoon in the batter slowed. And as if some law of relativity had distorted the room, she realized nineteen years had passed in an instant. She had to squint to sharpen her focus on her boy's—or was it a man's—face grinning back at her in a rush to leave. Doris sensed that this day above all others was infinitely precious. She yearned to sit Rama down at the table and linger with him late into the morning, and to slow the passage of time while she still had the chance.

"Hope you brought your appetite down with you, Sweetheart."

Doris Schwain had a lot to say that morning, including the fact that a Doctor Myer had called and that he would soon provide a thorough evaluation of her condition. She said the doctor was upbeat and so was she. Her face brightened. "Your father will be coming over today. We are going to work out your school finances and then he has promised me a little surprise—something about Aero Meadows. I am so happy for him."

Rama nodded. He wished he could share her faith, but he was haunted by the glimpse of a man with a cane at the starter's shack, and again by the Rambler hurtling down Bluff Meade's driveway only minutes after yesterday's match was complete. He was unsettled at the thought of his father falling so easily while his mother invested her finite stores of hope so freely in his renewal.

He would say nothing to dampen Doris's good mood. Even if Hank had been gambling, there was no telling how much he had wagered. There was no point in getting too worked up over losses if they were small. But damn it, thought Rama, the point was not about his wins or losses—that was just a question of luck—the point was about his father's word. Rama feared his father was not to be trusted. It was a conclusion he had long avoided, even after taking an angry blow for innocently receiving a share of Lee's Trujillo's winnings. Such had been his childish adoration that it had once blinded him to his father's foibles, even those that were threatening. But it was not a child who sat at Doris's table this morning.

"Yeah Mom, I've got a heck of an appetite. Only had a leftover hamburger for dinner." He peered beyond his mother at four pancakes already browning on the griddle.

Rama was happy to change the subject from his father to his mother's good fortune. "Ivar came through, huh? He said he'd find you a doctor…probably be a good one. Did the paper come yet?"

Over an abundant breakfast, Doris fussed with the crossword puzzle while Rama looked through the sports section. He noticed an Argentinean golfer had prevailed at the British Open and recalled Mesquite Creek's old gaucho,

Carlos Taddio. Rama picked up the front page but quickly discarded it; the accounts of a new offensive in Vietnam—bad news for mothers who would give anything to share one more breakfast with their sons—remained unread.

"So, Mom, when is Dad coming by?"

"He said in the afternoon after he took care of some paperwork," replied Doris. "He's taking me out for dinner afterward," she smiled. "Going to make a real date out of it."

Doris touched Rama's hand lightly. "I am just so pleased that your father is coming to his senses. You know, I don't think we ever fell out of love; it's just that since the war he has grown so troubled, so distant…" She paused to catch her breath as if the memories alone were fatiguing.

Doris nudged the platter of pancakes Rama's way. "Maybe he and I are getting to the point where we can finally help each other," she paused, "in our weaknesses, if you know what I mean."

"Yes ma'am," said Rama, worried that he might know more of his father's weakness than he should.

"You know, your father is ready to give up that terrible little apartment and come home." Doris looked across the table to the empty chair and out the window. "It's worth a try. We won't get many more chances to be together as a family…in this house."

Doris noticed Rama didn't brighten at the thought. "Of course I'd get after him to help out with things. A few repairs are so overdue, and you are in over your head with golf and the garden."

Rama didn't want to pursue this conversation for fear he would subvert his mother's faith. Until now he had not realized how strong his protective instincts had become, nor had their companionship ever registered as so valuable. He felt deeply—from far beyond the reach of logic—that he and his father could not share such a place in this home. It was time for him to leave. It was going to hurt.

"Sorry Mom, I guess I could have done more, especially in your garden. I'm not much of a hand with plants and stuff," Rama replied honestly. "I know I've probably spent too much time at Bluff Meade lately."

"Honey, no. That just might be your destiny. Que sera sera, I always say."

"No, you always *sang*, Mom."

"You remember that?"

Rama would never forget. He stood up from the table and stacked a few dishes for a trip to the sink. "Patti Page, right?"

Doris lingered at the table with the newspaper. She heard Rama's voice ring out from the kitchen.

"I'm off. Got an afternoon bag. Be home about seven. Good luck with Dad."

She looked out the window as Rama, hunched over his old bicycle's handlebars, swooped out of the driveway toward Crutchfield Lane. He held the rusty old golf club before him, looking for all the world like Don Quixote. She had to laugh.

After he had disappeared around the corner, her laughter turned to tears.

———•———

"Where have you been hiding her?" asked a wide-eyed Jimmy Jim after cracking a pretty 240-yard drive with Rama's old brassie. "She's got a little magic left in her."

Rama told Jimmy the story of Carlos Taddio recovering the lost club from the rocks out at Mesquite Creek, Texas, in the dead of night. "First time I swung it, Jimmy, a train whistle blew right in my downswing…swear to God."

"Yeah, you've always had a good imagination, Schwain."

The two golfers, armed with Rama's brassie and a collection of Jimmy's fish sticks, headed out for a quick thirty-minute circuit of their course. Jimmy, who had played some almost-good-enough golf before giving up the quest for glory in favor of greens keeping, enjoyed winning four-bit bets from his young friend while generously showing off a few pointers. But today he found the going against Rama a little harder than before.

"Damn, Schwain, you play much better than this and I'm gonna have to bring a jar of quarters along."

A congenial smile sprang from his broad burnished face. Years in the weather had augmented his handsome Indian features with a rich helping of folds, crags, and creases. The friendly face wrinkled in admiration of Rama's growing skill and in thanks to the Gods of Golf for finally delivering a challenging partner to share what was left of his game. He liked to think his lessons had done some good.

"Shit, you'll be in the chips like old Wedgy at the rate you're going," laughed Jimmy.

"Yeah, I heard he won yesterday."

"Won? Let's just say he walked off with the money," Jimmy sighed. "Wedgy has a way of doing that. Charlie interfered with Ivar's winning putt…cost Ivar two strokes. I wonder how much that little trick with Ivar's flag-stick cost Wedgy?"

Jimmy set the bucket of sticks back in the maintenance shed and hopped aboard a small tractor to get on with the day's mowing.

"You don't think Charlie and Wedgy were in cahoots, do you?" asked Rama.

"I don't know, Rama; they kicked old Wedgy's ass out of here for a reason way back when," Jimmy shouted over the tractor. "I wouldn't put it past him. And that Vestal kid…forget about it. It's bad enough that people lose their money when the game's on the up and up. Shit, the starter told me some poor vet lost big on that little match. Imagine how that poor bastard feels?"

The tractor lurched forward. "You know, I always feel like Arnold Palmer when I start this thing up," Jimmy laughed at the memory of Arnie's Pennzoil ads. "Gotta get seventeen and eighteen done before they realize I've been fucking off. Adios."

Rama watched the tractor rumble off, and although he stood in the warm July sun, he felt a chill as he turned toward the caddie shack. The fleeting sight of his father and now Jimmy's report was a disturbing coincidence. It didn't help his mood either that Ivar, the most honorable man at Bluff Meade, might possibly have fallen victim to collusion between Charlie Vestal and this Wedgy character. He hated to believe that Charlie would have blocked that putt, but that wasn't even the point; now he feared that his father might have been robbed right along with Ivar. The sunny day turned suddenly black.

As Rama approached the clubhouse he passed a couple of members and their caddies heading out onto the course. The two caddies carefully maneuvered to avoid eye contact with him. He usually would have made an effort to capture their attention, but today he wasn't in a mood to patronize anyone.

"Rude snobs," he muttered. "What's their problem?"

He entered the caddie shack, hoping to leave his gloom at the door, but the boys in the shack went out of their way to avoid him, too. Even Agunstus was short on words. The caddie master looked uncomfortable at his desk and made a show of sorting through some papers before Rama pinned him down.

"Well hello to you, too," Rama frowned. "What's with everyone down here? Nobody will even look at me."

Agunstus stirred slightly, hoping to avoid mentioning the petition Charlie had talked the other caddies into signing against Rama's membership in the caddie corps. The caddie master glanced nervously around to be sure the other caddies were gone. "Look, Schwain, that petition idea…that wasn't official. You can tell them all to take a hike. They don't really have a leg to stand on. I do the hiring and the firing."

Rama looked at Agunstus blankly; he didn't know what petition the man was talking about. Agunstus had mistakenly attributed Rama's dark mood to rejection by his peers.

"As a matter of fact, it's bullshit," cried Agunstus, jumping to his feet. "Charlie's little power play has gone on long enough." The caddie master strode to the bulletin board and, with some satisfaction, tore Charlie's carefully worded petition from the cork. "Don't worry, Schwain; you're still on for three o'clock with Guidance." Agunstus began to ball the paper up when Rama stopped him.

"A petition? I never heard anything about a petition? For what?"

Agunstus reluctantly tossed the balled-up document to Rama. "Like I said, it's bullshit."

Rama read the wrinkled petition and learned that he was not wanted at Bluff Meade—at least not by his fellow caddies. He recognized every name signed to the bottom of Charlie's elegant document. And to think the day had started out so nicely.

"Toss it, Schwain," suggested the caddie master. "And forget it."

Rama stuck the rumpled paper back on the board with the remaining thumbtacks, his fingers quivering slightly with the effort. "Tell Ivar Guidance to take more time in his back swing today…and to keep his elbow in," Rama said quietly. He walked to the door considering the usual box of donuts on the way, but his appetite wasn't what it used to be. He left empty handed.

Agunstus stood alone in the caddie shack as the door closed behind the best caddie he had ever seen at Bluff Meade. Some members were going to be plenty upset at this loss. "Crap," he cursed. "Damned if Vestal didn't have Rama figured." Agunstus remembered Charlie, freshly embarrassed—or so it appeared—by the incident on eighteen, saying that Schwain wasn't the type to put up a fight. And now it looked as if the vindictive caddie was right.

Outside the caddie shack, Rama angrily fussed with his bike's kickstand as Agunstus rushed out the door, holding an envelope.

"Come on, Schwain, don't quit. I can sort things out with these punks and with Charlie soon as the little chicken shit gets back from Political Action Camp. You're not the only one who's pissed at his behavior." The caddie master nearly pleaded. He knew there were several influential members of Bluff Meade who wouldn't be happy if he let Rama slip away and they all had to return to the lackluster games they had suffered before the charmed caddie entered their world.

Rama said nothing. He couldn't imagine fighting Charlie Vestal for a crime he couldn't prove, and he wasn't going to linger in a place where over a dozen signatures said he wasn't wanted.

"Hang on, Schwain; before you disappear take this envelope. It showed up on my desk this morning."

"Great, more fan mail." Rama scrunched the letter into his hip pocket, and dropped his full weight onto the pedals. With the midday sun on his shoulder and his future thoroughly adrift, he rode past the regal facade of the great clubhouse. Rama wished he had left the imposing old building where it had always been in his mind: an unapproachable white mansion populated by nameless people harboring untold stories. He wished he had remained just another passerby down on Crutchfield Lane.

Ivar, Jimmy, and even Pep were the happy counterpoint to a drumbeat of selfish souls plodding through the good life and lousy golf at Bluff Meade. He would miss the game he had come to respect with Ivar and to understand with Jimmy Jim. Maybe he could pick it up again on a municipal course someday—strictly for fun. The days of generous tips and wealthy customers bidding for his services down in the locker room were over. The handicaps of the members he served would rise again to their rightful levels of mediocrity, and Roland Bandon would ponder the change—another mathematical anomaly—right under his nose.

In his heart Rama always knew his departure from Bluff Meade was inevitable; a mere game could not shield him from the realities of the world indefinitely. Education, employment, and Vietnam each possessed its own gravity—he would soon feel their pull, but for the moment, as he soared down the magnolia-lined driveway armed with the old night lessons club, he felt a curious sense of freedom and anger at being cut free of the comfortable gig at Bluff Meade.

He stopped at the intersection with Crutchfield, unsure whether to take a left back toward home or a right toward everything else. As he straddled the bike, he felt the letter Agunstus had given him stuffed uncomfortably in his pants pocket. At this moment of indecision, the unopened letter begged to be read. Rama hopped from the bike and ripped open the envelope:

Greetings Mr. Schwain:

*I am departing soon on a professional tour of
California and the Southwest, and am in need of a
qualified caddie. Your friends Dustin Pepper and
Wessel Waddley have highly recommended your services.*

*I would like to offer you the opportunity to apply for
this lucrative job if it doesn't conflict with your
present commitments.*

*If interested, I will be reviewing candidates at the
Kings Kreek Golf Center on Monday afternoon.
I'll be waiting,*

W. Byrne

Rama glanced up from the letter into a group of inconsequential clouds drifting against the sky. He tried to remember either Pep or Wessel talking about a Mr. Byrne, but he drew a blank although the name seemed familiar. The offer sounded interesting, especially under the circumstances. Rama reckoned it was about one o'clock, still plenty of day left to ride the ten miles or so over to Kings Kreek and get home by dark. He slid the letter back into his pocket and tucked the old brassie behind some shrubs beneath Bluff Meade's welcome sign.

The chugging of a feeble engine suddenly filled the air as a tired old Renault turned into the drive. Rama ducked out of sight as the car labored up the hill. The car's driver, Ivar Guidance, was anxious to meet Rama on the tee and to put the bitter taste of his loss to Wedgy behind him. As his generous bene-factor climbed the drive, Rama rose high on his pedals and sped down toward Kings Kreek, anxious to see what W. Byrne's employment "opportunity" was all about.

Chapter 37

"Late...damn it!" Hank pounced on the accelerator. A glance at the dashboard confirmed he was already ten minutes behind schedule. It wasn't like he had a good excuse, not unless sleeping off a half-bottle of Old Crow would fly as an alibi for showing up late for his date with Doris. But after yesterday's disastrous loss, who could blame him? He had gone from the heights of expectation to despair in less than twenty-four hours.

Hank's depressed condition wasn't improved by the fact that he had fallen asleep in front of the television. A bleak parade of daytime programming had fouled his dreams as he sprawled on his sofa. Waking to a bankrupt reality from the announcer's cheerful dribble offered no relief. The thought of trudging through the motions of what should have been a pleasant date this evening now felt like a cruelty. Faking happiness under the hopeful eyes of Doris would be a terrible fraud.

Saturday morning's optimism that Sunday's match would deliver him from Monday's debt had moved him to add a glider ride at Aero Meadows and a fine dinner to today's agenda. But now, thanks to Rama's inexplicable abandonment of Ivar Guidance, he was a loser again. The ransacking of Rama's college fund and the foolish purchase of the glider could no longer be reimbursed or explained away. The right thing—the healthy thing—Hank recognized, would be to face the music and admit his errors in judgment. He shivered at the thought of such honesty. Doris would be hurt, and God knows she had been hurt enough, but he guessed she could handle it. But could he?

A donut and a cup of instant coffee fortified him against a hangover and mixed emotions as he swung the Rambler into Monday morning's traffic. Although late he was up and moving in a busy world, even though it threatened him like a noose.

—•—

Doris had spent half a day in limbo, unsure whether she should attempt to start anything productive or just give in to Hank's promise of a great date.

She chose to give Hank the benefit of the doubt, even though he had disappointed her in the past. After tiring of the *New Yorker,* she wandered through the garden to take stock of summer's blossoms. Her face brightened when the Rambler finally pulled into the drive.

Even from the depths of his bluest thoughts, Hank couldn't resist Doris's smile, nor could he restrain the bright shades of affection that persisted after such a beleaguered relationship. He watched her return from the garden; her smart, mod slacks and a sleeveless blouse seemed bold acquisitions to a usually conservative wardrobe. He smiled that she had dressed so fashionably just for him and hoped that his double dose of toothpaste, a quick shave, and a shower would hide his rugged condition. As Hank stepped onto what was still his own driveway, he felt like an intruder.

"You're looking very handsome, Mr. Schwain," Doris chirped.

"And you, too…" Hank stammered. "Beautiful, I mean."

Doris allowed him a kiss on her cheek, then suggested he inspect the flowers while she grabbed a sweater.

"You did bring Trent's registration papers?" Doris asked. "Perhaps we can look over their tuition fees while we eat. Heavens, I have such an appetite."

Hank was not particularly eager to hurry the moment of financial truth and mentioned that the surprise he had promised had to be claimed before dark.

"Oh, we can hurry, Hank. Take me to Ringlers if you like. Burgers would be like old times, huh?"

Hank nodded and held the Rambler's door open for Doris. Even as he rushed to face the music, Doris was serene in her ignorance of his losses. On their last get-together, he had vowed a break from gambling's grip and a return to his boyish passion—flying. She had no reason to believe he had strayed. Hank nearly cringed at her confidence.

"Damn, you *are* looking gorgeous, Doris. How are you feeling?"

"Good days, bad days. Starting today I have a new doctor, but best of all, Rama seems so happy lately. Do you know your son earned an eighty-three-dollar tip yesterday? Can you imagine?" The thrill at her son's good fortune was palpable. "And you're here…guess that would make this one of the good days."

"Eighty-three bucks. How'd he do that?"

"One of the fellows at the club made a hole-in-one yesterday. One of Rama's players. How lucky can you get? One in 12,000 odds, Rama said."

Hank struggled to show enthusiasm for the great event. But he wished he could have asked what the odds were that his man, Ivar, would be distracted on the seventeenth hole and lose his lead, thanks to Rama's man's damned ace.

"Son of a gun, whatever that boy touches just seems to turn to gold."

Hank struggled to hold his tongue. If he could have, he would have jumped on the brakes and screeched to a stop. He would have turned to Doris and yelled, "But why not me? Why did he fail me?"

If he'd had the courage, Hank would have released the strings that held all his lies in place and watched them vanish in a freshening wind. He would have revealed all his deceptions and buried his head in her lap and cried tears of absolution onto her bright boutique slacks.

"Imagine that, a hole-in-one," he said vacantly.

In a minute Doris's '88 had rumbled past Ringlers. "We've got a little time; we can do better than burgers...how 'bout Chicken in the Rough?" suggested Hank.

"Sounds good to me, Dear." Doris tossed the folder for Trent Institute of Landscape Technology to the dashboard and settled into her seat. She smiled at Hank. "You brought your checkbook, right?"

— • —

"Landscaping...who would have imagined Rama in landscaping?" Doris exclaimed over coffee and spumoni. "My gosh, there was a time I couldn't get that boy to mow the lawn without an argument. I thought he was only going to Trent to make his gardener mother happy, but since he has become friends with that Cherokee fellow up at the club, he has taken an interest in golf course design.

"Those classes are costly, Hank, but the fellows at Bluff Meade have pulled a few strings and made this affordable for us: $7,500 not counting the deposit. We just have to fill out these financial need forms. Shouldn't be too hard to make us look needy I fear," Doris chuckled. "Of course, you've already sent the deposit."

"Yeah, I sent a check back in June...or early July." Hank couldn't bring himself to say the check was bad.

"Funny, I don't think Rama has seen any registration materials from them since then. They are going to need half of the balance with these papers. Maybe I should call."

"No, Doris, you've got enough troubles. I wrote the check...I'll look into it. You just concentrate on that new doctor." Hank anxiously slipped the forms from their folder. "Why don't we get started, then? I've still got a surprise waiting for you." Hank pulled the incriminating checkbook from his pocket. "Send half the balance with these papers, eh?"

"I wish we could pay it all," Doris sighed. "I hate to take charity."

"Why? It's what those rich guys always do. They get deals on everything."

"I suppose," said Doris. "At least at this rate we can support Rama for two more years; isn't that right?"

Hank looked into the useless checkbook. "Yep, fifteen thousand should about cover it." A great burst of stomach acid caused him to gag for a moment.

He feared cowardice was consuming him. Without another word, he grabbed the dinner tab and stood to go.

———•———

The Oldsmobile settled to a stop outside Aero Meadows's hangar. Hank hopped out in nervous anticipation. "Now, just stay right here for a minute," he said. "Got to make a few arrangements."

Doris's eyes swept the line of small aircraft. The red Piper Pawnee had returned to base and was parked out on the tarmac near a silver glider. The craft had been freed from its tethers and her canopy propped open awaiting a pilot and passenger for the afternoon's final ride. Doris watched an orange windsock fluttering about its pole as Hank crossed the tarmac. For a moment he appeared free of all failings. She was enchanted to see him stride across the very turf of his dreams.

"Well, chalk one up for you, Bub," the pilot sang out to Hank between slurps of tepid coffee. The pilot glanced toward the woman sitting in the automobile. "Is she a looker?"

Every female obscured by shadow, distance, or clothing appeared to fit the pilot's fantasy specifications until reality revealed otherwise. Doris's colorful sleeveless blouse and bare arms attracted his attention. He winked at Hank.

Hank looked at the pilot with disdain. "Christ, she's my ex...I mean my wife," Hank said as if invocation of the word *wife* would cast away any prurient interests. "We're kind of getting back together. It's our first day out in a long time."

"And you're taking her up just before sundown. Damn, that's romantic. Should soften her up good."

"I'm not taking her up. Shit, you know I'm not a pilot...I'm just getting back into it." Hank trained his best negotiating eye on the pilot. "But listen, I'm a little tight on the old budget after buying this thing, so can we...?"

The pilot cut Hank off in mid-haggle. "Can we give her an economy ride?" he grumbled. "Christ, no wonder I ain't getting rich in this damn business."

The pilot looked out the hangar to the lengthening shadows. He noticed the grove of locust trees by the parking lot fidgeting in the wind, but he said nothing about the weather. "If you've got twenty-five bucks I can take your true love for a ride she'll always remember, but only got time for about 1,500 feet."

"That'll do," said Hank. "But one more thing: She doesn't know I bought the Little Crow."

"So don't say a word; I get it," the pilot snickered. "Damn it, you do have some budget problems there don't you, Bub? Well, your secret's safe with me. Now get your girl out of that Olds so we can have a good look at her."

———•———

Doris gasped at the frightening "pop" as the pilot released the towline clamp and hurled the glider into a steep left bank. If giving her twenty-five dollars worth of thrills was the objective, he could have leveled off and landed right then. She had already had that much value just from the anticipation of going aloft, but from the moment the glider's tiny wheel left Aero's tarmac and its rumble was replaced by the elegant rush of air over smooth metal skin, Doris's excitement could only be assessed as priceless.

She felt a fluttering sensation as the fragile craft was buffeted in the tow plane's slipstream. Was it her heart or the glider? When the craft was released from the tow plane and the intrusive whine of its engine, the sensation of flight escalated from merely exciting to sublime.

Doris looked to the north where the Mississippi glimmered in the afternoon's amber light. Trees lining the west bank cast gray shadows across the burnished water. Far up river at the edge of her vision, Doris thought she saw buildings of gold marching across the horizon: St. Louis, she wondered…or El Dorado? From her silent perch, she looked down upon two great red-tail hawks flying closely about the crest of a tall tree—the changing-of-the-guard on a huge nest they believed hidden in the branches of their towering white pine. She felt tears of joy for the birds' intractable service to the chicks lodged deep in their nest.

The glider carved several thrilling curves in the unsettled afternoon sky. "Havin' fun, Tootsie?" called the pilot over the slipstream's roar as he engaged the spoilers. "Now you'll have to hold on; it's a little too breezy for a silky landing."

Doris was disappointed. It had only been a couple of minutes since they had been swept up behind the tow plane, but she obeyed and clung to the harness at each shoulder. The pilot turned into his final approach and the glider rattled in protest.

"Is this normal?" Doris shouted impulsively.

"Never sounded like this before," replied the pilot at the top of his voice. "Shit, hope she ain't comin' unglued."

The fluttering was now definitely in Doris's chest. She held her breath as the landscape below threatened in its proximity.

—•—

"Here they come, Schwain," the mechanic called to Hank, who sat at the picnic table struggling with the Trent forms. "They're looking good…the landing could be *interesting*, though."

Hank stopped for a moment, but he didn't look to the sky. Instead he extracted his checkbook and considered his actions. Perhaps he could buy some more time. He might fool Trent for a few more weeks, but not Doris. Without another thought he dashed off his second bad check to Trent. He tucked the check in with the paperwork and licked the return envelope irrevocably shut before stepping out to watch his wife's first landing.

Doris was paralyzed with fear that the flimsy little aircraft would undo itself in mid-air. The pilot wasn't making their last seconds of flight any easier with his frantic pleas to "just hold together baby" and "get us down in one blessed piece." The hangar lay just ahead and Doris could see the greasy mechanic and Hank standing at the edge of the landing strip. Then, with a sickening feeling, the glider seemed to stall. She gasped and waited for the unthinkable plunge to the ground. For a moment she understood the horror that had always haunted her husband.

But it was just a trick. The pilot had brought the glider in higher than usual, knowing that in a strong headwind he would have minimal ground speed and could descend with little forward progress—like an elevator. It was a dangerous trick: If the wind slackened, they really would fall from the sky. But after thirty-eight years of flying in this corner of the Volunteer State, the pilot was certain of mid-summer's afternoon air. After he had given his passenger a good fright, he trimmed up the rudder. The rattling stopped and the glider simply settled to the ground.

After the Little Crow was safely on terra firma, the pilot threw open the canopy. "Whew wee...made it back alive!"

Doris still held her breath in fear and amazement at the unexpected elevator-like landing and in wonder at the hawks and the golden city. Hank walked casually to the open craft to help his wife deplane. He was stunned to see her ashen face and noticed her white knuckles still clinging to the harness.

"You okay, Honey?"

A feeble smile and some color returned to Doris's face. She still couldn't manage speech. Hank looked accusingly at the pilot who held his hands up in surrender.

"Hey, Bub, you wanted to give the little lady a ride she'd never forget... voilà," replied the pilot as he helped Doris undo her buckles.

"Just kidding around up there to make it interesting. Fun, huh?" he asked. Before Doris could answer he looked at the trees bowing gracefully beside the runway and turned to Hank. "It was getting a little bumpy up there. Probably gave her a little more than your money's worth."

The pilot stepped out of the glider and began a slow inspection circuit around the craft just for good measure. Satisfied that all was well, he slapped its wet skin.

"Worth every damn dime, this little bird is," he winked at Hank.

Chapter 38

Rama peddled hard to leave Bluff Meade Country Club behind. The one-two punch of the other caddies' rejection and the nagging disenchantment with his father fueled a furious ten-mile ride down to Kings Kreek Golf Center to find Mr. W. Byrne and perhaps a ticket out of town. A cool, encouraging breeze cut through his damp shirt as he approached the bizarre structure that served as the King's pro shop.

The owner of Kings Kreek, in an epiphany of marketing brilliance had long ago decided that the entire building housing his business should resemble a crown and had constructed an appropriately regal facade bejeweled with shattered mirror shards, soda bottles, and chromium hubcaps. But the golden paint and the sparkling glory of the architectural oddity had since decayed to a condition unworthy of royalty. As a child, Rama had always admired the crown from the window of his mother's car but until today had never entered the Kingdom. He paused at the golden door before charging inside to find an icy soda and the whereabouts of Mr. Byrne.

After pulling a Coca-Cola from the icy waters of the King's beverage chest, Rama approached the counter with a quarter and a question. The counter was manned by an old fellow dozing over a copy of *Golf Digest*. His shaggy gray hair peeked down from beneath a red plaid tam-o'-shanter as he nodded over the magazine—threatening to drool on the industry's latest swing tips. Rama rattled a plastic cup full of scoring pencils to draw the old fellow back from his dreams of lush fairways and par-or-better women. The old proprietor raised his head and brightened for a second.

"Was that you I just heard rooting around in the cooler?" he asked. "Suppose you paid, eh, matey?" If there was any golf royalty left in this old fellow's bones it was obscured by a sallow face and a liberal sprinkling of liver spots.

"Not yet," Rama replied as he slipped his quarter across the counter. "You sure keep 'em nice and cold."

"Fit for a king, matey. So what are we working on today—short game or long game?"

Rama wished he were working on a game, but game improvement was off his agenda for the time being. "Neither one, sir. I'm just looking for Mr. Byrne. He said to meet him here."

"Oh, you're looking for Wedgy…aye aye," said the old man. "He's staying over in the campground. Been there for a few days already."

"Did you say Wedgy?"

"Don't know a lot of other W. Byrnes," huffed the proprietor. "You might find him on the range."

Rama was shocked. He hadn't guessed what the *W* stood for. If Ivar had ever mentioned Wedgy's last name, Rama hadn't heard. So there he was, after a hot sweaty ride looking up the very hustler who, if Jimmy Jim was right, had cheated Ivar and might have won some—maybe lots—of what Rama still believed to be his father's hard-earned money. It was a small and unfair world.

"He's not on the range. Is he on the course?" asked Rama.

"Wedgy is wherever Wedgy wants to be, matey. Doesn't pay me to keep an eye on him," said the old man, anxious to return to his dreams. "He was camping just down the lane alongside the course in those willows. You'll find him."

Rama left the old man in the crown and rode past the range into a thick poplar grove. After a few hundred yards the trees receded to make room for the King's par three course. A half-dozen campsites dotted the clearing around the first tee. One was occupied by an old pickup truck with a homemade camper, its inhabitants still homeless a generation after the dustbowl; another was occupied by a blue Lincoln Continental pulling a Luv Bug trailer.

The driver of the Lincoln sat on the end of the picnic table dangling his feet and swatting golf balls scattered in the grass beneath his toes. Several beer bottles and an empty shag bag lay on the table beside him. Rama stopped his bike and watched in silence as the sturdy, itinerant golfer took slow, effective swings with only his left arm. No question; Wallace Byrne and Wedgy were the same shifty character. Wondrously, Wedgy managed not only to contact the balls from his perch on the picnic table, but he skillfully lofted lazy, one-handed shots from the thick grass, through the crook of a willow tree, and high into the air. One by one the balls landed about fifty yards beyond and, more or less, within the vicinity of a small domed green. A few managed to find a resting place near the bright yellow flag.

"Don't you ever hit the tree, Mr. Byrne?"

Wedgy swung around to face the intruder. A smug grin gave way to a gravelly laugh. "Well, well, let me guess: Mr. Rama Schwain, the legend of Bluff Meade. The trees…can't say that I ever hit this one, but I've hit my share of others."

Rama took a few steps forward and looked through the crook out to the constellation of old golf balls scattered around the green. He turned back toward Wedgy. The shopworn golfer perched on the picnic table didn't appear threatening, nor did he fit Rama's image of a golf hustler. If Wedgy had made much money at his chosen trade, including yesterday's victory over Ivar, it didn't show except for a single, substantial gold ring on his right hand.

Wedgy eased himself down off the table. His feet had cramped up as they dangled, and now with his considerable weight upon them, they protested. He grabbed the shag bag off the table and headed for the constellation, walking as if on nails until his feet limbered up.

"C'mon while I fetch those balls," Wedgy said, wielding the shag bag. "I'm guessing you're looking for a job." Wedgy zipped the bag closed with a jerk and looked up at Rama. "Or are you coming down here to whine about that little fuck-up on eighteen yesterday? There are folks that think I actually put Ivar's caddie up to screwing with that putt. Christ, somebody should give that kid some credit. We're all in deep shit if his generation can be bought off for a lousy buck."

Rama hadn't come to discuss the putt. Although he was angry at Charlie for the petition, he was just as anxious to believe that the rival caddie would not commit such a blatant crime, and he was more than willing to believe Wedgy's lie. A fellow couldn't be blamed for winning, even as the consequence of another's blunder.

Wedgy, having dispatched the truth, was eager to receive a demonstration of the Gift Dustin Pepper had drunkenly revealed in the Bunker Room last night. "You up for a little game? Maybe some pitch and putt?" Wedgy asked. "Just around the green."

"Well, I don't really play," Rama answered cautiously.

"I've heard from a few of your customers up on the hill that you're one hell of a caddie. Got a knack for it. Shit, you've gotta play," insisted Wedgy.

Rama just shrugged. He, too, could toy with the truth. Instinctively, he held his cards face down, unsure where this game might lead.

Wedgy walked gingerly across the grass to the first ball, lying about thirty feet off the green. "Well, if you *did* play, you'd be mistaken not to work on these short shots. They've kept me in business." He dropped the shag bag and waggled his wedge, then popped up a crisp little lob that stopped ten feet short of the hole.

"Shit, closer would be a damn sight better," he swore. "The older we poor bastards get, the more we need these shots. Up and downs keep us going 'til some luck comes our way…like somebody forgetting to pull the other guy's flagstick." Another gravel laugh escaped the hustler's lungs.

Rama was inclined to believe Wedgy. His apprehensions softened as he watched the over-the-hill golfer work his way around the domed green— pitching, popping, bumping, scuffing, running, and lobbing balls toward the elusive yellow flag in a tedious effort to forestall the inevitable decline in his final bastion against unemployment—his short game. The efforts didn't appear to be paying off. Too many balls came to rest too far from the pin for Wedgy's liking. But as Rama's appreciation of the hustler's sincere efforts bloomed, his empathy for the ragged old fellow's vulnerability warmed, and as it did Wedgy's stroke became pure and faultless. One by one the balls found their way closer and closer to the flag.

Rama watched intently, hoping to absorb Wedgy's technique around the green as Wedgy fell happily under the spell of the Caddie's Gift. Wedgy was taken with the unusually unerring perfection of his own shots. He moved quickly, setting up his stance and posture with the relaxed efficiency of a good pianist knocking off a Chopin etude.

After about forty balls crowded around the flag, Wedgy grabbed the shag bag and admired his work before plucking up all the balls. He felt a spasm of laughter stirring deep in his belly, and finally had no choice but to stand there beneath the willows' waving shadows and let his disbelief go. The gravel fell away and he laughed with the clarity of new organ pipes.

"Now that's more like it. A short game like that would put a fellow in the chips," he beamed. Pep and Wessel had not been bluffing; it was true what he had heard about this caddie. With Rama on his bag he might hold the game's quicksilver skills in his grasp another season or two longer. No doubt about it, Rama had passed Wedgy's examination.

"Yeah, Hogan's got nothing on you Mr. Byrne," Rama replied, and for the moment he was probably right.

"Got two beers left," said Wedgy. "Let's celebrate."

Rama accepted a cool Pabst from Wedgy's ice bucket. The world that only an hour ago had turned against him had now turned back toward new possibilities. "Celebrate what?"

"My new caddie," exclaimed Wedgy with a raised Blue Ribbon.

Rama's liberation was immediately tested. "Who said anything about caddying?" he protested. "Here in town maybe, but you're going on the road, right?"

"Yep, but what difference does that make? I'd cover most of your expenses," said Wedgy. "Now don't tell me you rode all the way down here if you weren't interested."

Wedgy lowered his toast and took a long, noisy slurp from the beer. He belched deeply before continuing. "How old are you? Nearly twenty? Just about a full-time caddie 'til you lost your job, right? Now where in hell does that leave you?"

Rama looked at Wedgy suspiciously, "How do you know I lost that job? I just quit an hour ago."

Wedgy looked away uneasily. He dropped a ball onto his sand wedge and bounced it off the face several times like a rubber ball on an elastic band. "Well, I try to keep up to date. I heard about Charlie's little mutiny," he said. "I figure you had too much pride to stick around for that abuse. You haven't got any better plans, I'd wager."

Rama was taken off guard by Wedgy's assessment. "Not for the rest of the summer anyway, but I might be going to school in the fall." The *might* still troubled Rama because he still hadn't heard back from Trent Institute or his father. He had never ventured to connect his father's troubles to the school's unresponsiveness.

"School?" Wedgy screwed up his face as if he'd tasted something bitter. "Come on, Rama. Just between you and me: You don't look like the college type. The money gets real good out here in the fall—about the time we hit the Sun Belt."

The old golf hustler popped up his ball from the shiny clubface and caught it in mid-air. "Rama, it's the seventeenth of July. Ain't it getting kind of late for *might* be going to school? I'm betting there's some bullshit in your background. You really need a change of scene…a job. Now use your head. If we start working together, we'll both win."

Rama sipped self-consciously on his beer and stared out through the willow branches into the King's shaggy fairway. He recalled his mother telling him that she was planning on reuniting with Hank. Rama had often imagined the moment his father might take his place back in the family. The reunion had once played hopefully in his young mind—the welcome resumption of a secure childhood. But afternoons shooting hoops alone in the driveway with a hopeful ear tuned to the sound of each car decelerating from Crutchfield had long ago proved too discouraging a test of his faith. His father's car rarely arrived, and H-O-R-S-E with an imaginary partner had its limits.

Over time the sketch of Hank's return was rendered with less-welcoming detail: the smell of cigarette smoke rose from armloads of rumpled clothes; a poker table and a homely leather recliner protruded from the Rambler's tailgate. In this picture Rama did not rush to help his father unload the car parked on his basketball court.

Wedgy followed Rama's eyes out into the shadows of the empty fairway. The two sat quietly, lingering over the last of their beer. Wedgy bided his time wisely and took a deep breath. "Just chipping the ball around in the evening like this reminds a fella what a pure joy this game can be." It was almost as if Wedgy had picked Chandler Stone's romantic vision of the game's essential pleasures from Rama's mind.

"I've been out early mornings when the air is clean and sharp, when even a crappy little course like this one is charmed with a Cypress Point-kind of mystery—for a few minutes anyway—before it disappears like a vampire with the sun," gushed Wedgy. "Takes your mind right off your troubles…most of 'em anyway."

Rama could relate to the mystery. He felt increasingly comfortable with Wedgy's proposition. Suddenly, in a flash of color a flock of yellow finches rose from the shiny green rhododendron foliage and flickered like tiny flames to the fairway.

Wedgy noticed a longing in Rama as the sensitive young man peered up the fairway toward the flame-birds. At that moment Wedgy knew exactly what Rama needed to hear.

"Rama, when you get out on the road and you're scouting some fine forgotten course at first light…" Wedgy's eyes wandered off into his own fantasy. "Sometimes being in the middle of nowhere with no one to bother you is exactly what a man needs, huh?

"Take yours truly, for example. As long as I can get out every once in a while—just me and a long shadow—seems like I can keep the flame alive… money or no money. Now I don't suppose those wooly old farts out in St. Andrews ever intended for someone to make a living at a shepherd's game or to screw up their lives trying, but here I am—I'm on the road and I'm free. I've got a trailer for three-quarters of the year, and a little house up in Sage Hills, Washington, that the damn mice are probably chewing into pulp right about now. I'll be honest: I'm making a buck at it…but it's not getting any easier at my age."

Wedgy fixed his most persuasive expression on his would-be caddie. "You know that we're peas in a pod, Rama. For Christ sake, we were both tossed out of Bluff Meade; that damn near makes us a team. Face it: You need to get out of Dodge and I need a regular caddie with a little inspiration and a lot of whatever it is they tell me you've got. Hell, look at those chips I just hit. Christ, I could throw a hula-hoop down around the lot of them. *That's* what I'm talking about. There's no way that is business as usual, and that is exactly the business I'm after, Mr. Rama Schwain."

Rama was mesmerized by Wedgy's sales pitch. He hadn't expected the beer-drinking hustler camped along the area's worst golf course to be so loquacious. He remained silent as Wedgy continued.

"Like I said, I'll pick up the tab for your motel room when it's practical, but mostly you'll be bunking in the trailer. Then I'll tip you twenty dollars a round in competition and pay you 5 percent of the winnings. And sometimes that ain't bad."

Wedgy fiddled with the wrapper on a new pack of Pall Malls. "Starting tomorrow," he announced, "I am chasing this dream south down to Shreveport, Baton Rouge, then through Houston, San Antonio, and El Paso. Got plenty of old friends along this swing who are happy to give me their money and plenty of strangers who don't know any better.

"Then we're going to Albuquerque, Tucson, Phoenix, and Palm Springs to get through the winter. There's usually plenty of pigeons roosting with the snowbirds out there." Wedgy laughed while looking to see if Rama was tickled by ornithological humor, but Rama only listened.

Wedgy continued his travelogue undeterred: "Might even play up the California coast. There are always some sailors or marines betting over their heads in 'Diego and Oceanside. And if I can still scare up a few old connections in Hollywood, we might brush shoulders with some fame at Riviera. God willing, we might even get a few rounds out on Seventeen Mile Drive…perhaps pick a few touristas' pockets while they gape at the view."

Wedgy grew reverent as he contemplated the Pacific pilgrimage. "Now talk about long shadows, Rama. Imagine Cypress Point at sunset…or Pebble… or Pelican." The old hustler had just about talked himself back onto the road but still had to tangle with a Coleman stove and a half-pound of dangerously under-refrigerated hamburger for dinner.

"Train leaves here tomorrow, Rama."

Rama was unfamiliar with the golf courses and most of the locales Wedgy was describing. Up to that point he had set foot on only two courses and had struck only one shot in competition. There was honesty in Wedgy's affection for the game and romance in the thought of chasing the summer out into the desert and then off into a Monterey fog bank.

Rama worked hard to keep his interest and his ignorance concealed. He set his empty bottle down on the table, a little giddy from the beer and from the romance of Wedgy's westward tour. He imagined the freedom on the road, but he also imagined his mother returning exhausted from the garden. Who would wake her or cover her against the night's draft if she fell asleep on the sofa? Or who would help her if she fell further ill…unless his father stepped in?

The evening threatened Rama with a long dark ride home. As intrigued as he was by Wedgy's offer, it was time to move on to the more substantial world beyond the out-of-bounds stakes of Wedgy's endless course.

"Thanks for the beer, Mr. Byrne," Rama said. "I don't think I can leave home now, but it looks like you'll do okay with that short game. You've got other applicants for the job, right?"

The old hustler looked irritated that he had wasted his breath and a perfectly good Pabst. He snatched away Rama's empty can and tossed it into the woods. "Applicants," he scoffed, "yeah, got *dozens* of 'em."

Wedgy raised his voice: "Christ, kid, if no one ever left home, where in the hell would we all be now?" One of the dust bowlers peered out from their rig across the clearing with interest in the "feller that drives the blue Lincoln." The Okie apparently had the answer.

"Damn it, Schwain, you disappoint me. You'll have to go sooner or later, but don't be like most people and just creep from one safe place to another… or get pushed out because you've got no choice. Shit! Then you might as well stay home with your Momma."

Wedgy tossed his shag bag and club into the back seat of the Lincoln. "I was just bullshitting about other try-outs for this job. There are plenty of greedy kids looking for a tip if I get too tired to haul my own bag. It's just that none of them are gonna have that spark of yours."

Wedgy turned a disappointed face toward the first shades of dusk. "Bet you've got quite a ride back, eh?" he gestured toward the bicycle leaning against the picnic table. "Stow that thing in the back of the trailer. I'll run you back to mommy and daddy."

Rama bristled. "No, it's not that far. And I can come home *as I want*. It doesn't matter."

"Hey Rah Rah, it doesn't matter to me either, but I've been thinking about that old hamburger and figure I'll be driving out for a good steak anyway. Go ahead, stow the bike before I change my mind."

Rama wasn't really looking forward to another ten-mile ride. He threw the Luv Bug's door open and found just enough room to wedge the bike in beside a tiny bed, then slammed the door shut against his handlebars.

"Mr. Byrne, you don't even have enough room for yourself in there. If I had gone with you, where was I meant to sleep...in the Lincoln?"

Wedgy looked at Rama incredulously. "That is one spacious car, kiddo. Way more room than you'd need for a good night's sleep." Wedgy's ruddy face turned up in a smile as he slid behind the wheel. "Come on, let's get you home."

Soon the ponderous automobile was laboring up Crutchfield past Bluff Meade's entrance. Wedgy saluted as they passed. "Turned out that match with Guidance was one of my best stops all year. I usually just play there to watch that crooked crowd of white-collar hypocrites eat a little roadkill. There's no money in it; everybody knows I'm gonna win, but this year I got extra lucky. They tell me this one fellow shows up and he's foolish enough to put down six grand *against* me. Poor bastard must have figured he knew something these other fools didn't."

Rama felt blood surge into his face as his loyalty to Ivar was offended, but he kept cool. "You didn't meet the guy?" Rama asked suspiciously.

"Didn't need to. Sometimes I tell the starters—the ones I trust—that I'll take a sure bet like that if they can find one. Trouble is, a bozo like that doesn't come round very often, but they keep an eye out anyway. It's worth 5-percent to them. All they told me about this clown was that he had a bad leg and a load of cash."

Wedgy whistled like an incoming mortar while his passenger stared straight ahead in silence. "You can imagine, I about shit myself after that windfall. It is kind of funny, though," Wedgy added. "There's a car salesman up the river a ways—the very thief who sold me this fine automobile—and damned if I didn't see him in the gallery a couple of times. Sure as hell had a crippled leg, too. Makes me wonder if he was the big loser."

Wedgy attempted to punch up some music on the Lincoln's radio, but two of the push buttons were jammed. He laughed as the radio finally responded with a passage midway through the "Egmont Overture." "Ah, maestro Beethoven...so what the hell would a damn car peddler have been doing throwing that kind of cash around when from what I could tell talking to him up on the lot, the damn fool didn't know shit about the game."

Rama looked perplexed: "Beethoven sold cars?"

Wedgy forged on: "Anyway, it could have been somebody else lost all that dough—maybe the place was just overrun with cripples this year." Wedgy chuckled at the thought. "At least one of 'em made my day."

Wedgy noticed that a sullen look had darkened Rama's face. "Guess you don't take kindly to jokes about gimps, eh?" With that he turned his attention back to Rama's employment.

"Now come on, my offer is still on the table. You've got something special on the golf course, but it won't mean squat if you're in some damn philosophy class. Hell, even Jesus said don't hide your candle under a bushel… remember?" Wedgy slapped the blue dashboard for emphasis and Beethoven short-circuited.

Rama listened with rising anger and confusion. How ironic could it be that a fellow who had taken a man's money was now begging that man's son to be his caddie? Obviously, Wedgy hadn't made the connection. Rama focused beyond the windshield and tried to imagine what to do.

Lee Trujillo had once returned a portion of Hank's losses, and as far as Rama was concerned Lee had a more honest claim on that money than did Wedgy to Hank's six thousand. Maybe he could simply ask Wedgy to return Hank's money in return for caddying services. But Rama knew such a proposal would not fly, even if he knew Rama was "the gimp's" son. Rama realized he was going nowhere. He knew he couldn't face or live with his father, and it was looking doubtful that Trent was going to admit him. But he had far too much pride to return to Bluff Meade. It looked like Wedgy's was the only offer on the table. Rama needed Wedgy as much as the old hustler needed him—an unsettling symbiotic relationship.

On the last mile before he and Wedgy arrived at the Schwain home, Rama resolved that he would sign on to Wedgy's caravan. While the down-sliding hustler profited by the rejuvenation of his golfing fortunes, Rama would take what Wedgy had to offer, learn what Wedgy knew, and wait for a chance to recover what had been stolen.

—•—

"Make a right turn off of Crutchfield, just past the old filling station," said Rama. He watched for Hank's car. If he were to best the wary old hustler somewhere down the road, the fact that he was Hank's son and had an obvious motive for trying to claim back his father's losses had to remain veiled.

Although Rama was still grinding on the terms of an arrangement with Wedgy, he still hadn't said yes. Wedgy feared his sales pitch was running out of time.

"Okay, okay. Maybe the Luv Bug is a bit too snug and there ain't much privacy in the back of this rig," Wedgy agreed. "I'll take a cut out of yesterday's winnings and get a decent trailer. If it's comfort you're after…shit, it'll be just like staying home."

Rama watched breathlessly as his house came up on the right. To his alarm his father's Rambler was parked beside Doris's Oldsmobile. He did not reply to Wedgy's offer.

Wedgy turned to close the deal. "So what do you say? The Pacific Ocean is a mighty spectacular sight in the fall."

"Fourth house on the left," Rama blurted. "The one with the Impala in the drive. Just pull up along the curb." Rama misdirected Wedgy two doors past his house. He didn't want Wedgy to see Hank any more than he wanted Hank to see Wedgy. Although he had a huge bone to pick with his old man, Rama didn't want Hank to assume he was in cahoots with the same fellow who had ravaged the Schwain fortune the previous day. He had been down that road before.

"Don't get out. I'll get the bike," Rama ordered as he hurried back to the trailer. With his bike in tow he signaled Wedgy to take off, the sooner the better. But Wedgy still needed an answer. He executed a U-turn then pulled the Lincoln to a stop beside Rama to play out one last hand.

"Okay, Rama: Eight percent of the winnings and a bigger trailer. I'm pulling up stakes tomorrow afternoon about three. That's the best deal you're gonna get anywhere, kid. Sleep on it." The tail lights on the Luv Bug followed the Blue Lincoln into the darkness.

A moment before, attracted by the familiar rumble of a 430 V8, Hank stepped to the living room window. He had watched as Wedgy's car pulled away from the curb and onto whatever route he guessed the cheating son-of-a-bitch golfer was bound. And there in the street, to Hank's utter disbelief, stood Rama.

Rama had noticed his father in the window before walking the bike back to the garage. The house seemed so different, so alien this evening that he almost knocked before entering. He was reticent to face his father now that he was certain of the man's deception and its high cost, but he was embarrassed at his father's weakness as well. Above all, he was fearful of disturbing his mother's abiding faith in her husband's renewal.

If it were true that Wedgy had bought the car from Hank, Rama guessed that Hank knew who had driven him home. Rama knew that his father would be disturbed by the circumstances of his son's arrival with the hustler, but he also knew that his father couldn't reveal any knowledge of yesterday's match for fear of revealing his costly backsliding so soon after his well-publicized reformation.

Rama closed the door behind him and stepped into the living room. His mother was seated on the sofa with a cup of tea held to her chest. His father was returning from his post at the window.

"Look who's home," Doris chimed. Her face was alive with satisfaction that her two men were both under her roof for the first time in a long while. She recalled the pair of birds she had seen circling their nest earlier that afternoon and brimmed at the thought. She would not understand the dance of inquiry and evasion her husband and son would soon perform. Hank wanted to know what Rama knew of his losses, and Rama wanted Hank to know that *he* knew, yet neither man wanted to trouble Doris with the truth when she was so happy for their reunion—even one charged with doubt.

"Rama Sweetheart, there's coffee in the percolator and some cake on the counter." His mother moved quickly through the essential courtesies to the real news. "You'll never guess what happened today. Your father bought me an airplane ride. My oh my, what a thrill."

"Well, it was a glider, not an airplane," Hank explained.

"My gosh, Rama, it was just gorgeous. I swear we could see halfway to St. Louis. Maybe you can talk your father into a ride," she said, smiling at Hank.

"Oh hell yeah, we'll get you up right away," Hank replied with authority. He approached Rama with the intention of rapping his son playfully on the shoulder, but his hand dropped into a feeble handshake as he entered Rama's cold aura.

"How are you, Chief? What you been doing last couple of days?"

"Been working at the course, Hank. You know...Bluff Meade." It was the first time Rama had ever addressed his father by name.

"Damn, that was some ride you came home in tonight. Got lucky hitch-hiking, eh?" Hank asked nonchalantly.

"Oh yeah, that was Wallace, one of the rich old guys from the club, or at least he used to be."

"Hell of a car," said Hank. "Is that Wallace one of your customers?"

"No, he was just in town for a big match up at Bluff Meade," Rama replied casually. "He was playing against one of my customers, Ivar Guidance—the guy I told you about the other day at lunch. Yeah, it's some car huh, suicide doors...blue interior. Did you ever get a Lincoln like that up at your lot?"

Hank hesitated. "Hmm, I don't recall. They're kind of rare." He quickly changed the subject from the car's origins. "So you caddied against your boss, then?"

"No no; I didn't caddie for either one in that match, but I wish I had. Wallace did all right money-wise, so I hear."

"Yeah?" asked Hank feigning disinterest. "What does a match fetch up there at your little club?"

Rama looked at his mother. She seemed engrossed in the dialogue. "You need a reheat on that tea, Mom?" Doris signaled yes.

"Well," Rama continued, "they don't get in too deep there from what I know—a few hundred." He watched his father's face fall slightly. "But like I said, he did all right this time. Wallace told me he won nearly six thousand dollars on a single bet against him. Can you imagine that?"

Hank reached for a pack of cigarettes and busied himself tamping a smoke. His mother gasped slightly. "Rama, my heavens, I had no idea they bet that kind of money on a golf game."

"Not usually, Mom, but somebody came in out of the blue and put down all that money against the favorite. Kind of a stupid high-risk bet, but the guy probably could afford to lose it—no big deal to him, I guess. The word up at the club is the fellow was an outsider, didn't seem to know much about the players. Might have been a war vet."

Rama took the tea cozy from the pot and poured a fresh cup for his mother. "Heavens, Rama, have you been drinking?"

"Just a beer, Mom, with Mr. Byrne…just one. We were practicing some chipping and got to talking about things," Rama said with a glance toward his father. "It's not the first beer I ever drank."

Doris forgot about the beer. "Well, the other fellow—the veteran or whatever he was—he lost all his money? My gosh that's terrible."

"Yeah, there's no chance to win it back like in cards or craps. It's pretty bad," Rama agreed. "Don't you think, Hank?"

Hank Schwain concentrated on knocking the ash from his cigarette into a plastic Big Star ashtray. "Well, there's always a few risk-takers out there," he answered vaguely, defensively. "Sometimes they win big, too."

"But gosh, Hank, for that much money you'd think he had to have known something about Ivar's chances. Everybody at Bluff Meade knew Ivar wasn't up to Wedgy's snuff as a golfer."

Hank squirmed at his son's implication that he had been unwise. He wanted to punch the wall and demand to know why his son had not been on Ivar's bag and why the unbeatable Ivar had been left so vulnerable. He wanted to justify his bet on Ivar as a sound investment with a high rate of return. And what about that irregular ending with the flagstick; how could he be held accountable for that? But Hank couldn't speak; his lips were sealed in defense of a deception.

"Didn't you say your friend Ivar had been winning a lot lately?" Hank asked facetiously. "Maybe that poor fellow who lost picked up on that fact somewhere along the line." Even now a trace of pride at his willingness to take a risk soothed his remorse for having been so foolish. Calculated risk, Hank thought; wasn't that what success was built upon?

Rama was relentless: "I guess the poor guy should have remembered that Ivar's winning streak was with me on his bag."

Hank momentarily forgot his supposed ignorance. "Well, where were...?" He choked upon the incriminating pronoun.

"Were who?" Rama echoed suspiciously.

Hank had grown weary of the treacherous conversation. "Yeah, where the hell—why the hell—are you even involved in that lousy club up there if it is riddled with gamblers and money-grubbers?"

"Well shit, Dad," Rama cursed even as his mother cringed at his new vocabulary. "Those fellas can afford to lose. To them it's just entertainment."

Hank pondered the word: Was entertainment all that the gentry of Bluff Meade played for—just a lark, irrespective of wins or losses? Hank's experience included clenched fists and a sour stomach as a horse came up short, a card turned up wrong, or a winning putt failed to drop...no matter how much money was on the line. Why? Maybe *his* father was to blame.

As a young boy, Hank had watched his father place innocuous two-dollar bets on harness races out under the lights at Moses Lake. "More entertaining when you got a few bob on them nags," his old man always said.

With the leathery hands of his wheat-farmer father steadying him, Hank would sit on the splintered railing along the track while the light-bulb numbers on the board blinked across the infield like bright constellations in the dry, dark sky. He recalled how beautiful bands of purple streamed from the depleted sunset far into the night's canopy above the racetrack. The taste of dusty turf and manure churned by iron horseshoes mingled with the smell of wild mustard growing along irrigation canals.

The memory of those nights forged a sensual link between a child's joy and the thrill of a bet. The spectacle of the races and the cheers from his father's lusty voice as the great animals swept so closely by were sublime entertainment. But now the bets were larger, the consequences more threatening. Somewhere along the line that innocence had been misplaced; there was little entertainment left in his desperate crush for a payday.

"Entertainment," Hank spat the word back at his son, "shouldn't include letting a caddie get away with blocking a winning putt."

———•———

Like the ashes from his dying cigarette, the words falling irretrievably from his lips revealed Hank's knowledge of the match. He felt nauseated and dizzy, as if that cigarette had been his first. If there was ever any doubt, now his son knew him to be a liar. His self-respect disappeared like a last puff into thin air.

Rama was not pleased to know the truth, nor was he pleased that his father knew it. He had achieved all he could from this encounter; he could not change Hank, nor would maneuvering his father into a humbling admission before Doris give Rama any satisfaction. Rama's first reaction was hope that his father would spare him and Doris any further untruths. His second reaction was anger.

Rama's heart raced as a cauldron of emotions churned within his chest. He trembled as he approached Hank. His last vestige of respect and honor for his father had now been washed away in a flood of revelation. Hank was now a stranger, but Rama wisely appreciated that his mother's happiness was deeply entwined with this stranger's character.

Rama felt that a payday was due him: for lost time, for untold stories, for unshared dreams, for unignited inspiration, and for lost love. His hands clenched. A blow might clear the air or balance the scale tipped so far off-kilter by the angry fist he had received long ago in the bottomlands beyond Mesquite Creek. It would be only fair, but such violence might destroy his mother.

Rama's arms remained at his side, his fingers uncoiled. He moved within a whisper of his father. "Since when do you have six-thousand bucks to lose? Whose money was that, Hank?"

Hank was stunned at his son's question, but he still found a way around the truth that he had depleted most of Rama's college money, that he had penned a rubber check to Trent Institute not once but twice, and that he hadn't sold a car besides the blue Lincoln in two weeks.

"Calm down, it was just a loan…Calcutta Finance," Hank whispered.

Rama cringed at the name. During Hank's poker parties with his buddies from Big Muddy's, Rama had overheard stories about Lew Raybon's late-night collection tactics. Crouched with his head against the bedroom window, Rama had learned most of his dirty jokes and founded much of his sexual imagery on the content of the used car salesmen's rude discourses. When tits and pussies weren't the subject of choice, Lew Raybon stories often were.

"Calcutta! Shit, Hank, are you trying to get killed just to make a few easy bucks? What did you put up for collateral?" Rama asked, fearful of the answer.

"Possessions…" Hank replied vaguely, "whatever would add up." Hank did not mention the glider or that it was in Rama's name. The aircraft was a secret—an impossible, unaffordable dream that Hank had clung to stubbornly through far too many setbacks. "Nothing to sweat. I have six months to return the money."

"Shit, I heard Calcutta takes a lien on their customers' houses, too."

"Don't worry, Chief," Hank said in a low voice with an eye on Doris, who seemed engaged in a new issue of the *New Yorker*. "That ain't legal…old Lew always tries to scare folks with that house repo bull."

Hank's voice returned to full volume and blew away any reservations Rama had about caddying for Wedgy. "Don't worry, son. Business is looking up and your mother and I were just talking about taking in a boarder when you drove up. That'll go a long way toward paying your college debt."

His debt? A boarder? Rama felt a shiver from the second revelation in as many minutes and turned to his mother. "Dad *and* a stranger moving in? When were you going to tell me?" he asked.

"Honey, we just decided," Doris replied sincerely. "We were just going to bring it up, but you and your father got into such a discussion."

Rama directed his father to step outside. He was through with whispering. "Why not take two boarders if it'll pay more bills, damn it, because my room is gonna be up for grabs. I'm leaving tomorrow."

Rama gripped his father's shoulder. The peaceful spirit that had generously passed to so many upon golf's peaceful greens and carefree fairways was momentarily trumped by power of a more elemental sort. "I swear that if you put Mom's health below your greedy bullshit, I will make you pay her back, even if you have to sell your gold teeth to Calcutta."

Hank looked at what had once been his bashful little Rama. Doris was right: She used to tell him that your kids are always a step ahead of you, and now, dumbfounded by his son's threat, Hank could see it was true. He gathered his breath to reply but before he could form a word, Rama released his grip and stepped back into Doris's living room.

"Mom, it is so cool that you all are finally getting back together." Rama turned to hide his face; he never could successfully float a lie before his mother.

"And yeah, I would like a ride in one of those gliders someday, Pop." Rama winked at Hank's reddening face. "What do you say?"

Hank attempted to form a casual answer, but his astonished mind gripped his vocal cords and he barely stuttered, "Sure."

In a moment, Hank had drifted back to the bedroom and Rama was sitting on the arm of the sofa beside his mother. She dropped the *New Yorker* into her lap and looked attentively at a wiser and stronger son. She thought she had seen the change that morning when he came down for breakfast, but it seemed more evident now. She intuitively knew they had a lot to talk about, but before he ever spoke, she knew where the conversation would lead. She had seen that, too.

"Sorry, Mom…guy business," Rama apologized. "What about your ride today? Could you really see halfway to St. Louis?"

Chapter 39

Halfway to Natchez, Rama fell asleep to the slapping of worn recaps against cracked asphalt. Even with the sun hanging high in the sky above his first day of freedom, he still could not resist the slide into unconsciousness. His last night at home had been just too exhausting.

After exchanging angry words with his father, he had enjoyed a lingering reminiscence with his mother that stretched deep into the night. There was nothing he could have said to adequately comfort her; Doris Schwain was already grieving for her departed son.

Without revealing motives for leaving that might have condemned his father, Rama had attempted to explain his desire for freedom in the same vague terms that a million young men before him had pitched to teary-eyed mothers.

"It's just time to move on," he had declared romantically, like some golfing Kerouac, as he tried to recreate Wedgy's image of a continent of beautiful courses stretching west toward Cypress Point.

Rama had explained that he would be caddying for a golf professional but offered no description of Wedgy's character or of Wedgy's damning connection to Hank. Mustering all the conviction he could, he had assured his mother that it was respectable work and a great opportunity, and that when Trent Institute finally came calling, he would leave the golfing adventure behind.

By three o'clock in the morning, Doris had made peace with the reality of her son's departure. "At least you aren't going off to that wicked war." She kissed his forehead as if he were still a child and, bearing a mother's lonely burden, drifted down to the room where her recently returned husband lay snoring. The remainder of the night was barely sufficient for Rama to pull his resolve and a duffle bag together.

All too soon, Rama had found himself uttering his final good-byes at the front porch as Doris clung to the wrought-iron railing for support under the weight of the inevitable. Hank had raised his eyes from his morning coffee long enough to offer his son a ride: "in case the bastard's too damn cheap to pick you up."

But Rama had preferred to ride away from home under his own power and take one last pass down Crutchfield along Meade Creek. The innocence that had so often lightened him as he sped down that shady stretch was absent now, and in its place Rama labored under the weight of awareness that by searching for some uncertain justice against Wedgy he had been skating on thin ice; sooner or later the draft board would notice that he had slipped through the cracks between Trent Institute and Vietnam.

He had pedaled up the drive to Bluff Meade to rendezvous with Wedgy and to leave a good-bye note for Ivar but had stumbled into the old gentleman by chance. Ivar had been pleased to see his gifted young caddie again but had been alarmed to learn of Rama's plans to travel with the notorious Mr. Byrne. After admonishing Rama to watch his step around Wedgy, Ivar had insisted on providing his ex-caddie with something to fall back on…just in case. He signed his name to a blank check and tucked it into Rama's shirt pocket.

"If you get into any trouble, make this out for whatever you need to sort things out…and that includes coming home if need be."

Rama recalled how Ivar's face had taken on a mischievous look, startling in its departure from the old fellow's usual dignified demeanor. "Or… if you ever see that our friend Wallace has talked himself into more match than it appears he can handle, offer the biggest damned bet he'll take… against him of course." He patted Rama's shirt pocket. "Use this check; the risk is on me."

After a moment's deliberation Ivar plucked the check from Rama's pocket and dashed off six thousand and no hundredths.

"Didn't want you to sell us short, my boy."

With business behind them, Ivar and Rama had talked until Wedgy arrived. They mused about Jack Nicklaus's recent emergence from his supposed slump and the merits of the great one's unorthodox chicken wing. Ivar assured Rama that like Jack's swing, everyone has to find his own way and that despite Charlie Vestal, there would always be a place for Rama Schwain at Bluff Meade.

As Wedgy's blue Lincoln cruised up the driveway like a shark, Ivar reminded him: "Whatever you do, keep this check and your intentions a secret."

Wedgy grinned with satisfaction at the sight of Rama seated beside Ivar on the trunk of the old Renault. When Rama had called that morning to accept the job as his caddie, Wedgy had pumped his fist at his powers of persuasion and at his good fortune for stealing Ivar's strangely gifted caddie away into a life of gamesmanship somewhat less honorable than what Ivar and his gentle friends regularly practiced.

Wedgy swooped gleefully up the magnolia-lined driveway. "The record shows I took the blows," he sang as he stepped from the Lincoln to greet the unlikely pair.

"Now, don't think I was trying to beat you out of your money *and* your caddie, Ives." Wedgy crafted the half-truth with remarkable alacrity. "Our friend Rama called *me*."

Ivar hadn't been impressed or fooled. "Wallace, you've been fishing for a miracle ever since I've known you. Once you heard Dustin Pepper shoot his mouth off about our handicap stats I knew you had fixed your sights on Rama. Can't say that I blame you," he sighed. "If you're going to hire a caddie, you might as well hire the best…and he is as close to a miracle as you're likely to see."

"Couldn't have said it better, Ives," replied Wedgy. He looked at Rama. "Toss your bag in there, wonder boy, and we'll motor on to greener *cashtures*."

In a final gesture of good will, Ivar had slapped him on the back and declared his faith that Rama would pick his way through Wedgy's minefield of vices—perhaps even elevate the shady old hustler.

"Whatever you do, Rama, keep Wallace honest. If he stiffs you for a tip, blames you for a stroke, or won't eat from the same menu as you, I want to hear about it. And Rama, my boy…keep his hands off the flagstick."

Before allowing the duo to depart, Ivar had peered into the baby blue leather interior of Wedgy's car. "Not a Presley Lincoln, that's for sure," he winked, offering his hand to his nemesis, who limply returned the unexpected gesture. Ivar's wink dissolved into piercing scrutiny.

"You take care of that young man, Wallace. There is a lot of good in him… you might learn something."

"God-damned romantic. Don't worry, Ives, he'll be fine. And hell, this little junket beats the shit out of touring Southeast Asia."

Wedgy settled in behind the wheel, but Ivar stopped him again. "One more detail, Wallace: Evidently you promised my young friend a more spacious trailer and an 8-percent slice of your winnings as terms of this forthcoming employment."

Wedgy squirmed anxiously in his seat.

"Just so you'll know, Wallace: That is a promise that, if broken, will slam the door on any profitable matches at Bluff Meade in the future."

Rama remembered how Wedgy's eyes had rolled skyward. "Christ, kid; you didn't tell me you had an *agent*." Then without another word the old hustler ignited the engine and started down the driveway. Before the clubhouse disappeared, Rama hollered a final request of Ivar:

"Keep an eye on my mom."

A moment later, as Wedgy slowed before pulling onto Crutchfield, Rama had bounded from the car to Bluff Meade's Welcome sign and recovered the battered old Night Lessons brassie from the shrubs.

"What the hell does this look like—a scavenger hunt, Rama? You got any other clubs stashed away?" Wedgy had laughed while glancing at his passenger suspiciously. "Sure you don't play, son?"

Rama had remained poker-faced as Wedgy accelerated southbound into a new morning. "Play? Who says I ever played?"

—•—

Now, five hours south of the Tennessee border, Rama slept deeply—a blessed relief from the relentless barrage of Frank Sinatra songs that Wedgy bellowed into the steamy Mississippian atmosphere. With the rush of wind and Old Blue Eyes's spirit through the convertible, sleep hadn't come easily. As they hurtled past depleted fields, sharecropper shacks, and through murky swamps, Rama had felt untethered and alive. But inevitably, the fresh air of unlimited possibility had pulled his imagination into its slipstream and he had given in.

He dreamt of flight and of a little child singing at his first taste of freedom. The child teetered on a bicycle as he coasted down his family's driveway. The dreamer could see the colored stripes on the child's jersey and a smile on his mother's face. The child's song still rang clear:

"Momma, I ride. I ride."

But, as always, the lens of recollection twisted and that smile flattened when the scene's bittersweet detail came into focus: There was no car in her driveway, and her lawn crept shaggily across the empty concrete. The woman glanced with concern toward something down the street even as she watched her son's first joyous bicycle ride. From the iron railing of her front porch, a crow watched *her* with black eyes. Inside, dinner was burning.

—•—

Rama bolted awake as the Lincoln hammered the plank decking on a bridge above an inky bayou. Wedgy was working his way through a pack of smokes as he piloted the Lincoln south. Rama looked into the waters below and wondered how far they would have to go before he saw his first alligator.

Silent now, Wedgy pondered the misfortune of his next golfing partner and the prospect of a new travel trailer. He remembered Yogi, a friend of a friend who dealt in recreational vehicles in Cloudsborough, just down the road several miles. Although Ivar's departing edict had carried some weight, Wedgy knew he would have to house Rama somehow, and he was already weary of the mildew that had set up housekeeping in the Luv Bug. He figured a stop at Yogi's Camper Land was in order.

Wedgy leaned forward as if he might miss Yogi's sign if seated too casually. On the far end of Cloudsborough, Yogi eventually came into sight—a poor likeness of the famous cartoon bear that smiled from a sign above a gravel lot populated by shiny Airstreams and lesser trailers. Wedgy hummed a Nelson Riddle chorus as he skillfully maneuvered the bug into its final resting place.

As Wedgy fussed with the hitch, he glanced up at Rama. "Next time you see your old buddy Ivar, be damn sure you tell him that selling this classic teardrop really hurt."

"Sounds like you're trying to make a liar out of me, Mr. Byrne."

"Lying? Well it *is* a skill…just like any other. Takes practice, son," Wedgy chuckled.

Rama let the exchange slip away. His attention had been diverted by something familiar—like the attraction he had seen years before on that trip through Texas with his father. It was a spherical water tank painted in the likeness of a golf ball—a gaudy lure for passing duffers.

"Mr. Byrne, look at that."

"What, that shitty little course? Christ, I doubt there's a soul on that track who'd even put a dime down on one of those crappy holes," replied Wedgy.

Rama looked again. He hadn't noticed the battered municipal golf course below the tower. "No, I mean the big golf ball…pretty cool, huh?"

Wedgy cast a disparaging look toward the water tank. "Not exactly the Colossus of Rhodes, kid."

In the distance a lone groundskeeper struggled with a reluctant mower and overgrown fairways. Wedgy frowned. "Not exactly Augusta National, either." He couldn't have summoned more of an understatement. The battered nine-holer wandered predictably around a couple of stagnant ponds and through some geriatric elms; it certainly wasn't going to find its place in a coffee-table book and would never attract the wealthy or the critical golfer.

"Don't get lost, Schwain. I won't be long."

The itinerant golf hustler's joints cracked in three places as he worked out the kinks from a half-day on the road and tucked his shirt back into place before heading for Yogi's sales office.

Rama guessed Wedgy would be occupied for a while and figured a walk beat the Lincoln's sticky seats. With luck maybe he'd find a cold soda at the golf course across the highway. After two jammed quarters he was rewarded with a Coca-Cola from a battered pop machine out on the golf shop's porch. As he savored the cool drink, Rama was taken by the muni's rustic charm. Wildflowers littered the rough with snatches of color while a variety of birds expressed satisfaction with the unkempt landscape. The fairways were marginally mown, but the greens were surprisingly well tended.

Rama walked idly to the highest point on the golf course—a mounded crescent of earth surrounding the ninth green. The promontory towered a mighty eight feet above the fairway, providing a view of any action out on the course. But there was precious little activity that afternoon, just a threesome about 150 yards up the fairway.

A weeping willow shaded Rama as his senses sharpened by his first day of freedom gradually turned from the comforting odor of cut grass to the three golfers.

"Oh God, just give him one good shot…please."

The bright voice of a young woman startled Rama from behind. He gasped as the sizzle of icy soda nearly boiled through his nostrils in surprise.

Chapter 40

Rama recovered his composure and turned to face a pretty blonde girl who appeared to be about his age. She seemed oblivious to his presence and gazed intently at the group up the fairway. A light breeze stirred the willows and her flowered blouse in graceful synchrony. For a moment he wasn't sure if she had actually been talking to God or to him.

The girl must have heard his thoughts. She turned. "Have you been watching? Has Ricky been doing okay?"

"Uh no, I don't know Ricky. I just stopped by," Rama said. "Is this some kind of match or something?" He looked around to see if anyone else was following the golfers' progress, but there was no one except the girl.

"Watch the fella in the white tee shirt; he's my brother. I so hope he's having a good time. I know how golf can tick you boys off, but he so needs a good game…or just one good shot. God."

"Everybody needs a good shot," Rama said as he focused on the three young men up the course. "What about the other ones?"

"They're all his golf buddies. I know they're rooting for him. They've been trying to get him out here to cheer him up for a while now. He's been so down he didn't even watch the Masters this spring…and that's his favorite."

The sister of the tee-shirted golfer raised her fingers in a good luck sign. "Ricky's had a real bad spell. He and Monica just had their first kid—a boy—about six months ago. Would have been my first nephew," the girl explained. "But the little one took sick. God, they were up nights with him…and then to the hospital and all."

The pretty girl looked at the sky. "The little guy didn't make it."

Rama felt the love for a lost child and a grieving brother stream from Ricky's sister. But the Cloudsborough girl was not the crying kind. "My brother took it harder than Monica did. We laid the little one down, said our prayers, and now we've got to pull Ricky through. I guess you never know how somebody's gonna handle a loss, huh?"

She looked at Rama and a smile brightened her strong face. A couple of locks of golden hair danced across her cheek. "You rooting for him now?" she asked.

Rama thought about Chandler's disappearance back at Mesquite Creek and of Carla's bitterness after the loss of Dickey and Glendora. Theirs were the only deaths Rama had ever known, and he had only learned of them through the ramblings of an old man. Just the same, he wanted to tell her he understood and tuck the loose hair behind her ear and maybe kiss her soft cheek.

"I'm pulling for him. I'm on his side, yeah," Rama replied. The two strangers turned together to watch Ricky and his buddies play up.

The first buddy must have hit fat. A huge divot exploded from his wild swing and the ball moved less than a third of the way home. The second buddy under-clubbed, and after an apparently decent swing, his high-flying ball descended into a pond guarding the deep oblong green.

The two observers by the green had no idea of Ricky's mood or if he were having a good game. For his sake they hoped he was counting his score in non-numerical values. Rama smiled to himself as he recalled a fellow he and Ivar had played with who had sketched tiny cartoon-like faces in lieu of a number in each of the eighteen frames on his scorecard—each face reflecting his mood following his performance on that hole. The fact that Ricky was in the company of his friends and in the caress of a glorious day would score high in such a system.

Rama hoped that Ricky, after enduring the pain of losing a child, would place no special weight on himself for the success of a mere game or the outcome of this final approach shot. Perhaps the hopeless attempts of his friends to reach the ninth green had taken some load from his thin shoulders.

———•———

Ricky saw his two friends exhale in disgust at their failed shots. He noticed their chests rise then hold in anticipation of his fate. He looked to the pin; it was set in the front, not far past the bank of the menacing pond and its sheltering willow. Behind the pin, the green stretched back and up through two distinct shelves. Ricky noticed his sister and someone standing beside her. Maybe a new boyfriend, he thought. He tried to focus on her companion's distant features when a soft gust rippled the willow's graceful boughs above the pond and sent fallen sycamore leaves into motion across the fairway. Ricky watched the world come to life and for the first time in weeks, his heart glowed. Five words came to mind; he had heard them before—something to do with the Old Course—and now they had meaning:

As we breathe
there's hope.

His attention turned from his sister to the upcoming shot. The green was favorable—he could go deep. God knew how Ricky loved to show off for his sister; maybe this was the time. Ricky glanced at his buddies, each locked stoically into a golfer's mute refusal to acknowledge a companion's pain, especially if heaped tragically upon bad luck. How he loved them for their friendship, he thought, and for their futile swings. Ricky wondered: Did they realize, like he did so clearly now, that there was always tomorrow, that life was just a...

Ricky completed the thought with his club.

From his place by the green, Rama saw the flash of Ricky's true temper.

———•———

Ben Hogan wouldn't have allowed such a poorly dressed young man on the same course with him, but here stood a young tee-shirted disciple, balanced purposefully at the end of an artful swing. All eyes watched, and all hearts longed for as perfect a result.

Perfect was, in this case, subjective. Old Ben would have cursed under his breath and poked at his divot in frustration if his ball had flown forty feet beyond the flagstick. Ricky, on the other hand, had made good contact and had stayed out of the slimy little pond. Forty feet away or not, he had hit the green and that was perfect! A forty-foot downhill putt through two descending shelves was the very least of his worries on this wonderful day.

The sister looked at Rama with an unspoken question.

"Yeah, it's good. It's on the green...I'd be happy with it," Rama replied. "Though it's a bearcat of a two-putt for par."

Soon, Ricky and his friends were on the green. Ricky surveyed his situation: A long descending putt at the end of nine holes on a humble muni before a gallery of two—what could be better? It felt like Sunday at the Masters.

Ricky was still away—considerably away. With a comical heave of his chest he acknowledged the impossibility of the putt and the presence of his sister and her friend, then with a smile turned resolutely to the task at hand. Wouldn't Sis love to see a par, he thought, as he stood over the ball again? But the peace that had swept over him moments before on the fairway collapsed without reason under another insistent wave of grief.

Ricky stood back up to collect himself. Through vision distorted by shimmering tears he could make out his sister's blonde hair and the stranger's skinny stature. He wiped his eyes with the back of his hand—never forgetting how fertilizer could burn—and stepped back in to putt. His vision returned as he crouched low to read his line.

The afternoon sun's extreme angle revealed every dip, divot, and ripple in the old green's surface. He could see the faint impressions of past footprints—the ghostly traces of yesterday's players. He read the green for the complicated line to the hole, but saw far more. Ricky perceived a parade of the courageous souls who, like him, had played through life's tragedies and across this very green in search of comfort. The phantom record of their passing was etched in the tight Bermuda turf. He felt them: The ones who even in the grip of sorrow at lost fortunes, lost crops, and lost loves had set their feet upon this green to peer down the same treacherous slope, to face down their demons, and to gather themselves like he did now to unravel its mystery and take their shot at a hopeful tomorrow.

With the grain of the green cast so clearly, Ricky could see the game's purpose that so often lay obscured by golf's ponderous opaque numbers. The challenge in its simplicity and its difficulty offered solace to all who surrendered to its grace...whether they be stymied by a chunk into the second cut or staggered by a more profound tragedy.

With clearing vision and a warming heart, Ricky stroked the putt. The ball was pulled to the hole so surely that a chorus of "Oh my Gods" rang up while it was still twelve feet out. The joy that followed as the ball rattled in the cup would have put a Masters victory to shame, yet nobody even recognized at first that he had scored a birdie.

Rama looked at the girl rejoicing beside him. "No doubt about that one, huh?" he smiled.

"Oh my God, *thanks*," she cried and touched Rama's hand for an instant—as if certain of his contribution—before racing onto the green to hug her wonderful brother.

—•—

Rama retreated from Ricky's green, happy for the young man's small victory but slightly askew at having a girl of such spirit and charm slip in and out of his afternoon so easily. Such must be the ways of the vagabond, he mused romantically. He considered turning back, maybe to intercept her in the parking lot, but discarded the notion as too hopeless for one only minutes away from disappearing forever. Instead, he strolled back to the putting green behind the pro-shop and waited out Wedgy's return while putting some abandoned practice balls with the toe of his sneaker. A couple even dropped home with a satisfying clank.

The crunching of gravel under large tires interrupted Rama's idle practice; maybe Wedgy had returned, he thought. He emerged from behind the pro-shop to see a gray military bus creeping across the parking lot. Every window framed an anxious young man's face. Although the bold letters on the bus's flanks read U.S. Army, its passengers still sported the hair and the clothes of civilian kids out for an adventure. A spasm of interest spread through the bus as the young men noticed a pretty blonde girl in white shorts and blue flowered blouse talking with a trio of lucky bastards out on the golf course.

The bus abruptly stopped. As it idled rudely its door lurched open and discharged the driver. The fellow's fatigues hung heavy with sweat, and although in uniform, the listless man bore no resemblance to the hardened men who staffed the boot camp to which he was headed. He had enlisted only after losing his civilian gig driving cattle from feedlots to the slaughterhouse, but somehow the joyless fellow had found a comparable niche in the Armed Forces.

The driver descended the steps and headed with determination to the pop machine. He noticed Rama lingering nearby but said nothing as he worked the vending machine like a favorite old pinball table. In seconds he was popping the cap off a Dr. Pepper.

Catching Rama's eye he grunted, "Stay away from that Luva'Lime shit... tastes like dirt."

The driver had to stay on schedule but could never resist making this stop on the run down to Biloxi. A good cold drink and the torture his refreshment inflicted upon the thirsty draftees locked in the steamy bus broke up the monotony of the tedious drive. He took another long slug off the bottle and scowled at Rama.

"What the hell is fresh meat like you doin' on the loose? Got room on the bus here for ya, college boy." The driver didn't wait for a reaction, but hocked a heavy wad of syrupy spit to the ground and strode rapidly back to his bus.

As the dismal vehicle made a one-eighty back to the highway, Rama could see the boys' faces again—all eyes still clung to Ricky's sister walking with tantalizing femininity to her car. A shiver coursed through Rama. An unexpected cloud had momentarily blocked the sun, casting a deeper shade across the bus rattling from the parking lot.

Rama's knees nearly buckled as the truth darkened his heart: Out of all the detestable driver's human cargo, three of those boys dreaming of the delights beneath the blonde girl's blouse would never know a lover in their short lives.

—•—

With the cursed bus whining through its gears and into the distance, Ricky's sister returned to her red Volkswagen bug and fired the faithful little engine to life. Rama, still frozen in place beside the pro-shop, listened as the VW's rev erased the sound of the bus disappearing to the south. He was startled as the car suddenly stopped before him. The girl's bright face dispelled the shadow of the doomed boys. He tried to smile.

"You're looking kind of lost," the girl observed. "Where y'all headed?" Her happy blue eyes worked their magic, and Rama felt the glow of her company and of his freedom on the road.

"Monterey...Cypress Point, I think," he smiled.

"Where's that...Arkansas?"

"No, California," Rama replied, now the worldly wanderer. "On the west coast."

"Wow, fun," she said.

Laughter attracted the girl's attention and she turned away to watch her brother and his friends lingering on the tailgate of a pick-up truck—joking over a few beers and passing a joint. Rama couldn't see the smile lighting her face, but he noticed how her hair parted at the back of her head into cascades that tumbled to her shoulders and around her neck. Between the two streams of gold, her soft skin flowed over the subtle humps of her spine before plunging southward.

Wow, fun, he thought.

"You traveling in the Lincoln?" she asked, turning back to face the wanderer just as Wedgy pulled into the lot with a shiny new trailer in tow.

Rama smiled in the affirmative.

"What do you *do*? Are you on vacation?"

"No…professional golfers," Rama declared in a Wedgyesque half-truth.

"Wow, fun."

The Lincoln's horn broke the spell spinning between Rama and the girl. They simultaneously chimed "See ya" and laughed at themselves.

Wedgy's sunburned face leered at the pretty girl in the VW. "Can't leave you alone for a minute out here, Rama," he quipped, unaware of how much life had passed while he had been talking the trailer salesman out of half his commission.

The red Volkswagen revved like a toy and was gone.

"Hop in, Romeo, got to roll," said Wedgy as he gunned the Lincoln's engine impatiently. He looked forward to a string of prosperous golf courses down the road and to a parade of overconfident weekend warriors lining up to hand over their misguided bets to some grizzled old golfer who, empowered by his caddie's special gift, just happened to be having "one of those days" every day.

Chapter 41

Doris awoke late in the morning with the names of her favorite flowers on her lips. As her fragile world came into focus, she wondered if she always talked in her sleep. Perhaps she would ask Hank when he returned from Big Muddy's that evening, assuming his day's fortunes left him in the mood for such small talk.

She slipped from the bed and went to the kitchen to start the coffee. Her hand quavered at the tap and her eyes fell to the garden beyond the window. Heavens, she thought, it could use some attention. The perennials begged not to be forgotten—pleading through the kitchen window for her to find the energy to give them another chance. Maybe it was grief at Rama's departure or simply the advance of her illness, but it seemed that she had worsened since he had left. She knew it would be selfish to beg him to return, but it didn't seem right that the door to her home revolved in one sad motion that received her husband just as it expelled her son.

Her thoughts returned to coffee and to the memory of the garden in full bloom. She smiled at the vision of color and blossoms—images as encouraging as the first report she had recently received from her new doctor. Doctor Myer was a visiting physician from Atlanta who had been working with associates at the University Hospital in Memphis. His first exam was revelatory. Tired old Doc Stasson had long insisted she was the unlucky heiress to a relatively benign variant of muscular sclerosis, but Doctor Myer wasn't so sure. He had taken great interest in her head and in particular the hidden scar that had testified to her fall at the petroglyphs. He had brought the full power of diagnostic imaging to bear on her behalf, even taking a few passes with the mysterious new ultrasound machine.

She could see the blue cathode-ray tube reflecting in the doctor's glasses as he peered into its flickering glow. He huddled with a technician, called in another doctor, and muttered of things medical. Doris took great comfort in the notion that her well-being was high on Doctor Myer's priority list, ranking higher than the recreation promised in the Palm Springs retirement brochures that once littered the old doctor's desk.

Although Doctor Myer had dared venture no diagnosis without more thorough test results, he had explained that he suspected a structural dys-function—from an injury, he guessed—that might mimic other disorders. The good news, the doctor suggested, was that such a condition might be operable. He assured her that the lab at his clinic in Atlanta would have results in seven days or so that would at the very least preclude other possibilities.

"Just be patient," the doctor said.

"I already am," Doris joked.

Doctor Myer laughed along, embarrassed at stumbling into that one. He turned to go but another question crossed his mind. "How long did you say you have suffered this condition?"

Doris thought back to the summer she sent Rama on the road trip with Hank and added several years onto that. "About twelve years or so."

The doctor looked perplexed. A dozen years did not square with the pathology he was considering. He would have expected more severe symp-toms by now. He worried that she might be sliding into an accelerated decline after an inexplicable remission. The thought troubled him as much as the possibility of a medical anomaly excited him. He promised he would be in touch, but despite his upbeat appraisal, Doris could see that the doctor looked more concerned than when he had first greeted her.

He pulled a pad from his coat and scribbled off a prescription. "In case those headaches become…uh, significant."

He returned the pad to his pocket, but on second thought drew it back out. This time he carefully printed a number and handed the slip to Doris.

"My personal telephone number," he said, "just in case."

"Thank you, Doctor. Mr. Guidance said you were thorough."

Doctor Myer disappeared into the buzz of the busy hallway and Doris gathered herself for the drive home. She glanced at the two slips of paper be-fore tucking them into her purse. But something in the doctor's hurried script startled her and she looked again. Morphine, it read.

———•———

By the end of the month, Hank's fortunes at Big Muddy's remained in the doldrums and he and Doris were forced to take in a boarder. Siran, a Libyan exchange student, moved into Rama's room. But along with Siran came Siran's sister, and along with the sister came the cuisine: garlic, eggplant, garlic, grape leaves, goat, garlic, and more garlic. God only knew the source of the strange odors that now challenged the Betty Crocker atmosphere of Doris's kitchen. If for no other reason than the smell in his house, Hank regretted that he hadn't found the motivation to wrestle his debts under control and leave gambling safely in his past. But from the moment he had peeked under the lid of a large, steaming pot one evening after work and was greeted by a goat's head, he questioned his reliance on Siran's contribution to the mortgage.

But odor be damned. Hank rose earlier to soldier on against the weight of his own blunders. And, against her body's protests, Doris rose bravely beside him to chase away the scent of Siran's cooking with a bubbling percolator of Maxwell House and a skillet of Hank's favorite breakfast—the one breakfast entrée that could hold its own against the north-African odors still prevailing in their morning kitchen—Spam and eggs.

The extra time Hank spent at Big Muddy's was paying off, but too slowly for Lew Raybon's liking. Hank would have paid more than Calcutta's usurious interest on his first month's installment, but he had to pay his home mortgage as well. Lew had somberly reminded Hank that the entire principal and interest were due in less than four months.

"Don't make this any harder on yourself," Lew warned. "Next month you pay 25-percent or *we've* got problems…you dig?"

Hank nodded grimly as he slid his first check across Lew's desk. He dug. At least he had made the minimum payment, he thought with diminishing satisfaction. Lew gave Hank a receipt, then waved him out of the office. The loan shark made a note to dispatch an "appraiser" to the Schwain house for a look; then he sat back in his chair and held up Hank's check to the light. He rubbed his thumb across the signature to test the ink. Old habits die hard.

———•———

Hank was already in the Rambler and halfway home when he checked his watch: Almost five thirty, he thought, still enough time to have a look at the Little Crow and get home for dinner before Siran fouled the atmosphere.

The Crow was proving to be a heavy burden. Weighed against the threatening costs of his loan and Doris's medical bills, selling the glider made obvious sense. He couldn't kid himself forever; how was he going to fly? He couldn't even afford the tow aloft. But somewhere between the practical considerations of relinquishing a foolish indulgence and the boyish thrill of merely sitting aboard the aircraft as if astride a giant dragonfly, he was moved to stay his dreamy course.

The pilot from Aero Meadows didn't make clinging to a dream any easier. When Hank arrived, the pilot ambled out from his picnic table and his pornography to confront the stranger skimming an open palm along the aircraft's smooth wings.

"Oh shit, it's just you, Schwain," the pilot grumbled, pissed at having been stirred from his afternoon fantasy. "Except for the cane, I wouldn't 'a recognized you all dressed up like that."

Hank glanced down at the crease of his trousers. "Just got off work. Muddy keeps us looking slick. Sells more cars, he says."

"Well since you're here, Schwain, tell me: Are you planning to actually fly this little bird someday?" Hank's platonic relationship with his glider was costing Aero considerably in lost tow fees.

"You're gonna have to get her airborne before she grows moss." Then without waiting for a reaction, the pilot added that he was raising the hangar fee by fifty dollars a month. "And it's not just you," the pilot assured Hank. "Money is tight all around."

Hank swallowed hard. After Lew's increased pressure, another fifty dollars to lodge a plane he couldn't afford to fly was the straw that pushed Hank to the conclusion that this month's mortgage payment would have to wait. When he returned home, rather than toss the troubling mortgage bill into the waste can like a common dead-beat, he tucked it carefully between the pages of Doris's family Bible for future consideration. Judging by its dusty gilded pages, Hank guessed his secret would be safe in the Good Book.

He slipped the Bible back onto its shelf, muttering an appropriate little prayer for some god-damned better luck and for God almighty to direct a few car-crazed fools up the road to Big Muddy's.

———•———

Wedgy and Rama rolled into a vacant campground deep in the harsh creosote bush and yucca landscape west of San Antonio's hospitable hill country. Within minutes the songs of Frank Sinatra as interpreted by Wallace Byrne rang out from the CruiseAir trailer. The cosmopolitan spirit of Old Blue Eyes softened the awful emptiness of the sixty-mile horizon.

Wedgy may have wanted to wake in a city that never sleeps, but he welcomed the hushed landscape and the chance to relax. The busy swing through his fertile hustling grounds from Dallas to San Antonio had proven profitable but dangerous. This was golfing country not to be trifled with, and being on top of his game and his gamesmanship every waking minute took its toll. Two generations of players bred upon blustery weather, burgeoning courses, and bulging billfolds had created a constitution of power, control, and cocky confidence that flowed from the elite, to the avid, and down to the casual player. There were scratch players lurking at every two-bit track who could humiliate the unwary hole for hole. And there were a fair share of accomplished tee-box thespians who could work the limp, the look, and the lie into a treacherous combination of acting and golfing skills.

Attempting to hustle his way through such country was akin to skipping happily through a minefield, but Wedgy had done well due as much to his wary judge of character as to his magically rejuvenated game. With the Caddie's Gift lifting Wedgy to heights well above his apparent ability, he found it easy to talk gullible competitors into additional strokes or to charm them into risky side bets. Still, it was hard work trying to out-play and out-think the skilled

Lone-Star linksters. Wedgy had had enough drama for a couple of days and relaxed gratefully in this quiet refuge beyond any traces of humanity.

The old hustler stretched out on the trailer's sofa, a cold longneck pressed against a searing tennis elbow. After belting out another Sinatra classic, Wedgy fell into an expansive mood and proceeded to explain the foundations of his matchmaking philosophy to his traveling companion.

Rama listened passively. With nothing on the surrounding plains to distract him, and with a hot skillet of Sloppy Joe keeping him close to the propane stove, he was a captive audience.

"Now the first thing you gotta know in this business is who *not* to play against. Sure, there's plenty of pigeons," as he called his easily defeated, well-heeled prospects, "but Christ, there's some big-league players down here, too. If you're going to make a few bucks in this damn state, you'd better keep your eyes open to avoid being one of them flying rats yourself."

Wedgy moved the cold bottle to his forehead. "Then you'd better know the signs of a ringer. If a man's got too much tan on his forearms or his cheeks, watch out—he's been spending a shitload of time in the sun and I guarantee he ain't been choppin' cotton.

"If he's got a pale left hand: he wears a golf glove a lot. Got a calloused right hand: he plays a lot. If he's playing single and asks for a match…avoid the SOB like a rattlesnake."

Rama stared into the sizzling skillet, paying only shallow attention to the pages reeling from Wedgy's book of knowledge. He was more concerned with numbers—the elusive count of dollars now overdue him after several weeks of valuable service to Wedgy. Rama noticed Wedgy had always been careful to propose stakes or offer side bets discreetly into the ears of the competition and beyond his caddie's earshot. Without a clear idea of the stakes, Rama couldn't know what shares should be trickling down to him or how they squared against the 8-percent he had been promised. He couldn't calculate it but felt he was being swindled.

It wasn't that Rama really cared about stacking up his own nest egg at the expense of Wedgy's victims, but whatever assets Wedgy accrued, Rama felt a part of it justifiably belonged to him. He was learning every day how easily the weak or the unwary were baffled by Wedgy's song and dance. Rama wondered how his own father had been attracted and if he had put up much resistance. Wedgy didn't know it, Rama hoped, but there were thousands of dollars of Schwain money in the old hustler's coffers, and Rama was damned if he was going to be cheated out of any more.

Wedgy sniffed at the aroma from Rama's skillet. "How 'bout sprinkling a little Tabasco on that poultice while you're at it?" Wedgy stretched out his legs and kicked off his shoes, wincing involuntarily at the pain in his rapidly stiffening ankles.

"Old damned age," he groaned. "You been listening, Rama?"

"Oh yeah…I'm all ears."

Wedgy peered suspiciously through half-closed eyes as he settled back on the sofa. "Just trying to pass on a little experience, my boy…in case you get serious about the game one day."

Wedgy drained the remainder of his Lone Star. "You got to learn this stuff, Schwain. There's always somebody better than you out here. Take the guy who's got the 1-iron in his bag—nobody *plays* with a 1-iron—or the fella' who's playing solo on a workday but he's *not* a doctor. You've gotta be ready to walk away from those sharks or demand an embarrassing number of strokes. Shit, it's your money. Don't plunk it down till you know who these dudes are and if you can out-play or out-think them."

Your money. The old hustler got that part right, thought Rama. He slid the pan off the stove and flipped open a quartet of hamburger buns.

"Then you gotta know who *to* play against," Wedgy continued. "Once you've eliminated the hustlers and the ringers, then you work the rest of 'em for as many strokes as they'll give and as much money as they'll go…kind of a balancing act."

Wedgy held his two hands palms up in a pantomime of Lady Justice balancing invisible weights in each hand. "Their pride against their ability. Their fear against their greed," he chuckled, then added, "and your need against their disposable income.

"But it's not always a cakewalk, kid. You can spook a pigeon or scare down a nice fat bet if you don't negotiate *artistically.*" Wedgy savored the word like a decent bourbon. "Of course it's always a little easier if you look like a washed-up old reprobate."

Wedgy laughed as he stretched across the sofa and opened his arms in surrender to his own description.

"Then sometimes you just stumble into some dick who's so starry-eyed that he thinks his game will finally come together for him just when the chips are down. And sure as shit, he'll toss down way too many chips. Don't get me wrong; optimism isn't a bad thing, Rama, but it sure as hell can't knock six strokes off a handicap overnight." He winked at Rama. "It takes something more potent to do that trick, eh?"

"Come and get it," Rama announced, glad to interrupt his incorrigible mentor.

Wedgy hobbled over to the stove and grabbed a plate of dinner. They ate in silence. In the blessed quiet Rama had a moment to consider his unusual employment. Except for his elusive compensation and the fact that he hadn't seen even a glimmer of a chance to invest Ivar's money against Wedgy, Rama had to admit that with Mississippi, Louisiana, and three-quarters of the state of Texas behind them, this adventure had been educational and at times enjoyable. Except for Wedgy's relentless fixation on that which lined other people's billfolds, or his musical preferences, or a snore like a rutting bison, he had his fair share of charms.

On the course, his chatter and his facility around the greens were a wonder. While watching Wedgy work, Rama was reminded of a skilled cutlery pitch-man he had once seen on the midway of a county fair. The fellow performed miracles of high-velocity knife work as he soared through his rap and a parade of ripe tomatoes like Charlie Parker through a whirlwind of thirty-second notes. Off the course, Wedgy could spin stories or spew anecdotes that compressed the empty stretches between lonely towns or distant buttes. But he wasn't just a walking golf primer. The old hustler was well educated and could reel off credible nuggets of information on history, philosophy, roadside geology, and the very nature of the stars shimmering in the night sky.

Curiously, the knowledge associated with Wedgy's previous career counted for little. Rama never heard a peep's worth of wisdom on securities, bond ratings, or stock options. Increasingly, he was content in thinking that if he could just get his fair share, he might follow Wedgy's hustling show all the way to California unless he got the chance to put Ivar's bankroll down against Wedgy, or unless he heard word that Trent Institute had summoned him to class—whichever came first.

After Wedgy had consumed two helpings without offering any recognition of the food's flavor—good or bad—he popped the top off another longneck and resumed Rama's lesson.

"Like that starry-eyed dick I was talking about…or the overly hopeful fool who can't tell Grimm's from Dale Carnegie…or the positive thinkers who've talked themselves into thinking they can conquer the game with good intentions alone—Lord, they're the dreamy boneheads who really piss me off.

"Remember one thing, Rama: This game is mastered from the ground up—from down in the dirt, they say. If you get a chance to play one of those eggheads, you've gotta bury him so deep that he'll stay out of the golfing gene pool for good. Kind of a Darwinian public service. And hell, you never know; maybe the bastard will discover a future in bowling."

Wedgy wiped away a trickle of Sloppy Joe with the back of his hand. "But you've gotta respect those guys a little. They don't know it, but what they really want is to pay *you* for the privilege of beating *them*."

Rama was intrigued by Wedgy's rant. He recalled a game that morning in which Wedgy had relieved a self-important over-achieving member of the Abilene Rotary Club of a sizeable sum in a match on his home course. "What about the guy back in Abilene? Did he belong in or out of the gene pool?"

"That puffed-up small-town political hack?" Wedgy laughed at the memory of the man's open-mouthed humiliation. "Out of the pool…way out!

"It wasn't so much that the fool was stupidly *optimistic*," Wedgy said, remembering the victory with satisfaction. "It was that he was stupidly *egotistic*. There's a difference: The unrealistic guy can be talked into an unrealistic bet for the whole round—say a fifty-buck Nassau. He'll just hope that somewhere along the line his ship will haul itself off the reef and come in. But that wasn't the case with today's Elk, or Odd Fellow, or whatever the fuck he was. He just couldn't back down from a bet. For a poor bastard like him it's a pathological problem, so it wasn't real hard to get him to leap at a chance to win back his losses and press the bet over and over and over like a damned fool." Wedgy rapped his beer bottle on the table to emphasize the repetitiveness of the fellow's miscalculations.

"God love him, but he just couldn't believe that some old fart who'd looked so hopeless on the first four holes could suddenly be challenging him. He probably figured I had stumbled into a temporary lucky streak when I tallied up a most unfortunate run of birdies.

"The poor fellow is probably still trying to drink off that thrashing. He didn't know he was strolling down the garden path…didn't know what league he was in when he tangled with us," said Wedgy, granting Rama his due.

There was no doubt in Wedgy's mind that Rama had transformed his game. With that thought, Wedgy leaned over to the refrigerator and without leaving the sofa recovered a bottle of Scotch. He pulled two glasses down from the counter.

"That's about enough for one night's lesson, Schwain. Let's drink to the fools…and to our little team."

Wedgy was sincere. Before Rama had climbed into the Lincoln three weeks back, the intervals between games in which his performance had remotely justified his moxie had been growing lengthy. He had known the lackluster games would eventually expand into a continuum of frustration and to a hopeless retirement. Why, Wedgy wondered in a rare reflective moment, had the Lord seen fit to deliver Rama to him, of all people, when God should have known he would shamelessly play the charmed caddie for every damn cent his magic was worth? Like they say: The Lord moves in mysterious ways.

Wedgy sipped his Scotch and tried to put his finger on the *mystery* in what Rama actually brought to his game. The hustler knew nothing about Dickey Stone or the Caddie's Gift. He only knew the outwardly unexceptional young boy in jeans and an untucked madras shirt fussing at the CruiseAir's propane stove looked anything but heaven sent. Rama's effect had nothing to do with technique. Wedgy felt that he still swung with the same quirky motion he always had. He still took the same little scab of a divot. If Rama couldn't actually affect the ball or the club—a concept that was too far into Uri Geller territory for his liking—he reasoned Rama's influence came to bear just *before* the swing.

A couple more shots of Black Label had lubricated Wedgy's powers of reasoning and he understood that it was there, in that instant over the ball when confidence rules the stroke, that Rama's effect intervened. But there could be no confidence if he hadn't some faith in the outcome of the shot. If faith begat confidence and confidence begat performance…then faith begat performance.

Wedgy's tipsy reverie conjured up an image: a colorful ribbon tying the intended and the actual together with an impossible connection that stretched between the present and the future with a loop up through the imagination. The ribbon was faith and it rippled erratically.

Ah, the wonders of logic and good liquor, thought Wedgy. He realized he had had it backwards for years: playing faithlessly as his performance plummeted. It was an illuminating concept, but if Rama's magic was rooted in faith, how could such an awkward young fellow inspire such a potent force? Wedgy was still puzzled but raised his glass again.

"Here's to faith…in God knows what."

His musings might have been philosophically helpful, but he had drifted beyond his intellectual comfort zone. He needed a smoke. He fumbled drunkenly with a new pack's wrapper and lit up a cigarette. Wedgy preferred the empirical, and walking on nicotine's solid ground he returned to more prosaic thoughts.

He smiled at today's performance. How valuable had it been to once again confidently pull the driver and wail for all he was worth into a shallow left dogleg with faith that the draw would find traction in the atmosphere? Or to launch a loose and fully swung flop high above a short-sided pin? Or to stand over a downhill lie and face a two-hundred-plus carry across an inhospitable arroyo to a domed green and calmly propose to his trembling opponent, "What do you say we press that bet?"

Wedgy tamped the pack against the trailer's bulkhead and offered Rama a smoke. Rama waved the offer off and Wedgy returned to a dissection of the Abilene match.

"So once our Mr. Odd Fellow lost a couple of holes…" Wedgy's hand mimed a car careening off an imaginary highway and into an abyss, "he was on the road to ruin. That big old head of his just got in the way."

Rama wondered if Wedgy really understood human nature as clearly as it appeared, or did his bluff go on forever?

"I know what you're thinking, Rama: Bluffed on the first tee and bamboozled on the next, why didn't old Odd Fellow figure the hustle was on?"

"That's pretty close," Rama lied.

"Sure, if he was smart he might have figured it out. He could have cut his losses and gone quietly back to the city council meeting. But our Odd Fellow just couldn't tuck his tail between his legs—that would have been against his nature. Anyway, he probably figured there wasn't room down there for it and his big old cojones."

Wedgy laughed heartily, then replaced the void in his lungs with a breath of blue smoke. He exhaled a plume through the window above the sofa and out into the dusk gathering around the solitary trailer. The tobacco made him swoon for an instant, forgetting himself. "So damned if the Odd Fellow didn't get in deeper and deeper. Eight hundred dollars on a fifty-dollar bet...how sweet it is."

Rama sipped tentatively on his Scotch. A true appreciation of the liquor's complex flavor was still years away, but he had been appreciating Wedgy's hustling lesson. The instruction was a far cry from the reverent lesson old Carlos had given him using the club that lay, even now, under his bunk in the CruiseAir.

Despite his doubts about Wedgy's honesty to him, Rama agreed with Wedgy's characterization of today's competitor. "Puffed-up political hack" might have been too kind, Rama thought, and with good reason. Just before he and Wedgy had hit the road westward, Rama had dashed to the men's locker room for a final pee. He almost collided with a man propped against the pay phone—none other than Mr. Abilene. Rama had seen him earlier in the bar, drinking off his losses in the affectionate company of a woman a third his age. Now, Rama stood at the urinal eavesdropping unwittingly on one end of a deceivingly apologetic phone conversation.

"Yeah, honey, just now finished up with the surveyors. Got a lot of ground to cover. Probably be out here again next week..."

"No, we walked it...the site's gonna be a moneymaker," the man spoke into the receiver with whiskey breath and absolute dishonesty, a far better liar than golfer.

"You get the wagon in there for service, Sweetie? Good girl."

"Uh no, I might be a little late...you know these builders. Like to tip back a couple while they talk turkey."

Rama heard the man's feet shifting uneasily on the tile floor. "Give 'em both a kiss for Daddy.

"No, no, honey; this is how they do business now-a-days..."

"Yeah. Love you, too."

Rama heard the receiver land heavily back on the hook and the man's footfall trailing quickly back to the bar and to the girl.

He was surprised to have tasted a delicious pride for his part in hustling the sleazy fellow. In fact, he wished Wedgy had squeezed this pigeon a little harder, but then realized it hardly mattered. It was unlikely the adulterous hack was picking up the tab for his own golfing debts.

—•—

Rama stepped out onto the trailer's stoop. He considered bumming a smoke off Wedgy after all, but the evening's air carried the scent of mesquite and faraway rains. It would be a shame to blanket such perfume. Darkness was descending rapidly and stars randomly winked to life, leaving a sky populated by partially completed constellations. As he looked into the heavens, the number $850 burst like a nova in Rama's thoughts. Wedgy had absent-mindedly laid the smoking gun on the table when he revealed his winnings. Rama ran the numbers, figuring that he should have earned sixty-eight dollars and change for his share, not to mention the caddie fee, but he received only twenty-four dollars. Like everyone else in Wedgy's world, Rama was being screwed; at least now he knew by how much—nearly two-thirds.

Thirty miles away, the headlights of a car cresting a hill on the horizon sparkled through the atmosphere's prism. Maybe old Odd Fellow was coming after them, thought Rama. He imagined a Wild West encounter with the enraged golfer and his posse before recalling that the fellow had other "business" on this night.

Rama returned to his math, calculating what losing two-thirds of his share might mean over the long haul, especially if Wedgy ran into some real money. His father's six thousand dollars came sadly to mind. He imagined, with a shade of guilt, how he would pocket $480 if Wedgy found someone that foolish.

Rama closed his eyes and tried to put money from his mind. He thought about his mother's health. He wondered if she and Hank had actually taken in a boarder yet. Standing out there on the CruiseAir's stoop, he realized that in three weeks on the road he had not written a single letter.

Rama heard Wedgy hoot in glee from inside the trailer. The old hustler had found a song on the radio, something about trains carrying lonely hobos back to Abilene. His rough-edged baritone rode the music out through the trailer door:

Rama smiled at the irony in the lyric. He thought of some soulless home out in the Abilene suburbs—the unfaithful Odd Fellow's home—and two children sleeping with peaceful ignorance of their father's crime against their mother. In the glow of the TV she fretted through an amusing exchange between Johnny Carson and Bob Hope. Rama's heart ached for the three strangers, but an unspoken voice directed him from being swallowed by the sufferings of others. There was too much pain for one spirit to bear. He could only do his best in a tawdry world.

Rama smiled at the music and at Wedgy's swaggering accompaniment. At least the old hustler wasn't parroting Old Blue Eyes again. He listened, and there in that lonely place Rama found comfort even in the voice of one who had wronged him. But soon enough Rama would have to confront Wedgy and rock the boat, regardless of how far they had sailed together into the Southwest's desolate sea.

Chapter 42

Hank guessed it was LBJ's damned war, but whatever the reason, people just weren't in the market for a decent used car lately, at least not at Big Muddy's. Two weeks after Calcutta Finance had tightened its terms on his loan, a stingy used car market had left him no closer to having the funds to make his next payment than he had been when he first left Lew Raybon's office.

Lew's calculated display of tooth had achieved its effect. Hank found himself growing more nervous with every customer who wandered through the lot without as much as a double take at the inventory. He wondered if Johnson's Asian adventures were finally getting to folks, or was it just him? What in hell's name was wrong with the world when he couldn't even get a young buck to pony up the cash for a damned muscle car?

What was wrong in *his* world was clear. He worked through a distressing mental checklist as he steered the Rambler up River Road: wife sick, son alienated, business lousy, in debt, and mortgage unpaid.

His dismal tally was interrupted as a flock of geese rose from the muddy bank and sailed out across the silver water. Hank let his mind ride for a moment on the birds' shiny backs out to where the buoys marked the barge channel. He envied their freedom. Then, loosing its grip, Hank's mind fell back to his list. Somehow he would have to break bad financial news to Doris. Her piano had to go.

He hoped she would understand that selling the instrument was just a one-time liquidation to get over the hump. He would remind her that she never played the bloody thing anymore. They had bought it for Rama, but the only interest he had ever shown in anything was in carrying somebody else's golf clubs. Hank planned on telling it like it is: that with her out of a job, and with their budget strained by rising medical bills, something had to give. But that wasn't exactly the way it was. The fact was he had gone out of his way to snag her medical bills so that he might manage the account. He had convinced himself that it was necessary to relieve her of unneeded stress, but his true concern was that by claiming a heavy burden from the doctor's fees while making minimal installments, he could obscure the impact of his secret payments to Calcutta. The medical bills would take second fiddle to the more insistent creditor, Lew Raybon. And if necessary he could cite the doctor's bills as a reasonable excuse for selling off a few of their treasures, piano included.

Then there was the mortgage. The chill of panic could almost be mistaken for the cool river breeze that blew in through the Rambler's window. Hank shivered. The Auto Retailer's Mortgage Company would not be particularly understanding at the prospect of playing second fiddle for the second straight month to Hank's other financial commitments.

If he tucked another unpaid bill away in Doris's Bible, he knew ARMCO would take an active interest in the house's market value. If the financial shit really hit the fan, Hank imagined one of their wire-rimmed clerks and Lew Raybon arm wrestling for the title. Of course, ARMCO would have the law to enforce its claim. Hank shuddered to think what that alternative left for Calcutta Finance to enforce its claim.

Hank told himself to calm down; he had walked this tightrope before. Business was bound to improve. But he forgot to consider that his previous high-wire exploits had never threatened the very roof over his head. What the hell, a good night at the track could set everything straight, and that piano was liable to fetch a couple months' relief.

As he guided the Rambler to his driveway, Hank noticed the flag on the mailbox was down and a few letters still lay inside. Doris must have had a really down day not to have made it out for the mail, but even so, by now Siran should have brought it in.

Hank gathered the mail, glancing over the envelopes with apprehension as he walked up the driveway. He breathed a sigh of relief: nothing from ARM-CO or Doctor Myer. But his heart swelled at the sight of a generous envelope addressed in Rama's hand. Hank clung to the threads of affection that held against his and Rama's falling out. It was not lost on Hank that Rama had carefully avoided dashing Doris's hopeful image of him when he so clearly had the chance to do otherwise.

"I'll be damned," Hank muttered, "wonder how he's doing out there?" Whatever his son was up to, it was good news to receive a long-awaited letter from Rama—especially now, he thought. This might make it a little easier to break the bad news about the piano.

Hank strolled into the living room. Doris was asleep, settled deeply into her place on the sofa. A seed catalog, a cold teapot, and a jumble of newly written letters attested to the time she had spent on that spot. He tossed the letters onto a pile of mail growing on the coffee table. An envelope from the Admissions Office – Trent Institute of Landscape Technology lay at the top of the stack. He never noticed.

The sound of the mail landing on the table awakened Doris. She smiled weakly at her husband, who approached with a letter in his hand.

"It's from your prodigal son," Hank said. "I'm surprised Siran didn't drop it off for you earlier."

Doris's face fell slightly. "Siran has found an apartment in town."

"Oh, Christ." Hank's emotions teetered between alarm at another financial setback and relief at purging the house of goat essence. "Did he say why?"

"Something about a religious aversion to SPAM."

—•—

Rama sat in silence on a stone bench near the first tee at Sunset Hills Golf Course and contemplated the dark folds of the Franklin Mountains. For once he had time on his hands. After a morning on the range, Wedgy had told him he was going into El Paso to catch up with some old cronies and left Rama up at the golf course with the admonition to stay out of harm's way. He'd be back in time for the afternoon match he had arranged the previous evening.

Looking at the empty terrain beyond the course, Rama realized that if Wedgy's activities in town got out of hand he could be stranded here, ten miles from their camp and the CruiseAir trailer, which, for now, was home. But as Rama pondered his vulnerability, he remembered Lee, the Mexican golfer for whom he had caddied long ago at Mesquite Creek. Lee had once told Rama to look him up if he ever got down to El Paso. That was a few years back, Rama thought, but it was good to know he might have some connection in town, regardless how tenuous. Of course if Wedgy ran into too much trouble, Rama always had Ivar's check and the Greyhound bus.

For now Rama was savoring the solitude. He had enjoyed few breaks from Wedgy's chatter since Memphis. At first, the nearly constant stream of shady enlightenment flowing from Wedgy's ruddy face fell on less than receptive ears. Rama had no intention of following golf's darker path. But as Rama's distaste for the corruption of what Ivar referred to as "the Royal and Ancient Game" grew, Rama started paying attention to Wedgy's methods and watching for chinks in the hustler's defenses. The thought of someone beating his boss at his own tricky game had served to keep Rama awake across the featureless western stretches when Wedgy would hand him the wheel and doze away into a dreamy world of junk bonds and cooked books.

Rama still had about three hours until Wedgy's expected return; he dangled his bare feet above his empty tennis shoes and gazed idly across the sunny golf course and its bordering hills. The tenth fairway, an intensely manicured buffer between him and the raw desert landscape, lay just a few steps away. The fairway struck Rama as an unnerving green swath parading awkwardly against the earth's rocky contours. Despite the attention lavished upon its turf and its flowered tee boxes, it offended Rama's vision.

Rama had nearly forgotten he had such a vision, but from his earliest days when his mother's garden was a place of wonder, he had been fascinated with landscapes. Only later, with the discovery of the gap in the laurel hedge revealing Bluff Meade's seventh hole and its artful topography, did he realize the fascination focused particularly on golf courses. His mother had noticed, and it was she who had directed him to Trent Institute.

Summer had come and was rapidly going, but still no word had arrived from home regarding Trent. Nothing ventured, nothing gained, Rama figured. But the registration fee *had* been ventured and was meant to have secured his enrollment. Rama feared his education was slipping through doubtful hands. At least here on Wedgy's so-called tour he was receiving some exposure to golf-course architecture, even if the unimaginative municipal tracks to which Wedgy was generally relegated consisted of poor landscape and precious little architecture.

The comforting rattle of a set of clubs and the squeaky wheels of a pull cart intruded on Rama's thoughts—or had they been daydreams? He raised his head, and a friendly voice confirmed it might have been the latter.

"Mighty fine day for a siesta, eh?"

Rama turned to face the voice. Before his brain could process the image of the golfer approaching, Rama could feel a grin forming across his face. The smile formed contrary to Wedgy's rules of engagement: "Never warm up to anyone around a golf course. You don't know who my next opponent might be, so always keep your eyes open and play close to the vest. It's like war with these guys—like over in 'Nam—you never know which of the black pajamas is gonna stick a Punji up your ass. It doesn't hurt to be a defensive prick, Rama; but at the very least be diffident."

Rama never had been clear about the diffidence instruction since he hadn't been anywhere near a dictionary for weeks, but on this sleepy afternoon it would be virtually impossible to be anything but friendly in the presence of the cheerful fellow smiling back at him. He was the incarnation of the character from a children's game where the head, the torso, and the legs of different characters can be rearranged to form entertaining new possibilities—possibilities that most definitely did not include the likes of Wedgy's Viet Cong.

The fellow wore a rose satin cowboy shirt complete with mother-of-pearl buttons and a generous helping of rhinestones. Even in daylight they twinkled like a night at the Ryman Auditorium. The fellow had cut the sleeves just below the elbows to free up his swing. Somewhere someone mourned the desecration of a famous country singer's discarded wardrobe.

He wore khaki plus-fours, and below the cuffs tanned calves disappeared into argyle socks that in turn plunged into red Globe Trotter tennis sneakers. Balanced impossibly on the fellow's tightly barbered head sat a straw fedora; where its jaunty trout fly should have hung dangled a leviathan bass plug.

"Or are you working on the *mental* game?" laughed the golfer at Rama's trance. "Guess that might beat the hell out of hauling all these tools around." The fellow flipped an obscene gesture toward his squealing pull cart.

Rama laughed out loud, completely abandoning his post in Wedgy's diffident army to the twinkling green eyes in the golfer's brash face. "No…I was redesigning the tenth hole," replied Rama with uncertainty.

"An architecture student, are you? Where the shit were you guys when we needed you? Are you playin' today?"

"No, but I'm gonna do some caddying later."

"Well, then you'll see for yourself," replied the golfer. "The only thing the bozo that built this course knew was how to drive a dozer and how to make a left turn. Fives are too short. Threes are too long. Damn course is paradise for the southpaw lay-up artist. Damn layout takes half the clubs right out of your hands, and the slopes bounce half the balls and most of the luck out there into Gila monster land.

"Oh, and did I mention the greens will put you to sleep? Of course, you might like that part," the golfer cackled cheerfully.

Rama chuckled at himself and at the odd course critic. "So why do you bother to play here? You look pretty happy."

"Happy? Whew, at least you didn't say queer." The golfer wiped an imaginary bead of sweat from his brow and flicked it from his fingertips. "It's like Everest: because it's here. This is the nowhere corner of Texas. There ain't a lot of other choices unless you want to join up in a proper club back in 'Paso."

The golfer looked serious for an instant. "Not a real comfortable option for yours truly." He extended his right arm to Rama. "Tyler Grant…and you be?"

Rama didn't reply for a moment; his eyes were drawn to a snakeskin pattern of scar tissue curling about the golfer's fingers—two of which were shortened by a joint. "Rama Schwain," he blurted at last.

"Yep. Gnarled those digits up pretty bad—electrical shocks, mostly," explained Tyler, anticipating Rama's question. "Got a few too many RF burns trying to keep XERF's transmitter tickin'. For the most part, we kept the Wolf on the air till he packed up for Hollywood."

Rama sensed that he was in the presence of celebrity. "Do you mean Wolfman Jack? You worked for him?"

"We were part of the posse, you might say. Ha. Damn near took a bullet for the bastard down the river at Acuña. Enough history. Did I hear you say you were caddying?"

"Yeah, this afternoon." Rama was fully awake now and reluctant to let go of the story that the unusual fellow displaying his scarred grip seemed so quick to abandon.

"Well then," Tyler suggested, "how 'bout just going around the front nine with me? Give you five bucks for your trouble. Son of a bitching cart is losing its bearings, though—you'll have to loop it. We'll have you back to your nap in an hour and a half or less. I play fast…I don't fuck around out there." Tyler's stubby fingers fished for the bills in his wallet. "What do you say? Where else you gonna get paid for scouting the course?"

Rama couldn't argue with Tyler's logic, and the pay was good. The offer might have been even more generous if the eccentric golfer had known the transformation his game would soon undergo—but Rama was not in the business of selling his treasures.

"Why not; it'll be fun," Rama replied, as the starter called the Robbins threesome and the Grant single to the tee.

"That'd be us," said Tyler. He tapped down his straw fedora into firm footing and offered Rama a pre-round handshake; this time Rama noticed the tattoo of a wolf and a lightning bolt peeking from beneath the cut-off sleeve.

"Let's do battle."

Rama and Tyler were first on the tee box. Rama busied himself cleaning grit from the grooves in Tyler's well-worn Wilsons. Tyler didn't ask for advice but took his place at the middle tees and drew his 3-wood. He squeezed off a volley of vicious practice swings as he waited for the Robbins to show.

Finally a group of three well-fed and well-dressed male golfers in two gleaming golf carts glided to a stop near the black tees at the back of the tee box. Tyler and Rama looked back from the blue tees at the late arrivals. Dressed in nearly identical pastel golf shirts, pleated slacks, and bright white saddle golf shoes, the men appeared to be the equivalent of the uniformed gentleman golfers of an earlier time. But these were no gents; they made no effort to approach or respect the single golfer on the tee ahead. They chattered rudely as they milled around their tee.

Tyler's glance would normally have been sufficient request for quiet, but it went unheeded as loudly whispered references to his unorthodox appearance floated teeward on a current of intolerance. Rama felt the atmosphere turn electric. "Crappy way to get started," he muttered.

But Tyler was not all that unused to charged electric fields, and he turned to face the troublesome trio. He squinted to make out the identity of the Robbin's group.

"Let me guess: Ralphie, Ben, and Carl? Damned, I can barely tell you Chamber of Commerce boys apart. Who dressed you fellas? Did your wives all go shopping at Penny's together? Hell, I thought this was a game for rugged individuals."

Tyler's voice then assumed a stern tone that belied the carefree demeanor Rama had witnessed earlier. "You boy's know you're breaking the rules, right?" The threesome were muzzled by the audacity of Tyler's confrontation. Tyler didn't wait for an answer. "The rules say we all should compare the ID on our balls before we begin. So pull 'em out and let me have a look. You do have *balls*, don't you, 'cause you sure don't have manners. And by the way, you gals are kidding yourselves if you think you belong back on the tips."

The Robbins boys were gathering their wind to protest, but this was one strange bird and they knew not to push him. Tyler continued: "While you think about it, fellas, I'll just hit away…my ball is marked TG. But you'll never get close enough to see it." Tyler calmly positioned himself behind the ball. Rama wished he had taken the driver; the farther this one flies from the Robbins, the better, he thought.

Tyler looked up at Rama from his address. "I know what you're thinkin', but I don't need the driver here," he said placidly. His 3-wood came back in a majestic arc. The jewels on Tyler's shirt shot tracers into the sky. The golf ball obediently followed his wish and flew twenty-five yards farther than any drive he had ever hit. Tyler lingered for a moment after the shot and examined his club in disbelief.

"Holy…got a piece of that one, eh caddie? Ha. Ha." Tyler trotted deliberately after the ball while Rama stood in confusion on the tee. The Robbins were up next; shouldn't Tyler wait? After about fifty feet, Tyler turned back toward the tee. "Come on, caddie; those bigots won't mind if we go to the front of the bus. Just walk up the middle of the fairway; they'll never hit it anyway," he hollered.

Rama ran forward, wishing he had the courage to turn back to savor the astonishment that surely must have been playing across the faces of the threesome falling silently into the distance.

"Guess we kind of broke the rules by teeing off first, huh?" Tyler chirped as Rama caught up. "The poor bastards—they're gonna have to play the tips just to save face. Christ, they'd have been away the whole damn round anyway… would have slowed us down big-time. Like I said, an hour and a half round. I don't fuck around."

Tyler followed the gratifying opening shot with strokes registering at or near the top of his ability. The adverbs fell happily into place on the list of his all-time golf shots: satisfying, pure, perfect, confident, precise, heroic. As they approached the ninth and Rama's final hole, Tyler regretted that his magic caddie would soon return to the pumpkin patch.

A deep sinkhole intruded into the ninth fairway in such a way as to make driving through the hazard out of the question for mortals and laying up short highly unrewarding for anyone desirous of a birdie.

Tyler had Rama check and recheck his scorecard. Each tally registered the same answer: Thirty-one, miraculously one under after eight holes. One more par would yield the Holy Grail and the best front nine he had ever played. Tyler had declared earlier that only making par would validate his criticisms of the course, but now, having played the track at that level, he felt more respect for the architect. Maybe old Mr. D-9 wasn't so crude after all.

To make this the front nine of a lifetime, Tyler knew he would have to carry the sinkhole's cruel carbonate walls. He couldn't recall having ever tried, but neither could he recall having ever played a round of golf with faith like this. Maybe he should hire a caddie more often, he thought. Maybe he should rethink that five-dollar tip.

Tyler had promised to get Rama back in an hour and a half. Even with the geological and psychological chasms staring him in the face, he wasn't going to dawdle now. Mindful of Tyler's decision, Rama already had drawn the driver.

Tyler made a practice swing, and another, then two more. That is one swing too many, Rama thought. Tyler had abandoned his routine as fear of failure was suddenly calling the shots. The ball sparkling on the ninth tee was destined inevitably for oblivion.

"Hold up, Tyler...hold up," Rama interrupted.

Tyler stepped back from a tense stance and looked at Rama with irritation. "What the..."

"Didn't you see that?" asked Rama. "A coyote about ten yards past the hazard. Sorry, I was afraid you'd hit it...could've messed you up."

"Ha," replied Tyler, tamping his fedora back down tightly. "Little bit bright out for those critters, don't you think, Rama?"

Rama glanced at a phantom wristwatch to hide a knowing smile.

Thus distracted from his spiraling doubts, Tyler reloaded and confidently struck the ball to the hard green turf beyond the hazard. His heart soared as the ball settled into a place from which he had never played a second shot—a very good place. From his new perspective, nothing could stand between him and finishing the ninth hole at even par. And nothing did.

Tyler Grant had just finished the front in four strokes less than his previous best. Facing the back nine, he knew enough about the value of golf's silly embrace of routine and superstition to know that he didn't want to burst the fragile bubble in which he was operating so effortlessly, and that included losing the noble young man carrying his bag.

As they walked from the ninth green Tyler fondly clasped a disfigured hand on Rama's shoulder. "Ain't no way I'm letting you desert me now, Buddy. You've gotta stick this one out...I'm making hay here. Christ, I've never had such fun."

Rama had heard it before at Bluff Meade. Still, it always warmed his heart to assist people in their grasp of the simple, glorious thing to which they aspired. Rama felt exhausted at the rapid-fire pace of Tyler's great game. His spirit was depleted from the will of balancing his player on the high, slender wire of achievement. Less than ninety minutes had elapsed; he still had time to rest and prepare for Wedgy's return. Tyler's golfing fate would have to find its own way.

"Can't do it," Rama apologized to the rampaging golfer. "Don't worry, you'll do great on the back. You left a few putts back there so you know there's room to go lower. Just stay ahead of your Chamber of Commerce buddies."

"Well…shit. Then I'll tell you what," offered Tyler. "I'll post the scorecard up on the bulletin board. Whatever happens, at least you'll know. And if I break my best score, there'll be a twenty pinned behind the card." With that he plucked the card from Rama's shirt pocket and replaced it with a ten-dollar bill. He tapped his hat back into place and moved rapidly down to the tenth tee. Only the bulging black eyes of the bass plug dangling from his brim would witness the brave fellow's solitary test of faith on the back nine.

Chapter 43

Rama dozed in and out of sleep with the pulse of the proverbial western wind. He had settled into a comfortable chair on the clubhouse deck, hoping Wedgy would blow back in time for their afternoon match. The soft chatter of groups playing across the nearest greens, their voices rising and falling with the breeze, had lulled him to sleep. An insistent cawing of crows interrupted the dialogue from the green and stirred him from visions of Carlos Taddio's ball-hoarding ravens.

Rama woke to find Wedgy's Lincoln sitting in the parking lot. He had snoozed two hours away after leaving Tyler at the turn. He scrambled to his feet and headed to the clubhouse in search of his boss; the bar would be his most likely bet. Hurrying past the pro shop en route to the bar, Rama noticed a busy bulletin board tacked lavishly with notices for men's club meetings, poker parties, lost clubs, honey-do services, and all manner of communications vital to enriching the lives of the addicted.

There, tacked in a relatively clear corner, was a fresh scorecard signed by Tyler Grant. A carefully rendered seventy-four indicated the golfer had failed to make par by two strokes. Rama felt a surge of guilt for sleeping through the eccentric fellow's critical back nine but smiled as he turned up the card and found a twenty-dollar bill—a promise kept by an honorable man whose two-over-par, although disappointing, was two strokes better than he had ever scored before.

Rama stepped into the blinding darkness of the bar. For a few moments he could make out only the flicker of TV screens and the swirling lights of a dozen animated beer signs. The room smelled of great hamburgers and grassy shoes. As expected, Wedgy lingered near the bar, working his way through a frosty pre-game draft. His back was turned halfway to Rama as he faced another figure in the dim light. Bright flecks winked in the dark as the man facing Wedgy tipped his own glass high. Cowboy jewels, straw hat…damned if Wedgy hadn't stumbled upon Tyler. Rama shivered with certainty that the connection was bound to stir trouble.

Tyler spotted Rama. He was disappointed that he didn't have par or better to crow about, but in case the charmed caddie hadn't seen the card on the board, he would put him straight pronto. But before Tyler could speak and give away the fact that he and Rama had played together, Rama signaled him to silence with a slashing-of-the-throat gesture rendered with enough vigor to make him pause. Feigning ignorance of the identity of his boss's oddly dressed drinking companion, Rama approached Wedgy and good-naturedly harangued him for forgetting he was meant to play today—an hour ago, to be exact.

Tyler noticed the ruse immediately. Wedgy did not.

"Jesus, since when does my caddie call the shots *off* the course?" Wedgy laughed. "Settle down, kiddo. Turns out we got our match right here."

Rama turned to face the shadowy recesses of the bar room.

"No, right *here*," scolded Wedgy. "This here is Mr. Grant…like president Ulysses S. But damned if I got his first name."

"Tyler Grant." Tyler offered his scarred hand to Rama as if they had never met.

"Excuse my feeble mind, Tyler," said Wedgy. "I never forget a score but I've got a lousy head for names. This is my nephew, Rama Schwain. My sister told me to keep an eye on him for a few months 'til he enters seminary school. He'll be carrying my bag today just for something to do."

"Schwain?" asked Tyler.

"Yes sir," replied Rama, holding back a chuckle at his new relationship to Wedgy and at his alleged academic pursuits.

"Tyler is playing a friendly little Nassau with us today, Rama," explained Wedgy, careful to avoid mentioning the value of the wager. "He was kind enough to step in for Mr. Monroe, the men's club president, who was planning to take me for some real money—or so they tell me—but got the trots or some god-damned excuse."

"Uncle Wallace!" Rama gasped in disapproval at his "uncle's" irreverent language. "Perhaps you and Mr. Grant could refrain from cursing today."

"Right…so sorry," Wedgy apologized, pleased at Rama's creative initiative. "Luckily, Tyler was gracious enough to stand in for the stricken presidente and has saved us from driving all this way for nothing. The starter has got us going out in about thirty minutes. Is that right, Tyler?"

Tyler nodded and took a long slow drink.

Wedgy tossed Rama the car keys. "How about fetching my clubs? I'll meet you up on the first tee after Mr. Grant and I negotiate a level playing field over another brew." Wedgy tipped the rim of his glass toward his opponent who gently clinked in return. The bartering was on.

Wedgy drank in the sweet possibilities of the round ahead. The oddball apparently didn't have enough marbles to dress himself or to put on a pair of spikes; in all likelihood the fellow's grasp of golf would be as tenuous, and those ravaged fingers weren't likely to help.

It turned out that Tyler had a firm negotiating hand, and although Wedgy worked their age differential, his unfamiliarity with the course, and a variety of fabricated ailments for all they were worth, his marble-challenged drinking partner wasn't giving an inch or a stroke. Wedgy grudgingly granted his opponent two strokes after Tyler had cited the beating Wedgy had given a fellow in Abilene just the other day. Evidently golf news traveled like the wind out in these parts.

Wedgy slid his empty glass across the shiny oak bar. "Enough fraternizing with the enemy. Now that you've robbed me, I gotta piss. Don't want to march to my doom on a full bladder," he whined. "See you on the tee." Then he slipped back downstairs to the locker room. Hanging on the bulletin board was a clipboard with the latest handicap postings for the Sunset Hills Men's Club. Wedgy was surprised at the number of near-scratch players who called Sunset Hills home. Deep into the second page he found what he was looking for: Grant, Tyler – Handicap 12.6.

Wedgy smiled. Nearly thirteen strokes separated his weirdo competitor from par and about eight strokes from his own handicap. "Jesus, I shoulda given that queer bastard a couple more strokes just to make it interesting." Wedgy wandered out to the tee with the confidence of knowing that after giving Tyler two strokes, he still had a theoretical six-stroke advantage.

—•—

The problem with theories is that they are theoretical. An unforeseen factor or a whim of nature can dash them into the rocks of reality. So it was with the perception of safety in Wedgy's calculated advantage. Who could have known that the Caddie's Gift that had buoyed Wedgy would today, on the strength of Rama's admiration for Tyler's honorable spirit, shine its beneficial light on Wedgy's opponent instead.

As the supposed cakewalk Wedgy had imagined got underway, Wedgy's game slipped to pre-Rama levels. He grew increasingly fearful that the magic had for some reason run its course. Tyler monotonously hit fairways and avoided trouble with a game that was well above his posted handicap. When he missed greens, he chipped irritatingly close to the hole. It looked as if Tyler were playing far over his head, thereby canceling out Wedgy's theoretically superior game. Wedgy clung to a single-stroke lead as the couple stepped to the ninth tee, but his confidence was shaken.

Tyler had gained the honors with an exceptional putt on the eighth hole and now faced the same carry that he had successfully managed across the sinkhole earlier that day with Rama. Taking his practice swings prior to the shot, Tyler firmly believed he could carry the rugged gap again. Wedgy did not and hoped to parlay his doubts into some money and momentum. He felt certain the added pressure would condemn the tenacious Tyler to failure.

"What do you say we double the bet here, Grant old boy?" Wedgy offered abruptly. "I'm standing one up before my shot, but if you make yours and I miss mine then we double the Nassau for the first nine. If we both go over—or in—then the bet is off. You've got everything to gain, Grant…maybe earn a few bucks to buy some decent shoes. The pressure's all on me."

Rama had seen it before: Wedgy's offer on a critical hole had often worked to unsettle his competitor. Of course, Wedgy had usually screened out the strong minded to improve his odds in these gambles; today it appeared he had underestimated his competitor.

Tyler chuckled to himself. Before today this was a bet that would have been pointless to consider because he had always laid up. But now, after successfully negotiating the sinkhole that morning with Rama, he felt an embrace from the very game that had stymied him so badly in the past. "You're on, partner," he replied.

For the second time that day, Tyler found the rare earth beyond the hazard. Two for two, he thought. He tamped down his hat to keep it from tumbling off as he bent to snatch away the tee lying like a tiny bleached bone on the tee box.

"Pressure's on, Wallace," Tyler parroted Wedgy's gravely voice as he stepped clear of the box. He looked at Rama. "Better say a little prayer for your uncle, Reverend."

Wedgy's shaken confidence climbed up the Richter scale as his tee shot bored into the wall of the sinkhole. He cursed loudly at his folly, then snapped his fingers for a new ball.

As Rama placed a shiny Skyway-Pro in Wedgy's impatient hand, he noticed the old hustler's eyes had darkened in accusation, as if it were his caddie's fault he had just failed to carry the abyss. "Whose side are you on today, god damn it?" Wedgy hissed. "That queer SOB has been sandbagging the hell out of me. Christ, he's playing seven or eight strokes below his cap."

Rama had no answer. The magic was in his spirit, but never under his control. He looked at Wedgy dispassionately. "Boss, the drop area is left of the green about twenty yards."

"Screw it," declared Wedgy. He teed again and in anger hit his third within a dozen feet of Tyler's ball. Wedgy dropped his club to the turf for Rama to collect and charged toward the footbridge.

In five minutes the front side was history. Tyler had finished with a thirty-seven, two shots more than that morning but still had a good chance at making par for the round. The shot into the sinkhole had erased Wedgy's lead, and its penalty stroke should have put Tyler ahead by one, but Wedgy angrily reported a five for the hole instead of a six as he stalked toward the tenth tee.

"That's a push for the front. It's still your honors," Wedgy barked, attempting to get the group's attention on the next hole.

Rama looked at the card, then back at Wedgy who was moving rapidly away. That was a six, not a five, he thought. Tyler, engrossed in his own quest for par didn't seem to notice, but the stroke meant the difference between tying—which Wedgy claimed—and Tyler's winning the front.

Rama hurried to catch up with Wedgy. The once-powerful shoulders were hunched slightly as Wedgy moved quickly from the suspicious hole. Rama had always been a willing medium for the spirit behind his gift. He knew he had been exploited since learning of the Bluff Meade men's auction for his services, but he had no intention of abetting one who now crossed the line between hustling and cheating. Like Tyler's bet, Rama's integrity was now at stake.

He arrived at Wedgy's shoulder just as Wedgy arrived at the tenth tee. Tyler was still bringing up the rear. Rama leaned into the hustler's ear and confronted him in a whisper: "This is *Texas*…you can get shot for that."

Wedgy played dumb. "For what? Does it look like I've got an ace up my sleeve, partner?"

Rama was insistent. "Tyler's a little distracted now, but before long he'll count up those strokes. He won't buy your bogey five. I wouldn't get him mad, Boss."

"Shit, what's the faggot gonna do, butt-fuck me? I'll tell him we take two off the tee where I come from."

Rama put his foot down. "Bullshit. There's no *we* in that bogus story. I'm just as responsible as you for your score's accuracy. Correct your card now or I'm leaving you to your crappy game. It's only a few bucks for a Greyhound to Memphis. At least you've paid me that much."

Wedgy groaned at the thought of his vulnerability without Rama's magic. He envisioned more lackluster games like the one he was involved in now. He looked back at Tyler who was ambling up the path with the scorecard in his palm.

Rama smiled with a self-assurance that Wedgy hadn't seen before. "You can still win it back on the back nine," whispered Rama. "If you play good enough."

Wedgy groaned again and faced the music.

"Oh shit, Grant, think I got it wrong. Did you put me down for bogey back there? It was double." Wedgy's innocence was unconvincing. "Guess I got too pissed at losing one in the damned Grand Canyon to count 'em up proper."

Tyler glared at Wedgy with little tolerance for his arithmetic lapse. "Not only a six, hombre, but you owe me for the hole, the side, and the push," replied Tyler sternly. "Guess I'd better pay a little more attention to you two from here on out."

Tyler hadn't heard Rama's appeal to Wedgy and looked at Rama as if double-crossed. "Suppose that gives me the honors," he snapped as he stepped to the tee, his wolf tattoo peeking from beneath the sleeve of his cowboy shirt.

Rama ached to distance himself from Wedgy but remained silent as Tyler went through his pre-shot routine. Rama and Tyler were both rooting for a seventy-one. Tyler swung viciously, sending the ball deep down the tenth's broad, artless fairway.

As Tyler moved forward, he paused beside Wedgy who lingered at the ball washer. "Thought I was gonna have to kill you there for a minute. Ha ha," he whispered with chilling sincerity. Wedgy froze, speechless, and watched his invigorated competitor stride confidently up the fairway.

Tyler proceeded to break par for the first time in his life, collecting not only the entire Nassau, but two other side bets Wedgy had concocted to try and stop the bleeding along the way. Wedgy, on the other hand, was hot, burning in a furnace of humiliation and anger even as he swallowed a bitter double-dose of defeat and disrepute.

After the match Wedgy peeled $250 from his bankroll like an automaton. Although he was in no mood to make small talk with the odd-looking golfer who had just cleaned him out, he had to ask if the fellow really had broken par for the first time. Was Tyler the real hustler? Wedgy didn't expect an honest answer, but he could read between the lines.

"Some of us play this game on the straight and narrow," Tyler replied. "A hustling shithead like you doesn't deserve an answer, but hell yes—a seventy-one. That's about thirteen under my handicap. Damn right, best game ever. Ha, ha."

Wedgy muttered a forlorn oath. Tyler's answer squared up with his 12.6. Wedgy couldn't have cared less about Tyler's scatological characterization of him, but he was irritated that he been suckered by a phony vanity handicap, and that somehow he had let an easy one get away.

"Must be that lucky *nephew* of yours, pal. I've played twenty-seven holes with him today and ended up one-over. Can you believe that?"

Wedgy stopped. "Twenty-seven?"

"Counting the nine he looped for me this morning. Guess he needed the money," said Tyler. "Shit, he's about the best caddie I never had. Ha ha."

Wedgy winced at Tyler's irritating laugh and at the sting of betrayal. He regarded Rama's gift as a trade secret, to be concealed as well as exploited by him alone. He fumed silently, but his anger soon collapsed under the weight of opportunity.

"Well screw Rama Schwain," Wedgy sniffed. "If you think a GD caddie makes that much of a difference just *being there*, how 'bout we go around again tomorrow without him? No caddies. No handicap strokes."

Tyler was brimming with confidence and a mighty thirst. Without wasting any time in deliberation, he accepted Wedgy's offer thinking that the least he could do was lose half of today's winnings as long as he didn't take any side bets.

"You're on," Tyler answered, "but I'm gonna watch you like a damned buzzard."

Chapter 44

Ivar Guidance waved off the mint julep and sipped on a cold ginger ale while surveying the world from Bluff Meade's sunny patio. He pressed the icy drink to his forehead and watched through the glass as the players down on the eighteenth green plunged in and out of a frosty, distorted world. His dignified posture gave way to a lazy slump as he settled into one of the white wicker rockers that marched along the patio's perimeter.

He had arrived earlier that morning to play a solo nine and savor a few quiet minutes before his guest arrived. It was not that he needed more time alone. Since his wife died, he seemed to have no shortage of that. It hadn't been a full year since Rebecca had passed away. Just last summer she was here, then by winter she was gone. His friends had assured him that the speed of her decline was a blessing, that it had spared them both protracted anguish. But the swiftness of Rebecca's passing made the silence in their home especially difficult to endure. The company of friends and the competition on the golf course had helped. In fact, in those dark days Ivar almost wished Wedgy was still at Bluff Meade to routinely challenge him as he had in years past—if only to provide relief from the terrible loneliness.

At times like this a family would have been welcome, but Ivar and Rebecca never had children. After a decade of fruitlessness they considered adoption, but well into middle age, with a demanding stable of business and other obligations, they both agreed that a child deserved more attention than either could give. Instead, they became generous benefactors for children's causes. But now, Ivar questioned if it were a blessing *not* to be saddled with the demands of a family or if it were a curse to bear her memory and his life alone.

His heart churned heavily in his chest. He wondered if he were still laboring under the strain of that last steep fairway or under another wave of grief. The waves came and went, and when they came, he thanked God for Bluff Meade and the ridiculous game that had lured him with its promise and so often dashed him into its hazards. Even from the worst lie and in the deepest bunkers he had always found comfort on the course. It was what Rebecca would have wanted.

Ivar smiled at the thought. Would she have really wanted him to face a buried lie in a pot bunker or a chip from deep grass to a descending green? She had been far less cynical than that.

They had golfed through many dewy mornings and sultry afternoons together, lost in their own travails against ninety's Holy Grail but linked in the joyful futility of it all. Even now, Rebecca's baby blue bag with its immaculate Patty Berg signature clubs stood forsaken in the garage where she had last parked them. If they had known the finality of that round, perhaps they would have lingered over the eighteenth green a while longer.

Ivar gazed into the splendid September morning. Rebecca had never bested ninety-two, but he smiled—as she always had—at the memory of that round. She had achieved that score from the ladies' tees at Augusta National. Regardless of its modest number, it had been the round of a lifetime, played upon the most legendary of courses. Breaking ninety would have to wait…

"Oh, Honey…" whispered Ivar across his ginger ale, "if only you could have played with Rama."

———•———

"Pardon me if I'm late." A cheerful voice startled Ivar. He felt a blush creep across his face as he was caught gazing through a ginger ale glass darkly.

"No, not at all. I just finished up a tad early," replied Ivar, collecting himself from his slump.

"Well, I hope you didn't rush through for me. You look a little pale."

Ivar stood up courteously, regaining his courtly demeanor. His silk shirt had absorbed a hint of sweat, but the collar remained crisp and the fabric still hung handsomely from his shoulders. He offered a firm friendly hand. "Thanks for coming by, Doctor Myer. If you've got an appetite, brunch here is heavenly."

After seeing that his guest was comfortably settled with iced coffee—the good doctor had declined a morning cocktail—Ivar got down to the business of Doris Schwain's diagnosis.

From his chatter with Rama along the fairways, Ivar had learned of Doris's condition and of her husband's inability to secure the help of a specialist. He had taken a paternal interest in his charmed caddie's fortunes and sometimes wondered if his concern for Rama's life beyond Bluff Meade was just another charity or a latent expression of fatherhood.

"Doctor, I understand you examined Mrs. Schwain recently?"

"Yes. In fact, we're awaiting test results from Atlanta now. You asked us to leave no stone unturned, Mr. Guidance, and we have not." The doctor always understood the financial implication in Ivar's request.

"I appreciate your thoroughness, Doctor…and we now know what?"

"We know your interest may have saved her life," the doctor replied with sincerity. "Although her symptoms appeared at first to be a type of congenital sclerosis, I now believe she is suffering from the complications of some trauma to the back of her head—an aggravated sclerosis, so to speak."

"And that's bad, I take it?"

"Yes. If there is an advancing tissue of any sort within the cranial cavity or in the basal regions," Doctor Myer noticed concern ripple beneath Ivar's attentive expression, "it can eventually impede certain neurological functions and possibly pressure the brain stem...all bad scenarios."

"You said she had suffered an injury to her head?"

"It appears it was a blow, but Mrs. Schwain is shy to elaborate."

Ivar shuddered at the implications of Doris's reluctance. The thought of *another* woman passing prematurely from this mortal coil with a life of dreams left unfulfilled was disturbing. "How critical is time?" he asked anxiously.

"She has suffered for an unusually long time, Mr. Guidance, and that is troubling. If our diagnosis is correct, she is in remarkably good shape considering the time this tissue may have been building. I fear her condition could spin out of control rapidly if circulation to surrounding tissue is compromised. Frankly, I'm surprised it hadn't years ago."

Doctor Myer met Ivar's inquisitive eyes. "But, it does seem that in the last few weeks her symptoms have been worsening. Would you know if Mrs. Schwain has recently suffered any traumatic events that she might have failed to share with us?"

Ivar didn't know Doris that well but knew of one significant event. "Well, yes; her son moved away in the middle of July. Could that make a difference?" He recalled what a negative impact Rama's departure from Bluff Meade had made to the silly game he and his associates were once again suffering beneath. He wondered whether he should share that information with the doctor for fear that it signified nothing more than an intriguing golf superstition.

"Yes, family issues could certainly create some stress." The doctor lingered over his next sip of coffee.

Ivar smoothed out a bothersome wrinkle in his sleeve and changed the subject. "As I told you: Do all you can to help, Doctor. And remember to keep all Doris's medical bills between you and me, period. It's my good deed in a naughty world," smiled Ivar. "I happen to know Mr. Schwain is suffering through a difficult spell, too."

Doctor Myer reminded Ivar of the potential cost of such a generous gift, but Ivar waved off further talk as a waste of breath and ruinous to a perfectly good appetite. He chose instead to divert the subject to his other interest besides golf and charity...flying.

In the most bustling days of his career, Ivar had purchased a 4-seat Cessna 310 airplane for business travel in the Southeast. It wasn't long before he had added flight lessons to his schedule and his pilot had been obliged to look for another gig. Now with some of the fire in his belly extinguished by time and with the loss of his favorite passenger, Rebecca, boring holes in the clouds had lost some of its appeal. Ivar had fallen back to earth and to golf as his primary escape. Funny, he thought, now he had to look for excuses to take to the sky just to keep his hand in and his hours up.

"You are speaking at Vanderbilt on Tuesday, is that right, Doctor?"

"I have a short presentation, yes," said Doctor Myer modestly.

"I have some business in Nashville as well. I am flying over on Monday. The weather looks to be ideal for a novice like me," Ivar laughed. "If you are interested, I could use the company."

Doctor Myer took Ivar's novice comment in the humorous spirit that Ivar intended, and although the doctor had rarely flown in small aircraft, there was no one whom he would trust more when hurtling through Tennessee's skies.

<hr />

"Hope I didn't get your tit in a wringer, Rama?" Tyler Grant smiled apologetically as he encountered his favorite new caddie outside the bar room at Sunset Hills. "I told your cheatin' boss that you played that front nine with me. Now that poor bugger doesn't know which side you're on."

Tyler pulled a twenty-dollar bill from his clip. "I figure I owe you a little something for that last round."

"But I wasn't caddying for you."

Tyler laughed. "Yeah, I suppose tipping the other fella's caddie might look a little suspicious. But shit, that was the best round of golf I've ever played, and Christ, the second best was the round just before that, and you caddied for *half* of it. I don't know how, Rama, but you've got something to do with it. It's like working near a fifty-thousand-watt transmitter when she's lit. I can just feel it."

Tyler tucked the bill into Rama's shirt pocket. Rama wondered if the unusual golfer had been putting on an elaborate hustle and now, somehow, he was just Tyler's foil. Rama extracted the bill, remembering the painful experience with Lee's tip and his father's violent reaction.

"Sorry, mister Grant. Maybe next time."

"You aren't going anywhere yet, Rama. Your boss wants another shot at me tomorrow, same time, same station. And dig it: no caddies. Better keep the tip; it's only money." Tyler parked his clubs outside the bar and disappeared inside to celebrate his good fortune and to pick a bone with his friends in the Chamber of Commerce.

Rama returned to Wedgy's car, relieved that instead of preparing to leave town so late they were heading back to the campground for another night's stay. He was happy he wouldn't be trapped in the car for the long trek out to Albuquerque until Wedgy had a chance to reclaim his losses and his sense of humor. At the moment the old hustler was locked into the blackness of a serious golf hangover, a condition in which an accumulation of the ugly and the unjust draws a vacuum that greedily sucks a golfer's hopeful spirit into a bleak, damp place—the Scotland of the human psyche. Wedgy's blank, joyless mood was aggravated by Rama's alleged treason.

Rama tried to explain that he couldn't help it if Tyler had been moved to play better by whatever mystery had so often elevated Wedgy's game and that he couldn't be blamed if some people were just more receptive to magic than others. Rama didn't venture to explain that the same spirit that might guide a man to take scissors to a jeweled cowboy shirt or inspire a fellow to adorn himself with tokens of Bobby Jones, Slammin' Sammy Sneed, and Meadowlark Lemon might also be a spirit that wouldn't easily confuse rational with right but would readily embrace the mysteries of life, however absurd they might appear.

"Save your philosophy for the professors, Rama. I'll be taking my damn money back from your receptive friend tomorrow, and there will be no mumbo-jumbo involved," said Wedgy. "And that means you won't be anywhere near the son-of-a-bitchin' golf course."

Rama couldn't have been happier. He was relieved to be excused from another greedy game and glad to drop the uncomfortable subject of his effect on golfers. He feared that becoming too analytical would eat at the gift's mystery just the way thinking works its corrosive effect on the golf swing. Most of all, Rama was relieved to put Wedgy out of his sight for the better part of a day.

His thoughts then turned from the prosaic to the practical. If a fellow as unlikely looking as Tyler and as modestly accomplished as his handicap indicated could so easily take $250 from Wedgy, then the secret to defeating the wise, wary old hustler lay in finding a competitor who in his unlikeliness would blind Wedgy's judgment when the lure of Ivar's six-thousand-dollar bet was dangled before his eyes. Then after Wedgy had taken the bait, Rama would cast the full grace of his gift to the unlikely competitor by serving as his caddie.

This was the game for which Rama would now watch. He would remain alert for the most appropriate competitor and muster the gall to abandon Wedgy's bag when the deal went down.

—•—

The next morning Rama woke to the fiddles and trumpets of ecstatic Mexican music. The speakers in the Lincoln's rear shelf throbbed not more than twenty inches from his head. He had not relished the idea of sharing the trailer with Wedgy after yesterday's unhappy events. Luckily the mild, sage-scented evening ensured a comfortable night in the grand car's back seat.

Rama had slept unusually well, in fact. He remembered watching through the rear window for falling stars before slipping into unconsciousness. He never heard Wedgy stirring from the trailer or turning on the broadcast from Juarez.

"Buenos días, Schwain. I told you the seat wasn't so bad, remember?"

Rama sat up on one elbow and looked out the car windows as low yellow light streamed through the pepper trees that struggled to shade their campsite.

The golf hangover still hung around Wedgy like a persistent swarm of gnats. "Haul your ass into the trailer. I'm making breakfast this morning."

Rama wasn't about to turn down a meal and slid briskly from the blue leather seat. The homey smell of coffee and bacon greeted him as he entered the CruiseAir. Wedgy labored at the tiny range, trying to cook away his irritation over a terrible performance yesterday and an odd sense of desertion today. In an unusual act of servitude, the old hustler set a cup of coffee on the Formica tabletop. Rama felt like a prisoner facing his last meal.

"Don't get used to it," Wedgy said. "Thought I'd get a good breakfast in me before tackling your odd-ball friend, Tyler." He glanced at Rama. "In case you don't remember…you're not invited."

Wedgy scraped a pile of scrambled eggs onto a plastic picnic dish and set it on the table. "After I'm through with our little rhinestone cowboy, I'll be taking a sabbatical—won't be back for three days. Don't worry, you've got the trailer and plenty of food." Wedgy chuckled. "I told you this job beat the hell out of school."

"Guess that explains the breakfast," Rama scoffed. He wasn't sure whether to be alarmed at being unexpectedly stranded at the desolate campground or elated at having a three-day break from Wallace Byrne. "So where are you going?"

"Mexico."

"What do you do down there?"

"What *can't* you do down there?" Wedgy smirked. The prospect of what he did down there seemed to have a tonic effect on the poisons still circulating in the old hustler's brain. A smile flashed across his wrinkled face. "You know, Rama, they got fishing poles for rent up at the camp store. That should keep you occupied."

Rama looked disgusted. "Hey that'll be fun, pulling the same old catfish out of that pond for a couple of days. Boy, if I could just afford the pole."

Rama was convinced that this was as good a time as any to make a stand for his pinched wages. If there was any money to be recovered from Wedgy, it had better be extracted now. God knows what might become of his bankroll in Old Mexico.

He pressed: "I've been broke since you started hanging on to two-thirds of my share. Come on, Mr. Byrne…we had an agreement. Ivar even witnessed it."

"Keep Ivar out of it, Schwain. Some thanks I get for making your damn breakfast," Wedgy grumbled. "Jesus, kid…you're telling me I owe you two-thirds of your share? You've been counting? Hell, you're lucky not to be in school or dodging Punji sticks…and you're grousing about a few bucks."

"A few bucks is all I need, now," insisted Rama. "And yes sir, I *have* been counting, and the missing part of my share comes to $1,120…and you wonder why the magic doesn't work?"

Wedgy reluctantly pulled out his billfold and counted off eighty dollars. "That should get you off my back," he snarled. Wedgy escaped the breakfast nook and quickly packed for his Mexican weekend. He grabbed his golf bag and stormed out the screen door to load up the Lincoln.

Rama followed him out. "Why don't you leave me the shag bag and your clubs? Maybe I'll take up the game…since I'm on vacation."

"Not a chance, Schwain. No one is messing with my sticks—not on this iron ground," snapped Wedgy. He loaded his clubs into the trunk with finality but emerged with the shag-bag, a couple of salvaged irons, and a pitching wedge. "Don't say I never did anything for you," sniffed Wedgy as he tossed the gear on the ground beside the car.

Wedgy grabbed the old Night Lessons brassie from the trunk and chucked it to the pile. He slid behind the wheel and looked back at the skeptical young man standing on the trailer's stoop. "Three days…now don't go nowhere, Rama," he laughed. "And don't forget the breakfast dishes, eh, amigo?" The Lincoln roared to life, and Wedgy headed for the border.

Chapter 45

Hitchhiking to the Greyhound bus station in El Paso and buying a ticket back to Memphis seemed like a reasonable response to Wedgy's departure, but bolting from Wedgy and his chronic greed didn't square with Rama's scrappy nature—not when there was still the matter of recovering Hank's losses. But lingering in this place for three days with nothing to do until Wedgy's return might be pushing his patience. Maybe Wedgy was right; perhaps he really could work on his golf skills. His game hadn't received any attention since his last round in the back-of-beyond at Bluff Meade with Jimmy Jim almost two months ago.

Rama unzipped Wedgy's shag bag and disgorged its sunburned contents. A collection of dehydrated balls clattered down the metal snout and settled in the dusty grass at his feet. After plucking a pocketful of the most promising from the pile, he spent the better part of the morning working them around the pond as bullfrogs screamed in dismay at the intrusion. After enduring wedge shots over and around their heads for an hour and a half, the creatures had all retreated to the center of the pond. A dozen eyes poked through the algae and watched Rama's technique with the keen vision of insect hunters.

The rust in Rama's swing quickly fell away as his anger with Wedgy subsided. Gradually, as he chased the balls around the pond, the balance and the elusive timing that produce grace and power revisited him. And as his strokes improved, Rama pictured Carlos Taddio smiling in approval.

After working up a good sweat, Rama sat on the picnic table and lit up one of Wedgy's cigarillos. He was happier than he had been for weeks. The smoke tugged at his stomach for a moment, then flooded him with a sense of good will and indomitable confidence. The bullfrogs thrashed back to their stations along the bank. As the commotion in the pond settled down, he noticed the old Night Lessons club still lying on the ground where Wedgy had tossed it.

A shiver ran up his back. In a moment the brassie's dry leather grip was back in his hands. Rama felt the radiance of possibility that still shone from the club after so many years. He swung it cautiously at first, and then faster, with blooming audacity.

"Enough of this wedge stuff," Rama said to himself. He teed a ball on a scrap of bark and took aim at a spot over a cactus patch far beyond the pond. It appeared to be about two hundred yards to clear the thorns. Rama waggled the club, then unleashed a swing that startled him in its velocity and in the unexpected volume of its lash through the air.

The ball easily carried the pond and the cactus. Rama saw a flicker of white ricochet off a rock outcrop a good thirty feet or so past the farthest thorns. He put down the club as though he had been caught stealing. The stroke was shocking…too good to be an accident. He imagined a new future spreading out like shock waves from that perfect swing, a future that did not include wasting his gifts on the selfish or caddying for Wallace Byrnes. In fact, with the confidence of the tobacco in his blood and the lively club in his hands, Rama realized the winds of defeat that had blown so freely through his family would stop here. He would not go another step down Wedgy's or his father's selfish roads.

Rama's thoughts circled back to his mother and her visit with Doctor Myer, and her excitement at the promise of a hopeful new diagnosis. Rama pictured how much sweeter his return would be if he arrived to find her in good health. But a troubling pang of guilt displaced the tobacco's artificial glow. The thought of leaving her so quickly in his anger at Hank now struck him as merely selfish, and he feared that he might never fit into the Schwain household again. For the first time since he had climbed aboard Wedgy's Lincoln in the lot at Bluff Meade, he felt a tug toward home.

Rama fetched a soda from the trailer's fridge and sat on the picnic table. He considered another practice session, but banging the ball around Sunset Hills's green slopes seemed a more fruitful alternative than terrorizing the denizens of the slime pool again. It was high time he played a real round.

—•—

"Are you going to be able to get back to camp before dark?" asked the elderly couple as Rama climbed from their Roadmaster at the entrance to Sunset Hills. "There are skin-walkers in these parts, they say. We'll be coming back from Carlsbad around eight o'clock. We'll keep an eye out for you, Son."

"Thanks, but don't worry about me. I'm not sure when I'll be heading back, but I'll find a ride okay." Rama had no doubt about the couple's punctuality, but he didn't worry over superstitions like skin-walkers. He waved them on their way and turned to the clubhouse with a heady sense of independence and with four old clubs rattling on his shoulder.

The golf course looked inviting in the morning light. His breath quickened in anticipation as he approached the pro shop counter to book his chance at destroying par.

"Can't get a single on for a couple hours, kid. Full up," the clerk apologized. Rama's enthusiasm flagged slightly at the thought of waiting. He asked about rental clubs and felt his pluck wane further when told they were all taken. The clerk noticed Rama's disappointment. "Hell, you only need a few more clubs to round out that *fine* set you're carrying. The range master can scare up another ten sticks for you if you ask him real nice." The clerk slid a couple of range tokens across the counter. "His name is Levi."

Rama was discouraged by the logjam on the tee sheet but soon readjusted his sights to the range. He had all the time in the world, it seemed, so why worry? But when Levi told him they were out of balls, Rama wondered if maybe he shouldn't have taken his chances with the frog pond after all. He didn't bother to ask about the ten clubs, thinking he already knew that answer, too.

"They kinda put a rush on us this mornin'; we can't fetch them balls back fast enough…not short-handed like we are 'round here today," said Levi. "The damn retriever tractor broke down, wouldn't ya know. Hell, I'd send the range boy out with a couple a' shag bags, but he come up sick today or some such horseshit."

The range master looked at the deflated young man standing before him. He considered the antique brassie, a pair of irons, and the pitching wedge resting on Rama's shoulder.

"Them's all the clubs you got, Son?"

Rama shrugged.

"Well *that* I can fix," smiled the master. "You shag in a couple of plump bagfulls, and I'll fix you up with a full set."

Levi pulled two shag bags from beneath the counter. "You just go out there past that 250 marker and shag up whatever you can find. You'll be safe," he laughed. "These yokels ain't liable to bean you out that far. Besides, they'll be running out of ammo pretty quick; then you can shag in closer. You fetch in a half- dozen bags and I'll write you up for a free game, too."

In a couple of minutes Rama was looking back at the firing line from the no-man's land beyond the 250-yard marker. The occasional report of a well-struck shot rang from the stalls, and even less frequently Rama heard the thud of a ball landing in the dust nearby. The range master was right; only a few balls threatened him as he filled his first bag. He was walking back toward the mound to retrieve the empty bag when a particularly crisp driver rang out. A few seconds later a ball thumped the earth and rolled past only three feet to his right.

Someone got lucky and caught one flush, thought Rama. But in a few moments another ball traced the first ball's trajectory within several feet.

"Shit, Levi said I'd be safe out here," Rama muttered. He quickened his step, keeping a sharp eye on the tees as he headed to the center of the range. Another sharp report exploded from the tees, and a towering ball started toward the net draped along the right edge of the range. It seemed to pose no danger, but before he knew it the ball had executed a left turn and was bearing down on him with unsettling purpose. Rama danced away from the incoming missile, then peered back up-range. A shed roof shaded the golfers and he couldn't make out much detail on the figures flailing away in the shadows, but he noticed a cluster of folks gathered around one stall. Laughter, presumably at his expense, floated from the tees.

"Crap, some guy is putting on a clinic and I'm the target," growled Rama.

He plucked up a few more balls along the right side and started back across the range to retrieve the full bag. Before he arrived on the opposite side, one more ball skidded across the ground in a flurry of dust and another soared over his head. Rama felt as much anger as he did amazement that anyone could be so accurate at such a distance, but he didn't appreciate being a goose in a shooting gallery.

The range abruptly went dead as the last of the marksman's balls ran out. The laughter stopped and the little crowd dispersed. Rama hurried to the dense clusters that populated the 150-yard latitudes to collect as many balls as quickly as he could. With both bags bulging, he returned to Levi to claim his rental clubs and to complain at being a target.

"Hell, if Lee had wanted to hit you, he'd have hit you," replied Levi. "Clubs are out in the shed; help yourself, Buddy."

Fifteen minutes later Rama had picked through a haystack of steel and hickory orphans and built a set of the best unmatched clubs the lost-and-never-found had to offer—Sunset Hills's version of Jimmy Jim's fish sticks. Then he settled at a sunny table in the coffee shop with a view onto the putting green to have a soda and to wait. Down on the green, a group of men assembled around a black-haired, bronze-skinned man for a group putting lesson. Rama scrounged through last month's golf magazines and sipped at a Luva'Lime. The flavor was brighter and more refreshing than he remembered. Damned if Dustin Pepper hadn't finally got it right.

Suddenly, the door to the coffee shop swung open and the putting instructor, eager at the prospect of lunch, stepped inside. Without hesitation a broad smile broke across the fellow's face in recognition of the madras-shirted young target he had chased around the range earlier. And it was a face Rama had seen before.

"Uh oh, I suppose you'd like a couple of shots at me, eh amigo?" the man laughed. "Lucky they ran out of balls or I might have chased you around all morning. You added some entertainment to my little show."

"They told me I was safe out there at 250."

"Well, thanks for making me look good. Usually you'd be safe anywhere in *front* of me," laughed the man heartily. The broad smile pushed at his cheeks and his brown eyes twinkled with good nature.

Then Rama made the connection: "You're Lee…from Mesquite Creek," he declared with certainty.

"Since the Open everybody seems to know I'm Lee," the man said, "but I'm sure as hell not from Mesquite Creek."

Then Rama's thin, shy face and his shaggy brown hair struck a chord of familiarity in Lee, and he remembered: "Well, I'll be...Mesquite Creek, you say? Damned if you're not the kid who carried my bag when Donaldo got the trots way back when." Lee chuckled at the old war story. "Jesus, I was sick, too, eh, amigo? Haven't touched pozole since. But hey, I remember: You made that putt for me...that crazy, damned eighty-foot putt. We about fired up the Alamo again with that controversial victory."

Lee extended a strong hand. "Did I get the story right? I've been telling it for years now. Christ if I can remember your name. Are you hungry?"

"Yeah," replied Rama. "And no...it was only about sixty feet."

In a few minutes Rama was sharing lunch with Lee Trujillo, the gallant and generous golfer who had struggled against food poisoning and a scorpion's sting in the same unfortunate round in June of 1959. Here in the late summer of 1967, the name Trujillo was beginning to gain some traction. He had finished strong in the US Open and was on the verge of making his run as one of golf's elite. For the moment he resided at the enviable position between anonymity's freedom and achievement's rewards.

The stress of tournament golf and the demands of a growing celebrity had not robbed the congenial fellow plowing through a cheeseburger basket of his good humor.

"So how's your game coming along? You hadn't touched a club before the time I caught up with you on that range." Lee smiled at the memory. "You were trying to make off with my 7-iron."

"No sir, it was the 6."

"Yi, yi, do we have a memory? You took a couple of good swipes at it for a beginner, as I recall. I thought you might have been a natural. My game came around pretty good, all things considered, once you got on my bag." The memory of Rama's effect on that performance lingered with clarity.

"So what is your name again and how is *your* game?" Lee asked. "And what in God's name are you doing shagging balls way the hell out here?"

Rama introduced himself and explained that he hadn't even looked at a golf club for eight years since their amazing day together. He explained that he had recently been caddying for the rich guys at a club in Memphis. He told Lee that he had learned a few things about the game from playing with a Cherokee gardener on an improvised little course some evenings after work.

"Me and Jimmy called those games *Night Lessons*," said Rama. "So much for my career."

"But you're having fun, right?" asked Lee. Even one of golf's greatest hadn't lost sight of what was important.

Rama hesitated in the face of the $64,000 question and then realized he hadn't asked Lee about *his* game. "I remember, the lady at Mesquite Creek said you were going to be someone to watch," Rama recalled. "Guess she knew what she was talking about."

"That would be Carla Stone," Lee recalled. "My God, haven't seen her for a while. Now there's one tough cookie. Always seemed too good for that golf course of hers, though. I guess she kind of got marooned out there after some bad breaks."

"You mean losing her kids?"

Lee nodded. The memory of the Stone children seemed to haunt everyone who frequented Mesquite Creek. "You know, if I ever make it to the Masters, I swear I'll ask Carla to come along. She used to go there in her younger days—so I've heard—back when she knew Mr. Bobby Jones himself. It'd be good to see her rolling up Magnolia Lane some sunny morning. Hell, I'd even buy her a green sombrero if I thought she'd wear it," Lee laughed at the thought.

Rama remembered the story of Carla's lost children and her husband's tumble from a seat at golf's finest tables to an unknown fate in the Texas wilderness. The Schwain family seemed blessed by comparison.

"Is she still there? Do you get up to Mesquite Creek anymore?" Rama asked.

"Not like I used to," Lee replied with a touch of nostalgia for days when he could play a decent round with a couple of the Mesquite regulars, then enjoy a first class platter of brisket, a couple of cold beers, and a good long bullshit session on Carla's back porch. "Hell, there were some pretty good players up there—even that Boney fella'. I worked with him on his game the next year. All he ever needed was to drop the elbow, lose a few pounds, and kick the brownie habit and he'd a'been a real competitor."

Lee and Rama both smiled at the incongruous thought of Boney's bulky face smudged with chocolate laboring over an amazing, graceful swing.

"I've moved on. The fellas back there figured I got too good for them…just weren't as hospitable as before." Lee shook his head at the price of fame. "To tell you the truth, Rama, I don't think that crowd ever forgave me for taking that game away on your putt. Shit, I don't blame them. It wasn't according to Hoyle, but hey, it was according to Carla, and up there she's all that matters."

Lee turned his attention back to his lunch companion. "And so…here you are running around this godforsaken corner of the state with a shag-bag in your hand. What gives?" Lee wasn't going to let Rama's story end at golfing with a Cherokee gardener.

Rama still felt shy about violating Wedgy's hush-hush edict when it came to speaking to strangers about one's golfing activities, but Lee hardly seemed a stranger. Judiciously at first, Rama began to report on his life's recent turns. But once he got started, he spilled all the frijoles, including his strange winning run with Bluff Meade's players, his mentor Ivar Guidance, his father's unfortunate wagers, and his tour with the conniving Wedgy Byrne.

Perhaps it was the disarming smile, or the memory of Lee returning Hank's money way back when, but Rama also felt bold enough to reveal his desire to find a good match against Wedgy. He even alluded to a wealthy backer but stopped short of mentioning Ivar's six-thousand-dollar check.

Lee gestured for silence. "Tone it down, Rama. Are you looking to bet against your boss?" Revenge didn't seem to fit with the young man's character. "Just be sure you aren't caddying for him if you do…that would be unforgivable. You could get yourself hurt."

Rama explained. "No sir, I'm gonna quit working for him anyway. Heck, he may already have fired me. I don't know…he's in Mexico. But how can I find someone to take him on? Maybe if you weren't so famous you could…"

"Hold on, Rama. You aren't asking me to hustle your boss, are you? You understand I can't take a match like that anymore. I'm a professional. Got way too much to lose nowadays, and besides, them's the rules, amigo."

"Yeah, I guess," said Rama. "But I was thinking maybe you knew somebody around here who could. I figure Wedgy will only fall for a guy who *looks* like he's got no game. He's not easily fooled."

"That so," said Lee, already searching through a checklist of disheveled but respectable players. "Well, I know this one guy, Tyler Grant."

Rama laughed. "Wedgy already lost to him once. But you've got the right idea."

"I'll think on it."

The two acquaintances turned their attention to finishing their lunches and leafing blankly through the dog-eared golf magazines that littered the table. Rama had talked enough about himself and was happy to quiz Lee about life on the tour. It soon became clear that Lee could talk ceaselessly as long as he had an audience, and maybe he didn't even need that. Rama wished they were in Bluff Meade and that Lee was spinning his golfing tales for Ivar and Dustin.

Suddenly the door to the snack bar burst open and a man leaned inside. "Is there a Schwain in here?" he barked. Rama raised his hand. "Schwain, you're next on deck, with the Brown threesome…sorry the loudspeaker just went on the fritz or you'd have known," the man apologized. He started to withdraw his head from the doorway, then looked at Lee and stopped.

"Hey aren't you that Mex…"

"Yeah, Chi Chi Rodriguez," deadpanned Lee. "And I don't do autographs, amigo."

Rama hopped up from the table. "Gotta go!"

"Talk about *hustling*," laughed Lee. "Next time I'd recommend a little less talking and a lot more time for a good warm-up. Go on, I'll bus your dishes."

The next couple of hours flashed by. Rama was too rusty and too excited to get off to a good start, but by the fourth hole he had become familiar with the salvaged clubs and had settled into a comfortable groove. The Brown threesome represented three generations of wind-burned western golfers. The younger of the three, a couple of years Rama's junior, offered Rama a competitive fulcrum from which to leverage his game upward. In return, Rama offered the Browns an invisible, transcendent gift that achieved the same effect. The foursome whooped and hollered their way around the front nine in some kind of all-time-family-best score. The eldest Brown appeared well on his way to shooting his age, and Rama felt like part of the family.

Solidly on the Brown bandwagon, Rama managed to par two of the last three holes on the front nine, just missing a birdie at nine by a lip-out. He had hurried from the ninth green to make a quick stop at the snack bar with the youngest of the Browns when a golf cart approached. Stout brown arms and a broad smiling face gave the driver away: Lee Trujillo was back again.

"My, my, aren't *we* having fun." Lee's eyes danced. "I noticed you just missed that birdie, eh? Maybe peeked a little, Rala."

The threesome looked at Lee in astonishment. Trujillo was already a familiar name in this part of the state. The middle-aged Brown searched for a pen, hoping for an autograph.

"Now, you all gotta pick the pace up just a touch," Lee laughed as he mimicked a marshal, waving the Browns on to number ten. He held Rama back for a moment. "I think I've got the match you are looking for, and damned if it's not back at good old Mesquite Creek. Carla said she'd be happy to set something up. She figures her crowd can finally get a little of their money back from you after all these years," Lee winked at Rama, "if you know what I mean."

Rama felt flush; his fantasy match was within reach. But how was he going to derail Wedgy from his southwestern tour and get back up to Mesquite Creek, and who could Carla have possibly lined up so quickly as Wedgy's opposition?

"I know what you're thinking, Raja. Believe me, it'll be a good match," Lee said hastily. "You just tell your fellow Wedgy that he can feast on those pigeons up at Mesquite Creek. Tell him they've got too much money and too little brains—how can he lose? Show up by Friday. Carla says they can get a good little purse and some interest drummed up for a Saturday afternoon tee time. I'll be there, too…but don't tell anyone."

Lee throttled the golf cart and caught up with the Browns. "Now Raja, my friend, you're holding these nice folks up." Lee laughed and reached behind the seat for a paper sack containing several golf balls he had previously signed. "Anyone need a souvenir?" he asked, and then tossed a couple of balls to each Brown generation.

"Get there early enough on Friday and I'll give you a little lesson. Maybe you can buy me some of Carla's brisket for the trouble, eh Raba?" Lee turned his attention back to the threesome, standing open-mouthed in the presence of the nearly famous. Lee revved the cart and cranked the wheel to go. "You all have a great back nine, but you're gonna have to pick up the pace. *Hasta presto.*"

The cart sped back toward the clubhouse, leaving three golfers holding their autographed golf balls and staring at Rama as if he were some kind of celebrity. The youngest one, still bobbing breathlessly in the wake of Lee's departure, spoke first: "You're friends with Lee Trujillo? But didn't you say your name was Rama, with an *m*?"

"Yeah, that's Lee," said Rama smugly. "He always gets my name wrong."

Chapter 46

Enough was enough, Hank thought as he waited for the percolator to prepare a fresh cup of courage. The night had offered only fitful dreams of blind passages through rocky landscapes. Grateful to awaken, he hoped coffee and the rising sun would promise a more fruitful direction. When the brightness had crawled over the horizon and the caffeine had slipped into his veins, he would fire up the Rambler and drive over to Aero Meadows. He had business there.

Yesterday, faced with a choice between paying the credit union or Calcutta, he had again tucked the mortgage bill—the second unpaid bill in as many months—into Doris's Bible and delivered a cash payment on Calcutta's loan into Lew Raybon's thankless hands. Fear of Lew's collection methods had trumped the mortgage company's more civil tactics, but Hank knew he was only buying time. The fine people at ARMCO could put the hammer down in their own assiduous way.

Today, the financial pot Hank had set on the fire had warmed past simmer; threatening medical bills, a gambling debt, and the foolish purchase of a glider had finally sent it to a boil. The fact that neither used cars nor Doris's piano were selling wasn't lowering the heat.

Hank nursed his second cup all the way to Aero Meadows's ramshackle airfield. The pilot there had said he'd always buy back the Little Crow at cost, and today, regretfully, Hank had decided to take the disagreeable fellow up on his offer.

One last tepid gulp pried Hank from the Rambler and nudged him toward the hangar. He imagined the pilot and the mechanic sitting at their picnic table as usual and hoped they were in a receptive mood. But as he approached he was surprised to see the hangar door shut tight.

"Shit. They picked a hell of a day to sleep in," Hank muttered.

He glanced up at the sky. Ribbons of high-altitude clouds reflected the autumn sun's golden glow in fiery streamers that pierced the brightening blue of a soon-to-be-glorious day. Hank ambled out to the flight line and lingered amongst the assortment of small aircraft tethered to the tarmac. The gorgeous sunrise glinted from canopy glass and polished aluminum while the shadows of struts and props flowed across graceful, aerodynamic surfaces. At the end of the line, the Little Crow waited for a long-overdo tow and a chance to show her stuff. Hank fumbled in his jacket for a smoke. He snapped the lighter shut with a clink and walked down the line to kiss his dream good-bye.

It had almost seemed worth it, he thought, to have owned the little aircraft—even for a short time. He had never flown it solo, yet just knowing she was out here tied so close to the sky had drawn him nearer to the day when he might soar above the hedgerows like the dusters back in Othello. But it was, he feared, the hopeless dream of a man who couldn't clear life's ordinary hurdles let alone the bounds of gravity. It was a selfish fantasy that put his son's future and the roof over an impossibly understanding wife's head in jeopardy.

The screech of stubborn bushings disturbed the quiet morning. Hank turned back to the hangar to see the mechanic struggling to slide the great door open. Aero Meadows was now open for business and he could get on with the inevitable sale. Hank considered jogging over to help, but discarded the notion as he remembered the man's caustic attitude. He crushed his smoke into the tarmac and reluctantly started for the hangar door. But he never made it.

"Praised be, have you been slummin' at the Big Star again?" rang a full, familiar voice.

Marcile Gold stood beside her Thunderbird, tapping a white-booted foot with mock impatience. The singer was dressed for work in blue satin pants and a red leather interpretation of a flight jacket complete with faux fur collar.

"Least you didn't get rolled this time," she laughed in a voice husky with second-hand smoke.

"Yes ma'am, I even drove here *myself,*" replied Hank. He warmed at the sight of the woman. His wife had been so weak for so long he had almost forgotten how vibrant a female could be.

"That's a fact; I saw the car…you're still a Rambler man," Marcile laughed once more. "God doesn't make mornings much finer than this, huh, Hank. I *did* get your name right, huh?"

Hank nodded as his eyes roamed Marcile's colorful costume. "You got an elephant like a memory, Miss Gold."

"So you like the patriotic look? Well, don't strain your eyes, mister. You've got a wife if I recall," Marcile scolded Hank with a coy smile. "I sprung this little outfit on my public last night. I thought I'd better put a flag-waving get-up like this in my show. You never know when Lady Bird might want yours truly to strut her stuff up on Pennsylvania Avenue."

Marcile's brown eyes twinkled from within a corona of show-stopping eye shadow. The glint of blue iridescence reminded Hank of hummingbirds' feathers and his mother's delight as the entertaining little visitors buzzed the glass feeders she had suspended before the sweeping wheat vista beyond her back porch. Yes, he liked the look.

"Good morning for flying, I suppose," Hank replied.

"Lord yes. Gotta air out good after last night." Marcile cast a loving look toward Hank's glider. "You taking her up this morning?"

A pang of regret formed a lump in his throat. "No, sorry to say." He looked intently at the ember at the end of his cigarette and flicked a few ashes free.

"No, I've got to sell her off. Times are tight."

"Sell her? Hells bells, you just *got* her. Shit, have you even soloed yet? I suppose you Rambler men don't jump into anything half-cocked," laughed Marcile playfully. "Honey, now don't toss off that dream of yours so easily. You might not get another go-around. Just get that bird off terra firma at least once, *then* think about your bank account."

Hank was a pushover for any persuasive argument, but this time he wasn't going to be so easily deflected—or so he thought. The Little Crow had to go.

Marcile's face lit up as if last night's spotlight had found her again. "You got fifteen bucks, Honey?" she asked. "For the tow. You and I are going up as soon as I get that jack-off artist's face out of them *Playboys* and into that tow plane." The fire of her nightclub persona had not yet passed from her face.

"Are you with me, Hank?"

Hank could not deny her. He nearly shouted amen but was moved instead to admit that he had no money for a tow.

"Christ, Hank; if that's all it'll cost me to finally get your booty up into the blue yonder, well I guess this one's on me."

After enduring another round of the tow pilot's irritating wisecracks and sloth-like preflight preparations, Marcile walked Hank through a brief review of the glider's controls while the pilot fiddled with his plane's vital organs. Finally satisfied with his craft's airworthiness, the pilot strolled over to the Little Crow, spitting sunflower seeds out the corner of his mouth as he approached.

"All systems are go, go, go Big Mama," he reported. "C'mon, let's roll Schwain's rusty little dream out."

Hank and Marcile took their places in the Crow's cramped cockpit. Hank felt his companion's powerful legs pressing through the back of his seat, then he felt the first jerk of the tow line as the tow craft took up the slack and made a run for the sun hovering low above the lush Mississippi bottomland.

Marcile hummed a few bars of a Steve Cropper riff as she let the magic of the morning's ascent wash away whatever strain still lingered from the long night's performance. In a few hours she would find sleep easy and inevitable.

"You still with me Hank, Honey? Now watch it; here comes a little whoop-di-doo."

Hank nodded apprehensively.

She pulled back the stick and the tow plane fell away as the sky filled their vision. The tow line released with a discomforting bang—like a crowbar against Little Crow's thin flanks. Marcile dropped the nose and watched as the damp forests of Mississippi, Tennessee, and Arkansas rose back into view. A hard left turn moved them safely from the menacing steel cable.

"All right, Hank, let's get our money's worth out of this ride. Put your right hand on the stick and your feet on the pedals—gently—and we'll have some fun."

Marcile walked Hank through the basic motions of non-powered flight. As she spoke, he remembered similar words from an instructor at the Sedalia, Illinois, glider base only a few days before D-Day and his rendezvous with St. Claude's unforgiving spire. How much easier soaring seemed now, without the scent of twelve young men's fearful sweat or Old Crow's worried glances…and without the horrible darkness.

Following Marcile's lead, Hank executed two reasonably smooth turns, then leveled out in the direction of a large barn. He recognized the Bull of the Woods logo scrawled across the roof from his wild ride with the foul-mouthed pilot two months earlier. Marcile waited for the glider to crab out of line or to porpoise, but it didn't.

"Damn, Hank, you've done this before," she cried. "Think you can line her up for a landing?" She didn't wait for an answer. "Head her out over the barn and do one more nice even turn downwind. I'll take her from there." She tapped him on the shoulder. "And you wanted to *sell* her? Lord, lord, Hank; it's only money."

Hank only heard the word *landing*. Marcile's directions struggled for his attention against an upwelling of fearfully recalled images. Today was sunny and beautiful. A flatbed loaded with cotton bales moved along a red dirt road below, but Hank saw a nocturnal cyclist in a pool of lantern light, moving silently through his memory along a dark French lane. The Bull of the Woods barn shimmered ahead in the bright Tennessee morning, yet Hank saw the stony face of St. Claude's Virgin Mother lurking in dark recollection. Should he turn or should he wait to clear the spire? He already knew what bronze and stone could do to fabric, wooden struts…and flesh.

"Turn…hold on…turn?" Hank struggled for a decision while his copilot, Old Crow, waited for an answer in the radium glow of the glider's instruments.

⎯•⎯

"No, Crow, you take it…take her now," Hank called out in alarm. An instant later he felt a strong brown hand on his shoulder.

"Okay, sugar. Relax. I got the stick." Marcile's cheerful voice erased Hank's tragic memories. "You didn't think I was really gonna let you land, did you, Honey?"

Hank sunk back into the seat. The fearful sweat he smelled was his own.

"You were doin' fine—maybe a touch slow on the turn there," Marcile said calmly. "But why the hell were you callin' me Crow?"

Hank did not respond. He felt the crippling grip of failure looming just as it had when it first settled over him in the wreckage at St. Claude. Was he cursed to always come up short in the final approach to success? His mind began to construct a new trap of hopeless thoughts from which there would be no escape, even as the most glorious moments of this splendid morning flight with Marcile were ticking away. The very experience that he had once breathlessly imagined as a young would-be duster pilot was sweeping past like the treetops below.

The thump of Marcile's palm against his shoulder brought Hank back to reality. "Glory be, loosen up, Sugar. You can't fly all hunched up like that. Put your hand back on the stick...lightly. Remember?"

Hank obeyed, and his dark fears vanished in the bright cockpit.

"Okay, just feel it while I turn her back upwind into the final approach." Marcile's voice tempered in a thousand nightclubs was just as powerful when delivered softly over the shoulder of an audience of one.

"Now, just tap the stick and get us in line here—hardly any pedal, Honey."

One hundred and fifty feet below, the faded white stripe of Aero Meadows's runway crossed the glider's path at a slight angle. Almost any angle off-line could mean trouble. Hank tapped the stick and watched the lines converge as the glider barely banked into the course correction.

"That's it, Sugar. Straighten out now," Marcile urged.

Hank flicked the stick back upright as the glider leveled out. The runway was directly ahead and rising to meet them as the Little Crow settled gently from the sky.

"God-damned perfect. You are a nat-ur-al, Hank. Now don't let her slip on us. We're nearly home."

Hank nervously over-pedaled and the glider yawed slightly. The air slashing across its skin made the bird protest in a metallic rattle.

"Kiss the rudder...soft on the pedals." There was a sense of urgency in her voice; it was vital that they be squared away at touchdown. She was about to take the controls, but the craft's heading and its course came back into sync before she touched a go-go boot to the rudder pedal. Apparently Hank understood the kissing concept.

The Little Crow's wheel announced touchdown with a bang as the landing wheel's suspension bottomed out. A loud rolling commotion reverberated into the craft's tin-can recesses as the wheel picked up the tarmac's rugged surface like a phonograph needle. Marcile tapped Hank on the back, this time in congratulation.

"And I wasn't gonna let you land? My oh my!" Marcile chimed. "You were born to fly, Rambler man."

Hank flipped open the canopy and the scent of berry thickets beyond the runway welcomed him home. Wobbly with relief, he stepped down to the tarmac. The glider's single wheel rested precisely in the middle of the white line.

Hank raised his wide eyes back up to the patriotic character stepping from the cockpit.

"Glory be, we're on the stripe! Don't look at me, Rambler man. I took my hands off the stick after we made that final turn. That landing was all yours."

Hank felt the unfamiliar pulse of a victorious heart beating in his chest. Maybe the glider was worth the financial hardships. Surely the value of fanning the embers of his hopeful but hapless desire to fly would count for something in the world beyond Aero Meadows.

Of course, he suspected Lew Raybon wouldn't see it that way.

Marcile climbed from the Little Crow. "This is where I get off, Honey. Got a check ride to take on a new bird." Her eyes were focused ahead on a cobalt blue tail dragger waiting for her down the flight line. "This is what I came over here for. I'll be flying solo before long…under full power, hallelujah! Stick around; we might get you a real flight."

"Next time, Marcile. Thanks anyway, but I gotta go."

"Go? What in God's name did you *come* for?"

Hank couldn't answer. He had intended to sell the glider at cost, then hurry home and pay at least one of the bills from the Bible. And he owed Doris a few hours in her garden, but with this flight—more importantly, this landing—echoing in his heart, his plans were adrift.

"Well, we'll sure as shit make a pilot out of you one of these days." Marcile smiled broadly. The morning sun ignited brunette highlights in her shiny black hair as she turned from Hank in favor of her cobalt dream. Hank cinched down the tie-down lines at the glider's wingtips and made a mental note to take in one of her shows as long as the venue wasn't the Big Star. He could stand only so much entertainment.

The pilot and the mechanic watched Hank limping back down the tarmac toward the hangar. They knew he had come to talk turkey and that they would buy the glider back for less than they sold it. The two characters sensed that Hank was desperate, so they waited, coolly expecting Hank to park his cane and take his usual place at the picnic table before rambling on about his strained finances. But Hank just raised his cane in recognition, passed up the cold coffee and the clutter of nudie magazines, then disappeared behind the hangar and into the parking lot. He fired the Rambler to life and left just as indebted as when he arrived, but considerably richer.

The pilot took a sip of greasy coffee. "Walk on by, you rude son of a bitch. Why would he bullshit us like that?"

"What are you grumbling about?" asked the mechanic. "You didn't really want that glider back, did you?"

"Oh hell, it's not that…I'm talking about our buddy Schwain sayin' he hadn't flown since the war. What's he doing…playing dumb to get out of a few bucks for a license? Christ, he can fly like a champ."

"What makes you think *he* was flying?" the mechanic answered with eyes raised above the morning paper.

"Christ, have you ever seen Miss Gold set that bird down within five feet of the line let alone smack dab on the stripe?" replied the pilot. "Old Hank there might just be the real deal."

—•—

The Rambler's radio played a Marty Robbins tune as the 'real deal' blew on down the road from Aero Meadows to Big Muddy's AutoTorium like a leaf. Hank was too easily tossed by the winds of fortune, and he knew it. His resolve to liquidate the glider in favor of settling some accounts had been blown away by Marcile's encouraging spirit. His remarkable landing may have put some ghosts to rest, but at a price: He was in deeper debt than ever and desperate for a good day on the lot.

"Christ, I could use a few breaks about now," Hank sighed over the sappy violins that passed for a decent fiddle in Marty's tune. Alone in the car with the Nashville Strings or some such abomination, his plea resembled a prayer.

Big Muddy's receptionist, positioned strategically at a tiny desk in the AutoTorium's display window, crossed her legs and pulled her miniskirt tight around recently expanded thighs as Hank limped onto the showroom floor. She teased her strawberry tresses and struck her best Nancy Sinatra pose.

"Got a call, Hankie," the girl reported, "about an hour ago."

She held up the pink message slip for his retrieval like a mail sack for a speeding train. He snagged it in passing, making brief contact with her warm fingers. Hank glanced at the note carefully rendered in flowery script:

Call dockter Miyer B-4 lunch.

—•—

"Mr. Schwain, thanks for calling back so promptly. I wanted to speak with you before we alarm your wife," the doctor said. "I have reason to believe she is suffering latent complications from an old head injury."

Hank squirmed in his office chair. "That doesn't sound so good." The same pulse that marked this morning's intense final moments before touching down now pounded out a fearful tempo. Hank thought of their trip to the petroglyphs.

"No, it is not particularly good. Scar tissue seems to have spread recently and could be encroaching on sensitive regions around the base of the brain and the pituitary gland. Her symptoms are a sign of the neurological and glandular dysfunctions resulting from the sclerosis."

"So…you got a pill for these problems?" Hank asked anxiously.

"There are possibly effective pharmacological treatments to retard the sclerosis, but frankly, we may be facing more intrusive measures. However, surgery in that region carries risk. We should avoid it as long as she is reasonably healthy."

Hank tried to respond but only managed a croak from his dry throat. Somehow the word *risk* when brought into a medical discussion implied far greater consequences than the risks with which he was acquainted. Hank knew the doctor was speaking about death in language as direct as he dared.

"Drugs or surgery will be very costly. However, I am happy to tell you that a benefactor, who prefers to remain anonymous, has pledged to cover the costs from this point forward. Your wife would have access to the best treatment possible; and should surgery be necessary, our clinic in Atlanta is second to none."

"A benefactor? Who would take on such a cost?"

"Ethically I can't reveal the person's identity; however, if you are uncomfortable with their anonymity, I can have them contact you."

"No, I am happy for any help. I just want the best for my wife, of course." But even as he spoke, Hank considered the implications of this windfall. His insurance was stingy at best, and God knows how much this treatment could run. The Schwains' share of her medical bills had already strained a meager income previously drained by his adventures. Maybe now the money that would have gone to medical bills could begin paying back what he had lost. As long as the benefactor's gift was secret, Hank might erase his incriminating debt under the guise of paying medical bills.

Maybe his prayer in the car had been answered.

"Doctor Myer, if you don't mind," Hank said politely, "I would like to keep the benefactor business between us...Doris has a lot of pride and wouldn't be happy accepting charity. You understand?"

"Of course, I'll leave such matters between you and Iv..." The doctor stammered on the brink of revealing Ivar Guidance's identity. "We will begin planning a treatment program, and in the meantime call us if there are any changes in her condition."

The doctor's voice softened to a less-professional tone. "And how's your boy doing?" Doctor Myer had a passion for golf that had been stirred by several rounds with Ivar but had been sidetracked by a demanding medical career.

"Rama? Last I heard he was just a caddie. A good one, they tell me." Hank was taken off guard by the sudden interest in his son. "But no, I haven't heard from him...not for a while."

The doctor bid Hank good day and left him holding the phone in one hand and a call slip in the other. Hank felt relief at the unexpected subsidy but also self-loathing at his readiness to work yet another angle. He looked through the office window to a father and his teenage son stalking the lot for a good affordable car. He wondered if he would ever hear from his son again. Had he done so much to poison their friendship?

Hank dared not answer, knowing that the checks to Trent Institute had still not been covered. He would have to make things right, and soon. But intentions, like talk, were cheap.

Chapter 47

Three days had passed and Wedgy still had not returned from Mexico. Wednesday afternoon's shadows crept across the thirsty landscape surrounding Rama's camp as locusts ramped up their voices from the thorny brush for one last aria before their curtain fell. The relentless drone and Rama's anxiousness over Wedgy's whereabouts constricted time's passage to a tedious trickle.

Rama looked up from his fifth reading of last April's *Popular Science* to the clock above the CruiseAir's tiny stove. It was 5:30. The scent of hamburgers sizzling on a grill somewhere in the campground reminded him that he was hungry and that the fridge was empty. Rama considered begging dinner from his fellow campers but chose to preserve his dignity by falling back on Wedgy's last can of beef stew.

Earlier that day he had played twenty-seven holes and conned some impromptu instruction and a pimento sandwich from a scratch member of the Sunset Hills Men's Club. His game's improvement was encouraging, but with doubt rising as to his and Wedgy's fortunes and with his appetite soaring, his mood had tumbled to the point that he was ready to eat the stew straight from the can.

The week was running out fast. It was already Wednesday and Rama knew Lee Trujillo would only wait at Mesquite Creek through Friday. Then, can opener in hand, he heard the signature growl of a Lincoln V8 and the thump of a spent suspension bottoming out on potholes along the campground's rugged driveway.

The car ground to a halt beside the trailer, and before the trailing dust cloud caught up, Wedgy raised his sun-burned head above the windshield and called for help.

"Opener. Bring me a fucking church key…por favor!"

His eyes were red within and without and were rimmed with dark smudges of sleeplessness. Dehydration, sun, and wind had all taken their toll on his cheeks and his pitiful lips. A green streak of a once-upon-a-grasshopper striped the old hustler's wrinkled forehead.

Rama was disturbed at Wedgy's distressed appearance, but was pleased that the very son-of-a-bitch whom he plotted to lure to justice on the greens of Mesquite Creek was back in one piece. He grabbed a bottle opener from the picnic table.

"Muchos gracias." Wedgy climbed from the car and swatted clouds of dust from cheap leather pants and a simulated Hawaiian shirt. Rama half-expected the weathered tourista to sport a sombrero, but if Wedgy had actually stooped that low, the hat probably had blown away many miles ago.

"Gringo beer. Gracias, Christo Redemptor," Wedgy cried as he pried the cap off a Texas longneck still cold from the first cooler he had encountered north of the Rio Grande. Half the beer disappeared immediately in a gurgling that nearly drowned out the locusts.

Wedgy looked at Rama. "So how's the fishing?" He laughed until choking himself off with another swig. "Hell, with all that blue gill action, you probably never noticed I'm a day late."

Wedgy threw his head back like a coyote and belched. "Like they say: Time flies when you're havin' fun."

Rama wondered if Wedgy's haggard appearance testified to fun in any respectable sense of the word. Wedgy pulled another beer out of the sack and stood it on the table. The bottle nearly toppled under his unsteady hand.

"On me." He fished in the sack and extracted a warm tin-foil package of a half-dozen tender tamales and slid it in Rama's direction. The scent of cornmeal and savory pork quickly extinguished all Rama's thoughts of a canned dinner.

Wedgy didn't speak much after that but drank his beers in quick, thankful succession. His thirst finally sated, he fetched a Mexican cigar from the Lincoln's glove box. The tobacco product resembled the dried turd of a large desert animal. Its odor was not far removed from its appearance.

"I hate to admit it," Wedgy mused, "but I might be getting a little over-the-hill for that much fun. Shit, I'm lucky to have gotten me and the car out of that Chihuahua madhouse in good health. Left a shitload too many pesos back there: some bad bets on jai-alai and the damned cockfights…and a couple of greedy señoritas. Christ knows what I *can't* remember."

Wedgy took a long, disgusting drag on the smoldering object in his teeth. "All I know is we're putting our little golfing show back on the road…pronto. Drink up, Rama; we've got work ahead. We've got to rustle up a few cash cows down the road."

The sky above them turned from azure to cobalt. Wedgy looked up to see Venus blinking brightly into view just beyond sunset's lingering traces. Through a slackening hangover he made a fatigued, silent wish that he be spared from chasing a young man's profession into the uncertain fringes of a game that once had been so noble.

"Next up, Rama: Albuquerque and Santa Fe." Wedgy spoke without enthusiasm. Deep under the dry cortex of an aching brain, he dreamed of his ex-wife setting the dinner table with a flowered centerpiece.

The locusts quieted as the stars came brightly out above their camp. Rama was starting his third beer when he realized that if he were to maneuver Wedgy toward his comeuppance in Mesquite Creek, the time to act was now.

"Can't play Albuquerque…not for a few days, anyway."

Wedgy's stomach groaned in disbelief.

"I heard it on the radio and from a couple of folks driving south," began Rama convincingly. "A storm dropped down from Colorado. Dumped on everything over two thousand feet. Broke records for September in New Mexico."

"Shit you say? Albuquerque? Snow?" Wedgy asked woozily, aware that his carefully planned parade westward into the high country where golf, fresh air, and disposable income were tied so tightly together could be knocked out of kilter by an early fall.

"It might be a lucky break," Rama offered, quick to play his hand after laying down the Albuquerque card. "I overheard some rich players over at Sunset Hills talking about all the action up at a course north and east of here: Mesquite Creek."

Wedgy puffed a series of terrible, distorted smoke rings into the sky, listening carefully.

Rama worked the sales pitch he had learned from Lee: "They said the crowd up at Mesquite Creek have got too much oil money and too little brains—perfect for golf. This one fellow, Lee, says they can always work up a big pot for a Saturday match if you can get there in time to strut your stuff on Thursday or Friday."

The stogie had begun to turn too foul even for Wedgy, and he tossed the glowing *turdarillo* into the dark. "Where did you say? Mosquito Creek?"

"Mesquite Creek…about half a day from here," Rama answered.

Wedgy chuckled drunkenly as he watched the cigar's ember glowing tenaciously in the dark. He was happy to know that Rama and hopefully that caddie voodoo were still on his side. Wedgy considered Rama's suggestion for a change in plans. He guessed he could forgive that round with Grant, the rhinestone cowboy, in return for a good idea. Following the money to this Mesquite place seemed reasonable. "Well, this car probably ain't shit in the snow anyway," Wedgy concluded, shivering beneath his Hawaiian shirt.

"Viva Mosquito Creeko."

—•—

With Rama gone and only a couple of postcards in his place, Doris found her mind a din of unanswered questions and sad memories. During the long days when the empty house rang with silence, she wished that Siran and his entourage had found a way to overlook Hank's Spam-related culinary offense that had sent them to more culturally agreeable lodging. She missed the sound of unfamiliar music and the impenetrable chatter of foreign voices drifting down the stairs. The empty nest had become an anchor hurtling to unknown depths, and she was determined to cut the rope while there was still slack. *Business Opportunities* in the classified section might be a start, she hoped.

The day's newspaper still lay at the end of the driveway. Hank had left early that morning for a meeting at Aero Meadows before going in to work, but he hadn't retrieved it. Walking unsteadily down the front steps, she wished for an upturn in Hank's fortunes and maybe a job for herself that would accommodate her physical limits. How silly to cave in to a little setback like this brain thing, she thought. People get on well with much worse.

She gathered the morning's mail. "Nothing from Rama," she sighed. But there was a letter addressed to him from Trent Institute. It looked serious. She turned from the mailbox and was stooping to collect the paper when the pain hit: an excruciating bolt in the back of her head that ran down her spine and out to her legs. The world fluttered and she was disconnected.

Before the cement in the driveway came up to meet her face, Doris had a fleeting image of President Kennedy recoiling from that terrible, precise bullet and then the lady in pink attempting to climb from Zapruder's 8mm frames to another reality.

If she had been shot, Doris never heard the report, nor did any neighbor see her fall. When she came to, she stared into the same glorious colored bands that streamed across the morning sky from which Hank and Marcile had just descended. Doris wondered if she had died, but she recognized Rama's old bicycle leaning against the garage. Tattered twines of net hanging from his basketball hoop fidgeted in a gust of soft autumn wind, and she could clearly pick out the smell of roses and recently turned soil.

No, she was alive, and she was determined not to be seen lying helplessly like this. She gathered herself onto an elbow and then carefully to her feet. As if in a dream, Doris collected the newspaper and the letter from the driveway. She was back inside, before the bathroom mirror, dabbing at the bruise on her temple and considering the frightful attack on her well-being. Then, as if a few frames had skipped, she was running her hands across the books in her shelves. Dreamily she extracted the grandest book from the shelf and fell into Hank's easy chair with her mother's old Bible in her lap.

In fearful times, Doris often sought out a favorite psalm for comfort, but this morning the thought trapped in an inaccessible corridor never got through. Doris cracked open the heavy book aimlessly, allowing it to part at the satin bookmark and then again where two hidden mortgage bills cleaved the gilded pages. It seemed to Doris that those crude papers didn't belong in such a sanctified place, and she dropped them to the floor.

The desired passages seemed impossibly lost in the great book, and in frustration she slid the opened Bible onto the coffee table. The mail seemed more accessible, so she picked it up and settled back into her chair. An envelope addressed to Mr. Rama H. Schwain stared up at her; its return address and logo begged to be noticed: Admissions Office, Trent Institute of Landscape Technology. Final Notice!

The telephone in the kitchen demanded her attention, too. It jangled on its hook several times before Doris realized it was ringing. Her instincts told her to take the call. She tucked the Trent Institute letter into the Bible where she thought she had found it and then closed the book with a thud. The phone's insistent ring summoned her into the kitchen. It rang several more times before she finally pulled the receiver from the hook, but only the revving of an automobile engine emerged from the earpiece. Doris listened, waiting, as her kitchen rolled on heavy seas.

A familiar voice asked, "Mom? Hello, who's there?"

When Doris realized she didn't know the answer, she returned the phone to the hook.

—•—

Rama lost his dime and his bearings with the phone call. As the phone in his mother's kitchen rang repeatedly, he gazed absently from the phone booth to the dry hills above the campground. With vision distorted through a web of broken glass left by a vandal's bullet, he caught the black shape of a buzzard floating effortlessly above the rolling hills. The bird's jagged image jumped from one sliver of glass to the next across the shattered window.

Rama shivered with foreboding when nothing greeted him on the other end of the line but vacancy followed by a sudden return to the dial tone. He turned from the booth determined to try again, but he was out of change. Wedgy gunned the engine impatiently, muffling Rama's intention to ask for another coin. Perhaps he would call from somewhere farther down the road… maybe get a better connection.

"That was quick," scoffed Wedgy. "Suppose your mom hasn't got a good word to say now that you've run off with the golfing circus, huh?"

"No sir," Rama replied. "No, she didn't say anything. It was a bad connection…I think."

Chapter 48

A man and his son plotted an evasive course through the lines of Big Muddy's patched and polished automotive offerings. They tried to avoid the salesman who limped awkwardly in pursuit, but Hank Schwain was on his turf and he knew all the moves. He was already certain which car the teenage boy desired, even though the pair dared not linger over the '59 Impala for fear that he would pounce. He stalked his prospects as if he needed nothing less than their life's blood. Hank was as desperate to close a sale as was the young man eager to climb behind the Chevy's wheel.

Just before he moved in to applaud the boy's wise choice and to begin dickering away the tiny bargaining margin Big Muddy had built into its bloated sticker price, the father paused at a blue Ford Futura, a thousand dollars less than the Chevy.

Hank was cheered that the boy was clearly unimpressed, but to his chagrin the man's interest in the Ford wasn't just a ploy. Hank stopped at a Mercury Meteor several yards away, feigning interest in its sticker while he gathered his wits.

"You see why I hate this car-shopping shit?" the teenager's father hissed under his breath. "Look at him: Acting like he's never read the sticker on that Merc before…hell, he probably wrote it. You'd think that son of a bitch could leave us alone to think."

When Hank finally sprung, the prey put up little fight at first. The father tried to explain the virtues of the Ford, but his son had already settled on the car that set his teenage heart aflutter. The inevitably of the youngster's choice weakened any bargaining power his father might have had. Perhaps if the boy had seen the bastard title and the content of the crankcase he might have had second thoughts, but in this case, love was a blind and wonderful thing—or so Hank thought. The father tried at first to bargain on the Chevy, but Hank, certain of the pure persuasive power of the young man's passion, wouldn't budge. The father had no taste for further negotiation and abruptly put his foot down, insisting that since it was his money, the Futura would be the wiser choice. The father was right, of course, but Hank was too slow to derail the train of thrifty logic that threatened to shrink his only commission of the last three days. The Futura it was.

At the conclusion of the transaction, the father—a self-described Ford Man to the bone—returned to his Galaxy while the boy fumbled with the worn keys of his powder-blue disappointment. Hank returned to his desk to face the music; he knew he had let a good one get away…and so did Big Muddy.

Hank busied himself with the paperwork from his picayune sale. He was comforted by sunlight streaming from the showroom through his office door, but abruptly the beams were eclipsed. The documents before him dimmed. He knew the source of the shadow and faced the man who blocked the sun—Big Muddy, better known as BM by his terrorized sales force.

An expanse of shiny dark suit coat highlighted by a contrasting pink silk shirt filled the entire door. Through the chink between BM's hips and the door-jamb Hank could see the receptionist peering after her boss from the safety of the showroom. She wore the same voyeuristic face he had seen at prizefights.

Hank knew a visit from BM meant an employee had taken liberties with his commissions or had suspiciously favored a customer. Tampering with BM's profits could result in serious repercussions. Hank was confident that although outwitted by the Ford Man he had played straight-up out on the lot, but he knew his lackluster sales figures had left him teetering close to the brink of unemployment.

Hank attempted to speak but was cut off by a simple gesture from his employer's giant hands. BM might have made a good major league umpire—he had the "outta-here" move down pat. Without uttering a single word, he signaled Hank out and over the brink.

Under Big Muddy's impatient glare, Hank grabbed the few effects that belonged to him. He lingered for a second on the old photo of Doris posing on the beach in Gulfport in her full twenty-year-old glory. The receptionist settled back into her seat and pretended to update her address book. She avoided Hank's eyes as he grabbed his final commission envelope and disappeared into the lot for the last time. Her Nancy Sinatra hairdo heaved in sympathy as she sighed at Hank's departure. She was happy not to have missed the action and relaxed in her seat feigning business, only to be startled back to rigidity by the heavy hand of BM reaching down from above. With powerful fingers he pinned her address book to the desk. She watched in terror as he rotated the book 180 degrees back to right side up.

Without a word the dark-suited specter traced Hank's steps through the showroom door. As he watched Hank Schwain put the embarrassment he called a car into motion, BM dialed up his friend Lew Raybon. After some routine business and sports chat, BM mentioned that one of Lew's clients had just lost his job at the AutoTorium.

"Thought Calcutta should know," said Big Muddy. "So...do you think that Jew Koufax is gonna come back for one more year?"

—•—

No harm done, Hank thought as he pulled the Rambler onto the highway. It wasn't the only car lot in town. Although resilient, he had seen one too many setbacks. Driving back toward the city, an unnerving thought occurred to him: He had no destination. The Sixteen-Ton Tap Room seemed as good a landing as any other.

Except for the cash commission he had collected on his way out the office door, Hank might not have been compelled to try his hand at craps. He had intended only to console himself with a beer and a bowl of boiled peanuts. The bones weren't on his side, either, and like flesh in the food chain, a chunk of the Ford Man's cash that had just fallen to Hank continued quickly down to the bottom-feeders gathered at the craps table.

Hank had the good sense to get away while he still had a few bills, but as he pulled the Rambler back onto the highway toward a menacing tower of clouds and home, he cursed his helplessness in the alluring face of chance.

He twirled the radio dial and landed on the curious, meandering guitar-organ interplay of one of the hippie rock bands the university radio station seemed to favor lately. When he got to the song's description of a killer's pre-dawn prowl through a family's bedrooms, Hank decided he'd had enough and spun the dial again until he found George Jones squeezing every possible nuance of sadness from a simple lyric of regret at a tragically collapsed home life.

"That's more like it," he sighed as he comforted himself with thoughts of Doris's dinner menu.

—•—

Doris lingered aimlessly in the kitchen. She was unsure whether a daydream had somehow been interrupted by the voice of her son or if his telephone call from Texas had been a dream. Her eyes fell unsteadily on the panes in the patio door; there was no doubting the reality of the vista beyond the glass. A colossal storm formation was rising in the southern sky. Gray bands streamed from below as early evening sunlight illuminated the angry clouds with a breath-taking palette of molten tones.

No dream could be so beautiful.

Her head throbbed as she reached up to touch her temple. She was alarmed to discover a swelling bruise, yet she had no memory of any event that might explain the wound's origin. Alone in the quiet kitchen she rummaged through the pantry, pondering the mysterious injury and what she might toss together for dinner. Perhaps I should call Doctor Myer in the morning, thought Doris as a rumble intruded on her tangled thoughts. She stopped to consider the sound. Was this noise in her head or was it thunder from an electrical storm flickering in the distance? It was neither.

The Rambler rolled to a stop in Doris's driveway. Hank gunned the engine to scare several crows from her flower beds before dragging himself in for dinner. In the course of the drive home, Hank had tried to forget his losses at the craps table and strained to focus beyond his unemployment to some new opportunity, but his vision returned only darkness. The credits and debits of life threatened to pull him apart. Why had the credits always seemed so insufficient? Even now he weighed the heartening value of this morning's flight against the glider's costs; the return of his wife against the departure of his boy; his responsibilities against his compulsions; a happy future against his wife's fragile health. Hank tried to ignore that which suggested the balance had moved irretrievably into the negative, but how? He had just been fired for making a sale.

The Rambler disgorged its discouraged driver. As Hank approached the front porch, he realized the door was open and the house was silent. He shivered. No radio. No hi-fi. Not even Doris's voice. She loved to sing, and even when she was feeling poorly he would hear her voice from the kitchen. More than ever he needed its assurance this afternoon. He called her name. No answer. When he stepped inside, he realized the house was devoid of the welcoming odors he had anticipated on the drive home. Tonight's dinner, he feared, might be one of his wife's weaker efforts.

He peered into the living room and noticed papers strewn on the floor. When he stooped to gather them he realized they were the unpaid mortgage payments he had tucked into the Bible. His blood ran cold. He had been discovered. Any thoughts of sharing the tale of his perfect touchdown at Aero Meadows that morning were swept away in a tide of guilt. He cringed as he imagined what Doris must think of him now, only a few weeks after his pledge of reformation. Not paying the bank was bad enough, but how would he explain this deception?

Hank Schwain had built a house of cards whose foundations were constructed of debts and denial. He was certain it was toppled now, and God knows what else might be destroyed in the flimsy structure's collapse. He braced himself and poked his head into the kitchen expecting the worst. Doris stood silently at the refrigerator, holding the door wide open and staring quizzically into the appliance, lost in a confusion of ingredients. Hank choked on his own voice as he announced his arrival, but she had not heard him over the hum of the aged fridge and the distant thunder.

"These damned bills…" Hank began to face the music, holding the evidence in a quivering hand. "I didn't want to worry you, Honey." He still hadn't noticed her bruise.

Doris looked at Hank blankly, overlooking the papers in his hand in favor of explaining dinner's absence and the lump on her temple. "I've fallen a little behind on my house work." She touched her wound lightly, satisfied that she had made all things clear.

Hank gave his wife a timid hug then pulled his head back to focus on the bruise. "Damn, Honey, it looks like you've taken a few laps in the Roller Derby." He fetched a bottle of antiseptic and dabbed at the abrasion while waiting for the axe to fall.

"Hank, something came over me out on the driveway and next thing...I'm sitting here watching a thunderstorm. I must see Doctor Myer tomorrow."

Doris sighed heavily, then gathered herself to get on with dinner. "I guess I fell...I'm sorry, what were you saying before I started blabbering?"

If Hank had realized her lapse of consciousness had hidden his deception, he might have tucked the bills away into his jacket and proposed a run into Melrose for hamburgers. But thinking he had been discovered, he dropped the bills on the counter next to the empty dinner plates and began spinning his defense.

"Believe me, I haven't forgotten about these. I plan on talking to the bank about 'em real soon. Jesus, it's tough enough these days, Doris." Hank couldn't bring himself to mention his depressing relationships with Calcutta or Big Muddy. "But your health just has to come first," he said, blending just enough honesty into his lie to achieve a semblance of sincerity.

"If it weren't for these medical bills..."

Doris stopped him. "Oh, I'm such a bother," she said before realizing she was looking at unpaid mortgage bills. But as the nature of the documents became clear a fire began to consume her tolerance for Hank's confession, and in its heat her clarity returned. If amnesia had not already threatened the durable memory of Hank's goodness in her heart, this revelation did. Hank's vices imperiled not only their home but also their future together. And worse, it swept away her trust. Doris slumped at the one-two punch.

"Oh no. No, Hank," she cried. "Our home isn't yours to lose like one of your bets. I'd rather be sick and have a roof over our heads than be well and on the street."

Doris felt pain rising in her head and in her heart, and with it another terrible thought. "What about Rama's account?" Doris looked at Hank as if he were a stranger. And in his silence she realized not only was she in jeopardy, but now her son's future was at risk. She rose from the kitchen chair where she had wilted and demanded Hank's attention.

"Is this why we haven't heard from Trent?"

Hank shuddered. How could the same day that had seen him roll perfectly into the center of that thin white line now see all his lies, and his security, blow up in his face? He waited for the next question like a condemned man awaits his sentence.

"How much money is left in Rama's fund, Hank?"

Hank could not lie again. "A couple of thousand."

Doris's dropped back to the seat again as if a phantom bullet had struck her. "Have you settled with Trent Institute…yes or no?"

Hank's false constructions had now totally collapsed and it was time for the simple truth: "No ma'am."

Hank waited for Doris's next move. In a moment he would explain all his good intentions and his incredibly bad luck. She would understand. Together they would rebuild from an honest foundation…he hoped.

But Doris said nothing. She raised a trembling arm and pointed toward the front door.

———•———

Doris pressed her forehead against the patio door. The cool glass eased the pain but did little for the turmoil in her heart. She had seen her husband frustrated and scared before, but never so sad. It had taken all her resolve not to follow him to the driveway and withdraw her eviction. She listened to the growl of the Rambler's tires turning onto Crutchfield Lane and to the crack of crazy thunder. The storm had grown into a full electrical maelstrom. It was no kind of night to send Hank away.

He watched the storm lashing the hills above Bluff Meade as he dropped into the curves hugging the creek. The familiar laurel hedges swept past like a black shroud as he sped recklessly into the night. Regardless of his speed, the cost of his deception and self-delusion was inescapable; there was no denying or outrunning the truth. It wasn't gambling or the unreasonable desire to realize his flying dream that condemned him. It was the lies.

An awful emptiness and a searing bolt of shame stabbed at Hank's heart. His debts would be paid in the currency of loneliness and poverty. He had been there once before. He doubted he could face it again. But like the unfathomable course of the jagged bolts overhead, Hank's emotions surged out of control. He grinned crazily through his despair and cursed as lightning illuminated the torn gray clouds.

"Not a total fucking loss…got my money's worth. At least I flew the Crow once!"

For a moment Hank consoled himself in the knowledge that even though he owed a debt to ARMCO, Calcutta, Trent, Doris, and her doctors, they couldn't take away the fact that he *had* flown again and that he had landed the Crow right on the stripe. At least there would always be one memory that lingered fresher and brighter than the nightmare flight over St. Claude.

The image vanished in a deafening clap of thunder. His thoughts fell back to the costs of the Little Crow and to his most inflexible creditor. For an instant his smile flickered with satisfaction: Not even Lew Raybon could recover a nickel of Calcutta's funds where he was bound. Somewhere ahead the Mississippi churned beneath the steel deck of the Interstate Bridge.

—•—

As Hank approached the bridge, raindrops the size of marbles freed themselves from over-burdened clouds and fell like bombs. Recklessly, he pulled the Rambler from the pavement and onto the sidewalk, then lurched into the deluge. He stumbled with purpose up the on-ramp.

Concrete gave way to steel grating as the structure rose above the water. Hank bowed his head against the storm. As he limped along the railing the raindrops exploded in countless numbers on the rusty steelwork, yet his vision was drawn hypnotically by the few drops that whizzed past his temples and passed cleanly through the steel grating. He watched them plunge unaffected to the waters below. What were the odds of that, he thought—a strange notion for a mind consumed by a more sinister concept.

"One in a thousand," he barked into the building rainstorm. The wind tearing at structural steel and the booming of passing cars drowned out his pronouncement.

"One in a million…fuck it," he laughed, knowing he would never have to consider the odds again. He never was much good at numbers anyway.

When he guessed he was above the channel, Hank stopped and leaned against the railing. His right foot searched for purchase on the lowest rail, then he hoisted himself up and leaned out over the railing. Swirling rain plummeted to a vanishing point somewhere well below the river's murky surface. Nothing separated him from the water's empty promise and from an end to his torturous insufficiencies.

The abyss was within reach. Hank closed his eyes. There was nothing to stop him now…except a blast from the air horn of an approaching barge.

He raised his drenched face to look upstream. A tug pushing six grain barges was working its way south along the channel, Baton Rouge bound. Its pilothouse towered on steel struts above the barges' rusted decks. Amber light from its windshield glowed through the storm's gloom. Hank could see the shape of a figure at the helm holding a mug of hot coffee to his lips. He imagined the warm sanctuary of the pilothouse: It would smell of cigarettes, electrical gear, and gumbo. The pilot would smile as he followed the channel south, his thoughts on simple things: the shifting sandbars and that Cajun roll-in-the-hay waiting downriver. Hank stood transfixed in the rain as the barges slid beneath him. The pilot's bright haven of humanity approached through the rain; it would pass only a few yards beneath his feet.

Looking up from behind brass and polished rosewood, the barge pilot caught a glimpse of a man leaning over the bridge's railing. On an impulse, the pilot stepped out to the gangway and raised his grimy white coffee mug in recognition of the hardy soul up on the bridge.

"Haallloooowww," he bellowed hard into the storm.

Hank froze in what might have been his last tracks. "Hello," he whispered in surprise. The tug churned beneath, and as it passed, Hank Schwain imagined he smelled good tobacco and filé spices.

Hank stepped back from the brink. As he regained his footing he noticed an unusual heart-shaped pattern on the railing. There, in peeled paint and pigeon droppings, lay a distinct valentine—imperfect but beautiful in its improbability. Suddenly, Hank's dark impulse was consumed by the craving for a good cup of coffee. As quickly as he could without snagging his cane in the walkway's steel grid, Hank left the valentine and the abyss behind. He fished for the keys as he approached the Rambler, still parked astride the sidewalk. Funny thing, he thought, shuddering in the chill, why did he even bother to lock it? As he fumbled with the key, Hank noticed a citation from the Bridge Authority tucked under the windshield wiper.

"You're shitting me." The ticket was too much—a bad joke on a bad night. In an algebra of emotion, the product of two negatives was a positive. Hank's face cracked into an unlikely smile. Standing in the rain along the bridge's busy approach, he was consumed in laughter. In gales of crazy mirth he purged all thoughts of death, divorce, and a lifetime of lost bets to howl instead at people's insensitivity.

"You'd think they'd come looking for a man who'd abandoned his car on the ramp of a god-damned bridge. Wouldn't you?" His laughter turned into a curse. "Nah, just write out a ticket for a dead man…the assholes."

Hank's damp clothes balked on the vinyl upholstery as he slid into place behind the wheel and hung an abrupt U-turn back toward town. It was better to be alive and a little pissed than looking up at the keel of gumbo-man's tug. But it occurred to him that, except for the river, he had no destination when he had fled from Doris's door…and he had none now.

Hank tossed his wallet to the seat beside him and took stock: Eight dollars—not enough for a decent room and a meal, but at least he could drink. The Raccoon Roadhouse coming up on his right would see to that. The Rambler splashed through images of the neon 'Coon reflected in puddles on the roadhouse's flooded lot. Hank left the motor running and returned with two six-packs and a bag of warm hushpuppies. A man had to eat. If he couldn't bed down somewhere comfortable, at least he had a dry car, a snack, and plenty of cheap beer.

He drove carefully through the storm, working his way across town. The beer, the radio, and the Rambler's heater created a comforting cocoon for his shattered emotions. But by the fourth beer a breakdown had set in. Hank found himself raving against the demons who had brought him to this desperate point: Big Muddy, Ivar, Wedgy, Ike, Hitler, Churchill, The Ford Man, and Rama.

"And the god-damned Little Crow," he added angrily as he pinched a can between his knees and jabbed a church key into its aluminum top. Nobody was spared Hank's anger and blame—except Doris.

———•———

Hank practically dared the state troopers to add another setback to this day's bad fortune as he drove recklessly through the first six-pack. Ahead the ghastly mirrored edifice of the Kings Kreek Golf Center materialized in the beam of his headlights. Hank hurled a half-empty beer can across his hood and watched with satisfaction as the can slammed against the gilded flanks of the King's creation.

"And fuck golf, too," he cried with special emphasis at the memory of his costly encounters with the supposedly noble game.

As the royal facility slid back into darkness, a motorcycle cop passed him in the opposite direction. A shock of adrenaline surged up Hank's spine. Drunk and Disorderly might get him shelter for the night, but it would be a shame to waste that last six-pack. He watched in his mirror for the tail lights of the cycle, but the cop must not have noticed his crime.

"Close one, shit-head." The Rambler threatened to rise onto two wheels as Hank cranked the wheel into the first right turn that offered harbor from the incriminating highway. Hank fought the car back to stability then drunkenly crammed the pedal to the worn red carpet and reached for another beer. A weathered sign raced quickly to greet him: *Aero Meadows Air Park – Glider Rides and General Aviation.*

"Wouldn't you know it," Hank laughed. On an intoxicated run from the bridge into an aimless night, he had stumbled into his destiny.

———•———

A broken neon light above the hangar cast the word *Aero* on a blue beam into the dark. As Hank skidded to a stop on the tarmac, the dark silhouette of the hangar and the gleam of wet aircraft were framed between swipes of the Rambler's worn wipers. One of the craft on the flight line was his glider, the Little Crow—the one he should have sold today. The fragile aircraft tugged at its tie-down lines under the urging of the weather. He regarded the glider darkly through the lens of cheap beer and foul humor. The Crow fidgeted as if it were alive—the embodiment of crushed aspirations that Hank couldn't get out of his life. Unlike the other antagonists on his list, this one was within his power to destroy before it damaged him any further.

With the Rambler idling and the radio turned up loud, he switched off the headlights and surveyed the deserted facility. The swirling rains repeatedly froze, swirled, then froze again as the beam from a lone security light was interrupted by a swaying branch. The stroboscopic effect cast the stormy flight line in horror movie illumination. Hank yelped in sinister delight: Here was the perfect place for the mayhem brewing in his drunken brain.

Ain't no law against wrecking what's already mine, he thought.

The Jefferson Airplane soared from the Rambler's radio. "Somebody to Love" raged with impatience as Hank grabbed the tire iron from the tailgate and headed toward the flight line. His feet splashed on the tarmac as the speaker blared. He fingered the tool's wet iron shaft in his right hand and howled along with Balin and Slick's stratospheric vocals. The beer can clutched in his left collapsed under his murderous grip.

Hank soon stood before the fragile aircraft like a priest before the lamb. He considered for an instant whether shattering the windshield or crushing the elevators would be the best first blow. He chose the glass and raised the iron, but before delivering his first strike his intentions were derailed by a tiny light peering back at him from within the cockpit. A string of goose bumps charged up his arms.

"Jesus Christ!" He jumped back involuntarily. Something—someone— was on board.

The Airplane's song had thundered to a wavering whammy-bar finish followed by a rare moment of dead top-forty air as a DJ somewhere in a lonely cinderblock studio fumbled for his next disc. In the silence, Hank heard only the rain pelting the glider's windshield and the creaking of the wings against their tethers. With his weapon held high Hank's intentions were exposed, but no sound or reaction came from within the cockpit. He nearly stumbled as he leaned in for a better look—the blue light remained.

"Out of my damned plane...glider. Now!" he commanded.

There was no response from the Little Crow, but the radio returned to life—this time with a swampy, electric baseline running like syrup beneath a slippery guitar riff while an organ figure descended on warbling Leslie speakers to a dark sensual groove. It had been a while since he last heard it, but even to a drunken man bent on destruction the music's dark bayou brew was beguiling. Then, in perfectly late timing the voice swung in behind the music's smoky beat. It was Marcile Gold.

The low-country masterpiece from which her enchantress persona emerged to mystify a million listeners and launch a rowdy roadhouse career, was on the air:

> It's just Blue Light Voodoo
> Damn that witch
> Got a way with you

"Gold, you damn spook. Leave me be," Hank cried in confusion that the woman who loved this little aircraft was singing directly to its would-be executioner. As the song unfolded, Marcile sang Hank's grip loose from the iron and coaxed a smile back onto his rain-streaked face. She was irresistible. The tire iron rang like a bell as Hank dropped it to the wet pavement.

Unarmed now, he peered closely through the Plexiglas at the alarming blue glow. "What the hell…"

Hank almost laughed as the song charged into its chorus and he recognized the origin of the light. The glider settled between gusts, and as it stilled the fuzzy blue reflection resolved into the mirror image of a word: *Aero*.

"For God's fucking sake," Hank gasped, then cackled against the storm. It was a reflection, a fragment of Aero Meadows's broken neon sign. Hank laughed at his fear and at his drunken apprehension. "Blue Light Voodoo, my ass." But though he discounted the song's power, Marcile Gold's music had just saved the Little Crow.

The wind gusted abruptly and the glider rattled in response.

"You wanna fly? Shit, that's two of us."

Hank released the tethers holding the craft and then drunkenly grabbed her tail and rotated her into the wind. He flipped open the canopy and dropped into the forward seat. With the canopy closed, the storm and the music fell away. Hank peered into the night as he took the stick.

Years ago the glider instructor at Sedalia had shown him how you could practice stick technique by "flying on the ground." If the winds had sufficient lift to hold both wings off the ground, a pilot could hike the glider up onto its keel and keep it balanced there by controlling the lift on each wing with the flaps. It was good practice, the next best thing to really flying. Drunk and crazy, Hank figured he could use a "flight" right about now.

The storm kicked up a squall of rain that swirled out across the tarmac and slammed the untethered glider's left wing hard to the ground as it lifted the right. The disconcerting impact shocked Hank and reversed the effect of his last several beers. With another crash, Little Crow's left side rose and the right wing hammered the tarmac. If Hank didn't fly her soon or tie her back down, the glider would bash herself to pieces in the storm. Only a few moments earlier he was prepared to destroy the craft; now he fought for her survival.

With a left turn to nowhere, Hank eased the stick left and watched the right wing clear the soaked tarmac. He over-corrected at first and bumped the left wing down, then reversed the process with a lighter touch. After three tries the wild pilot and his glider struck a balance; he could hold both the aircraft's wings safely off the tarmac for ten seconds or so. The wind shifted and he worked the flaps again. When he had achieved level flight once more, he worked the pedals and the craft rotated like a weathervane in and out of the wind. The grounded glider pilot whooped as if he had executed a perfect barrel roll.

Hank closed his eyes and flew the Little Crow by feel, keeping her level long enough to soar in his imagination across the black channel to St. Claude, to the eve of June 6, 1944.

He circled the statue of the Holy Mother and plucked the spirits of thirteen lost soldiers right from beneath her sorrowful granite nose. Mission accomplished. Then, in a pool of blue light he and Little Crow soared in the balance between uplifting and depressing forces—flying on the ground until the storm passed.

Only when a pair of headlights approached up Aero Meadows's driveway did Hank return to earth.

Chapter 49

Rama endured a sizeable portion of the Frank Sinatra songbook as the Lincoln headed northeast into the heart of Texas. Wedgy was in full voice, none the worse for his randy adventure in the foreign lands to the south. He crooned in satisfaction that they had avoided Albuquerque's foul weather and in anticipation of the loose, lousy, and loaded players awaiting him in Mesquite Creek.

It was just as well that Wedgy was in a musical mood; Rama harbored troubling thoughts about the strange phone call with his mother just behind and the hope of hustling Wedgy somewhere still ahead. He had resolved to try her phone again when they got to Mesquite Creek, but for now he would have to simmer in guilt and doubt, comforted only in the thought that the trip with Wedgy would end soon. He had longed to see the cypress groves along the Monterey coast but, one way or another, Mesquite Creek was going to be his final stop. His future beckoned with or without an education from Trent Institute, but without a student deferment he was on borrowed time. With the war's appetite for young men growing, the lack of response from Trent was increasingly disturbing. He could not have known how long Hank's line of creditors had stretched and how close he was to joining the young men who marched from high school straight into Vietnam's steamy jungles.

Rama lingered on these uncertainties as he watched a green smudge on the empty horizon resolve into a stand of thirsty cottonwoods lolling above an inviting pond. To his relief, Wedgy pulled the Lincoln onto a couple of dry ruts that led out to the oasis.

Brittle grasses whisked at the Lincoln's undercarriage as they rolled to a stop in a crude picnic site beside the pond. The place had long been maintained as a getaway for the nearest prairie-locked ranchers and their families. A stone barbecue with an iron grill and a weathered picnic table branded with the interwoven initials of lovers spoke of happy afternoons for generations of folks who lived somewhere beyond the windmills whirling on the horizon.

"Take five," declared Wedgy.

The would-be Old Blue Eyes took a long leak through the barbecue grill, his stream thumping heavily against ancient ashes. "Adds a little something to the flavor, eh, Rama?"

Rama said nothing but looked away, offended on behalf of the ghosts of picnics past. He slid from the car, gratefully stretching his legs as he strolled to the water's edge. Cattails had taken root in the beach to the delight of a coven of red-wing blackbirds who sang happily to one another while clinging precariously to the reeds. Rama's mood brightened as he noticed a scattering of flat stones around the pool's banks. The ghosts slipped away as Rama, an accomplished skipper, picked up one of the stones and in a well-practiced motion sent it on a low, flat trajectory that kissed the tops of the pond's tiny ripples once, again, and again until twelve rings of ripples radiated on the water's surface like pearls in a graceful strand.

"Twelve. Pretty good, kid."

Wedgy's thirsty voice scared the blackbirds from their reeds and up into the temporary refuge of the cottonwoods. He had watched the young man's loose, athletic skipping technique with the discerning eye of an opportunistic gamesman. "Hope you don't swing a golf club that well," Wedgy laughed. "You might be a threat. How much you want to bet I can skip a golf ball better than you can skip a stone?"

Without waiting for an answer, Wedgy opened the Lincoln's trunk and extracted a throwaway 5-iron. It was one of the clubs he had left for Rama to practice with back at camp near Sunset Hills. Wedgy paused when he noticed green stains on the face of the club; he didn't recall grass anywhere back at the campground. He slid his thumbnail through the grooves. Traces of rich turf confirmed that Rama must have gotten around while he was in Mexico— probably back to Sunset Hills, thought Wedgy. Odd for a kid that claims he rarely golfs.

Wedgy grabbed a couple of battered balls and turned back toward the pond. "Twelve, huh?" He smiled as he waggled the club. "A buck says I can beat it."

Rama looked at Wedgy. "With a golf ball? Okay, one dollar." He figured this was an easy bet, but he knew that no matter what, the old hustler would always be a tough competitor. He hoped Lee Trujillo and Carla were lining up some mighty stiff competition at Mesquite Creek.

Wedgy dropped a ball onto the bank, but it nestled too deeply for his liking. He pinched some thick mud from the bank and formed it into a little cone then placed his ball on the impromptu tee and tamped it down with his fingertip.

"They used to tee 'em up like that all the time before some black guy came up with the tee. Can you believe that...a nigger?" Then, with all the serious-ness of a man aiming at a club championship, Wedgy stared down his shot.

He looked for a gap between the cattails and pictured a low stinger across the pond's widest point. He rolled the clubface shut and gripped far down the shaft. A flat half-swing spanked the ball a microsecond before splattering the mud tee. Like Rama's stone Wedgy's ball touched down lightly, but it skipped farther. It didn't touch the water again until it cleared half the pond. Rama was sure Wedgy would run out of water and would have to cough up a dollar—a fitting preview of the payback to come—but the ball was spinning in such a way that it quickly lost velocity and scribed eleven more rapidly compressing skips. Rama was left with the number thirteen dangling from his lips.

"Still got it," Wedgy declared gleefully. But remembering Rama's magic, added sarcastically, "or was that you?"

"Son of a...gun," Rama nearly cursed as he patted his hip pocket for his billfold.

"Nah, forget it, this one's on me. You should have known I only make bets I can win. That's a lesson you'd better learn," Wedgy winked at Rama, "if you ever plan on doing any hustling." The grassy 5-iron was still on his mind.

Wedgy laid the club across the picnic table. "Sit down; I'll buy you a drink."

The old hustler fetched two reasonably cold Coca-Colas from his ice chest. He set one before his caddie and, to Rama's amazement, drank the other instead of a beer. In a moment of unguarded camaraderie, Rama couldn't help but pursue a lingering curiosity about the old fellow's past. "You never told me about your family. You got one?"

Wedgy groaned, his utterance muffled inside the bottle's thick green glass. He pulled the mute from his lips and recited a brief outline of his immediate family history.

"Had a wife, but she bailed out when the IRS, the SEC, and the great state of Tennessee lowered the boom." Wedgy watched a blackbird glide back from the cottonwoods and across the pond to an impossible perch on one of the cattails.

"Had a daughter. Died of leukemia. At least she croaked while I was still on top of my game. Thank God she got to see her daddy in clover."

Rama winced at the unexpected revelation of a dead child. With some trepidation he asked if Wedgy had a son.

"Oh yeah," Wedgy replied scornfully, "I've got a son...somewhere. Might even be in the war you're dodging, but I doubt it. He's a god-damned hippie."

Wedgy leaned his back against the table and stretched his feet as far as he could to dispel any more kinks before returning to the car and the final stretch toward Mesquite Creek. He took another drink and belched loudly. A bullfrog answered immediately, bringing a sad smile to the old hustler's wind-burned face.

"He's on his own, and if he's drafted…hell, he brought it all on himself. Blew his own dad right out of the water. Pretty much put the Byrnes out on the street, and for sure kissed his education good-bye."

"What'd he do?"

"Turned on, tuned in, dropped out, got soft, got stoned…got a conscience. Shit, I don't know," Wedgy grumbled. "Figured he was gonna change the world's evil ways…and do it on my dime. The bastard guessed he'd start with his old man. Said I was financing war mongers. Shit, I was just selling some sweet securities to the highest bidder. It wasn't my concern what the companies did, long as they looked profitable. But he never understood. Most folks don't."

Wedgy's face turned gray at the thought. "So he copies a bunch of my records right under my fucking nose and makes a tidy little package for the Feds. Figured he was among friends. Christ, the shitheads probably gave him some of that lysergic acid their buddies in the CIA cooked up."

Wedgy sighed as a dragonfly attracted by the polished steel of the 5-iron alighted on the shiny club head like a priceless jewel.

"Can you believe it? The hippie fink told me he did it to *save* me."

Rama thought about the freedom of roaming from course to course through an extended summer that stretched under a giant blue sky from the Great Lakes out to Monterey just to play a game he loved. Even if the old hustler's motives or his accommodations were a little tawdry, how else could he live a life where he could linger at the simple pleasures and discoveries the game and the road regularly provided—like this charmed oasis?

"Well, maybe it *did*," Rama replied. Where else could Wedgy count tee times and happy hours as his only deadlines or conduct business in bright daylight on soft lawns?

Wedgy looked at Rama with fleeting respect. Damned if the young man didn't have a point. There were times when he couldn't deny a golfing life was far better than the high-risk high-stress business dramas that had consumed him in his successful past. It could be argued that his son had saved him, but if only for the time being. Loneliness and age threatened the freedom he enjoyed now and would likely soon call for a new game. Wedgy raised the Coke to finish it off, and with the mouth of the bottle poised a couple of inches from his lips, a coy smile wrinkled his red face.

"Did I mention he was a motherfucker of a golfer?" Wedgy mused as his vision strayed to one of the distant windmills. "I wonder if he still plays."

Rama, the birds, and the bullfrogs all remained silent.

Softened by Rama's innocent question, Wedgy expressed an interest in his caddie's family for the first time since they had been on the road. "There's a reason malcontents like me roam around the country without a thread tying them to anyone, but what's your excuse? You've never said diddly about your old man other than you were in a big hurry to get out of Dodge."

The eyes that spotted traces of yesterday's turf on a battered club now stared directly into Rama's eyes. "So what's your story?"

Fearful of revealing his father's identity and the motives that would damage any chances of ambushing Wedgy, Rama's mind clanked to a halt. Before he compromised himself, he fell back upon the stock answer he had used since childhood to characterize a rogue father and to maintain his own pride:

"Dad was a pilot but got injured in a plane crash on D-day."

"Oh crap, that's rough," said Wedgy. "What does he do now?"

Rama let his guard down when a little lie would have kept his father's and his connection invisible. "Sells cars at the AutoTorium."

Wedgy's face perked with interest. "Which one? There are several you know."

"Big Muddy's…on Highway 61."

The words had just left Rama's lips when he recalled Wedgy once mentioning with satisfaction that the fool who lost six grand to him was the same fellow who had unloaded the questionably pedigreed Lincoln on him. Rama feared that if Wedgy was paying attention, the connection between him and his father had just been revealed.

"No shit? Much of a living in that?" asked Wedgy with a devilish smile. The old hustler had been paying attention, having engineered the line of inquiry out of curiosity whether Rama's heritage might explain why he would lie about his playing skills and practice on the sly.

"He does okay sometimes," Rama said. "But he hasn't worked in months."

If Wedgy Byrne was anything he was nobody's fool, and Rama knew that if his motives tipped Wedgy off to an impending trap, the old hustler might never take the bait. Rama, uncomfortable with the blatant lie, quickly slid from the picnic table.

The route to Mesquite Creek wandered another four hours beyond the bright horizon. Wedgy pulled the Lincoln back onto the highway, then launched into a hearty, twenty-minute rendition of "Very Good Year." The performance might have lasted longer had the Lincoln's transmission not chosen the umpteenth coda to give up the ghost.

Rama felt more relief than alarm as the car coasted to a halt in the empty rangeland. At least the singing was over.

"Damn Ford crap!" Wedgy cursed as he threw open the door to investigate the problem. Smoke from beneath the car told him all he needed to know: He wouldn't be leaving this spot under his own power.

He slammed the hood shut and looked at the sky. There were about three hours 'til sunset, less than that to the golf course. He was beginning to have his doubts about the wisdom of continuing forward when he realized it was a shorter tow to Mesquite Creek than it was back to whatever cow town they had blown through several hours ago.

"I'd like a piece of the son of a bitch who sold me this heap of garbage," Wedgy swore. He restrained himself from accusing Rama of having a genetic link to the aforementioned SOB.

Rama guessed by Wedgy's relatively civil response to the car's breakdown that his lie about his father's tenure at Big Muddy's had left some doubt in the old hustler's mind. "It's the tranny, right?" Rama asked.

Wedgy nodded. "Smells like it."

Rama was in no mood to linger there with Wedgy. Up the road Lee was priming the boys for a match with "Wedgy the Gypsy Hustler" or some such nonsense to hype the traveling golfer's mystique. Rama remembered Lee's advice to get there on Friday. There wasn't much time to waste being broken down. He grabbed a jacket from his bag and, as an afterthought, pulled the Night Lessons club from the trunk. Better to go for help than wait for it to come to them, he figured. The less time he spent with a frustrated and suspicious hustler the better.

"If I get a ride right away, I can get some help back out here tonight," said Rama. "If I don't make it back, well at least you've got a place to sleep."

In the absence of a better plan, Wedgy nodded his approval and extracted two twenty-dollar bills from his wallet. "Here, you might need to bribe a driver to come out this far," said Wedgy.

He pressed the cash into Rama's palm, certain that he wouldn't see the young man again. At least, thought Wedgy, his conscience at stiffing Rama out of much of his pay would be eased by forty bucks. But Wedgy wondered, if Rama did return there would have to be a reason why he would help out a fellow he knew all along had screwed his father…unless there was something in it for him. Maybe something up the road at Mesquite Creek? Wedgy guessed that if Rama came back it would not be out of a sincere desire to repair the Lincoln. His caddie's return would put Wedgy on high alert for a hustle.

"Nice while it lasted, eh, Rama?" said Wedgy with a wave.

Rama walked a few paces along the broken shoulder to put some distance between him and the Lincoln. He swung the old brassie to loosen up and to take his mind off the depressing collection of trash woven into the brush along the shoulder. Lady Bird had not yet succeeded in beautifying this empty corner of her great state.

"Don't worry…I'll be back," Rama called.

"That'a boy," muttered Wedgy.

Chapter 50

Half a mile down the highway Rama stopped to blast the seedpods of a noxious weed into oblivion but was interrupted in mid-swing as a white Fairlane wagon pulled to the shoulder. The driver, a balding fiftyish plumbing salesman in exhausted blue slacks and a weary white shirt, signaled Rama aboard.

The man lounged behind the wheel, his right arm draped lazily across the back of the seat as if he were settled into a couch to watch all six reels of *Ben Hur*. His shirt was unbuttoned at the neck and his tie loosened till it sagged far below the collar. Two majestic golden pheasants attempted to flee the approach of an unseen hunter but were forever stymied by the necktie's blue silk confines. The fellow smiled at the prospect of having some company.

"Well hey, looks like you're a golfer."

Rama hesitated at the clutter of catalogs and demo fixtures occupying the passenger's seat. The headline across the cover of a toilet seat flyer greeted him cheerily: *Tops for Bottoms – Luxury Seating*.

"The back seat, son…golfers gotta ride in the back of *this* bus." He laughed at his unwitting snub, hoping the hitchhiker could take a joke. He had nothing against golfers, but as far as he was concerned, even Jesus Christ would have had to settle for the back had he been thumbing north to Mesquite Creek.

Rama obliged and slid in behind the passenger's seat. The salesman turned his attention to the highway as six tired cylinders heaved the Fairlane back onto the blacktop.

"Is that your rig with the trailer back there? Where you headed?"

"No, it's my partner's. I'm going up to Mesquite Creek to get some help." Rama squirmed uncomfortably on the dirty vinyl seat. Two months on the Lincoln's plush leather had spoiled him.

The man glanced back at Rama. "Where'd you say?"

"Mesquite Creek. It's up the road a couple of hours. It's a golf course…just turn off by the giant golf ball."

"A giant ball?" A look of confusion crossed the salesman's face but dissolved as he recalled some local history. "Oh yeah, I think I know where you're talkin'."

As the wagon reached cruising speed the driver's fingers settled onto the wheel, drumming out the rhythm of a tune from the swing era that still sounded fresh in his head. "You had me kinda lost there with your giant ball. That damn old eyesore has been gone for a spell. Blowed away by a twister a few years back."

The driver laughed at the thought. "Swear to God, somebody up there has got a sense of humor. The twister tore that damn thing up by the roots, flipped it head over heels, and left the ball on the ground and that shaft pokin' up in the air like—swear to God—some giant damned genitals."

"The high-school boys had a field day with *that* thing. Couldn't resist spray-painting their buddies' girlfriends' names on that big old dick. Painted hair on the ball…you can imagine." The driver chuckled at the memory. "Swear to God, the fellows from the Baptist church brought in some torches and scrapped the damned thing out of sheer embarrassment."

"How will you know where to turn off then?" asked Rama.

"Oh hell, they put up a picayune little sign, but you gotta watch out or you'll shoot right by it."

The salesman's fingers settled into a lazy shuffle on the steering wheel. "Yeah, I can take you all the way…*mess keet* it is."

Rama and the salesman arrived at the turnoff and plunged into Mesquite Creek's arroyo while the sun still reddened the sky. As the Fairlane rolled down the steep gravel drive, Rama watched as they approached the clubhouse. It appeared as if nothing had changed in eight years. Out on Carla's veranda, a group of regulars shared frosty beers in the rosy evening light. He had once enjoyed a cold soda on those very boards, and he had sat in quiet admiration as Lee Trujillo and the others replayed the high- and low-lights of some long-lost round. Rama hoped he would recognize at least one of those fellows in this afternoon's gathering.

The wagon rolled to a stop and the driver hopped out anxiously. He scanned the lay of the peaceful green land. "Swear to God, I always wondered what was down this draw." He straightened his tie and turned to more pressing business.

"Don't suppose you know a shortcut to the shitters, eh chum?"

Rama remembered that, too. He pointed at the front door. "Just take a right at the wild boar…*swear to God*," Rama laughed. He watched the salesman climb the weathered steps and disappear through the old doors; golf clubs still doubled as doorknobs. Rama hoped the stuffed boar, like the giant golf ball, hadn't taken flight over the intervening years. He imagined the salesman, filled with watery coffee, frantically searching for a non-existent boar as a waypoint to the pisser. Rama smiled as he dismounted and turned toward the golfers up on the veranda.

He ducked through the willows that still wept above the putting green. Ahead, late orange rays bathed the group gathered to watch the hopes of their friends, still chipping and putting their way around the eighteenth green, fade as surely as the daylight.

Nothing looked much different: The vines had crept a little farther across the adobe walls, and a few more louvers had fallen from the shutters up on the widow's watch. Rama wondered what changes time might have brought to Mesquite Creek's players; had a whirlwind toppled any of them, too, or blown their features askew? Would he recognize anyone?

Even as the men watched his cautious approach to their perch, Rama searched their faces for a familiar smile or a hint of recognition: Boney, Mirage, or Donaldo, but he came up without a match.

By the time Rama stepped onto the veranda, the men had already cast him as another hungry traveler seeking the source of the barbecue scent that swirled on the late afternoon breeze, or perhaps the son of a tourist looking to limber up over a basket of balls. A rusted old brassie seemed an odd choice for a session on the range, they thought, but accustomed to a strange game, they easily accepted the unexplainable and returned to their chatter.

"Any of you fellas seen Lee Trujillo around here today?" Rama ventured.

One of the golfers answered with a laugh. "*Everybody's* looking for Lee Trujillo these days. Hey, if you're looking for an autograph, I've got a pocketful of balls with his John Henry in my bag." The golfer watched Rama to see if he was buying the story.

"Cheap," he added.

A second golfer let Rama off the hook. "Nah, he was here earlier. Played a little and took off for his sister's house." The golfer spoke with an air of importance for just *knowing* the comings and goings of one of the game's emerging stars.

Rama asked if Carla was still around. It was as much a question of her fate as it was a query into her immediate whereabouts. The golfer told him that she had gone home and would be back early in the morning. He turned back to his beer and the sunset. "You can set your blasted watch by that old gal."

Rama was reluctant to drop a request for serious roadside assistance onto a group so comfortably settled into their ritual, so he turned to the clubhouse. Finding a familiar face or maybe a club directory would be his next step, or so he hoped, until he met the playful brown eyes of a dark-haired young woman smiling back at him from behind the pro-shop counter.

"Tarzan!" she exclaimed at the sight of the taller, more robust edition of the thin, brown-haired boy who had once helped her change a tire on the beverage cart during one of Carla's Sunday tournaments. The girl was now a beautiful woman with a memory as quick as her smile. Apparently, the turbulent sea of gulf and great plains air that clashed above Mesquite Creek was good for the brain. Rama's murky Memphis memory lagged far behind as he struggled to place a name with the pretty face.

"Missie, Mella," he tried in vain.

"Melyssa, with a *Y*," she replied helpfully and reached across the counter to offer Rama her hand. Rama eagerly accepted a handshake that was at once feminine and deceptively strong. He remembered what a tomboy she had seemed on the day of that strange match with Lee—the day the scorpion had demanded Rama's intervention. The clash of masculine and feminine forces still coursed through her like the convergence in the atmosphere above, and its contrasts made her all the more alluring. Rama remembered the promise of her young body bouncing beside him in the cart that day. That promise had been answered lavishly. Rama was left with a simple, aching question: Why couldn't she have lived in Memphis?

Melyssa released his hand and told Rama she wasn't sure if she ever did get his real name. "But Tarzan is perfect."

The two easily charmed each other and reminisced with enthusiasm far beyond that warranted by a brief childhood acquaintance. With dusk settling upon the auburn landscape outside the pro-shop windows, Rama reluctantly cut their reunion short and returned to the business of rescuing Wedgy.

He explained his situation and, to his relief, Melyssa said her uncle Michael ran a repair service for trucks, pumps, and compressors. "All sorts of industrial crap…you name it," she said. "If he's not drunk, he can help out for sure. But I'll call for you…should get better results." She winked and his pulse quickened.

After invoking all the family clout and charm she possessed, Melyssa returned the telephone to the hook. "He'll be here to pick you up in fifteen minutes," she said. "I told him your partner had cash…" she looked at Rama expectantly.

"Oh yeah, plenty."

Melyssa began hustling through her shutdown checklist. She headed out to collect the beer bottles the sunset crew had left on the veranda. "I'll see you tomorrow then?"

"Oh yeah, absolutely," Rama gushed. "If you see Lee Trujillo before me, tell him Rama and Wedgy will be camping in the parking lot…in a trailer." With that, Rama disappeared to await Melyssa's Uncle Michael out by the drive.

A new moon lingered above the horizon as the rocky silhouette framing the golf course deepened. Darkness threatened to swallow the young man standing alone by the drive. He tightened his grip on the Night Lesson's club and mimicked the swings of the greats: Arnie's dip. Player's step. Trevino's lurch. The old persimmon brassie whistled in the night—happy to be home.

Ten minutes later a pair of headlights appeared at the top of the drive. A flatbed truck with a homemade boom and winch pulled to a noisy stop beside

Rama. Its diesel rattled like it had lost its bearings. A dome light flickered to life in the cab, and beneath its weak glow a skeletal figure with a crew-cut waved Rama inside.

"Where to?" the driver asked before clamping his teeth into the business end of an Abba-zaba. He tore a chunk of taffy free and offered the remainder of the bar to his passenger.

Rama waved off the candy, even as circuits of recognition tripped into action—he knew this fellow.

"Just head south at the highway. You'll see a blue Lincoln and a trailer on the left shoulder...about eighty miles," Rama said. The tow truck driver seemed unfazed by the estimated distance.

Rama strained to recall the man's identity. The fellow's eyes were too sunken to be read from the passenger's seat, but in that sepulchral face and in his penchant for taffy, Rama had clue enough to make the connection: Melyssa's uncle had been Boney's caddie. Rama struggled to remember his name but could only picture desert images.

"Sure nice of you to go this far out of your way," Rama said.

"Especially at night, huh," agreed the driver. His eyes never left the hazardous climb back to the highway. "But whatever 'Lyssa wants, 'Lyssa gets."

The word *mirage* finally lodged in Rama's mental stream like a twig against a stone.

"Of course, I don't work for free," the driver said. "But workin' after dark ain't a problem—in fact, it's always more interesting along here at night. It don't matter; I'll charge you 'bout the same as daylight." His wiry arms guided the awkward rig out onto the pavement and cranked its stiff wheels left—southbound. The tow truck's headlights burned a bright corridor into the night ahead.

Melyssa's uncle watched the tortured asphalt of the lonely road carefully for threats to the old rig's suspension, but he managed to keep an eye on his passenger, too. Melyssa hadn't said who Rama was, but the young man's face seemed familiar, and so did the old club he tapped nervously against the toe of his tennis shoe.

"That brassie...she's a bit of an antique," the driver observed. "I think 'Lyssa forgot to give me your name."

Rama remained silent until he realized what antique the truck driver meant. "Oh, the club! Yeah...for sure. It's way over twenty years old."

Rama did the math. He figured eight years since Carlos had entrusted him with the club, plus eleven years prior to that when the Stone children had been felled by the lightning and the club had been abandoned up on the sixteenth tee's promontory—that made nineteen. He guessed the club had been in Chandler's bag for a good number of years before that.

"Let me guess, she's a Walter Hagen?"

"No, it's Scottish…handmade, I think," replied Rama. He never really knew the origin of the club; the club-maker's name had been obscured by wear, but the words *Dornoch, Scot*…were clearly readable in the sole plate.

Rama looked down the rusty metal shaft resting between his legs. "Yes sir, it did get a little beat up laying in the brush out here all those years."

"Out here?"

"Yeah, out here…it was Chandler Stone's club. He left it laying up on the sixteenth tee the night before the children…" Rama paused, wondering for the first time since Carlos had told him the story of the children's death if it were even true.

"Got zapped." The driver completed Rama's sentence. "So you've heard about the accident. Small damn world."

The cab fell silent except for the buzzing of a loose shift knob. The two travelers stared into the dark, mute at the eerie convergence. Doubts rose in Rama's mind: Shouldn't he be exploring the night life around Trent's campus about now instead of clattering down this lonesome road with a skeleton at the wheel?

Suddenly, a jackrabbit, terrorized by the tow truck's approach, darted frantically through the headlights a hundred feet ahead and disappeared into the blackness. In an instant the ghostly white shape of an owl descended from an invisible perch and swooped across the road in pursuit to heap horror upon its terrified prey.

"Holy hell, did you see that? What'd I tell you? There always something interesting along here at night."

Rama shuddered at the rabbit's fate, and the cab fell back into silence until the driver's brittle voice broke the stillness as a significant date returned sharply to his mind. "June something…longest day of the year I think it was," he mused. "Yep, nineteen years now. A hell of a day that was. Nothing's really been the same around here since that lightning bolt."

The driver looked at Rama and the Night Lessons club, trying to put some sense or purpose to Rama's presence and his connection to the Stone children's tragic fate. He could only fall back on the cliché again: "Damn small world I'll tell you, son, but the timing is about right. Matter of fact, it was June 21, 1948, when those kids got fried."

Rama froze on the seat. Something in the driver's recollection stabbed at him like an icicle. Some explanations were in order. Maybe if he explained how Carlos Taddio had ushered him around the course on that odd night and how the old man had revealed the secret line for the sixteenth green's impossible putt, or how Carlos had presented him with Chandler Stone's club before disappearing back into the night, then, perhaps, the man piloting the tow truck through this strange night could fill in the blanks. Maybe this chilling revelation would make some sense. June 21.

But it was too much to ask. Rama was already reeling from the unfathomable connections between him and the people of this remote track. But mainly he was reeling from the driver's abrupt declaration of the date of the children's deaths: The twenty-first of June, 1948.

That was his birthday.

—•—

The tow truck driver studied the young man sitting beside him. The soft features of a child's face still lay below the maturing lines and whisker stubble of a nineteen-year-old man. The pieces fell into place. "Well, I'll be go to hell. I recollect…you were the kid caddying for Lee the day he tangled with the scorpion. Do you remember? That was me on Boney's bag." The driver seemed enthralled at the memory. "And that crazy putt…that was you? Shit, there's still folks wantin' to lynch Carla for letting you take that son-of-a-bitching stroke."

Rama smiled although still in shock at the coincidence of Dickey and Glendora Stone dying on the day of his birth.

The driver's bony right arm hovered above the seat, awaiting Rama's handshake. "I'm Mirage. Let me guess: You're gonna caddie in that match Lee's been talking up for this Saturday. How'd you ever come to be on the Gypsy Hustler's bag?"

"The Gypsy Hustler?" Rama almost gagged at the ridiculous moniker. But he had to admire Lee's promotional creativity. "Well, if that's what you want to call him…I don't know about caddying, though; I'm sort of done with that."

Locked in the truck with the Gypsy's very own caddie, Mirage saw an opportunity to get a tip on the upcoming match. "How good is he really?"

"Nothing short of fantastic," Rama lied without hesitation, still clinging to Wedgy's rules of engagement. "Almost never loses that I can remember."

Mirage grinned broadly at what he guessed to be Rama's blatant disinformation. "Of course, of course," he chuckled, letting the matter drop. Odd, he thought, here was a caddie that was *not* sandbagging for his man. It seemed that everything would remain strange on this evening.

As the truck bore deeper into the darkness, Rama's head bobbed with drowsiness. A gallery of gray forms streamed by just beyond its beams. The fleeting shape of a small horse flashed at the edge of recognition—on the fringe of certainty. Rama pondered the grainy image lingering in his mind like the TV news programs that had zoomed into each 8mm frame to conjure the ghostly shapes of assassins on the grassy knoll. He imagined the horse bore a rider: a gaucho crouched against the evening's chill.

"Did you ever know Carlos?" Rama asked.

"Taddio? The old Gaucho?" Mirage replied with surprise. "Before or after he died?"

"After he died?" Rama was thoroughly puzzled.

Mirage poked around in a canvas bag on the front seat and extracted a Nesbitt's orange soda. "Got another one if you're thirsty."

Rama declined.

"People thought the old fellow kicked the bucket a few years after Chandler vanished," began Mirage between long tugs on the soda. "But folks dawdling on the back nine after sunset said they thought they'd seen him on that little pony of his…like an apparition. He became Mesquite Creek's own little ghost story. Word got around, and a Fort Worth TV station even sent a crew out at Halloween for the 'Ghost Gaucho' story."

Mirage sighed at the thought. "A load of crap. Most of us who knew Carlos thought he'd probably gone back to Argentina. Shit, what did we know? One day, here about eight years ago—probably round the time you won that match for Lee—damned if the old coot doesn't come riding up, right off the golf course…in broad daylight! Just him up on the back of that little pony. In flesh and blood. End of ghost story.

"But here's the damnedest thing," Mirage continued. "Somehow while he was 'dead' old Carlos learned how to paint. I mean paint real good like a genuine artist. He started working up in that room above the clubhouse and stowed all his work up there. The crow's nest, they called it."

Rama remembered the crow's nest and how Carlos had given him its key on the night they had set up the course for Lee and Boney's match. Rama still recalled how Carlos had said something about the answer to Chandler's disappearance being in the crow's nest.

Mirage dropped his high beams as the first car they had encountered in an hour flew past. "Well, my friend, those paintings made him famous…but by accident. You see, the next time the TV folks came by to do their ghost story, their damn ghost was alive and kicking. But the producer lady got to talking with Carla Stone and learned how Carla had discovered the secret studio after some kid, clear out of the blue, had given her a long-forgotten key to the crow's nest. She never said anything about the kid other than—get this—he claimed to have been given the key by the gaucho…in person.

"Well shit, you can't write this stuff. That was too much for TV to resist. They knew a good story when they heard one, so they took the crew up in the crow's nest and there they were: A shitload of paintings of Glendora, Dickey, Chandler, and Carla—the whole Stone family—all of them posed along a wild old golf links strung along the edge of some rocky coast. It wasn't no Texas seashore, that's for sure.

"'A treasure trove,' the TV lady said. Then she went on about Carlos's colors: the reds of Glendora's hair; the intense green turf; the purple heather and the yellow broom. A 'primitive palette,' she called it. And she put it all up on the air.

"Right off, her station got swamped with interest in the ghost's work, and next thing you know, Carla is turning people away. Carlos had told her the paintings were only for the family—Carla and Chandler—they weren't for sale. Hard to believe, but for once Carla Stone turned her back on a buck."

Mirage shook his head in disbelief at a story he already knew. "So she's still broke. Still runs the course on a shoestring, and still tries to scalp off a few bucks with the book on her little tournaments. Still waters down the drinks. It's tough, but people seem to be losing their interest in golf matches way out here. Guess television is hard to beat, huh? Flick a switch and there he is: Arnie. Anyway, she's hurting for cash these days."

Mirage drew in a long breath after exhaling the story. "If it was me, I'd put old Carlos in front of an easel and crack the fucking whip," he laughed. His skeletal fingers tweaked the dial on the radio and settled on the irresistible swing of Bob Wills, sprinkled lightly with static from an unseen thunderstorm.

"Is he still around?" asked Rama.

"You mean, Carlos? Yeah, but I think he's on his last legs. He still gets in a few licks up in the crow's nest. Guess he's painting everything now: flowers, clouds, even got a damned good one of a locomotive scaring up jackrabbits out on the Santa Fe-Colorado line. He's just stacking them up, and the rich folks are just itchin' to shell out for them. God damn, he's near a legend and Carla's a pauper just by holding out."

Mirage's voice fell silent as the vibrant music of fiddles and mandolins filled the cab of the tow truck. Somewhere in the dark, the radio signal penetrated lonely casitas hidden up empty ranch roads. Somewhere in the dark, the music filled hearts brimming with passion or breaking with regret under neon lights from Wichita to Corpus Christi. A transmitter's 5,000-watt signal and the soul of American music held the two travelers in its spell for another ten miles without interruption by a single approaching headlight.

Mirage listened to the music and to the echo of own voice. He knew his reputation as a man of few words and was surprised at the ease with which he had regaled his passenger. The same magic that possessed Rama to make that putt and lifted so many to such heights now had his voice under its sway. Without waiting for a question, the skeleton's words rose one more time.

"Do you remember Carlos's little pony, Niña? I hate to say it, but I helped the old spook put her down a couple of years ago. You'd a thought Carlos had lost his best friend. I don't know what'll become of Mesquite Creek when Carlos follows that beast into the ground. Maybe this Trujillo kid will get folks excited about golf around here again…or Carla's gonna have to give it up— maybe open a gallery."

Mirage finished his soda and slipped the bottle beneath the seat. "Or maybe it's like it says on the clubhouse door: *As we breathe there's hope.* Maybe that's true. Did you hear how well Lee did at Baltusrol this year? That should stir up a little local interest…a little *hope.*"

"Fifth place, wasn't it?" Rama offered eagerly.

"So you're a fan!" Mirage observed with some pleasure. "Makes sense… you were his caddie for a couple of holes." Mirage laughed at the odd circumstance of Rama's taking the bag from Lee's stricken caddie. "Least you can tell your grandkids you looped for Lee Trujillo."

Rama smiled at Mirage's passion, but his mind was still on the mysteries of Mesquite Creek. "Mind if I ask you one more question?"

With a few more miles to while away and his tongue so comfortably limber, Mirage nodded.

"What became of Chandler Stone?"

Mirage slumped at the sixty-four-dollar question. He wished he could give this young man—the very soul who by unfathomable twists of fate now carried Chandler's own club—a decent answer, but the truth was as opaque as the red water racing down Mesquite Creek after a cloudburst.

"All I know was he drifted away. Most folks think he took his own sad life after the kids passed…and that his bones are scattered somewhere out there in the chaparral."

Mirage savored the mysterious story and for a moment imagined himself a drifter-storyteller from a John Ford Western. He felt the urge to cup his hands around a flaring match and light up a blunt. Then, with the scent of tobacco in his imagination, he remembered Chandler smoking a briar pipe and joking with his friends on the veranda while his children fussed on the green with putters as long as they were tall.

"Chandler Stone always loved this country," continued Mirage as they rolled farther south. "He could have hitched up with his friend Bobby T. Jones, but he never liked Atlanta or Augusta. He sacrificed a lot for Mesquite Creek, but he said the horizon and the humidity back East were just too close. People knew how he felt—or so they thought—and I guess they figured that he couldn't leave here dead or alive. But, my friend, I have my doubts."

Rama held his breath so he wouldn't drown out the whisper to which Mirage's dry voice had fallen. The skeleton had run out of orange soda. "Like I told you, I helped old Carlos put that pony of his down. The damned old pain-in-the ass wanted to bury Niña at the edge of the arroyo, out there by number sixteen. Shit, he coulda got twenty-five bucks to render her out. Anyway, I was the only fella' with a backhoe around here…"

Mirage slapped the dashboard of the tow truck. "Still am! So I got the job: gravedigger.

"We got poor little Niña in the ground, and I was fixin' to cover her up when Carlos remembered the saddlebags. He said he wanted to bury her burdens along with her, so he fetched the bags from the back of the flatbed we'd hauled her in on. He said some kind of a Gaucho prayer and tossed 'em in. When we were all done, he drove the flatbed back to the maintenance shed and I followed with the hoe.

"I guess it came from the saddle bags…just a little slip of paper, but it caught my eye as it blew off the flatbed. I hopped off the hoe and picked it up. You're probably thinkin' old Lady Bird's litter-bug thing got to me, eh?" Mirage smiled with respect for the First Lady.

Mirage looked sheepishly at Rama. "Well, it wasn't my business, but I read it. As best as I could tell, it was part of a letter from Chandler—a good-bye letter maybe. I couldn't make out a date or nothing, but it spoke of making his way back to a wee hut and tending sheep for some fellow up in the highlands, wherever that is. Chandler was probably crazy with grief when he wrote that crap, but I remember one thing for sure: Part of the letter was like a poem and it stuck with me." Mirage peered down the darkened highway and recited what he recalled:

Alas I welcome the fine foul weather from the firth
far more than the towering storms of sorrow
that prowl these hopeless plains

"That, I'll never forget," whispered Mirage. "And his wee hut in the highlands…it's always made me wonder what else was on the rest of that letter and what else Carlos knows."

The words echoed in Rama's mind, and he thought he might remember, too.

Buoyant Texas radio dominated the remainder of the drive, and soon the disabled Lincoln and its trailer loomed up on the left shoulder. A faint amber light glowed from the trailer's windows. As the tow truck scribed a U-turn on the lonely highway, Wedgy Byrne stepped through the trailer door.

The tails of an unbuttoned shirt flapped above a pair of worn Bermuda shorts reserved for private consumption. In a hurry to greet the approaching truck and face his long-awaited rescuers, Wedgy had slipped his feet into a pair of street shoes without socks or lacing. Milk-white skin below the shorts and ghastly expanses of exposed belly shone brightly in the truck's cruel headlights.

"Put down your fucking high-beams, asshole," rang the appreciative voice of Wedgy Byrne.

"Jesus," gasped Mirage at the unhealthy sight.

"Behold: The Gypsy Hustler," declared Rama.

Chapter 51

"No...Hank Schwain does not live here!" Doris raised her voice in agitation at the rodent of a man who stood on her front porch. The detestable character insisted that not only was it Hank's residence but that her husband was unemployed and needed to talk to Calcutta Finance about their lien on his house. Urgently!

Doris feared that Hank had really done it this time, but she didn't let on. She lied that Hank's name had been removed from the title to the property and that they had, in fact, been divorced years ago.

"You're barking up the wrong tree," she said as sternly as possible. The unnerving encounter triggered a rush of opaque fog that expanded across her vision. "You'll have to leave."

The rodent stepped menacingly toward her.

"Siran, come down here!" she called to her non-existent renter. She clung tightly to the door to maintain a defiant posture as long as possible. "This man is threatening me."

The rodent fell for her bluff. "You tell Mr. Schwain that we need to speak with him." Then he turned toward the street before Siran made his appearance.

The aperture in Doris's consciousness squeezed her vision down to a peep-hole and then winked shut as she tried to focus on the rodent's departure. She passed out still standing her ground in the doorway, and fell mercilessly into an umbrella stand en route to a hard landing on the floor.

The Calcutta collections agent heard her fall but sprinted to his car, never looking back to see if she was hurt. He roared onto Crutchfield without pausing for the stop sign.

From the entry floor Doris heard the car's growl, then the telephone. The ringing from the kitchen triggered a fantastic floral pattern that materialized from the darkness in her mind, then dissipated with each ring's decay.

With every unanswered ring, Rama, listening from the phone in Mesquite Creek's pro shop, became more concerned about his mother's well being. After a dozen rings he returned the receiver to its hook and slid the phone back across the counter to Melyssa.

"Can I try one more number?"

"Oh yeah, as many as you need." She was happy to help. Her uncle Mirage had said Rama and the Gypsy Hustler hadn't pulled into the lot until about one that morning. He warned his niece that they were liable to be a little cranky. But other than being worried about his mother, Rama seemed fine. The Gypsy was nowhere to be seen.

Rama dialed again. "Hank Schwain please…I know he works there."

Rama listened to an account of his father's latest misfortune as reported by Big Muddy's receptionist, still terrorized by her near-miss the day before. As Rama hung up, Melyssa watched a new level of concern cross his face.

"Can I make one more call? Sorry, Carla's gonna kill you when she gets the phone bill," said Rama.

This call found its destination: Guidance Industries. Ivar's secretary said Mr. Guidance was not around, but that she would relay a message to him promptly. Rama explained that he was concerned for his mother's health and asked if Ivar could send someone to drop by the Schwain residence to check up on Mrs. Schwain.

Rama read the course phone number from the hub of the rotary dial. "I'm at Mesquite Creek Golf Club in Texas. He can leave a message for me at the pro shop when he has some news."

"Trouble?" asked Melyssa.

"Just worried about my mom. She's been sick."

His eyes drifted to the grill room where morning golfers at tables along the sunny windows worked their way through breakfast. He recalled sitting there once, watching his father trace dollar signs on a frosty mug.

"If I get a call back…"

"Yeah, I'll find you," Melyssa assured him. Then she remembered the note Lee had left at the counter. "Oh, here…from Lee," she said, happily changing the subject.

Rama:
Glad you made it. If you are still looking for a good match for Mr. Byrne meet me on the range after my clinic. Bring your clubs! Lee

Rama was cheered to see Lee had followed through on his promise to find some competition for Wedgy. The thought of Wedgy's impending Waterloo was heartening.

Rama raised his face from Lee's note to meet Melyssa's inquiring brown eyes. He was startled at their depth and intrigued at their promise. Even as a young girl she had stirred his nascent desires; somehow eight years had not diluted the chemistry.

"When is Lee's clinic?" he asked.

"One to three this afternoon."

Rama hesitated. "When do you get off?"

"Right around sunset usually…just after the last guys get in a drink or two." She looked at Rama with a sly smile. "Why? Don't tell me you want to hit balls in the dark?"

Her smile turned into a playful laugh. "I've heard about your Night Lessons."

Rama imagined innuendo hidden in her laughter. "Lessons…yeah, that might be fun."

Melyssa's eyes sparkled as she leaned across the counter and lowered her voice conspiratorially. "I'll borrow a few beers. We can *practice* up on the sixteenth tee. You help me run the drunks off this evening. That'll get us out of here a little earlier."

Rama attempted to restrain his eyes from drifting into the hint of cleavage her posture offered. He left Melyssa to her duties while a warm glow kindled in his chest. Here it was again: the first blush of love, unfettered by doubts, or fears, or personal politics—the wondrous sensation so casually waved off as infatuation by a world of jealous cynics who should be so lucky as to have such a reckless, divine emotion pulling their hearts into foolish and joyful places.

———•———

Rama had time on his hands that morning. He clambered up the rocky slope above the clubhouse to take in the view. The panorama was wide and serene. The first fairway gleamed brightly in the September morning sun. Beyond, number two stretched far into the distance.

The second fairway had once been Mesquite's airstrip, but even though flat and featureless, it still gave golfers fits by virtue of its interminable length. The grill room had hosted many debates about the hole's par rating: par five vs. par six. It was a five, but when the wind blew into the faces of golfers confronting the second's daunting distance, there were few who could ever reach the 620-yard hole in three blasts.

From his perch on the rocks, Rama could hear voices rise now and then from the course on a steady breeze that combed the rough's shaggy grasses toward the northwest and set the putting green's old willows swaying like hula skirts. Below, he could see Wedgy's trailer parked beside the maintenance sheds.

He enjoyed the solitude for several minutes until Wedgy appeared at the trailer's door like a large predator emerging from hibernation. The decidedly ungypsy-like fellow sucked down the morning's first cigarette in six mighty breaths. He spat impressively, then grumbled off a few morning epithets concerning his caddie's absence and disappeared back into the trailer.

A few moments later Wedgy reappeared, dressed in his snappiest golfing regalia. The old hustler grumbled about losing his caddie as he loaded his bag on a pull cart and headed for the first tee. Rama stealthily descended from the hill and raided the trailer for his clubs.

Carla was confident that the opportunity for a golf clinic with Lee, a contender for the US Open, would guarantee her some extra business today and would drum up even more interest in tomorrow's match. Lee had hastily pulled Wedgy's exotic moniker "The Gypsy Hustler" from thin air when asked about the proposed competitor's background. Carla had always admired Lee for his game, his humor, and his honesty. She trusted his judgment as well so the Gypsy was in, but she was still unsure who he would be facing.

Wedgy was unaware that any advance public relations had been done on his behalf, and he nearly laughed in Carla's face when she innocently addressed him by his alleged title. But he instinctively recognized an opportunity for self-promotion and screwed his face from the edge of hilarity back to the aloof scowl of his new persona.

"I've been called that, yes," he sighed with a trace of Bela Lugosi standing in for a gypsy accent. "At your service, dahlink."

—•—

Rama saw Wedgy and Carla speaking up on the porch. He remembered that she always took a piece of the action from any bets she booked. He imagined they were discussing terms or that Wedgy was charming the would-be Augusta debutante with worldly tales spun off his slightly threadbare cuffs. If Wedgy knew of Carla's Augusta National connection, his fiction would likely have adapted to include a privileged romp around the exclusive track with Mr. Bobby Jones himself, or some such nonsense. Rama chuckled, wondering how long Wedgy could sustain the Eastern European accent. To Rama, the Gypsy sounded for all the world like Dracula.

Rama planned to stay out of Wedgy's sight until after his secret meeting with Lee up on the driving range. When Lee's clinic and the line of autograph seekers wound down, Rama headed toward the range.

The whine of automobiles climbing the drive up through the arroyo tapered off as the day's business concluded. As the Gypsy's scheming ex-caddie ascended the path to the empty range, he heard the familiar voice of Lee and another co-conspirator.

To Rama's astonishment, Lee was accompanied by Boney Carlisle. Eight years of brinkmanship on the turf and in Texas roadhouses had not diminished the man's robust stature. He still sported an expansive laugh, a quick smile, and a penchant for cheap cigars. Boney had long been Lee's foil on the links, but any animosity he harbored from years of regular beatings at Lee's skilled hands had long since given way to respect for Lee's immense talent and good humor. In fact, Boney's game had grown stronger under Lee's tutelage. Boney was a golfer to be respected, even if he looked anything but respectable.

Rama grimaced. This was Lee's vaunted competitor? But Rama remembered his specifications for the Wedgy-beater: The fellow had to have game, but he had to look hopeless. Rama's face lit up in a smile. There was no doubt about the look.

"Rama, you remember this hombre, do you not?"

Rama nodded. "How could anyone forget you, Mr. Carlisle?"

Boney let out a whoop. "You even remember my name! So our ace in the hole against the big bad Gypsy is none other than Rama, the master of the sixteenth green, eh?"

"That was eight years ago. Don't you guys ever forget a putt around here?" Rama said as Boney's calloused hand met his. Rama returned the handshake with the same vigor with which it was offered. Boney had hardened up considerably, he thought.

"Glad to see you two remember each other," said Lee.

Rama thought he saw the obvious: The match Lee was cooking up with Wedgy was against Boney. Rama wondered if that was the best Mesquite Creek had to offer these days. He also wondered if Lee understood how badly he wanted to see Wedgy bested, or how tough a competitor Wedgy was when money was on the line. In the last two days, the check Ivar had given Rama to cover a match had practically burned through the tired leather of his billfold in anticipation of the perfect match.

Lee felt Rama's doubts. "Don't look so worried. Boney has taken me to the wire a number of times. No, he's not exactly Gorgeous George, but if you're hustling, you sure as shit don't want to look better than you play." Lee chuckled and slapped his old friend on the belly. "No offense, Bones, but there's gold in them thar hills."

Boney blushed at the reference to his geography.

Lee continued with conspiratorial glee. "No, we're gonna give your Gypsy fellow a game he'll never forget. But all bets are off if we can't get him to go up against Boney."

Rama could guess the rest. "You need me to talk Boney's game down and Wedgy's confidence up, right?" He considered the task uncomfortably.

"Si, at least enough to keep him interested until somebody waves an irresistibly large bet under his nose," replied Lee. "With your money of course. But we don't want to scare him off. We'll nudge the bet up as high as possible. You've been there, Rama. How far do you think he'll go?"

Rama thought about the money in his billfold and about his father's losing bet. "I've seen him go six thousand on one bet," he announced.

Boney whistled.

Lee imagined the match could get interesting, especially if any of the magic that seemed to follow Rama around rubbed off on Boney as it had on him years ago. Maybe he'd even put a little of his own money on this one.

Lee turned to Rama. "Okay, let's get to work. Name a club, any club," he said, taking Rama by surprise.

Rama quickly recovered. "4-iron."

Lee pulled the prescribed club from the set Rama had rescued from the bucket at Sunset Hills. He looked it over with dismay and gripped the tired handle. "Ouch," he muttered, as he handed the club to Boney. Lee picked a ball from the wire basket and dropped it at Boney's feet. "Show your stuff, amigo," said Lee. "Gotta see what we're working with."

Boney tugged at his cigar, then laid it carefully on the turf. He settled over the ball, interrupting his usual routine with an acerbic comment regarding the club's condition.

"They're all I've got," Rama apologized.

Boney drew the club back in a wider, smoother arc than Rama had remembered. The forged steel head made better contact than Boney or Lee ever expected. "Swweeet!" Boney exclaimed.

"Yeah, I'd take about twenty yards off that shot without our little *brujo* here," said Lee. "Okay, Schwain, pull another club. Gotta make sure this Rama-effect ain't no fluke—not with cash on the barrelhead."

Rama pulled the pitching wedge, but before he handed it to Boney he suggested a target: "That big red boulder on the left side. About 135 yards, I'd guess." They traded clubs.

The big man seemed confident in the wedge and swung it freely a few times, grunting his approval, then sent the ball as high as it traveled far. The ball caromed off the top of the boulder and nearly rolled back to the tee.

"Jesus, that could've been an ace!" exclaimed Boney. "Lee, I thought you've been bullshitting about Rama's magic all these years." Boney looked at his mentor in happy disbelief.

Lee smiled at Rama. "Boney's not bad, huh? I told you: He's taken me to the wire a few times. So…would you put your money on him against the Gypsy?"

"Well, it depends who's on his bag," Rama replied smugly.

"Okay, Bones, bring it tomorrow…don't forget your clubs. But while you're here go talk some trash to our Gypsy friend," Lee laughed, enjoying the game-within-a-game more than Rama knew.

Lee patted Rama on the shoulder. "Now, it's put up or shut up. We can't go any further on good intentions. You said you had some backing…"

The two golfers looked expectantly at Rama. He had to show his cards before they got in any deeper. They watched as Rama pulled the Guidance Industries check from his billfold. "Six thousand dollars," said Rama.

Boney whistled again.

"Ivar says any bank in Texas will cash it, no questions asked," explained Rama. "Ivar doesn't lie."

Lee took the check and inspected it. He had no reason to doubt Rama. "Boney, can you get this cashed today? Otherwise this pot is gonna shrink considerably tomorrow."

"Yeah, my bank still trusts me," shrugged Boney. "Just don't write it out to Boney…it's Thomas Carlisle."

Rama hesitated. What would Ivar think? Could Boney pull it off? Would he even return with the money? Rama knew that Ivar would defer to his judgment; God knows Ivar wanted a piece of Wedgy as much as anybody.

"Shit, amigo, don't worry about Señor Carlisle," said Lee, sensing Rama's reticence. "He is even more honest than he is ugly."

Rama chuckled and made out the check.

Boney retrieved his smoldering cigar and drew it back to life, then plucked the check from Rama's fingers. "Don't you worry; this little nest egg is gonna force the old Gypsy to put *his* money where his mouth is."

Boney turned to descend to the clubhouse. "I'll see you gentlemen tomorrow. Got business down in the bar. Rama, you take care of that mojo. And Lee…just stay away from the pozole."

As Boney hurried off to the grill room lounge to intercept the Gypsy, Lee proposed that he and Rama work on a few swings. "Heck yes," Rama replied, oblivious to the plan developing around him. How often did a fellow get a free lesson from a US Open contender?

———•———

Ivar's Renault backfired as it decelerated down Bluff Meade's magnolia drive. Several golfers out for their Friday round looked up in irritation as Ivar swung left onto Crutchfield, destined for the Schwain residence. His secretary had caught him at the club and relayed Rama's message. When he pulled into the Schwain's empty drive and noticed the front door ajar, the hackles on Ivar's neck rose like quills. In a moment he was kneeling over Doris, who lay entangled with the umbrella stand.

She was lost in a state of consciousness somewhere between the hardwood floor and a windblown ride in her fiancé's new convertible. Ivar checked her breathing—it was fine—but her breath carried fragments of loving words for a handsome young man from the wheat fields of Washington.

Ivar carefully removed one of the umbrellas from under her leg and considered his next move. Doris woke slightly and smiled as her eyes comprehended a man's face above hers.

"Hank. Hank…at the petroglyphs. It wasn't your fault."

"Of course not. Of course not," Ivar replied softly. "We're going to get you some help directly. Now just lie still." In a moment he was on the phone with Doctor Myer.

The doctor told Ivar he would arrange her admittance to the hospital immediately. Soon thereafter they would have to transport her to his clinic in Atlanta and that he should contact Doris's husband to make arrangements.

"Is Mrs. Schwain ambulatory, or should I send an ambulance?" asked the doctor.

Before Ivar could respond, he was startled by a sound in the doorway. He twisted into the coils of the phone cord as he whirled around to find Doris brandishing an umbrella in a gallant but feeble effort to defend herself from the second intruder of the day.

"You! Out!" she cried. "I'll call...my husband." She raised the weapon in support of another hopeless bluff.

"Doris...Mrs. Schwain, hold on, I'm here to help," Ivar blurted. "I've got Doctor Myer on the line." He raised the receiver as if offering visual proof.

"What...who are you?" Doris was shaken but standing and thoroughly confused. "How do you know Doctor Myer," she asked. "Or me?"

An electronic cricket chirped in the receiver. "Ivar, what's going on?"

Ivar ignored the voice. "Your son, Rama...he's my caddie," Ivar explained. "He asked me to check on you. He is a very worried young man."

Doris felt weak at the mention of her son. "Rama? How is he?"

Ivar relaxed and lowered the phone. "He is fine, I'm sure. I haven't spoken with him directly, just got his message." Ivar returned the phone to his ear.

"Well, doctor, she's on her feet. She's making sense now. Maybe I can get her to your clinic sooner not later."

"How soon?"

Ivar considered the frail and disoriented woman standing in her kitchen. He remembered Rama singing the praises of his mother's gardening and of her fine singing voice. Rama had even spoken of her selfless support of his father's dreams. Here was a woman, Ivar realized, whose dividend for her loving investments was long overdue.

"How about this afternoon?" Doris Schwain's welfare was not going to linger on the shelf any longer. "Can you begin her treatment tomorrow? I'll see what I can do about contacting her husband."

Doctor Myer was already in Ivar's debt for the flight to Vanderbilt. He would rise as far as possible to meet Ivar's request, but accommodating him tomorrow was a stretch. He began to point out the travel issues when he realized Ivar Guidance would jump into his plane at the drop of a hat.

"Alright, Ivar; I'll arrange admittance for this afternoon, but we'll have to wait and see about the schedule...if surgery is necessary. Contact me when you have arrived in Atlanta."

Ivar hung up the phone and turned his full attention to a very bemused woman. "Mrs. Schwain, I'm Ivar Guidance. Can I get you a cup of tea?"

Doris nodded. And in a moment he had settled down at the kitchen table beside her.

Chapter 52

"Horses for courses, my Limey friends used to say," grumbled the Gypsy Hustler to anyone who might be listening at the grill room bar. He had just walked in after judiciously crafting a sloppy eighty-one for his first and only practice round on Mesquite Creek.

"Damn track just doesn't suit my game," he added, remembering to pepper his speech with a hint of his best Transylvanian accent.

Wedgy's round had been a model of skillful sandbaggery: convincing hooks here, a flubbed sand save there, weak lag putts, and an Oscar-worthy pair of yipped six-footers—all accompanied by a stream of virulent, self-critical epithets. The performance had been conducted before the gullible eyes of a mouthy threesome to whom he had carefully attached himself in hopes that they, in their loquaciousness, were likely to be the best publicists for what he hoped they perceived as the Gypsy Hustler's over-rated game.

He had tromped from the green in studied disgust and asked if any of the hapless three were drinking men. "Let's settle up these skins over something cold," he suggested. The threesome was in full agreement. Wedgy's pre-game machinations were all going nicely; now, if someone would just get "Flowers On the Wall" off the bloody jukebox...

In the glow of the illuminated liquor bottles that had graced the shelves above the bar since the locust plague of '59, Wedgy collected several fifty-cent skins from each of his opponents. He had figured by engineering a poor enough round he could spread the fiction of his vulnerability and fatten to-morrow's pot against him. But Wedgy was crafty enough to maintain a slight edge over his practice-round competitors. Losing money—even four-bit skins—never came easy, even if the loss was a small investment in creating a lucrative illusion. He hoped the chatter with his companions would chum the waters of Mesquite Creek's patrons and bring greedy gamblers to the surface for the real game where they could put some serious money on the barrelhead.

To Wedgy's delight, the jukebox soon gave up on the Statler Brothers. Boney Carlisle stepped back from the Wurlitzer after punching up a trio of Otis Redding, Gene Pitney, and Roy Orbison tunes. He seemed satisfied with his eclectic choices as Otis's Muscle Shoals rhythm section cranked out a slow burning groove. Nearby, the Gypsy and company slid coins across the table to settle up their accounts. With a new musical atmosphere and a couple of shots of Old Crow to fortify him, Boney was primed to get to work.

Returning from the jukebox, Boney casually stopped beside the four-some's table and scoffed at the meager coinage scattered before the Gypsy.

"Well, you fellas got off *easy*," Boney began sarcastically. "Takin' on the one and only Gypsy Hustler...my God, what were you thinking? What'd you lose? Four...maybe five bucks? Oh, the pain of it."

The three pigeons each felt they had done pretty well to have stayed within three or four strokes of such a player. They snarled at Boney with resentment for his intrusion, but Boney wasn't concerned with their games or their admiration. He was courting the Gypsy. The ponderous golfer picked up the four-some's scorecard and studied the tally with dramatic interest.

"Cleaned you boys out...with an *eighty-one*? Holy hell!" Boney groaned in mock regret for the health of his friends' egos, but he restrained himself. He was playing the same game as his would-be opponent, and he feared over-acting. He flicked the scorecard back to the table and turned to the Gypsy.

"It's like St. Peter said after Jesus knocked in that ace with the help of a squirrel and a dust devil: 'Did you come all this way to play golf or are you just going to fuck around?'"

Boney extended a hand and introduced himself. "T. Carlisle...people who *think* they are my friends call me Boney. Welcome to Mesquite Creek, Gyp. If you're looking for higher stakes..." Boney drummed a forefinger on the pica-yune stack of quarters. "It can be arranged."

Wedgy sized up the huge, foolish man looming over the table. You're damn right I am, he thought. It was just like Rama had promised: Fools with lots of money. Hell, maybe there was a God.

Wedgy returned the big man's handshake. He felt the calluses of a player and reminded himself to be careful.

"Wallace Byrne," he offered. "I don't know where this Gypsy shit came from. I just enjoy a good little go-around like everybody else." He smiled deceptively.

Boney grunted with studied disinterest and found a seat alone at the bar.

Wedgy scooped up his quarters and picked up the tab for his golfing buddies. "It's been mighty fun, fellas. Maybe we all can break eighty together one day." Wedgy laughed at that improbability as he rose from the table with a chorus of protesting joints. His friends seemed somewhat less than amused that their illustrious new friend was abandoning them in favor of courting Boney.

The closing notes from Booker T's Hammond B-3 receded like a gentle tide as the jukebox searched for "Twenty-Four Hours from Tulsa." Wedgy flashed a hand signal to the bartender to reprise Boney's drink and to bring him the same. If he had known Boney's cocktail included a shot of Luva'Lime Soda, he would have demurred.

Wedgy slipped onto the stool beside Boney as Gene Pitney's ode to a prostitute rang feverishly through the room.

"To tell you the truth," Wedgy confided when the drinks arrived, "I just might be talked into another round tomorrow…if I ever find my god-damned caddie."

Like one luckless gambler did years before, his fingers traced a dollar sign on the sweaty flanks of his whiskey sour. He sipped and wondered how this Carlisle fellow could purposely ruin good liquor with this foul green soda. Shuddering at the flavor, he asked his drinking partner if any matches ever got interesting out in these parts.

Boney rested the cool rim of his glass against his upper lip, artfully timing his response to the Gypsy's obvious opening. The liquor and the lime filled his nostrils as he took stock: that this Gypsy so easily divulged his name and seemed so easily drawn into a game worried him. He reminded himself to be careful as he questioned the risky plan Lee was orchestrating; they might be dealing with a master. But Boney was confident that Lee was as good a judge of character as he was a tournament golfer, and after a couple more sips he resolved to stay with Lee's script.

"Would five hundred dollars be interesting enough?" asked Boney. "There's some betting fools in the oil trade around here that might want in on the action, too…if it gets fat enough."

Wedgy was disappointed in Boney's number but guessed he could push it up 50-percent with a deft word or two. "Well, I'm partial to the Nassau: A bet for the winner of the front, the winner of the back, and the winner for the whole enchilada…spreads the wealth around. Let's say we make it a tidy 250-bucks. If you play well you can still get your five hundred with two-fifty to spare, and I'll have more incentive—like your guy said to Jesus—not to fuck around."

Boney helped himself to a cigarillo from a box on the bar. "Okay, Gyp. You got yourself a bet. Probably should have my head examined for taking on someone with your reputation without getting a few strokes up front. But it's all I can afford. The side bets might get spirited, though; there's always folks around here more than willing to bet on yours truly."

Boney scratched a match into flame for another smoke. Mission accomplished for now, he thought. The Gypsy Hustler was nailed down to a match. He would leave it up to Lee to elevate the stakes with some serious cajoling and some blatant cash-flashing tomorrow, assuming the Guidance Industries check in his pocket was really negotiable. Of course, Boney knew he still had to beat this fellow straight up, but he had a cocky—bordering on obnoxious—confidence, and he knew what the Gypsy didn't yet know: that Rama Schwain would not be caddying for his old boss but would be looping for Boney Carlisle. Such were the best-laid plans.

Boney blew a blast of blue smoke into the air. "Yeah, win or lose it should be fun." He gave his competitor a firm pat on the shoulder. "See you in the morning, eh? I've got to get my ass down to the bank. That money sure as shit doesn't grow on trees."

Wedgy tried to smile at Boney's departure, but the pat on his shoulder had spilled half his drink. Still, he was pleased; he had sealed the deal for what the he guessed would be a $750 cakewalk against the ungainly Mr. Carlisle. Wedgy treated himself to a fresh drink.

"Leave out that lime crap this time around," he instructed the bartender. Then he ordered an early supper, comforted in the certainty that he'd win enough to get the Lincoln repaired and back on the road and, if those betting fools he'd been promised materialized, perhaps much more. Wedgy hungrily consumed his meal, unaware that he had also swallowed the bait.

Even as Wedgy was working his way through his barbecue platter, Boney Carlisle was hustling to gather his clubs and hit the road. He would have to hurry to make it to the bank in time to negotiate Guidance Industry's check. He nearly ran as he left the locker room, past the stuffed boar, and out the door, trailing smoke from his cigarillo like a locomotive.

Boney's train came to an abrupt halt as an old man in a derelict golf cart intercepted him in the parking lot. He held his breath as he pondered the craggy face of the old man smiling at him from beneath a flat, black brim. It was Carlos, the "ghost" of Mesquite Creek.

"Sir, you shall not need of thee bank this day." Gold winked from the ancient man's mouth.

Boney held his cigar and his thoughts in suspense as he wondered how the strange fellow knew his intentions.

"Sir, please…sit." A thin, wrinkled hand patted the seat beside him. "You ride with Carlos Taddio."

Boney's eyes followed the old hand. Two tall stacks of hundred-dollar bills secured with leather bootlaces lay on the vinyl seat. Like the Gypsy back in the bar, Boney was easily hooked. Without protest he took a seat beside Carlos.

The cart coughed back to life, and the unlikely twosome disappeared to a far corner of the back nine to a quiet place where Carlos's frail voice could hold his passenger's ear. Maybe the bank would have to wait, thought Boney.

—•—

A three-quarter moon was already torching the dusky eastern sky as Wedgy stepped from the grill room onto the porch. Shadows from the crags above the clubhouse crawled down the rocky slope like molasses, casting the path back to his trailer in gloom. He finished his after-dinner cigarette as he made his way home. Upon arriving at the trailer, he stumbled into a set of cast-off golf clubs that, in his haste, Rama had left propped against the front stoop.

"Stupid fuck is trying to break my neck." Wedgy tossed the bag aside. "Dodges me all day…for what?" The empty evening would not answer or reveal that Rama had spent the better part of the afternoon absorbing the secrets of Lee's skill and coupling it to the same magic that had elevated so many others' games. Nor would it reveal that Rama had no intention of returning tonight.

Wedgy reluctantly brought the clubs inside. No point in breaking Rama's neck, too. "Not that he doesn't deserve it."

Instinctively, he inventoried the clubs, a habit of anyone who had ever run afoul of the fourteen-club rule. Thirteen, he counted. Rama's ancient brassie was missing. Wedgy pulled one of the second-hand irons from the bag and held it in the glow of the porch light.

"I'll be god damned." He was surprised to see that the irons had recently been polished to a soft sheen along the top line and across the center of the face—"rubbed up" as the old timers called it—an unusual technique of Scottish caddies that was abandoned long ago as more sophisticated metals came into use. But there were those who insisted a good rubbing-up added a special magic to the game. Wedgy shivered. Somehow Rama's old fish sticks looked formidable.

—•—

"Sometimes it gets spooky out here," confessed Melyssa.

She took Rama's arm and leaned into him as much in response to the descending temperature as to her ascending affection. Together they walked beyond the clubhouse's farthest light and entered the darkened course. Rama raised the old brassie as if preparing to joust with any apparition that might loom up from the shadowy fairways.

Melyssa had pulled a woolen sweater over her blouse and had taken a bottle of Drambuie from the grill room bar to ward off the night's chill. She carried a blanket and a canvas bag containing a couple of dozen old range balls. The bag bumped happily along one hip as she pressed the other against her companion.

Rama pressed back gratefully. He had only flirted with the occasional cart girl or waitress on the road with Wedgy. The girl on the course at Cloudsborough had stirred him enough to fire his imagination for several nights, but she had faded. Back home in Memphis, Rama circled a loveless eddy, trapped between the current of friends flowing off to pursue their dreams and the still waters of a life bound closely to his ailing mother. But tonight, with the scent of oleander welling up from the barranca and the touch of Melyssa's thick dark hair spilling onto his shoulder, love was a vibrant possibility. The girl's deep feminine spirit cast away any doubts he harbored. Her spell demanded his full attention, and he effortlessly complied.

Walking together down the middle of dark fairways, they glowed like novae in a twinkling universe. The force animating their attraction ran deep. Even as children brushing past each other eight years ago en route to separate, distant futures, they had felt the special gravity between them. Somehow, it brought them to this moment. A pretty young woman like Melyssa could most likely have been anywhere else: bound to the fortunes of a hard-working local man or stolen away by a visiting golfer's promising vision.

So, too, could Rama have taken any path other than the twisted one that had led him back to Mesquite Creek. But here he was, intoxicated by her un-likely, laughing presence. And she was equally delighted that he had emerged from a distant memory. Together they plunged into the dark without caution, yielding happily to the attraction tugging at them now as surely as it once had in their childhood.

Attraction had not always come so easily for Rama. He recalled awkward, juvenile attempts to connect with girls he had adored from the safe, agonizing distance of his imagination. He had not been blessed with the confidence to approach the shining creatures with anything resembling élan or spontaneity, but had crafted scenarios for "accidental" encounters or perfectly scripted dates in which his young Romeo would spin off reels of cool, casual conversation. Too often, paralyzed by shyness and strangled by nervous dialogue that refused to conform to his vision, Rama had returned home from his encounters crushed by self-consciousness and convinced of his eternal exclusion from love's joyous club.

But it was not so in Melyssa's presence. Her glowing spirit easily found an opening through his bashful shell. Even as they walked together, his mind drifted back to the boy shuffling home after one particularly humbling after-school rendezvous. He had avoided the questioning eyes of his father out of reluctance to admit his defeat or to fabricate a success. Wouldn't Hank be happy now to know that a young woman as charming as Melyssa had found his son to be worthy of her affection?

The squeal of the cork from the Drambuie bottle startled Rama from his thoughts and chased a covey of quail to a roost deeper in the sheltering brush. Rama and Melyssa had reached the arroyo lying between the fifteenth and sixteenth holes.

"Oh crap, I've never gone down through there after dark," Melyssa whis-pered into Rama's ear. Her lips brushed his skin like a warm kiss. The two stood together where the path from the fifteenth green plunged into the dark. Instinct pricked at animal regions of their brains and raised objections to descending from safe, high ground into the near-blindness of a gloomy scrub thicket.

"Spooooky," Rama crooned.

Melyssa laughed nervously and offered the bottle for a sip of courage. "After you, Tarzan."

Rama took a slug from the bottle and returned it to her keeping. Before she tossed her head back to drink, Rama caught the gleam of excitement in her eyes. The warmth of the sweet liquor prompted her to tighten her grip on his arm and to nudge him into the first step downward.

"I rode through here once…on Carlos's pony," Rama said with surprising volume. His fearless voice almost startled him, just as he subconsciously hoped it might frighten away any dangers lying ahead.

The rocky butte that cradled the soft ground of the sixteenth tee loomed against the starry sky as they picked their way carefully down the narrow path. Dark forms of mysterious bush and sinister cactus lurked in the shadows, provoking their imaginations.

"You rode with Carlos?" Melyssa asked in disbelief.

Rama slowed to explain. "Yeah, it was the night my dad and I stayed for Boney and Lee's match. Eight years ago, the night after all the locusts…do you remember? Carlos took me around the course. I rode Niña right through here. He even showed me how to putt the green at number sixteen when they've set the pin at the bottom."

Melyssa gasped. "I *do* remember. That's the putt that won the match after Lee had been stung by the scorpion. Wow, don't tell anyone else that you'd already seen that line. There's a few that are still pissed off that Carla let you take that putt." She nudged him onward.

Melyssa regarded the drop into the arroyo as an adventure and, like clutching a boyfriend at a horror movie, was happy to share it with the young man who moved her so easily with the gentle force of his magical appeal. She feared she had become hardened by years of waving away the obvious empty advances of Mesquite's golfing gentry.

If crossing the spooky arroyo prompted Melyssa to tighten her grip and to press closer, then Rama was all for some good healthy fear. But he recalled a puma crouched on rocks by the sixteenth green on that strange night, and an icy flash of alarm stabbed at him. That encounter, although years ago, still raised hackles on his neck, betraying his brave new persona.

"Ever heard of mountain lions out this way?" Rama asked, in full voice.

"I think the ranchers killed them all off, way back," Melyssa replied. "They even had pumas up the canyons back then. At least that's what Carlos told me." With that the girl froze, pulled hard on Rama's arm, and hissed into his ear.

"Wait. What's that? On the trail…you see it?"

Rama shuddered. He tightened his grip on the golf club and peered into the darkness. He hoped Melyssa didn't hear his heart pounding so fearfully.

"Stay back, 'Lyssa," Rama said firmly as he pushed her back in an instinctive act of defense. He looked down the trail but his vision came up empty, even though he expected to see the puma's shadowy form.

"See what?" he asked.

Melyssa tipped her forehead against Rama's temple and whispered delicately in Drambuie-scented breath that felt like down against his neck.

"The *Jabberwocky*," she giggled.

Rama didn't know his English literature, but he knew he had been fooled.

"Shit, Melyssa," he groaned in relief. "Not fair!"

Melyssa laughed and he exhaled the breath he had held back in defense. Maybe he would have been less gullible had he not remembered the puma he had once seen so near this place. Perhaps he would tell her that story and more, but some other time; he didn't want to appear too fantastic. She was already having trouble believing he had ridden with Carlos. Rama forgot the cat and stepped bravely down the trail toward the butte rising against the starry sky.

———•———

Deep in the shadows not more than a dozen paces away, the graceful progeny of Rama's puma moved silently through the brush. Her sleek coat avoided the faintest contact with brittle foliage that might reveal her presence. She moved like liquid into the deeper reaches of the arroyo and into obscurity. Her bloodline carried knowledge: the skill to deceive hounds, a wariness of traps, repulsion at the poisoned carcass, and avoidance of the ranchers' lead slugs. But like her grandfather, she had been drawn against her instincts to the brink of detection to glimpse the face of the magic one.

The cat's curiosity had brought her within several silent paces of ruining the innocent punch line of Melyssa's little joke.

———•———

Two lingering blasts of an eastbound freight's forlorn whistle hung in the air like frosty breath as Rama and Melyssa emerged from the arroyo to climb the stone path to the sixteenth tee. The spirits of Glendora and Dickey Stone welcomed Rama's return to their beloved place as Melyssa opened her bag and dumped a dozen golf balls to the grass. The orbs looked ghostly in the light of a three-quarter moon.

"Ladies first," Melyssa announced as she took up the old Night Lessons club. "Tell me what you think."

She took a confident, graceful stance and swung the club a few times to chase the hesitance from her limbs and was soon rewarded with the satisfying whoosh of velocity. Rama could see she was not a newcomer to the game's primary skill.

After several swings she turned to Rama. "This club..." she began, searching for words to describe its indescribable liveliness. She squinted into the dark reaches of the fairway below as if the appropriate language resided there.

"This club...it's unreal. Where did you get it?"

Rama explained its origin and said the club was probably just happy to be home, or at least in her sweet hands.

Melyssa teed a ball and struck it with a swing that was a seamless melding of form, function, and femininity.

He was stricken as effectively as was the golf ball. Mesmerized, he watched her shot swallowed by the darkness as a poem's final phrase is absorbed into silence. The sharp report from the persimmon club head trailed off in a faint echo against the walls of the arroyo. "You never said you could play," Rama gasped.

She laughed. "It just rubs off on you working around this place."

Before Melyssa had demonstrated her skills, Rama had imagined showing her a few tips. But the shopworn old trick of using a hands-on teaching technique as an excuse to cozy up to an aspiring female golfer had been yanked from his deck. He watched as she launched a half-dozen more missiles against the stars. When she was satisfied, she extended the club to Rama.

"Here, fire away, Tarzan."

Fire away he did. Even though self-conscious in the presence of one obviously schooled in golf's elusive arts, he swung well. The priceless lesson with Lee that afternoon had ironed out a wrinkled quilt and had happily spared him the embarrassment of watching hopeless clunkers careen from the tee while under the scrutiny of a beautiful girl.

She was not without criticism: "You could drive as well as you putt..." she said, referring to the game-saving putt she had once witnessed from her refreshment cart, "if you would turn your hips back earlier."

Rama's swing—a patchwork of Ivar, Jimmy-Jim, Wedgy, and now Lee's instructions plus a helping of Shell's *Wide World of Golf* telecasts—had its share of flaws, but he never guessed that one of its remedies would be a woman's touch.

It was Melyssa's bold tomboy attitude coupled with an alluring face and considerable charms that first captured Rama's attention. Now her surprising swing joined the list of attributes. Melyssa stood before him and demonstrated the turn she was advocating. The twist of her sweater around a limber waist suggested an enticing, flexible body beneath the fabric. Rama overlooked the concept and simply savored the motion. The magic one was only human.

Melyssa tapped a ball into place and asked him to take a stance. Then, in a reversal of the teaching trick *he* had imagined, she stood behind him and placed her hands on *his* hips. He felt her belly against his lower back as he bent slightly over the ball. He might have been bashful about this position if he hadn't felt such a rush of excitement.

"Now turn, Tarzan."

Rama rotated to the top of his swing. She turned with him like a warm shadow. Her hands monitored his position as he coiled to the deepest point in his swing. Poised at the top he felt Melyssa's breasts pressed beneath his shoulder blades.

"That's nice," she said quietly. Rama couldn't have agreed more.

"Now start your turn from down here before you move your arms," Melyssa said. Her hands tightened on his hips and he felt her palms urging him to rotate around his lower spine. She thrust her right hip to his rump to emphasize the action.

The voice of his teacher was warm and moist against Rama's neck. "Work on this...it'll help," she giggled and relaxed her grip as she backed away slightly.

Rama dutifully tested the lesson, swinging across the surface of the turf. The motion of his hips and the delayed arm action gave him the sensation that his swing felt at least as good as the great golfers' swings looked. When he put Melyssa's advice into play behind a ball, the soft, lively feel of his club's contact told him there was more than mere sensation in her lessons.

Rama turned around to face the smile awaiting him in the moonlight. He lay down the club and picked up the Drambuie. They shared a couple of sips and surrendered to the warm waves flowing through their limbs as alcohol and passion mingled. Still holding the bottle, Rama touched Melyssa's hair. His palm dropped gently upon her shoulder and his fingers curled to the curve of her neck. Her skin was surprisingly warm under his touch.

She did not resist as he drew her face slowly to his in an exalted first kiss that moved quickly from tentative to torrid. After a minute of her impossibly tender lips and the consuming excitement of their tongues, Rama pulled away a few inches to take a breath and to see if Melyssa's eyes reflected his joy in the incredible moment.

They did. The tiny world between their faces was charged with anticipation and was filled with the air of kisses scented by an essence from the Isle of Skye.

—•—

The retreating puma stepped from the barranca onto a secure stony shelf where she froze, listening to the night. Her rigid ears turned toward new sounds. She tasted new scents. She raised her muzzle toward the brightest light in the sky and softly growled in longing for her next mate, still a quarter moon away, prowling in male solitude somewhere in the distant chaparral.

—•—

"You are beautiful," Rama whispered. He had never spoken such words. There seemed little else he could say.

"You, too," Melyssa replied breathlessly.

The girl reached for the blanket and quickly spread it on the teeing ground's deepest grass. They rejoined their kiss, shielded from the chill in the warmth of the thick blanket. Rama's hands moved inevitably across Melyssa's sweater to the yielding fullness of her breasts. Their hearts pounded together as she explored the growing stiffness beneath his jeans and he, the exquisite rigidity of her nipples. Their clothes would soon have to go, and their golf lesson would yield to a more insistent Night Lesson.

Melyssa and Rama enjoyed each other lavishly—youthfully. After the fever had subsided, the evening's chill brought them grudgingly to their feet and launched them, still clinging together, on a slow walk back through the night toward the glimmer of the clubhouse lights.

—•—

Behind them, and beyond perception, the downward sweep of the sixteenth fairway brightened miraculously in the amber light of a midsummer's evening. Long, hazy shadows of cottonwood streamed across the grassy slope beneath the butte as a young boy and his sister charged down from its tee. The girl's red hair trailed behind like a comet's tail as she raced, laughing, with her brother to locate the balls most recently offered to the empty fairway.

There would be a new buffalo nickel for each ball recovered. Their father had promised it!

As they ran, their crystal voices carried up the fairway and spilled down into the arroyo. In the still, cool air of a September night, such a sound could play tricks on a listener. On such a night, even the sound of children's ghosts might travel amazing distances, perhaps as far as heaven.

Rama stopped at the faint sound, like delicate glass chimes from a mile away. He strained to hear its tinkle against the quiet night. No, it wasn't chimes. This sounded like laughter.

A shudder jolted Rama involuntarily, and Melyssa looked at him quizzically.

"Another lion?" she asked softly.

Chapter 53

Wedgy awoke Saturday morning to a cacophony of birdsong and a nagging hangover. He cursed himself for the boozy headache but had no one to blame for the birds. Since first light, an unusual migration had been moving up Mesquite Creek's green bottomlands in pursuit of the first wave in an invasion of locusts, the most recent onslaught of the insects since 1959.

He grudgingly shuffled through the fog of last night's whiskey sours to kick-start his percolator into bubbling up a dose of Maxwell House. Only when the scent of cheap coffee touched his nostrils did he awaken sufficiently to notice the sofa where Rama slept was still empty. Not only had his caddie made himself unavailable for practice all day yesterday, he had also apparently stayed out all night. Rama's absence irritated Wedgy, but such irresponsibility wasn't without its benefits. The old hustler welcomed any reasonable excuse for docking Rama his share of their winnings, especially those they would plunder today from that odd excuse for a golfer, Boney Carlisle.

Yet he felt an unexpected shiver of vulnerability. Saving a few bucks on caddie fees was one thing, but facing today's match without Rama's undeniable gifts could be trouble. Wedgy quickly shook off the gnawing doubt. He lit a cigarette, poured a cup, and fell onto the sofa with an ashtray on his chest. With the birds gathering outside and the occasional rap of a locust against the trailer's tin walls, Wedgy considered his caddie's future. Ever since Sunset Hills, Rama hadn't been the same. Now, perhaps, he mightn't be worth the cost of room and board.

"When all's said and done, the kid's probably just as phony as his old man the war hero," Wedgy muttered over the bitter cup, discounting the unbroken string of victories he had won with Rama before tangling with that queer Grant fellow. Wedgy slurped at his coffee then flicked on the radio, hoping to find a decent weather report.

Rama woke to the locusts' rising chorus as dawn strained to resolve the patterns on the room's wallpaper. The dreamy reality of a timeless night secreted away with Melyssa in one of the guest rooms above the clubhouse obliterated all intruding worries. He lay blissfully unconcerned with issues such as Trent Institute, the draft, or his caddying obligations. If for only a moment, he had found contentment that could serve as a model for the rest of his life.

Rama began to voice these feelings to Melyssa when he realized he was alone. Her warmth still lingered on the sheets as he rose on one elbow to await her return. The bathroom was down the hall; in a moment she would slip back into bed and they would welcome the morning together. But the sheets cooled and Rama slept no more.

He felt a spasm of abandonment but comforted himself with the thought that Melyssa had work to do even before morning's first light. It was the nature of a golf business that catered to dew sweepers. She probably had an important schedule to keep, he guessed. Unfortunately, he was right.

Rama quickly showered and made himself as presentable as possible but feared his appearance in broad daylight might be less enchanting to Melyssa than it had beneath last night's moon. An inexplicable melancholy haunted him as he made his way downstairs into the pro shop to catch up with the magical girl.

An energetic young boy staffed the counter where Melyssa had worked yesterday. A contagious smile lit the boy's face.

"Playing a round this morning?"

Rama was staggered slightly at Melyssa's absence. "Maybe later…thanks. Haven't seen Melyssa, have you?"

The boy displayed several crooked teeth in a sincere grin. "Yeah, she's gone. Her uncle picked her up about an hour ago."

Rama felt his heart plunge. Mesquite Creek's clubhouse suddenly lost its charm, as if a shade had robbed all color from the light. For the first time in months, Rama felt too far from home. Before he could ask the circumstances of her departure, the boy blurted, "You her boyfriend?"

Rama wanted to say "No, I'm her *lover*," as if words could replace what had so suddenly slipped from his grasp. Instead, he was reticent to even claim that title. "Yes, we're friends."

"Are you Rom Swan?" the boy asked uncertainly.

"Rama Schwain? Yes."

The boy pulled a large envelope from beneath the counter. His eyes traced the letters written in a pretty feminine script. "Oh…RAMA, yeah that's right." A blush consumed the freckles from his cheerful face. "She said you were her boyfriend. This is for you…lucky."

Rama took the envelope, grateful to have some link to a romance so ephemeral as to already be a memory. The envelope bulged. If this was a Dear John letter, he feared it was a lengthy one.

Rama drifted off to a table to sip a cup of coffee and read whatever tragic words awaited him. His head spun as he slit the top of the envelope with a butter knife. The envelope contained a bundle of what looked like Polaroid photographs accompanied by a short letter written on Mesquite Creek stationery. A piece of heavy, rigid canvas had been slipped behind the photos, apparently to protect the envelope's contents. He paid the canvas no mind but quickly slid the letter out and unfolded it.

Rama had no idea how Melyssa had struggled through regret and sleeplessness to craft the letter he now held in his hands. She had grown up at Mesquite Creek and had come to know Carlos before he dissolved from flesh and blood into a ghost story. She had heard his strange prophesy that a "magic one" would come again with the locusts and bring rest to the unsettled souls hovering above Mesquite Creek. Now, as she tried to craft a good-bye note, the first insects were already landing on the clubhouse's veranda. Melyssa tried to make sense of what she had once thought were only the visions of a mystic old man. Carlos may have been a crazy, dreamy artist, yet now she believed his prediction. She tried to recall his stories but couldn't remember that he had ever mentioned that *she* would be stricken with affection for the "magic one."

For eight aimless years, Melyssa had spent the best of her considerable energy in the service of Carla's obscure golf course. She had waited out the rising and falling attentions of a dozen or more interested boys. For what? It wasn't fair that Rama had lingered in the past until they had only a single day together before she would leave for her future. And it wasn't fair that after all this time she was rewarded with only one wonderful night and a blank sheet of stationery.

Rama sadly considered the letter. Melyssa's handwriting reflected her spirit. Her hand was strong, the characters rendered in firm strokes on precise invisible baselines. Calligraphic flourishes sprouted like wildflowers: The *I*'s were dotted with tiny circles and the *T*'s crossed with hopeful ascending strokes. It began:

Dear, Dear Rama,
I hope you are not mad...

Rama had hoped to savor Melyssa's message like he had her warm kisses, but an angry voice stopped him cold.

"God damn my eyes, if it's not Rama Schwain. Takin' a little break from porkin' the cart girl, are we?"

Before bursting into the grill room for a decent breakfast, Wedgy had aborted an attempt at crafting pancakes in his trailer after discovering weevils in his Krusteaz. With bugs in his food and a storm of their ilk threatening to burst from the skies, the Gypsy Hustler was in no mood to empathize with his AWOL caddie's heartache.

Rama looked up from Melyssa's letter and glared at the intruder like a cat over its kill. Wedgy realized this was not the acquiescing young man with whom he was familiar. But the incorrigibly cranky fellow was not easily put off. With the golden eggs safely stashed in a strong-box beneath his trailer's sofa, Wedgy played rough with the goose.

"Don't look at me like that," Wedgy growled. "For Christ sakes, I forgave you for fucking me up at Sunset Hills, and now after you talk me into driving all the way out here, you disappear on me. I never took you for a quitter."

Wedgy pulled a chair back from the table where Rama sat. The legs screeched in alarm. "I pay you good money…for what? You don't have to scout the course or walk off the yardages, you don't have to read my greens, and you don't have to take the heat for pulling the wrong club." He dropped heavily into the chair. "You just have to *be* there with your…*voodoo*."

Wedgy could hardly believe his own words. Even now it seemed too strange to be real that he, a pragmatic businessman/golfer, had ever bought into the notion of some supernatural effect upon his game. "It's just good vibes, man," his son would probably have said, automatically accepting the unreal with the naive hippie faith in the fantastic that was so infuriating.

Wedgy imagined his son panhandling on Haight Street or grooving in the Redwoods at Big Sur, supported by a payoff from the Securities and Exchange Commission for his cooperation in the W. Byrne investigation. As Wedgy shivered at the image of his traitorous son, his hangover disappeared in a surge of anger. Suddenly he was especially hungry to humiliate somebody on the golf course, and if he could rob him, too, all the better.

Rama kept his cool for the battle ahead. He folded the letter and carefully returned it to its bulky envelope. He could feel Wedgy's heat from across the table and the hustler's curious eyes scanning the envelope like a beacon.

"Mr. Byrne, the last time we played you said you didn't need my help. You went back to replay Tyler on your own…remember?" Rama pulled the package closer, resolving not to engage Wedgy further if possible. All he wanted was to be by himself.

But Wedgy was in the mood for engagement. "Shit…so I get into a little scoring mishap with that damn fruitcake after you and him had your secret little round together. Sure I heated up, but believe me, you'll *know* when you've been fired."

Wedgy felt that he had said quite enough on the subject and it was back to business as usual. "Soon as I grab a bite you can stow that letter you're wilting over and meet me on number ten. That back nine's a killer; might need your help playing through there one time."

"Oh by the way," Wedgy added, "got a halfway-decent match at two o'clock with some character named Boney. He says the boys around here will likely bump the action up a bit. Know anything about that?"

Rama answered cautiously. He was never comfortable with blatant deception. "Yeah, I heard that Boney has a lot less game than gab…and a lot of rich friends. Guess that's what you were hoping for, isn't it?" Rama forced his eyes to meet Wedgy's. "You'll do fine against Boney…no matter who's on your bag."

Wedgy looked at him curiously.

"Because it won't be me," Rama declared.

Rama had tried to picture what Wedgy's reaction would be when his ex-caddie appeared on Boney's bag later that afternoon. Rama hoped that reaction would unsettle the Gypsy Hustler's concentration as Lee had planned.

Wedgy was startled at Rama's bold announcement but was not accustomed to accepting anything at face value. "Bullshit, you're not going anywhere, Schwain. It's a pity," he sneered, "that when your magic comes out a little flat for a couple of games you can't handle the consequences. Listen up, Schwain: Losing is part of the game…for caddies, too."

"But cheating isn't," Rama said with finality.

"Come on, Rama. You're sounding more like my damn son every minute," Wedgy laughed. "There's a fine line between dishonesty and gamesmanship. Christ knows I've been down that road before."

Wedgy wrinkled his brow and leaned forward in his chair. "You want to talk about honesty, Rama? I heard the weather report this morning: Sixty-five degrees and partly sunny in Albuquerque…not a sign of that early snow you mentioned. So why am I out here? To go head to head with some kind of ringer?"

Rama shivered, certain he had blown his cover and fearful Wedgy would back out of the match.

"Ringer? You said you were looking for a good match. You might be walking away from a lot if you walk away from Boney. The guys I've heard talking say the real money out here is on the side bets. I'm surprised that you are worried about beating that guy, of all people! It's not my fault that Boney is the best that they could come up with on two days' notice. He's no ringer. You don't need my help to kick his ass."

Wedgy smiled at first. He appreciated a good lie now and again, but not a betrayal. He was oddly disappointed that after two months of studying with the master, Rama couldn't do a better job of setting up a trap. Wedgy lowered his voice to a fatherly tone. "Let me give you a little advice, son, just in case you were planning on making a buck in this match or in this business: You'd be a damn sight better off if you just settled into a nice honorable profession selling broken-down cars to the poor bastards who make their living out on the road…you could be a salesman maybe, like the miserable deadbeat who sold me the damn Lincoln.

"You're just a chip off that old block. I don't need a loser caddying for me anyway!" Wedgy spat out the words as if an insect had flown into his mouth. He'd had enough and was ready for a greasy breakfast and the chance to disembowel this Boney character on the golf course—but only for the $250 Nassau they had agreed to last night. Regardless of what Rama had said, Boney could be better than he appeared. And if he wasn't, Wedgy doubted the locals had enough cash to engage in a side bet that would make beating him all that worthwhile.

He lowered his eyes to his coffee. "So how are you getting home?"

"Not through Cypress Point, that's for sure," replied Rama.

—•—

Rama felt a jolt of relief at severing his ties with Wedgy Byrne. He rose from the table; breakfast could wait. The hustler softened slightly at the realization that the caddie who had brought him some two-dozen victories and had tolerated miles of admittedly interminable Sinatra medleys was jumping ship. Sometimes you just have to cut your losses, Wedgy thought, offering his hand in resignation.

"If you're smart, Rama, and if you've got any money left, put it down on me. By the way, that money I owe you…that should about cover you sending me out here on this god-damned detour from Albuquerque." Wedgy looked hurt as Rama withdrew his hand. "I never said you had to like my style."

"You never said your style included paying off another guy's caddie to "forget" to pull the flagstick either," snapped Rama as he left the table. "Charlie Vestal never could keep a secret."

Wedgy watched Rama go, then signaled for a waitress. Anything she could bring would be better than Rama's lousy news. As he watched the girl flit between tables he recalled Rama's words: "another guy's caddie." That other guy would be Ivar Guidance. Damned if his old friend wasn't somehow still in the picture, thought Wedgy…behind Rama's fumbled hustle, perhaps?

"Christ, Ivar, don't you *ever* give up?" Wedgy hissed.

The waitress just approaching Wedgy's table looked startled as if she had just stumbled on a snake. Wedgy ordered an omelet, then settled over his cup to think. The words of a long-lost Dutch friend came to mind: "The ape comes out the sleeve," old Jaap would say when the truth was revealed. Perhaps this ape was still hidden, but Wedgy guessed it had something to do with Ivar's money. That might explain Boney's eager challenge and Rama's bogus weather report.

A smile warmed Wedgy's face like the heat from his coffee. Sometimes he savored the complexities of the hustle more than the game itself. He had a feeling the betting would get interesting this afternoon.

"Now we're really playing some golf, eh, Ivar?" Wedgy whispered across his cup.

—•—

Ivar Guidance thought he was having a heart attack, but it was just exhaustion. He slumped into the embrace of the hospital's unforgiving vinyl furniture, and there in the bleak light of the waiting room he finally got some rest. Several paces down the hall Doctor Myer was conducting a pre-operative exam on Doris Schwain; Ivar had been banished to the benches to await its outcome. It was just as well. He was wrung out from the strain of answering Rama's call to assist his mother. His labors had included helping Doris prepare for a hasty trip to Atlanta, readying his plane, attempting to locate Hank Schwain, and finally flying the route to Atlanta—all in the course of twenty-four hours. It was one too many straws on Ivar's tired back.

Right there in the hospital would have been as good a place as any to faint dead away. But the cool synthetic furniture had restored him long enough to summon the stamina to grant one more big favor to a thankful and very scared Doris Schwain. She had learned only hours earlier that Doctor Myer planned brain surgery Monday morning. She had argued for time to gather her family about her, and that still included Hank. Once again her affection for Hank—forged on timeless summer days with a handsome young dreamer—rose above her disappointments. The doctor had declared he would permit no further delay beyond Monday. The danger in waiting was too great, he had said; another attack could be fatal.

The surgery itself was risky, he had explained. But doing nothing would be like accepting a sentence of paralysis or death. The new scanning equipment available to him at this hospital had revealed the tale of an old injury to the back of her head. It wasn't scar tissue or sclerosis that imperiled Doris. It appeared that a sliver of bone had worked its way close to catastrophe. It had to be removed with precision from the surgically unfriendly environs near her brain's lower reaches.

"A little like pick-up sticks," Doctor Myer had described the dangerous surgery in a poorly chosen analogy.

At the news Doris had turned to Ivar in fear and loneliness. She had asked that he do whatever he could to reach Rama and Hank and to arrange their transportation to her bedside in two days. Ivar had reassured her, but even as he promised to get her boys together, he reminded himself to leave future altruism to the young.

He snoozed in the waiting room until woken by Doctor Myer's tap on his shoulder; Doris was all clear for Monday's surgery. Within hours Ivar was airborne again, en route to performing one more serious favor.

—•—

Home was swooping up to meet Ivar as he lined up his approach on the south runway. The uneventful flight into Memphis had given him time to consider the consequences of his promise. He feared the task of delivering Rama and his father to Doris's bedside would be substantially more involved than merely placing phone calls. He knew Rama was in Mesquite Creek, somewhere deep in the heart of Texas. The elder Schwain was presumably in town but far more remote. Ivar knew a good set of charts could deliver him to Rama's locale, but nothing could navigate to Hank Schwain's defeated soul.

Ivar was resigned to fetching the Schwains and flying them back to Atlanta, but his Cessna 310 could make the trip to Texas and back to Georgia only so fast. By Ivar's reckoning he would have to land three times during the course of that trip to refuel, and he still had to get some sleep tonight. That left little time to search for Hank today. If he couldn't be found, so be it; at least she would have her son at her bedside.

Ivar resolved to give finding Hank one try. As he taxied to the Guidance Industries' hangar and flashed a thumbs-up to his ground crew, he imagined his best single chance would be found where the most gamblers gathered during the day: Volunteer State Studs and Stables. Ivar hoped the stables—a front for illegal horse racing—would be "exercising" its horses today.

Within an hour after landing and with only a bag of Krystal Burgers to fortify him, Ivar pulled the Renault to a stop at the track's valet parking area.

"Just leave her right here if you'd be so kind," Ivar told the parking attendant. "I'll be back out shortly…and I'll be in a hurry." Ivar tucked a ten-dollar bill into the attendant's palm and pulled the keys from the ignition. The boy watched the old fellow in the leather flight jacket stride away toward the grandstands, certain he had just done business with his first hit man.

"Hank Schwain please meet your son, Rama, at the west gate. It is urgent." The announcement reverberated twice in two minutes above the buzz of the greedy crowd. Five dollars had convinced the PA announcer that there really was an emergency and that the page couldn't wait. Ivar couldn't know how Hank would respond or if he was even on the premises, but hoped the prospect of Hank's meeting his son would be compelling. Ivar would give Hank five minutes to show himself.

Hank was on the grounds but had nearly missed Ivar's page in the hubbub of gamblers and the snapping of Howell Juitt's shoe shine rag. For the first time in more than ten years, Hank had not come to the stables to play the ponies, as Ivar had guessed. He had come to return the two dollars he owed Howell, the venerable shoe-shine man who for so long had been stationed outside the Paddock Room's entrance. Howell had always been a friendly voice in the stables' heartless mob.

A day and a night had passed since Hank had peered from the bridge into the Mississippi's pitiless waters. After he had recoiled from that hopeless precipice, he reeled through despair, then anger, and finally into a drunken epiphany at the stick of his Little Crow. Like a dancer balanced upon the aircraft's single wheel, he had flown into the stormy night as far as the whiskey and the tether at the craft's tail would allow. The ascent from the windblown tarmac of Aero Meadows and into his imagination had been seamless: banking above dusty wheat fields and soaring over green carpets of sugar beets, just as he had imagined as a young man.

He had just throttled up to clear the tips of a poplar windbreak when the cold beam of a flashlight grounded him. The cop had been curious about the Rambler that had been seen lurching up Aero Meadows's drive a few hours earlier.

The next morning, released on his own recognizance to the streets of Memphis, Hank had called the only person he thought would understand. He asked Howell Juitt for a lift and a couple of bucks for gas for the Rambler, which had run itself dry while he had soloed through his memories.

"Now you call me if I can ever hep', you hear!" Hank recalled Howell once saying. "Long as you got a dime, you can always find me...the only Juitt in the book!"

Now, looking into the kind eyes of Howell's wrinkled black face, Hank didn't even hear the thunder of the horses' hooves or the frantic two-minute call to book final bets. He couldn't have cared less about the races. He was finally free. But for the barge pilot and the blue light, Hank might have destroyed himself and his dreams. He had been spared again and he knew it.

Hank had neither the will nor the audacity to sidle up to fate herself and again test her beneficence, not even for a lousy three-to-one on a five-dollar bet. Not when he had already come so close to flushing away the greatest odds anyone is ever granted.

Life could go on, but he had to square with Howell Juitt first. Howell tucked Hank's two bills into his shirt pocket with a grateful nod. He had always liked the crippled fellow who had so often taken a seat at his shine stand. Howell never fathomed the cane-toting fellow's restiveness but more than appreciated that the handsome vet always understood the value of a well-buffed pair of wingtips.

When it came to horseflesh, Howell had long been Hank's primary well-spring of wisdom, and Hank had often come to drink. But Howell's value to Hank was not bound by things equestrian; in fact, after Doris and Hank had separated, the old fellow had often been a priceless, solitary voice of reason in Hank's troubled ears. Unfortunately, Hank wasn't often receptive to reason. A dozen times he had watched that earnest onyx face preach its sermon on, as Howell called it: "*The Bank o' Life*," but Hank had never really listened. He had heard the rich Delta drawl, the cadence of a satisfied spirit, and a lively heart slapping in syncopation with the brush and the rag. But Howell's exhortation to understand that life's experiences were far more valuable than cash had regularly fallen on deaf ears.

To Howell's way of thinking, time was the only capital we were issued at the beginning of life's game. "The rich child and the po' child each gets dealt 'bout the same...like that 'Nopoly money, heh?" he would smile. Howell explained that a fella could trade that capital in for joyful experience that he could deposit in life's bank, or he could trade it in for or cash. But there were no guarantees he'd get either.

"Hell, you can waste yo' time on *misery* fo' that matta'…it's yo' choice."

But it was important for Howell to make one thing clear, and he would pull the rag taut across his customer's shoe for emphasis: "Joy and love are the pree'ferred deposits in the Bank o' Life. Y'all hear me? A happy minute is like a dolla' bill, and that minute's got the same value all 'round no matter if you rich or po'. Listen up: The rich man's happy minute sippin' champagne from the tail of his million dolla' yacht ain't no mo' valuable than the po' man's happy minute skippin' stones 'cross a glassy little pond or kissin' on his sweetheart.

"Y'all hear me?" Howell would ask before releasing the tension across Hank's shoes.

"So a fella's gotta be mindful how much time he gonna spend chasin' down them big-ticket items…'cause the time he spends in chasin' is charged against him, and the joy he gets from what he owns may not be worth any mo' in the Bank o' Life than what the po' fellow got for a whole lot less time.

"Now sir, I believe y'all should think on that," Howell would suggest with compelling sincerity. "You can spend yo' time makin' money any old way, but there's one thing old Howell Juitt can tell you fo' sho' mister Schwain…"

"The Bank o' Life don't take cash."

This time Hank heard. He was about to ask Howell's opinion as to where dreams fit into his banking philosophy when the loudspeaker first announced that a Rama Schwain was waiting at the west gate. Hank signaled Howell to quiet the rag for a moment until the announcement repeated.

"Who's this Rama fella' that's lookin' for you?" Howell asked suspiciously. After picking up Hank outside the police station that morning, Howell figured he was entitled to pry.

"He's my son."

"For Christ's sakes, in all these years you neva' said a word about havin' a boy," Howell exclaimed. "You gonna have to get straight with me one of these days, Schwain…you hear!"

"Man, I am sorry," replied Hank as he slipped Howell a five-dollar tip. He grabbed his cane and started warily for a reunion at the west gate but turned back toward the shoe-shine philosopher.

"He's nineteen, going on twenty…hell of a golfer, they tell me."

Chapter 54

Ivar glanced at his watch and tried to recall Rama's description of his father. He remembered Rama had once mentioned his father's combat injury from a glider crash on D-day—a crippled leg. Spotting a man with a limp at the west gate would likely be all the proof Ivar would need. But five minutes had passed and no one with any visible disabilities arrived.

Ivar wrote off the attempt to catch up with Hank as a good try and spun on his heel to head back to the parking area, but his eyes, still sharp from years of reading greens and making VFR landings, noticed a man ducking behind a group of idle race fans. Ivar realized the man had been watching him.

Hank was wary of who might have summoned him. He had heard that Calcutta Finance had asked after him when he left Big Muddy's and worried that they might be luring him into a trap. But if Rama had gone to this much trouble to find him here, something might be seriously wrong. He had to find out. He soon realized there was no Rama, but there was a white-haired man who seemed to be looking for someone, and he looked familiar although Hank couldn't quite place him. At least this fellow didn't look like the Calcutta Finance type, but Hank wasn't confident enough to find out.

Obviously, Mr. Schwain has some reservations about this rendezvous, thought Ivar, so he approached the man he reckoned to be Hank as if oblivious to his identity or his furtive behavior. Ivar noticed the man carried a stout ironwood cane.

"Mister Schwain?" Ivar asked quietly. "Your son, Rama, caddies for me."

Hank looked at Ivar incredulously. "Are you talking to me? It's damned funny, but you're the second one today to mistake me for some guy named Swan…must be the cane, huh?"

"Rama told me you used to fly." Ivar smiled disarmingly.

Hank relaxed for a moment. This white-haired fellow definitely wasn't a Calcutta goon. And he was right: Rama did caddie for an old gent up at Bluff Meade. Then the pieces fell into place. Hank recognized the face. The gentleman standing before him was the golfer who had lost his six thousand dollars to Wedgy Byrne.

"What the hell?" Hank was dumbfounded. Had his world become this small? "What's wrong…where's Rama?"

"He's okay. Come with me…I'll explain outside," said Ivar, "in case someone else is looking for you."

The parking lot attendant watched as Ivar and Hank approached. The boy wondered why the old hit man would want to off some poor guy with a bad leg. Just didn't seem fair, he thought. The boy's gangland fantasies were shaken when Ivar slipped him ten bucks and asked him to "keep an eye on my friend's red Rambler Wagon for a few days 'til we get back." The only damage Ivar Guidance inflicted on Hank Schwain was sharing the Krystal burgers cooling in a paper sack on the passenger's seat as they rushed to the airport.

——•——

Wedgy meandered through Mesquite Creek's pro shop after having washed down a decent western omelet with a bad Bloody Mary. He stepped out onto the veranda overlooking the course, and as sunbeams flooded the first holes in gold, he belched in appreciation and groped for a smoke.

Rama had taken the opportunity to gather his gear from the trailer while his irritable ex-employer ate breakfast up at the clubhouse. Feeling utterly desolate, he plucked the weevils from Wedgy's pancake mix and attempted to salvage breakfast.

Finishing off the last of Wedgy's coffee, Rama sat on the stoop and opened Melyssa's envelope again; the bundle of photos and her letter still awaited his attention. He turned first to her note, reading as the sun cast bright rays on the sad reality of a good-bye letter. It was sad, but it wasn't hopeless:

Dear, Dear Rama,

I hope you are not mad that I didn't say goodbye.
I had to leave early and I couldn't stand to wake you,
if I had I might never have left. I start classes next week
in North Carolina. Carlos and Carla paid my way.
Carlos finally sold some paintings, God bless him.

Oh I wish we had more time. Last night was
heaven. I hope you feel the same.
Who knows, Tarzan, I might even fall in love with you…someday.
Don't be sad (but I am…). Here's my address at Trent Institute, please write
me… PLEASE!!! And send me your address.
Forgive me for sneaking out.

Love, love, love
Melyssa

PS: Carlos took these Polaroids of the greens for you. For some kind
of a test he said. Maybe they'll be helpful.

Rama read the letter several times to confirm that this amazing girl felt as strongly about him as it had seemed last night. He read it again to assure himself that there wasn't some trick to this. She was going to attend Trent Institute of Landscape Technology—impossible! Rama sat in the sun on the trailer's stoop and burned from within with a curious mixture of jealousy at her good fortune and helplessness at his father's bungling of what might have been acceptance into the same school as Melyssa. If he had only known he might have done something different, maybe demanded copies of Trent's correspondence when his father was backpedaling. But Rama would have been tortured far worse if he had known his acceptance letter and subsequent financial aid forms had been deliberately slipped unopened between the pages of Doris's old Bible. The venerable old book held the key to Rama's future with Melyssa and would likely remain unread until Easter.

Rama groaned in discomfort and considered scrambling through Wedgy's liquor supply, but sloshed down the last of the coffee instead. The sooner he got home now, the better. Maybe he could still salvage something from the wreckage of his application attempts.

He pulled his wallet and counted fifty-four dollars, more than enough for a ticket to Memphis. He could flag down the hound at the top of Mesquite's driveway. Dallas, Texarkana, Little Rock…home. He knew the stops and recalled the faces of retirees, soldiers, elderly black women, and ranch hands peering from its green windows as he and his father traveled that highway years ago. It was time to hit the road again. Boney and Lee would have to understand.

Rama scrawled a note on the back of Melyssa's envelope justifying his departure. He left his mother's address and phone number for his conspirators to contact him if they made any money against Wedgy. These instructions were the least he could do as trustee of Ivar's nest egg, but like Ivar, Rama would have to have a little faith in the other's honesty.

He turned his attention to the remaining contents of the envelope. There was a set of eighteen Polaroid instant photos—one for each green at Mesquite Creek.

Rama fanned them out on the stoop beside him, then examined one closely. The photographer must have risen early and taken his camera to the course before the dew had been swept from the greens. Their color had faded, but Rama could see the silver of the dew and scribed into it the graceful curving tracks of four putts, each shot from a different point around the green's fringe.

The tracks all converged near the cup, and some disappeared into the hole. Some lines were straight; others curved as the ball fell with the slope of the damp greens. At the bottom of the photo someone had scribbled the hole number in Spanish, followed by a letter. Apparently this set of photos had a companion set with different hole locations.

"Carlos, you wise old goat," Rama whispered. Like any golfer who gets out early, he knew that greens can be read from the tracks of previous putts in the dew. With these snapshots Carlos had made a valuable record of the breaks from a variety of points across all Mesquite's greens. Rama wondered if Carlos himself had made the putts; they were all so remarkably well struck. And what of the sixteenth green, he thought, fanning quickly through the Polaroids.

That photo depicted several putts scribed into the dew around a flag set in the lower section of the green—the same hole location he had confronted eight years ago. Rama was enthralled to see one track originating from the upper tier of the green. He already knew this line, the same line Carlos Taddio had demonstrated for him on that mysterious night. He smiled at the memory, but a wisp of regret at his father's unhappiness at the circumstances surrounding the heroic putt haunted him even now. But a second equally difficult putt from the upper tier was captured in the photo as well.

This putt's line originated from a point tucked so inaccessibly into a lobe of the green that the ball could not even be started toward the rocks like Rama's notorious putt. This putt had to be struck with one's back to the flag and one's shoulder to the rocks. On this line the ball was in danger of dying even farther from the hole than it started, but if it reached the highest corner of the green without being snared by the hungry fringe, then a single, subtle undulation might coerce the ball into a curving path along the green's perimeter and back downhill to converge with the trajectory of Rama's memorable putt and an equally amazing chance at the cup.

The golfer who had staged the photos had executed a credible attempt at this putt. The photo revealed he had been a little too tentative out of fear for the fringe, and his line had passed about four feet above the hole. It must have been the last shot of the morning because the golf ball still rested at the end of the dewy track like the head of a comet.

Rama stared at the Polaroid, then realized the photo had to have been snapped a good twenty feet above the green to include the putt's entire track to the hole. His smile returned as he pictured Carlos standing in Niña's stirrups at the top of the hill or perhaps even climbing to the first branches of the yellow oak above the green. The old fellow must have figured this photo would be worth the effort to someone someday.

Rama wondered if the photos were common knowledge to the regulars up on the veranda, or had Carlos left him something really special he might share with Boney to help defeat Wedgy. A noble idea, he thought, but it occurred to him that if the flags were in different positions than those in these snapshots, the images would be useless today. If things were like they used to be at Mesquite Creek, the only person who controlled the hole locations was Carlos Taddio, and Rama hadn't seen a trace of the old gaucho since he arrived yesterday.

Rama tried to tuck the photos back into the envelope, thinking that referring to them during a round might not be legal anyway. The last thing they needed to do with Ivar's money on the line was get Boney disqualified. The bundle jammed against a scrap of rigid canvas Melyssa had used to protect the photos. He pulled the obstruction free and was startled to see that it was much more than a scrap—it was an oil painting. Apparently it was true: Carlos had loosened the grip on his creativity. Rama wondered if this art was intended for him.

The painting's subject proved there could be no more deserving recipient. A handsome dark-haired man posed self-assuredly before the grill of a green Ford station wagon—one boot on the chrome bumper. The man held a black cane with one hand and rested the other on the shoulder of a skinny brown-haired boy dressed in faded jeans and a colorful madras shirt. The boy smiled at his father's touch although his knees were knocked as if he might have to pee.

Rama gasped in recognition. Somehow Carlos had captured the Schwain's arrival at Mesquite Creek. Their clothing was accurately rendered, as was the car...even several fat grasshoppers paused on the Ford's blistering hood. Rama could recall the humidity of that sweltering afternoon, the strain on his bladder, and the hum of the swarming locusts. The artist had rendered the two figures perfectly, even though they had never posed so fondly.

Rama felt his eyes welling up. The sudden departure of Melyssa and now this astonishing reminder of another lost love were perhaps too much for one morning. Somehow Carlos had captured it: the last day of a boy's adoration of his father—the final happy day before the man's hand would slam unjustly across the boy's innocent face. Strangely, Rama remembered how much he still loved his father.

He reached to dab at his eyes and was startled by a familiar old voice.

"It is true, sir...that they are thee holes for this day. Thee photos may be useful, no?"

Rama looked up and there, seated at the controls of a three-wheeled golf cart was Carlos Taddio. The old gaucho had withered considerably in the intervening eight years—more than his black Wranglers and turquoise cowboy shirt suggested. Carlos hunched slightly at the old cart's tiller but smiled as brightly as in that magic moment when he first realized Rama wasn't Dickey Stone's ghost. The same flat-brimmed black hat he had worn that night shaded his tired eyes from the brightening day.

Rama rose to his feet. "Carlos!"

He held up the painting in acknowledgment of its impact yet still in complete wonder at its purpose. His mind coursed with questions. Something incomprehensible flowed in the air between them; something invisible like a heat devil that has not yet pulled a puff of dust or a sprig of sage into its vortex. Before Rama could ask why or even mouth the word *thanks*, the old man's brittle hand rose from the tiller and motioned him to settle down.

"Rest please, sir. You have yet much work." Carlos had noticed Rama's traveling bag on the stoop. "You must remain. Much lies upon thee course this day. You must remain…to save thee children."

The gaucho's boot, inlaid with a hand-tooled puma, fell upon the accelerator and the Cushman coughed to life. The old fellow smiled deeply at Rama and gestured to the painting Rama still clutched.

"Perhaps Carlos shall paint you and Miss Melyssa next time, sir," he said in a voice barely audible above the worn engine.

Rama remembered the Polaroids and began to form a question, but Carlos interrupted. "Use them with wisdom, sir."

The cart backfired as Carlos aimed it down the rough gravel drive. Rama could make out the word *Niña* handwritten in fine script across its fenders.

Save the children. The words so heavy in Carlo's speech were troublesome. Perhaps the old gaucho had become demented by the years and the heat, and his thoughts were to be taken lightly. But if he had known more art history, Rama would have realized that Van Gogh and so many others like him weren't exactly pictures of mental health. He shrugged off the encounter and took one last look at the little painting before stowing it in his bag and starting the trek up to the highway to meet the Greyhound.

But the painting looked back.

Mesmerized, Rama focused beyond the texture of canvas and the surface of hardened oil. He peered through his own memory and a new image appeared in Carlos's masterful strokes: the happy, confident face of his father. Momentarily suspended in a peaceful inner place, Rama heard the whispers of the children.

Much lies on the course, Carlos had said. Rama realized that one who could paint with such truth would only speak the truth. He understood Carlos was right: He had a job to do, yet he didn't know exactly what. With faith in an unfathomable outcome, Rama turned back to face the game ahead.

———•———

The crowd gathering on Carla's veranda for the match had grown until the timbers groaned in protest. Lee had delivered a good crowd for a mid-September Saturday. Long, late-summer chore lists waving in female hands had been disregarded in favor of just one more day at the golf course. The presence of a contender from the US Open and a match with the enigmatic

Gypsy Hustler were just too much to miss. Many a chore and many an irritated wife were washed aside in the wake of golf aficionados streaming to Mesquite Creek.

Carla noticed the hubbub and smiled with satisfaction. "I think that's about enough of my help for one day," she told the new girl she had been training for Melyssa's job. "You'll be fine, Sweetheart. If you need me, I'll be in the cage."

Carla nodded toward the old teller's cage she had installed as much for its utility as for the air of legitimacy it had added to her gambling operation. From behind its steel bars, Carla plied her bookmaking trade. Her services made it convenient to offer or cover a bet while her careful records ensured that misunderstandings were kept to a minimum. The only bullets ever fired at Mesquite Creek were from her starting pistol.

It had been a while since she had had a good match come her way—one that attracted a real crowd. With interest noisily growing for today's contest, she expected a decent take and a good fee regardless of the outcome. She fastidiously dusted off the little marble counter, changed a dead light bulb, and wiped tarnish from the bars. She erased all traces of the last match's betting lines from the blackboard and chalked in a new table in which to list the odds and the day's bets—offered or taken. Finally, the wiry would-be debutante opened her ledger to a blank page and wrote in careful hand: *Byrne versus Carlisle.* Then rising to her toes, she reached up and flipped over a sign hanging above the cage window: Place Bets Here.

Carla settled down with a book to await her first customer. This would make the fourth time she had read *Gone with the Wind.*

The crowd on the deck spilled out onto the green spaces surrounding the opening tee and the finishing hole. Since yesterday there had been an undercurrent of speculation on the relative strengths of the two golfers' games. The fact was, nobody had really seen much of the Gypsy Hustler, even though reports from three men who had played with him yesterday revealed him to be less accomplished than his billing might warrant.

"Oh he was just getting the feel of our odd little course," Carla had explained as much in defense of her marquee player as in support of a more lucrative betting line.

"Boney will have his hands full—don't y'all take the Gypsy for granted." Carla talked up Wedgy's game and posted odds of four to one in his favor to intrigue the wise majority of the crowd who would likely make reasonable bets on what they knew. And what they knew was that Boney had been playing some very fine golf in the last few months. They knew squat about the Gypsy's record.

What Carla wanted was to draw out a few large bets from the risk-takers and to generate a decent pool and a respectable purse on the backs of the average bettors. In Carla's matches, the purse was built from a 10-percent surcharge on all the betting action: eight for the winner, two for the house. The contestants were still free to bet between themselves or with the gallery. Even if a golfer couldn't drum up a side bet, at least he was assured of 8-percent for his victory. And of course Carla would take her 2-percent.

After several hours, Carla's ledger book was filling with bets favoring Boney Carlisle. No one had bet lavishly, but the total action added up to a decent take for the winning golfer. Wedgy had watched Carla's blackboard closely. Several folks had offered attractive bets against the Gypsy Hustler. Had he not been suspicious of a possible trap, Wedgy would have taken those bets on himself, but he remained cautious and resolved that he would only play to the $250 Nassau against Boney. Any other action would be between members of the gallery. If he won, the 8-percent would be a nice bonus.

There were also a few savvy gamblers who hadn't taken the Gypsy's reportedly poor practice round at face value and had posted bets in his favor; to Carla's delight, there were more than enough reckless Boney fans to cover them. As the action between these factions was logged into her book, it became clear this was going to be the biggest payday she had enjoyed in years.

Carla should have known after all these years that nothing ever came so easily to her thirsty endeavor down in Mesquite Creek's arroyo. The hair on the back of her neck prickled to life as a forbidding groan replaced the happy chatter of the gallery now gathering in anticipation of the coming contest.

The sound of sinking hearts filled the air as Boney Carlisle made his entrance on crutches, his left foot dangling like dead poultry. Now suddenly, it looked as if all bets were off.

Lee and Rama looked at their man in disbelief.

So much for Rama's ringer, thought Wedgy.

"Son of a bitching, damned *gopher*." Boney barked his epithet against burrowing backyard animals with studied gusto, loud enough to override the din of disappointment sweeping the crowd like a dust storm.

"Twisted it good…damn it," he continued. "I'm out unless someone works a miracle."

Wedgy had been in business long enough to recognize the scent of a common household rodent. "Out? Shit no, Carlisle! There's some damn good cripples in this game. Swing from your crutches, and I'll grant you a stroke every other hole."

Boney was amazed that the Gypsy Hustler offered even that. At nine free strokes he started to think about tweaking his swing to accommodate the crutches, but it was a new game plan now—a charade—one that Carlos had convinced him to accept. His job now was *not* to play, and neither Lee Trujillo or Rama Schwain knew it.

"Jesus, you can't be serious. Forget it. I'll get you next time, Gypsy," replied Boney.

The would-be gallery came alive with unflattering remarks regarding Boney's encounter with the gopher hole, including several unsavory references to his own holes. Boney scanned the crowd and found Lee staring at him, the Mexican's familiar broad smile having given over to a seething grimace.

Carla, having just arrived on the veranda to start the match, looked alarmed. She had just locked her safe and now suddenly faced an uppity gallery and a possible run on her bank.

"Hold your horses Gypsy, Boney…everybody!" The voice of authority. The word of the committee. The hammer of the law resounded from Carla's wiry body.

"Attention patrons! Since Mr. Carlisle has evidently lost his footing, I will refund your bets in the order I received them, unless…" She paused, looking to the sky as if something in the endless azure expanse might still deliver her match. "Unless someone else is willing to challenge the Gypsy?"

Silence prevailed.

"If so, we can figure a handicap and rework the odds. You can withdraw your bets or adjust them. We can still make a good match out of this." Carla knew she faced losing what would have been a satisfying slice of a very hefty pie. If nobody stepped up to take Boney's place, she would drag her feet in paying out the refunds in order to sell every extra drink her girls could rustle up. It would be better than nothing.

The crowd grumbled in unison, but no one stepped forward to take on the Gypsy Hustler. It was clear that Carla would soon be returning the disgruntled patrons' money. Fifty or so people surged from the pack to vie for first place in line at her cage. The gallery was in danger of descending into a mob.

Boney wasn't surprised. Carlos had suggested the anguish ensuing after his withdrawal from the match would provide the opening for an unlikely proposal. He shook off the crowd's displeasure and hobbled up to the veranda to get their full attention.

"Whoa there. Hold on, everybody," he cried. "Carla has the right idea. But since none of you chicken shits will step up to the Gypsy, even with handicap strokes, then I propose another match."

The crowd murmured in anticipation that Boney might propose that his old rival Lee engage the Gypsy in battle—a match made in heaven for the denizens of Mesquite Creek—but Boney threw them a curve…a screaming down-and-away slider.

"Wouldn't you all like a real entertaining contest?" he began.

"Yeah…with Trujillo!" replied a scattering of voices.

Boney ignored their sentiments. "A match with drama and uncertainty… one that might be wild to watch and wilder to wager?" He waited for the crowd but they looked at him with vacant eyes. "I propose a grudge match: the Gypsy Hustler against the one person here who would like to see him defeated most." The crowd stirred.

Boney extended his crutch like a broken wing toward Wedgy. "If the Gypsy here if willing to accept, of course."

"Accept what...who?" hollered Wedgy. "*Everybody* wants to kick my ass, so who in hell are you trumpeting, Carlisle?"

Wedgy had already begun thinking about his chances farther west. Boney's mishap had spared him whatever trap Rama or Ivar might have set up against the ponderous ringer.

But without missing a beat, Boney answered. "I wager that Rama Schwain can beat you straight up in stroke play."

Wedgy almost laughed at the image of the old Dutchman's ape peeking out the sleeve. "Carlisle, you're not only clumsy, you're nuts. You can make all the proposals you want but you can't make him play...besides, Rama is my caddie, for Christ's sake."

"That's not what I hear," replied Boney. "I happen to know you and your caddie parted ways this morning. I've got reason to believe your ex-caddie has enough game and more than enough motivation to make this match interesting...and I'm ready to put good money on it."

The color drained from Lee Trujillo's face. He knew Boney had an unstable streak, but somewhere between their meeting up on the range yesterday afternoon and now, the big fellow must have finally snapped. Lee patted Rama on the shoulder for assurance that this wasn't what they had planned. "Forget him, Rama, this wasn't in the cards...I swear," he whispered. "I'll get your money back before Boney does something foolish. Then maybe I'll kick his fat ass myself."

Lee noticed Boney making his way toward them and thought he might get the chance to make good on his promise. Rama was shocked, feeling like he had just gone from being a spectator to a participant in a surreal play. Crawling into a prairie dog hole seemed like a good alternative to hanging around this odd scene. He wondered why he had let Carlos talk him into sticking around for this insanity. If he hurried, he might still catch the next bus to Texarkana. Mesquite Creek had gone nuts.

Rama gathered himself to reject the preposterous idea of a match with Wedgy but was dumbfounded when Boney, with a seriousness belying his crazy proposal, whispered to him: "I've got a message from Carlos Taddio: '*For thee children...you must play, sir.*'"

Lee and Rama stared at the messenger in disbelief.

—•—

Must be the water up here, thought Wedgy. Rama was right, these guys really were loco, but Boney's offer to put money down on Rama was too enticing an opportunity to wave away. Sure, the young man might have snuck a little practice in here and there, and according to what he had heard through the grapevine, Rama had taken some secret instruction from an Indian gardener at Bluff Meade, but he could not possibly be enough of a threat to justify anyone investing in his victory. This Boney fellow must have a loose screw. Wedgy realized he had better take that bet before Boney came to his senses. Maybe he could salvage something from this trip after all—if Rama would play.

"Okay, Mr. Carlisle. I'll take some of your money, say somewhere to the tune of five hundred dollars," replied Wedgy. "I'm in if Schwain has got the gumption to put that *revenge* you're talking about on the line. But I'd sure hate to soil a perfectly decent player-caddie relationship."

Wedgy was still thinking of recovering the would-be winnings of his Nassau bet with Boney and of making an early departure for Albuquerque. But he was thinking small. When Boney responded that he was thinking about something in the thousands of dollars, he had to quickly reconsider his priorities.

"Thousands?" gasped Wedgy and several dozen spectators simultaneously. Wedgy nearly pissed. He would hogtie Rama to get him on the course now. He turned to Rama, who stood frozen at Lee Trujillo's side. "What do you say, Schwain? See if that practice you've been sneakin' in will do you any good. Nothing like testing oneself under pressure...it'll be fun."

The gallery's mass migration at the imminent collapse of the Boney-Gypsy match abruptly stopped. All attention turned to the one person who could keep things interesting.

Rama was paralyzed in a struggle between his nature and Carlos's cryptic words—between self-doubt and the desire to best Wedgy. He never thought it would come down to him. It would be easy to say no. Who could blame him for bowing out of a preposterous match. He attempted to mouth the word but his voice was gone. He cleared his throat and was about to speak when he noticed Carlos Taddio parked in the shade of the willows. Even at a distance Rama sensed that the old man's eyes were fixed on him in anticipation. Rama's throat softened. "Alright, I'll play," he said with resignation. "If Tyler Grant can beat you I don't see why I can't either, Wallace."

The crowd looked perplexed—happy that the match was on but troubled that the Gypsy Hustler's real name might be Wallace.

Wedgy quivered in anticipation of easy money, but he composed himself and looked to the man leaning on his crutches. "Well now, Boney. You said something about thousands...care to get specific?"

"Yes sir...thousands," Boney replied. "But you would be the first to admit Rama would be a long shot, eh, Wallace?"

Wedgy could see a wrangle for odds coming and quickly turned to minimizing his own advantage. "Well, maybe not *that* long. You said yourself you had reason to believe in Rama's skills, and I've got reason to believe he has been working on his game a lot more than he's been letting on. Enough to make me cautious."

Wedgy fixed Boney with a put-up-or-shut-up stare. "So about how much are you really talking to make it worth my while, Carlisle?"

Boney glanced at Lee, who was still pale but spellbound. The big man teetered dramatically on his crutches and fumbled to extract a fat roll of bills from his pocket.

"Alright. I've got six thousand bucks on Rama," said Boney. "But before you slobber all over yourself, Gyp, I'm only offering this much dough if you are ready to take a little risk—eight-to-one. Like I said, Rama is a long shot."

Wedgy recalled the "fools and their money" line again. No doubt about it—the folks out here were crazy. He doubted he could lose to Rama Schwain; however, at eight-to-one, an improbable loss could be devastating. It was time to wave off this odd encounter, but the siren song was too strong: six thousand dollars. He hadn't made that much in one deal since Ivar Guidance's loss, and he had to cheat for that!

"I'll give you two-to-one," Wedgy said automatically.

"Damn, Rama ain't no Jack Nicklaus," replied Boney sarcastically.

"Shit, three-to-one."

"I thought you were a hustler, Gyp. Didn't you see the crappy clubs in his bag? Inferior equipment has got to count for *something*."

"Alright Carlisle, five-to-one," Wedgy agreed nervously. "And I'm losing my damn patience."

"You really *are* worried about your old caddie, huh? Where's your confidence, Gyp?" sighed Boney as he straightened up on his crutches as if to begin the hobble home. "Guess this was just a bad idea…maybe get you next year."

"Six-to-one. SIX-TO-ONE or I'm stowing the god-damned clubs."

Wedgy felt a bead of sweat snake down his temple. He hoped no one noticed. The entire crowd held its breath in silent anticipation of Boney's reaction. Only the buzz of brittle wings from the first dive-bombing hoppers in a new wave of the plague pierced the calm.

"That's good enough for me. We've got a match," beamed Boney.

Wedgy recovered from the initial shock of the bidding frenzy and seemed unconcerned that he had just put thirty-six grand on the line to win six. But his certainty that it was Ivar's money made it worthwhile. He noticed Rama appeared equally dazed.

"Come on, Schwain, don't look so shocked. I always knew you had a little game hidden away there; those grass stains on your clubs had to count for something. No doubt about it; it's an impressive little scheme you've cooked up with the crutches and all…just hope you haven't got yourself in a little too deep for a beginner."

A devilish grin sprung to Wedgy's face. "The easy part is over. Now all you've got to do is play golf…real well."

Before Wedgy could subject Rama to a withering round of gamesmanship, Lee escorted his young player to the practice green. "Don't even listen to him, Rama. Move on to Plan B, amigo. Let's practice your chipping."

"Plan B?" Rama asked. "What ever happened to Plan A, Lee?"

Lee shrugged his shoulders. "I'll go fetch your clubs."

In a moment Rama was standing at the practice green looking at his clubs. The Night Lessons brassie and the clubs he had scrounged from Sunset Hills were rubbed up and gleaming brightly in the sun. He looked into Lee's confident brown eyes. "Lee, how did you get these clubs so clean so fast?"

Lee looked at Rama blankly. "Never touched 'em, amigo."

A dozen chips later, the clubs rattled in Lee's bag as Rama fell in step with his caddie's stride to the first tee. But he stopped Lee for a moment and extracted his putter to roll a few practice putts. Rama walked alone to the putting green where he had first tasted Mesquite Creek's strange magic. From a spot in the shade of the willows swaying above the green, Carlos Taddio watched him putt. The old fellow was weary at the effort to pull against the events of lives that fall like dominoes into the most absurd patterns. Rama was poised to finally enter the game. It had been eleven years.

Carlos closed his eyes and listened to the soft clink of practice putts into the cup. "And still with thee touch of Dickey Stone."

Chapter 55

Ivar cranked the Renault sharply into the municipal airport's General Aviation entrance and raced down to Guidance Industries' hangar. On the ride in from the horse track, he had informed Hank of Doris's medical condition and her urgent request to see her family. As it became clear to Hank the lengths—and costs—Ivar was taking to assist a stranger's wife, he grew suspicious of the seemingly sincere gentleman's motives.

"So what's in all this for you?"

"No compensation or monetary gain, if that is your concern," replied Ivar with a rare hint of impatience. "I assure you I am placing no financial burden on your shoulders. The fact is, Mr. Schwain, I probably have more wealth than any man deserves." Ivar explained that he was simply doing a favor for his caddie, who had asked him to keep an eye on his sick mother while he was away.

"True, it has become a bit more involved than I ever expected," Ivar admitted with a weary smile, "but I am overdue to give something back. My wife, Rebecca, would have wanted it this way. Besides, that son of yours has done wonders for my golf game, and that's worth a lot up where I play."

"Bluff Meade, right?" Hank said, picturing Ivar and his wealthy friends happily dueling for sums they could easily afford to lose. "But this flight has gotta be costing you…"

"Well, Mr. Schwain, I really need an excuse to fly now and then."

Once at the hangar, Hank watched with interest as the languid pace of his host accelerated in the presence of his ground crew. With little wasted motion or worry, Ivar and his crew readied the plane and hastily planned a flight to Mesquite Creek and back to Atlanta via Jackson, Mississippi. They checked the weather bulletins for the trip and it looked good: The air was clear and calm; the visibility excellent. The only issue was daylight. The Cessna 310 could make Mesquite in about four hours, but Ivar preferred a little slack for any delays and to ensure a safe daylight landing.

"You've got a little under six hours until sundown at Mesquite Creek," his crew member said as he reviewed the charts. "You should be in good shape."

Ivar seemed satisfied. "Is she ready to roll out?"

"Fifteen minutes and she's all yours, Mr. G. Even packed a few sandwiches in the Coleman." The crewman was proud of his thorough service and turned to Hank. "Corned beef okay by you, sir?"

"Me? Yeah, great," Hank stammered, clearly enthralled by this exposure to private aviation and the crew's courtesy toward him. His doubts about Ivar's intentions vanished.

The crewman gathered the charts and jogged them into a tidy package for Ivar. "Now a couple of those charts are dated 1963—best I could get on short notice—so just keep your eyes open. Damned TV towers have been popping up all over the Midwest. Don't want to tangle with one of those SOBs."

"Very good, we'll be watching," Ivar turned to Hank. "You heard the man. We'll have to keep our eyes peeled up there, eh co-pilot?"

Hank didn't answer. He was thinking about the night over St. Claude and the Holy Mother's stony gaze as his glider was torn open on her spire.

—•—

In thirty minutes Ivar and Hank were approaching 8,500 feet. As predicted, the air was perfect. When the plane was slipping through the atmosphere like satin, Ivar turned to Hank. "Rama says you were a pilot. Why don't you take her for a half-hour or so?"

Hank was startled. "Me? I only flew gliders, and that was over twenty years ago."

In fact, it had only been a few days since Hank had flown with Marcile. Had it *not* been such a beautiful flight and such a perfect landing he might have sold the glider, and some of his troubles would have been over. But he dared not speak of that flight or his financial troubles. Ivar seemed to know too much about him already.

"I've never flown under power," Hank added.

"Well, there's no time like the present, Mr. Schwain. Put your hands on the wheel."

Ivar talked Hank through a few basics and demonstrated the appropriate instruments to ensure straight and level flight. In a couple of minutes the old fellow was relaxing in the pilot's seat with his arms stretched behind his head as Hank held her steady.

"She has a mighty forgiving spot for you, Hank…your wife, I mean," Ivar said, chuckling over the ambiguity.

Hank tried to chuckle along but was troubled by Ivar's insight.

"Doris seems like a good judge of character, Hank."

It was not in Ivar's heart to question Doris's measure of the roguish fellow he had just plucked from the racetrack. In years of business he had seen scoundrels, evil-hearted and heartless men. But the fellow chewing on his lower lip as he scrupulously kept the aircraft's wings level seemed none of these things. In fact, an air of vulnerability—of tragedy—hung around Hank.

Ivar suspected that the root of Doris's resilient affection for Hank lay in the past, and he was right. Doris still cherished the hopeful heart of the wheat farmer's son who, twenty-four years earlier, had boarded a Trailways bus out of Moses Lake for some dubious flying experience for Uncle Sam, only to return brokenhearted.

"You are a very lucky man to have a woman like Doris. Doctor Myer says she is going to get a new lease on life if this surgery works out…and so should you." Ivar scanned the landscape below. The VOR receiver and thin line of state highway 67 heading southwest to Texarkana confirmed their heading as they soared above the great expanse of Arkansas's forests.

"A new lease, a second chance…we should all be so lucky," Ivar said wistfully. "I lost my dear Rebecca last year. No surgery could have saved her."

"Jesus, I'm sorry to hear that," Hank shivered.

"I appreciate it. Now, if you don't mind I'll take the wheel 'til we get around Texarkana traffic."

Once they were south of town, Ivar dialed the OBS to a new heading that would take them over Tyler and Waco with little or no course change for about an hour and a half. He brought the plane back onto that heading and returned the aircraft to Hank's control.

"Alright, Hank, you'll have real easy going for about ninety minutes. If you get bored flying straight and level just let me know."

The green blanket below was breaking up into a collage of crops and pastures as the plane raced onward. The radio was quiet. Except for a widely spread collection of small clouds floating just above and an occasional airliner cruising far overhead, they were alone with their thoughts and a comforting stream of small talk.

Following a heading over unfamiliar country took faith and confidence. After an hour the vastness of the country below began to unsettle Hank. He fidgeted at the wheel, glancing nervously from their heading to the VOR receiver and back out to what he guessed was highway 31 running to the north. He tried to suppress a pang of acrophobia. Surely with all this space—all this possibility for error—he was bound to get something wrong.

"I didn't think I would, but I guess I *am* getting a little bored," Hank tried to conceal his nerves.

"Well I wouldn't doubt it…you've probably never had more than a few minutes of straight and level flying. Let's try a couple of turns here, just to wake you up."

Hank looked at Ivar with doubt. Just last night on the tarmac at Aero Meadows he had soared in his imagination, and now he had the chance to make that dream a reality. But an upwelling anxiety at the vastness of the airspace and the intimidating complexity of the controls sapped his courage.

"Don't worry, Hank, you've flown gliders…you are halfway there." Ivar exchanged his slump for a commanding posture. "Now here's what you'll do: Just turn the wheel a wee bit right and give her a little pedal and just a tug to keep her nose up. I'll watch the directional gyro…then when I say go, you'll reverse the wheel—gently—to level her back out. Sounds like fun, eh?"

Hank tried to speak but his throat was dry beyond words.

"We'll start with an easy little right turn. Three, two, one…now!"

Hank repeated the motions as described. The plane was far more responsive than he could imagine, and in a moment Ivar was at his ear directing him to level out.

"Wilbur and Orville got tired of their glider mighty fast, too," Ivar laughed. He nudged the prop controls forward to increase the rpm. "Okay, here's the fun part: the power. Push the throttles forward to get the feel of it, and just pull back on the wheel a tad."

Hank obeyed and fell under the spell of a new sensation. He watched the horizon drop away as the plane climbed into the sky. "Whoa," he exclaimed, forgetting his anxiety as a darker shade of blue descended into their vista. Hank imagined that if he held the wheel back they would simply fly off into space.

"Can't do that in a glider, eh?" Ivar declared. "Now, just tip the wheel forward and we'll see where we are."

After Hank complied, the plane was level with the base of the neighboring clouds. He could see the small feathery islands and their shadows skimming across the fields below in synchronous pairs. A puff of cloud hovered directly in their path. Before Hank could voice any concern for the impending collision, Ivar declared somberly, "You have a choice to make, Mr. Pilot: Fly around or crash on through."

Hank shivered at the C word.

Ivar noticed the look of alarm creasing his companion's face. He had heard Rama mention his father's crash, but he didn't know of the boys who had perished at St. Claude's Chapel or of Hank's guilt at not avoiding the menacing obstacle. The crash was simply a vaguely heroic incident in Rama's family history; Hank's black cane and his limp its only hard evidence.

Ivar knew there were war injuries less visible than those that had crippled Hank's leg—injuries far beyond the reach of scalpel, splint, or sutures. He recognized such wounds might fester in the heart of the most unblemished veteran.

"Okay, around the cloud it is," Ivar declared. "That might be more fun anyway. Bank left, real easy there, Sky King."

Hank lurched awkwardly into a left bank. Ivar reached in and steadied the plane as it passed the cloud on their right. But then, rather than return to the heading for Waco, Ivar returned the stick to Hank and issued another command.

"Let's do a long easy right turn back around the cloud, what do you say?"

This turn was executed with less hesitation, and the plane banked smoothly. Hank waited for Ivar to ask him to level out, but the old fellow slid the throttles forward and said to pull up the nose a bit more and to let her keep climbing.

Looking out the right side of the windshield, Hank watched as the cloud dropped away. He held his breath as they banked upward and around the towering white structure in one smooth, exhilarating spiral. A smile crossed Hank's face, and in his heart he felt a fleeting sense of command over the elements that had once cast his dreams into the unforgiving hands of gravity. Here on the very day he had finally said good-bye to the ponies, and only hours after Howell Juitt had instructed him in the Bank of Life's simple terms, the Bank had paid its first dividend.

—•—

Ivar ignored the scenery and watched his instruments until their heading approached the centerline. "Okay...level her out now."

Hank returned from the spiral right on course but two thousand feet higher than where they had started. The vista had expanded to include the tops of early afternoon storms building far to the north over Oklahoma. A grin betrayed Ivar's satisfaction at his student's performance.

"That concludes our lesson for today," Ivar said with a glance at his wristwatch. They had been aloft about two-and-a-half hours. "We've got a plane to catch," he laughed as he took the controls back from Hank. He figured a final heading for Mesquite Creek and descended to 4,500 feet. The VOR navigational beacons were getting sparse, and he would finish the flight using good old-fashioned pilotage. A good pair of eyes, an accurate chart, decent weather, and, in this case, a highway leading directly to their destination should make visual navigation a pleasure.

Ivar was confident that their heading, along with a little guidance from the highway and Mesquite Creek's landmark water tower, would deliver them to the old landing strip beside the golf course. His eyes swept the instrument panel. It was all good news.

"If you don't mind, Hank, can I trouble you to hold this course while I fetch us some chow?" Ivar tapped on the directional gyro. "We should be intersecting a highway soon. It runs at about forty-five degrees across our heading; you can't miss it. Give me a shout soon as you spot it."

"Sounds great," croaked Hank through a dry throat. He realized he hadn't had a bite since he'd choked down a sleeve of miniature donuts from the vending machine outside his room at Beale's Budget Inn that morning. While Hank held the plane on course, Ivar rummaged through the cooler the crew had stowed behind the seats. Hank's eyes widened as Ivar climbed back into his seat with two corned beef sandwiches. Not only had the diligent crewman been wise to provide a snack, he apparently knew the difference between a good sandwich and a great one.

The two ate well. Ivar interrupted the feast as the two-lane highway running westward towards Mesquite Creek came into view. He put the craft in a due-west heading that paralleled the highway. Since they were flying toward the descending sun and Hank wasn't equipped with decent sunglasses, Ivar said he would keep the controls. "You can't be too careful up here, Hank, even if you are living a charmed life."

Hank laughed easily as he yielded the wheel. Their conversation had covered many topics but it never touched on Ivar's recent match with Wedgy Byrne. Hank nearly burst from holding back the revelation of his suffering at that loss. "You talkin' about me? Charmed? Not hardly."

"Well, Hank, you walked away from a virtual death sentence in that crash at Normandy. *That's* charmed. Of course, you weren't flying alone...did any others perish that night?"

Three words rattled up Hank's constricted throat: "Twelve helpless boys."

Hank had deflected the questions about St. Claude a thousand times, but here in the cockpit of Ivar's plane droning securely beneath scattered clouds, he spoke of that which he had never dared voice.

"Thirteen, counting Walter Crow. I called him Old Crow...he was my co-pilot. If I had listened to him I might have put us down sooner—safer—before hitting the steeple."

"My lord, Hank," Ivar gasped, "I am truly sorry for you...for those fellows. But do you know there were over two thousand casualties during your glider assault? You are not alone in your regret, but how could those tragedies have been avoided? You boys were damn near sacrificed by being dropped in confusion into strange country in the dark. From what I know, hundreds of your comrades died from hitting nothing more than the good old French soil, not to mention trees, anti-glider poles, other gliders...and steeples.

"It's not your fault, Hank. You. Those boys. Old Crow...you're all *heroes*."

Ivar's voice was warm with understanding and the glow of camaraderie abounding in the plane's sunny cabin. "Were you with the 101st or the 82nd?"

"101st Airborne Division," replied Hank. "Troop Carrier Command I think the brass called us."

"The CG-4A...that's what you fellows flew, isn't that right?"

Hank nodded.

"You know, Hank, you fellows are a rare breed. You're the first one I've met." Ivar slipped on a pair of custom-crafted pilot's sunglasses, the earpieces disappeared beneath his sweeping white locks. To Hank his host looked both aviator and angelic, as if he could fly the perfectly behaved little aircraft straight to heaven.

"I would be honored to know more about that night, Hank. If you feel like talking…I'm all ears."

In the silence following Ivar's request there was only space for truth. Hank began with the draft letter. He covered the sketchy training in Missouri, then the fearsome rise into the dark void above the channel. He recounted the last moments of serenity as a cyclist passed below in a pool of lantern light, and the terror in Old Crow's plea to land before they reached St. Claude's Chapel. Hank described the statue's looming face, the wrenching sound of torn fabric and broken struts. His voice quavered as he spoke of the cries of his men suddenly falling, but he neglected to share the unspeakable thud of their impacts and the chaotic roar of air like the devil through his disintegrating aircraft.

Hank's story, in its reverent passage from one aviator to another, was transformed in its telling from a tragedy fraught with lingering despair into a harrowing war story. The telling carried Hank and Ivar another thirty minutes down the road toward Mesquite Creek, and into trouble.

Chapter 56

As Rama approached the putting green, he noticed Carlos Taddio sleeping in the shade of the willows. The old gaucho slouched in his cart, while wavy shadows swept his face. Momentum was pushing Rama toward the first tee with only time for a few hurried putts; otherwise he would have awakened Carlos to ask him about the painting. And he would have returned the Polaroids. But Carla was already calling the golfers and the gallery to the tee. Carlos's photos would have to wait. Rama hurried on, but before he could stow the envelope containing the snapshots back into his bag, he encountered Lee.

"I thought you'd be putting by now, not carrying the mail." Lee patted Rama on the back. "What in hell's name are you doing with that envelope?"

"It's full of photos," Rama replied reluctantly. "Of the greens. He was planning to give them to Boney, until Boney messed up his ankle."

"He?"

Rama pointed at the old man sitting in the cart across the green. "They just don't seem fair."

"I don't have a clue what you're talking about. Let's have a look." Lee thumbed through the Polaroids, pausing to examine some particularly testy putts he had once encountered.

"What do you think, Lee. Are they legal?"

"Hell yes, they're legal," Lee declared unofficially. "And damned handy. I haven't seen a good caddie yet that didn't diagram the greens. But photos in the dew…shit, why didn't I think of that?"

"Probably too dry in El Paso, amigo," Rama grinned.

"Bingo," Lee chuckled. "Ya got a sense of humor, you're loose. That's good, *amigo*."

"And about to puke," Rama confessed to nerves as he approached the stage for his showdown. Wedgy already paced the boards. Over a pounding pulse, Rama thought about Carlos and his insistence that he play "for thee children." How, Rama wondered, was this impending humiliation meant to serve children who died nineteen years ago? "Crap, whose idea was this?" he whispered to Lee.

Lee searched for an answer, but except for Boney's crazy outburst he was clueless.

—•—

An American eagle clutched a quiver of arrows in its menacing claws and looked straight up into the clear blue Texas sky, then fell to earth. Carla and Wedgy examined the silver dollar lying on the brittle turf.

"Tails. The Gypsy's honor," announced Carla before vacating the tee.

Wedgy, caddieless now, extracted a driver from his bag. He prowled the box looking for a comfortable line up the 438-yard right dogleg, a line that would avoid the harrowing bunker in its crook. Before he placed his tee, he passed intentionally close to the sidelines where Lee and Rama stood waiting.

"Just for the record, Schwain: It wasn't my idea to embarrass you in public. So what the hell are you doing out here?"

"Just playing for fun," Rama tried to lie casually. Playing for a crazy old man's mysterious purposes would have been a more forthcoming reply. Wedgy's question was better asked of Carlos Taddio.

"At least I don't have anything to lose…not like you, Byrne."

Wedgy replied with a powerful opening drive. His great expectations were rewarded with a flight that cleared the first bunker but then suffered a lousy break. As the ball bounced off a patch of iron turf and dove into a hidden pot bunker, Wedgy spat out a routine oath.

With zero fanfare but with a furious flapping of butterflies, Rama sent a mediocre drive—his first in competition—bounding down the fairway, leaving 205 yards to a slight green. Arriving at his ball sixty yards earlier than Wedgy, he had the dubious honor of executing his approach shot with the entire, lively gallery at his shoulder. His ball never became airborne but managed to stay on target, running through the dry rough to a stop just above the hole on the green's left flank. Jimmy Jim had always said that straight was half the battle.

Coming up the fairway, Lee lingered to watch Wedgy lick his chops: 145 yards from home with a good lie in a dry bunker. The hustler confidently chose a pitching wedge with the intent of artfully crafting a high-trajectory, low-spinning shot that could escape the bunker and run up the final reaches of the fairway to lightly kiss the green. He wasn't nicknamed Wedgy for nothing. But under the scrutiny of Lee, a US Open-caliber golfer who strategically lingered nearby, Wedgy fell into the trap of performing, not executing. His shot was robbed of its anticipated altitude, and so impaired bounced to a landing far short of the green's leading edge.

Three puffs of dust blew across the fairway in the wake of Wedgy's mistake. He turned to swear at his caddie for not advising a more lofted club, but as a robust expletive escaped his lips he realized he was carrying his own bag.

Lee quickly stepped forward from his perch near the bunker's right side and grabbed a rake before Wedgy regained the presence of mind to tend to his own housekeeping.

"Don't worry; I've got it," said Lee as he stepped into the sand to rake over Wedgy's tracks. "Rama can't help you today."

Wedgy watched suspiciously as his opponent's caddie completed the job and was startled when Lee addressed him in a low voice softened to remain within the bunker.

"Oh, by the way: What he's *doing* out there," Lee pointed out, "is lying twenty yards closer to the pin than you." Lee handed Wedgy the rake and stepped from the bunker in pursuit of Rama's ball.

Three strokes later Rama walked from the first green. The nervous young novice to pressure golf was thrilled to have matched his disgruntled competitor's bogey. Wedgy was considerably less than pleased to have missed an opportunity to press Rama from the opening hole, especially if there was a chance that the young Schwain really *did* harbor a decent game. Wedgy clenched his teeth and suffered the indignity of posting a five to match Rama's score.

———•———

"Like I said, you're a natural." Lee snatched Rama's putter away, then wiped the club's face with his towel just to make himself feel needed. "First hole, first tee nerves, and you still had a tap-in for bogey. You've already got the old boy thinking about those six-to-one odds." Lee slipped the putter into the bag and pulled the Night Lessons brassie.

Rama blinked in wonder as the sun glinted off the club's shiny persimmon finish. "Is that my...er, Chandler's, old club? When did you spruce her up?"

"Don't look at me. Hell, I never thought *you'd* be playing," Lee replied. "Somebody's on your side, though. What the hell, a little shine can't hurt, eh amigo...specially on this next bruiser?"

Wedgy had already hauled his clubs to the second tee and wasted no time in setting up. Nor did he waste any precious energy trying to fiddle with his competitor's mind. He reasoned the intimidating hole would speak for itself.

It did. Rama looked at the blistered sign posted at the tee box: 640 yards from today's tees. Then he looked down the long straight fairway; he could scarcely make out the flag's yellow dab against the sage and sky stretching beyond.

"Jeez, I don't remember this," gasped Rama, suddenly losing a substantial quantity of the confidence he carried from the first hole. He remembered how he had once watched from Melyssa's refreshment cart as a younger Lee and his sickened caddie scrambled miserably to keep up with Boney and Mirage, back when it was a short par four.

"No, I guess you wouldn't," Lee agreed. "This hole used to be the old airstrip that ran alongside the course."

The neglected airstrip hadn't seen a plane or an FAA inspector in ages. A couple of years earlier Carla had finally given up on the notion that any Augusta glitterati would ever drop in for juleps again. Those days had passed with Chandler. She had routed the course back through the airstrip and voilà: a rangy par five with the distinction of being the longest in the state—a dubious honor when a golfer was struggling against a headwind or a hangover.

Lee lowered his voice out of respect for Wedgy, who was taking his final stance. "So much for good course design, eh?" he whispered. "At least the wind is with us. You can get there in three, Rama...one stroke at a time." He placed the brassie in his young player's reluctant hands. "Am I right?"

"Yeah...right," said Rama absently, but the sensation of the grip in his palms snapped him back to form. He noticed a new suppleness in the old leather. "What did you do...?"

"Slept with her," replied Lee. "A sweaty night in the old sack with yours truly has put new life in many a grip."

Rama frowned at Lee, uncertain if he were falling prey to a tale or receiving a warped but worthy club maintenance tip. Lee laughed at Rama's innocence.

The laughter was too loud for Wedgy's liking. He backed away from his ball and glared at Lee. The tee box fell silent as he mumbled a few final filthy swing thoughts and launched a low, running drive that made a mockery of the hole's dimensions. It appeared the Gypsy Hustler was shaking off the first bogey.

Wedgy strode from the stage like Bob Hope at Bing's clambake, a Frank Sinatra tune on his lips. He interrupted the first chorus of "All I Need Is the Girl" with a sneer aimed at Lee, who only moments earlier had intimidated him in the bunker.

"Now don't make me report any poor etiquette to the USGA, eh Mr. Trujillo? It could cost you if you're thinking about going pro."

The mental jousting between Lee and Wedgy was not entirely lost upon Rama, but it did nothing to calm him into allowing his swing to unfold naturally. Refreshed grip or not, he still only managed a strangled takeaway and an ineffective lunge. His ball sputtered to rest only halfway to Wedgy's heroic drive.

"Sorry," Rama said as he handed Lee the club.

"Sorry...for what? It's only one shot, my friend, only one." Lee slapped Rama on the shoulder. "Hey amigo, there are few places in golf for doubt, but there is *no* place for guilt."

Rama couldn't help but smile as he saw the trademark Trujillo grin working its magic. "It's a crippling damn emotion. I should know...I was raised a Catholic."

The sum total of Lee's advice upon arriving at the ball's disappointing position was a breezy homily about having all the time and all the space he needed. The reference to space was accurate: Rama could barely make out the flag fluttering on its bamboo pole. But time was another matter. With a gallery gathering on every shot, he would always feel a sense of urgency. He had heard how the great players had turned the scrutiny of the crowd into a positive force by playing to show off their skills, but his skill was in helping *others* play well. Rama had never glimpsed how or why.

But now, no matter how convoluted his entrance into the game had been, he was a golfer. And like all golfers, he needed help. To a young man standing above his ball with a 3-wood scavenged from a waste can of lost clubs, the how or why of things seemed too cerebral a question. One swing at a time, he recalled. The threadbare old advice seemed appropriate today. The imponderable questions could be saved for another time. Rama's eyes strained ahead. No point in forcing this, he thought; the par five that had once been an airstrip was wide, flat, and forgiving.

Rama did not remember the swing that followed or recall seeing one of his 3-wood shots ever sail so far, but here he was: The recipient of the very gift that had delighted so many others in his company.

"Muy bueno," smiled Lee. "No guilt in that blast."

Wedgy felt a collegial sense of appreciation for Rama's beautifully struck ball. Sincere words of praise begun to form on his lips, but upon recognition of such magnanimous emotions, he spat the unspoken words away like a clot. In his sullen mind there was no room for the hippy-dippy sort of sensitivity that his son might have embraced—not when there were four figures on the line.

Wedgy plunged silently up the fairway to play from his superior position. Before the gallery could assemble and distract him, he pulled his 3-wood and fired a two-hundred-plus shot up the airstrip. A third stroke would, and did, put him on the green in three.

Rama looked troubled. Even after his solid second shot, the remaining yardage was more than any one club could produce. Lee advised a middle iron lay-up to a safe position for a high-percentage pitching wedge to the green, but Rama felt he could reproduce the previous stroke and be within a chip of the cup. He retained the 3-wood, but this time *trying* got the better of him. Feel and touch that had so naturally freed the previous swing now dodged away. The stiff stroke that followed nearly cast the club from his hands and pulled the ball into the brush left of the fairway. A dispiriting search eventually located his ball in the clutches of an impenetrable fist of cactus from which there was no escape except to declare an unplayable lie. He dropped a new ball and played his fifth shot, now 140 yards from the pin.

"Well, you get to hit iron to the green after all," kidded Lee in hopes that Rama would learn fast. "That cactus should be a little lesson in playing the odds. Comprende?"

Rama blushed. Although mortified, he remained receptive to the magic and hoisted a high, graceful shot that flew to a perch on the upper side of the green. The flight was as gorgeous as its resulting lie was treacherous. He now faced a long, slippery downhill putt.

"Holy shit," Lee groaned. Even from their position in the fairway he could see its difficulty. "We best be checking those photos to figure the break on that crazy putt."

With his ball lying on the green in three, Wedgy moved firmly into his comfort zone. He watched his young competitor struggling to read conflicting signals from the green's tricky surface.

"Guess that mojo just don't work on you, eh, Rama? How 'bout ten dollars for a two-putt or better just in case you get lucky?"

Rama scowled. He knew better than to get sucked into Wedgy's side games. Without a word he turned his attention back to the upcoming putt.

Lee examined a Polaroid of the green. He could see that Wedgy faced a cross-slope putt from two-thirds the distance of Rama's downhill roll. The Gypsy Hustler appeared likely to win the hole, but not necessarily the two-putt.

"I'll take that bet," Lee said.

"You've got a lot more guts than your boy here," Wedgy beamed in reply.

Lee suddenly feared he had created a monster by putting Wedgy back into his wagering element.

The golfers stalked their putts like prey, Rama more out of show than out of know-how. As he finally squatted behind his ball and sighted down the confounding slope, Lee fell in behind him. "It starts to run a little right before it straightens out and speeds up…so find a spot about six feet out and aim just above that. Easy does it."

Rama had his doubts. "It looks straighter down to me."

"Trust me, Rama. Remember that cactus you just dropped from?"

"I know. Sorry, but I just don't see it…you sure?"

"Rama, you don't have to sink it. I've got ten bucks on a nice lazy lag up to the hole then a tap-in, so watch your speed." Lee hoped that pictures didn't lie.

Rama had passed the photos off as a well-intentioned but improper gesture intended for Boney. He crouched over his ball, Arnold Palmer-style, as the gallery murmured like dry wind through the mesquite. He imagined a putt rolling along the line Lee had suggested, but he had his doubts. This putt would have to be taken on faith.

The gallery gasped as Rama's putt threatened the cup but ran past the hole, missing the mark by two inches and coming to rest only two feet away.

"Clean it up," barked Wedgy in disgust. Now he would have to two-putt just to save his own bet. After Rama tapped in for a disappointing seven, Wedgy launched his attempt. The ball never climbed high enough and his putt dropped well below the hole. He followed that with a fusillade of angry references to unnatural sexual acts and then a solid ten-foot rap back up the slope, only to be thwarted by a lip-out.

Lee was now ten bucks richer and Wedgy still had to be careful not to four-putt lest he be anchored early in the round with a leaden seven. He composed himself quickly, as only a man who had become accustomed to the plunges from anger's searing heat to golf's icy concentration could. After two holes fraught with niggling difficulty, an irritated but well-tempered Wedgy stood only one stroke ahead of Rama's twelve.

"Not that I don't trust you, Wallace," said Lee, assuming the duties of gamesmanship for his young player, "but if we could settle up now before we forget..."

Wedgy slapped a rude grasshopper from his cap. "You'll get yours when I'm through with Rama."

"We'll see," replied Lee with utter lack of concern for the ten bucks. As far as he was concerned, Wedgy had already paid his debt in the streak of frustration that hopefully had distracted him from the business at hand.

Wedgy had anticipated an easy round on a balmy autumn afternoon. Even though the trace of evidence that Rama might have been working on his game since they had been on the road together suggested the possibility that Rama could actually be a challenge, Wedgy really had not expected Rama to do more than embarrass himself. He almost blushed at the thought of taking Boney's six thousand dollars so easily—borderline larceny, he thought.

Losing the two-putt bet to Lee seemed to bring the errant pieces of Wedgy's game back together. His stony concentration and alarming silence on the next five holes were as much a testament to his respect for a game that might be disguised beneath Rama's unpolished surface as to the recurring fear that age could catch up with him and dash his round at any moment. He imagined that he could lose his swing in one snap of the Devil's fingers, and like the outfielder in *Damn Yankees*, he might stumble onto the warning track, suddenly, unquestionably over the hill while in pitiful pursuit of that unreachable fly ball.

Chapter 57

By the seventh hole, Wedgy's lead had grown to a four-stroke advantage. The effort to increase the margin had taken some grind out of the old grinder, but as Wedgy stepped to the eighth tee—a par three—his moxie returned like salt water to a well.

"Seven over par after seven holes, that's *bogey*, kid. Not bad…but probably keep you out of the Hall of Fame."

Wedgy was relieved that the prodigy he had conjured Rama to be in the most insecure corners of his mind was really just a mediocre player. He was painfully aware that his own one-over score was mediocre as well, yet he faced the eighth hole with confidence that his game was back in hand. Wedgy was clearly back in his mouthy, malevolent element, and his competitive spirit had been rekindled. He confronted Rama with another wager: Closest to the pin, on what he called a little old par three.

Rama regarded Wedgy with disbelief. "One ninety five into the wind, over that cactus, and with nothing but rocks around the green isn't exactly a 'little old' par three. Count me out."

"Christ, Schwain, if you haven't got the gonads for a side bet, the least I can do is get my money back from your caddie. Tell him I'll go double or nothing."

Rama turned to Lee whose money Wedgy was proposing to double. "You don't mind keeping your money on this one, do you, Mr. Trujillo?"

If Lee was even a little concerned about Rama's four-stroke deficit, he didn't show it. "No, Rama, that ten bucks is going to buy us both a damn nice victory dinner. I'm not risking it, or your confidence, over this prickly hole."

Wedgy bristled. "For God's sake, Trujillo, how do you think you're gonna get anywhere on the tour with that cowardly attitude?"

Lee's smile slipped from his face. His blood boiled easily at the suggestion of cowardice. "When the time comes, *Gypsy*, I can throw my money down with the best of 'em. If I was on your bag, I'd tell you to pay more attention to the hole and less to your competitor's caddie…this hombre can bite."

Wedgy faced the troublesome par three uncertain if the hombre in question was Rama or the hole. There was no doubt that the hole demanded attention. Like an Alistair McKenzie design, its green was shallow, forcing the puzzle to be best unlocked with a high fade to the right even though its distance put less lofted clubs in most players' hands. The bold might attempt to hoist a 5-iron, but Chandler Stone, being far less wicked than his hole indicated, had given the timid and less accomplished an alternative. A smudge of fairway blossomed to the right of the green providing a small, safe harbor from rock and spine. The cactus still had to be confronted and conquered, but even if the player couldn't muster the finesse to shape a shot to hold the green, he could still score par from the harbor with a good chip and a putt.

Wedgy discarded the notion of settling for par. With his challenge to Lee's courage still fresh and the assessment of his own powers tinted by vanity, he drew his mid-iron and attempted the cut shot. All eyes watched the valiant ball rise, stall, and plunge into the cactus.

In the ensuing hush, two voices rang out. The first was Carla's: "For those of you unfamiliar with Mesquite Creek, there is a drop area yonder," she declared without pity. The second voice was Rama's: "4-wood to bail out?" he asked Lee.

"A very *soft* four." Lee backed away nodding his approval.

Carla's lost husband had posed an unambiguous question of the player's ability, and his hole demanded an honest answer. When the moment of truth came, Rama swung from what he thought was a three-quarter back swing, but his fear of a prickly fate depressed a biomechanical throttle that over-powered his platonic intentions. The excessive stroke that resulted put his ball on a trajectory destined for a rocky collision beyond the hole.

"A tad strong," quipped Lee as he followed the ball's flight.

In addition to skill and justice, luck sometimes holds equal sway over the maddening game. The luck was that Rama's ball bounced high and *backward* to fall improbably on the green. The injustice was that it took three putts to get in the hole—three putts executed under the burden of having just witnessed Wedgy's chip from the drop area skip across the fringe and roll down the green with devastating certainty into the cup for par. To Rama, the rattle of the flagstick sounded like a slap in the face of reason.

"Seems kinda unfair don't it, amigo?" Lee asked as he took the putter from Rama's flaccid hands. He recognized that such a stroke of injustice could easily destroy a player.

"Unfair will kill you, Rama...stop thinking about what's just or unjust. Your opponent gets a few free passes, and before you know it you start thinking it's divine retribution. If you believe that, then you've got yourself playing against God Almighty, and sure as shit...he's always on the *other* guy's side.

"Rama, I've seen perfectly decent golfers collapse because they really believed it just wasn't meant to be, that they were up against something bigger than them, and that made it okay to give up. Well, my friend, they are partly right: We are all up against a foolish, impossible game, and it truly is bigger than us. Of course we fall short or we'd all be shooting in the fifties. But if falling short of that standard is reason to give up, Christ, we shouldn't even tee it up."

Lee looked into Rama's face searching for a spark of hope—seeking to make his point. "Listen Schwain, you will fuck up…and you will get some breaks, but don't ever talk or think about unfairness. That's a slippery damned slope for a golfer."

Rama knew Lee was right. He had seen Wedgy maneuver weaker players into one no-win situation after another until they collapsed in a cascade of self-pity. They even smiled as the phrase "just not my day" slipped from their lips. Rama was abundantly aware that he was now down five strokes and Wedgy was approaching the tee with an air of inevitability. He knew the game would now be played across the folding terrain of his cerebrum as surely as it would across the brittle turf of Carla Stone's unforgiving course.

—•—

The ninth fairway curled left around a grove of scrawny oak trees. A high drive could carry them and strip the short par five of its defenses. Wedgy, already protecting a five-stroke lead, didn't feel the need to gamble with the trees, but he did feel the need to talk.

"Don't mean to bother you again, Lee," said Wedgy, obsequious to the point of puking. "You were right to pass on that last bet. Looks like your boy can find a way to lose a hole even *with* a couple of lucky breaks."

Lee tipped his head close to Rama's as they stood watching the old hustler prepare for his shot. "And they say I talk a lot."

As Wedgy resumed his pre-shot routine, Lee watched every nuance of the Gypsy Hustler's address.

"He's playing it smart," Lee whispered. "Check his stance. He's set up for a safe shot right up the heart of the fairway…could be he's not as confident as he lets on."

Suddenly Rama felt like gambling. "Okay, Byrne, make it twenty bucks… just this hole."

"That's my boy," replied Wedgy. He reshuffled his feet and changed his aim from the safe shot up the fairway, to one flirting with the trees along the left side in hopes of negotiating a cut shot from left to right. But before he could pull the trigger, a couple of grasshoppers fluttered to the turf near his ball. Wedgy stepped from his stance to crush the offending insects with his driver, then readdressed the ball. The momentary lapse of concentration altered his swing sufficiently that it failed to get his ball airborne. He watched helplessly as the white speck burrowed into the oaks.

Rama was already at Wedgy's heels, pressing the aggravated golfer to collect his tee and yield the tee box—a rude tactic he had learned from Wedgy himself. The old hustler left quietly, and a reenergized Rama struck a decent drive into the very heart of the fairway. He turned back from the tee wearing a smug grin as Lee rushed up to take his club.

"Nice, very nice. But don't get too cocky."

Wedgy, taking a leaf from Arnold Palmer's scrambling book, drilled an impressive recovery from beneath the oak's menacing branches that seconds earlier had appeared to confine him to nothing more than a sideways bump to the fairway. His dandelion duster whistled to within pitching range of the green.

Rama scrambled to trade his short-lived conceit for concentration, and to neutralize Wedgy's sudden advantage, but his head jumped up in anticipation of another stellar shot. He managed only a thin, ineffective stroke.

The scramble continued: Wedgy wielded his namesake club with legendary mastery once again to place his third shot fourteen feet below the hole. And Rama, after missing the green on his third, managed to find the green on his fourth, but his ball lay on the high side, sixteen feet from the pin.

Wedgy putt first and walked away with a birdie and Rama's bet—and, he hoped, with Rama's last gasp of confidence.

Rama stared down the terrifying putt. A miss would likely roll off the green and ensure another two strokes to get home in a fatal seven. He stood up straight and took a long slow breath. His vision swept the peaceful green fairways, the white clubhouse, and the red crags beyond. The willows swayed above the putting green where Carlos, still seated on Niña's vinyl seat, appeared to be rapt at the proceedings.

Rama remembered Carlos's Polaroids still tucked somewhere in Lee's bag. If he ever needed help reading a putt it was now. He imagined a line etched in dew, sweeping safely to the cup. How easy might it be to follow such a path, but here on a sunny, late summer afternoon, the break would defy detection. With nothing more than instinct, Rama took aim.

From his place at the flag, Lee disapproved of Rama's direction. He cleared his throat like a cannon to stop the action. He dropped the flagstick and walked up the green to counsel his man. "Looks like you're playing a lot of break here, amigo. You're liable to miss high." He pulled the photos from his hip pocket to illustrate his point, but Rama waved them away.

"No, they're just not fair. Pull the flag…I've got this one read, Lee. Believe me."

Lee complied, but glanced at the photo just as Rama took his putt. Sure enough, the ball trickled along the higher curving path as the Polaroid depicted. The ball was moving left and picking up velocity when the hole swallowed it up for a par. His five felt like a victory at the US Open, even though he had lost the hole to Wedgy's four. Rama was down by six strokes going into the turn.

———•———

Chandler Stone had framed the turn with back-to-back par fives: number nine in and number ten back out. Depending on the wind, one hole could always be reached in three strokes while the other would invariably put up a serious tussle.

Wedgy retained the honors from the previous hole, but he mounted the tenth tee box well aware of the importance in the pivotal putt Rama had just sunk. The young man had just brushed aside the heaviest pressure of the match. Too often Wedgy had seen the shape of a game warp under the force of a single stroke. He faced the tenth knowing *his* recovery from the oaks was pure luck. Even after his birdie he couldn't shake the hiccup on the ninth tee from his mind. Grasshoppers were no excuse for losing concentration, and the seed of doubt planted in that off-balance stroke could easily bloom into a crop of poor shots, just as Rama's confident putt could bring him more good fortune.

The first signs of restless afternoon winds arrived as Wedgy, still standing at the tee, pondered the mercurial nature of confidence. The leaves of the sycamores alternately flashed their leaves' bright undersides and dark green tops in a complex code: dark, short-bright, long-dark, long-bright. The wind will be a factor, they signaled. Then, as if in reply a dust devil picked a cloud of grit from a broad waste area that yawned beside the fairway. The ghostly apparition whirled its way toward the hole and for a moment blew in favor of the player—just as Chandler had planned so long ago.

Wedgy didn't wait for the devil to play through and hastily fired a fine drive into a solid position from which he might have a bona fide try at hitting the green on his next shot. An eagle was certainly in the Gypsy's equation.

Lee and Rama agreed that they would be satisfied with three shots to the green no matter what Wedgy did, so the old Night Lessons brassie stayed in the bag in favor of a 4-iron. Rama's second shot—this time with a comfortable 5-iron—delivered him to a lie just short of a finger of unplayable wasteland that intruded into the fairway's heart. Rama faced a 139-yard 9-iron over the waste to an easy green and another great chance at par or better.

Wedgy watched his opponent's careful lay-up with respect and growing fear of Rama's emerging ability. The old hustler looked at his target: 200 yards to a large green with ample room to miss long—a prime chance to deliver a near-fatal blow to his troublesome ex-caddie's chances. A birdie was a reasonable outcome here, which would elevate his lead from six to eight, with only eight more holes.

Wedgy strangled the urge to wish Rama *sayonara*. Such a gesture would be far too juvenile, so he turned his attention to gripping the 4-wood and taking dead aim on a yucca that stood somewhere out of range but precisely in line with the green's left flank. With a little natural fade and a two-putt, Wedgy could begin to focus on collecting the absurd wager that Boney had recklessly placed on Rama Schwain.

Wedgy might have been better served by his intellect had he gauged the air's turbulence between the tee and the green with the same intensity with which he had pictured the forthcoming financial bonanza. The neurons employed in the calculation of his anticipated winnings might have otherwise considered the wind's effect on a lofted shot, but oblivious to the tempestuous hazard, Wedgy became its victim. He watched in dismay as his ball was swatted from the sky to an unknown and never-discovered crash landing in the intruding waste area.

"Sort of like that little par three down in Augusta," Lee explained to Rama in a voice just loud enough to be overheard by the sulking Wedgy Byrne. "Yes sir, that windy little hole can just about ruin a round if you don't pay attention." Lee's brown eyes strayed to Wedgy's for confirmation that such sarcasm wasn't cast on the waters in vain. Wedgy's upraised middle finger confirmed it wasn't.

Rama's lay-up paid off. He pitched his third shot onto the green, then relaxed for five minutes as Wedgy attempted to find his ball in the waste area. When Carla signaled time's up, Wedgy paced angrily back up the fairway to play his fourth shot. He reached the green in four and guessed he'd make up at least one of the lost strokes with his putter but found that lost ground gone forever as Rama one-putt for a birdie. Wedgy's intended coup de grâce never materialized, and in one hole his lead fell from an expected eight-stroke Himalayan summit to a surmountable four-stroke mogul.

Wedgy's neurons flashed again: Thirty-six thousand dollars at risk here, they warned. And although it was a pleasant, dry afternoon, he began to feel damp in very private places.

Rama felt a blush of promise. Maybe it was the spirit of Dickey Stone urging him to conquer the course by mastering his confidence. Maybe this was the path to achieving the mystical goals of which Carlos had so cryptically spoken. Whatever it was, he sensed something fateful in the air.

Chapter 58

"**R**ebecca, it wasn't meant to end like this. It's just not fair," Ivar pleaded. "This can be fixed…I have the money."

"No, it's alright, dear. Just keep an eye on the camellias…they should be beautiful come spring." Rebecca Guidance smiled as she drifted from the moorings of the boathouse at Boca Grande. The tide would gently pull her into the gulf and soon she would just disappear somewhere out beyond the zinc dredge.

She sat comfortably in the dingy, turning away from her husband of forty-seven years to resume her assault on the *New York Times* crossword puzzle. Ivar was left on the dock's lonely planks. His wealth and his long tenure as her loving companion were of no further value.

Without looking up from her newspaper, she called across the growing divide: "Sweetheart, do you know a four-letter word for selfless affection or holy affinity?"

Ivar was frantic.

"Rebecca…the motor has an electric starter now. You don't have to pull that cord anymore; just push the button. It's easy. Come back…please," he begged the woman floating far out of reach to bring the little boat to dock.

"We'll go out for crab cakes tonight," he cried helplessly.

Crab cakes and cold beer were his wife's favorite. Maybe she could delay eternity for one more good meal together. But Rebecca drifted on.

A sad, silent minute passed before her voice drifted back across the silver water for the last time. "And sweetie, the word begins with *L*."

—•—

Ivar snorted twice before bolting partway back to consciousness. The old gentleman remained lost on the cusp between reality and dream for a few dizzy moments when the answer came into focus.

"It's love…L.O.V.E.," he called to the spirit of his dear Rebecca, but his words were swallowed in the drone of the Cessna's twin props.

Hank Schwain was startled at Ivar's outburst but relieved that his host—and pilot—was awake. Although Ivar had just begun to snore, Hank wondered how long he had been dozing.

So did Ivar. He had heard about pilots sleeping beyond the point of no return and was relieved that he had awakened in time—just barely in time. He was embarrassed that he had slept at all, but it had been a long and fatiguing couple of days with the whole Doris Schwain episode. With the plane's engines synchronized to hypnotic perfection and with a belly full of corned beef, sleep had come too easily.

The *L* word reverberated in his mind, and a pang of loneliness stabbed at his heart. He would be thankful when he could really sleep.

"Can you take her for a couple of minutes, Hank?"

Ivar consulted his chart. He glanced anxiously at the instruments and peered down at the highway streaming westward far below. "We're good. Right on course...probably just a little east of Mesquite Creek." Ivar appeared confident but briskly waved Hank back off the wheel and reclaimed the controls, immediately nosing the aircraft downward. At 1,000 feet he leveled off on a course paralleling the highway one-quarter mile to the north in order to leave clearance for any freelance fliers who might be navigating directly above the road. From their vantage Hank and Ivar could pick out fence posts and determine the makes of cars rolling along the highway below.

Ivar tried to relax. "This is the juicy part, Hank. There are no directional signals in or around Mesquite Creek. In fact, we are out of range of the nearest VOR beacon up in Brownwood so we'll be flying right along the road until we see our landmark. Keep your eyes peeled for their water tower. Soon as we spot it we will fly a little reconnaissance over Mesquite's airfield. If we don't like what we see, we'll ascend to 3,500 and fly due north until we pick up a heading on our alternate strip in Abilene...about thirty minutes out and well within our range. If push comes to shove and we get into a fuel situation, we've always got the strips at Brady and Brownwood."

"Ten-four," replied Hank, confident that his pilot had it right. "I'm all eyes."

Ivar peered anxiously at the highway below. The hot asphalt picked up the low rays of the sun, reflecting like a dazzling ribbon sweeping to the west. He shivered in silence, chilled at the consequences had he slept a few minutes longer. Above the nearly featureless land stretching before them and without a navigational signal, it would have taken some dead reckoning just to approximate their position if he had over-flown their destination.

"Your son told me you and he have been out this way before, is that right?" Ivar watched Hank's face carefully for any nuance of doubt in his reply.

Hank nodded as he watched a small aircraft passing below and to his left—clearly not a danger.

"Do you remember a spherical water tower?" asked Ivar. "'Unusual markings,' it says here on the chart."

Hank drew his mind back from the panorama below and searched his memory. "Unusual markings, huh? That would probably be the big golf ball they rigged up alongside the highway...must have been eighty feet tall. Might have been a water tower once. It'll get your attention, that's for sure. It got ours that day."

"Just to be absolutely certain, Hank. You didn't see your big golf ball while I was napping? You would have told me, yes?" asked Ivar. A good pilot couldn't be too thorough.

"Oh, shit yeah, I would have told you. I've been watching every inch ever since we joined up with the highway. We're not there yet," Hank replied confidently.

Ten minutes crawled past as Ivar ran the numbers in his weary mind. No matter how he figured it—airspeed, groundspeed, elapsed time, and distance— he was certain that something was amiss. The tower should be, or should have been, clearly in sight by now, but only a trio of radio antennae stabbed at the hazy afternoon sky.

"Now, Hank, you said the tower was on the left side of the highway when you were westbound, correct?" Ivar's voice had taken on a very business-like timbre. "And it looked like...?"

"Like I said, a golf ball...on a tee," recalled Hank. "Had dimples painted on it as I remember. Is there a problem?"

Ivar could only be direct. "Only that we should have already spotted it. Makes me wonder about the accuracy of the chart."

The exhausted old fellow was speaking calmly but was gathering himself to face a possible crisis. Ivar was certain he had not snoozed past the landmark, but numbers indicated they somehow had over-flown the charted position of the tower. And worse, by flying low and north of the highway they had missed seeing any glimpse of the alleged golf course and its private airstrip through the folds in the bluffs that sheltered Mesquite Creek down in its arroyo.

Ivar's plan allowed fuel to fly to Mesquite Creek with reserve to hop over to Abilene to refuel in case fuel wasn't on hand at Mesquite or if there were an emergency. But if they were flying beyond Mesquite, as Ivar suspected, the additional flight time was consuming the reserve. He realized that if he didn't spot the great ball or Mesquite Creek's airstrip soon, he would have to abandon the planned landing and head to Abilene with some urgency.

He scrutinized Hank's safety belts. "Take up the slack there, my friend."

His fuel calculations were a secret, but his concern was not. "I am dropping to five hundred feet and doubling back for a closer look along the south side of the highway. Remember, we're eastbound now, look sharp on your right for anything you recognize."

Hank guessed turning back was a bad sign.

Ivar put the plane in a steep bank and nudged the wheel forward. The highway wheeled around 180 degrees and rushed up to meet them. The window on a safe landing at his back-up destinations would soon begin slipping closed; they couldn't search for Mesquite Creek for long.

"Any of this look familiar?" Ivar felt dampness collect under his headset. He waited a few interminable moments for Hank to declare a visual on the phantom water tower but there was no answer, only the droning of the engines and Hank's heavy breathing. With every breath, the margin of safety for reaching Abilene diminished.

Ivar slammed his fist on the console.

"That's enough of this goose chase," he barked as he pulled the wheel back to commence a ninety-degree turn across the hostile wastelands to the north. "At least I know where Abilene is."

Hank noticed the color drain from Ivar's face as the old gentleman pulled the plane up into a left turn. A navigational oversight and exhaustion were taking its toll.

"Goddamn it, someone is going to hear about these worthless charts!" It was the first time Hank had ever heard Ivar curse, and it was the last time Hank would hear that voice on this flight.

Ivar's hands suddenly went slack and slipped from the wheel. His chin dropped down to his chest.

"Ivar! Fuck…what's wrong?" But with the plane banking up and left Hank couldn't wait for an answer. He grabbed the wheel and pushed it forward instinctively to slow the plane's ascent, then he gingerly rotated the wheel clockwise to bring the highway—his only reference point—back beneath them.

"Ivar…are you with me?" Hank watched for a reaction. None. He thought he saw the old fellow's chest rise slightly, but he dared not take his eyes off the earth below for long.

Hank's mind clogged with thoughts, but oddly, not all of them fearful. Although he had been thrust into an unforgiving emergency he felt a curious relief, as if he had been presented with a clear opportunity to succeed or fail. For once in Hank's life there was no further room or time to second-guess his options, to calculate the odds, or to hedge his bets. And judging by the treacherous rocky terrain that loomed below, failure appeared final. The chance to get his feet back on the ground and to repay those whom he owed so dearly was a welcome risk, regardless of the odds stacked against him and his unconscious pilot.

He glanced at Ivar again to see if the old fellow wasn't just testing his reaction to an in-flight crisis. He half expected Ivar to resume his command, but the pale cast of the gentleman's skin and his head bobbing with the aircraft's every bump were unnerving. If this were a test, failure would be absolute.

A surge of confidence washed over Hank. "I'll get you home, Ivar," he called above the droning engines with hope that his resolve was more substantial than adrenal.

Hank had brought the plane around successfully, and that was a start. Flying level and eastbound, directly above the highway, he watched the ground slide below them. The giant golf ball was still nowhere in sight. They were still lost. He focused on a moment during the drive he and Rama had shared along this highway back in 1959: The locusts smearing his windshield, and Rama flicking the door lock up and down, as he waited for their car to stop so he could take a leak somewhere along road below.

It had been the ball that diverted them from the highway and down that winding drive to Mesquite Creek. He almost smiled at the memory, but doubts were building like a furious black cloud as nothing familiar came into view. Perhaps they were damned. Perhaps his redemption from gambling and from guilt at the loss of the boys above St. Claude was only to be granted in his final hour.

Hank's vision of damnation suddenly vanished with a flash of recognition of an unexpected object passing below! His heart leapt gratefully as his eyes fixed on an old thresher parked along a gravel road winding to the south. He had hardly noticed the rusty hulk on that day, but now, even from 500 feet it was familiar. He was certain that betting on this landmark would pay off.

"Almost home. Hang on Ivar." Hank pulled Ivar's harness taught.

With no sign of the giant ball, Hank would take his chances with the thresher. He looked to the south and saw the drive disappear down into the folds of an arroyo. This was the place. It was time to act.

Hank didn't know the range of Ivar's plane, or how to navigate to Abilene. He wasn't even sure how to use the radio, but he knew he would attempt to wrestle this plane down to a walk-away landing on Mesquite Creek's abandoned airstrip while he had some fuel and control. The alternative would be surrender to paralysis and deal with mother earth on her harsh terms when she inevitably came to meet him.

Hank wasted no time in banking the plane to the south and down the arroyo.

—•—

"You ain't no stunt pilot! That's too much stick, Ramblin' man...too much nose."

Marcile Gold's voice rang in Hank's mind. She had harped on his heavy hand during their glide together over Aero Meadows. With a miraculously restrained touch Hank eased the nose back up to avoid the crags of the arroyo. The plane reacted favorably; chalk one up for Marcile, thought Hank. A new surge of adrenalin laced with hope jolted him as the sheltering red bluffs receded and the welcoming greens of Mesquite Creek's Golf Course opened before him. The sun twinkled off the tops of a hundred pickup trucks and dusty cars parked willy-nilly beside the clubhouse, and he noticed the unmistakable shape of the widow's watch rising above the clubhouse's green roof.

Hank raised a thumb in victory. "Found it, Ives."

Ivar had said they would give the airstrip the once-over before committing to a landing and proceed to Abilene if he didn't like what they saw. Hank realized that the empty forbidding lands stretching north didn't offer a novice pilot that option; one way or another Mesquite Creek would be the end of the line.

Hank's turn from the highway brought him around to the southwest and eventually back across the golf course. Its population of cottonwoods, oaks, and pepper trees cast long shadows across the fairways in the afternoon's hazy light. Hank looked for the promised airstrip but saw nothing except fairways and greens.

"Son of a..." he swore. This was one time when a man could do without fairways and greens. He had seen the old strip with his own eyes eight years ago, but then again he had also seen the giant damned golf ball. He continued across the course at 500 feet. The second hole out from the clubhouse was unusually long and straight, and judging by the snapping of the flag, ran directly into the wind.

Hank recognized the lay of the land below. "Jesus, that's our airstrip. It's part of the damned golf course now!"

Beneath them stretched the remains of the old runway. Except for a fairway bunker and a raised green, the fairway was the only long, level expanse on which he had a prayer of landing—assuming the turf was firm and the neighboring pepper trees kept to themselves. Hank thought about landing back up on the two-lane highway, but the encroaching telephone poles, eighteen-wheel oil tankers, and Burma Shave signs seemed more hostile than the golf course.

Down here an emergency landing might irritate a few duffers, but this place was a soft green bird in a hard, anxious hand.

—•—

Carlos stirred from a shallow dream. It was not the rising and falling of warm sunlight through wavering willow shadows that woke him. He turned his head to the north and listened. It was unusual to hear aircraft in the vicinity of Mesquite Creek. It had been many years since the last of Chandler's friends from Georgia had soared to and from what had once been a firm turf airstrip. Carlos held his breath. He heard one now.

It was not Carlos's inclination to ever discount coincidence, irony was the province of signs; so it was that with the distant sound of airborne engines he pondered what could be the meaning of an approaching aircraft in the same hour that Rama would finally return to the sixteenth green to satisfy the vision of the Stone Children's return.

After eight years, the dominoes of life had fallen into place to bring the souls of Dickey and Glendora back to their place of ascendance. He feared any event that might now interrupt the progress of Rama and Wedgy toward the sixteenth's charmed green. The old gaucho knew that further intervention in the affairs of these players was beyond him. Niña's engine turned over with a huff of protest as Carlos guided the cart to the highest vantage on the course, the promontory above the sixteenth tee. If there was a threat in the approaching aircraft, Carlos wanted to confront it on that magical tee.

— • —

By the tenth hole Boney Carlisle had seen enough. Rama was down six strokes and Wedgy appeared alive with piss and vinegar. Boney thought about the six-thousand-dollar bet he should be playing for and the troubling fact that there was nothing in Wedgy's game he couldn't have bested. What the hell had happened? The charm by which Carlos had bewitched him into abandoning Lee's plan for the match now seemed like a foolish dream.

Boney reminded himself that his phony twisted ankle was real to the crowd and that he had better remember to continue playing the cripple until he was finally back in his car and roaring out of Mesquite Creek in disgrace. But Rama's two-stoke rally on number ten put a stop to what had been Wedgy's irresistible advantage, and it derailed Boney's desire to escape to his car. After eleven, twelve, and thirteen, Wedgy still guarded a five-stroke lead with five holes to play, but Boney believed Rama still had a fighting chance. The car would have to wait.

Boney hobbled along to join the anxious gallery and watched as Rama took the fourteenth tee, to the annoying accompaniment of a low-flying aircraft.

— • —

Wedgy's thoughts of a crushing blow to Rama's competitive heart had been abruptly swept aside by Rama's crucial birdie at number ten. But Wedgy still nursed the desire to scorch the earth under Rama's feet rather than merely outplay him. He would bury Rama on the course and inter any evidence that he, a pragmatic, seasoned competitor, had ever considered the absurd notion that his game could ever have risen on the fairy wings of some sort of voodoo like the Caddie's Gift.

Walking from the thirteenth tee, Wedgy renounced the very magic that had buoyed his game all summer and had delivered another lucrative season unwarranted by his eroding skills.

Before Wedgy even found the green on the fourteenth hole, he was in jeopardy of losing a stroke to Rama. He faced a short chip across a receding green while Rama lay only ten feet below the hole. But Rama would have to work to capitalize on his advantage. His putt would have to follow a line along the crest of a barely perceptible ridge to the hole; off-line either way would send the ball far from any good chance for a two-putt par. Rama, like most reasonable folks, was happy just to be on the green in regulation. Wedgy choked back a common euphemism for sexual intercourse as he solemnly trod the path to the green where he discovered he had missed on the high side.

The chip down to a green that slopes away is one of golf's must dreaded shots. Without a caddie, and eager for a scapegoat, Wedgy looked with angry eyes to the aircraft whose engines had been disturbing his concentration for the last minute. The plane appeared as it banked in a wide, wobbling arc above the course before disappearing again behind the red bluffs.

"Sons of barnstorming bitches," cursed Wedgy. "What in hell do they think they're doing?"

As the gallery quickly assembled around the green, Rama realized he had a chance to close the gap to striking distance. He lay about five paces closer to the hole than Wedgy's position on the fringe. The difference was indisputable, but in a voice borrowed from a summer of watching the old hustler needle his victims into mental errors, Rama observed, "Looks like you're away." The phrase was delivered with artful timing and studied nonchalance calculated to put tooth in such a simple statement.

Wedgy wouldn't give Rama the satisfaction of a reaction, but his powers of concentration couldn't adequately process the downhill break across the green's treacherous geography while simultaneously accommodating his own vanity. The poorly struck chip ran only halfway to the hole before the slope of the invisible ridge nudged it left to a lie requiring a complex cross-slope second effort.

To the rising chagrin of the old hustler, Rama again declared his superior position, but this time without a word. Borrowing another of Wedgy's ungracious behaviors, Rama merely shuffled his feet and looked at an imaginary wristwatch as if agitated with the valuable time Wedgy's putt and all its associated surveying would consume.

Lee leaned into his player and whispered, "Couldn't have said it better myself."

"Laugh it up while you can, Trujillo," growled Wedgy. He was losing ground and he knew it. He walked indignantly to his ball and sized up the ugly putt. Worst I'll do is lose one here, he thought.

Thus comforted, Wedgy stepped into his stance and tried to focus on the high point of the anticipated putt. His mind cleared of doubt and an image of the ball curling into the cup materialized in its place. All systems go. But the drone of the aircraft intruded again into the silence cloaking the fourteenth green. The image of his would-be perfect putt wavered like a mirage and dissipated in the heat of reality. Wedgy's fourth stroke came to rest sixteen inches short.

"That's good by me, don't you think, Mr. Trujillo?" said Rama.

"Hell no!" scolded Lee, the bad cop to Rama's good. "It's not match play. With six grand on the line—make that thirty-six if old Gyp loses—nothing's a gimme."

Wedgy hastily jabbed his ball marker into the turf and snatched his ball away. He was due for a little stroll and walked several paces beyond the green before stopping to look back in horror as Rama's ten-footer slid along the ridge top then disappeared into the hole for a birdie. Wedgy still had a return putt just to make his bogey.

As Wedgy stepped to the ball, the plane, now lower and louder, appeared again for its second pass above the fairways.

"What is this, a son-of-a-bitching air show?" While the plane banked overhead, Wedgy's bogey dropped into the cup. His lead had spiraled down to three.

———•———

Lee could never face the fifteenth hole without feeling phantom pains from the scorpion's incendiary sting. It was that sting that had eventually put Rama on the green in Lee's place. He still carried the memory of the scorpion hole and a fear of the fairway's rocky right edge high in his consciousness. Like a hook at Pebble's eighteenth or a slice at The Road Hole, this was one out-of-bounds that Lee respected viscerally.

Even though it was a dogleg to the right in which a faded drive would safely earn an easy 9-iron approach, Lee always teed off with a cautious iron up the left side, then took his chances with a strong 6-iron into the green. Such was the legacy of one poisonous creature.

Rama remembered the hole and the size to which Lee's hand had swollen on that raucous day. The crowd had become hostile after the phenomenal Mexican golfer had bowed out on the next green. Rama recalled how Carla had given him the nod to finish out the sixteenth hole in Lee's place and to etch his name in Mesquite Creek's bitter history.

Although stricken, Lee had lingered that day to watch Rama's amazing putt before hurrying off for medical attention. He had stopped at the clubhouse long enough to peel off a generous portion of that day's winnings and leave it for Rama.

Like Lee, Rama would never forget the scorpion. But it was the sting of Hank's hand, delivered in misunderstanding at Rama's possession of Lee's "refund" that, even now, left a divide of mistrust between them—a phantom pain as real as Lee's.

Wedgy fidgeted conspicuously as Lee counseled Rama in playing the hole conservatively. Their deliberations were cut short as the troublesome aircraft returned for its final pass.

The descending plane's engines roared indignantly at those who valued the peace and quiet of the ancient game's respite from modern contrivances.

But with its right wing banked alarmingly close to the treetops, this reckless performance was far more than an affront to golf's decorum. This was no prank. Something was amiss. Rama shivered at impending disaster. As the plane approached, he noticed the logo on the tail: A compass with a stylized G at its center. He had seen it before on Ivar's golf bag—Guidance Industries.

"Jesus, it's Ivar," Rama gasped. The plane roared across the adjacent fairway, revealing a brief look into the grim face of the man desperately seeking an emergency-landing site. But the face that looked back wasn't framed in Ivar's familiar white locks. This face was chiseled in trauma and crowned with damp dark hair. It was his father.

A few minutes earlier, as the golfers had battled to trade birdie for bogey, Hank had put the plane into a sweeping right turn and turned his attention to Ivar.

With the plane circling safely above the course, he felt for the Ivar's pulse; at least the poor fellow was alive. He opened a couple of buttons on Ivar's shirt and slid open a cabin vent. Air, scented with the hopeful odor of mown grass and bay laurel, filled the cabin. But that was all he could do for his host.

With the plane stabilized, Hank had taken stock: He guessed the fuel that might have taken them to Abilene would give him a few more minutes to get the feel for the plane; to take several passes over the golf course and settle himself for the inevitable.

The wing waggling and porpoising may have looked like confident grandstanding from the ground, but Hank nearly bit a hole through his lower lip as he searched for mastery of the 310's controls—and for courage. As the seconds crawled past, his pulse kicked to a thunderous tempo. The reality of committing to a dangerous landing and accepting its potentially incomprehensible outcome had triggered the terrible memory of St. Claude. He struggled to control his breath; he would not let the granite face of the Holy Mother condemn him to another tragedy.

Hank guessed that somewhere on the soft green grass below his son had joined the hundreds of others whose faces now turned up as he buzzed the treetops. He wanted to open the window and shout down "I will not die without a fight," in hopes that his son would finally know his courage.

The plane passed across the fifteenth tee box. A group had gathered there around a caddie and a couple of golfers, and indeed, they all were looking up. But the face of one of the players—his shaggy brown hair falling back onto a bright madras collar—rose above all the others.

"Rama!" Hank shouted into the din, but only Ivar, who still drifted in the dingy with Rebecca, could have heard.

Separated by altitude and velocity, he knew he might never touch his son again, yet he warmed with his good fortune at having made contact. As long as he had any control over this aircraft, the barriers of physics might not be as persistent as the selfish barriers that had separated them in the past. A smile flashed across Hank's face before he plunged back into crisis, and for an instant he wondered if Rama would ever stop dressing like a kid.

Rama gasped in amazement as his father swept overhead. He couldn't imagine the impossible tangle of fate that brought Hank to the skies above Mesquite Creek. Although his father was in obvious danger, he nearly cheered for his old man's good fortune at being airborne at last. He couldn't imagine what fears Hank faced or what circumstances had placed him at the controls of the plane sweeping overhead. But he clearly saw that frightened expression, and in that fleeting moment of recognition more understanding passed between them than they had ever allowed. And in that instant a life's worth of forgiveness flashed.

Hank pulled his eyes back from Rama's bright face and straightened the plane back out. He could not circle forever.

Chapter 59

Hank banked the plane awkwardly across the chaparral beyond Mesquite Creek until the golf course wheeled back beneath him. He leveled out for one last look before attempting to set her down. To his relief, the Cessna fell easily into line. Perhaps the time spent "flying" the glider on the ground at Aero Meadows the night before had paid off.

Then, most improbably, a stream of reassuring logic encouraged him: He had landed the Little Crow with Marcile Gold; he could put this bird down, too. He visualized stepping onto the golf course, embracing his son, and getting help for Ivar. The roar of the engines that had been so distracting now softened into a comforting drone. They were working for him, not against him. The locusts were another matter. Their numbers swirling above Mesquite Creek had increased steadily all day, and now as Hank gathered his courage the creatures began splattering on the windshield. He ignored the threatening occlusions; this plane would be on the ground before they could blind him.

Hank scanned the controls. He discarded most of the instruments from his mind to focus on the basics, almost as if this craft *were* a glider. This wasn't a check ride; he didn't have to land pretty or for points—he just had to land. If he didn't stall, kept the wings level, deployed the landing gear, kept the prop out of the turf, and cut the throttle before he ran out of fairway, he might just walk away.

Hank came around downwind of the intended landing strip. A twosome had pulled their carts to safety, leaving the long par five wide open. Judging by his experience at Aero Meadows, it seemed of adequate length. If not, it appeared that he could scoot across the green to an adjacent fairway and coast to a safe stop if he dodged those pepper trees.

Tension clamped Hank's neck as he banked the plane upwind. The troubling group of trees shading the second tee rose to meet him like sentinels to another world. The thought of nipping the trees consumed his attention as he descended, but the thought was cut short by a voice.

"Hank, your gear. Don't forget the landing gear!"

He looked to see if Ivar was stirring, but the old gentleman still floated in the waters off Boca Grande. The back of Hank's neck bristled. The voice had a familiar Oklahoma drawl…it was the voice of his old flying partner Walter Crow, but Old Crow hadn't come to gab.

"Oh, Christ," Hank yelped, then slammed the controls. The obedient mechanism deployed the gear and locked into place with a comforting thump as he skirted the treetops.

The loftiest twigs of the pepper trees slapped against the bottom of the craft. Hank feared they would grab the wheels, but in a second the trees were behind him. In a flash the image of crop dusters flirting with the very tips of hedgerows shot through his mind, and he smiled like an oily pilot skimming his fields.

Hank backed off the throttles to let the plane settle, resisting the fatal urge to nose down out of impatience. He steadied himself with the pulse of "Blue Light Voodoo" sounding in his brain. But suddenly a flurry of loud impacts startled him from Marcile's swampy groove as the plane plowed through a dense squadron of locusts. Green explosions further smeared the windshield as he dropped toward the fairway.

"God-damned bugs," he swore, forgetting that his first arrival at Mesquite Creek had been similarly greeted. He was almost home.

Then another voice sounded in the cabin: the groggy murmuring of Ivar Guidance.

"Bugs…in my plane?"

"Stay put, Ivar. Brace yourself," Hank barked, now only seconds away from meeting the thirsty turf. He struggled to follow Marcile Gold's admonition to stay loose. But he had no room for error now, and unlike his flight with Marcile, he had no graceful brown arms to save him.

Hank worked the controls as gently as his taut muscles could manage and leveled out. There was nothing more he could do. Time stretched every elastic moment to the breaking point as he waited for impact. Every second he was airborne was nearly one hundred feet less fairway to receive them. He had lost track of time—instants felt like eras as the elevated green at the end of the fairway raced to meet them.

Rama and the entire gallery watched in horror as the daredevil plane nipped the pepper trees and dropped to a lurching touchdown followed by a harrowing run out to the end of the fairway. The engines revved down to a whisper as the plane in sudden, breathtaking silence carved across the second green and well into the third fairway before coming to rest in the fallout of pulverized turf.

Carla's horror turned quickly to anger as the plane skipped to a stop with the number two flagstick protruding from the landing gear like a lance. Although happy that nobody, and none of her precious pepper trees, were hurt, she was dismayed at the trails of torn turf. The pragmatic Mrs. Stone was none too thrilled by the reckless landing, but she was particularly unhappy that play had ceased with four holes to finish and less than an hour 'til dark. There would be hell to pay if this match and its unexpectedly weighty purse were not settled promptly.

She was more than ready to read the pilot the riot act but was equally curious as to what kind of fool would attempt a landing where none had dared venture for so many years. Chandler's bare-bones airfield had once seen barnstormers draw large crowds for rides and exhibitions. Back then it had been used as a stop for aircraft when their ranges were shorter and when hops over from Dallas or up to Tulsa might require a fuel stop.

Chandler had hoped that small aircraft would ferry wealthy golfers to his course's remote location, but the harrowing drop into his stingy strip sealed the airfield's fate long before he had drifted away on the winds of grief. Carla eventually ordered the rerouting of the second and third holes through the old runway, but in its day, with the Chandler Stone/Bobby Jones friendship in bloom, the airstrip shepherded the likes of Hagen, McKenzie, Ross, Nelson, and other luminaries safely from the wide Texas sky to try their hands at the curious track laid lovingly on this harsh country by one of Dornoch's own children.

For a moment Carla imagined that the door on the little airplane would swing open and reveal the boyish face of Bobby Jones and his red-headed host, Chandler. In a daydream she imagined the Scotsman's hopeful green eyes scanning his fresh new fairways for his bride. She would hurry to the plane, wave good-bye to the wondering gallery behind her, and leave the roughnecks to book their own bets and pour their own beers. She would leave the course to ravenous thistle and jimson weed—and to Carlos—as she settled into the embrace of her long-lost Chandler on a one-way trip to Augusta's golfing Colorado…but not today. Carla's last real hope for Chandler's return had expired in New Orleans eighteen years earlier.

She had been tending to the thirsty crowd in Mesquite Creek's grill room lounge one Saturday afternoon when she overheard one of the patrons telling the other members of his foursome that he recognized the face of "that Scottish feller" in a picture back in Carla's pro shop. That "feller" Carla knew was Chandler. After striking up a conversation, she learned that the patron was a brakeman on the Gulf-Colorado line. One day not long before, in the Brownsville yard while walking his train for hot boxes he had encountered a feller who looked like a dead ringer for Chandler Stone. The brakeman explained that "being a fair-minded person, I didn't call the bull but told the feller he'd better beat it out of the yard. I asked him where he was bound and he told me New Orleans. I pointed out a string of boxcars I knew for a fact was Orleans-bound. Away he went."

Carla had tried to act blasé at the brakeman's story. But the next day she had driven out to New Orleans. She spent three days in the presence of police, hobos, the Salvation Army, the *Times-Picayune*, and a dozen other institutions seeking out leads on the presence of a Scottish drifter while tacking up missing-persons handbills. She had returned to Mesquite Creek, but her phone never rang. In its silence her final hopes turned to dust. There was some satisfaction in the effort; she had to try something even though she sensed it was a wild-goose chase. Most likely, Chandler, blinded by sorrow, had stumbled out into the barranca and run into a rattler or even a hungry puma. It hurt then and still stung today, but if he were dead…so be it. And if he had been so spiritually damaged that he could overlook her grief and her loneliness, then she could look beyond him, too.

"Taxi that piece of junk off my blessed fairway," Carla yelled to the face framed in the cockpit windshield. Hank's ashen features and the dark swath of sweaty hair were nothing like Bobby's visage, but he stared back with Jones-like joy at a world now thankfully at rest beneath his feet.

Carla strode toward the plane and gestured to the open waste areas west of the fairway. "Move it. Pronto. You're gonna kill somebody with a stunt like that," she shouted in frustration. "Who the hell…"

Rama caught up with Carla halfway to the plane and took her arm, imploring her to relax. To her amazement he explained that the intruders were kin: "My father and Ivar Guidance…I think."

Carla recovered her wits. "Well, if you're right, your crazy father owes me some repairs…and who in Heaven's name is Ivar?" she called as Rama raced ahead to greet his father.

Rama waited beside the plane as Hank, who was having more trouble deciphering the latch than he'd had with the aircraft's controls, fumbled with the door. The lock finally released, and Hank, leaning heavily on his cane, climbed down the wing to share an overdue embrace with his son.

"I saw you at the window," Rama cried. "You were flying. What happened… why'd you land here?"

"Could have been a prettier touchdown, but what were we supposed to do?" laughed Hank. "Look, we've got to get some help for Ivar; he's fainted or something."

As he spoke, a pale white figure loomed behind Hank's shoulder. "Your father can be a bit over-dramatic, Rama. I'm just fine. Perhaps a little dehydrated," said Ivar. "And your father is too modest…*he* landed the plane."

Though still shaky, Ivar, sensing Carla's understandable displeasure at landings on her golf course, quickly turned to damage control: "Our sincere apologies, ma'am, for the unscheduled landing. If we did any damage, please let me know." He reached for the doorframe to steady himself before dismounting.

"But why are you here? What's wrong…is Mom okay?"

"Your father and I came for you, Rama. Of course, we thought there was a landing strip here. It's a long story, but she is going to have serious surgery and wants you at her side," explained Ivar. "Perhaps someone could give an old fellow a hand stepping down."

Carla wasn't so polite. "No you don't. I said get that piece of junk off my fairways and I meant it. I've got a course to run and a match to finish."

Ivar shrugged and turned back inside the cabin. "I'll see if I can oblige you, ma'am. Hank, keep those folks clear of the props."

In a moment one engine roared to life, then the second sputtered fruitlessly. Suddenly the first engine died as well. In a moment a ghostly Ivar Guidance reappeared in the door.

"Jesus, we never would have made it to Abilene. She's flat out of fuel."

Carla frowned. "We'll get some of the fellows to push you out of harm's way or the morning foursomes are liable to pound your plane like a hailstorm. And nobody is pushing anybody anywhere until Rama hustles his lucky butt back onto the tee and finishes up the last four holes. We're running out of daylight."

Ivar perked up. "Did you say *Rama* is playing?" The old gentleman was as confused with events on the course as were Rama and company dumbfounded by the descent of an aircraft into their midst. "Hank, you'd better go watch. I don't think you've ever seen him play." Ivar waved Hank off to the match. "I'll keep an eye on the plane."

As ludicrous as were the circumstances, Hank was anxious to see his son in action when, for once, he had no money invested on the outcome. Here, for the first time since Knot Hole baseball when Rama had given up twelve humiliating runs in one endless inning, Hank would cheer for the success he had once dreamed for his son. Just as Rama had once pictured his father as a hero, on this day both their dreams might come true.

Ivar leaned back against the wing, still suffering from rubber legs. For a moment Carla looked more concerned about this tall, ashen stranger's health than her own business. "Stay put; I'll fetch you a cart and an iced tea."

"You are far too kind," Ivar replied, still slightly disoriented. "This is Mesquite Creek then? My charts showed a water tower and an airstrip."

"Well you're a few years late, mister. I tore out the airstrip, and a tornado did in the tower." She offered her hand like a debutante receiving gentry. "Mrs. Carla Stone."

Ivar shook Carla's hand gently. "I am so sorry for any damage. I will be more than happy to compensate your repair efforts." He bowed: "Ivar Guidance at your service."

Carla laughed at his formal speech and genteel manner. She hadn't seen this sort of man since her last trip to Georgia. "Damage? Well, sir, you may have noticed this is not your perfectly manicured track. You could land a B-52 out here and not kick up much of a divot." She smiled coyly. "The damage to the green isn't too severe. Hell, half of these duffers won't notice the difference."

Carla, like hundreds of people before her, had softened at Ivar's honest, trusting heart. "You take it easy right there, Mr. Guidance, until you've at least had some iced tea. I'll see if I can't find old Doc Otnes to give you the once-over. I've got to tend to this match and keep an eye on that Gypsy Hustler."

Ivar perked up. "Who is this Gypsy fellow? Sounds like a pro wrestler."

"A stage name I guess you could call it…for Mr. Byrne."

"Not *Wallace* Byrne?" The color poured back into Ivar's face so rapidly it startled Carla. He felt no urgency to hurry over to watch Wedgy weasel his way into another poor loser's mind, and barely—always just barely—stroll off with the fellow's money. Ivar felt sad to think of Rama's pure spirit tethered to such deception for the better part of the summer.

"How's old Wedgy doing?"

"You know him, too?" Carla continued to be amazed by these men's relationship. "Well, he's doing all right. He's up by three strokes with four holes remaining. Rama's giving him a damned good fight, though."

"Rama? *Our* Rama is up against the Gypsy?" Ivar's tired eyes brightened as he made the connections: Rama was playing the Gypsy, and the Gypsy was Wedgy

"Who else?" replied Carla. "Know any other Ramas?"

Ivar experienced a sudden surge in vitality. "If you don't mind, ma'am, I'll take that tea later. Perhaps you'll accompany me to the fifteenth tee. I believe Mr. Byrne…er, the Gypsy…will be glad to see me." Ivar relished the fact that that would *not* be so.

At the sight of his nemesis approaching, Wedgy anxiously slammed the heel of his club into the tee-box turf. "Ivar, for Christ sakes…if you can't fly 'em why buy 'em? I hope you didn't go to all that trouble just to come watch *me* lose 'cause you're in for some costly disappointment."

Ivar smiled at Wedgy's customary sarcasm but was glad to have found a familiar face so far from home, even if it was Wedgy's. Amazing what a near-miss will do to one's judgment, he mused.

———•———

The song of the locusts had only been an intermittent chorus since the insects first reappeared, but now it had modulated into a steady whine as the horde settled into Mesquite Valley. Hank swatted one from his thigh as he watched his son tee the ball. The bug was pulverized in a green swoosh across his pants, the victim of a torrent of adrenaline still coursing after Hank's landing.

Rama was pumped, too, although continuing the hole seemed vastly un-important in light of his father's unexpected arrival. Life-and-death trumped six grand and his desire to extract justice from Wedgy. But Lee, Carla, Boney, and a dozen other gamblers betting on the long-shot ex-caddie didn't see it that way. The outcome had real value to them. And to Wedgy, facing a five-figure loss, the match was deadly serious. He fidgeted as Rama methodically visualized his shot from behind the ball.

"Damn, let's get this over before the fucking bugs run off with us," Wedgy grumbled.

Rama had learned from Wedgy that controlling the pace helped control the opponent's emotions, so he patiently waited for a few curious stragglers to return from inspecting the aircraft. Finally he calmed himself, putting the idea of his father as a spectator from his thoughts. As his mind cleared, he threw the old persimmon brassie into the slot and delivered a two-hundred-yard drive safely past the dangers that lurked or crawled along the arroyo on the right.

Wedgy seemed confident, but with the presence of Ivar Guidance now disturbing his rhythm, his swing separated into several disconnected segments. When the club head arrived at the ball his arms were still on their way down, and the resulting slice, and possibly a sizeable portion of his lead, seemed destined for a thorny fate in the scorpion's domain. But fate granted a lucky bounce from a boulder entombed somewhere in the hazard. Resurrected, the ball flew to a resting place not more than three paces from Rama's ball.

Ivar groaned at Wedgy's impossible luck. "Mercy, has he been this charmed the entire round?"

"Don't complain about anyone's luck, Mr. Guidance." Carla gave Ivar a vexed look. "I believe you've had your share recently, have you not?"

Ivar couldn't argue, nor could he resist the urge to get into the game that only a minute ago he had cared nothing about. Before Wedgy started up the fairway, Ivar caught up with him. "I assume you are still a sporting man, Wallace. Perhaps you'll grant me a chance to earn a little something back from our "mishap" with the flagstick?"

Wedgy suspected Ivar was already invested in this match, but a few more bucks couldn't hurt. "You mean you want to throw good money after bad? Sure, Ives; what are your stakes?"

Ivar began to name his poison when Hank stepped forward. He hadn't saved the old gentleman's life just to see him fall beneath Wedgy's wheels again. Any wager with Wedgy was liable to be a bad investment.

"No, Ivar is not interested…no bets," Hank interrupted.

Wedgy looked at the intruder with disbelief. How could it be? This was the used car hawk who had sold him the Lincoln back at Big Muddy's. The pieces fell into place. The pathetic fellow counseling Ivar *not* to bet was Rama's father.

Wedgy looked at Hank indignantly. "Who are you, Mr. Schwain, to tell my old friend Ives not to make a friendly wager? You would do well to bet *for* me for a change. Might be more lucrative than the used car game."

Hank bristled. "I'll be damned if I'd ever wager on you, and God knows I'll never bet against my son."

"Really?" sneered Wedgy. Irritated at the sanctimonious proclamations of the newly converted, Wedgy was moved to pick at the scab recently formed over Hank's old wounds.

"Then how about this, Schwain? You wager something, anything, on me and if I lose I'll pay you back double." Wedgy raised his right arm. "But as God is my witness, if I beat your son I'll give you 20-percent of all my winnings on all the bets I've taken out here today."

Wedgy listened with satisfaction as the gallery hummed over the reckless offer. He hoped this little wrangle with Hank would rattle Rama for keeps. Just another lost stroke or two and Rama would be blown completely out of contention. Wedgy waited for Hank's reaction, and in the silence he feared that a few folks in the gallery might demand the same bet if he didn't move on quickly.

"So, what'll it be? It's a win-win bet for you this time, Schwain. No gambler worth his salt would pass this one by."

Rama's blood ran cold. The prospect of a no-lose bet with a huge pay-off might well push his father back from the healthy place into which he had somehow finally landed. He feared he had recklessly allowed Ivar's seed money, intended for a good match against Wedgy, to end up foolishly at risk in a doubtful match that tested both him and his father.

Rama's heart pounded as Hank considered Wedgy's devilish proposal. This had not been his intention when he passed Ivar's check over to Boney, nor was this what Ivar had in mind.

Ivar was speechless. He wished he had never brought the cursed subject up; he should have known Wedgy would work a wager to some devious end. Yet as he waited for Hank's reply, he was as amazed at Wedgy Byrne's audacity as he was at his old rival's foolishness.

Carla watched as the men, whose relationship still remained murky in her mind, negotiate what appeared to be dark waters. Her mind spun as it tried to fathom their history or, more important, how she could claim a piece of Wedgy's win-win bet with Hank.

Hank had never heard of such a bet: 20-percent of the winnings—a virtual gift, considering his son was down by three with only four holes to play. The sizable gallery ensured that his slice would come from a substantial pie. It would be the payday of his life. He looked at his son who had spent the day battling uphill against heavy odds. Rama had already pulled his 6-iron and waited for his reply to Wedgy's bet before taking the hike up the fairway.

Rama watched his father's face soften in contentment and glow with pride as his response to Wedgy became clear. Rama had seen the expression before: on the faces of his teammates' fathers as they cheered their boys' efforts on the baseball diamonds of weekends long-passed—games he remembered only for *his* father's absence.

—•—

"The Bank of Life don't take cash!"

Howell Juitt's words rang back to Hank from the shoeshine stand. He took his cane into his hands and made a vicious cut at a phantom fastball. "Play ball, son," he hollered.

"No deal, Gypsy."

Wedgy slammed his driver back into his bag. "A fool and his money, Schwain…you'll never get out of that car lot." With that rejoinder, he took an angry first step up the fairway toward his second shot and into retirement.

Chapter 60

As Rama headed up through the barranca toward the sixteenth tee, he was well aware that with three holes to play he was still down three strokes but was oblivious to the spiritual machinations swirling around him. He could not have known that the spirits of Dickey and Glendora Stone were poised to find rest once he reached the sixteenth green. He knew only how much sweeter would be the taste of victory following his father's brave refusal of Wedgy's wager. But victory seemed remote this late in the round; at least he still had the honors. And he had the special ground of the sixteenth tee under his feet. The memory of the night lessons with Carlos and last night's glory with Melyssa strengthened his claim to whatever magic might be left him. This was his spot.

He punched his tee into its turf and took his shot.

Had the Gulf-Colorado & Santa Fe's long lonely whistle blown through the ball's flight as it had eight years earlier, the convergence would have been the stuff of sentimental fiction, but the whistle never came. Yet even without the high lonesome sound, Rama's drive was majestic. Wedgy answered with a defiant blast, propelled by pure surliness. After each player had taken his second shot, they both faced an approach to a green that no one who played Mesquite Creek could ever forget.

Rama remembered it well: the kidney-shaped green perched near the top of a hill. Its two-tiered putting surface fell away from the approaching golfer— the rear tier lower than the front. The fiendish affair was hidden from the fairway and protected by a great yellow oak that loomed above the green's left flank like the Grim Reaper, his scythe raised and ready to ruthlessly chop any fade, lob, or good intentions to earth. It was a hole to be played conservatively with the flag forward, and tackled with a prayer when the pin was cut on the lower tier. Even played well, bogey was a good score.

Both players' lies after their second shots seemed adequate, but their third strokes would be perilous, blind wedges to a target that defiantly snubbed its green nose at all comers.

Rama's shot would be from the right side of the fairway; Wedgy's ball was farther left. Both players lay seventy-five yards short of the hole, which lurked invisibly on the lower tier. Rama's position was preferable: A line from his ball to the hole would pass over the front lobe of the kidney. If it fell short it would still land on the green and with a good bounce had a chance of trickling down-hill where it might find a resting place adjacent to the hole.

From Wedgy's position, a shot to the flag would have to pass over the crook in the kidney. The oak guarded that route. Its silver bark was pocked with the signatures of foolish gamblers.

As fate would have it, both players attempted wise shots, but both still found misfortune in the tree. A sloppy over-the-top swing pulled Rama's "safe" shot into the branches. With a clattering of balata against oak, the ball rattled down through the limbs before being kicked improbably out into a corner of the green's upper lobe, a location that offered nothing even resembling a line to the hole far below.

"Lucky fuck," growled Wedgy, unaware that even though Rama had found the green, he would have been better off if his ball had stayed up on the hill beneath the tree. "For anybody else, that tree is an obstacle."

Wedgy would not count on such a warm relationship with the tree, so he abandoned all thought of a towering, risky wedge above its menacing branches. Instead of that imprudent line to the pin, he settled for a flop to the green's mid-section that connected the upper and lower tiers like a chute. If it landed in the chute it could run down to the hole as if in a rainspout on a putt-putt course, but if it strayed right, it would find the jagged stone outcropping where Rama had once faced the puma.

Incorrectly assuming his opponent had a realistic putt, Wedgy gambled on the risky flop shot. For once the magician of the lofted metal failed to draw the rabbit from his hat. He hit his wedge thin. The ball rebounded from the slope leading up to the green and shot to the right on a beeline for the rocks. When it came to rest it had settled behind the outcropping, blocked from any subsequent shot at the flag. Checkmate. Nobody appeared likely to gain a stroke at sixteen, which in effect was an advantage for Wedgy.

Arriving at his ball, Rama considered his position on the upper tier's cul-de-sac while Lee surveyed Wedgy's lie. "The Gypsy's ball is exactly where you lay when you scrambled for par on our big day, amigo...remember?"

"No, Lee, that is exactly where *we* scrambled. You chipped it on, and I got lucky with the putt."

"You are modest to a fault," Lee laughed. "You've got to learn to be an ass-hole every once in a while. Take all the luck you can get...just make 'em think it's skill." Lee pointed to his head. "Keep the other guy guessing and you'll surprise yourself. Believe me, your good fortune on that day took more than luck, my friend."

Lee's encouraging voice momentarily washed the pressure from Rama's mind. The Hispanic cadence graced every phrase with an optimistic ascending note. "Now what kind of magic is *this* putt gonna take, eh?" Lee quipped as he scrutinized Rama's conundrum on the upper tier. He traced the sign of the cross on his chest for good measure.

Wedgy regarded the rocks blocking his route to the flag. Rebuffed by his latest failed flop, he abandoned any thought of hoisting a shot over the forbidding outcrop. He settled for a chip back onto the green's upper tier. His ball came to rest on the green as he had planned but farther from the pin than Rama's.

"The Gypsy has about the same line as you," whispered Lee. "Pay attention, Rama. Read his putt carefully."

And what a putt it was: an eighty-foot line through a twelve-foot descent around a 120-degree counter-clockwise bend and along a right-breaking roll to the flag. Wedgy lay four, one stroke shy of par. Nonplussed, he gave the ball enough chutzpah to get it into the chute and begin the rotation—but perhaps too much chutzpah. When the ball stopped, it was in the far left corner of the green's lower tier and eighteen feet beyond the hole. Wedgy stood on the upper reaches of the diabolical green muttering sincere curses at all things Royal and Ancient.

Rama's ball—laying three—was trapped in the upper tier's cul-de-sac with no direct line to the lower tier. After watching Wedgy, he realized a smart strategy would be to simply putt the ball to the most accessible point along the line that Wedgy's putt had just taken. Then, with Wedgy's miss to guide him, he could adjust his velocity on the next putt to correct the errors of Wedgy's unschooled attempt and, he hoped, cozy up to the hole for an easy third putt. If he did this right and Wedgy missed his eighteen-footer, he would gain a stroke and pull within two of the lead.

Rama's mind was charged with clarity. Success on this hole seemed reasonable…until he remembered Melyssa.

He pictured her, up long before sunrise, scrawling a good-bye note to him and tucking Carlos's gifts into the envelope before hopping into Mirage's truck for a lift to Brownwood's bus depot. He remembered leafing through the snapshots of the dewy greens, and he recalled a putt similar to this: A single track that defied reason by heading *away* from the chute to the edge of the damp fringe, then curling into a descending path through the chute and into the hole's reaches. Rama embraced the unreasonable.

Lee's smile fell away as he watched Rama set up for that backward Kamikaze stroke. He had begun to believe that somehow this young golfer would wrestle a victory away from his antagonist. Lee Trujillo had been around his share of cynics and frauds in his young career, but before he made his run at history, he wanted to embrace the hopeful, happy, innocent ending—just once. But as Rama prepared to self-destruct, Lee realized he was just a self-indulgent romantic for encouraging Rama even this far. The truth was that the best and the truest man doesn't usually win, but the toughest man often does. Only in the rarest competitor do the three traits come together. Jack Nicklaus came to Lee's mind.

Lee knew Rama was light years from the best or the toughest in a world of grizzled competitors, but this crazy decision on the sixteenth's green was disconcerting and anything *but* Nicklaus-like. Yet Lee, who aspired to face the Golden Bear one day soon, had always sensed a true spirit in the modest young man he had once declared a natural. He would watch and learn from whatever lesson Rama's game might offer.

Depending on the outcome of this suicidal putt, Rama could get within range of Wedgy or blow himself out of the match altogether. There was no doubt that Rama also knew the consequences. At that crucial moment Lee remembered the Polaroids. Before Rama pulled the trigger, the snapshots were in Lee's hands. There, in the dew of an otherwise forgotten morning, a damp line confirmed that Rama's backward putt would be, incredibly, on the right track. Lee sighed with relief at Rama's crazy decision.

Wedgy saw things differently: "What the fuck is he thinking?"

He cracked the closest thing to a grin since his birdie on thirteen. His opponent was going to give another stroke away with the hare-brained putt he appeared ready to launch. But Wedgy's smile and Lee's relief were short-lived as Rama rose from his putting posture. In the silence of anticipation, all eyes watched Rama turn his head toward the great oak as if acknowledging some-one, then turn deliberately from the backward line to a more conventional direction. The gallery murmured its approval, but Rama revised his aim, not for lack of faith in the Rube Goldberg putt but in the genesis of its discovery. As he had stood over the putt, Rama had realized that the mental image he recalled from shuffling innocently through the photos presented the same test of honor. Accepting assistance that he had not devised or acquired through his own efforts was wrong, just as asking a competitor about the breaks, or marking the green to align a putt, or testing its grain by touch were deemed violations by the arcane but venerable dictates of the grand governing bodies of the game.

As Rama trod the sixteenth green the spirits of the Stone Children were poised to ascend to the bosom of God. Carlos's vision teetered on the verge of fulfillment. Rama would no longer bear the spirits of the Stone Children or carry the Caddie's Gift, but the scrupulous spirit of Dickey Stone would always instruct Rama's heart.

"A stickler for the rules," Mirage had said of Dickey as he and Rama had driven to Wedgy's rescue the other night. Now here, near the place of the ter-rible lightning that had stolen his life, Dickey Stone's spirit whispered into Rama's ear for the last time. A few seconds and an honest stroke later, Rama's ball rolled to a stop at the top of the chute. Still away, he considered his next putt. He studied the path Wedgy's ball had taken through the chute in its mis-guided roll beyond the hole. He adjusted accordingly, but no magical hand would guide his stroke. With a soft tap he alone launched the ball into the grip of the chute.

Several breathless seconds and two course changes later the putt tracked toward the pin with promise. Lee grabbed the flagstick and watched as Rama's ball dropped incredibly into the cup to register a par and to flick the trigger of pandemonium around the sixteenth green. Dozens helplessly pondered the plummeting value of their bets on the Gypsy Hustler.

Lee stood in silence, his eyes fixed again on the Polaroid and the proven track of the putt to which this inscrutable young man had purposely turned his back.

——•——

Wedgy needed to traverse eighteen feet in a single tap, but even that would only avoid losing two strokes. It was not to be: His sixth stroke slid by the hole. In a moment he reluctantly faced his seventh stroke, and for the first time in years he prayed. He asked God to spare him the blank stare of a snowman's coal black eyes.

His seventh putt rolled ingloriously home.

From his perch above the green, Hank welcomed Wedgy's misfortune without realizing the hustler's seven to his son's five had tightened the match to a single stroke. Hank didn't stand to make a red cent yet he cheered for Rama, who for irretrievable years had heard only the voices of his teammates' fathers rising from the stands.

Rama warmed at Hank's welcoming spirit, but as he turned to leave the green he was staggered by a vision of two blinding bolts and the Stone Children's final instant. Unaware that he stood on the exact spot where Dickey had been struck, Rama nearly buckled under the vacuum of an inexplicable loss. He was overcome with a spasm of grief as the children's spirits raced from the company of his soul to find peace. It was as if the pain of losing a brother and a sister had been compressed into one wrenching moment, but the grief was washed away as he was embraced by the majesty of the grand spiritual circle.

The void in Rama's heart was filled with joy at his father's revival. His legs, which a moment before had fallen slack, now carried him in a sprint back up the slope beneath the yellow oak. As he crested the slope he saw Carlos's cart disappear behind a fold in the landscape as it raced toward the next hole. The old gaucho had been watching the predicted drama play out on sixteen. To the southeast, the remnant of a tropical storm breathing its last after a dry run up from Corpus Christi was hurling a bank of ominous clouds heavenward. The sound of locusts stilled as the gulf air charged inland.

The lightning would soon return.

Rama felt the eerie tingle of electricity in the air and feared for his partners remaining down on the putting surface. "Lee. Wedgy…come off the green." His voice was firm as he called the others away. It was not the happy chirp of a fellow on the receiving end of a miracle.

Chapter 61

Michael "Mirage" Jimson's pick-up truck careened along the path skirting the old livestock pond that formed the seventeenth's chief hazard. Bullfrogs surveyed every motion on the neighboring tee and screamed like crazy children in terror at Mirage's approach.

"If I didn't know a whole lot better, I'd swear I saw an airplane sitting on the third fairway," Mirage joked. He tugged at an Abba-zaba and made a pointless effort to smooth out his graying flattop as he caught up with Carla. The old friends exchanged late-breaking news, including the emergency landing and the game's score. Mirage assured Carla that Melyssa was safely on the bus to Trent, North Carolina.

"Can you do us another huge favor?" Carla asked. "Line up some fuel for Mr. Guidance's airplane." She read from a note Ivar had scrawled on a scorecard: Four hundred pounds of AVGAS, in new drums. "Of course, there'll be a few bucks in it for you." Carla tipped her head close to Mirage's thin, freckled face and whispered. "But first can you disable the Gypsy's car, the blue Lincoln Continental? Nothing serious, just so it can't start."

Mirage's face dropped at her odd request that he vandalize a guest's car.

"Shit ma'am, we just fixed the damn thing," he whispered.

"Just a little tweak," she said with a nefarious twinkle. "In case things don't work out the Gypsy's way, I don't want a premature departure."

Mirage winked yes. "But I won't get that fuel back 'til tomorrow morning." He stepped to the refreshment cart idling nearby and extracted an icy Nesbitt's Orange. "It's on Carla," he told the girl before climbing back into his cab. He glanced at Rama who stood on the tee anxiously waggling the Night Lesson's brassie as he awaited the truck's departure.

"Hit 'em straight, Schwain. Lyssa says she'll write you real soon." Mirage raised his orange soda to toast Rama's success and depressed the pedal to terrorize a few more bullfrogs on his way to Brownwood's fuel depot via Wedgy's Lincoln.

For Rama, Mirage's interruption was welcome relief. The reality of his climb back into the game and a possible victory looming only two strokes away weighed like a boulder on his nerves. He was already charged with confidence at the two-stroke swing in his favor. Now his heart surged with Melyssa's message and his father's happy spirit. His imagination soared recklessly ahead. He imagined facing the seventy-second hole of the US Open with a comfortable lead. And he pictured himself granting the defeated Wedgy a victorious handshake with one hand and collecting a $150 Nassau in the other. The picture was perfect.

Lee wasn't so happy. He watched Rama carefully and didn't like what he saw. The young man's routine and posture looked different. Suddenly Rama seemed too cocky. He couldn't share Rama's thoughts, but he guessed Rama had forgotten he was still subject to fickle luck and fallible skill, regardless of his heart's lofty elevation. Lee took advantage of Mirage's noisy retreat and stepped into the tee box to derail Rama's train of thought.

"Too bad you don't smoke, amigo," Lee said quietly, "or I'd offer you a reefer right now to calm you down…to bring you back to earth."

Rama drew a breath to protest the interruption, but Lee continued. "I know the signs. You are charged like a lightning rod. Too much adrenaline… and God know what else pumped you up on sixteen. But don't forget: You are still behind by one stroke, and the Gypsy might yet play his best hole."

Lee pulled the 5-wood Rama had scavenged at Sunset Hills and held it out to his player. "I know you've got a thing for that old brassie, amigo, but swap with me now or you'll blow the back right out of the hole. It is just as bad buried out beyond the green as it is in the slime you're so worried about carrying."

Rama remembered pulling the fairway club from a pile of forsaken clubs in the janitor's closet. It occurred to him that he had never hit this club in competition, but then again, he hadn't hit much of *anything* in competition. Lee was unconcerned with Rama's disappointment at the club selection.

"One shot at a time, Rama. Believe me, this will be perfect," insisted Lee with a comforting wink as he left the tee box.

In Rama's energized hands the ensuing shot seemed weak, but sure enough, it carried the pond, took one helpful bounce, then rolled to the far side of the green. Lee exhaled with relief. If Rama had kept the brassie, there would have been no satisfaction in being right but unpersuasive.

There were no birdies carded on number seventeen. Wedgy stoically scrambled a par to match Rama after missing the green. As the hustler stooped to retrieve his ball from the hole, his back popped in protest of the day's unexpectedly strenuous work. With a mere single-stroke lead, the six-to-one odds and his age were beginning to haunt him.

Lee stood with the flagstick, well within earshot of Wedgy's tiring joints. "Don't worry; it'll all be over soon, Gypsy," he said, as the old hustler walked from the green. Lee stopped as his words uttered in gamesmanship echoed away in sadness. A spark of compassion flared for the man desperately cling-ing to a lead and the trailing edge of a career.

Wedgy refused to acknowledge Lee but left the green with the soon-to-be-famous Mexican golfer's words haunting him like a prophecy.

Wedgy looked grim but determined as he watched Rama prepare to shoot from the final tee. The spark that he had come to expect from sharing the game of golf with Rama—even as a competitor—had vanished after the first nine holes. Somehow the young golfer had found the unlikely putt, the lucky bounce, and the poise to keep the game close, even though the smoke, the mirrors, and the magic were gone.

Someday Wedgy would have to tip his hat to Rama for his attempted hustle, not just for crafting a five-stroke resurgence but for a virtuoso performance of deception and tightly held cards that stretched from the day he had shown up at Kings Kreek until now. If Rama were hustling him, then surely he would propose a hearty bet on the final hole. But Wedgy didn't know that Rama's entry into this competition was another's doing and that this game was not the suspected hustle but was instead a struggle for dignity and three lost souls. The expected wager never came.

⸺•⸺

The final hole looked simple enough: a straight par four with only a hint of visible risk. But Chandler Stone, who had admired Donald Ross and had scratched many windy rounds from the Kingdom of Fife's sandy links with the master designer, was himself a master...of deception. Here, on number eighteen, he had paid homage to Ross, the most famous of Dornoch's children, by crafting a grievous domed green intended to heap an extra stroke or two upon the careless golfer's card. But that was only part of the puzzle. Chandler had positioned the tee so that a tree blocked the left center of the fairway in such a strategic manner that a simple drive up the fairway would be imperiled. To avoid the tree, golfers had two choices: They could work the ball around the obstacle to leave a shorter approach from the left, or they could play con-servatively up the right side of the fairway. But this approach had its costs as well. The angle on the "safe" shot was such that it robbed golfers of critical forward progress but left them a clear, although longer, 200-yard shot to the green dome. The physics of that shot dictated that the goals of aggressively carrying such a distance and settling down lightly upon the convex green were mutually exclusive.

Chandler Stone had been a fair and cunning man before he vanished. He had provided a third route to the green, but not one undertaken without a gamble. Chandler, the Scotsman-turned-Texan, had taken a page from Car-noustie, the great diabolical Scottish links, and had carved a new serpentine channel for Mesquite Creek. So like Carnoustie's infamous Barry Burn, the creek would scribe a loop in the fairway's right side. The land within the loop formed the shape of an orange segment, a distant and progressively narrowing tract of high-risk real estate that was reachable but not easily hit or seen from the tee. The risks posed by distance and dimension were compounded by unplayable scrub on the right and the creek along the left, more than ample reason to consider playing around the tree. But the reward for golfers hitting this confounding target was forty yards *less* distance to the green than their conservative brethren and a far better chance to loft a ball to a stop on the domed putting surface.

Rama had never seen the hole from the tee. His brief caddying stint with Lee eight years ago had ended on the sixteenth tee. Ignorance was bliss. At his low angle of view, the creek was foreshortened into invisibility and the orange segment seemed a plausible target, exactly as Chandler had intended.

He knew he would have no chance of making up the crucial stroke separating him from Wedgy if he chose the easy way out, and he knew he didn't have the skill to curl around the tree. What he *did* have was the course designer's own club in his bag and the confidence to spank the crap out of it in hopes of reaching the elusive orange slice.

Lee instructed Rama in the risks. Even though he knew the long shot across the creek seemed the only chance, he pointed out there was still a possibility that Wedgy would fail. Lee was still searching for a more convincing argument in favor of caution—a 3-wood perhaps—when Rama drew the Night Lessons brassie for one last swing.

Lee looked at Rama with disapproval, but Rama smiled back deceptively. He had seen Wedgy perform enough eighteenth-hole miracles that he doubted the old hustler would stumble now with a victory nearly in his grasp; that possibility seemed more remote than hitting the elusive orange segment.

"Here we go 'round the mulberry bush," Rama sang cheerily.

Lee stepped away, convinced Rama's intention was to draw the ball around the tree. Rama wouldn't make up any slack here, but he would stay out of the creek, and he would retain a chance at drawing even if the wheels fell from Wedgy's wagon. After Rama's stroke, the match would be Wedgy's to lose.

Rama stepped to the tee.

—•—

He once had towed the rubber as if he really were a pitcher. He knew better. Twelve runs had crossed the plate in a single inning. Why hadn't the coach pulled him off the mound? Wouldn't six walks have been punishment enough? Was twelve some magic number that might drive the lesson in failure home more soundly…was he to be transformed into a *better* pitcher if humiliation were heaped upon defeat?

Rama had learned a different lesson: to stay out of harm's way, to avoid crippling challenges, and to find contentment by watching others suffer their losses or celebrate their glories. Even now, if he had the power to view the layout of this hole from the perspective of hawks wheeling on a roiling afternoon thermal, he might have judged differently...more conservatively. From such a height the creek would have loomed larger and the orange segment narrower. He might have chosen to attempt the safer curl to the left as he had misled Lee into thinking he would; but this was a new day. Rama had heard Hank's deep voice wish him good luck from the front of the gallery, and he warmed at the thought of a victory for his father. It was no time for hedged bets.

Rama waggled his club, fully conscious that in his strong play and feisty run at Wedgy, he had already achieved more than he had ever expected when he conspired with Boney to beat the man who had cheated Ivar and defeated Hank. In that sense, he had already won. The pressure was off. He shuffled his feet out of the draw stance and lined up the right side over the intruding creek.

Lee swallowed hard.

A grin tugged at Carlos Taddio's wrinkled face as we watched from his cart.

Rama never questioned his decision. His club felt determined and lively as he coiled back and through to an inevitable persimmon explosion. All eyes watched Rama's ball race into the sky, soar across the creek, and dive to the grassy refuge of Chandler's promised land. Spontaneous applause rose from the gallery, even from a few members whose bets were now imperiled.

"Go, go, go!" shouted Hank like a fan watching a drive to deep center field. Rama let out a sigh of relief. Twelve runs were permanently erased from the family scoreboard.

"Around the mulberry bush, my ass," Lee scolded Rama even as he smiled like a fool. "Must have miss-hit that *draw*, eh amigo?" When Rama finally relinquished the Night Lessons club for the last time, Lee blew across its head lest he singe its cover.

———•———

Wedgy knew the quality of Rama's tee shot, but he would not follow that ball for love nor money. God knows there was plenty of both in play. The day before he had navigated the course on his sandbagging practice round and had learned the hole's travails.

He fussed grimly with his stance hoping to craft a low draw, but was interrupted twice as the growing population of locusts broke his concentration. He swept several insects from the tee box until he was happy with his chances. With a whoosh, his ball soared low and curled tightly around the landmark tree, snipping off a sprig of leaves. The foliage fluttered softly to the turf as Wedgy's ball turned up the fairway and bounded to a lie in the short grass. His drive's proximity to the hole cancelled much of the advantage Rama's heroic, high-risk shot had earned.

Wedgy's expression lightened for the first time since the rigid grinder's mask had fixed itself to his face. The gold caps on his teeth glinted as he smiled back at Lee, the US Open contender who labored nobly under Rama's bag.

"Hey caddie…it'll all be over soon," Wedgy sneered.

The old hustler turned up the fairway to stomp through another gathering of grasshoppers. The creatures skittered on rigid wings at his approach. He ignored the insects and searched the crowd for Boney, just to assure himself of the poor fellow's panic at a large impending financial setback.

When the hoppers had composed themselves again, Wedgy fired a stratospheric 8-iron that dropped to a stop eighteen feet above the pin. The hustler now lay on the final green in two after seventy-seven strokes. Wedgy looked back to Boney and then across the creek to Rama, who had watched the serene flight of that high beautiful stroke with reluctant appreciation. Rama tipped an imaginary cap across the fairway to his competitor.

Lee wasn't pleased. "Don't give up, Rama. Anything can happen yet…you know what game this is."

Although Lee referred to golf's capriciousness, Rama wondered what game truly was being playing across this remote track. In this, of all places, his father had just overwritten the terrible, crippling history of his encounter with St. Claude's unforgiving steeple. And just as his father had flirted with fate in landing on the fifth's fairway, Rama had fought back into contention even though burdened with the knowledge that his mother's future lay in question in a hospital a thousand miles away. Some game! Yet, he performed far above his head. The missing pieces of a shattered relationship with his father had fallen into place as readily as his ball had rolled into the cup all afternoon. Such might be victory enough in the game of life, but one look into Lee's intense brown eyes told Rama not to settle for that.

Wedgy had been temporarily rebuffed by Rama's resurgence, but knew exactly what game *he* was playing and held the trump cards of experience and the lead. He had been in worse spots and walked away a winner hundreds of times before. This was still his game, he thought.

The old gaucho watching from Niña's seat knew better.

Carlos knew that this match was bigger than the enterprise of strokes that so occupied Rama and the Gypsy. It was a larger purpose that first brought Rama and his father to Mesquite Creek. That Rama, sharing the peaceful spirits of the Stone children since his birth had come *again* with the locusts, and that his father had fallen from the sky, was beyond comprehension. Yet while working alone at night to move the hissing sprinklers and to cut tomorrow's pins, Carlos had come to understand the inscrutable sweep of a greater game.

Carlos had returned to Mesquite Creek and Carla's service after Rama had first appeared in the willow's silver shadows that night on the putting green. His soul and his painter's hands had been inspired by that encounter. From that night, along with the shower of images that had sprung from his canvasses, had come the vision that he had been chosen to guide Rama to the place of the lightning in service of Dickey's and Glendora's souls. He believed he had been charged with seeing those spirits on the journey to their green heaven. With the children at peace, all that had so long been torn at Mesquite Creek would be mended. Carlos prayed that even Chandler was still within reach of such healing.

He waited for Rama's next shot. Though the game was predestined, its outcome was most certainly not in his withered hands, nor was it in Rama's or the Gypsy's power. The game had nothing to do with stroke count. The game was truly a test, and its outcome had teetered on the photos tucked into Lee's bag.

After Rama had refused even the *memory* of the photos on number sixteen and had taken his remarkable putt, Carlos's vision had come to pass. The spirit of Dickey Stone had whispered in his ear that he and Glendora were free to go. Rama no longer required their support. As he had foreseen, Carlos ushered the Stone children's rise to eternal peace. But Rama, now stripped of his magic and the companion spirits that had attended him all his life, faced a final test.

———•——

"I know, I know…one shot at a time," replied Rama, trying to bolster his belief in the game's greatest mantra. Although he lay well positioned to attack the hole on his second stroke, Wedgy's excellent shot had delivered a powerful blow to his confidence. He would learn in later years that in golf, confidence could be erased by a lot less than a competitor's great play. It could be toppled with a feather.

Lee kept his distance but did not withhold his advice.

"Drop that pitching wedge down on the ball nice and easy. Don't look up. Guaranteed to get you on the green and keep you below the hole. Below the hole…and a makeable putt, that's the *only* game you're playing now, amigo," Lee said emphatically. "Keep your noggin down…*I'll* keep an eye on it. You'll *hear* when it plops down on the green. That's all you'll need to know."

Rama tried to visualize "drop and plop." What could be more effortless?

"Shake your arms out real good first," continued Lee, now both coach and caddie.

Rama self-consciously shook the tension like phantom droplets from his hands, then gripped the club. Lee was right: His arms were more limber, and in his downswing the club seemed to simply drop on the ball. When he finally did look up, the ball was already nearing the apex of its flight to a point twelve feet below the hole as prescribed.

Lee snatched the club away from Rama before they even left their spot in the crescent of Mesquite Creek. "Muy bueno. One little old roll to go."

Wedgy now shared the eighteenth green with his prey. He lay seventy-seven and Rama lay seventy-eight. Victory was within a single putt of inevitability, but the inevitable required an unenviable eighteen-foot putt: a single, steadily breaking downhill roll to the cup and into the chips. Wedgy almost smelled the cash and happily anticipated the road to sunny Albuquerque and foggy Cypress Point. A two-putt would work, too…as long as Rama did the same.

Mesquite Creek's hungry gallery crowded the fringe of the eighteenth green. Starved of big-time competition by their remote place in golf's universe, even no-names like the Gypsy Hustler and lackluster rounds flirting with the eighties were enough to feed their appetite as long as the story lines, the competition, or the money were compelling enough.

In this case, the money was far from right. The majority had bet on the Gypsy, but the odds against him winning were poor. His six-to-one odds had carried the day, and a gallery full of ten-buck betters was looking at making their money back plus some small change. But there were a few real gamblers looking to turn one hundred into six hundred. Their voices in support of Rama sounded like bassoons in a band of trumpets. The Gypsy contingent, once complacent in their low-risk bets, were now buzzing as loudly in fear of losing as the rising hum of invading grasshoppers.

Wedgy tried not to focus on the faces in the gallery, especially Ivar's or Hank's. For all Wedgy knew, Ivar had flown all this way and risked an insane landing just to watch him lose. His old nemesis had money and time on his hands, Wedgy thought jealously, but this time the gentleman had gone too far.

Wedgy smiled as he recalled writing his annual challenge letter to the good men of Bluff Meade Country Club. For years they had accepted their excommunicated brother's match, and for years he had extracted large sums from members whose pride had driven their judgment far off kilter. Ivar had often led the charge against Wedgy but time and time again had led his well-heeled troops into defeat. By now Wedgy was certain Ivar had money invested in today's outing. Once again he would be happy to send the privileged gentleman's hopes over the cliff, and if Rama's or his hillbilly dad's future followed, so be it. No one ever said it was a forgiving game.

"I'm gonna miss you out there in Monterey, Schwain. You might have had a future in this business…the Junior Gypsy or some such horseshit," laughed Wedgy as he circumnavigated the line of his winning putt.

He determined that his ball would break down the dome from his left to his right, but its main feature would be its speed. It could easily overrun the hole if struck too boldly. Wedgy had done his math, comforted in the knowledge that even if he two-putt, Rama still faced a 75-percent chance that he would miss his twelve-footer and lose or a 25-percent chance that he would make the putt and force an additional tie-breaker hole at best. Thus assured, Wedgy stroked his putt with confidence and watched it roll.

The grasshoppers had stayed off the greens all day. The lawnmowers had already consumed most of their fodder, and the fertilizers weren't especially tasty. The insect that fluttered down into the path of Wedgy's seventy-eighth stroke was an exception—only passing through—just pausing on the green to rest before another clattering flight to something more succulent. But before the creature could re-cock its leaping legs, Wedgy's ball struck. The insect easily deflected the ball, and the hopper immediately took flight as the thundering voice of one particularly unhappy human resounded over the green.

"Fucking bugs!"

Wedgy watched in horror as a perfectly struck putt was ruined. His ball was deflected about thirty degrees off course. By the time the insect had fluttered away, Wedgy's ball had stopped six feet across the slope from the hole.

"Interference. Did you see that…that's interference," Wedgy declared. He fished a coin from his pocket and pressed it into the spot from which he had just putt, then walked defiantly back to retrieve his ball.

"I wouldn't do that!"

The voice of Carla Stone, with riveting authority, stopped Wedgy in his spikes. His fingers hovered just above the ball.

"That would be a two-stroke penalty for not marking your ball. I don't think you can afford that," she said.

Wedgy stood up and looked at his antagonist. "What the…are you talking about?" He nearly gagged on the expletive remaining in his throat. "I'm not marking anything. I'm *replaying* the ball. Didn't you see that damned bug block my shot? It was an outside agency…I get relief."

"I am terribly sorry, Mr. Byrne, but you must play that shot as it lies. There was no OA involved in your putt."

"Bullshit. Everybody here saw the damned hopper."

"There is no denying the insect's interference," Carla said. She sensed a wave of support for Wedgy stirring in the crowd gathering around her. There was enough money teetering on the point of this judgment that she would have to turn quickly to a higher power for support.

Wedgy and the gallery watched as Carla pulled a small red, white, and blue book from her handbag. She thumbed through the pages until she found the clarification she was seeking. An air of authority—the word of the Royal and Ancients of St. Andrews, Scotland, as interpreted by the United States Golfing Association—infused her voice as she read from Holy Writ:

If a ball in motion after a stroke on the putting
green is deflected or stopped by any moving or
animate outside agency…

Carla raised her voice and glanced over her glasses at the plaintiff:

except a worm or an insect, the stroke shall
be cancelled, the ball replaced and
the stroke replayed.

Carla lowered the incriminating book. In this game Isaac Newton and his laws of gravity and motion appear to hold sway, but only until they collide with The Rules. To the recipient of an unfavorable ruling, no law is as unforgiving. "An insect is an exception," she concluded sadly. "And what did your ball strike on that last putt, Mr. Byrne?"

Wedgy turned away and approached his ball's officially-sanctioned position on the green. "A fucking insect," he muttered inaudibly at the vast injustice of the game and the foul humor of the Scots. "Christ, we got bugs in Texas bigger than the damn birds those kilts call *outside agents*."

Lee didn't need to tell Rama the obvious. If he sunk his twelve footer, he could force Wedgy to make his treacherous six-foot putt for no better than a tie and at least one extra hole. Lee pulled the Polaroid marked numero dieciocho from the bag and stuffed it in his hip pocket as they approached the ball. At first glance Rama's putt appeared to break to the left but was complicated by an almost imperceptible ripple in the tight green turf. The putt would doubtlessly react to the minute topographic feature, but how much?

Rama and Lee crouched behind the ball for a lengthy survey. The ripple didn't easily offer up a picture of its effect on a rolling object. Lee glanced up at Carla who was watching her wristwatch. After having slapped Wedgy for a strict and costly ruling, she would be bound to enforce a delay-of-game rule now if Rama didn't strike his putt soon. Much of that time had already ticked away.

From just over Rama's shoulder, Lee peered down the line of the devilish putt. "We're gonna have to putt this one quick, amigo. It's a tough read, but I've got one of the photos...probably make that break crystal clear," he said urgently. "We can't look at this putt all day. I know what you're thinking, but damn it, Rama, there's too much to lose. There ain't no harm in it."

Rama never took his eyes from the line he was studying. Carla concentrated on the face of her watch. Lee pulled the photo from his pocket. The pin placement on that damp morning had been nearly identical to today's pin location. The phantom putter had taken six tries at the eighteenth; several of the dewy lines had carved arcs directly into the hole, the rest were close. Lee's heart raced as he oriented the Polaroid with Rama's position on the green—and there it was: an identical putt to Rama's—its telltale line captured in the curious medium of silver oxides and morning dew.

Rama's putt would be pushed twice as far to the left as Lee had imagined. "Quickly, Rama, have a look; it's your exact putt." Rama didn't respond. Lee approached him with the Polaroid in his extended hand, like Eve's apple.

"Lee! Put it away," Rama snapped. "I have to read this one for myself. Now damn it, don't *you* worry."

Rama settled behind his ball and prepared to align the putter. He raised his head and smiled at his friend. "But thanks anyway."

Nearby, Carlos Taddio's foot hovered above Niña's accelerator as he watched the match play out on the eighteenth green. Rama still had a chance, and Carlos could become a wealthier man in a matter of two putts. But he had seen Rama wave off the photos and he needn't see any more. Only in deference to the struggling golfers did he *not* depress the pedal and chug off to the shade of the willows while they finished their silly match.

The game he had waited eight years to complete was already finished.

Chapter 62

Rama looked at the line one last time and sent the putt on a path higher than most would have imagined. The ball lost inertia as it encountered the ripple and glanced slightly to the left, leaving it on a perfect line. Whether it had sufficient velocity to reach the pin was the only question. The answer waited like held breath as the ball paused at the cup, then with nothing more than its dead weight to drive it further, tumbled over the lip.

Carla jotted a seventy-nine on her scorecard.

Dignity alone kept Rama from a juvenile display over his first broken eighty, but the green still hosted an incomplete round. Wedgy could force extra holes if he sunk a fiendish six-footer across the slope. The old hustler tried to forget Carla's ruling on the grasshopper and struggled not to think of the consequences of missing. Thirty-six thousand dollars would clean out most of his year's winnings and force him to stay on the road well into the winter. He winced at the thought of endless rounds in the company of plaid shorts and cheap shits down in the Sunbelt or, God forbid, Florida.

Instead of visualizing the tricky break, he imagined pulling the Lincoln into his driveway and jacking the trailer off its weary wheels. He could picture himself settling onto his porch swing, if it still worked, and studying the employment pages with a good cup of home-brewed coffee. From that moment forward, his golf clubs would gather rust with a shed full of forgotten gardening tools.

After all this time and trouble, he almost *wanted* to miss the putt and force his hand. It was then, in the fatal grip of ambivalence that Wedgy took his stroke. His ball refused to hold its intended line above the hole and drifted a quarter of an inch below the cup. No force of nature could pull that ball back up the fraction that separated Wedgy Byrne from an extra hole and perhaps a different future. As the ball settled to rest, the match came to an end. Wedgy could second-guess his lapse of purpose forever. Rama had won.

Like horribly wounded soldiers who leave their bodies to escape intolerable pain in war, Wedgy rose above this peaceful green battlefield and watched as his hand plucked the ball from the turf in defeat and held it like a curious relic. Thus discorporate, Wedgy was unaware of the fatigue of his itinerant life. He did not feel the painful kink that had been binding up his back all afternoon. He was temporarily unaware of the sore arches, the swollen elbow, the tender ankles, and the searing sunburn. He saw Lee's and Hank's hands fly upward in celebration but heard no cheers—no sound at all—as if he were watching silent grainy figures from an old newsreel flinging their hats skyward following Francis Ouimet's grandest stroke.

Rama stepped through Wedgy's muffling shroud and offered his hand. Wallace Byrne's returning handshake startled Rama in its lifelessness. Winning was not as he had imagined. Rama had once learned from a friend on his baseball team that the Japanese allowed—even preferred—the tie game. Their mature culture had learned to cherish the draw as another sort of perfect game. He knew that concept would never fly in Texas, but for now he understood.

As Wedgy came around, he searched for words that might preserve his dignity, convincing himself that he had been betrayed into a complacent effort. "You fooled me, Schwain," were the only words he could muster. He winced at his pathetic, selfish response, knowing Rama deserved *congratulations* for fooling him, for such was always the essence of a hustle. He couldn't deny that, for now anyway, he was no different from the countless pigeons who had similarly bellyached at being misled into defeat at *his* hands. But Wedgy Byrne's tail wouldn't remain between his legs for long.

"Don't start thinking you'll make a career out of seventy-nines, Schwain."

Rama's empathy for the old hustler muzzled his reply. In deference he pointed out that Wedgy had brought out the best in him, but doubted Wedgy would take that as a compliment.

Wedgy didn't. He took it as a sign that losing to a seventy-nine had put his livelihood in a precarious state and that being out-maneuvered by Boney Carlisle into such a ridiculously overblown wager had alerted him to his judgment's worrisome poverty. Wedgy looked every minute his age as he trudged silently from the green.

———•———

To say that the thought of slipping quietly behind the wheel and easing the Lincoln's rebuilt transmission into drive hadn't occurred to Wedgy would be misleading. Leaving Mesquite Creek like a fugitive was an option, but one that would incubate no further when he discovered his car was detached from the trailer and was undergoing a most untimely washing.

Mirage Jimson grinned like a Halloween skeleton from above a fresh coat of suds. "Complimentary wash for all our overnight guests." Mirage fired a few sunflower seeds to the ground. "Don't worry, Gyp, I'll have you ready to roll about the time you get all your loose ends tied up. Hell, I've got to get on my way, too...still got to line up some flight fuel for that daredevil."

Wedgy had never tried to beat a debt—at least not by running—and it was with mixed emotion that he realized Mirage had removed that option. He muttered uncomplimentary nothings about Mirage's helpfulness as he hobbled on sore feet across the gravel lot to his trailer. Feeling empty and sick, he transferred a discouraging portion of his strong-box contents into a paper sack and trudged back up to the clubhouse. As he handed Carla the bag through the bars of her cage, he thought he might faint under an unexpected spell of déjà vu: The woman behind the bars could just as easily have been the Securities and Exchange officer handing him the government's charges, and Rama could have been his son slipping the knife between his ribs. It all felt the same.

After her ledger was satisfied, Carla smiled kindly. "I do hope you'll come play again some time, Mr. Byrne. Now, if you're hungry, dinner and a pitcher of beer are always on the house for my players." She reached through the iron bars and patted the back of his hand in sympathy even as she calculated her cut.

"Next!"

Wedgy watched grimly as a short line of winners formed at the cage. It was no comfort that he, the Gypsy Hustler, had once been the favorite. He had seen enough and almost collided with Boney Carlisle as he turned for the door. Now that the chips had all fallen, the big man seemed to favor his injured ankle far less. In fact, Wedgy doubted that the crutches supported any weight.

"Enjoy your son-of-a-bitchin' loot," Wedgy sneered. "You owe a lot to that god-damned grasshopper."

Boney seemed confused. "Loot? Oh, the money…it's not mine. And the ankle is feeling a lot better, thanks."

Not Boney's money? Wedgy's head was spinning as he entered the comforting darkness of the Grill Room lounge. As his eyes adjusted to the gloom he was fearful that he would encounter Ivar and possibly even Rama's car-salesman father, but the bar stools were unoccupied. Fortified by an Old Crow on the rocks, he meditated on the reflections of illuminated liquor bottles in the cut glass mirror. His weathered face stared back from between the colored bottles as the phase-shifting musical hook of Eddie Fisher's "The Big Hurt" swept through the room like a jet.

It's not mine. Boney's disclaimer echoed discordantly in Wedgy's brain. Of course not, thought Wedgy. Nobody out here in this sun struck place had that kind of money. No doubt—it was Ivar's money, just as he had suspected. And it would be Ivar who would keep the lion's share of the booty he had just handed over to Carla. Wedgy found it hard to believe that a man of means like Ivar could have a taste for revenge so acute that he would risk life, limb, and a sexy aircraft just to get in on the action.

"The rich get richer…Ives, you bastard," Wedgy swore into his drink. Before the alcohol could impair his mathematical skills, he tried to tally up the years he had pummeled Ivar. Perhaps he might find some comfort if those totals, when stacked against this single massive loss, balanced out in black numbers.

—•—

Boney Carlisle couldn't remember ever having held so much cash. He limped away from Carla's cage with the same grocery bag Wedgy had carried in—only Carla's fee had lightened the load. But he wouldn't have the money for long. Out on the sunny veranda, Lee waited to relieve him of Wedgy's hard-fought losses. But Lee was unaware that he waited in vain. Neither he nor Rama were the beneficiaries of these winnings. Boney's real partner lurked in the dim of the clubhouse's deserted foyer.

As we breathe, there's hope…it's Kool inside.

Boney smirked at the accidental message some jobber for a cigarette company had created by rudely slapping a decal containing the ubiquitous Kool slogan and its penguin mascot beneath the ancient, optimistic phrase that had always graced Mesquite's entry. He stepped into the foyer and propped his useless crutches against the stuffed boar. "Damn, you're one hell of a gambler, old man. Who'd have given that Rama kid a chance in hell." Boney chuckled at the thought of their ruse. "Jesus, I thought Lee would choke when I showed up on those damn crutches."

Boney raised the bag to Carlos. "It's all yours."

But Carlos waved the winnings away. "Sir, you have acted well for Carlos Taddio, and with much faith."

Boney smiled humbly. "I wouldn't have played along with your crazy plan on *faith* alone, old fellow. Only your promise to cover Rama's losses if Wedgy won got me up on those crutches.

"Here, take the bag, Carlos. I've got some explaining to do for some folks out on the veranda."

Carlos gently pushed the bag away. "No. Thee game is not finished, sir. You must not share our secret."

He grabbed the crutches and handed them back to Boney. "Sir, you are yet thee lame one today. Deliver thee money to Rama. Say no words of us. He must believe thee money is Ivar's…only then, like water, shall it flow to thee most thirsty place."

Boney always thought the old gaucho was crazy, but turning one's back on thirty-some thousand dollars with no more explanation than this flowing water mumbo jumbo confirmed his suspicions. Still, Boney did as he was told; there was nothing crazy about the substantial "teep" Carlos had slipped him yesterday.

As Carlos disappeared out the front doors, Boney tightened his grip on the sack and tucked the crutches under his arms. He hoisted his "lame" foot for one last act. What *was* crazy, he thought, was the windfall this Ivar fellow was likely to collect from Rama. Boney had never cashed Ivar's check, and as far as he could tell, Ivar hadn't otherwise wagered a dime on Rama. And crazier still, neither Rama nor Ivar would ever know it.

—•—

Like bandits gathering outside of town, Boney rendezvoused with his conspirators at the rockers on the veranda. "It gives me great pleasure to present you with these *groceries*, Rama," Boney laughed. "You will especially like the greens."

Lee flashed his trademark grin, still unaware of Carlos's investment. "We're all square now, eh amigo?"

Rama reluctantly accepted the bag without looking at the contents. "Lee, you never owed me anything." Rama recalled the thank-you note that accompanied Lee's refund on Hank's lost bet eight years and one locust cycle ago.

"Oh that," said Lee. "That was your fair share of the take. Let's just say *this* is for returning my putter that day. That flat-stick has been worth its weight in gold the last couple of seasons. I'm gonna win an Open with that putter yet. No, Rama; this money is all yours."

Rama had his doubts. It was Ivar who had provided the funds, and it was Boney who had jacked the odds. And wasn't it Lee who had engineered the whole unlikely enterprise?

Rama counted off ten fifties and handed them to Boney. "Is that enough for a tip?" he asked, certain that Ivar would approve.

Boney instinctively reached for the bills but stopped as he remembered he still had Carlos's "teep" tucked away in his locker. "No, it's not necessary. But thanks…I already got paid."

Rama shrugged and offered the bills to Lee, but Lee also refused. "No way, amigo; you might hurt my professional status," he smiled.

Rama slipped the money back into the bag. If he couldn't get a taker maybe he could get an answer. "Lee, back at Sunset Hills you told me you could get a good match for Wedgy up here. Was I who you had in mind?"

"Took a little doin', didn't it?" Lee chuckled. "No…it was intended to be Boney's game, a good game from an unlikely player like we'd planned, eh… until our friend took a little tumble. I swear the only thing I knew, Rama, was that you were a natural, but I wouldn't have put you in that match." Lee's smile settled into a thoughtful expression. "You had me a little worried. Jesus, Rama, we dodged a bullet with your seventy-nine. Boney would have made our victory a little less dramatic."

Lee clapped the big man on the shoulder. "Isn't that right, amigo?" Boney winced as he bit his lip to hold in the truth as he had promised Carlos. If only his partners knew how good a "game" he had really played.

"Never a doubt," said Boney with a wink. "I would've knocked the wheels right off the Gypsy's damned wagon."

Lee laughed as he fished for the keys to his car. "I'm afraid I can't celebrate with you all; I've got an early tee time in El Paso tomorrow." He offered his friends a handshake. "Bones, maybe we'll get a game in next trip. I'll give you twelve strokes, maybe more if that ankle's still bothering you. It's the least I can do…you saved my image. After I talked this match up for three days, my reputation would have been banged up pretty bad if you hadn't suggested Rama. But nobody would have put a dime on that match if you hadn't put Ivar's money where *your* mouth was."

Boney grinned as he followed Lee down to the drive. "No problem, amigo. Your rep is safe in these parts. Hell, they'll be naming streets after you before long, my friend."

Lee clamped a firm bronze hand on Rama's shoulder. "And don't you quit on that Melyssa, either." He whistled a long note in her praise. "Maybe you should send her that scorecard for a souvenir."

———•———

It had been far too long a day for Ivar Guidance. After the match he had begged a ride on the refreshment cart to his plane. In the day's remaining light, he conducted a casual inspection. Carla had assured him that Mirage would arrive with fuel first thing in the morning. Barring any damage from Hank's landing, and assuming there was adequate length on her fairways, they would be airborne by ten o'clock tomorrow morning.

Ivar steadied himself as the cart turned away from the aircraft and headed up the third fairway, back toward the clubhouse and a good night's sleep. Carla had promised a comfortable bed in one of the guest rooms. As they bumped along, he looked up at his home for the night. The pepper trees' shadows stretched across the fairway in the final minutes before dusk erased them into nothingness. The odor of sage and mown grass, and the scent from the barbecue pit, mingled into a rustic perfume that comforted his tired old bones.

"Would you be so kind as to stop a moment?" He asked the girl. In the absence of the cart's clatter, he listened to the laughter from the veranda and the rustle of quail in the sage. The stately lines of the clubhouse, its generous eaves, and its curiously landlocked widow's watch were cast in the day's most congenial light, striking a familiar silhouette against the purple sky. He realized that here, in an unlikely green respite from the harsh plains, Carla's husband had constructed an adobe homage to Augusta, Georgia's, most celebrated building: the National Clubhouse. It was a building with which he was familiar. His business associates included several National members, and together they still occasionally trod that perfect track.

Ivar closed his eyes. The beauty of the evening coaxed an easy smile from his lips. After waking up intact and alive, every moment would be worth that much more, even without his Rebecca. From the perspective of a new life, the rough and tumble course before him seemed as alluring as Augusta's resplendent emerald showpiece.

"Sir, are you alright?" The cart girl feared for the health of the old fellow whom she heard had fainted at his airplane's controls that afternoon.

Ivar's eyes opened to the peaceful scene. A coven of bats launched into the twilight above the course and cut erratic mute figures against the sky. "Yes, quite alright…just a little bushed. You are so kind for asking." He flicked his fingers forward: "Carry on."

As the cart approached the clubhouse, Ivar was sidetracked by the voice of Rama Schwain calling to him from the porch. He pressed two dollars into the cart girl's hand before bidding her good-night.

Rama approached, still clutching the Waddley's grocery bag

"I thought you were too tired to stay up."

"I could never fall asleep, Rama, unless I had checked up on the old girl again. She seems none the worse for wear. And I was treated to a beautiful moment just now…glad I lingered." Ivar looked at Rama curiously. "And you?"

Rama looked around to be sure he was out of earshot of the golfers lounging on the veranda.

"Do you remember the check you left in case a good match against Wedgy came along?" asked Rama. "Well, it was riding on the match today. But the odds got bumped up a bit. Don't worry…you did okay." Rama hoisted the sack. "This is all yours."

Ivar was in no hurry to take the bag Rama offered. It looked heavy. "My, oh my, this has been one red-letter day. Do you know how long I've been waiting to see Wallace take his medicine? Darned if I almost had to die to see it happen."

He took the bag from Rama and was startled at its bulk. "Quite a bit of *medicine*, I gather."

Rama was glad to be rid of the cash and was anxious to catch up with his father. "Get some sleep, Mr. Guidance, unless you plan on having Dad fly us all the way home."

"You know…that is not such a bad idea." Ivar's eyes twinkled in the twilight. The current of pride beneath Rama's voice was a greater reward than Wedgy's comeuppance or even the weighty contents of the grocery bag.

Rama didn't want to detain Ivar any longer, and he bid his amazing and most generous friend goodnight.

When Ivar reached the stairs that served the guest rooms, he stopped under the glow of a sputtering yellow insect light and opened the bag. He was startled to discover that the cash within was far more than his investment. Ivar sat on the bottom step and roughly counted out the money. When he got to twenty thousand he stopped.

"My Lord, the betting did get a little steep." He extracted several stacks of bills and stowed the bag in his room, then made his way to the liquor-bottle lights of the Grill Room lounge.

Wedgy never noticed Ivar enter. The old hustler's focus had not progressed beyond the meaningless patterns shifting through the ice cubes in his third Old Crow. There was a good chance his attention would have remained trapped in the ice of subsequent cocktails had he not been disturbed by the entrance of his old nemesis.

No one who had witnessed Wedgy's loss or had grimaced at the brutal twist of fate the offending locust had foisted upon him would have dared enter the hostile aura surrounding the stricken golfer. He drank alone. Even offering well-meaning remarks would have been akin to driving into a blasting zone with a CB on full gain.

The explosive Mr. Byrne was better left in solitude. But Ivar had suffered sufficiently at Wallace's cagey hands for so many years that he had earned the right to interfere in his rival's most gloomy reveries. He had even once been Wedgy's friend.

"Tough luck on that outside agency call, eh Wallace? What goes around comes around...karma, my Indian friends call it."

Wedgy's expression softened from murderous to merely irritated as he raised his eyes in recognition of his well-appointed old associate.

"Karma can kiss my ass, Ives. You like that oriental mumbo-jumbo? How about a little haiku to put it all in perspective: *Hoppers are a bug, bad luck a bitch, this day I played like total shit*," Wedgy sneered. "Go tell your Buddhist pals to take a seventeen-day fast...from water...see how their karma holds up."

Wedgy scowled although he was actually feeling better in Ivar's company. He patted the empty stool beside him. "You must be thirsty after nearly ditching your damned aero plane." He tapped his glass with a finger. "The whiskey's not bad, just stay away from the Luva'Lime sours."

Ivar took a seat and ordered a Brandy Alexander and a paper sack. As he waited for the bartender to bring his unusual request, he noticed that Wedgy smelled like a man who had sweated through a day's hard labor, not a mere round of golf with a mid-handicapper.

Ivar raised his glass to meet Wedgy's. "Can't say that I'm *not* glad to see you got your gluteus maximus trounced for once—especially by my protégé."

Wedgy set his glass on the bar. "You want me to toast my own misfortune?"

"Well, Wallace, it's not like you've never had an interference intervene on *your* behalf." Ivar knew Charlie Vestal's flagstick trick back at Bluff Meade was as doubtlessly engraved in Wedgy's brain as it was in his. "At least that grasshopper on the last hole had no bad intentions."

"Ives, it's not like you lost so much on *that* match...not like what I got stiffed today. Rama and that damned Boney fella were in cahoots with that Mexican caddie to clean me out. But you tell me, Ives, since when do oil-patch cowpoke hillbillies like Boney have six thousand dollars to bet on a lousy amateur match?" Wedgy looked at Ivar suspiciously.

Ivar felt a pang of responsibility for Wedgy's suffering. "Guess they might have had some financial backing, eh?" Ivar could not resist smiling; he never had been much good at poker.

Wedgy held his cocktail at mid-sip. His green eyes tracked across the space between the two old rivals to peer into Ivar's mischievous expression. But before Wedgy could muster a suitable oath, Ivar pulled the bills from his jacket and dropped them into the empty sack. Wedgy looked on in disbelief.

"That should be somewhere near ten thousand bucks, about a third of your losses if I have heard correctly," declared Ivar. "Do try and be a little more savvy with your odds-making in the future. Six grand at six-to-one…really, Wallace. You were a member at Bluff Meade once; your bad judgment might still give the place a bad name."

"Christ, Ivar…so it *was* you! I thought you flew in here to fetch Rama back to his momma."

"Wallace, if you don't want to accept this refund…"

"Refund?" Wedgy pulled the bag closer to his chest.

Ivar continued: "I did fly here for Rama, and I *did* send him off with the resources to recover a few of the dollars you and Charlie hustled back in June with that stuck flagstick ruse. But this affair with these Mesquite Creek high rollers talking you into the stratosphere…that was none of my doing. Like I said, Wallace: karma."

Ivar's confession was well-intentioned but inaccurate. His check had never been cashed, but he didn't know it then. All accounts were being settled with proceeds from Mesquite Creek's "ghost artist," Carlos Taddio. But believing himself magnanimous, Ivar lifted his glass again and finished his confession: "I am near exhaustion, but I couldn't sleep if I took that much of your money, Wallace." To Wedgy's surprise, his old friend discreetly pulled another two bundles of bills from the sack and slid them along the bar to a point just beneath his chin.

"Just swear that no one knows it has returned to you, Wallace."

Ivar glanced around the bar to be sure no one had seen him slip the cash to Wedgy. He planned to share the remainder of this windfall with Rama but knew if the young man thought Wedgy had been reimbursed, he might fear Wedgy had simply thrown the match as part of a scheme. Ivar knew Rama wouldn't accept what he could so sorely use if he thought the match wasn't on the level, or if the money wasn't truly from Wedgy's pockets.

Wedgy looked Ivar in the eyes. The unexpected refund had disturbed the old hustler, who responded with a weary handshake. "Your secret is safe with me, Ives."

Ivar stirred the remains of his Alexander. "I expect to see you next July at Bluff Meade. Don't worry, Wallace; we'll find you a fair match," Ivar said sarcastically. "Unless, of course, Charlie is on the bag."

Wedgy rolled his bloodshot eyes. "Caddie or no caddie, I'll still have my way with you, Ives. If I'm still in the business."

Ivar tossed a twenty-dollar bill onto the bar to cover the drinks and tip, then shuffled from the room with all the dignity he could muster, stopping momentarily at the jukebox to spend a single quarter that had troubled him in its solitude. He released the coin into the slot and punched up three tunes. Before the first disc had landed on the turntable, Ivar was gone.

In Ivar's absence Wedgy pondered his uncertain future while from the depths of the Wurlitzer, the crystal voice of Doris Day cheerfully resigned herself to accept whatever will be.

Chapter 63

Carlos Taddio retired to his room above the clubhouse, comforted by old photographs and the certainty that his visions weren't those of a man touched by the moon. After years of faith that this blessed day would arrive, he was spent. He feared his time might now be numbered in only a few fleeting seasons, that he would never see his sisters and their children or the skies above the Pampas lands of Argentina again.

In the fading light he studied their faces.

A written correspondence consisting of nine letters in thirty-eight years comprised a sketch of their lives since they had last been together—before he sought fortune in Texas. And with the letters had come photos: first the images of glorious brides, then shining dark-haired children, and later, proud adolescents. The photos had turned faintly orange under the spell of poorly fixed emulsions and time's relentless passage.

The letters had found their way into the bottom of a lemon crate that held Carlos's most sacred belongings, but the tired old images were still tacked to the frame around his mirror. The old gaucho regularly blessed each head, and although he had never seen or spoken to any of the children, he knew them all by name. Every evening he lit a candle for them all, including one special flame for his brother who had drowned trawling off the Falklands.

Just as Carlos prayed for a family whom he would never see again, he also prayed for the Stone family, once so close in Mesquite Creek. Nineteen years ago his prayers for the health of the children, Glendora and Dickey, had been rebuffed by a single terrible bolt. Yet thereafter he had prayed for their souls and for their father, Chandler's, return from wherever in the world he had chosen to find solace from his storms of sorrow.

For the first time Carlos hoped he knew that place.

His understanding began with a poem he had found in Niña's stall the day after Chandler's disappearance. It was, he supposed, a farewell message, but certainly the poem describing his sorrow was not a suicide note. Carlos kept the note in his saddlebag for many years. It seemed no more than a beautiful expression of Chandler's emotions in a heart-rending time—until three months ago when he had chosen to clear out some space in the widow's watch for his latest canvasses. Behind a heavy wooden chest he had discovered some old papers and a clipping from a steamship line's schedule. Six columns of departures and arrivals from a list of cities populated the list. He never would have lingered to take a second look except he remembered a story Carla had told of a railroad worker announcing that he had seen someone who looked like Chandler down in the Brownsville yard. Carla had said the fellow sent the Chandler look-alike up the Missouri-Pacific line to New Orleans.

That is what caught his eye. One column in the schedule began with a departure from New Orleans. That might not have been compelling, but as Carlos traced the cities the vessel would call, he realized that ship's destination was Glasgow, Scotland. After checking an atlas, he realized only 140 miles separated the docks in Glasgow from Dornoch, Scotland—Chandler's birthplace. Carlos sighed at the thought. It was wearying, but the image of Chandler riding the rails out of Brownsville to a refuge in Scotland gave him the strength to catch a bus to Abilene where a long day in the library yielded the names and addresses of constables and directors-of-golf at villages and links along the coast and firths of eastern Scotland. If Chandler were alive, his old servant could imagine him in no other land.

Carlos recalled he had sent five- or six-dozen letters detailing his desire to connect with a Chandler Stone. The letters described Chandler, his interest in golf, and the fact that he often wore a red scarf. To his amazement, he received six replies. Five were courteous answers empathizing with Carlos's plight but regretfully stating they had observed no such individual. But one letter was hopeful. It was from: Director of Golf - Kintyre at Turnberry. The director recounted that he had seen such a fellow. The man often came to the golf course, not to play but to walk the seaside paths where he wouldn't interfere with play. He suggested Carlos contact the MacKenzie family on Glafyn Road. In the director's words, "Apparently your friend took on work there as a gardener ten years or so ago. Old man MacKenzie fixed him up with some living quarters and as far as they know, though he don't say much, 'Red Scarf' is a fine, sad man." To Carlos's delight, the director included a proper address.

With Rama Schwain's noble performance, Carlos sensed that the events swirling around the young man marked the mechanisms of a grand apparatus—a divine engine turning incomprehensibly to grant an old man his final prayer for a fractured family. He believed he had played his part. He had found a way to get Rama into the game and onto the sixteenth green where a thousand prayers for the peace of the children's souls had been answered. Might it be too much to ask the same for Chandler Stone?

His tired hands touched the matchsticks to this evening's candles, but not without effort. As the wicks came to light, he knew that with a destination for his final painting, he could not rest. He would have to complete his work before spring lit the prairie with black-eyed Susans, and while he still had the strength to hold a brush and possessed the eye to blend a palette. If God were to answer his prayer for Chandler's return, such grace would be granted only through the brushes of the lost Scotsman's truest friend. It would take such a masterpiece, a convincing vision of the children's eternal peace and Carla's longing, that should it ever fall before Chandler's eyes, it might enchant his broken spirit and see him home.

The old hands touched one more candle…for Rama. Carlos smiled in gratitude that Rama's pure spirit had provided harbor for the children's souls. He whispered a simple prayer of thanks with a wish that Rama should no longer labor beneath the burden of old lies.

—•—

The unfamiliar glow of achievement still illuminated Hank with persistence that lasted into the fine September evening. The threatening storm had been consumed in a mass of dry air flowing in from the west. After passing his winnings on to Ivar, Rama caught up with Hank, who lingered at the plane like a sentry. The only real dangers to the craft might be marauding boar, coyote, or whirlwinds—improbable threats—but Hank felt he owed the aircraft at least as much protection as she had granted him. In addition, he had discovered that the airplane's resting place near the trees lining the third fairway was a tranquil spot to enjoy one of Boney's cigars.

"Haven't seen you light up a stogie in years," remarked Rama as he encountered the tobacco's welcoming aroma. Since childhood he had never been able to separate that scent from memories of tagging along with his father on hikes up abandoned railroad tracks near their house.

"Kind of a victory smoke I guess, eh Chief?" Hank exhaled a well-formed smoke ring and watched it dissipate in the dying light. "Didn't realize what a big deal your game with Wedgy was…guess I was lucky to see you in action."

"No, I was lucky to see *you* in action." Rama patted the aircraft's cold wing with his hand.

"How 'bout a puff? I bummed it off that Boney fellow, the one on the crutches. We gimps gotta help each other out, you know." Rama smiled at his father's comfortable wit.

"Hell of a day, no doubt about it, Chief. Your old buddy Ivar had fainted dead away," Hank explained as Rama tested the smoke. "What else could I do?"

"You could have clipped off a couple of those pepper trees or panicked and augered into the dust somewhere out there." Rama waved the cigar at the expanse of forbidding landscape looming in the dark. "That's what most people would have done…under pressure, with no practice! Shit, what has it been, Dad, twenty-four years?"

Hank looked at his son and felt a wave of nausea sweep him at the thought of Rama's innocent acceptance of so many deceptions. Carlos's prayer for Rama's deliverance from lies tugged at Hank like a gust; after his deliverance from the skies there was no room for further deceptions. The moment for truth had come. With a chorus of frogs singing in the creek nearby, Hank did not hold back. He revealed that he had squandered most of Rama's college funds on purchasing an old glider and on gambling, even after he had professed to having stopped. He had fallen into debt with Calcutta Finance to cover the deposit on Trent Institute's tuition but had lost that, too, on a bet against Wedgy when Ivar was supposedly a sure thing. His job and a few crucial mortgage payments had tumbled in behind. And most painfully, Hank confessed that he had even hidden the financial burden under the guise of Doris's costly treatment, most of which was being paid through Ivar's generosity.

"Christ, Rama, I even sent Trent a rubber check hoping to buy time to fix this mess up, but things just got worse."

Hank spoke with as much satisfaction as remorse, relieved that all the cards were on the table. He raised both arms in surrender. "There, now you *really* know your old man. Guess you already figured out some of this crap and that's why you left home. I can't blame you."

Hank paused to look at the first stars winking to life above. "I could have died with all this on my mind…" Hank shivered at an image of Heaven's gate: Saint Peter attempted to crack open the book on Hank Schwain, but the old angel seemed to be laboring under the load.

"I've still got to square up all my accounts, Son. I sure don't believe this machine got me to the ground in one piece just so I could step back into the same old pit." Hank took the cigar back from Rama and blew a puff into the night. As the blue smoke drifted upward, his eyes moistened. He drew a quavering breath.

"There's another thing that's been eating at me all along…that I smacked you when you had that Lee fella's money in your pocket." Hank's hand dropped softly to his son's shoulder. "I've always been sorry that I didn't trust you… you've got to know in case something happens to me one day." Hank waved at the sky. "You never know, one of those shooting stars just might pick me off some night."

Rama laughed softly at his father's imagery. He understood the thread of humor that ran deep at Hank's core. "Come on, Dad, that's one in eight billion… why worry?"

Rama was uncertain what to make of his father's revelations. At this tender moment forgiveness seemed appropriate. How could he express disappointment or anger when staring straight into the face of vulnerability? He hadn't asked for a confession, just the sharing of a cigar in the afterglow of both their triumphs. And forgiveness didn't require a list of penance, a ledger of infractions, or a confessional in the corner of a dim church. It merely required an appreciation for life—all things would flow from there.

"I guess you were always trying for that payday. It's a whole new ball game now, huh?"

Hank agreed but didn't answer; he had one more story to tell. He gazed at Venus hovering in the western sky.

"Your mother's problem..." His eyes remain fixed on the glimmering planet. "It isn't a disease. It's an injury that didn't have to be."

He continued without waiting for Rama's inevitable question.

"It was on a Sunday. We were just teenagers, your mother and I, and I made her climb up a damn rocky draw out in the Palouse to see some old Indian writing...petroglyphs. You know, like cave paintings. The Injuns had scratched antelope, birds, fish, and each other on a big rock slab that rose over a real pretty little flat up the sides of the draw. That flat...really just a broad ledge was hard to reach, but it was worth it.

"A spring at the base of the rock kept things extra green and cool." Hank sighed at the memory. "Thick grass, birds singing...a couple could get mighty comfortable up there." His eyes turned bashfully back to the sky. "The rock pictures were sort of a come-on, you know what I mean?"

Rama thought about last night with Melyssa on the sixteenth tee's grassy carpet. "Yeah, I do."

"Damned if I didn't haul your mother up there. We were a mighty healthy couple."

Rama held his breath, enthralled at the insight into his parents' courtship. Muffled Duke Ellington music coming from their bedroom had been the extent of his knowledge of their romance.

"We'd had a nice afternoon...our first real fling, wouldn't you know it. But coming down the slope, I wasn't paying attention and let your mother get ahead of me. She tangled with some rotten rock and lost her footing. The poor thing took a hell of a tumble down the scree and banged the back of her head pretty bad." Hank was glad that in the fading light, Rama couldn't see the goose bumps the memory still raised on his arms.

"I never should have taken her up there—not a nice girl like her. And I should have been hanging on to her better. It was like we were getting punished for being so damn..."

"Passionate? Come on, Dad; you weren't the first guy to sneak off with his girlfriend. Mom just had some bad luck."

"Well, that's for sure, but I was scared. I was scared at how bad she might be hurt, and at what I was going to tell her parents and all. So I cleaned her head up good and got her comfortable. She didn't *look* too bad, just a little wound under her hair, but she was woozy and it was getting dark. I knew I was in deep shit, but she was too dizzy to try that slope in bad light, so we stayed up there Sunday night. The next morning she had a headache but felt okay. You'd never have known about that cut behind her head unless you went looking for it.

"We tore on out of there at first light, and went straight to school, like nothing ever happened on Sunday. Our folks were fit to be tied that afternoon after class, and I was scared about being out all night with a girl. She was scared, too, but her head didn't seem to be bothering her at first, and she never said boo about it…never saw a doctor. I told her folks the car had broken down. We both took a tongue-lashing but that was that. Just a couple of horny kids.

"But a few years on she starts having her spells. She never said boo about the old injury and the doctors were content to shrug her symptoms off as fatigue, women's problems, diet…hell, the last guy even said sclerosis. I always supposed they knew best, but now this new fella' Doc Myers thinks the injury has been the problem all along. I hope he's right, cause that means he might just fix her up, but it'll also mean I caused your mother a lot of misery. I should have had the balls to fess up to the whole story and see that she got to a doctor soon as we got off that mountain."

Rama warmed at his father's courage, although he wasn't comfortable with his guilt. "You didn't cause anything, Dad. Any guy in his right mind would have taken a girl up there if it was as nice as you say," he proclaimed with some bittersweet authority. "I would have. And Mom could have had that wound looked at. She could have made up an excuse. That's not your fault."

Rama knew it could not have been easy for his father to share this story. It was bad enough that he had the fates of those soldiers from St. Claude tangled within him, but carrying his wife's suffering as well…it was a wonder he hadn't become hopelessly bitter or succumbed to worse vices.

"Mom doesn't hold it against you, does she?"

Hank thought about his wife and the years of tolerance for all the lost wages and lonely nights. He shivered at the inequity. Blame or regret rarely reared its head, even as his gambling had mutated from a pastime to a cancerous obsession.

"I guess you haven't heard. She tossed me out just a few days back—over unpaid bills. Can't blame her, but I promise I am going to straighten things out starting this week." Hank noticed Rama's cigar had gone out and, with a graceful move, expertly flicked the metal lid from his Zippo and held a flame for his son.

Rama pulled the cigar back to life with breath held during Hank's testimony. "Yeah, I know you will, Dad. Just don't sell off your gold teeth," Rama grinned, recalling their angry encounter the night before he followed Wedgy's promises down Highway 61.

Hank laughed at the memory and at his son's bravado.

Rama puffed up a cloud from the resuscitated smoke and let his last doubts float away. He knew that all the words of promise were meaningless when talk was cheap, but this evening his father's words had never had more value.

The quiet of the evening passed between them like a chalice until Rama's voice broke the silence. It was his turn to speak of romance. "Dad, do you remember the black-haired girl who drove the refreshment cart last time we were here?"

—•—

The twin engines of Ivar's Cessna roared to life even before the dew sweepers had taken to the first tee. Ivar had slept well but had been awakened by the crunch of Mirage's flatbed on the gravel drive. The reliable scarecrow of a man had arrived with two drums of aviation fuel as promised. In ten minutes Ivar was giving the plane a thorough run-up check while Mirage sat in the co-pilot's chair, tugging on the day's first Abba-zaba.

Carla arrived at Carlos's room below the crow's nest studio and placed a pot of maté on a wooden chair by his bed. She listened to the engines' drone as the old gaucho sipped himself awake.

Carlos had opened his tired eyes to a new day and listened to the sound that had replaced the locusts' whine. It would be a good day, he thought. One candle still flickered by his mirror.

He would make the rounds of the course and water a few hot spots until his energy flagged. If he had the strength, he would climb the stairs to his studio and resume his final work. He smacked his lips and thanked Carla for the drink; even now its earthy flavor still reminded him of a home he would never see again.

"It shall be a good day for you in thee sky, Señora." Carlos smiled at the rocky crags turning to flame above the driving range as the sun's first rays collided with the ragged outcroppings. "Thee new jardinero, he is a good man, and thee flowers will be kept well. Perhaps you may again meet your amigas at thee Nationale de Augusta."

Yesterday, after concluding business following Rama and the Gypsy Hustler's match, Carla had found Carlos parked beneath the willows. She sat beside him on Niña's vinyl seat and broke the news: She and Ivar Guidance had found a common connection in Georgia. She would be leaving for a while.

Carla explained that the exhausted old pilot who had climbed down from the airplane yesterday had proven to be a gentleman of the caliber she had once known. Even after such a harrowing experience, his genteel demeanor and courtly carriage struck a chord of familiarity—like that of the gentry she had charmed at Augusta when Chandler was still carefree and Bobby Jones was still vital.

Over a plate of pecan pie following Rama's match, her conversation with Ivar Guidance had turned to that era. Ivar had listened attentively and recognized several of the names Carla dropped. Being a humble man, he did not press the fact that Guidance Industries had business affiliations with numerous members of the elite golf club. She learned that Ivar merely had to inquire as to the condition of the greens and his associates would take that as a polite inquiry as to the possibility of a round on the National, should an invitation to play be proffered.

So it was, Carla learned, that Ivar had become a frequent visitor to the storied grounds. Years ago during a storm delay, he had even exchanged idle chatter with Ike himself, sipping club soda as they discussed the mystery of the Hogan Secret—even the president couldn't get a grip on the definition of *pronation.*

Carla's dreams of sitting in the shade of billowing oaks and watching gentlemen, including the occasional golfing luminary, parading to that first grand tee had long been abandoned. But suddenly, here was a new link to her irretrievable past.

Ivar Guidance had heartily enjoyed Carla's company and her masterful dessert. The renewed vision of a forgotten fantasy had lifted ten years from her face. Believing her to be a widow had piqued Ivar's interest in the possibility of romance after Rebecca.

Tempted by the attention of a wealthy gentleman, Carla, too, felt the tug to a new world. She had feigned hesitation at Ivar's suggestion that she join them on the return trip to Atlanta and perhaps to visit the grail of golf, whose wrought-iron gates apparently still opened to him. Yes, Carla thought, a visit to Atlanta with a sojourn over to Augusta would be a welcome vacation. She had cautiously concurred that if properly escorted she might accept such a proposal.

The plane would leave by ten o'clock next morning, Ivar had said. The old gentleman had assured her of the best accommodations and the most appropriate of manners. She already imagined the dogwoods and the magnolias, though she feared the blossoms would be gone in September.

—•—

"Yes, Carlos, perhaps I will meet my amigas again." She patted his frail hand. "But I will only be visiting. It has been so very long they may all be gone."

Augusta had most improbably come calling again. Carla feared that in the presence of a fine man with a world of possibilities swung wide again, she might resist returning to this solitary speck of struggling turf. Whether blown away like Chandler on his "storms of sorrow" or plucked up by the wings of the Cessna revving so promisingly on the fairway down below, she knew that any departure might be a final good-bye.

Carla felt a pang in her heart. She feared the old fellow might not live to see her return, and for him to die here with his entire second family dead or gone seemed like the height of cruelty to one who had labored to sustain the spirit and the vitality of Mesquite Creek since his reappearance eight years ago.

Carlos smiled at his old friend. His prayers had put him at peace. "Go, Señora Carla…be well prepared. All is in good hands."

Carla thought the reliable old greens keeper was speaking of the golf course. She poured him a fresh cup of maté and stood to go. She noticed an unfinished painting resting on one of the old gaucho's easels. She had never seen it before.

"The children," she gasped, "and their father. It will be one of your most beautiful." Before her emotions got the better of her, she slipped out his door with an adios.

Carlos finished his maté and dressed for the departure. He pulled his finest white satin shirt down over his meager frame, then strained to pull on a festive pair of soft leather trousers and to fasten a grand silver buckle. He struggled against his favorite snakeskin boots; only the flat-brimmed hat and bolo tie were easy. He pulled the slide up halfway, leaving the amber rattlesnake rattle hovering above his heart. If he died on this day, Carlos Taddio wanted to be dressed for the angels.

The regal old man stepped to his window and threw open the louvered sashes. He watched the plane in the distance taxi back to the center of the first fairway. From there he could see it would have a good run up number one, past the mounded green, then down number two—more than enough runway to get aloft, he hoped.

Long minutes dragged by, but presently Carla, Hank, and Rama approached the plane. Several onlookers, Boney and Mirage among them, stayed back as the three passengers stepped forward to board the little aircraft. Even with aged eyes, Carlos could see the white-haired man in the cockpit window.

Carlos raised a shaky hand and scribed a cross in the frame from which he watched. "Go with God," he whispered.

Rama turned suddenly as if tapped upon the shoulder. He looked back to the clubhouse and spotted the old gaucho, outfitted in his finest regalia. Rama smiled and waved in a long, slow arc to make certain those old eyes would pick out his good-bye signal.

He was surprised that Carlos was at the window. Following the match yesterday, the old fellow had appeared especially frail. Rama wished he had spent more time with Mr. Taddio, but Carlos always seemed to be content with just what he had, or didn't have, and now that included time. Rama vowed he would be back. Only after seeing the old gaucho's hands rise in recognition did he feel free to depart.

Carlos saw Rama and Hank enter the plane, and then turned his attention to the third passenger, Carla Stone. Her right arm was also raised to wave, but she didn't face the clubhouse or the group of well-wishers. She faced the plane. From Carlos's vantage he could see she was speaking to the passengers, but he could not hear her speech. He watched Carla step back from the plane. The door snapped shut, and without hesitation the aircraft began to bounce slowly out across the rough fairways.

It was moving at a gallop as it veered past the first green, then jogged into the expansive second fairway. The plane would need every inch of the ample playing surface. Carlos heard the engines scream, and for a moment the plane looked to be in need of a third fairway. It charged toward the end of number two and raced up the gentle slope that supported the green. At lift-off speeds the backside of that green, which was a demanding-enough chip, would be disastrous if they weren't airborne. But the plane leapt from the fringe and into the morning sky.

Ivar quickly executed a long rising curve to the east. The craft would fly effortlessly to refuel in Jackson, Mississippi, and on to its destination in Atlanta.

Carla released the breath her lungs had held during the risky take-off. She wiped at the dampness in her eyes. "Stirred up some grit," she complained. Mirage and Boney understood. The would-be debutante turned back to the clubhouse—to Carlos and a sense of promise stirred by the painting on his easel. There was work to do.

The plane had delayed the morning's tee times as Carla had guessed it might. She had directed the starter to arrange a shotgun start on six different holes. He waited for her signal now. The gray-haired dame of Mesquite Creek walked to the top of the stairs near the veranda. She opened her handbag and removed a thirty-eight revolver. Its ivory handle gleamed in the glorious morning's light. She checked the magazine and slid one bullet into place, and as the dark speck of Ivar's plane was swallowed in the distance, she raised the gun.

In a split second, the report of a single shot rang out across Mesquite Creek's empty fairways.

Play had resumed.

Chapter 64

Doris thought she was with angels, but as the last traces of anesthesia faded, the glowing aura of the figures attending her dissolved into mere terrestrial forms—her son and husband—but far more wondrous creatures than the heavenly hosts. She smiled weakly, certain she was the recipient of a miracle, but as amazing as Rama's and Hank's arrival at her bedside was, she had received a greater stroke of fortune on the operating table. Doctor Myer had found a threatening but operable tumor at the site of her head injury where he had only expected sclerotic tissue or perhaps a dangerous bone fragment.

The doctor had described the find to his assistants as a serendipitous occurrence. For many years, the attention of his predecessor, Dr. Stassen, had been diverted from further exploration at the site of the head injury by the notion that such old trauma was an unlikely cause of Doris's current symptoms. Consequently she had suffered through fruitless, misguided diagnoses as the tumor, though benign, had progressed under the shield of misunderstanding to a debilitating proportion.

Doctor Myer had taken a reasonable risk when he challenged the old perception of Doris's illness and opted for an aggressive surgical approach. After encountering the tumor, he ratcheted up the odds further by attempting its removal. Only in relief after the operation's successful outcome had he felt free to marvel in the irony that the old doctor was partly right: Doris's wound had in itself been non-threatening, yet oddly, it had proved her savior by chance. He knew he had stumbled upon her would-be executioner by accident. Unwilling to claim any more credit than that which his skill with the scalpel warranted, he admitted to Hank that medicine harbors its share of luck. "Funny, but that old rap on the noggin might actually have saved your wife, Mr. Schwain. We mightn't have found that mass until too late."

Hank's heart leapt as he received the news that Doris would recover fully. He appreciated the doctor's nod to the workings of luck in his profession. The odds seemed to be rolling the Schwains' way at last. It was a long, long shot that he and Doris both had received a second chance in the last thirty-six hours. Hank resolved to make the most of this reprieve. It wouldn't be easy, but the damage he had left behind in Memphis had to be undone, and with Lew Raybon involved, it had to be undone soon.

Hank was encouraged as Doris's eyes brightened and she spoke with unexpected strength.

"Hank, honey, thank goodness you're here. Was the flight good?"

"Couple of rough spots, sweetheart. But Ivar has a mighty forgiving plane." Hank left the tale of his emergency landing for another day. No point in overloading the poor woman with drama.

Doris raised her hand to Rama. "And my prodigal caddie...it has been two months. I only remember dreaming of your voice on the telephone." She shivered at having been so distant. "You did call, didn't you?"

"Well, never enough, Mom."

"Mr. Guidance tells me that you roused him after my last spell." She remained amazed that Rama could have divined her needs from so deep in the heart of Texas. She patted his hand lightly. "Looks like you've been in the sun too much, sweetheart. Oh...and did you hear from Trent Institute?"

Hank gasped. He had already revealed to Rama his mishandling of the college funds and was prepared to make amends however insufficient, but he was fearful that the whole truth was best disclosed to a stronger woman.

Rama understood. "Well Mom, Trent's roster just filled up. Ever since Arnold Palmer, there's been more interest in golf course design. Don't worry, though; they put me right on top of the list for next year." It was a convincing, cheery fabrication. Hank gathered his breath to blow the burden of such a deception from his son's innocent shoulders, but Rama stopped him.

"It's okay, Dad. Next year will be soon enough."

Doris sighed, "Que sera sera. We could all use a good year...together." She beamed brightly 'til the incision in her head protested. "Who'd have thought we would begin in Atlanta?"

She was so moved by the moment that she asked Rama to fetch her old Bible and to read from the Twenty-Third Psalm. "For your fallen mother," she added with a trace of the wit Rama so admired.

The book lay at her bedside, still unopened since she groggily bookmarked it with an envelope during that awful spell. Rama obligingly reached for the Bible and took a seat on the foot of her bed. The book fell open to a sealed envelope addressed to him. To his amazement the return address sported a familiar crest: The T- square and spade crest of Trent Institute - Admissions Department.

In the heat of family reunion, a chill stabbed at his heart. Hank had already confessed he had bounced the tuition check, so Rama knew this letter could only be bad news. Discreetly, he put the envelope aside lest its contents disturb Doris. Then he read from the ancient poems of a lonely shepherd until she fell asleep, secure in the company of her family.

Hank dialed through the TV channels, settling for several minutes on a rerun of "The Millionaire." Soon he tired of the fantasy and switched off the set. "That show is just pure bullshit. You up for a game of checkers, Rama?" Hank started for the door. "Think I saw some games down in the waiting room."

Hank's exit was followed by a flurry of polite knocks. Rama welcomed in a well-rested, smiling Ivar Guidance. The previous day's hardships had worn the old fellow to a ghostly state, but now he looked fresh and stylish in tailored blue slacks, a sunny silk polo shirt, and alligator-skin loafers. He carried a hob-nail vase and a generous bunch of fresh flowers.

"A delightful day. We should be teeing it up somewhere, eh Rama?" Ivar spoke softly in deference to the sleeping woman as he arranged the flowers artfully in her window. "I suppose you've heard the good news?"

"Well, if removing a tumor is *good* news, yes sir."

"Well, of course, that is a checkered sort of good tiding." Ivar frowned slightly. "But the tumor was benign, and your mother should be right as rain. But heavens, I should leave the details to the doctor; I am stealing his thunder."

Ivar glanced at the sleeping woman, then back to Rama. "Where is your father?"

"Just slipped out to find a game to pass the time."

A crease formed in Ivar's brow. "A game?" he asked ominously.

"No, no, just checkers…to play here with me."

"Good…got to bind that man to the mast when the sirens come calling."

Ivar seemed reassured. He had developed a bond with Hank, as much in their common passion for flight as for the fact that the troubled gambler he had snatched away from the racetrack had saved him from certain death. Ivar knew Hank had unresolved financial obligations and could ill afford to back-slide onto gaming's thin ice.

He gently closed the door to the busy hallway. "Your father is taking the bus back to Memphis tonight. He says he has loose ends to tie up before we can fly Doris home. I thought I should tie up a few ends myself." The old gentleman pulled a small envelope from his pocket. "I've been thinking about that money you won from Wedgy. As generous as it was for you to consider it as a return on my investment, the fact is…you earned it."

Ivar handed the envelope to Rama. "Don't worry; I've recouped my bet and then some." A sly smile betrayed his merciful gift to Wedgy, but he said nothing. "The rest is yours, Rama. I am certain you will put these funds to good use."

Ivar mimicked a little golf swing, Johnny Carson-style, to divert attention from Rama's stammering reaction to the gift. "Now act dumb, my boy, when Myer—I mean the doctor—brings you the good news about your mother. That's the part these fellows enjoy most: the god-like proclamations. I certainly don't need to give the good doctor a reason to be peeved at me; he and I have a round later today and he'll be unhappy enough before that's over."

Rama searched for words in the face of Ivar's generosity but stumbled short of a coherent phrase.

Ivar was content to do all the talking. "Myer won't be unhappy for long. I have an invitation to take a turn around The National course tomorrow morning with the good doctor in tow. That's liable to smooth out any ruffled feathers...don't you think?"

"My God, yes." Rama was amazed that Ivar could speak so nonchalantly of "hopping over" to Augusta for a round at the most storied of American golf courses...as if he were knocking off a quick nine at a muni.

"You keep a good eye on the patient 'til I return. We'll fly back to Memphis in a couple of days when Myer gives Doris the thumbs up."

Ivar bent over the bouquet and fussed with several of the flowers till he was satisfied, then started for the door. Halfway there he turned back to the young man now holding two envelopes. "Now, if you need to cash that check right away, my bank has a branch just four blocks up the street. I have made arrangements for you; just bring your driver's license.

"And one more thing: The bakery by the bank has the world's best peach pie," Ivar added as he slipped out the door.

Rama sat alone on the bed. His mother's breathing was regular and deep. There was no point in playing hide-and-seek with the contents of the envelopes in his possession. He was in no hurry to read the denial letter from Trent Institute, so he slipped his thumbnail under the flap of the Guidance Industries envelope first.

A flash of color peeked through the torn paper, and he plucked a check, like a petal, from the envelope as if rough handling could undo the fragile chain of events that had led to this unlikely compensation. He held the check to the light, admiring the decorative engraving before the value written in Ivar's careful hand registered on his brain: $18,950.

Rama lost his breath. He gasped as he recalled the parade of Wedgy's pigeons and befuddled hackers, including his father, who had been the reluctant source for this booty. Then he pictured himself on a shopping spree, cashing in the chips for his gallant effort against Wedgy: new golf clubs, a Dynaco stereo kit, a Mustang convertible, or a trip to North Carolina to catch up with Melyssa.

The other envelope—the Trent letter—begged for attention, too. Rama tore the envelope open and unfolded a tidy personal letter to Mr. Rama Schwain:

Third and Final Notice:
Our admissions department has reported that the deposit on your
registration fee and tuition payment check #3515 for $3,500 was returned
for insufficient funds. We are certain this was an oversight and apologize

for any inconvenience. To ensure proper enrollment of Rama Schwain, please immediately submit a cashier's check or wire funds to the Registrar's Office as shown at the top of this letter. We must inform you that if payment is not received or other arrangements are not made by noon Sept. 13, Mr. Schwain's admission will be revoked. We look forward to your prompt attention to this matter.

Rama's heart sunk as his eyes snapped back to the drop-dead date. Why hadn't his mother mentioned the letter earlier? It was a bitter disappointment, but the letter only confirmed what he already had guessed: That he was out. A glance at the front page of the newspaper lying on Doris's breakfast tray told him he was wrong. The paper's masthead registered like an electric shock. It was the eleventh. He still had two days and plenty of money to put his life back on track.

Rama heard Hank's voice chattering with someone down the hall. He remembered the "loose ends" his father was heading home to confront. He feared that if those ends were serious enough to warrant a red-eye bus trip all the way back to Memphis, and if his dad was as indebted to Calcutta Finance as he had confessed, then Hank faced a daunting and dangerous task.

Rama cringed at his dad's predicament, then realized that he, too, was vulnerable. He wondered how his ticket to school lay lost in the pages of a holy book as an unholy war searched like a hungry demon for boys unprotected by the grace of a student deferment. Rama was in jeopardy of being 1-A, but he could not ignore the looming consequences of his family's bleak financial circumstances—not now, not when he had the currency to help. For the second time in the hour, he imagined that there was always next year for school—not to comfort his mother, but to assure himself. His education would have to take a place with the clubs, the hi-fi, and the Mustang on a someday wish list while as Carlos predicted, the money would "flow like water to thee most thirsty place."

Rama rolled the Trent Institute letter into a ball and fired it across the room toward a wastebasket. His ticket to a different future—possibly one as Melyssa's classmate—rattled around the rim and skipped to the floor.

"Nice shot, Meadow Lark," quipped his father from the doorway. Hank juggled a box of checkers and two bottles of cola while holding his cane under his arm. "Did you know the Coca-Cola really is better in Atlanta?"

The two played while Doris slept, but Rama's tactical blunders revealed a mind distracted by larger matters. The abrupt shift in mood finally prompted Hank to ask what was the matter.

"Trent turned me down." Rama strained at the untruth as he sought to remove paying Trent from the daunting list of financial repairs that awaited Hank back in Memphis. "Guess I didn't measure up."

Hank felt a huge load rise from his shoulders—one less obligation to face in the next few days—but he took little comfort in being off the hook at the cost of his son's disappointment.

"Jesus, Son, I hope it wasn't my fault."

Rama shook his head no. He didn't trust his lips with a lie.

After several more careless moves, Rama finally conceded the third game and excused himself to take a walk. As he found his way up the busy street to Ivar's bank, the clatter of the city offered a welcome change from the hush that had hovered over so many of the fairways he had trod with Wedgy, Ivar, and the others. He welcomed life beyond the country clubs' pastoral facade.

As he entered the marbled bank lobby, Rama hesitated under the tug of self-interest, but soon converted Guidance Industries' check into fifty one-hundred-dollar bills for his mother and a $13,000 cashier's check to the order of Mr. Hank Schwain. He kept a few hundred to cover the pay Wedgy had shorted him during their summer together.

Rama was in no hurry to return to the hospital; his mother was in good hands and he was sick of checkers. So when he passed Addie Mae's Peach Palace, he stepped inside. The scent of buttery crust, cinnamon, and sweet fruit filled his head as he peered into the bakery case, yet his attention was elsewhere. He still imagined that his sacrifice would repay his mother's losses and give his father the funds to handle his most critical debts. The elegance in the fact that these accounts would be settled with money hustled from a hustler brought a smile to his face, even as the delights in the case came into focus.

The round woman behind the pies beamed back at her smiling customer with the assurance of one who knows that she always offers the world her very best.

—•—

While Rama was at the bank, his mother had awakened and asked Hank for a glass of water. Returning from the sink, Hank kicked the crumpled Trent letter across the floor. While Doris drank, he scooped up the ball to try his own bank shot, but the T-square and spade winking from one crumpled surface prompted him to unfold the letter. In a moment Hank realized that his son, having already been victimized by his father's failures, was now protecting *him*. Hank tucked the letter into his pocket.

In a few minutes Rama returned carrying a couple of take-out boxes from Addie Mae's and a get-well card for his mother. Hank noticed his son's attitude had brightened since their checker game. The walk must have done him some good.

As Rama entered the room Doris sat up in bed, tucking a pillow behind her back without assistance. "Heavens, I must have fallen asleep. I'm so rude… where were we? How was your golfing adventure?"

She asked with uncertainty what a caddie stood to gain on such a tour. She was unsure whether Rama had even played let alone beaten his boss, but it didn't matter; her smile burned a magnitude brighter than it had for years.

"I played him once, and did alright; Dad even flew in for the match," Rama laughed as he handed his mother the card and the pie boxes. "Now this one's for now, and that one is for…later."

Doris read the card and peeked into the "now" box. It contained the cash.

"Rama," she gasped, unaware that she was being repaid for funds that ultimately had been borrowed from his education account. "What is this?"

"Best pie in the world they say, Mom," Rama laughed at her surprise. "No, I ran into a foolish old golfer and his money…I figured you could use it more than me."

Hank watched wordlessly as Doris discovered the cash. He realized that Rama could have paid her anytime but had purposely paid her now while he was watching. The thought occurred that Rama intended he understood that she was one less obligation to repay as he faced his creditors back in Memphis.

Hank recalled Doris's premonition of their son's saintly nature: "He's a special one, Honey," she had told him many times, "your dream come true." Perhaps he had passed off those motherly words as too rhapsodic, but now they rang true. He turned to face the sunlight streaming in through Ivar's bouquet. A bus to Memphis awaited tonight. The work of drawing blood from a stone awaited him tomorrow.

<hr />

Rama stood in the cold sodium light of the Greyhound terminal's platform and waved his father good luck. Hank watched his son diminish to a speck before turning from the window. As the bus merged onto highway 78, a rising moon gave chase to the hound's northwestward run.

The bus smelled of stale cigarettes, sweat, and a hopeless application of air freshener. The atmosphere reminded Hank of the Big Star Club, and he shivered at the thought of past misjudgments. Rolling along every tedious asphalt inch to Memphis would be a far cry from soaring across the hardwood forests in Ivar's private aircraft. He could have waited to make the flight back with Ivar and company several days later, but he needed time to smooth the ruffled feathers of the credit union's mortgage department, set up a payment plan for Doc Stassen's unpaid medical bills, find a new job, and get the glider on the market before Calcutta Finance caught up with him. Hank's agenda would take all his salesmanship and all the sympathy he could charm from his stature as a Purple-Heart vet. Given his scarcity of resources, a mastery of smoke and mirrors would be crucial at the potentially hostile negotiations that lay ahead.

Rama watched the bus disappear into the dark streets. He never questioned Hank's need to return to Memphis, nor had he any doubt of the sincerity in his father's confession at the plane two evenings ago. But he had wondered if his father's will would be strong enough to ensure success without a more negotiable currency than good intentions. He had hoped $13,000 would help.

Like Carlos's water flowing to the most thirsty place, the wealth now flowed to Hank through an undiscovered cashier's check tucked into the pages of a *Stranger Than Science* paperback lying deep in a bag of goodies Rama had prepared for his father's trip home. He had said nothing of the check, fearing Hank's pride might prevent him from taking money that appeared to be his son's. Instead, Rama made his father promise that before he reached Memphis, he would read the amazing story of the day it rained frogs.

—•—

Hank had tired of the endless interplay of dark forest and silver farmland streaming by in the moonlight. He considered reading the frog story, but before he fetched the book he drifted off to a shallow sleep to the comfortable tempo of two colored men sharing stories in the seat ahead of him. When the stories turned to golf, he was certain he was dreaming.

Soft, baritone fragments of conversation escaped the muffling upholstery and pierced his consciousness—fragments enough to piece together that one of the fellow's brothers had been a caddie at Augusta National.

"He would die for those folks…that's what Jessup always reckoned," said voice number one. "He allowed that they was on one side of the street, sure enough, and he was on the other…and that was that. But when they all got into a game together, they was like brothers—the caddies and their men against old man par.

"Christ almighty, he loved the game they played over there in 'Gusta. And he got to know every blessed inch of that track. He knowed how the balls was gonna roll or hop up, and those folks got to trust that *he* knew. Some of them fellas would pay pretty handsome if Jessup could talk 'em around them holes in a few less swipes. Can you imagine payin' out good money for that?

"The funny thing is, Jessup really could make those fellas play better. And it wasn't just knowin' the lay of the land, if you know what I'm sayin'. He had a *spell* about him. Jessup said there was other charmed ones like him, but from what he'd heard, the spell was 'bout as rare as one of them double eagles. There wasn't no doubt; it was bona fide voodoo. And to think old Jessup never even played their game…just carried the bags and helped conjure them little balls into the holes."

"Glory be, I'd like a shot at that job," sighed voice number two.

"Ain't that the truth?"

Voice number one was just hitting his stride. "Now this one fella used to be so ever-lovin' good at the golf that he didn't need nobody's spell—likely had his own. Nobody could touch him, 'least not 'til his spine went out on him. Jessup says he got to know that fella—Jones was his name. Guess he 'bout owned the place. They'd talk up the game from time to time out by Jones's little buggy. Jessup said that Mr. Jones told him there was a lot of mysteries in the game and that Jessup had a fair share of the mystery about him. Jones said it was a pity old Jessup couldn't have played with him as a golfer not a caddie, but rules was rules down there.

"Guess that didn't bother Jessup. He loved the loopin' as he called it. And like I said, he'd die for the place. But 'ventually he got him a bad leg, and they let him go. Some of them rich fellas took up a little retirement collection for him. Along with years of pretty good tippin', old Jess had him a nice little nest egg. Then 'bout a year later…sure as I'm talkin' to you now, old Jessup gets himself a sliver of worn-out land up around Greenville. Before you can say Jackie Robinson, he's scraped out a range for the golfin' folk up that way. Gave lessons and everything."

Voice number one begins to chuckle at the thought of his brother's audacity. "Now listen up, he called himself the 'Caddie to the Stars.'" The old voice cracked in rattling laughter that snapped Hank a little wider awake.

"Blessed be, the old boy does have a good imagination," the voice laughed again. "But I suppose there was a jot of truth in it…carryin' the bag for the likes of all them big wheels like he did. Even President Ike, so he said. Anyhow, these days Jessup says he's got it made, 'cept for the bum leg. Says he's got this old world licked and he ain't gonna let it go for a whole long spell…that he's gonna get what most of them Sunday golfers is always going after."

Voice number two sounded puzzled. "Now what in Hades would that be?"

"To break one hundred!"

Voice number one waited for a chuckle of appreciation but heard only the pounding of ten rubber tires on uneven Georgian pavement. "Years…one hundred *years* is what I'm talkin' 'bout. And Jessup says he's got a scheme to get him there certain.

"Now listen up. Jessup was fixing to order a couple of dozen bushels of golf balls for that little range, but it turned out that one of the old boys back at 'Gusta National had a line on a golf ball company that had messed up on a whole load of balls. Jessup's man told the golf ball fella' to donate 'em to Jessup's church and take himself a sweet deal on his taxes."

"Lord, some of those folks is might cagey that way, ain't it so?" declared voice number two.

"That's a fact…it's why they're so damn rich," agreed number one. "So bingo, Jessup writes the fella' up a receipt from Godly Golf or some such horseshit, and gets himself a whole damn shed full of balls, more than he'll ever need for his little range. Next thing, he scrapes him out a pretty little wallow and runs the creek through it so the folks can hit them balls about 150 yards 'cross it. Funny, them golfers seem to favor flyin' *over* the water 'cept half the time they fly *into* it, you understand?

"One hundred years…that's his plan," continued voice one as the passenger behind them stirred. "Every morning before Jessup opens her up for business, he goes out and plucks ten balls from that shed, pulls an old 7-iron club down from a peg, and tries to smack all ten of 'em over that water. Then he just goes about his business. Now he figures that if he hits ten balls every day, in forty years his shed's gonna be empty and he'll be a hundred years old—just like that.

"Jessup allows that if he just takes it one day at a time and all he's gotta do every day is find a way to hit those ten balls…then he's bound to get there. And he don't believe he's putting the Good Lord out too far to grant him so *little* when he's seen all them folks at 'Gusta that's got so much…just wants the strength to get his ever-lovin' bones up outta' bed every mornin' and whack them ten balls. And he don't care if the balls fly the wallow or if they even get off the tee. It's not like he's asking for money or a pretty wife…it's just a simple wish."

—•—

The listener behind the seat was wide awake now, he couldn't help but try his hand at running Jessup's numbers in his mind. He leaned forward, just clearing his face above the backrest.

"Hey fellas," Hank said softly.

"Oh my, mister, excuse us. Bet we was talkin' too loud? We'll tone it down a twist." The old storyteller was comfortable with deference.

"No, no…you all are fine," said Hank. "But I couldn't help listening—sorry to interrupt—but how long has this fellow been hitting those balls now?"

"Whoa now, you *was* listening up, mister," laughed the storyteller, happy for a larger audience. The old man's eyes twinkled in the Greyhound's cabin lights. "Well, let's see now, I was just there for my brother's eightieth birthday… he's been at it since he was sixty-five."

The storyteller's voice dropped into a mumble as he did the arithmetic in his wise old head. "So that's an aught on 365 for one year, another aught for ten years, that's 36,500, then half that for 18,250 and add 'em…thirty-six and eighteen is fifty four…mmmm, two-fifty and five is seven-fifty."

The storyteller raised his voice like an adding machine spooling out a paper tape. "That would be 54,750 balls so far, sir." Then he paused—his eyes focused beyond his own reflection in the coach window. "And old Jessup's still got to whack another 73,000 balls out across that wallow to make it a century."

Hank whistled. "Lot of balls. Lot of practice. I suppose your brother's a pretty good golfer by now, eh?"

The old storyteller laughed deeply. "Well, I suppose he's getting' mighty damn decent with that 7-iron."

Hank and the storyteller laughed softly 'til the rumbling of the wheels again filled the coach. "Hey mister?" Hank whispered again over the seat. "How'd you get so damn quick with the numbers?"

"It's like that golfer, Jones said: 'It's just a gift.'"

Hank sank back into his seat and listened as the two old fellows moved on to craps, crops, horses, and women. Hank dozed on the timbre of their comforting voices until the bus pulled to a stop in Tupelo with the first light of day already glinting off the window frames.

"Forty minutes," cried the driver before he vaulted from the handrails and through the doors like a gymnast.

Hank rambled through the bus station before realizing the peach pie he had shared with Rama and Doris was long gone. A real breakfast of grits and country ham sounded irresistible. The cafeteria was just about to open; the glass globes of coffee had just been set out on their warmers. He would be first in line.

He passed the storyteller and the other colored gentleman who had been riding with him. The two were standing by a vending machine counting change in their palms and considering the option of coffee, tea, or chicken broth from paper cups. They carefully avoided looking into the cafeteria for fear of seeing the steam rising from fresh scrambled eggs and bacon beneath warm amber heat lamps.

Hank yielded his place in line and doubled back to the two gentlemen. Several sleepy travelers shuffled by on their way to breakfast. As Hank approached, the storyteller and his companion looked up in recognition of their neighbor from the bus.

"The ham is smelling mighty good, don't you think?" Hank smiled.

The two fellows looked embarrassed. Hank quickly opened his wallet and pulled two five-dollar bills from his meager traveling cash and pressed them into the storyteller's palm. "Here's a little something…for your story." He felt the nickels and dimes through the bills as he held the cash in the wiry old palm for an instant. Hank sensed the storyteller's dignity, and before the old fellow could speak, he silenced the expected proud protest with his own story.

"My son was a caddie, like your brother. He has the gift your Jones fellow was talking about, but now he's a player."

The storyteller's eyes twinkled. "Well glory be, it's a funny world. So how good is your boy?"

Hank was unaccustomed to scores or handicaps and searched for a word to describe Rama's game. "He's a winner."

A warm wide smile grew across the storyteller's fine black face. "Good for him. Damn good, Sir."

Hank stepped into line with his traveling companions to share a morning meal laced with a common interest in racehorses and an uncommon connection to extraordinary caddies. Later, outside the bus depot, as the morning brightened pink against the limestone storefronts facing the empty street, the two black men went their way and Hank returned for one last stint in the stuffy Ameri-Cruiser.

One day at a time, like Jessup, seemed a good plan, Hank thought as he settled back into his seat to face the monotonous ride to Memphis. Perhaps the hours would go by a little faster with the help of some light reading. Rama's insistence that he read story of the raining frogs came to mind as he reached into the sack for the paperback.

Chapter 65

tranger Than Science. It was an appropriate title. The stories of meteorological anomalies, raining amphibians, spontaneous human combustions, and in-plain-sight vanishings were not far from the fiction of Hank's intended deliverance from his creditors. Negotiating new terms with next to no money on the table would take a miracle on par with the fantastic stories promised in the book.

Hank cracked open the pages to the frog story expecting relief from relentless financial woes, and indeed, that is what he found. His eyes flicked across the slip of paper tucked improbably into the pulp pages without realizing it was anything more than a bookmark. Then, in a breathless revelation, he realized it was a cashier's check. It was current and made out to him for $13,000, enough to settle most of his debts.

Still short of breath, he became aware that by the grace of his son, he would be spared scraping before humorless creditors and would be freed of the dangerous renegotiation of Calcutta's terms...if he cashed the check.

But Carlos's water sought its place, and before Hank thought of other debts, he remembered the Trent collection letter he had discovered yesterday in Doris's room. Today was the last day Rama's enrollment could still be salvaged.

It did not require a mathematical gift like the old storyteller's to calculate that thirteen thousand would not cover all Hank's pressing debts *and* his son's tuition. Something would have to give. It was the thirteenth of September. Rama's enrollment could only be saved by noon today, but noon would come and go somewhere along this red clay highway. He looked out to the loading dock; the bus driver was lingering outside the cafeteria, still picking his teeth. Soon he would climb aboard and slam the door on Rama's last chance at entering school this year and avoiding a damning induction letter from Uncle Sam soon thereafter.

Hank leapt from his seat and bulled back up the aisle through the boarding passengers. With a strange, urgent grace he clattered on his cane out across the platform and into the lobby as he raced for the Western Union office. The morning operator, like a sloth dangling from a Eucalyptus branch, looked up at Hank sleepily.

"How much for a telegram…to wire some money?" Hank gasped.

"Depennnds…where tooo…how looong…and howww much," the operator drawled. He eyed Hank's cashier's check suspiciously. "And we only take casshhh. There's a farmers' bank across the street…just opening for the day."

The loudspeaker was announcing final boarding for the Memphis bus when Hank arrived back at the Western Union window. He rapped on the glass until the telegraph operator stirred from a siesta.

"Soooo, where are we wiring this loot?"

"Trent Institute, Trent, North Carolina." Hank pulled the Trent letter from his pocket. "Wire $3,500 to the Registrar's Office…here's the name and address." Hank tapped the address on the letter anxiously, then snapped his fingers for action like Sergeant Bilko. "Pronto!"

Hank glanced back to the loading dock. His driver had just emerged from the bus after having counted heads and appeared agitated that he was one short. The driver consulted his watch and glared at the door into the terminal through which his tardy passenger had better emerge soon. Clearly no one would delay this man's bus for long. Hank scribbled a brief explanatory note to the Registrar and submitted it to the telegraph operator.

He slipped the cash across counter, tapping his foot nervously. "Are we done?"

The operator methodically counted the money. "No, you owe another six bucks…for the note."

Hank was near bursting. He tossed down the cash, grabbed up the receipt, and dashed out to the dock just as the driver was slamming the door shut on the Memphis-bound coach.

—•—

Back in Memphis, Hank, like a character from Rama's strange science book, levitated in the zero gravity of a payday he had never earned. After wiring Rama's tuition payment, he still had cash to pay the overdue mortgage and take care of Doris's medical debts. Only one balance remained in arrears—Calcutta's—but Rama's winnings could not stretch that far.

He owed Calcutta six thousand dollars, but his only asset was his glider, the Little Crow. He hoped that if he avoided Lew Raybon and Calcutta's goons long enough, he might sell the glider before they raised hell with him. He knew the Crow wouldn't fetch six grand but guessed that if it fetched a large enough chunk of the debt, he might persuade Calcutta to grant him some time to raise the remaining balance. Hank resolved to visit Aero Meadows tomorrow to test the market.

Upon arriving back in Memphis, he hailed a cab from the bus depot to the horse track to reclaim his car. As the cab zig-zagged across town, he imagined what might have befallen a relatively nice car abandoned at a seedy race track for five days. To his amazement, the Rambler was still there and still intact. The parking lot attendant approached with sinister curiosity.

"Boy, you is in luck. Another day and she's in the chop shop." The attendant got down to business. "You hurried out of here so fast with that rich dude five days back…hell, I thought he was taking you for a ride if you know what I mean. Shit buddy, you got me to thank for not towing this rig off the lot. I was *worried* about you."

The attendant dangled Hank's keys at arm's length.

There was no resisting the inevitable. Hank peeled a twenty-dollar bill from his remaining cash. The operator seemed pleased and dropped the keys into Hank's hand. "See you around, huh?"

Hank fired the Rambler to life. "Not likely."

—•—

When Hank finally pulled into the driveway of Doris's house that evening, he noticed that the grass was long overdue for a mowing. He chalked up another item on his list. To his relief, a loose brick in the front porch still offered up a front door key. He was about to slip inside, intent on composing an ad for the glider, but a letter tucked beneath the front door stopped him abruptly. In the glow of the porch light he could see the envelope was addressed to Mrs. Doris Schwain. The return address read: Calcutta Finance Collections Dept.

Hank's blood boiled at the thought that those predators had anything to do with his wife, but his blood chilled as he recognized it was his poor judgment that had drawn her into Calcutta's sights.

He ripped open the letter in anger. Only the laboring of a refrigerator in dire need of a defrosting broke the awful silence of his home as he sat at the empty dinner table and read Calcutta's decree:

> If the sum of six thousand dollars is not delivered to our office by Thursday, collection actions will be undertaken immediately, starting with, but not limited to, the sale of an aircraft known to be in the possession of Mr. Hank Schwain at Aero Meadows Air Park. In lieu of a cash settlement, Mrs. Schwain, you are hereby directed to appear at Aero Meadows with title to the aircraft on Friday at noon for a fair assessment of its value. Be prepared to surrender the title and pay reasonable transaction fees. You will be responsible for payment of any shortfall should the assessed value be less than six thousand dollars.

"Fair assessment," Hank groaned. He could not imagine *fair* and *Calcutta* in the same statement. Nor could he dodge this confrontation with them forever.

The next morning he rummaged through his papers and eventually found the Little Crow's title and certification papers. If he could not sell the glider back to Aero immediately, his only hope would be to attempt to convince the rude pilot and his mechanic to favorably assess its value at or near what Hank owed Calcutta, then offer Lew Raybon the glider in exchange. If Lew accepted, at least Calcutta would be off his back. And if he refused, Hank hoped Lew would at least give him a couple more days to drum up another buyer.

He thought this logic seemed reasonable as he reached for the phone to give the boys at Aero a heads-up on his plan.

—•—

"Six thousand dollars? Are you nuts, Schwain?"

Hank thought he heard sunflower seeds splatter against the receiver. "Jesus, Schwain," barked the pilot, "what do you think...we got a hot-line to Fort Knox over here? Maybe I can make a few calls for you, find you a hot prospect." The pilot's offer was voiced with the unmistakable tang of pessimism. "Or maybe we could scrape up 3,500 in a couple of days and take her back off your hands...best I can do," the pilot offered.

"Forget it, try the calls."

Hank returned the receiver to its hook. Thirty-five hundred wouldn't cut it. If something better didn't come along quickly, he could probably bargain up to four thousand with the Aero pilot, then walk into Lew Raybon's office and surprise the loan shark with a respectable amount in cash. He imagined that Raybon, with good intentions and a wad of green staring him in his steely face, might settle on a partial payment and terms for the balance as his notice to Doris had suggested. But then Hank recalled the stories of Raybon's harsh collection tactics; he feared that good intentions and settling were two concepts Lew might greet less than enthusiastically, especially on this account.

Hank fretted over his plan with the help of a Busch recovered from the depths of Doris's refrigerator. The watery beer momentarily washed Lew's evil face from his mind. In its absence Hank pictured an afternoon ahead in which to test the job market for experienced auto salesmen, or whatever else he could find. He fetched the paper and scanned the want ads as he finished the beer. A few leads looked promising. He headed back to the bedroom, hoping that Doris hadn't tossed away his good clothes after he had taken up residence at Beale's Budget Inn that horrible night. Soon Hank was spruced up into job-hunting mode, ready to tackle another task on his road to correction.

Hank returned that afternoon empty-handed but full of hope: He had secured two follow-up interviews and several more leads. He settled back on the sofa and tried to visualize how to he might conjure dinner from the sparse contents of Doris's refrigerator. As he relaxed, a nagging detail slipped into his mind. He had been gone from Beale's for nearly a week, and his rent was due today. What few possessions still remained there would be in jeopardy of re-possession. Rather than take chances on wrestling his own TV back from some crazed bargain hunter at Value Village, Hank figured he had better square up with Beale sooner not later. He'd get a bite of dinner on the way home.

After Hank had reclaimed his things from the apartment, he popped into the manager's office to settle up. The aroma of curry and garlic drifted like fog from the living quarters behind the Beale's front office. He considered asking for a sample of the manager's supper but thought better of it, recalling the bizarre ingredients his ex-tenant, Siran, had once simmered into his curries. Hank tossed the keys and his rent across the counter and stepped back outside for a breath of clean night air. He smelled the river's mossy banks and the per-fume of tulip poplars hiding somewhere in the dark.

Had the curried atmosphere in the manager's office not conjured such potent memories of Siran's ghastly cuisine, he might have been more attentive as he walked back to the Rambler. Before he realized anything was amiss, an Oldsmobile Ninety-Eight with tinted windows pulled up behind his car. Hank stepped back in fear as both doors on the Olds flew open and two large, awk-ward men stumbled out. He froze in confusion, unsure whether he was being confronted by goons or if a couple of welding supply salesman out for a night of cheap thrills on the wrong side of town had just drunkenly double parked behind him.

If they were the former, anonymity apparently was not an issue: Goon One wore a windbreaker with a poorly silk-screened logo for Muddy's Barge Inn. Goon Two sported a stylish deep blue rayon bowling shirt with what was presumably his name—Wyatt—embroidered above the pocket.

"Hold it there, Schwain," the bowler commanded in his most goon-like growl. The fellow looked as if he might be stepping out to pick up a couple of bucks between games by roughing up a few "customers" before returning to the alley for league night's final frames.

Hank was surprised to hear his name, then realized for whom these fellows worked. His initiative in the plan to settle the Calcutta account had just been stolen. He stood his ground against the advancing bowler. Wyatt pulled up tentatively and glanced over his shoulder for his partner, who seemed preoc-cupied back at the Olds.

"Where you been keeping yourself?" asked Wyatt, one eye cocked toward his car. Without backup, he stopped six feet short of his usual intimidating arm's length. "Ronnie, get the fuck over here."

Hank's reply remained in his throat.

Ronnie struggled to free himself from his windbreaker. "Shit, my damn jacket's hung up in the freakin' door," he cursed, then glared at Hank while puffing up his chest menacingly. "And don't you wise-ass Wyatt."

Wyatt the Bowler looked angry. "Damn it Ronnie, he ain't even said a word, you clumsy turd."

"I wasn't talking to you," said Ronnie.

Wyatt tried to salvage his bravado. "Now listen up, Schwain. You haven't been trying to dodge your *fiduciary responsibilities*, now have you? That wouldn't be smart...since everybody knows where you live," he said ominously.

Ronnie finally tore free from his windbreaker. "Crap, I won a dart tournament for that jacket."

Wyatt ignored his partner's unprofessional carryings-on and focused on Hank. "Now you wouldn't be toting around Mr. Raybon's six grand on a night like this would you, Schwain? You could lose it real easy in this part of town if you're not careful."

"And it ain't yours to lose," chimed Ronnie.

Hank was peeved that he had allowed himself to be ambushed, especially by the likes of these idiots. "Hold on, damn it, guys. I don't have money like that. I gave up on gambling, and I've been out of town on a real no-shit emergency. But if it's Raybon's money you're looking for, I've got an aircraft I'll sell...or I'll make a trade."

"Calcutta don't take pawn. We are a *finance* company," Wyatt sounded offended, "and we are collecting *cash* payments this evening."

Ronnie, having freed himself, snatched up a Louisville Slugger from the backseat. His tee shirt hung unprofessionally about his black jeans. He tapped the bat against his knee and sneered at Hank. "Yeah, cash, jerk-off. We don't make trades." He held out his hand and snapped his fingers. "Let's have a look at your wallet."

"He means business," advised Wyatt. "Drop the cane."

"Yeah, suppose he does," agreed Hank. He had serious reservations as to the peaceful nature of Ronnie's business even though the flowery graphics on the bat-wielding goon's tee shirt seemed contradictory: *'Trust Jesus '67 – Tent Revival.'*

Hank dropped his cane to the pavement. It wasn't the first time Calcutta had robbed him, he thought as he reluctantly withdrew his wallet and pulled out the only cash he had: $180. "That's all I've got, period," said Hank, relieved that the goons hadn't caught up with him yesterday while he was flush with cash—before he had wired Rama's tuition and settled up with the bank.

Ronnie reached forward and snatched the bills. "Let me see that wallet, too, you lying sack of shit."

Hank tossed it over reluctantly. The bowler extracted the cash and searched for a hidden pocket or maybe a spare Trojan, then tossed the wallet in disappointment back at Hank's feet. "Now don't think this pocket change is gonna keep Raybon off your back. He still expects the whole six grand. He'll consider this an overdue little service charge." Wyatt the bowler smiled as he taunted Hank with the cash.

"And you did get our note? Tomorrow evening: six o'clock? I strongly recommend you be there. Don't even try no negotiations, understand Schwain? Six o'clock—with cash—or the firebugs might get into your house." The bowler suddenly seemed more businesslike. "Bugs are mighty bad this year...you know what I mean?"

Hank nodded. Wyatt glanced at Ronnie. "Make sure Schwain knows we mean business."

Hank turned to look at the man in the Jesus tee shirt, and as he did Wyatt swooped in behind and put him in a powerful arm lock. Hank cried out in pain as his arm curled behind his back.

Ronnie gripped the bat and moved in on Hank. His usual target was the side of the knee. "Leave 'em just a little crippled and nobody gets hurt," he often said with logic as twisted as his speech.

He raised the bat, but Hank, who listed upon his good leg, presented a perplexing target. If he hurt that leg, thought Ronnie, then Schwain would really be disabled. He had his morals: He couldn't cripple a cripple, so he turned to the Rambler and delivered a vicious blow to the windshield.

An impressive explosion of glass rained upon the driver's seat. Hank groaned under Wyatt's hold and was suddenly set free.

"Son of a bitch," he cried.

"Put it on your insurance, Schwain. You got off easy," said the bowler, disappointed in his partner's restraint. "Ronnie, let's split." He was anxious to leave before the curry eaters, alerted by the breaking glass, called the cops.

"Six o'clock, Aero Meadows."

Calcutta's strong-arm duo returned to the Ninety Eight and lurched from the parking lot with Ronnie's windbreaker streaming from the passenger door like a banner for Muddy's Barge Inn.

Chapter 66

Glass fragments were still falling from the Rambler's windshield as Hank rolled into Doris's driveway intent on getting some rest. The broken glass and Calcutta would have to wait 'til tomorrow. He'd sleep on a real bed tonight, he thought as he walked up to what had once been their bedroom with the caution of one who feared he might stumble upon a ghost. The door yielded to his touch and the bed beckoned; it had been a long day, and falling onto Doris's comforter sounded appealing. His eyes skipped around the treasures of her life: the cut glass vials of perfume, a bright scarf he couldn't recalling having seen her wear in more than ten years, a crude glazed ceramic cat Rama had sculpted in first grade, and a pewter-framed photo of him and her arm-in-arm at a nearly forgotten gala for wounded veterans back in Nashville. A weary sigh slipped through his lips at the thought of that happy evening at the Maxwell House.

Hank gently eased the door closed like one might fasten the cover on an old pocket watch, then slipped back downstairs to sleep on the couch. But sleep never came. His mind wouldn't leave the thoughts of things undone. Eventually he got up, and under the glow of the front porch light limped along behind the mower to return the lawn to decency while happily irritating those neighbors who dared not criticize him now for tending to that which had all-too-often been ignored.

At 9:30 Hank rose from what remained of a night of anxious dreams. While prowling through the cupboards for coffee, he noticed a blinking light on the answering machine. He hadn't heard as much as a tinkle from her phone, but messages were waiting. His heart surged with anticipation; perhaps Aero had come through with a buyer for the Little Crow. But as the messages unwound: a marketing survey for breakfast cereal, a chatty message from an old friend at Waddley's market, and a call from Rama, he accepted his fate. There was no buyer.

It wasn't all bad. Rama had called to say Doctor Myer had favored Doris convalescing at home. There was a good chance Ivar would be flying them home that afternoon if the doc gave the all-clear.

Hank spent the day working down an ancient honey-do list in preparation for his wife's arrival while praying for someone to show some interest in his glider. By three o'clock he could wait no more. He would have to go to Aero Meadows and make his best pitch at selling back the Little Crow before Calcutta arrived at six o'clock.

Before leaving he fetched the mail. A robin's-egg-colored envelope addressed in fine female script to Rama "Tarzan" Schwain lay on top of the stack. Hank smiled at his son's good fortune, recalling Rama's proud, slightly bashful attempt at describing his feelings for the dark-haired girl and his pointing out that she was the same girl he had encountered there as a child eight years earlier. He lingered at the memory of such a durable attraction and the power it could wield in the heart of a young man.

He tossed the mail onto the kitchen counter, then hustled out to catch up with the pilot and his mechanic at Aero Meadows before they abandoned the picnic table and their *Playboys* for the day. Aero would be his last chance at cashing out the glider and avoiding a painful outcome with Calcutta. If he didn't hurry, the disagreeable duo would sweep the sunflower seeds from the hangar floor and roll the door closed for another day, leaving Hank to face Lew Raybon with no cash *and* no options.

Hank hurriedly bundled up the documents proving the glider's ownership and airworthiness. He would have to put an aggressive sell job on the pilot to buy her back, even if it meant accepting their $3,500 offer. Hank rubbed the bruises on his neck and reached for a pencil to scribble a note for Rama and Doris in case they arrived home while he was gone:

> *At Aero Meadows. Am meeting*
> *Calcutta at six o'clock to make*
> *a deal on glider. Home by eight I hope.*
> *Welcome back.*
>
> *PS: Rama get ready for school, you*
> *are in and your tuition is all paid up.*

He left the note on the dining-room table and walked out to his car. In the light of day, the broken windshield looked to be in worse condition than he had remembered; in fact, it was in danger of disintegrating with any good bump. He found Doris's dandelion claw and raked the loose glass from the window frame. The shards fell in a shower like cheap jewels to the driveway.

Wind whistled through the void, stinging his eyes as he picked up speed down Crutchfield Lane. Bluff Meade's fairways winked through the openings in the laurel hedge as tears streamed in protest from his eyes.

He arrived at the hangar around four o'clock. Down at the end of the flight line the Little Crow stood tethered in the glow of amber sunlight, seemingly as anxious as its owner had once been to get back into the air. Hank sighed with regret that somebody might actually take the bird off his hands today, but he was more than ready to release his selfish grip on an unrealistic dream.

For the first time since he had stumbled into Aero Meadows after his bad night at the Big Star, Hank arrived to find the mechanic on his feet rather than burrowed in the organs of a dismembered plane or in the pages of a centerfold. Today the man paced like a panther while he held his hand to his jaw.

"Fucking Corn-Nuts," he groaned in pain. "Damn it...chalk up another cracked tooth."

"I've been trying to tell you, Cheney, just stick with the sunflower seeds. Look, I got all my teeth." The pilot flashed an enameled smile—flaunting his superior dental condition with evil glee.

"Screw your perfect choppers, Crawford. You got to give me a lift to the dentist...pronto."

Hank stood in the doorway, holding his documentation sheepishly. He hated to bother the two men, and he hated overhearing their real names, but time was running out. He had to make a move. He mustered all his salesman-ship and burst through the door.

"Hey boys, you're in luck. Looks like you'll get to buy the Schweitzer back on the cheap today," Hank announced, fairly dripping conviction. He held his FAA papers aloft like a kid hawking newspapers on the curb. The two men fixed utterly uninterested eyes on him.

Hank reminded the pilot of his offer: "Forty-five hundred you said yester-day. You're getting the Little Crow back for less than I paid, but I'm afraid I've got no choice...I'll have to take it."

The mechanic fished through his pockets for a bottle of aspirin and fussed with the cap. "Forty-five hundred? Crawford, that's bullshit. I never agreed to that." He glared at the pilot. "We ain't spending a dime now. This damn tooth will cost a grand before it's crowned up and all."

"For God's sake, Cheney...if you had any sense about what you crammed in your damn maw..."

The mechanic interrupted: "Screw it, Crawford. The company pays med-ical and dental, remember? You'll yank your damn pecker out of joint one of these days and then I'll be paying for your dick doctor. Come on, you're taking me to the dentist..." The mechanic let out a genuine cry of pain. "Pronto."

Hank guessed that was a no.

The pilot looked apologetically at Hank. "Sorry Bub, if it was up to me…" he started, then thinking better of further talk, began closing the shop for the day. "Maybe we can work something out later, Schwain."

Hank felt the icy jolt of desperation as his cash cows wandered from the killing floor. Calcutta would arrive in two hours.

The pilot turned back to Hank. "Hey, Schwain, if you need to use the shitter, better get to it. We're locking up here in a minute."

Hank shook his head. "Thanks, but I'm just waiting to meet a guy about the Schweitzer at six. You were gonna appraise it for me, remember?"

"Sorry, I can't help you out, Bub, but we got an emergency in old Cheney's mouth. A fella did call this morning, though. Said he knew you. He asked a few questions about your glider…didn't seem too savvy about aircraft." The pilot smiled. "Don't worry, though; I didn't say nothing about a price. If that's the guy that's coming over today, gouge 'em for all you can get, Schwain."

Hank felt his knees buckle at the impending arrival of Lew Raybon and the Calcutta crew. Gouging would be out of the question. Without a reasonable appraisal and some professional support he was at the mercy of Calcutta. His last card was nearly played out; now he could only hope that Lew could be talked into an appreciation of aircraft.

The pilot bid Hank good luck and was gone with the stricken mechanic. Hank was left to his fate. Only the creaking of aluminum skin and the rumble of the hangar door in the afternoon's first winds disturbed the temporary calm. His thoughts ran freely back to Doris and the good life he had promised her. He was pleased to find the torturous compulsions that for so long consumed him were at bay and that his mind had returned to the same desires he had entertained as a young man. Doris still lay at the top of that list.

With the incomprehensible assistance of Carlos Taddio and Rama, he had satisfied most of his debts in coin, cash, and confidence; now he faced the prickly matter of Calcutta Finance. How many ounces of flesh would they deem appropriate payment for stiffing them? Whatever the price, Hank knew it would be the last payment due on a life he had mortgaged for a vacant promise. Tomorrow he would be free.

An hour passed. Then, as if his thoughts had conjured it, a black Cadillac convertible materialized at the far end of the driveway. Lew was a few minutes early and he had not come alone.

Hank clutched the papers for the aircraft as if they were weapons, then walked out toward the glider preparing to take the initiative with a convincing pitch for accepting Little Crow as down payment on his account. He struck a business-like pose at the side of the glider and prayed his sales instincts from years on the lot at Big Muddy's would carry him across this financial tar pit.

The Calcutta Caddy pulled past the hangar and rolled deliberately up the tarmac. Two men hopped out and with practiced menace flanked the object of Lew Raybon's attention: Hank Schwain, not the glider. Hank recognized Wyatt the bowler from last night; the other fellow, a garden-variety hoodlum in a motorcycle jacket, raised the hackles on his neck. When Lew's associates were deployed, Mr. Raybon made a casual exit from the Cadillac.

He was dressed in razor-sharp white slacks with a tailored, black silk golf shirt that hung perfectly from his bulldog frame. He stretched as he surveyed Aero Meadows's facilities, then took a deep breath of the humid air pooled above the runway's grassy infield.

"Fucking dump," he began, taking the high ground.

Hank couldn't argue but moved quickly to his game plan. "Can't judge a book, Mr. Raybon...but there are some fine aircraft here."

"Don't waste a second of my time with that sales shit," interrupted Lew. "Didn't get you anywhere at Muddy's, huh Schwain?" Hank withered: the checker player facing the Go master

"You have been mighty hard to catch up with of late. My boys got lucky last night. You haven't been avoiding us have you, Schwain?" It was a rhetorical question and Lew didn't wait for an answer. "You even left your poor sick wife to take the heat," Lew said sanctimoniously. "Don't suppose she told you about our *repossession* policy, did she?"

Hank tried to speak casually. "I've been out of town. An emergency."

"We noticed," snapped Lew. "Suppose you were raising a little money for me, huh?"

"Well Mr. Raybon, better than cash." Hank began to open the folder containing the Schweitzer's documents. "This aircraft is only going to increase in value. I hate to let it go."

"Increase in value? Hold up, Schwain. You think I'm investing in your damn plane to settle your debt?" Lew signaled his associates to step forward, tightening the noose. "Let me see those papers."

Hank handed the documents to Lew who made a show of examining the arcane FAA papers, logs, and certificates. "Forget it, Schwain," Lew replied as he crammed the papers back into their folder. "Even if I was interested, I don't see any experts around here willing to put a price on this piece of junk, and I'm sure as hell not taking your word."

Massive white teeth gleamed as the loan shark's face distorted into a dangerous smile. "Just good business, you understand?"

Hank understood.

"No, Schwain, I'm no airplane expert, and I'm not in the used car...sorry, used *plane* business, but I'll do you a favor. You sign the plane over to Calcutta Finance as a down payment, we'll call it 50-percent." Lew's smile descended to a smirk and then to a scowl. "Then I don't care if you have to rob a fucking bank. You'll bring me the balance in forty-eight hours or I'll take it out of your home."

Hank turned defiant, he had nothing to lose. "Lew, that's impossible," he protested. "That Schweitzer glider is worth way more than half my debt.

And what do you mean take the balance from my house…you can't do that. You've got no claim, no lien against it."

Lew pulled a cigarette case and propane lighter from his pocket. He offered Hank a smoke. The motorcycle tough stepped closer and Wyatt took up a new position by the open convertible. But still Hank refused.

"Suit yourself."

Lew snapped open the lighter and watched its flame roared like a tiny blowtorch. He lit his cigarette, but kept the flame alight, holding it up for Hank's consideration.

"Sure as hell don't need a bona fide *lien* to take a little something off the equity in your home." Lew lowered the boom congenially, hoping that all the shouting was over.

"It's been a bad summer for bugs, eh Schwain? There happens to be a bug in your neighborhood right about now. A crazy nut-case firebug that says shit like 'Leave 'em homeless and nobody gets hurt.' Crazy talk for a professional pyro, huh, Schwain? And I'll be damned if old Sparky isn't just waiting for a little toot on Wyatt's new CB radio to go ahead and do his thing, like the son-of-a-bitching hippies say."

Lew watched his speech work its magic. "The Schwain homestead is just off of Crutchfield…ain't it, Hank?"

Hank remembered stories about Calcutta's tactics. As he imagined visions of the new life he and Doris might have faced together being consumed in a cloud of smoke, he feared the stories were true.

"Christ, Raybon," Hank swore. "I've been your customer for how long? If you don't want the glider, don't take it. But give me a break; it ain't easy selling a plane. Give me a few more days. You'll get all your money."

"I never asked you to *sell* the fucking thing, Schwain. I only wanted my principal and interest in cash. Times is tough, and I've been losing on you for long enough. Now unless you've got the money, sign this damn title and get on your way…then you've got two days to bring me the remaining three grand or a buyer with cash."

Lew was through negotiating and nodded to Wyatt, who made a show of pulling up the CB handset from the Cadillac's dashboard. The coiled cord of the arson hotline danced under the tension.

Sweat tingled between Hank's palm and his cane. He considered the iron-wood clutched in his hand; it might make a good weapon, but it hadn't been tested under battlefield conditions. Hank weighed the possibilities of fighting back, but he had enough experience to know that when the odds turn too far against you, you simply fold. God only knew what armory the sullen motorcyclist carried. The bluff had to be used sparingly.

Hank counted up his chips. He had enjoyed his share of deposits in the bank of life—Howell Juitt would be proud. He alone had survived the crash at St. Claude, and he had been granted an imponderably faithful wife. Lately, he had received the generosity of Ivar Guidance, been granted a stay from death in a pilotless plane, and had finally found the jewel that was his son. With so much good fortune in the bank, maybe he could risk one more gamble.

"No deal, Raybon…I'll find you a buyer, but I'm not signing the glider over unless you accept it as full payment." Hank was resolute. "And by the way… burning the roof from over a sick woman's head is one lousy sales incentive, but if it'll make you feel better, burn it…I've got insurance. I'll take my lumps."

Lew considered Hank's bluff. "You're fucking nuts, Schwain. Sign this." He impatiently handed the papers back to Hank. "Nobody's going to cough up six G's for that tin can. I'll get what I can out of it, then we'll get what we can out of you. By the way, there's no way your insurance company is gonna cover you for storing gasoline in apple cider bottles. That was just damn stupid, Schwain."

"What bottles?" Then Hank sagged with the realization that Lew had all the angles covered.

Lew snapped his fingers. "Wyatt, bring us a pen."

Wyatt replaced the CB handset and fetched a cheap souvenir pen he had stolen from Lew's desk. It featured an image of a southern belle who would disrobe at the tilt of the pen's barrel. Hank shuffled nervously through the papers, stalling at the title transfer page for another idea. He wasn't ready to risk his and Doris's house, and he knew Lew knew it. Hank tipped the pen and watched as the belle's ruffled gown fell away, revealing a lurid figure.

Lew was growing impatient and snarled, "Your John Hancock, Schwain… now! While you can still write."

Hank lowered the pen toward the signature line and paused. Frozen with indecision, Hank nervously twiddled the pen to watch the strip tease as he searched for courage. The sheaf of documents obscured the action on the title transfer page from Lew. Satisfied that Hank appeared to be signing the aircraft away, Lew turned his attention back to the Cadillac to growl at Wyatt who fumbled with the CB handset. He nodded at the motorcycle goon and turned back to Hank, certain that in the motion of the pen he had finally been granted his signature.

"You finished up there, Schwain?"

But Hank hadn't finished and had no intentions of starting. His decision was final. He clicked the pen closed with finality, but before he could reply Lew snapped his fingers and the motorcyclist began removing his jacket. The ugly fellow advanced in anticipation of taking the glider's papers then teaching Hank a painful lesson on the importance of making prompt payment. But both he and Lew miscalculated Hank's resolve and overlooked the danger in the cane.

Hank would never know if self-preservation or self-respect moved him, but in that moment his earlier image of self-sacrifice dissolved in a surge of adrenalin.

"Fuck the lumps!" screamed his instincts. He wouldn't accept another defeat without a fight.

After a nanosecond's consideration of the odds, Hank Schwain took his last gamble. The ironwood cane driven by a powerful right arm caught the motorcycle tough square in the chin. The would-be biker, still ensnared in his own jacket, fell to the ground unconscious, his tongue a touch shorter than when he had arrived at Aero Meadows.

There was no turning back now. Hank turned to face an utterly surprised Lew Raybon. The loan shark took a step back out of respect for the crippled vet's uncharacteristic defense and unexpected skill. Like a man confronting an angry animal, Lew froze. He cursed his misjudgment as he considered the next move. He never thought that the meeting with a pushover like Schwain would get nasty, and now, when he needed it, his pistol lay tucked uselessly into his jacket back in the Cadillac.

Oblivious to the action, Wyatt groped for the CB handset that had just sprung from his hands and dangled like a yo-yo from the dashboard. Lew called to Wyatt for some support, but the number-two goon had advanced only as far as his boss when he realized his partner in mayhem was already down and that Hank possessed an unexpected facility with the cane.

Lew realized Wyatt wasn't going to tackle Hank so he took matters into his hands. "Alright, Schwain, don't make this any worse. Drop the cane, hand me the papers, or Wyatt is gonna call Sparky."

Hank took a bold step forward and Wyatt retreated. Lew Raybon stood his ground, facing down Hank from just out of the cane's reach.

It was with the glider's signing ceremony thus frozen that the music arrived.

—•—

Lew looked up at the sound, dumbfounded at the source of a familiar rock 'n roll refrain. Hank improved his stance from defense to offense, his attention remaining riveted to every movement of the loan shark's formidable body. Wyatt remained clueless.

From the end of the driveway the signature fuzzy guitar hook and drum riff of Keith Richards and Charlie Watts's most memorable moment announced a Stones fan was rolling up the driveway to visit Aero Meadows.

"Nobody move," barked Lew, unsure if Hank would listen. He knew no reinforcements were due him and could only guess that with the approaching car, Hank's position had strengthened. "We'll work all this out…it's just a fucking plane."

"Glider," snapped Hank.

Lew watched with one eye on Hank's cane and another on the metallic blue Riviera that moved rapidly along the runway. The driver seemed familiar with the premises and drove directly onto the flight line, stopping with a lunge of tight new brakes beside Calcutta's Cadillac as the Rolling Stones declared the frustrating impediments to achieving satisfaction.

The song stopped and the Riviera's door flew open. Hank's grip softened. Wyatt the bowler retreated another step from the face of this intrusion. Too many frames and too much watery beer last night had left him unfit for combat or comprehension. Lew squinted at the dazzling figure emerging from the Riviera.

"Hank Schwain…it's about time," rang a lusty voice.

Hank blinked in disbelief.

Chapter 67

Standing in funky grandeur beside her car, Marcile Gold regarded the stunned participants in the face-off on the tarmac. Jewels and rhinestones flashed glitz from a dozen prominent points, dazzling Wyatt who stood even more dumbfounded than usual at the sight. The thought of retrieving Lew's gun or activating the arson hotline never materialized in the star-struck synapses of his diminutive brain.

Since her latest visit to Aero Meadows, Marcile's hair had been straightened Mod-style. Festooned with silver beads, the sultry locks scattered like phosphorescent surf across the shoulders of an electric blue vinyl go-go coat.

Marcile's greeting rattled the silence that had fallen over the proceedings. She realized she had stumbled into a showdown and that Hank might be in danger, although by the looks of the man on the ground and the man with the bowling shirt who seemed reticent to step into the fray, Hank may have temporarily gained the upper hand. But God knew when one of those bozos might pull a pistol.

"Thought we'd join the party. But y'all look so *serious*. Looks like you need some new friends, Hank."

At that moment another door on the Riviera opened, and to Hank's amazement Rama emerged. Lew groaned in realization that the pursuit of any further punitive action against Hank was stymied.

"Are you all right, *Mister Schwain*?" called Rama. He saw no signs of mayhem on his father, but the unconscious fellow at Hank's feet revealed that violence hovered an instant away.

Hank looked at his son with uncertainty; Rama had never referred to him as *Mr. Schwain*. The young man was up to something. Rama puffed himself up as he approached his father. "Miss Gold called, looking for you just after Doris and I got home," Rama explained. "Some guy named Crawford had told her that the glider was up for sale. She was interested, so I told her you were here."

"The young man is right; I'm damn interested," Marcile declared. "Please tell me you haven't sold our Little Crow yet. She'd be wasted on these rubes. They don't look like real airplane enthusiasts to me, Sugar."

"Mister Schwain," Rama spoke with unusual authority. "Miss Gold is prepared to buy your aircraft."

"Damn right I'm prepared to buy her. Daddy was in the Tuskegee Airmen; I've *got* to fly…it's in my blood. I only let her get away for lack of funds—you know what I'm saying? Yes sir, I'm your gal unless these fine fellows haven't already sealed the deal." Marcile flashed a brilliant, twisted smile.

Lew's pulse quickened at a new opportunity. "Well, ma'am, in fact I just took official ownership of the craft from the brutal Mister Schwain. Look what he did to my assistant who simply attempted to fetch the plane's papers. Lousy business manners, eh?"

Lew looked with shallow sympathy at the unconscious biker, then snapped at Wyatt: "Come drag this sorry sack of shit back to the car." Without missing a beat, he continued. "But I might consider reselling if you have an attractive cash offer."

Lew had never relished the thought of needless arson or broken bones. He fancied himself a businessman, but with such difficult clientele his collection tactics were unfortunately necessary. He smiled broadly at Marcile and what appeared to be an unexpected chance to sign away what he thought was a white elephant, then collect his cash and get home to a stiff Manhattan. In the flamboyant woman he visualized a wild musician flush with easy money and a hereditary interest in this glider. A seller's market was at hand.

Hank held his breath, wondering what sparks would fly when Lew realized the Little Crow didn't belong to him.

Marcile looked at Hank who gave her an encouraging wink before she turned her attention back to Lew. "An attractive offer," she began. "Yes sir, I just might…if we can agree on what exactly is attractive. Luckily I was in town when Mr. Schwain put the word out that his bird was back on the market. I got over here soon as I could. Didn't want to miss the chance now that my ship has come in."

Marcile fairly glowed. "She's come in big time. You're looking at the opening act for the Rolling Stones next tour. I guess 'Blue Light Voodoo' really got to Keith."

Hank looked at Marcile. "Are you serious, Miss Gold? This transaction is kind of important."

"Serious? Hell yes, those British boys really know good music."

"No, ma'am; I mean about buying the Crow," he replied uneasily.

"Well, Lord yes! I was prepared to pay up now. Why would we drive on over here…unless of course we thought you were in some trouble?" Marcile winked. "To be honest, I was surely hoping we could have worked out a better deal. That six thou you're asking is a little steep, Stones or no Stones. But I'd have given you four-something in a heartbeat."

Hank's and Lew's hearts sank together. "Is that your offer? That's a freaking insult to this fine aircraft," Lew hissed, dismissing the flamboyant singer as a tease. "Schwain, you've still got two days to find me a *real* buyer. You won't get off so easy next time…you understand?"

Rama knew enough to know his father was in trouble if Calcutta's asking price wasn't met. If he could, he would simply buy this burden from his father like the others, but his winnings from Mesquite had run out. He knew Marcile was serious about the glider, but she hadn't survived in the music business without being shrewd. She wasn't going any higher than necessary. Rama knew that Marcile's resolve needed testing. He looked at Marcile as if deeply troubled. "Tell me that's not your best offer, Miss Gold. You're liable to lose your chance. It's Lew's plane and he's no pushover."

"Damn it, son," Marcile whispered, through a threatening grimace. "I've gotta give the fella a chance to counter. Now hush."

"I am sorry, Miss Gold, but I can't let that plane get away, it's just too good an investment. I've had some good fortune on the golf course lately and need to put the cash to work," Rama lied. Marcile was left uncharacteristically wordless at Rama's interruption.

Rama faced Lew and recklessly bid on a hand he didn't hold. "Okay Mr. Raybon, count me in on this auction. This aircraft is too good an investment…I'm sure Mr. Schwain must have been desperate if he valued the aircraft at only six thousand. But if that's what it is going to take to get it from you, then I'll go full price and it's still a steal."

Hank looked at Rama in alarm but dared say a word.

"Don't you worry, Miss Gold and Mr. Schwain," said Rama. "We'll work something out so you can still fly her from time to time."

Marcile looked perplexed. She never guessed Hank's son had money. She didn't buy his investment story, but it wasn't a stretch to think he might buy the plane to help out his father. "Damned if you aren't trying to bamboozle me, Rama. I should have shut up about that Stones' contract. Everybody's gonna want a piece of my good fortune before long. Shit, I've gotta get her back, and I ain't got time to screw around…I've got a show tonight. I'll go seven five cash, but then I'm out," declared Marcile with finality.

Lew looked at Rama in hopes of a higher bid, but Rama held his hands up in surrender. "Miss Gold, you won't lose on that deal."

Lew nearly swooned at the thought of an extra $1,500 for the afternoon's little drama. He looked at the wondrous Miss Gold. "You always carry this much cash?" he asked, clearly impressed. "Just peel me off seventy-five hundred and I'll sign this back over to you nice and legal. Can't screw around with the Feds, you know."

He stepped toward Hank, intent on gathering the papers and getting the transaction wrapped up. "Guess you're in the clear now, Schwain. Too bad about that fifteen hundred…could have been yours if you had put this thing on the market before you screwed with me. By the way, Schwain, I suggest you stay away from biker bars for a spell."

Lew snapped his fingers for the glider's papers but sweat rendered his digits silent. "Now, goddammit…the papers."

Hank looked at Lew with scorn, knowing who held the cards. "Don't worry, Raybon; you'll get your six grand in a couple of minutes. Just give me and Marcile here a minute to sign these papers and make up a bill of sale."

"These papers? You and her? What the hell are you talking about? It's my god-damned plane."

"Glider, Lew, glider…and no, it's not yours." Hank held out the transfer form. "Do you see my signature? No. I was fixin' to sign it over when your motorcycle buddy stuck his face in my business. Shit, you could have made fifteen hundred extra bucks if you hadn't been so antsy."

Lew lurched forward and grabbed away the papers. "Now you sign this son-of-a-bitch over so Tina Turner here and I can get this deal done. Then you can consider our business relationship over."

"Wyatt, get over here," barked Lew, still clutching the documents.

Wyatt snapped to action after depositing his comrade in the back of the Cadillac. A trace of blood from the motorcyclist's chin streaked his shoulder. "I should have beaten the crap out of you myself last night, Schwain."

Rama stepped into Wyatt's path. "Hold your horses. Does the name Ronnie Marletti ring a bell?"

Wyatt stopped in his tracks. Lew looked up at the confident young man standing beside Marcile. Rama continued: "I thought so…thought you guys were smart but I can't see how grabbing those papers is going to help pry a dime out of Marcile or a signature from Mr. Schwain…or help you defend an arson charge against your man Marletti."

Rama looked at Marcile. "Am I right?"

"I wouldn't pay these dudes a dime for a diamond, honey lamb."

Rama looked directly at Lew as he addressed Marcile. "And you *did* call the police after we surprised that prowler up at Doris Schwain's house?"

"Yes sir," replied Marcile. "Damn fool left a cider jug of gas behind and dropped his Zippo when he hopped the back fence."

Rama pulled a gold-plated lighter from his pocket and held it aloft. "Got his name engraved right here: *Ronnie Marletti – Muddy's Barge Inn.*"

Lew's lowest orifice clenched. Ronnie-fucking amateur, he thought. The two-bit thug would squeal the minute the cops looked at him crosswise. Damn it, good firebugs were getting hard to find.

"And did you tell the police there might be some criminal activity up at Aero Meadows?" Rama asked.

"Sure did."

"Well, good. Not that anybody's gonna try anything stupid now…but that driveway is the only way out of here," noted Rama.

The voice of rhythm 'n blues and reason picked up where Rama left off. She smiled disarmingly and held an open palm out to Lew. "The papers please, sugar. You're gonna have to trust *somebody*. Hank will pay you after I pay him… and sweetie, I'll take the Tina Turner comment as a compliment."

Lew hesitated, then slipped the Little Crow's papers into her hand. "I'm gonna watch you close, *Tina*."

"Close? Lord knows I'm used to that. Now if you boys would just scoot back a few steps…Hank and I can do our little deal for the Crow, then I'm solid gone before the police get up here and taint my image."

Marcile pulled a pouch from her purse and began to zip it open. Hank feared Lew would go for his gun in response, but when she extracted a handful of cash, the tension slackened. "I said scoot!"

Suddenly Marcile was alone with Hank. As Hank signed the title transfer, she counted out seventy-five hundred-dollar bills. "Now I expect fifteen of them back after that little trick your boy played jackin' the price up…let's call it a finder's fee," she whispered. She turned toward Lew, who sat on the trunk of his Cadillac and watched the transaction with covetous eyes.

"Won't you look at old Lew? The greedy bastard looks like my brother did the time he had just about boated a large-mouth bass in a derby—a $500 fish it was—and the slippery devil thrashed once, just hung in mid-air, then plunk… gone."

"Come to think of it…" Marcile adroitly slipped her fee from the bottom of the stack and into her purse. "Now if Lew tries anything fishy before we're done, most he can get away with is the six grand that's due him."

Then employing all her stage presence, she signed her autograph to the forms with a flourish. With the documents under her left arm, she raised her right hand into the sky and snapped her fingers.

"Next!"

Lew approached Hank, anxious that his payment was at hand and that the police might be close behind. He considered the chances of making a move for the extra fifteen hundred, unaware that Marcile had already outmaneuvered him there as well, but before such thoughts could mature Hank shoved a thick roll of bills under his nose.

"We're square now, Lew, but I think I'll keep Marletti's lighter for a souvenir. Hell, I can see his fingerprints from here."

Lew fanned through the bills like a machine. Then he considered the fellow who had crawled hopelessly into his office so many times before, begging temporary rescue from life's dark whirlpools. How was it that this pathetic character, Hank, had decked one of his thugs, sleight-of-handed the plane's title, and hustled one-and-a-half grand out from under his very nose?

The stiff Manhattan sounded better than ever. He almost shook Hank's hand but thought better of it. "It's your lucky day, Schwain." And Lew Raybon was right; the complex balance sheets in Hank's quest for a payday were finally satisfied.

Halfway to his Cadillac, Lew turned back to Hank. "One more thing, Schwain. You are black-balled at Calcutta. There's no skin left on your teeth, if you get my drift." The loan shark smiled imperceptibly. "But you gotta tell me, Schwain: How did you get so damn far behind the eight ball in the first place?"

"Golf," Hank replied. "I've never been real good at picking a winner."

Lew shrugged. "Golf? Shit! Everybody loses one way or another in that ridiculous game." He spoke with authority about the consequences of wagering and looked for a moment like a concerned father. "Golf…should be illegal," he said as he tucked the roll of cash into his jacket pocket.

"And gambling on golf?" Lew just couldn't let it go: "Next time just stick with the ponies."

—•—

In a moment Calcutta's Cadillac was burning down the drive. By the time the car arrived at the highway the biker had returned to consciousness and Lew Raybon had come to realize there never were any police headed his way. But with a thick lump of cash pressing against his heart he was happy, even if he had been outwitted. He would never take Miss Gold's "Blue Light Voodoo" tune, or the Rolling Stones, for granted.

Marcile watched with satisfaction as Lew and his crew raced away. "Guess he got what he came for…guess we all did, eh, Hank? If you're worried about losing the Crow, relax; you can take her up whenever you fancy. I trust you. Matter of fact, there's gonna be some good soaring weather later in the week. Bring Rama on over and we'll grow that angel some wings."

"Sounds fun," Rama said. "But school starts in a few days."

Marcile pulled a lipstick from her purse and touched up in anticipation of the night ahead. "It's getting on, fellas; you all should get going, maybe take some Chinese back to Mrs. Schwain."

Hank agreed. "Worked out pretty good last time."

The black woman in electric blue vinyl—a preposterous vision on a rural airstrip—walked rhythmically to her car. Silver go-go boots slipped across the cracked tarmac. With a wave of her hand and a twist of the Riviera's radio dial, Otis Redding's infinitely perfect rendition of "That's How Strong My Love Is" sent Miss Gold off to her next engagement.

Rama and Hank followed directly, squinting in the wind streaming through the Rambler's gaping windshield. Hank raised his voice against the roar: "You saved my bacon back there, Chief. If Marcile had stopped at four thousand, Raybon would have demanded your phony six and we'd both have been in deep shit. I wouldn't have put it past him to torch the house just to maintain his reputation."

"They wouldn't dare touch the house now, Dad." Rama flicked Ronnie's cigarette lighter triumphantly.

Hank maneuvered the car back onto the highway. As they accelerated, the wind took his breath away. "That was one hell of a move, making that bid. Or it was just plain crazy...I'm not sure which. But Lew and Marcile both bought it. Where did you learn to bluff like that?"

"I don't know...never thought that far. I just had to do something."

Rama recalled Wedgy Byrne sitting on the stoop of the trailer after dinner, blowing smoke rings out into the Texas sky. Rama would burn the paper plates and listen to the old hustler spin off reels of empty tales, but occasionally a memorable pearl would pass his sunburned lips. He was a scoundrel, but a literate one.

Once, with the plates burning brightly from the grease of that night's Sloppy Joes, Wedgy had smiled at what he called the *existential tempering* a man could receive by betting far over his head. The tension was good for a man's character, he claimed. Rama guessed that might answer his father's question. With the wind streaming through Hank's car, Rama raised his voice to quote his old employer:

"'You just haven't lived 'til you've bet a fifty-dollar Nassau with only two dollars in your pocket,'" declared Rama in a bittersweet nod to the Gypsy Hustler.

———•———

At the sight of the first Chinese restaurant, Hank followed Marcile's suggestion and pulled in. Soon, two bags of exotic delights were stowed out of the wind for the ride home to Doris. Halfway there, the odd, crown-shaped landmark of the Kings Kreek Golf Center loomed like a roadside curiosity worthy of Route 66. Rama remembered this was where he had signed on with Wedgy. The image of the skilled old golfer flopping balls up through the crook of the tree that afternoon strummed a nostalgic chord. Rama felt as if he had come full circle and was stricken with the desire to visit one last time.

"Dad, turn in here a second."

Without hesitation Hank turned into the royal structure's empty parking lot. Fragments of mirror embedded in stucco scattered the Rambler's headlights in crazy reflections. "What's up, Chief? Food's gonna get cold."

"I know, but let's check out the driving range just for a minute. Maybe hit a quick bucket...work up an appetite. Golf has been good to you, Dad. You should try." Rama bumped the Rambler's stubborn door open and tossed a jacket over the food bags for insulation. "Come on...just for fun."

"Just a few balls."

Hank was thinking of Twice Cooked Pork while he followed Rama through the crown and out to the little range. Bare yellow lightbulbs hung on old fabric cords—one bulb above each of eight tattered green mats. Several bulbs were dead.

Hank peered out to the yardage markers that beckoned in the gathering dusk. Years of impact and weather had reduced the readability of the hand-painted numbers to irrelevance. In a minute Rama returned from the shop with a rusty basket of balls and two cast-off 8-irons. He dumped half the basket's contents into a depression in the mat.

"They're yours, Dad." Above them, beetles clinked against the bulbs in suicidal flight. Rama offered a club to his father.

"No, Son; I'll just watch."

"We'll see."

In the yellow glow, Rama raked a ball onto the mat, avoiding the splintered rubber tee.

"Now, you stand with your left foot flared…" Rama proceeded to give his father a basic lesson while hitting a dozen balls into the range. The targets were nearly invisible now.

After several minutes the voice of the old proprietor rang through the door. "You fellas 'bout finished up?" Hank and Rama looked up, each wondering if this rugged fellow had ever been the King in Kings Kreek.

The King leaned comfortably against a long-neglected club-fitting display and sipped at a Dixie cup. The rattle of ice cubes promised the Dixie contained something stronger than water. He was dressed in dingy white caddie coveralls and sported a red plaid tam-o'-shanter plopped lazily on his head.

"Not that I give a damn," the King continued after a long, leisurely sip. "You got plenty of time; I'm not runnin' you off exactly. Shit, you can sashay out there and fetch 'em in and hit 'em again all night, for all I care…but you'll have to do it in the dark."

The King held up his cup to indicate the lights. "'Because I'm about finished. When I leave the lights go off with me." The old fellow belched and shook the cup to settle the cubes into the remaining liquor.

"What's your pleasure?"

Rama smiled from the bug-light's yellow pool. "Give us just a couple more minutes before you kill them, okay?"

"Ten-four," replied the King. He raised his cup to his customers in a toast: "And here's to Francis."

Hank looked at the old fellow. "Francis? Who is Francis?"

"Ouimet…God love him. First American to win our Open. Died a couple of weeks back…hell of a loss," mused the King.

Hank looked at his son and shrugged. "Three cheers for Frankie."

"Francis!" The King seemed royally offended and disappeared into his shop with the slam of a screen door.

Rama took advantage of the remaining time and directed his father into a grip and a stance. The elder Schwain took a few swipes at several balls and managed only to send them skittering a dozen or so sorry yards down range.

"Stupid. Stupid. Stupid," said Hank in a common and highly reasonable first reaction to the evasive golf swing.

"Try a few more, Pop. Relax."

Several more rigid swings followed. The last ball managed to get airborne and offered a hint of promise. Then the lights went out.

"Shit," said Hank, "just after I finally nailed one."

"Well at least you can say you tried it once," Rama pointed out philosophically. Chinese food was sounding better by the minute.

"No, I was fixin' to hit another one, damn it. Got it all ready to go."

Rama sensed a glimmer of interest. "Well, Dad, hit the crap out of it then. The King told us we could hang around." Rama sat on a bench behind the tee and smiled in the gloom—another night lesson. "At least this way nobody can see you mess up."

"But Christ, I can hardly see it," Hank complained.

"Sometimes that's not a bad thing, Dad."

Hank looked down. The worn range ball brightened in the gleam of distant lamps out on the highway and under the warm red light from a Coke machine purring behind them. The feeble illumination defined the spherical problem at hand.

"Straight left arm, turn away...and stay loose." Rama recited the usual mantra. "Keep your head down and don't look up, 'cause there's nothing to see out there in the dark anyway."

Rama went to the pop machine for a cold soda. With a silent apology to Dustin Pepper, he passed over the Luva'Lime in favor of the "friendly pepper upper."

On the darkened tee, Hank tried to figure out how to relax and stiffen the left arm simultaneously. Imagining it was hard enough, but *doing* it was ridiculous. It wasn't easy. There was nothing intuitive about it. Back in Mesquite Creek he had overheard golfers talk about how you hit down to go up, swing soft to hit hard, and that it was a thinking man's game but you shouldn't think too much. Ridiculous notions indeed.

And wasn't that what Lew Raybon had said about the game? But if a skill isn't intuitive, why should that make it ridiculous? Hank thought of nudging the Little Crow's stick left to start her into a bank, but returning it to center to remain in the turn. Like the conflicting notions of the golf swing, that, too, defied intuition, but it wasn't ridiculous. Intuition alone could fly a pilot into a death spiral.

Hank peered into the darkened range where the yardage markers lurked like apparitions. The simple promise of just hitting the ball soundly loomed invitingly. A few days had passed since he had wrested himself from fear and found a way to drop Ivar's plane to safety beyond menacing crags and pepper trees. In that moment he had chosen to survive, and had even found fun in it. The ball at his feet offered its own less-threatening challenge. Certainly he could conquer it.

Its flight would be a reflection of his will. If the swallows back home in Othello could float impossibly slow about his ankles on a summer afternoon, so, too, could he send this object soaring on such a fine evening. Like Jessup's brother desiring to merely hit ten balls every morning 'til he snuck up on the century mark, it wasn't too much to ask.

—•—

Rama had just thrown his head back to enjoy the cold soda when he heard the soft whack of steel upon Surlyn. He stopped and listened. Over the soft sizzle of soda inside his mouth he mentally counted: one, two, three...almost four seconds passed before he heard the distant thump of his father's ball landing in some dark, dusty spot far down the range. Rama yanked the bottle from his lips.

"Sounded good, Dad."

Hank didn't reply, but Rama heard the first spasms of mirth begin in his father's chest, then build until the first-time golfer laughed out loud with the silly pleasure of a pure stroke and at the contradictions in its execution.

"I didn't hear it. I couldn't see it. But yeah, I know it was good," replied Hank. "I didn't hardly feel it, Son...strange."

Rama leaned back on the rigid wooden bench. The beetles had moved on to distant lights, following the scent of nameless night-blooming plants that coursed into the sweet evening air. His father was a vague silhouette in the dark before him, but he saw the man more clearly than he ever had. At that moment he even knew his father's thoughts and shared his emotions. This was only a tiny piece of a great game or a great piece of a tiny game—another contradiction—but it was the moment that mattered, and for once they shared it.

On that forlorn little range, with their dinner cooling in the Rambler and with his father's premature glimpse of golf Nirvana still vivid, Rama could not have been happier. He and Ivar, and even Wedgy, had played the fine courses with perfect turf, flowered tee boxes, and lofty pedigrees.

Golf at its best or *Golf as it was meant to be* proclaimed their slogans. But the copywriters had it wrong—golf's best had nothing to do with flowers or agronomy. Rama had become familiar with the game's more substantial, humble attractions. This evening, flush with the simple joy of one long-awaited Night Lesson and his father's contentment, he felt the game's greatest reward.

"I suppose we should get that chow home to Mom, huh?" Rama said at length.

"Oh…yeah, hang on, Chief. I'm gonna go fetch a few more…try a couple more shots. Just a few."

Rama didn't care. While his father zig-zagged out in the dark to collect a few more chances at that inexplicable feeling, he slipped over to the pay phone and dialed home. He told Doris that everything was fine—better than ever, in fact—and they'd be home with Chinese food in just a few more minutes.

Rama settled back again and watched the shadow of his father pursue a new passion. There in the dark, Rama didn't even have to close his eyes to see Chandler, Dickey, and Glendora Stone playing up Mesquite's sixteenth fairway or to hear Carlos describe the magic in their games. Rama thought about his and Melyssa's torrid claim to that tee and to her promising letter that had greeted him on his arrival home earlier that afternoon.

And Hank Schwain hit golf balls.

He swung until the Moo Goo Gai Pan in the Rambler grew cold. He may have hit another thirty or so. No one was counting. Rama listened carefully to Hank's club make contact in the dark.

Indeed, this was the game as it was meant to be: Not many shots were pure, but they were all good.

Epilogue

Walter Cronkite could scarcely contain his emotions as he reported what would soon be the first steps of the first men on the moon. The television Carla Stone had rolled out onto Mesquite Creek's patio blinked his historic broadcast to the few golfers who cared more about human aspirations than their own struggles against par.

Carla wished Carlos were still alive. She recalled how the Christmas Eve message from lunar orbit the year before had so appealed to the old artist's imagination, and she tried to imagine his delight at this miraculous landing. She looked into the warm afternoon sky and felt compelled to watch the moon alone and in silence. Excusing herself from the company of Walter's audience, she left the patio and climbed to the widow's watch—the shuttered room in the cupola that Carlos had used as a studio after its tenure as her children's crow's nest had so abruptly ended.

Most of the paintings that once crammed the room were gone. Many had been sold and others sent to destinations ranging from the Falklands to Portpatrick on the Irish Sea—dispersed in accordance with instructions the old gaucho had left behind. Several remained: the ones Carlos knew were Carla's favorites—the images of the children and Chandler.

Carla pushed open the louvered shutters and found the moon's ivory disk still low in the July sky, but her mind wandered far from the Sea of Tranquility. "Glendora and Dickey would have turned 29 last month," she sighed through fragile breath.

From the window she could see the precarious drive leading back up through the arroyo to the high plains. Carlos had been gone only three months, but she knew already she could no longer endure the loneliness of Mesquite Creek. The fourth loss had been one too many, and for the first time the woman in the watch truly felt like a widow. The highway up on the plains would soon call her away.

Far up the slope, along the edge of the gravel drive, a sage hen burst from the underbrush. Its sudden motion caught the lonely woman's eye, and she forgot the men on the moon.

—•—

The moon was about one hour higher in the eastern sky over Memphis. Down in the Bunker Bar at Bluff Meade the lunar landscape was visible on a TV set the bartender had placed on a table for the historic moment. Ivar Guidance, Wessel Waddley, Dustin "Pep" Pepper, and Ivar's new pilot-in-training, Hank Schwain, had gathered to hear the venerable voice of America's space program report on Armstrong, Aldrin, and Collin's progress. But for the moment Pep only wanted to talk golf.

For the past three years he had made the pilgrimage to the British Isles—ostensibly as a business trip but really to attend The Open. He'd never had any luck, as he laughingly said, in interesting the limeys in Luva'Lime soda. But he always managed to get in a few rounds on the great links of the Scottish and Irish coasts. His friends at Bluff Meade Country Club often accompanied him, but this year he had gone alone. Pep seized the moment to rave about the last course he had played only a few days earlier—Kintyre at Turnberry.

"I couldn't help but go back there again this trip," he began. "The course lays in the rugged headlands beside the Mull of Kintyre. Few are more spectacular, believe me. But I also had to go and see about that crazy fella."

Pep's companions glanced back from the TV. They had heard part of the story when Pep had last returned from the British Isles.

"You all remember, right? Me telling you about slicing a ball over the cliff on number eight. A hell of a waste. It's a short par 4 and a man should make some hay there. Anyway, when I went to look down after it, I saw that fellow down on the rocks...do you remember—the guy with the red scarf?"

A feeble ripple of recognition greeted Pep's story, but he continued anyway. "Well, I don't recall if I told you boys the rest. I played it a month later, and even though I didn't hook it on that fairway second time around, I took a look over the edge anyway. My caddie asked me if I'd lost my ball or my marbles. He reminded me that I was in the fairway *for once*...the cynical bastard. Well, damned if that weird fool wasn't still down there—not golfing, not fishing, not gathering berries...just staring out across the sea to the west."

"Well, I was there just last week, and I hooked up with the same old reprobate caddie. We went around again, and when I got to that treacherous damned fairway along the cliffs, I asked him about the man in the red scarf."

"'Aye, crazy as a loon he was,' my caddie said. He told me that the fellow had come out there about eighteen years ago with nothing and had traded shepherding and greens work for his keep. He said the odd fellow lived in a potting shed on some gentleman's farm.

"'Daft bugger nae says a word fer ten years… maybe more. Aynd when he ain't workin' he's lookin' out to sea,' my caddie said."

Pep continued. "But no one out at Turnberry seemed too bothered about a strange bird in their midst. My caddie guessed old Red Scarf was far from the craziest loon they had spawned in those parts. He said folks there just tolerate them; they figure you never know what they have to offer. Guess that's why they got all them good writers. Then my caddie looked at me and said something odd: '*Dum spiro spero*, aye mate?' He really threw me with that. Turns out the phrase was Latin. Translates to "As we breathe, there's hope.""

"He claimed that is the slogan the hoity-toity Royal and Ancient Golf Club of St. Andrews—top dogs in the golf kingdom—have engraved on their clubhouse door. Pretty darned optimistic, but I guess they figure there's always a chance that as long as he's still kicking, a crappy golfer's game or a fella's life—even a loony like old Red Scarf—might still come around.

Pep glanced at the space-age drama unfolding on the TV. He still had the floor for a few more minutes and continued his story. "Damned if those boys up in space could use a good dose of *spiro spero* about now.

"Anyway, my caddie said that just a week before I got to Turnberry, a package from Texas had showed up at the Kintyre Clubhouse for a Mr. Stone. Damned if old Red Scarf doesn't claim it. It was the first time anyone knew his name. The next thing you know he's knocking around town as sane as you and me. Squares up all his accounts, gets a train to Glasgow, and poof…gone.

"They told me that folks went into his shed to snoop around after him, but it was clean as a pin and the only interesting thing anyone could come up with was the painting—a fine beautiful oil of a boy and a girl out on one of the North Country links…Dornoch, folks reckoned by the look of it."

Walter was explaining the hazards of safely negotiating a landing in the Lunar Excursion Module when Ivar Guidance asked Pep if the folks in Turnberry had a clue where the fellow went.

Pep signaled the bartender to bring a magnum of champagne—a toast to technology was in order—and to "crank up the god-damned volume…the *First Step* is at hand."

He turned quickly back to Ivar to answer his old golfing partner lest he miss history in the making.

"The caddie said all he'd heard was that the fellow was off to do some overdue repair work on an old course."

Ivar raised an eyebrow, "*The* Old Course?"

"No, no, Ives, *an* old course…somewhere in Texas."

—•—

"*That's one small step…*"

A muffled electronic voice spoke the first words. The broadcast echoed feebly up the stairs to her perch, but Carla Stone's attention had collapsed on the figure of a man striding down the drive. His confident step having stirred the hen from hiding now promised to do the same for her. Carla stood mesmerized at the window. She thought she recognized that step—like Chandler's highland gait—but the man descending to Mesquite Creek was still too far away to be certain. Her heart stirred with possibility.

"One giant leap..."

The man drew closer, then Carla saw the color. A splash of crimson. A signature scarf around the neck of the returnee.

About the Author

Don Anslow has morphed from a commercial copywriter to a novelist/part-time project manager. An odd combination, perhaps, but he claims his project work—often in remote locales throughout the western states—suits him fine. The work reveals intriguing settings and the character of many noble yet invisible people. He devotes much of his downtime to creative writing, posts on his blog, and battling blackberries. When not on the road, Mr. Anslow lives in Beavercreek, Oregon, with his wife, Shara, and whichever of the eight kids and seven grandkids might be passing through. He *claims* to be a golfer, but that has not been verified at this time.

Visit Don at www.donanslow.com, check his blog at www.somegumbo.com, or visit him on Facebook at https://www.facebook.com/donanslowauthor

www.ingramcontent.com/pod-product-compliance
Lightning Source LLC
Chambersburg PA
CBHW020821030726
47496CB00001B/30